THE COMPLETE
STORIES OF
ROBERT LOUIS
STEVENSON

Frontispiece from Katharine D. Osbourne's
Robert Louis Stevenson in California (CHICAGO, 1911).

THE COMPLETE STORIES OF ROBERT LOUIS STEVENSON

STRANGE CASE OF DR. JEKYLL AND MR. HYDE AND NINETEEN OTHER TALES

Edited, with an Introduction and Notes, by

Barry Menikoff

THE MODERN LIBRARY

NEW YORK

2002 Modern Library Paperback Edition

"Stevenson in the *OED*" and revisions to the Introduction and Notes
copyright © 2002 by Barry Menikoff
Biographical note copyright © 2001 by Random House, Inc.

Grateful acknowledgment is made to Northwestern University Press for
permission to revise and expand the Introduction and Notes and reprint the
glossary, all by Barry Menikoff, from *Tales from the Prince of Storytellers* (Evanston,
IL: Northwestern University Press, 1993). Copyright © 1993 by Northwestern
University Press. Used by permission of Northwestern University Press.

Grateful acknowledgment is made to Oxford University Press for permission
to reprint selected excerpts from definitions quoting Robert Louis Stevenson
from *The Oxford English Dictionary* (Second Edition, 1989). Copyright © 1989 by
Oxford University Press. Reproduced by permission of Oxford University Press.

LIBRARY OF CONGRESS CATALOGING-IN-PUBLICATION DATA
Stevenson, Robert Louis, 1850–1894.
[Short stories]
The complete stories of Robert Louis Stevenson: *Strange case of Dr. Jekyll and Mr.
Hyde* and nineteen other tales / edited, with an introduction and notes, by Barry
Menikoff.—Modern Library pbk. ed.
p. cm.—(Modern Library classics)
ISBN 0-375-76135-7
I. Menikoff, Barry. II. Title. III. Series.

PR5481 .M46 2002   823'.8—dc21   2002066022

Modern Library website address: www.modernlibrary.com

Printed in the United States of America

2 4 6 8 9 7 5 3

ROBERT LOUIS STEVENSON

Robert Louis Stevenson, a versatile and prolific writer best remembered for his novels of romantic adventure, was born in Edinburgh on 13 November 1850. The son of a prosperous civil engineer who specialized in the construction of lighthouses, he was expected to follow the family profession but ended up studying law at Edinburgh University. Still, when he was a young man his agnosticism and bohemian existence led to painful clashes with his strict Calvinist parents. Stevenson spent much of his life battling a severe lung disease (probably tuberculosis) and traveled constantly in search of a climate that would prove congenial to his health. His first full-length book, *An Inland Voyage* (1878), grew out of a canoe trip he took through Belgium and northern France; a later tour through the wilds of southern France produced *Travels with a Donkey in the Cévennes* (1879). Stevenson journeyed to San Francisco in 1879 to marry Fanny Osbourne, an American divorcée ten years his senior. *The Silverado Squatters* (1883) recalls the couple's eccentric honeymoon at an abandoned silver mine on Mount Saint Helena. After returning to Europe in 1880 the Stevensons moved about, living in Switzerland, France, and England.

"Fiction is to grown men what play is to the child," Stevenson once said. He launched his career as a storyteller with "A Lodging for the Night" (1877), a short story set in fifteenth-century Paris that recounts an episode in the life of French poet François Villon. He went on to write ghost stories, medieval romances, moral allegories, tales of psychological horror, and fables drawn from Scottish folklore. In 1882 he brought out *New Arabian Nights,* an extravagant series of adventures that pays tribute to one of the favorite books of his childhood. G. K. Chesterton remarked, "I will not say that the *New Arabian Nights* is the greatest of Stevenson's works; though a considerable case might be made for the challenge. But I will say that it is probably the most unique; there was nothing like it before, and, I think, nothing equal to it since." Stevenson's other compilations of short fiction include *More New Arabian Nights: The Dynamiter* (1885) and *The Merry Men and Other Tales and Fables* (1887). "[Stevenson's] short stories are certain to retain their position in English literature," judged Arthur Conan Doyle. "His serious rivals are few indeed. Poe, Nathaniel Hawthorne, Stevenson; those are the three . . . who are the greatest exponents of the short story in our language."

The publication of *Treasure Island* in 1883 brought Stevenson enormous acclaim. Written as an entertainment for his twelve-year-old stepson, the rousing tale of pirates and buried treasure proved universally popular. "Over *Treasure Island* I let my fire die in winter without knowing that I was freezing," recalled J. M. Barrie, and Henry James predicted, "*Treasure Island* will surely become—it must already have become and will remain—in its way a classic." "[Stevenson is] a master of narrative," observed V. S. Pritchett. "He places his scenes at a fitting distance from each other, with an unflurried order and particularity, so that we do not blunder into them but are quietly brought to the point where the view is best. . . . He is a writer of brilliant beginnings. He catches the sensation of being athletically alive, which is especially the gift of youth. In *Treasure Island* this sense of physical action is wonderful and youth's dominant preoccupation with its own fear and courage plays naturally upon it. The timidity, the pride, the caution, the heady excitement of youth, its day dreams and admirations, are wonderfully rendered." Novelist William Golding agreed: "When one turns to *Treasure Island,* one sees immediately that Stevenson was the professional knowing precisely what effects he wanted and how he was going to get them. Every chapter is shaped and fitted into the general structure like the timbers of a ship."

Stevenson soon enhanced his reputation with *Strange Case of Dr. Jekyll and Mr. Hyde* (1886), a psychological thriller that sprang from the deepest recesses of his own subconscious. A brilliantly original study of the dual aspects of human nature, it endures today as the quintessential Victorian parable of good and evil. "Robert Louis Stevenson has become immortalized by way of his private fantasy—which came to him, by his own testimony, unbidden, in a dream," observed Joyce Carol Oates. "The visionary starkness of *Strange Case of Dr. Jekyll and Mr. Hyde* anticipates that of Freud: there is a split in man's psyche between ego and instinct, between civilization and 'nature,' and the split can never be healed." Vladimir Nabokov considered it "his most wonderful book," comparing Stevenson's "shilling shocker" to *Madame Bovary* and *Dead Souls* as "a fable that lies nearer to poetry than to ordinary prose fiction."

A few months later, in another burst of creative energy, Stevenson completed *Kidnapped* (1886). Set in the Scottish Highlands during the aftermath of the Jacobite rebellion of 1745, this classic of high adventure interweaves the drama of Scottish history with the psychological moral growth of its adolescent hero, David Balfour. J. M. Barrie rated *Kidnapped* "the outstanding boy's book of its generation," and Mark Twain wrote to Stevenson, "My wife keeps re-reading *Kidnapped* and neglecting my works. And I have not blamed her; I do it myself." V. S. Pritchett reflected that "*Kidnapped* is far more than a boy's book.... [It] contains a universal statement about the loyalties and uncertainties of youth." And Stevenson biographer Ian Bell noted, "*Kidnapped* says as much about Stevenson as any autobiography. In David Balfour and Alan Breck he gave substance to two sides of his own character, adventurer and rationalist, man of duty and man of passion." Stevenson subsequently turned out three more tales embedded in the fierce loyalties and violent enmities of Scottish history: *The Master of Ballantrae* (1889), *Catriona* (1893), and the unfinished *Weir of Hermiston* (1896).

Though perhaps best known for his fiction, Stevenson was also a celebrated essayist as well as a popular poet. In collections such as *Virginibus Puerisque and Other Papers* (1881), *Familiar Studies of Men and Books* (1882), and *Memories and Portraits* (1887) he offered idiosyncratic views on everything from dreams, umbrellas, political activism, and jingoistic Victorian mores to the art and craft of fiction. "[Stevenson's] essays are tremendously bold in their biographical and interpretive outlines," said the *Times Literary Supplement*. "[They attest to his] human curiosity, his intimate, affectionate embroilment with behavior and character, his wonderful phrase-making and inventiveness of language." As a poet Stevenson enjoyed his greatest success with *A Child's Garden of Verses* (1885), an extraordinarily evocative picture of the joys and heartaches of childhood that appealed to both imaginative children and nostalgic adults. His other volumes of poetry include *Underwoods* (1887), *Ballads* (1890), and *Songs of Travel* (1896).

In 1888 Stevenson set sail from San Francisco for the South Pacific, where he spent the last six years of his life. *In the South Seas* (1896), a posthumously issued travelogue, vividly recounts his journey there. During this period he collaborated with his stepson, Lloyd Osbourne, on *The Wrong Box* (1889), a black comedy involving a mismanaged trust fund and a recalcitrant corpse; *The Wrecker* (1892), a story of modern crime and adventure on the Pacific; and *The Ebb-Tide* (1894), a dark tale probing the nature of evil that anticipates the fiction of Joseph Conrad. In addition he published *Island Nights' Entertainments* (1893), a collection of short stories that included "The Bottle Imp" (1891) and "The Isle of Voices" (1893), two tales based on Polynesian superstitions, along with "The Beach of Falesá" (1892), a masterful meditation on the growing gulf between native Polynesians and the white imperialists who had invaded their world. He also completed two works of nonfiction: *Father Damien* (1890), a famous defense of the Belgian priest who devoted his life to the care of lepers, and *A Footnote to History* (1892), a piercing examination of political turmoil in Samoa. Robert Louis Stevenson died of a cerebral hemorrhage at his estate in Vailima, Samoa, on 3 December 1894. The next day Samoan chieftains honored Stevenson, whom they hailed as *Tusitala,* or "Teller of Tales," with burial in a tomb atop Mount Vaea. *The Letters of Robert Louis Stevenson,* an eight-volume compilation of his correspondence, was issued in 1994 to mark the centenary of his death.

"Stevenson can claim to have mastered the whole gamut of fiction," judged Arthur Conan Doyle. "No man has a more marked individuality, and yet no man effaces himself more completely when he sets himself to tell a tale." And John Galsworthy stated, "As a teller of a tale Stevenson is the equal of Dumas and Dickens.... He had but one main theme, that essential theme of romance, the struggle between the good and the bad, of hero against villain.... Stevenson was so vivid and attractive as a person, so picturesque in his travels and his ways of life, so copious and entrancing in his essays and his letters, and so pleasing as a poet, that his general self overshadows him as a novelist. But compare with his novels all the romantic novels written since... and you will see how high he stands. Next to Dumas, he is the best of all the romantic novelists [and] of British nineteenth century writers, he will live longer than any except Dickens." His biographer, David Daiches, concluded that "Stevenson produced some of the most memorable fiction in our language.... He transformed the Victorian boys' adventure into a classic of its kind."

Contents

INTRODUCTION

Barry Menikoff

On 14 October 1877 the *New York Times* published a short story, "A Lodging for the Night," with no signature other than the name of the English magazine that had printed it a month earlier. The editor clearly had an eye for good copy, for three more stories were lifted from their English magazines over the next few years. Thus the *New York Times* has the distinction of being the first publisher of Stevenson's fiction in America. Some years later, just after Stevenson died, a *Times* reviewer recalled that first experience, raining plaudits on the newspaper for its perspicacity and shrewdness of judgment. Of course that was many years ago, when the retrospectives and encomiums were still fresh, and when every literate person shared a common conviction that Robert Louis Stevenson, whom the gods loved, was already a classic of English literature. Stevenson today is quite possibly the most anomalous figure in literary and cultural studies. In truth, Stevenson's versatility and productivity astonish anyone who happens upon the volumes of essays, travels, novels, plays, poetry, criticism, and correspondence that constitute one of the most extraordinary bodies of work in nineteenth-century English letters. But the variety and complexity of that work were nothing more than a mirror of the man. Stevenson was intellectual, bohemian, and consummately romantic. It is unreasonable to think he would not transmute the intensity of that personality into his work. Walter de la Mare said it best: "We actually see him in every line he ever wrote—that long face, those dark dwelling eyes, that straight hair, those tapering fingers."

Virtually all of Stevenson's contemporaries recognized that his claim on immortality—fame was not even the question—was made in his fiction, and particularly in the short story, a genre he defined both in theory and in practice. From George Saintsbury and Henry Seidel Canby at the turn of the century to V. S. Pritchett and Sean O'Faoláin more recently, Stevenson was synonymous with this new form. In 1914 Frank Swinnerton called him "among the best English writers of short stories." Five years later *TLS* reassessed the body of his work: "In the short story his art found a province narrow enough to dominate." Edith Wharton in 1925 considered him one of a modern English triumvirate, along with Henry James and Joseph Conrad. And John Buchan, at the end of the decade, affirmed all these judgments: "Stevenson was one of the best story-tellers that ever lived. He was a kind of bard who spoke in prose rather than verse, with all the bard's swiftness of narration and sudden bursts of lyric beauty. He was a great short-story writer." Stevenson's influence on the short story was pervasive. He became part of the consciousness of the modernist sensibility, and the poles of his short-story art can be seen in two later masters of the form—Jorge Luis Borges and Graham Greene.

The Complete Short Stories of Robert Louis Stevenson is for a new generation of readers, still open to experience and enthusiastic about the possibilities of magical art. In "Providence and the Guitar," Stevenson's brilliant riff on the theme of art and life, Léon Berthelini is a second-rate performer with an inflated sense of self-importance and a dated style. Nonetheless he is a genuine artist: he delights and instructs a younger couple who are having a marital conflict over the artistic life but are struggling resolutely to hold on to each other. Léon's wife advises the younger woman that a good man may be hard to find, and it is worth keeping the father of your child, even if he is not a very good painter. Painting, after all, is not everything. Léon, with his guitar, performs the noblest service of art—the affirmation of life. And Stevenson, the supreme performance artist, silently nodding in the direction of the reader, confirms both the reality and importance of the entire enterprise.

1

Few developments in contemporary fiction since the Second World War match the extraordinary rise in the status of the short story. Many of the most acclaimed writers in England, Ireland, Canada, and the United States are primarily short-story writers, who are recognized and acclaimed for their work in a genre that has historically been considered a second sister to the novel. But it would be a mistake to imply that the short story suddenly emerged from nowhere, or that nobody had paid it much attention before. On the contrary, it has an extensive and impressive history. We need only recover the origins of the form in the last quarter of the nineteenth century to recognize that the impulse that gave rise to its development was not fundamentally different from that which makes it such a viable form today. The short story evolved in tandem with the modern novel. They had in common a single objective: to reduce the size of the book and concentrate the art of the fiction. There is no question that a certain fatigue had set in with the reading public, as well as with the writers themselves. It is hardly coincidental that the two most successful fiction writers of the last two decades of the nineteenth century were Robert Louis Stevenson and Rudyard Kipling. The latter declared an end to the triple-decker novel, and the former considered it a feat of strength to complete one. For the Victorians, of course, at least the High Victorians, the triple-decker represented an achievement emblematic of high seriousness and moral integrity. To fill up three complete volumes with complicated stories that reflected the variety and multiplicity of ordinary lives was almost a vocation. Although it is a commonplace that the Victorian serial anticipated the contemporary soap opera in its kaleidoscope of characters, involuted plot, melodrama, and sentiment, it is equally true that the major Victorians were serious writers whose subjects were not conditioned solely by the marketplace. They were also driven by their compulsion to dramatize their profound if not obsessive themes.

What was the situation of the novel in the last quarter of the nineteenth century? Dickens and Thackeray were dead. Eliot had completed her important work. Trollope was writing his last novels. The only major novelist who was still productive was George Meredith, and Meredith, as everybody knows, was caviar for the general, a writer whom other writers could admire but whose work was destined to fail a larger audience. This was the situation when Robert Louis Stevenson began his career. If Harold Bloom's idea of generational rebellion is viable, then any serious writer coming of age with Stevenson might exhibit an antagonism to those monuments of powerful and daunting intellect, monuments of assurance if not indeed arrogance that were sold in three thick volumes to an elite audience for thirty shillings. In any event, nobody growing up in the 1860s and 1870s could fail to be awed by them. Certainly Stevenson was awed, perhaps even intimidated, although it is equally clear that he recognized exactly what they represented: a vision of the world that could only be contained within a formal text akin to the Victorian epic. It is hardly surprising that he considered Victor Hugo's *Les Misérables* the consummation of fiction on this scale, or in this manner. But it was not the avenue that he pursued, nor was it the avenue that was pursued after him. Stevenson realized that the Victorian novel had finally exhausted itself, that it was of a time, and a place, that had long passed. He had the remarkable ability to recognize both the achievement of the novel and its limitations. Just as he admired Walter Scott as a fellow countryman and a writer whose subject touched him personally, he also knew that Scott's fiction had played itself out, or at least that Scott's method was defunct. In brief, the age demanded an image of its accelerated pace; the age demanded the short story.

What was the status of the English short story when Robert Louis Stevenson first signed the initials R.L.S. at the end of "A Lodging for the Night" in the October 1877 issue of *Temple Bar*? For the most part it was moribund. The form was clearly not one that the English novelists had been able to master. Serial publication of fiction placed a premium on elaborate plots, and the continued dominance of the three-volume novel inhibited the development of techniques that would highlight the strengths of the short narrative. If one wanted models for shorter fiction there were only two: the Americans and the French. Stevenson was naturally attracted to both. For the Americans, Hawthorne and Poe were the dominating presences. That Poe had provided the theoretical underpinnings for the short story, or had elaborated a formal process that rationalized his own practice, was apparent to anyone. Stevenson read Poe avidly, and used him with impunity. The fascination with "doubles" (symbolized by *Jekyll and Hyde*) that runs as a motif through Stevenson's fiction is well known. In a letter to Andrew Lang, for example, he readily acknowledged his familiarity with one of Poe's masterpieces in the genre ("Yes, I knew William Wilson" [undated letter to Andrew Lang, Huntington Library, HM 2490]). The earliest reviews of Stevenson's short fiction are rife with references to Poe, who appeared to critics as the model and inspiration for Stevenson's tales of horror, and for that morbidity which was recognized early as a prominent strain in his fiction. Stevenson's affinity with the American theorist must be taken as a fundamental.

But it was Hawthorne that Stevenson was most intensely drawn to. The New Englander's stories of religious obsession and guilt, framed by the hard doctrines of Calvinism, held a special appeal for the writer whose own country was haunted by a staunch and unyielding Presbyterianism. Even tales of superstition and the supernatural found their echo in the terrifying stories of witchcraft told him by his childhood nurse, and which were among his earliest memories. Hawthorne also displayed a powerful moral strand that was absent from Poe but that struck a deeply sympathetic chord in Stevenson, who could never quite shake free of the strict faith of the orthodox. It is not surprising that from the beginning critics have commented, and not always favorably, on an abiding moral element as one of the salient characteristics of Stevenson's fiction.

Stevenson knew Cooper and Twain too, of course, and he chided Melville for his failure to transcribe accurately the Marquesans' speech in *Typee*. But the question is not how many of the American writers he knew. He read voraciously, omnivorously, and there is little he was unaware of. That Hawthorne was his intellectual model is as undeniable as that Walt Whitman was his emotional inspiration. Stevenson found in the outspoken poet a zest for freedom that was the antithesis of the crimped and dour Scots mentality. In Whitman, as in Thoreau, he found an idea, perhaps even an ideal, that was associated with America, an idea as persuasive as it was seductive to a young man growing up beneath the overhang of Edinburgh Castle, in the damp and darkness of a northern city.

If there is any single thing Stevenson might have learned from Hawthorne, it is unquestionably the use of light, a visual image that dominates Stevenson's fiction from his first published story through the final brilliance of *The Beach of Falesá*. But America did not represent "light" in fiction as opposed to the "dark" of Scotland. Rather, Whitman and Thoreau represented the elevation, indeed the exaltation, of the individual, and the idea of freedom that was so strong an element in Stevenson's personality. Yet the antithesis to that idea of freedom was just as deeply rooted in a man who read the stern Scottish religious writers with a certain degree of relish. Hence the overt "moralizing," the use of the word *sermon* to title his writings (*Lay Sermons,* "A Christmas Sermon"), and stories that often seem so strongly "moralistic" in their message or tone that modern readers are inclined to put them aside, or to dismiss them for that reason alone. Yet just as Hawthorne cannot be dismissed because of the moral message often attached to his stories, neither can Stevenson. His are no more moralistic, in the pejorative sense, than Hawthorne's, perhaps even less so. And this is because he was in certain fundamental ways a more self-conscious artist than Hawthorne, as well as a more broadly intellectual one than Poe.

As for the French, it is virtually a commonplace that Stevenson's connection with French literature and culture was as deeply rooted as his attachment to the country itself. From his laudatory remarks on Victor Hugo at the beginning of his career to his dedication of *Across the Plains* to Paul Bourget near the end, Stevenson retained an unshaken admiration for French writers. He even incorporated them in his own fiction. In *The Rajah's Diamond,* for example, he calls attention to Emile Gaboriau, the novelist whose stories of the Paris underworld established the *roman policier,* and whose detective, Lecoq, was a model for Prince Florizel in the *New Arabian Nights* stories. The French provided Stevenson with an abundance of material for his work. Among his earliest essays were those on Charles of Orléans and François Villon, just as his best-known travel book charts his journey through the mountainous Cévennes in southern France (*Travels with a Donkey*). Of course, the old and deep ties between France and Scotland were central to Stevenson's cultural experience and formed the substance of his longer historical novels. But aspects of those ties surfaced as well in the shorter stories that were set in France, either in their entirety or only in part: *The Suicide Club* and *The Rajah's Diamond,* "A Lodging for the Night," "The Sire de Malétroit's Door," "Providence and the Guitar," and "The Treasure of Franchard." Certainly the intellectual and aesthetic quality and even the daily texture of French life quickened Stevenson's imagination. But as a student of art it was the writing that drew his closest attention.

The French *conte* was the only alternative to the American short story, the only other model available to a writer determined to craft a form that had no modern equivalent in England. For the French short story, as opposed to its American cousin, "revindicated...the supreme value of form in composition and of that unity of effect which is twin to structural completeness" (Una A. Taylor, "The Short Story in France," *Edinburgh Review,* July 1913, p. 137). Taylor's description of the French short story, and in particular the short fiction of Prosper Mérimée and Théophile Gautier, reads like a primer for Stevenson's art: "Gautier sought his end in concentration, Mérimée in elimination of detail.... In the hands of both...the art of the French *conte* remained for the most part definitely objective" (137, 141). Of his familiarity with Gautier, Stevenson himself told a San Francisco newspaper in June 1887: "My special distaste is the use of any foreign word.... The great instance of the folly of reading to get new words was Gautier."

Stevenson found in the French *conte* the elements that were essential to the construction of the modern short story in English: the economical use of language, an economy that invariably encouraged a highly conscious concern for diction and phrasing; the linkage of incidents in a logical, ineluctable chain so that the ending, as Stevenson said in a famous letter to Sidney Colvin, is always implicit in the beginning; the habit of telling the story from outside the events, through either a third-person narrator or a first-person narrator who is virtually an objective observer, even when he is intimately involved in the story; and, not least, the compression of incidents and details into a focused and self-contained unit. Stevenson's search for compression and economy was clearly recognized by his contemporaries, although they often disapproved of the end result. One review of *Jekyll and Hyde* took the story to task for its failure to develop what was seen as a brilliantly original conception: "Perhaps, however, a larger audience will be found, in these days of hurried reading, for the condensed narrative presented by Mr. Stevenson than for a more elaborate story" (*New York Tribune,* 24 January 1886, p. 6). Stevenson himself was very clear about this aim in his art:

When I am making a point I try to do it in the smallest possible space. I do not think a reader should be expected to plod through pages of print to find out what I mean. The great difficulty I have is in compressing my matter. I can always tell when an author does not write over and over again. The most rapid and fluent writer cannot arrange the mass of material that goes to make up a book without having it out of order here and there. Order is the basis, the charm and the end of literature. Literature is an art that takes place in time. Therefore the main point is to be certain that you have everything in proper order. That you can never get in the first shot. That is my experience. (*San Francisco Chronicle,* 17 December 1894, p. 1)

Stevenson was by temperament aligned with the French in their emphasis on form and style in the short story. This is nicely illustrated, albeit in a small way, in an interview he gave to a San Francisco reporter in 1887, when he observed that the only writer who was doing anything at all as artistically exciting as Henry James was Guy de Maupassant. Although the remark paid tribute to the new direction James's fiction had taken in the 1880s, it was also a compliment to the facility and originality of Maupassant, who began his career at the beginning of the decade and whose work Stevenson was clearly following. He was always attuned to what the French were doing, and his ability to draw from them ideas, both formal and thematic, was a constant reminder of the catholicity of his reading and his taste. If the nineteenth-century police novel of Emile Gaboriau provided a model for the *New Arabian Nights* stories, the fifteenth-century *ballades* (and life) of Villon offered him a means to explore issues of poverty and wealth, art and life, in "A Lodging for the Night."

Stevenson sought to combine the elements of the French *conte* and the American short story in order to construct a new form that exhibited the best features of both. It is not that either had wonderful qualities absent from the other; rather, each had elements that spoke directly to Stevenson's artistic imagination and intellectual interests. In effect, he was determined to exploit the potentialities inherent in both. What Stevenson required was a form that would maintain the detachment and objectivity of the French with the moral implicativeness, even discursiveness, of the Americans. In a sense he was attempting something that had not been done previously; he was trying to meld together two distinct and in some ways contradictory modes. For the French, the form was primary: the narrative is the embedded chain of incidents that controls and unifies the story from beginning to end. The narration is made as objective as possible in order to forestall the author's intrusion into the story, and the manner is polished in all its details—economy of expression, concision of incidents, and exclusion of all extraneous or irrelevant data. What the French *conte* provides is a story admirable in construction and powerful in effect, in short, a magnificent artifice. For Stevenson, the appeal of that kind of art was considerable, for the writer is challenged by the material, concerned with presentation, and committed almost exclusively to problems of technical mastery.

With the American model, on the other hand, the moral issues in the story were of primary consideration. This was certainly the case in Washington Irving's stories, just as it was obvious in Hawthorne's. Indeed, if the Americans were guilty of anything in their short fiction, it was of making too much of the issues, of making the story nothing more than a vehicle for the moral. While this may not be the most interesting way to read Irving, and certainly not Hawthorne, it is nonetheless an approach that readers and reviewers invariably adopted. In the case of Hawthorne, the focus on sin and punishment made it convenient to read his short stories as moral exempla, aided by the summary conclusions often provided by the author. Although it is undeniable that the structural design of Hawthorne's fiction often concealed its complexity, rather like James's figure in the carpet, it is equally true that a reading of the exterior story frequently reduced it to a simple moral apothegm. Hawthorne, in effect, became the analyst of conscience. His subject and approach invariably focused attention on theme and deflected it from technique. Even Poe, whom everyone agreed was indifferent to moral issues, still paid them attention in tales like "The Cask of Amontillado," "The Fall of the House of Usher," and "The Masque of the Red Death."

Stevenson was at one and the same time the most deliberately artistic of new writers and the one most preoccupied with moral issues. The questions he confronted in his short stories were never without moral implications, whether it was equity and justice in "A Lodging for the Night" or prejudice and greed in "The Beach of Falesá." Indeed, even his adoptions of particular forms of the short story, such as the folktale "The Bottle Imp" or the parable "Will o' the Mill," exhibit the incorporation of moral issues within the form of the story itself.

Stevenson (like Henry James) found himself with two fundamental inclinations: the one toward technical artistry, which he saw in the
French, and the other toward moral analysis, which he found in
Hawthorne. The problem was to amalgamate the two, creating a fiction that was both technically brilliant and thematically complex. Instead of highlighting one or the other, as the French and Americans
did, Stevenson fashioned a short story that was moral in its impulse
and artistic in its execution; he created, in effect, the "moral art story,"
or the art story with a moral.

Perhaps no other writer exhibits a greater dichotomy between play
and purpose in fiction than Stevenson: fiction as play, and fiction as
purpose; art as pleasure and art as instruction. Stevenson is the quintessential embodiment of the Horatian ideal—the function of art is to
delight and instruct. The problem, of course, is that for most artists the
one or the other takes prominence. In the nineteenth-century novel it
appeared, for a time, as if the two purposes were united: in Dickens
there was pleasure, even fun, and there was instruction, or, more properly, social outrage. Yet it is clear that as the great Victorians developed
their art, they emphasized the one at the expense of the other: we
think of Eliot as a great moralist; of Dickens as two people, the entertainer of *Pickwick Papers* and the justiciary of *Bleak House;* of Thackeray
as a social satirist in the guise of a puppeteer. But in many ways these
writers were working in an ad hoc manner; they were not consciously
dividing their roles and determining the consequent effects on their
fiction. Hawthorne illustrated the same phenomenon. His primary
role was instructive in the widest sense. He may have complained
about his lack of audience, but he did not write to entertain or delight
that audience. As for Poe, if his conception of his role was complex,
the consequence for his art was less so. His stories had calculated effects, and whether he constructed them for that purpose or whether
the effects were simply a result of their design is beside the point.

But Stevenson's position was more subtle. For one thing, he was extremely sophisticated and articulate about the artistic process. He was
writing at a period when there was extraordinary ferment in France
and even Britain about the nature of art, and particularly narrative art.
He was involved in the historic debate that culminated in Henry
James's "Art of Fiction" and his own "A Humble Remonstrance." That
Stevenson's titles are so modest as to be virtually self-effacing is un-

fortunate, since they have encouraged critics to dismiss the arguments out of hand. Yet "A Humble Remonstrance" and "A Gossip on Romance" are far from modest inquiries into the nature of fictional art. Indeed, in "A Gossip on Romance" Stevenson anticipates Freud's commentary on creative writers and daydreaming, where the psychoanalyst argues that literature is nothing more than the legitimate expression of fantasies. When Stevenson says that fiction is play for grown-ups, he is merely using familiar language to describe the same idea. That perception of his—that fiction is an acceptable form of play for adults—is joined to another, that fiction is one of the few avenues for truth in the world because it is the only form that people will accept as entertainment, and therefore it is the only medium the truth teller has for his message.

Stevenson thus was caught in the position of wanting to entertain his readers, in that he realized he would have no readers without entertaining them, and at the same time was determined to convey his vision with the single-minded passion of a Hawthorne. Admittedly he had an arrogant and even patronizing view of his readers. Stevenson was under no illusions as to the abilities or interests or experience of the mass reading audience. And it is an open question whether his earliest fiction was even consciously written with that (or any) audience in mind. But there is no question whatever that he was always aware of what was owed his readers, and it is not for nothing that one of the central refrains that runs through Stevenson criticism is that he was a natural or born storyteller. The aptness of such a description was never in doubt during his lifetime, and it continued in force at least through the 1920s. Indeed, shortly after the news of his death, the *San Francisco Chronicle* headlined one of its biographical articles "Tales of the Prince of Storytellers" (23 December 1894). Stevenson's life had begun to assume a mythic quality; there were "tales" to be told of it that competed with—and indeed were bound and destined to compete with—the generated tales that constituted the work itself.

2

When we read Stevenson's short stories, we immediately sense the solitariness and loneliness of his characters. Francis Scrymgeour and Simon Rolles in *The Rajah's Diamond* are two early examples of figures who live in the midst of metropolitan centers but are nonetheless alone. Both are pursuing careers in the very center of European cities, one struggling against all odds for a secure position in an office in Edinburgh, the other driven by ambition for preferment in the church. They are intensely centered upon themselves and at the same time curiously unaware of the fact. Unlike James's "super-subtle fry," who know they are self-conscious and revel in that knowledge, Stevenson's figures (like those in classical tragedy) are largely unconscious of their obsessiveness. Even in a story like "The Pavilion on the Links," where the narrator admits to having been "a great solitary when...young" (137), the emphasis is not on the narrator's consciousness of his solitariness or even on his awareness of how distorting such a self-absorption might be. In *The Rajah's Diamond* there is a motif of voyeurism that functions as a mirror image for the voyeur's obsessive focus on himself, as if to gaze surreptitiously at others were the only escape from the prison of one's mind. That there is a sexual aspect to this gazing is clear in "The Physician and the Saratoga Trunk" when the young American cannot keep his eyes from the peephole. But on a deeper level Stevenson concentrates attention on an issue that was fundamental to a strict Protestant mind: the inward-looking self trying to discover an unblemished soul. It may be that the solitary and lonely self is the condition of the Calvinist mentality, a condition that was clearly reflected by the realities of Stevenson's Presbyterian upbringing and his Edinburgh experience. For him, the "long Scots faces" of the dour people he knew so well was a metonymy for their attitudes and their mentality.

A Stevenson story invariably has an individual at the center (either as character or narrator) and never seems to have more than one individual in it, even when there is a cast of characters who appear to fill out the pages. Moral issues, which are the heart of every Stevenson story, are always confronted in individual cases. From the start of "A Lodging for the Night," where Francis Villon is in a tavern carousing with his friends, to the end of the story, when he is alone in the street trying to toss off the experience of the evening, he is essentially alone in the world and forced to live with that condition. Philosophy, religion, art—all of which he is an adept at—can in no way alter or ameliorate his situation. Villon must live with himself, just as he has a vision of dying by himself, swinging from the gibbet like a piece of fruit on a tree. Part of the pain of Stevenson's depiction of the isolation of Villon, or of Cassilis or Northmour in "The Pavilion on the Links," is the realization that it is the inalterable condition of experience.

For Stevenson, mortality is destiny, inescapable, ineluctable—a vision that unquestionably drives many readers to attribute a distinctly morbid note to many of the stories. The doctor's speech in "The Physician and the Saratoga Trunk" spelling out his view of the flesh once the spirit has passed out of it can be read either as a cold-blooded commentary from a heartless materialist or as a plausible argument on the nature of man, an argument that must be acknowledged before one can determine how to address or answer it. The fact of death is so central to Stevenson's imagination that to shy from it at the start is to avoid wrestling with his subject and his art. Where is permanence? Over and over, he reflects upon this question through his surrogates. The young narrator in "The Merry Men" who discovers the shoe buckle at the bottom of the sea and silently discourses on the life of the man who wore the shoe, and in effect on human history, is another illustration of the way Stevenson promotes the idea of the transitoriness of life and perhaps the futility of all human pursuits. The contrast between life and death, which is another way of looking at this question, also recurs regularly in Stevenson's work. And it is the perception of death that makes the solitariness so bleak. It is curious, too, how little Stevenson's fiction is concerned with issues like ambition or success in the world in terms that would be recognizable to ordinary working people. Yet there is always an acute consciousness of the fact that these are indeed the issues that drive men's lives. The line in "Story of the Young Man in Holy Orders" about Rolles's struggle for success in the church and the recognition that his merits will have no effect on that success is only one of the wittier illustrations.

But the absence of incidents reflective of the ordinariness of life does not mean that Stevenson was simply trying to steal boys away from their Ovid and carry them into the world of romance, as he says in the dedication to *Kidnapped*. Rather, he preferred to concentrate on issues he considered more fundamental, or perhaps more revelatory of the human condition. The "adventures" in *The Suicide Club* and *The Rajah's Diamond* and the misadventures in "The Misadventures of John Nicholson" are merely the occasions for profound explorations of experience; they are certainly not the substance—let alone the meaning—of the stories. The swindling and fighting in "The Pavilion on the Links" are no more what that story is about than is the mystery surrounding the wrecked ship the subject of "The Merry Men."

This is not always apparent, because the engine that drives a Stevenson story is plot, moving forward through time with a series of incidents that are unpredictable and suspenseful. But for Stevenson plot is (on one level) just a technical device, a means to enthrall the reader while the serious issues are being explored. The excitement of a plot is the pleasure of the reading experience. Stevenson never denigrates that pleasure and always strives to sustain it, but it is finally an arbitrary, perhaps even a capricious, device. In *The Suicide Club* and *The Rajah's Diamond* the plots are extraordinary, straining credulity and calling attention to their own outrageousness. What is always at the center of the fiction is the idea. The core of a Stevenson story is intellect, either the intellect of a character or intellectual comprehension conveyed through the omniscient narrator. If we consider stories like *The Suicide Club, The Rajah's Diamond,* "A Lodging for the Night," "Markheim," and "The Merry Men," it is clear that intellectual issues are at bottom the meaning of the texts. It would indeed be surprising if one of the most widely read and scholarly of late-Victorian writers were to suddenly park all his knowledge and wisdom outside the circle of his fiction. Stevenson can be called a philosopher in fiction with far more justness than virtually any of his contemporaries, including Hardy and James. Some of his texts overtly identify themselves as philosophical, like "Will o' the Mill," where the protagonist watches from the perch of his rural retreat the whole panorama of men's lives cavalcading before him. Another, like "The Treasure of Franchard," wittily exposes the antics of a faux philosopher whose wildly extravagant vocabulary simply shows up his complete want of common sense. Others assume the manner of discourses, as the dialogue between Villon and Brisetout in "A Lodging for the Night" illustrates. Does the debate between the two about poverty and riches, circumstance and fate, honor versus degradation, constitute an inauthentic or undramatic use of fiction? Or does it rather, given its rich visual and linguistic context, powerfully illustrate the irresolvability of those issues?

Stevenson, developing his story from the character of a historical figure, cannot take Villon and make him other than what he was: a creative genius whose rough life contrasted sharply with his natural gifts and in all probability ended briefly and painfully. Whether he might have had a different life under different circumstances is really beside the point. He had the life he had, and he was the man he was. Hence the brilliance of the ending: Despite the long and contentious debate, the facing and challenging of complex philosophical questions, when Villon leaves and goes back out into the bitter-cold night, his first thought is for the loss of what he might have had: " 'A very dull old gentleman,' he thought. 'I wonder what his goblets may be worth' " (204).

The opening sentence of "The Pavilion on the Links" ("I was a great solitary when I was young") introduces the retrospective narrative, a characteristic mode of Stevenson's first-person texts. This method of delivering a story invariably implies two stories, the one a story of past events told in sequential order, the other the present story, which remains untold, except for our awareness of its presentness. In other words, a typical retrospective narrative is a story about the past which feels as if it were happening at the moment, thus achieving the immediacy and suspense of present action. But, in fact, all the events have long since vanished into the world of time and memory, recalled partly as a means of reviving the experience, and partly as a way of holding on to life. For Stevenson's retrospective narrators, the past is often the only life that has any vivacity, perhaps even reality, and the stories are told with a vigor and excitement that entrances the reader and makes him imagine himself caught in a wonderful or terrifying web of suspense. Through retrospective narration, Stevenson gives a deeper dimension to past events, keeping them alive in the memory of the survivor-narrator.

The portrait of Frank Cassilis, the narrator of "The Pavilion on the Links," is one that Stevenson periodically produced—a figure alone in the world, virtually living in the wild, whose gypsy life is reflected in his physical surroundings. The description of the countryside surrounding the pavilion captures the mentalities of Cassilis and his equally solitary companion, Northmour: "But there stood in the northern part of the estate, in a wilderness of links and blowing sandhills, and between a plantation and the sea, a small Pavilion or Belvidere, of modern design, which was exactly suited to our wants; and in this hermitage, speaking little, reading much, and rarely associating except at meals, Northmour and I spent four tempestuous winter months" (138). The image of a hermitage is an apt one, for in these situations Stevenson often identifies, or conflates, a disciplined, self-imposed isolation with a kind of religious asceticism. Indeed, along the sea wood not far from the pavilion, "one or two ruined cottages were dotted about the wood; and, according to Northmour, these were ecclesiastical foundations, and in their time had sheltered pious hermits" (140). There is a certain fascination with this life: a world where nothing but the sea and the links are to be encountered, a world with books for companions. This seems the ideal world sought by Cassilis.

It is hardly accidental that so many of Stevenson's protagonists are serious readers—Simon Rolles in *The Suicide Club* studies the patristic fathers, Villon in "A Lodging for the Night" is a student who quotes the Latin bible, and the Reverend Soulis in "Thrawn Janet" is immersed in theology. There is a complex association in Stevenson between the profound and disciplined study of deep books and the ascetic isolation of the (fictional) reader, a connection that leads to a kind of voyeurism, as if investigating the secrets of texts is the equivalent of surreptitiously looking into the secrets of others. It need hardly be remarked that the transference from the intense study of texts to the process of writing them is always present in Stevenson's consciousness, if not in the protagonist's or the narrator's. In some fundamental way there is an ineluctable connection between the self-imposed isolation of the fictional character, with all its attendant implications for personality and destiny, and the position of the creative artist in the world. The voyeurism referred to earlier that recurs in *The Suicide Club* and *The Rajah's Diamond* is nothing more than a fictional reality that inscribes the actual reality of the voyeurism that Stevenson practiced as a writer. It is a voyeurism that he himself viewed as a by-product of an obsessive self-absorption, a kind of narcissism that writers and artists were prone to by the very nature of their work. If Stevenson deliberately fought against this tendency in his own life, it was through the ceaseless pursuit of friends. There is no other writer who worked so hard and so steadily to sustain his friendships—each of his books had its requisite dedicatee—and whose marriage itself may even have been an escape from the prison house of the self. Stevenson lived with the fullness of friends and family in order not to succumb to the tyranny of self. Yet the pace and intensity of the work produced in those last few years in the Pacific were so profound as to virtually ensure his early death, from a sudden cerebral hemorrhage.

Stevenson's Scottish stories always draw on the most rugged features of the beautiful and harsh landscape, features defined by sheer cliffs and craggy rocks, by cold winds and roiling seas. He creates a setting so unremittingly desolate in "Pavilion" that Frank Cassilis declares, "The place had an air of solitude that daunted even a solitary like myself" (139). It is almost impossible to read this story without experiencing the bleakness of the country. It is not for nothing that Stevenson was consistently invoked by twentieth-century writers of handbooks on short-story technique as an exemplary master of "atmosphere" or "description"—terms that highlighted his extraordinary gift for evoking a mood from the most extreme physical settings. But it is not mood alone that conditions the narrative. For Stevenson, place is character, and the windswept links, barren of all vegetation except evergreen shrub, are an appropriate counter for the reclusive Cassilis and Northmour.

The consequences of isolation are manifest in the mental condition and the social behavior of the characters, in Minister Soulis in "Thrawn Janet," or Gordon Darnaway in "The Merry Men." Villon declares that "man is not a solitary animal—*Cui Deus feminam tradit*" (to whom God gives woman) (201–02). Of course, in the mouth of Villon, who is both rogue and poet, the words have a mordancy that almost belies their meaning: Villon needs a woman in the same way he needs meat and drink. Nonetheless, the central idea of the assertion is in fact Stevenson's answer to the damage inflicted on the self by voluntary or enforced isolation—love with the proper woman. In "Pavilion" Frank Cassilis marries Clara Huddlestone and has children, to whom in fact he is relating the events of the story. But Clara is already dead when Cassilis begins his narrative, so the focus remains on the solitariness itself rather than on the love that becomes a salve for that solitariness. In truth, Stevenson's imagination was energized more by the sense of failure his figures experience than by their prospects for love. In a real sense Cassilis and Northmour are outcasts, people on the edge of society, whose lives are separated from intimacy and connection, people who have deliberately removed themselves from the norms of domestic social responsibilities. Although joined by their common love for Clara, which motivates them to protect her father, they are not really against the Italians and are in effect fighting a false battle. As the pavilion goes up in flames—their redoubt against the world—nothing is left but the links scarred "with little patches of burnt furze" (184). The land has gone back to itself, and all the intruders are expelled from its midst.

It is a nice question how an only child, growing up in an indulgent upper-class Edinburgh home, could have so compelling a vision of the loneliness of men and women in the world. But for whatever reasons, it is a vision that controls a substantial portion of his fiction, and creates the atmosphere and tone that dominate his greatest short stories. In a way that is nothing short of modern in its invention and execution, Stevenson made the landscape an element that heightens the loneliness endured by an individual. It came to symbolize both the condition and the consequence of experience. "The Reverend Murdoch Soulis...dwelt in the last years of his life, without relative or servant or any human company, in the small and lonely manse under the Hanging Shaw" (410). The fusion of character and place is so simple, yet so vivid, that it can more easily be understood in our time as a cinematic technique, a graphic and instantaneous representation of subject and form. It is a technique that readers intuitively understood but rarely analyzed. Part of its effectiveness lay in the simplicity of the language, part in the evocation of mood, part in the rhythm itself, with its building up of a sense of finality, and ultimate emptiness, by the suggestion of imminent death and the total absence of human contact. It is a method Stevenson continued through his career, so that by the 1890s he was using coral atolls in the South Seas to illustrate the same terrible loneliness that he earlier identified with the wet and dark rock fastnesses of the Scottish coastline.

3

In "A Lodging for the Night" Stevenson introduces a theme that was to figure prominently in his fiction—chance, or the capriciousness of life. It is a philosophical issue that he treated wryly in *The Suicide Club* and *The Rajah's Diamond,* with comic pathos in "The Misadventures of John Nicholson," and with deep sobriety in "The Merry Men" and "Markheim." It is an issue that focuses on a vision of the world, even of the universe, and of man's place in the world. How do we live our lives? How do we plan for our work, our children, our posterity? Stevenson was an intensely driven man: the thought that he might die and leave nothing behind, that his name would have been "writ in water" and disappear unremembered into the oblivion of time, this was the spur that impelled him to write wherever he was, traveling steerage on a transatlantic boat, on a train across the United States, or on a ninety-foot sloop across the Pacific, coughing blood or running a fever, but never to be without a notebook and pen in his pocket, or a board to write upon in bed. Perhaps the desire for immortality and the refusal to go quietly, however futile that notion to a man who had absorbed Darwin into his consciousness ("Pulvis et Umbra"), compelled him to write unremittingly. For Stevenson wanted to leave behind a small, indelible mark on a stick, so that whoever came after, so long as the stick lasted, would recall and in the process revivify his name. Of course, this is nothing more than the artist's desire for immortality, and there is certainly nothing new here. But with Stevenson it was joined to the late nineteenth century's recognition that in the context of geologic time, the very notion of immortality was something of an anachronism.

It is clear that Stevenson does not approach this issue from the point of view of religion. Like Hawthorne, he draws on the grammar of religion for his subject and his vocabulary, but everlasting perdition, like eternal glory, is simply a trope that enables us to enter the circle where true meaning is explored and debated. Part of that debate has to do with what Stevenson (through Villon) calls "the riddle of man's life." For the pursuit of fame and immortality through writing is as arbitrary as any other pursuit engaged in by people high and low in life.

In "A Lodging for the Night" Stevenson draws together issues of art and immortality, poverty and wealth, and the transiency of all worldly pursuits, with the central idea of a universe ruled by chance. He begins with the first of his memorable opening paragraphs, from which I quote just the first two lines: "It was late in November 1456. The snow fell over Paris with rigorous, relentless persistence; sometimes the wind made a sally and scattered it in flying vortices; sometimes there was a lull, and flake after flake descended out of the black night air, silent, circuitous, interminable" (186). The opening sentence cannot be bettered for its utter simplicity and modernity. The voice is as dateless today as it was in 1878, and it is only the insertion of the year 1456 that gives the sentence (and the reader) a jolt. It has the effect of bringing alive the late medieval city, as if we were in the midst of it, able to enter its *mentalité* while still living in our much later time. Then Stevenson delivers one of the most powerful and evocative descriptions of a city covered in snow, whose whiteness provides a vivid contrast with the darkness of the night. And with the single word "vortices" he draws both on older theories of the universe that posited a rotational movement of cosmic matter around an axis and on nineteenth-century scientific theories that defined the term as a rapid movement of particles of matter around an axis. Thus the word itself merges the past with the present (just as historical fiction is a merger of different periods in time), while its meaning in each case is associated with natural laws or forces that are beyond man's control.

The snow, too, is beyond control, with its ceaseless and unpredictable falling, its complete sovereignty over the lives of the people. Francis Villon, who is educated, can speculate amusingly and just a bit blasphemously on its origins: "Pagan Jupiter plucking geese upon Olympus," or "the holy angels moulting" (186). But the illiterate poor, in contrast, have a sense of awe before natural phenomena, which is captured in a wonderful sentence: "To poor people, looking up under moist eyebrows, it seemed a wonder where it all came from." (186) They are of course looking up to the heavens, and implicitly looking up to God. But Villon is too sophisticated for such absolute and unquestioning faith. He is a "Master of Arts," and his ability to mix classical and religious allusions identifies him as an intellectual who does not take wonders for signs, or at least not for signs of God. Of course Villon's sly humor borders on the blasphemous, and he does not pursue the joke. It is fine for an educated man to play with words and ideas, but it is also dangerous, and not something to treat cavalierly. But in even proposing the question, as Villon does, with a slight anticlerical edge, Stevenson opens up the prospect of religious questioning. Although the story is not one of specifically religious questioning, it is one of moral or ethical questioning, and one that addresses the "riddle of man's life" (192).

The phrase appears when Villon, searching for shelter in the middle of the night, stumbles upon the corpse of a woman who has frozen to death. He goes through her pockets, which are empty, and then discovers two small coins hidden in her stocking. Villon's search is clearly a violation of the woman's person, although the issue is problematic since it touches on a view of death that recurs in many of Stevenson's stories. Simply put, if the spirit is gone, how can one violate the flesh? In "The Physician and the Saratoga Trunk" Dr. Noel insists to the young American whom he cajoles into accompanying a dead body back to London that it is only a "boxful of dead flesh," and nothing to be concerned about. Once death occurs, all that remains is animal protein. Villon states this theme when he remarks upon the woman's bad luck at not being able to spend her coins: "It would have been one more good taste in the mouth, one more smack of the lips, before the devil got the soul, and the body was left to birds and vermin" (192).

Stevenson's picture of Villon searching the prostitute's garter and stocking functions on two levels: on the first, it draws on the historic Villon's well-known fondness for women of all classes, not excluding prostitutes. That the fictional Villon would automatically lift the dead woman's dress to search her stockings suggests that this is hardly a new experience for him. Stevenson builds his portrait from what his contemporaries commonly believed about Villon, deriving their knowledge from their reading of the poetry as well as from a recent French biography, which Stevenson had used as the source for his essay on the poet in *Familiar Studies*. One of Stevenson's methods for constructing character, which he followed in his greatest fictions, is introduced here for the first time. The fictional Villon is built up from the historical Villon, a libertine whose poetry is dense with images of sexuality and love, however complex and problematic its ultimate view. Stevenson never directly suggests here that sexuality is a subject. He uses two vivid and implicative words in a simple subordinate phrase ("but in her stocking, underneath the garter"), and the reader must interpret all else, must recognize that the only way the fictional Villon could have uncovered the coins would have been through the intimate knowledge of women's bodies that was presumably possessed by the real Villon. The small scene is instructive for what it tells us about Stevenson's artistic principles: never disclose more to the reader than is absolutely essential, which is in fact a dramatic method adapted to fiction; and, in historical fiction, always base a complete understanding of character on a contextual knowledge of the historical personage.

The act of searching the dead woman's body to uncover the coins is distinctly psychosexual, and akin to the psychosexuality illustrated in Silas Scuddamore's peering through the peephole for a view of Madame Zephyrine. From a thematic point of view the sexuality has a furtive and secretive aspect to it; from the point of view of presentation, however, it is so unobtrusively managed that its meaning might easily escape the reader. The story could serve as a model for the kind of objective narration that Kipling became famous for and that Hemingway identified with *The Adventures of Huckleberry Finn* and Stephen Crane. That aside, Stevenson's association of sexuality and death, merely hinted at in this brief vignette, is further developed in *Jekyll and Hyde* and achieves a kind of climacteric in the death scene in "The Beach of Falesá."

Of course death is such an overwhelming subject in Stevenson's fiction that there is hardly a story that does not contain a death within the narrative. The issue is one Stevenson places at the center of human existence: we cannot understand life until we recognize and acknowledge the fact of death, that it may come when life appears most indestructible, and that it happens to the "poor jade" in the middle of the night as quickly and unexpectedly as it does to that fine figure of a soldier, Colonel Geraldine's brother. The issue of death is so central in Stevenson that it has often been mistakenly attributed to the genre, viewed as simply part of the machinery of "adventure" or "romance" fiction. Yet it is a mistake to see in Stevenson's treatment nothing more than an early version of Hollywood's action-adventure films where the audience becomes immunized against the realities of death. Quite the contrary: in Stevenson the depiction is so vivid, so graphic, that a *Chicago Tribune* reviewer of *New Arabian Nights* considered the stories so repugnant as to warrant comparison with Emile Zola.

But let us return to one of the central points of this discussion: the idea that life is capricious, and that chance rules in place of fate, or individual will, and overrides the physical and mental endowments of being and personality. When Villon looks at the dead woman, and the coins in his hand, he shakes his head "over the riddle of man's life. Henry V. of England, dying at Vincennes just after he had conquered France, and this poor jade cut off by a cold draught in a great man's doorway, before she had time to spend her couple of whites—it seemed a cruel way to carry on the world" (192). Arbitrary, sudden death, which snatches the highest and the lowest at the moment of their smallest pleasures or their greatest triumphs, is the subject of Villon's thoughts. And the juxtaposition of a king with a prostitute, the conquest of a country with the fierce protection of two small coins, highlights the issue as a philosophical and religious question and gives it a universal application. It also obliterates the distinction between king and prostitute, for chance is an egalitarian ruler, running the world for good or ill, indifferent to high and low, without regard for cause or justice or charity. Stevenson's citation of Henry V adds an appropriate ironic touch since it keeps the allusion local—the English king dying in France a little over thirty years before the action of the story, an incident that Villon could plausibly draw upon to illustrate the fortuitousness of fortune. But what Stevenson actually focuses on is not the casual nature of fortune but the tenuousness and fragility of life's glories or small pleasures. Villon reflects that it would be the better part of wisdom, or at least more satisfying, to leave this world in a moment of pleasure, for there is no guarantee that we will not be snuffed out before our long-prepared-for pleasure is enjoyed: "He would like to use all his tallow before the light was blown out and the lantern broken" (193).

Following the allusion and the reflection, "A Lodging for the Night" moves toward a dramatic debate concerning the nature of chance in individuals' lives. But the idea is there from the start of the story, in the depiction of Villon's debased and animal-like friend Tabary: "[He] had become a thief, just as he might have become the most decent of burgesses, by the imperious chance that rules the lives of human geese and human donkeys" (188). It is as if people are no different from animals, and certainly no better, and, what is most crucial, have absolutely no control over their lives: *imperious chance,* overbearing, dictatorial, domineering. Part of the brilliance of "A Lodging" is Stevenson's reconstitution in his own text of themes in Villon's poetry. Thus in Villon's *The Great Testament:* "The emperor asked him, 'Why are you a pirate?' The other replied, 'Why do you call me a pirate? If I could change my poor vessel for your throne, I would be an emperor, like you" (*The Poems of François Villon,* trans. H. De Vere Stackpoole [London: Hutchinson, 1913], p. 123). This observation is precisely the substance of the debate between Brisetout and Villon: "But if I had been born lord of Brisetout, and you had been the poor scholar Francis, would the difference have been any the less? . . . Should not I have been the soldier, and you the thief?" (200–01). Villon's argument throughout is that circumstances make people what they are. What is character but circumstance, or thievery but poverty, or virtue but the absence of hunger? The lord who takes Villon in from the cold, offers the hospitality of his home, addresses him with high sentiments, and extols the beauty of moral virtue believes that what he is saying is inherent in the structure of the world: that people are good or evil, follow truth or wrap themselves in falsehood, according to some preordained scheme by which absolute values like honor, integrity, and loyalty are rewarded. These beliefs are ingrained in the lord of Brisetout and fundamental to his vision of the world. Villon, who is intellectually more acute, better trained, and nimbler in argument, drives Brisetout to anger, for he undermines the nobleman's system of belief which assigns meaning and value, order and design to the world.

What Stevenson is doing here, and in other stories, is calling into relief a fundamental but unanswerable question about our experience: are we responsible for our lives or are they beyond our control? The question arises because so many elements of Stevenson's fiction appear to derive from it, or contribute to it. Thus the violence that is such a powerful and pervasive feature of Stevenson's work is frequently presented as impulsive and completely without warning. The murder of Thevenin is swift and unexpected: "Thevenin was just opening his mouth to claim another victory, when Montigny leaped up, swift as an adder, and stabbed him to the heart. The blow took effect before he had time to utter a cry, before he had time to move" ("Lodging," 190). The rapidity of the act reveals something of the personality of the historical Montigny who was a hard case, older than Villon by two years, born into a noble family (a detail Stevenson quietly incorporates in his text), twice sentenced to death, once for murder. The violence in Stevenson's fiction is stitched into the narrative, with the aim of making it as functional, and surprising, as life itself. Stevenson does not focus on the experience of death so much as on the act of violence, along with the victim's physical response. It is a quintessentially modern method, and one that might profitably be compared with Hemingway's, particularly in the interchapters of *In Our Time*.

Stevenson can never stop ruminating upon the question of how we live in the world when our lives hang by the slimmest of threads, when nothing but the merest chance keeps our small personal triumphs from being taken away. It is bound up with his view of history and where we stand in the universe. We pass from this journey or voyage— two terms descriptive and reflective of Stevenson's most elemental plot structure—into nothingness. "Life is a little vapour that passeth away, as we are told by those in holy orders" (220). Occasionally there are reminders of those long forgotten, such as the shoe buckle that the narrator discovers when he dives into the sea in "The Merry Men," a modern relic not all that different than Yorick's skull and one that poses the same question: is this all that remains of a man? If Stevenson were religious he might have had an easier time resolving the riddle. But Villon with his licentiate in theology, Simon Rolles with his church history, the Reverend Soulis with his sermons—none of them has an answer.

Of course, the question might be wrong; it need not be the one posed by Villon as to why there is suffering in the world, or why there are the hungry and the well fed, thieves and saints (or at least what approximate to saints, the righteous). There is no logic that explains why one suffers and another thrives, or why the two could not be switched, or why either's fortune can suddenly be snuffed out. In "The Sire de Malétroit's Door," for example, Denis's life is changed twice: first when he is caught inside the house and faces death in the morning, and second when he embarks on a new life with Blanche, having discovered his love for her in the course of the long evening. Critics who dismiss the story as sentimental would do well to see it in the context of Stevenson's other texts, for just as chance can destroy a life, so can it give a life, as it does for Denis. Similarly, there is no presumption as to what an individual may do in any specific situation. When Villon leaves Brisetout's house in the early hours of the morning, without robbing or murdering him, he reflects to himself, in a brilliant close to the story, " 'A very dull old gentleman,' he thought. 'I wonder what his goblets may be worth' " (204). That he leaves the house quietly may be a nice ending, but Villon could just as easily (and plausibly) have killed him. What is more to the point is that Stevenson, in the very design of his plot, allows for the open possibilities that constitute the realities of life: nothing is fixed or determined, and character and behavior, in fiction as in life, are conditioned by circumstances that are often beyond our control. Thus Stevenson might agree with Markheim that his life was bound at birth by the "giants" of circumstance and still reject the argument as nothing more than a plea for the failure of will. Character is not destiny, nor circumstance fate; but together they constitute life, and it is life that Stevenson's characters struggle valiantly, even desperately, to maintain.

4

"Jekyll and Hyde" has become a virtual synonym for good and evil, for the popular idea that every man has within himself an antithetical other self, and that the two selves exist in a state of unresolved tension or open conflict. The influence of Stevenson's story was powerful enough that as early as 1928 *Funk and Wagnalls New Standard Dictionary* cited "Hyde" and "Jekyll" as separate entries, as if the fictional creation were two distinct characters, each of whom could then be referred to the other. By the time of *Webster's Third New International Dictionary* (1961) the phrase "Jekyll-and-Hyde" enjoyed its own definition as an adjective: "of, relating to, or resembling a person who leads a double life or who has two apparently distinct characters one of which is good and the other evil." No subject in Stevenson would appear to have a greater general recognition; indeed, *Jekyll-and-Hyde* is an eponym that everybody knows, even if not everyone could identify its source. What is the explanation for such a widespread "understanding"? There is of course the broad interest in the traditional literary device of the double. And the modern psychological concern with questions of individuation, split personality, and ego formation undoubtedly go far toward explaining the fascination with a late-nineteenth-century story that was sold as nothing more than a cheap thriller but became the text for countless Sunday sermons.

Jekyll and Hyde, which Stevenson tells us came to him in a dream, dramatizes a subject that compelled the writer from the beginning of his career—the puzzle of duality in human nature. What is at the center of the exploration is the nature of human character itself or, put another way, the nature of the self. "Villon cringed, and brought up many servile words of apology; at a crisis of this sort, the beggar was uppermost in him, and the man of genius hid his head with confusion" (197). And from "The Merry Men," the narrator's first view of his uncle Gordon Darnaway after many years: "He was a sour, small, bilious man, with a long face and very dark eyes; fifty-six years old, sound and active in body, and with an air somewhat between that of a shepherd and that of a man following the sea" (332). Each example reveals Stevenson's fundamental belief that identity is neither obvious nor singular. Clearly Villon has a variety of aspects to his personality and cannot be reduced to either artist or beggar, any more than he can be identified solely as thief or student or lover or philosopher. In a sense

Stevenson shares Walt Whitman's conviction that each man is large and contains multitudes; indeed, it was his reading of Whitman's poetry, and in particular "Song of Myself," that inspired him to address issues of complex personality as directly as he does. The notion that men wear masks to cover up their inner selves can be traced as easily to Whitman as to Hawthorne, whose stories are rife with the image of the veil as a cover for the self.

Stevenson was always aware of the outer mask ("all men are better than this disguise that grows about and stifles them" [404]). In the description of Villon quoted above, the poet adapts to the situation, presents himself as a mendicant, and plays on the charity of the noble lord. But the artist in him is far from a mendicant; he is arrogant, contentious, sarcastic, and disdainful. Is the beggar then mere disguise? The answer is no, for one of Stevenson's convictions is that we assume the personality we don or practice. Villon, as long as he begs, is a beggar; he is a poet as long as he composes *ballades*—just as Simon Rolles is both thief and theologian, ascetic scholar and avid pupil of the secrets of the underworld. One does not exist to the exclusion of the other; the criminal and the religious coexist within the same individual. We are, in other words, what we appear to be.

In the sentence from "The Merry Men," Stevenson compares Gordon Darnaway to a shepherd and a sailor. The two could not be more dissimilar, the one rural, quiet, perhaps even contemplative, and the other placed in the middle of an active, violent, and perpetually changing world. The shepherd rarely wanders from his place, while the sailor is forever without a home. Stevenson builds up a complex picture of Darnaway in the paragraph, but here in an almost casual detail he divides his personality in such a way that he cannot easily be classified according to type. The elements of the shepherd are there in his rootedness, his care for his daughter, and his instinct for the isolation and quiet of his home. Yet he is also a man of the sea, surrounded by the sea, with potentialities for power that reveal themselves in the violent act that is at the center of the narrative. Although there may be qualities shared by shepherd and sailor, it is the stark contrast that is immediately called into question, a contrast reflective of Stevenson's portraiture. It is not always a division in personality that is crucial but the recognition that there are differing strands in any single personality, and that those strands cannot easily be separated. Stevenson's stylistic device ("between … a shepherd and … a man following the sea" [332]) is a linguistic fissure fundamental to his view of personality and, in a larger sense, to his perception of the world. By means of a simple preposition he exposes the modernist's sense of the world's uncertainty and ambiguity.

"The Pavilion on the Links" provides a striking illustration of Stevenson's presentation of personality:

> My wife and I, a man and a woman, have often agreed to wonder how a person could be, at the same time, so handsome and so repulsive as Northmour. He had the appearance of a finished gentleman; his face bore every mark of intelligence and courage; but you had only to look at him, even in his most amiable moment, to see that he had the temper of a slaver captain. I never knew a character that was both explosive and revengeful to the same degree; he combined the vivacity of the south with the sustained and deadly hatreds of the north; and both traits were plainly written on his face, which was a sort of danger signal. In person, he was tall, strong, and active; his hair and complexion very dark; his features handsomely designed, but spoiled by a menacing expression. (146)

There could hardly be a more dramatic example of duality in the early fiction. Just five years later, in *Treasure Island*, Stevenson introduced Long John Silver, whose capacity for calculated evil was offset by charm, courage, and even a kind of verbal felicity. There is no question that some of Northmour's "traits" were carried over to Silver. But the issue that is central to the portrait is the enigma of personality. How can Northmour be both handsome and repulsive, amiable and cruel? How can he possess the liveliness of the south and the remorseless vengeance of the north? What Stevenson does here is really quite simple: he adapts a divided personality to the larger aims of his narrative. Thus the division within Northmour mirrors the division that the text establishes between north and south, cold and warmth, dark and light, war and peace. A division within the self often reflects a division within the text, and the irreconcilable warfare taking place within the individual can only lead to a cataclysmic ending, in this case the fire that destroys the pavilion. Northmour's death, reported at the end in passing by the narrator, is symbolically identified with the demise of the pavilion, and his divided personality is nothing more than an image of the pavilion itself, a cold Scottish retreat of Italian design, a structure ill equipped and out of place yet curiously supportive of its residents and visitors. The visage is the visitation; perhaps we bring upon ourselves the destiny we seek to resist, just as we fail at the freedom we imagine we cherish.

Unquestionably the single story that most exemplifies duality in man, apart from *Jekyll and Hyde,* is "Markheim," originally published as part of a collection of "horror" stories in a volume titled *The Broken Shaft.* Stevenson used the form to focus attention on the divided self, and its implications for behavior and conscience. It is a story brilliant in its simplicity, its movement, and its psychological acuity. Markheim, a youngish man who has steadily resorted to more serious crimes as a result of his gambling debts, enters an antique dealer's shop on Christmas Eve, engages the flinty old man in conversation, then murders him with a long knife. He sets about to rob the store, which is closed off from the afternoon light and filled with clocks and mirrors of all sizes and shapes. In the process of moving through the house, he suddenly encounters another presence. This presence, or "visitant," engages Markheim in conversation, and the two debate the path that the murderer's life has taken. The visitant offers to help the murderer escape, but after the long colloquy Markheim decides to give himself up. As the dealer's servant girl returns to the shop, he tells her, "Go for the police...I have killed your master." Simple enough on the surface, the story is a stunning achievement on a number of levels—as a psychological study of conscience; as a discourse on good and evil; as a textual compression of time and space, light and dark. It certainly looks back to Poe and E. T. A. Hoffman, just as it looks forward to Henry James's "The Jolly Corner." But this is not a ghost story where the protagonist is visited by images of his past and future selves; rather it is a story where *memory* renders visible the past. Markheim vividly recalls his experiences as a child, experiences in which the morbid alternated with the joyous, where the open fields contrasted with the posters of notorious murderers hung up as sensational attractions at a Sunday fair. Stevenson takes for his subject memory and consciousness, twin images that generate the action and envelop the reader. Virtually the entire story takes place in the mind of the protagonist.

The question of duality can be readily placed in a modern context by substituting psychoanalytic concepts focusing on the ego, and in "Markheim" this approach would provide a plausible reading. Another way of examining duality is to approach it from the vantage point of good and evil—a common view of *Jekyll and Hyde*. But good and evil are more complicated, or perhaps more problematic, than a simple schematic division of the self suggests. Without question the nature of evil is one of Stevenson's major subjects, from his earliest fiction to his last unfinished texts. Although the treatment may not appear as profoundly philosophical as in Melville, where evil is immanent in the world, without origin or explanation, or as psychological as in Hawthorne, where the fall from grace is replicated in every individual's experience, it is in fact a fusion of both. Stevenson's focus on motivation and behavior foregrounds psychology, while his alternation of internal monologue with dialogic debate draws attention to the philosophical argument. Thus psychology and philosophy are joined for both dramatic and theoretic purposes.

What is the nature of evil? In "Thrawn Janet" the answer is complex. The devil is not the issue in this classic tale of witchcraft, but rather the minister's inability to perceive let alone acknowledge the fact of evil and its power in people's lives. This story, a masterpiece of linguistic realism, has always been considered among the strongest of Stevenson's achievements. He himself had a high regard for it, as he wrote to Lady Taylor, to whom he dedicated the volume of tales in which it appeared: "Of 'Thrawn Janet,' which I like very much myself, you say nothing, thus uttering volumes; but it is plain that people cannot always agree. I do not think it is a wholesome part of me that broods on the evil in the world and man; but I do not think that I get harm from it; possibly my readers may, which is more serious; but at any account, I do not purpose to write more in this vein" (*The Letters of Robert Louis Stevenson,* vol. 5, ed. Bradford A. Booth and Ernest Mehew [New Haven: Yale University Press, 1995], p. 365). Stevenson, reflecting on the completed text, wonders about his preoccupation with a subject upon which no definitive conclusion can be drawn. It is also interesting to observe his view of the creative process, that although the subject may be oppressive, its working out has no deleterious effect on the artist. (He acknowledges that the same assurance may not so easily be granted his readers, thus inadvertently giving credence to Plato's fear that the artist is a dangerous person because his work cannot be controlled and its effect on audiences is unpredictable.) What is daunting about "Thrawn Janet" is not the diabolic (or the horror) but the unknown, and the realization that there is a core of evil in the world that can be denied only at one's peril. In effect, the diabolic served Stevenson as a convenient frame for focusing attention on an aspect of life that appears to resist rational explanation. Although the villagers have no evidence that Janet is a witch, and the minister is a learned man whose courage is sustained by his belief in his own rationality, in the end neither Janet hanging from the thin tape nor the minister's resort to a theology of unremitting Calvinism offers any rational explanation for what occurred. If one wants a modern parallel for "Thrawn Janet," one can do no better than to consider the films of Alfred Hitchcock.

In "Markheim" Stevenson melds the issues of duality and good and evil in a story of conscience, redemption, and the narcissism of consciousness. Confronted by the visitant who appears to know him, Markheim exclaims:

> "Know me!" cried Markheim. "Who can do so? My life is but a travesty and slander on myself. I have lived to belie my nature. All men do; all men are better than this disguise that grows about and stifles them. You see each dragged away by life, like one whom bravos have seized and muffled in a cloak; if they had their own control—if you could see their faces, they would be altogether different, they would shine out for heroes and saints! I am worse than most; myself is more overlaid; my excuse is known to me and God. But had I the time, I could disclose myself." (404)

Markheim's plea is of course self-serving, blaming fate for his criminal conduct and his current condition. But if the argument appears nothing but an attempt at self-justification, it cannot be dismissed altogether. The belief that our outward life bears no relation to who we are is made with telling effect in this paragraph. It is as if "life" kidnaps us from our better selves, holds us in bondage to a behavior that is neither a genuine reflection nor an adequate expression of what we believe or feel. Markheim's cry is for the preservation of his own identity and against the false separation between our exterior and interior lives, of having our physical selves function as surrogates for our purer but captive spiritual beings. In a passage that has profound historical roots, Markheim declares the dilemma of his existence: "Evil and good run strong in me, haling me both ways. I do not love the one thing, I love all" (407). That sense of an individual at war with himself received its seminal expression in St. Paul's letter to the Romans ("But I see another law in my members, warring against the law of my mind, and bringing me into captivity to the law of sin which is in my members" [Rom. 7:23]), and in two telling descriptions in Sir Thomas Browne, whom Stevenson "sedulously" imitated when he was learning to write, and who as late as 1893 he continued to list in his private canon of revered writers ("With Mr Stevenson's compliments," undated letter, Parrish Collection, Princeton University Library): "The heart of man is the place the devill dwels in; I feele sometimes a hell within my selfe"; and "There is another man within mee that's angry with mee, rebukes, commands, and dastards me" (Browne, *Religio Medici and Other Works*, ed. L.C. Martin [Oxford: Clarendon, 1964], 49, 64).

This idea of inward division, that deep within the self there is a powerful disposition to evil that cannot be overcome simply by the mind's conscious desire for good—Milton's "hateful siege / Of contraries" (*Paradise Lost* 9:119–22)—is central in much of Stevenson's fiction. We have seen how pervasive the image of life as war is in Stevenson. Markheim's internal struggle represents a parallel version of the general struggle embodied in the social realm. In other words, just as life is a battlefield (in the words of Colonel Geraldine in *The Suicide Club*), Markheim and Gordon Darnaway and Northmour are engaged in a form of warfare within themselves, fighting to break out of the soul-destroying conflicts they face. There is a connection between the individual world and the social world, between the war within the self and the war in the larger world, for Stevenson's fiction is always set in the larger world and is never meant to be contained within the contours of the individual or egoistic consciousness. For the characters, the war within is frequently justified as the inevitable consequence of the war without, and the war without can be seen as a projection of the war within. Thus the battle royal between the "man-eaters" and the "voices" in "The Isle of Voices" serves symbolically as a clash between competing forms of ignorance and evil, and as a projection of the disturbed state of Keola's mind, his being torn between the laziness and greed that got him marooned on the island in the first place, and his desire to return home to his wife and his life in Hawaii.

It would be a mistake to think that there is ever a resolution, let alone a peaceful conclusion, to the unending Darwinian battle that is life. One of the reasons the endings to Stevenson's fictions are so problematic is precisely because they are not envisioned in any way as conclusions. The stories are texts whose deeper narratives are still unfolding, or which take different directions, following the fortuitous details that "complete" the action proper. Stevenson's Villon goes out into the night, wondering to himself whether (at the very least) he should have robbed his host of his goblets. That the real Villon disappeared from Paris shortly after a major robbery in Christmas 1456, and that his final end remains a mystery, gives a curious historical veracity to the text's fictional and formal logic.

But as St. Paul and Sir Thomas Browne and Milton tell us, the mind is all, and in the conception lies the crime. Thus the devil (if that is indeed who the "visitant" represents) tells Markheim that he is indifferent to his subject's crime: "[A]nd it is not because you have killed a dealer, but because your name is Markheim, that I offer to forward your escape" (406). He then makes the declaration that directly echoes Satan's "Evil be thou my Good" (*Paradise Lost* 9:110): "Evil, for which I live, consists not in action but in character; the bad man is dear to me, not the bad act" (406). This attitude defines the idea of character and the position of good and evil in the world. If it is not the act that defines the evil, then it must be the perpetrator of the act; if it is not in the deed itself, then it is in its imagining. This serves to shift the attention away from the action and toward the conception. In effect, the action itself might be nothing more than a sophisticated decoy, a divertissement, entertaining in its own right but not really the main event. Good and evil then are exclusively centered in the mind of the individual, irrespective of whether or not he commits a crime. Conversely, if the individual is well loved by friends and family, no crime he may commit alters their judgment of or their feeling for him. Dr. Noel's comment to the young man in "The Physician and the Saratoga Trunk" is a fair description of this position: "Credulous youth, the horror with which blind and unjust law regards an action never attaches to the doer in the eyes of those who love him; and if I saw the friend of my heart return to me out of seas of blood he would be in no way changed in my affection.... good and ill are a chimera; there is nought in life except destiny" (40).

Of course, this cannot be taken as an absolute statement of Stevenson's own position. But it is interesting for its philosophical dimension. Stevenson opens up the question of evil in terms of the nature of man, of his actions in the world, and of both in the context of time or "destiny." These issues are complicated, and neither the visitant nor Dr. Noel is a model for emulation. Yet their positions illustrate the kind of moral complexity that is articulated in all of Stevenson's texts. If good and evil are indeed a "chimera," then what is an individual's role in life? How are values like love, loyalty, honor, and courage maintained in a world devoid of meaning, yet one where evil is manifest? One answer is that the world is not empty, that evil does have its counterpart, and it is precisely that which gives Stevenson's characters their capacity to survive and their faith to continue living. If "Markheim" is a psychomachy, a struggle of good and evil for the soul of man, the ending is not on the side of evil: "If I be condemned to evil acts ... there is still one door of freedom open: I can cease from action. If my life be an ill thing, I can lay it down" (408). In many ways this passage strikes at the heart of Stevenson's belief that it is *thought* that determines character, the mind that makes the man, rather than the acts performed. It is not recognized often enough how much of Stevenson's fiction turns on protagonists who use their intelligence to survive, who indeed survive only because of their intelligence. The best-known examples are Jim Hawkins in *Treasure Island* and David Balfour in *Kidnapped,* the latter getting some very simple advice from his minister upon leaving home: "Be soople, David, be soople." But it can be seen in the shorter fiction as well, in "The Merry Men," as Charlie unravels the mystery bit by bit; in "The Bottle Imp," as the resourceful wife figures out how to dispose of the bottle and save her husband's soul; or in "The Isle of Voices," where the presumably ignorant Hawaiian sizes up the white sailors' inability to believe anything but their own stories and thus decides that the better part of discretion is not to reveal the mystery of Kalamake's lantern. This focus on intelligence belies a common perception of Stevenson as an adventure writer whose compelling stories exist solely on the level of physical action. But Stevenson is nothing if not intellectual, and his dramatic texts represent the embodiment of his ideas.

5

There are aspects of Stevenson's work that are even now only dimly recognized, particularly his treatment of love. It has been repeated unendingly that Stevenson does not write about women or sex, yet no reader of these stories would understand where that idea comes from. Love is at the heart of these tales. With an innocent young man like Silas Q. Scuddamore in "The Physician and the Saratoga Trunk," love may be nothing more than a blind infatuation, made mildly comic by its fastening on a woman of dubious reputation. With Frank Cassilis in "The Pavilion on the Links," it is a part of adult life, and a woman is someone to fight over, even to die for. In "The Bottle Imp" and "The Isle of Voices," love has all the cherished qualities of that most enduring of relations, a good marriage. But Stevenson was not his characters, neither innocent, nor roseate, and he was fully conscious of the role played by sexuality in the power struggle between men and women. In "Story of the Bandbox," Lady Vandeleur shrewdly remarks that one night's "adroit submission" to her husband can buy her many months of insouciant disobedience. It has not been noticed how often Stevenson portrays sex as a commodity of exchange, concealed behind the tapestry of marriage in "The Sire de Malétroit's Door," or promoted openly in *Jekyll and Hyde.* And so often sex and love become confused, as in "Olalla," where the narrator's illness places him in a house redolent with decay, one that could have come out of the pages of Poe, and with figures to match. Yet the atmosphere of death and degeneration in no way inhibits the narrator's sensuous description of Olalla's beauty, and by extension his own involuntary attraction toward her, an attraction that is the twin counterpart of her deep melancholy and inconsolable suffering. Love cannot surmount such pain and fatality, and Stevenson converts Olalla in the end to a symbol of human suffering.

One of Stevenson's most consistent habits is to depict love as an experience that emerges in a momentary flash, almost before the character fully apprehends it. "It was only a black dress that caught Dick Naseby's eye; but it took possession of his mind, and all other thoughts departed. He drew near and the girl turned around. Her face startled him; it was a face he wanted; and he took it in at once like breathing air." This as early as 1879, from "The Story of a Lie" (671). For Stevenson, love at first sight is not a quaint vestige of chivalric romance, but the visceral experience of men and women in the modern world, irrespective of whether the story is placed in medieval or contemporary times. Even Will, the detached and reflective philosopher ("Will o' the Mill"), cannot help but be instantly invigorated by the beauty and grace of Marjory ("he could see her face, as she leaned forward ... and the thought of her took its place in his mind beside that of dawn" [378]). A later narrator is "transfixed" with surprise at his first sight of the doomed Olalla. "Her loveliness struck to my heart; she glowed in the deep shadow of the gallery, a gem of colour; her eyes took hold upon mine and clung there ... we thus stood face to face, drinking each other in" (440). This kind of expression is a way of getting at the physicality that Stevenson associated with love, or, put another way, it becomes the language of sexual desire. Stevenson was a writer of plain prose, and his reluctance to treat women fully in some of his longer fictions was a deliberate response to the tight, stultifying constraints of Victorian publishing. Rather than deal with sexual relations opaquely, as Henry James and George Meredith did, he preferred to leave them out altogether, or cant them obliquely. But as these examples suggest, whenever Stevenson's males encounter women they are instantly affected both in their mind and their gut. They are virtually struck dumb, and are momentarily immobile. Given his passion for a clear and limpid prose, Stevenson cannot help but convey the eroticism with which the men gaze upon the women. Denis de Beaulieu, with only two hours to live, and trying hard to concentrate his mind, must still be admiring the body of Blanche de Malétroit, the woman he has been ordered to marry if he would save his life: "so plump and yet so fine, with a warm brown skin, and the most beautiful hair ... in the whole world of womankind" (219).

Unquestionably the most seductive description of love comes in "The Beach of Falesá," a graphic tale of violence, racism, and greed played out on a remote Pacific island, much like the one Stevenson settled on in the last years of his life. The narrator of the story, John Wiltshire, is one of the writer's most original creations. A trader, a self-exile, an alcoholic, and a bigot (his use of the word *kanaka* carries all the contempt of the colonial European for the indigenous Polynesian), this unpromising figure of a man not only becomes the story's hero but Stevenson's most tender lover. As the story opens with his arrival on Falesá, he is greeted warmly by a rival trader, Case, who insists that he must take a "wife" for his recreational pleasure, and offers to set him up with a native girl who is just coming out of the water. "She had been fishing; all she wore was a chemise, and it was wetted through, and a cutty sark at that. She was young and very slender for an island maid, with a long face, a high forehead, and a sly, strange, blindish look between a cat's and a baby's" (518). The picture of Uma coming out of the water, with her wet shift outlining the curves of her body, almost prefigures the matchless sequence seventy years later of Ursula Andress emerging from the sea wearing nothing but a white bikini and a hunting knife. And just as James Bond was taken with Honey Ryder, responding glibly to her query (" 'What are you doing here?' 'I'm just looking' "), Wiltshire is visibly impressed with Uma: " 'Who's she?' said I. 'She'll do' " (518). His language reflects the laconic and vernacular realism of the text, and is distinguished from the romantic description of the earlier stories. But the impulse is the same: the arresting physical appearance of a woman and the effect she has on a man.

When Wiltshire agrees to a fake wedding, replete with a sham and cruel marriage certificate, Uma shows up in regal splendor and unwittingly shames the coarse and homeless exile. For the first time, he sees her not as an island girl, fit for a night's pleasure, but as a proud and beautiful woman. Even his language changes, and becomes quietly poetic. "She was dressed and scented; her kilt was of fine tapa, looking richer in the folds than any silk; her bust, which was of the colour of dark honey, she wore bare only for some half a dozen necklaces of seeds and flowers; and behind her ears and in her hair, she had the scarlet flowers of the hybiscus" (522). After the ceremony, when they return to his house, Wiltshire continues to look upon this woman who has so profoundly affected him. "And what with her dress—for all there was so little of it, and that native enough—what with her fine tapa and fine scents, and her red flowers and seeds that were quite as bright as jewels, only larger—it came over me she was a kind of a countess really, dressed to hear great singers at a concert, and no even mate for a poor trader like myself" (523). This man who has lived for so many years among beachcombers and exiles, the wash of Europeans in the Pacific, yet has always held fast to the superiority of the white man, suddenly realizes that he has married above him, and that to a "native" woman. In one of the story's most stunning images, Wiltshire discovers that his sexual desire has been transformed into passionate love: "It had never taken me like that before; but the want of her took and shook all through me, like the wind in the luff of a sail" (524). Thus begins the redemption of a common man. And if John Wiltshire could be redeemed in the plot of a story, then "The Beach of Falesá" could be the emancipation of Robert Louis Stevenson. For with the publication of this raw and violent tale of contemporary passion and greed and race, the writer from Scotland finally cut his ties with the nineteenth century. In effect, he said good-bye to all those restrictions and inhibitions that shadowed and constricted all artists who wanted to confront the world directly. Stevenson, as Henry James said, was in the "final phase" of his career, and in the later words of Graham Greene, he had struck "granite" on those islands. His death, at the peak of his powers, was surely a decision of the gods.

Stevenson offers a kaleidoscope of people striving in the world, searching for love, the movement of men and women in the cities, the beauty and serenity of nature, and its alternative, rough, brutal, and threatening. And through it all man attempts to cut a passage for his life, through love, through work, much as Freud would say. Stevenson's stories are just such passages, "pictures" designed to hold the reader's interest, to suspend her in time while she follows the exploits of the Prince of Bohemia, or disentangles Kokua's dilemma in "The Bottle Imp." But more profoundly they are fables for our time, glimpses of time past and portents of the future. For Stevenson never saw life as a momentary flicker but viewed the living moment as an image of all moments in man's history. Thus he could write "historical" stories and make them seem contemporary; fantastic *Märchen* and make them truer to life than some of the grimmest realism of his contemporaries; and contemporary tales that were unparalleled in their authenticity and immediacy. The striking character of Stevenson's stories is that they wear well—that is, they can be read today with the same vividness as they were by his own readers. This is an extremely rare quality, one that he shares most notably with Ernest Hemingway, and among his contemporaries there are few, if any, who can match that achievement. His great co-equals, Henry James, Thomas Hardy, and George Meredith, are all time-bound, or put another way, one is always aware that the brilliance of their work is contained or constrained within the limits of their late-Victorian world. Although Stevenson shared that world, its "landscape" recedes into the background because of the intensity of the psychodrama and the immediacy of the connection that is made with the reader. *Jekyll and Hyde* may be late Victorian, but few contemporary readers—if they can hold the film versions in abeyance—become absorbed in that story because of the historical period. One of the reasons Stevenson has survived in the minds of readers around the world is because his insights into people's behavior, their needs and desires, their fears and secrets, are so completely understandable. The thwarted ambition of Simon Rolles, the cleric who cannot advance even though his talent is exemplary, speaks to everybody's sense of the unfairness, or inequity, in life and work. The desire of Will to have a life that is both satisfying and fulfilling, to marry the woman he loves, to accomplish something of value, is countermanded by his own self-centeredness and his blindness to simple reality: that he has driven away the one woman who truly loves him. Will could be seen, with little exaggeration, as an early version of John Marcher in Henry James's "The Beast in the Jungle," the one man to whom nothing was ever to happen, a beautiful mind, and a wasted life.

Robert Louis Stevenson's outlook was fundamentally modern. Both in the subjects that quickened his imagination and in the forms he devised for their expression, he stands at the very beginning of the modernist movement in literature. The individual isolated in a physical universe with no moral center; the fortuitousness that circumscribes and determines our lives, to the virtual exclusion of all will or desire; the existence of evil in the world and the mystery of its origin and nature; the intensity of sexual desire and the transformative nature of love, both of which are separate from the condition of marriage— these are among the issues in Stevenson's fiction that can readily be seen as modernist. Running through all of these issues is Stevenson's fundamental doubt—a quintessential modernist doubt—regarding the reliability of our knowledge, particularly as it affects our judgment of peoples' motivation and behavior. He demonstrates repeatedly how large parts of our lives are shrouded in shadows and darkness, where the ability to see, let alone determine meaning, is either dubious or problematic. In the beginning paragraphs of "The Sire de Malétroit's Door" Denis de Beaulieu searches for a way home ("It is an eerie and mysterious position to be thus submerged in opaque blackness in an almost unknown town") and winds up caught in a trap he can neither escape nor understand. The sense of being caught up in shadows and half-lights is so pervasive in Stevenson that we almost come to assume this as the condition of his world, a condition reflected in the wonderful opening line of "The Beach of Falesá": "I saw that island first when it was neither night nor morning." (513) Yet he is one of the great open-air writers, one whose description of landscape, mountain, valley, and sea has little competition. We might expect the majesty of natural settings to detract from the darkness endemic to the stories, but in fact it contributes to deepening the tone, for in the midst of great clarity there is essential ambiguity.

Perhaps the most telling illustration comes in "The Merry Men," Stevenson's magnificent "fantasia" to the sea: "A great change passed at that moment over the appearance of the bay. It was no more that clear, visible interior, like a house roofed with glass, where the green, submarine sunshine slept so stilly" (345). This is not simply an example of the discrepancy between the appearance of things and their reality. It reflects a deeper, more complex idea: that material things change, that essential reality is not inalterably fixed and thus graspable in its essence. If Stevenson's stories teach us anything, it is exactly the opposite: that strive as we might to secure the truth, the truth escapes us, or is simply undiscoverable. In "The Merry Men" the ocean is at one and the same time a graveyard and a wonder of creation, depending upon the moment and the observer. So when the narrator, having dived down into the sea and come upon the shoe buckle of a drowned sailor, reflects at length on the symbolism of the artifact, on the wrecked ship and all the lost sailors, "the full horror of the charnel ocean burst upon my spirit." But when he returns to shore, and after a brief prayer is refreshed, he looks with calm "on that great bright creature, God's ocean" (347), and reinforces the profound paradox of terror and beauty.

This ambiguity, which discloses itself linguistically as well as structurally, is central to Stevenson's vision of the world. There are few, if any, plain truths, despite Stevenson's formidable effort to make everything plain to the reader. This is one of the defining features of his fiction, that the lucidity of the style conceals the complexity of the meaning. Inevitably, this feature deceived casual readers into believing that the stories were nothing more than the sum of their plots, sustained exercises in easy entertainment. It also accounts for the criticism that they often collapse at the end, that Stevenson could not maintain the intensity and suspense that mark the extraordinary openings of his narratives. If the stories are viewed from the perspective of a modernist, however, then the endings are perfectly consonant with the epistemological doubt that dominates the artist's imagination. Endings, in particular neat endings, are fundamentally false to the reality to which Stevenson adheres, a reality faithful to all the uncertainties and confusions that constitute our living in the world. Stevenson's stories often end abruptly, but that abruptness means only that the action goes no further, that the characters continue on, if they do, in other places along other paths. The inconclusiveness of these endings is both dramatic and symbolic—the completion of the action on one level, and its subversion on another. For despite the brilliance and propulsion of the narrative, Stevenson refuses to falsify a central idea, that uncertainty and ambiguity are not only part of our language but conditions of our existence.

———

BARRY MENIKOFF is a professor of English and American literature at the University of Hawaii and one of the world's leading authorities on Robert Louis Stevenson. He also edited the Modern Library Classics edition of *Kidnapped*.

Binding for the English edition of *New Arabian Nights* (LONDON, 1882).

NEW ARABIAN
NIGHTS

THE SUICIDE CLUB

STORY OF THE YOUNG MAN WITH THE CREAM TARTS

During his residence in London, the accomplished Prince Florizel of Bohemia gained the affection of all classes by the seduction of his manner and by a well-considered generosity. He was a remarkable man even by what was known of him; and that was but a small part of what he actually did. Although of a placid temper in ordinary circumstances, and accustomed to take the world with as much philosophy as any ploughman, the Prince of Bohemia was not without a taste for ways of life more adventurous and eccentric than that to which he was destined by his birth. Now and then, when he fell into a low humour, when there was no laughable play to witness in any of the London theatres, and when the season of the year was unsuitable to those field sports in which he excelled all competitors, he would summon his confidant and Master of the Horse, Colonel Geraldine, and bid him prepare himself against an evening ramble. The Master of the Horse was a young officer of a brave and even temerarious disposition. He greeted the news with delight, and hastened to make ready. Long practice and a varied acquaintance of life had given him a singular facility in disguise; he could adapt not only his face and bearing, but his voice and almost his thoughts, to those of any rank, character, or nation; and in this way he diverted attention from the Prince, and sometimes gained admission for the pair into strange societies. The civil authorities were never taken into the secret of these adventures; the imperturbable courage of the one and the ready invention and chivalrous devotion of the other had brought them through a score of dangerous passes; and they grew in confidence as time went on.

One evening in March they were driven by a sharp fall of sleet into an Oyster Bar in the immediate neighbourhood of Leicester Square. Colonel Geraldine was dressed and painted to represent a person connected with the Press in reduced circumstances; while the Prince had, as usual, travestied his appearance by the addition of false whiskers and a pair of large adhesive eyebrows. These lent him a shaggy and weather-beaten air, which, for one of his urbanity, formed the most impenetrable disguise. Thus equipped, the commander and his satellite sipped their brandy and soda in security.

The bar was full of guests, male and female; but though more than one of these offered to fall into talk with our adventurers, none of them promised to grow interesting upon a nearer acquaintance. There was nothing present but the lees of London and the commonplace of disrespectability; and the Prince had already fallen to yawning, and was beginning to grow weary of the whole excursion, when the swing doors were pushed violently open, and a young man, followed by a couple of commissionaires, entered the bar. Each of the commissionaires carried a large dish of cream tarts under a cover, which they at once removed; and the young man made the round of the company, and pressed these confections upon everyone's acceptance with an exaggerated courtesy. Sometimes his offer was laughingly accepted; sometimes it was firmly, or even harshly, rejected. In these latter cases the newcomer always ate the tart himself, with some more or less humorous commentary.

At last he accosted Prince Florizel.

"Sir," said he, with a profound obeisance, proffering the tart at the same time between his thumb and forefinger, "will you so far honour an entire stranger? I can answer for the quality of the pastry, having eaten two dozen and three of them myself since five o'clock."

"I am in the habit," replied the Prince, "of looking not so much to the nature of a gift as to the spirit in which it is offered."

"The spirit, sir," returned the young man, with another bow, "is one of mockery."

"Mockery?" repeated Florizel. "And whom do you propose to mock?"

"I am not here to expound my philosophy," replied the other, "but to distribute these cream tarts. If I mention that I heartily include myself in the ridicule of the transaction, I hope you will consider honour satisfied and condescend. If not, you will constrain me to eat my twenty-eighth, and I own to being weary of the exercise."

"You touch me," said the Prince, "and I have all the will in the world to rescue you from this dilemma, but upon one condition. If my friend and I eat your cakes—for which we have neither of us any natural inclination—we shall expect you to join us at supper by way of recompense."

The young man seemed to reflect.

"I have still several dozen upon hand," he said at last; "and that will make it necessary for me to visit several more bars before my great affair is concluded. This will take some time; and if you are hungry——"

The Prince interrupted him with a polite gesture.

"My friend and I will accompany you," he said; "for we have already a deep interest in your very agreeable mode of passing an evening. And now that the preliminaries of peace are settled, allow me to sign the treaty for both."

And the Prince swallowed the tart with the best grace imaginable.

"It is delicious," said he.

"I perceive you are a connoisseur," replied the young man.

Colonel Geraldine likewise did honour to the pastry; and everyone in that bar having now either accepted or refused his delicacies, the young man with the cream tarts led the way to another and similar establishment. The two commissionaires, who seemed to have grown accustomed to their absurd employment, followed immediately after; and the Prince and the Colonel brought up the rear, arm in arm, and smiling to each other as they went. In this order the company visited two other taverns, where scenes were enacted of a like nature to that already described—some refusing, some accepting, the favours of this vagabond hospitality, and the young man himself eating each rejected tart.

On leaving the third saloon the young man counted his store. There were but nine remaining, three in one tray and six in the other.

"Gentlemen," said he, addressing himself to his two new followers,

"I am unwilling to delay your supper. I am positively sure you must be hungry. I feel that I owe you a special consideration. And on this great day for me, when I am closing a career of folly by my most conspicuously silly action, I wish to behave handsomely to all who give me countenance. Gentlemen, you shall wait no longer. Although my constitution is shattered by previous excesses, at the risk of my life I liquidate the suspensory condition."

With these words he crushed the nine remaining tarts into his mouth, and swallowed them at a single movement each. Then, turning to the commissionaires, he gave them a couple of sovereigns.

"I have to thank you," said he, "for your extraordinary patience."

And he dismissed them with a bow apiece. For some seconds he stood looking at the purse from which he had just paid his assistants, then, with a laugh, he tossed it into the middle of the street, and signified his readiness for supper.

In a small French restaurant in Soho, which had enjoyed an exaggerated reputation for some little while, but had already begun to be forgotten, and in a private room up two pair of stairs, the three companions made a very elegant supper, and drank three or four bottles of champagne, talking the while upon indifferent subjects. The young man was fluent and gay, but he laughed louder than was natural in a person of polite breeding; his hands trembled violently, and his voice took sudden and surprising inflections, which seemed to be independent of his will. The dessert had been cleared away, and all three had lighted their cigars, when the Prince addressed him in these words:

"You will, I am sure, pardon my curiosity. What I have seen of you has greatly pleased but even more puzzled me. And though I should be loth to seem indiscreet, I must tell you that my friend and I are persons very well worthy to be entrusted with a secret. We have many of our own, which we are continually revealing to improper ears. And if, as I suppose, your story is a silly one, you need have no delicacy with us, who are two of the silliest men in England. My name is Godall, Theophilus Godall; my friend is Major Alfred Hammersmith—or at least, such is the name by which he chooses to be known. We pass our lives entirely in the search for extravagant adventures; and there is no extravagance with which we are not capable of sympathy."

"I like you, Mr. Godall," returned the young man; "you inspire me with a natural confidence; and I have not the slightest objection to your friend the Major, whom I take to be a nobleman in masquerade. At least, I am sure he is no soldier."

The Colonel smiled at this compliment to the perfection of his art; and the young man went on in a more animated manner.

"There is every reason why I should not tell you my story. Perhaps that is just the reason why I am going to do so. At least, you seem so well prepared to hear a tale of silliness that I cannot find it in my heart to disappoint you. My name, in spite of your example, I shall keep to myself. My age is not essential to the narrative. I am descended from my ancestors by ordinary generation, and from them I inherited the very eligible human tenement which I still occupy and a fortune of three hundred pounds a year. I suppose they also handed on to me a harebrain humour, which it has been my chief delight to indulge. I received a good education. I can play the violin nearly well enough to earn money in the orchestra of a penny gaff, but not quite. The same remark applies to the flute and the French horn. I learned enough of whist to lose about a hundred a year at that scientific game. My acquaintance with French was sufficient to enable me to squander money in Paris with almost the same facility as in London. In short, I am a person full of manly accomplishments. I have had every sort of adventure, including a duel about nothing. Only two months ago I met a young lady exactly suited to my taste in mind and body; I found my heart melt; I saw that I had come upon my fate at last, and was in the way to fall in love. But when I came to reckon up what remained to me of my capital, I found it amounted to something less than four hundred pounds! I ask you fairly—can a man who respects himself fall in love on four hundred pounds? I concluded, certainly not; left the presence of my charmer, and slightly accelerating my usual rate of expenditure, came this morning to my last eighty pounds. This I divided into two equal parts; forty I reserved for a particular purpose; the remaining forty I was to dissipate before the night. I have passed a very entertaining day, and played many farces besides that of the cream tarts which procured me the advantage of your acquaintance; for I was determined, as I told you, to bring a foolish career to a still more foolish conclusion; and when you saw me throw my purse into the street, the forty pounds were at an end. Now you know me as well as I know myself: a fool but consistent in his folly; and, as I will ask you to believe, neither a whimperer nor a coward."

From the whole tone of the young man's statement it was plain that he harboured very bitter and contemptuous thoughts about himself. His auditors were led to imagine that his love affair was nearer his heart than he admitted, and that he had a design on his own life. The farce of the cream tarts began to have very much the air of a tragedy in disguise.

"Why, is this not odd," broke out Geraldine, giving a look to Prince Florizel, "that we three fellows should have met by the merest accident in so large a wilderness as London, and should be so nearly in the same condition?"

"How?" cried the young man. "Are you, too, ruined? Is this supper a folly like my cream tarts? Has the devil brought three of his own together for a last carouse?"

"The devil, depend upon it, can sometimes do a very gentlemanly thing," returned Prince Florizel; "and I am so much touched by this coincidence, that, although we are not entirely in the same case, I am going to put an end to the disparity. Let your heroic treatment of the last cream tarts be my example."

So saying, the Prince drew out his purse and took from it a small bundle of bank-notes.

"You see, I was a week or so behind you, but I mean to catch you up and come neck and neck into the winningpost," he continued. "This," laying one of the notes upon the table, "will suffice for the bill. As for the rest——"

He tossed them into the fire, and they went up the chimney in a single blaze.

The young man tried to catch his arm, but as the table was between them his interference came too late.

"Unhappy man," he cried, "you should not have burned them all! You should have kept forty pounds."

"Forty pounds!" repeated the Prince. "Why, in heaven's name, forty pounds?"

"Why not eighty?" cried the Colonel; "for to my certain knowledge there must have been a hundred in the bundle."

"It was only forty pounds he needed," said the young man gloomily. "But without them there is no admission. The rule is strict. Forty pounds for each. Accursed life, where a man cannot even die without money!"

The Prince and the Colonel exchanged glances.

"Explain yourself," said the latter. "I have still a pocketbook tolerably well lined, and I need not say how readily I should share my wealth with Godall. But I must know to what end: you must certainly tell us what you mean."

The young man seemed to awaken; he looked uneasily from one to the other, and his face flushed deeply.

"You are not fooling me?" he asked. "You are indeed ruined men like me?"

"Indeed, I am for my part," replied the Colonel.

"And for mine," said the Prince, "I have given you proof. Who but a ruined man would throw his notes into the fire? The action speaks for itself."

"A ruined man—yes," returned the other suspiciously, "or else a millionaire."

"Enough, sir," said the Prince; "I have said so, and I am not accustomed to have my word remain in doubt."

"Ruined?" said the young man. "Are you ruined, like me? Are you, after a life of indulgence, come to such a pass that you can only indulge yourself in one thing more? Are you"—he kept lowering his voice as he went on—"are you going to give yourselves that last indulgence? Are you going to avoid the consequences of your folly by the one infallible and easy path? Are you going to give the slip to the sheriff's officers of conscience by the one open door?"

Suddenly he broke off and attempted to laugh.

"Here is your health!" he cried, emptying his glass, "and good night to you, my merry ruined men."

Colonel Geraldine caught him by the arm as he was about to rise.

"You lack confidence in us," he said, "and you are wrong. To all your questions I make answer in the affirmative. But I am not so timid, and can speak the Queen's English plainly. We too, like yourself, have had enough of life, and are determined to die. Sooner or later, alone or together, we meant to seek out death and beard him where he lies ready. Since we have met you, and your case is more pressing, let it be tonight—and at once—and, if you will, all three together. Such a penniless trio," he cried, "should go arm in arm into the halls of Pluto, and give each other some countenance among the shades!"

Geraldine had hit exactly on the manners and intonations that became the part he was playing. The Prince himself was disturbed, and looked over at his confidant with a shade of doubt. As for the young man, the flush came back darkly into his cheek, and his eyes threw out a spark of light.

"You are the men for me!" he cried, with an almost terrible gaiety. "Shake hands upon the bargain!" (his hand was cold and wet.) "You little know in what a company you will begin the march! You little know in what a happy moment for yourselves you partook of my cream tarts! I am only a unit, but I am a unit in an army. I know Death's private door. I am one of his familiars, and can show you into eternity without ceremony and yet without scandal."

They called upon him eagerly to explain his meaning.

"Can you muster eighty pounds between you?" he demanded.

Geraldine ostentatiously consulted his pocket-book, and replied in the affirmative.

"Fortunate beings!" cried the young man. "Forty pounds is the entry money of the Suicide Club."

"The Suicide Club," said the Prince, "why, what the devil is that?"

"Listen," said the young man; "this is the age of conveniences, and I have to tell you of the last perfection of the sort. We have affairs in different places; and hence railways were invented. Railways separated us infallibly from our friends; and so telegraphs were made that we might communicate speedily at great distances. Even in hotels we have lifts to spare us a climb of some hundred steps. Now, we know that life is only a stage to play the fool upon as long as the part amuses us. There was one more convenience lacking to modern comfort; a decent, easy way to quit that stage; the back stairs to liberty; or, as I said this moment, Death's private door. This, my two fellow rebels, is supplied by the Suicide Club. Do not suppose that you and I are alone, or even exceptional, in the highly reasonable desire that we profess. A large number of our fellowmen, who have grown heartily sick of the performance in which they are expected to join daily and all their lives long, are only kept from flight by one or two considerations. Some have families who would be shocked, or even blamed, if the matter became public; others have a weakness at heart and recoil from the circumstances of death. That is, to some extent, my own experience. I cannot put a pistol to my head and draw the trigger; for something stronger than myself withholds the act; and although I loathe life, I have not strength enough in my body to take hold of death and be done with it. For such as I, and for all who desire to be out of the coil without posthumous scandal, the Suicide Club has been inaugurated. How this has been managed, what is its history, or what may be its ramifications in other lands, I am myself uninformed; and what I know of its constitution, I am not at liberty to communicate to you. To this extent, however, I am at your service. If you are truly tired of life, I will introduce you tonight to a meeting; and if not tonight, at least some time within the week, you will be easily relieved of your existences. It is now (consulting his watch) eleven; by half-past, at latest, we must leave this place; so that you have half an hour before you to consider my proposal. It is more serious than a cream tart," he added, with a smile; "and I suspect more palatable."

"More serious, certainly," returned Colonel Geraldine; "and as it is so much more so, will you allow me five minutes' speech in private with my friend, Mr. Godall?"

"It is only fair," answered the young man. "If you will permit, I will retire."

"You will be very obliging," said the Colonel.

As soon as the two were alone—"What," said Prince Florizel, "is the use of this confabulation, Geraldine? I see you are flurried, whereas my mind is very tranquilly made up. I will see the end of this."

"Your Highness," said the Colonel turning pale; "let me ask you to consider the importance of your life, not only to your friends, but to the public interest. 'If not tonight,' said this madman; but supposing that tonight some irreparable disaster were to overtake your Highness's person, what, let me ask you, what would be my despair, and what the concern and disaster of a great nation?"

"I will see the end of this," repeated the Prince in his most deliberate tones; "and have the kindness, Colonel Geraldine, to remember and respect your word of honour as a gentleman. Under no circumstances, recollect, nor without my special authority, are you to betray the incognito under which I choose to go abroad. These were my commands, which I now reiterate. And now," he added, "let me ask you to call for the bill."

Colonel Geraldine bowed in submission; but he had a very white face as he summoned the young man of the cream tarts, and issued his directions to the waiter. The Prince preserved his undisturbed demeanour, and described a Palais Royal farce to the young suicide with great humour and gusto. He avoided the Colonel's appealing looks without ostentation, and selected another cheroot with more than usual care. Indeed, he was now the only man of the party who kept any command over his nerves.

The bill was discharged, the Prince giving the whole change of the note to the astonished waiter; and the three drove off in a four-wheeler. They were not long upon the way before the cab stopped at the entrance to a rather dark court. Here all descended.

After Geraldine had paid the fare, the young man turned, and addressed Prince Florizel as follows:

"It is still time, Mr. Godall, to make good your escape into thraldom. And for you too, Major Hammersmith. Reflect well before you take another step; and if your hearts say no—here are the crossroads."

"Lead on, sir," said the Prince. "I am not the man to go back from a thing once said."

"Your coolness does me good," replied their guide. "I have never seen anyone so unmoved at this conjuncture; and yet you are not the first whom I have escorted to this door. More than one of my friends has preceded me, where I knew I must shortly follow. But this is of no interest to you. Wait me here for only a few moments; I shall return as soon as I have arranged the preliminaries of your introduction."

And with that the young man, waving his hand to his companions, turned into the court, entered a doorway and disappeared.

"Of all our follies," said Colonel Geraldine in a low voice, "this is the wildest and most dangerous."

"I perfectly believe so," returned the Prince.

"We have still," pursued the Colonel, "a moment to ourselves. Let me beseech your Highness to profit by the opportunity and retire. The consequences of this step are so dark, and may be so grave, that I feel myself justified in pushing a little farther than usual the liberty which your Highness is so condescending as to allow me in private."

"Am I to understand that Colonel Geraldine is afraid?" asked his Highness, taking his cheroot from his lips, and looking keenly into the other's face.

"My fear is certainly not personal," replied the other proudly; "of that your Highness may rest well assured."

"I had supposed as much," returned the Prince, with undisturbed good humour; "but I was unwilling to remind you of the difference in our stations. No more—no more," he added, seeing Geraldine about to apologise, "you stand excused."

And he smoked placidly, leaning against a railing, until the young man returned.

"Well," he asked, "has our reception been arranged?"

"Follow me," was the reply. "The President will see you in the cabinet. And let me warn you to be frank in your answers. I have stood your guarantee; but the club requires a searching inquiry before admission; for the indiscretion of a single member would lead to the dispersion of the whole society for ever."

The Prince and Geraldine put their heads together for a moment. "Bear me out in this," said the one; and "bear me out in that," said the other; and by boldly taking up the characters of men with whom both were acquainted, they had come to an agreement in a twinkling, and were ready to follow their guide into the President's cabinet.

There were no formidable obstacles to pass. The outer door stood open; the door of the cabinet was ajar; and there, in a small but very high apartment, the young man left them once more.

"He will be here immediately," he said with a nod, as he disappeared.

Voices were audible in the cabinet through the folding doors which formed one end; and now and then the noise of a champagne cork, followed by a burst of laughter, intervened among the sounds of conversation. A single tall window looked out upon the river and the embankment; and by the disposition of the lights they judged themselves not far from Charing Cross station. The furniture was scanty, and the coverings worn to the thread; and there was nothing movable except a handbell in the centre of a round table, and the hats and coats of a considerable party hung round the wall on pegs.

"What sort of a den is this?" said Geraldine.

"That is what I have come to see," replied the Prince. "If they keep live devils on the premises, the thing may grow amusing."

Just then the folding door was opened no more than was necessary for the passage of a human body; and there entered at the same moment a louder buzz of talk, and the redoubtable President of the Suicide Club. The President was a man of fifty or upwards; large and rambling in his gait, with shaggy side whiskers, a bald top to his head, and a veiled grey eye, which now and then emitted a twinkle. His mouth, which embraced a large cigar, he kept continually screwing round and round and from side to side, as he looked sagaciously and coldly at the strangers. He was dressed in light tweeds, with his neck very open in a striped shirt collar; and carried a minute book under one arm.

"Good evening," said he, after he had closed the door behind him. "I am told you wish to speak with me."

"We have a desire, sir, to join the Suicide Club," replied the Colonel.

The President rolled his cigar about in his mouth.

"What is that?" he said abruptly.

"Pardon me," returned the Colonel, "but I believe you are the person best qualified to give us information on that point."

"I?" cried the President. "A Suicide Club? Come, come! this is a frolic for All Fools'-Day. I can make allowances for gentlemen who get merry in their liquor, but let there be an end to this."

"Call your Club what you will," said the Colonel, "you have some company behind these doors, and we insist on joining it."

"Sir," returned the President, curtly, "you have made a mistake. This is a private house, and you must leave it instantly."

The Prince had remained quietly in his seat throughout this little colloquy; but now, when the Colonel looked over to him, as much as to say, "Take your answer and come away, for God's sake!" he drew his cheroot from his mouth, and spoke—

"I have come here," said he, "upon the invitation of a friend of yours. He has doubtless informed you of my intention in thus intruding on your party. Let me remind you that a person in my circumstances has exceedingly little to bind him, and is not at all likely to tolerate much rudeness. I am a very quiet man, as a usual thing; but, my dear sir, you are either going to oblige me in the little matter of which you are aware, or you shall very bitterly repent that you ever admitted me to your antechamber."

The President laughed aloud.

"That is the way to speak," said he. "You are a man who is a man. You know the way to my heart, and can do what you like with me. Will you," he continued, addressing Geraldine, "will you step aside for a few minutes? I shall finish first with your companion, and some of the club's formalities require to be fulfilled in private."

With these words he opened the door of a small closet, into which he shut the colonel.

"I believe in you," he said to Florizel, as soon as they were alone; "but are you sure of your friend?"

"Not so sure as I am of myself, though he has more cogent reasons," answered Florizel, "but sure enough to bring him here without alarm. He has had enough to cure the most tenacious man of life. He was cashiered the other day for cheating at cards."

"A good reason, I daresay," replied the President; "at least, we have another in the same case, and I feel sure of him. Have you also been in the Service, may I ask?"

"I have," was the reply; "but I was too lazy, I left it early."

"What is your reason for being tired of life?" pursued the President.

"The same, as near as I can make out," answered the Prince; "unadulterated laziness."

The President started. "D—n it," said he, "you must have something better than that."

"I have no more money," added Florizel. "That is also a vexation, without doubt. It brings my sense of idleness to an acute point."

The President rolled his cigar round in his mouth for some seconds, directing his gaze straight into the eyes of this unusual neophyte; but the Prince supported his scrutiny with unabashed good temper.

"If I had not a deal of experience," said the President at last, "I should turn you off. But I know the world; and this much any way, that the most frivolous excuses for a suicide are often the toughest to stand by. And when I downright like a man, as I do you, sir, I would rather strain the regulation than deny him."

The Prince and the Colonel, one after the other, were subjected to a long and particular interrogatory: the Prince alone; but Geraldine in the presence of the Prince, so that the President might observe the countenance of the one while the other was being warmly cross-examined. The result was satisfactory; and the President, after having booked a few details of each case, produced a form of oath to be accepted. Nothing could be conceived more passive than the obedience promised, or more stringent than the terms by which the juror bound himself. The man who forfeited a pledge so awful could scarcely have a rag of honour or any of the consolations of religion left to him. Florizel signed the document, but not without a shudder; the Colonel followed his example with an air of great depression. Then the President received the entry money; and without more ado, introduced the two friends into the smoking-room of the Suicide Club.

The smoking room of the Suicide Club was the same height as the cabinet into which it opened, but much larger, and papered from top to bottom with an imitation of oak wainscot. A large and cheerful fire and a number of gas jets illuminated the company. The Prince and his follower made the number up to eighteen. Most of the party were smoking, and drinking champagne; a feverish hilarity reigned, with sudden and rather ghastly pauses.

"Is this a full meeting?" asked the Prince.

"Middling," said the President. "By the way," he added, "if you have any money, it is usual to offer some champagne. It keeps up a good spirit, and is one of my own little perquisites."

"Hammersmith," said Florizel, "I may leave the champagne to you."

And with that he turned away and began to go round among the guests. Accustomed to play the host in the highest circles, he charmed and dominated all whom he approached; there was something at once winning and authoritative in his address; and his extraordinary coolness gave him yet another distinction in this half maniacal society. As he went from one to another he kept both his eyes and ears open, and soon began to gain a general idea of the people among whom he found himself. As in all other places of resort, one type predominated: people in the prime of youth, with every show of intelligence and sensibility in their appearance, but with little promise of strength or the quality that makes success. Few were much above thirty, and not a few were still in their teens. They stood, leaning on tables and shifting on their feet; sometimes they smoked extraordinarily fast, and sometimes they let their cigars go out; some talked well, but the conversation of others was plainly the result of nervous tension, and was equally without wit or purport. As each new bottle of champagne was opened, there was a manifest improvement in gaiety. Only two were seated—one in a chair in the recess of the window, with his head hanging and his hands plunged deep into his trouser pockets, pale, visibly moist with perspiration, saying never a word, a very wreck of soul and body; the other sat on the divan close by the chimney, and attracted notice by a trenchant dissimilarity from all the rest. He was probably upwards of forty, but he looked fully ten years older; and Florizel thought he had never seen a man more naturally hideous, nor one more ravaged by disease and ruinous excitements. He was no more than skin and bone, was partly paralysed, and wore spectacles of such unusual power, that his eyes appeared through the glasses greatly magnified and distorted in shape. Except the Prince and the President, he was the only person in the room who preserved the composure of ordinary life.

There was little decency among the members of the club. Some boasted of the disgraceful actions, the consequences of which had reduced them to seek refuge in death; and the others listened without disapproval. There was a tacit understanding against moral judgments; and whoever passed the club doors enjoyed already some of the immunities of the tomb. They drank to each other's memories, and to those of notable suicides in the past. They compared and developed their different views of death—some declaring that it was no more than blackness and cessation; others full of a hope that that very night they should be scaling the stars and commercing with the mighty dead.

"To the eternal memory of Baron Trenck, the type of suicides!" cried one. "He went out of a small cell into a smaller, that he might come forth again to freedom."

"For my part," said a second, "I wish no more than a bandage for my eyes and cotton for my ears. Only they have no cotton thick enough in this world."

A third was for reading the mysteries of life in a future state; and a fourth professed that he would never have joined the club, if he had not been induced to believe in Mr. Darwin.

"I could not bear," said this remarkable suicide, "to be descended from an ape."

Altogether, the Prince was disappointed by the bearing and conversation of the members.

"It does not seem to me," he thought, "a matter for so much disturbance. If a man has made up his mind to kill himself, let him do it, in God's name, like a gentleman. This flutter and big talk is out of place."

In the meanwhile Colonel Geraldine was a prey to the blackest apprehensions; the club and its rules were still a mystery, and he looked round the room for some one who should be able to set his mind at rest. In this survey his eye lighted on the paralytic person with the strong spectacles; and seeing him so exceedingly tranquil, he besought the President, who was going in and out of the room under a pressure of business, to present him to the gentleman on the divan.

The functionary explained the needlessness of all such formalities within the club, but nevertheless presented Mr. Hammersmith to Mr. Malthus.

Mr. Malthus looked at the Colonel curiously, and then requested him to take a seat upon his right.

"You are a newcomer," he said, "and wish information? You have come to the proper source. It is two years since I first visited this charming club."

The Colonel breathed again. If Mr. Malthus had frequented the place for two years there could be little danger for the Prince in a single evening. But Geraldine was none the less astonished, and began to suspect a mystification.

"What!" cried he, "two years! I thought—but indeed I see I have been made the subject of a pleasantry."

"By no means," replied Mr. Malthus mildly. "My case is peculiar. I am not, properly speaking, a suicide at all; but, as it were, an honorary member. I rarely visit the club twice in two months. My infirmity and the kindness of the President have procured me these little immunities, for which besides I pay at an advanced rate. Even as it is my luck has been extraordinary."

"I am afraid," said the Colonel, "that I must ask you to be more explicit. You must remember that I am still most imperfectly acquainted with the rules of the club."

"An ordinary member who comes here in search of death like yourself," replied the paralytic, "returns every evening until fortune favours him. He can even, if he is penniless, get board and lodging from the President: very fair, I believe, and clean, although, of course, not luxurious; that could hardly be, considering the exiguity (if I may so express myself) of the subscription. And then the President's company is a delicacy in itself."

"Indeed!" cried Geraldine, "he had not greatly prepossessed me."

"Ah!" said Mr. Malthus, "you do not know the man: the drollest fellow! What stories! What cynicism! He knows life to admiration and, between ourselves, is probably the most corrupt rogue in Christendom."

"And he also," asked the Colonel, "is a permanency—like yourself, if I may say so without offence?"

"Indeed, he is a permanency in a very different sense from me," replied Mr. Malthus. "I have been graciously spared, but I must go at last. Now he never plays. He shuffles and deals for the club, and makes the necessary arrangements. That man, my dear Mr. Hammersmith, is the very soul of ingenuity. For three years he has pursued in London his useful and, I think I may add, his artistic calling; and not so much as a whisper of suspicion has been once aroused. I believe him myself to be inspired. You doubtless remember the celebrated case, six months ago, of the gentleman who was accidentally poisoned in a chemist's shop? That was one of the least rich, one of the least racy, of his notions; but then, how simple! and how safe!"

"You astound me," said the Colonel. "Was that unfortunate gentleman one of the——" He was about to say "victims"; but bethinking himself in time, he substituted—"members of the club?"

In the same flash of thought, it occurred to him that Mr. Malthus himself had not at all spoken in the tone of one who is in love with death; and he added hurriedly:

"But I perceive I am still in the dark. You speak of shuffling and dealing; pray for what end? And since you seem rather unwilling to die than otherwise, I must own that I cannot conceive what brings you here at all."

"You say truly that you are in the dark," replied Mr. Malthus with more animation. "Why, my dear sir, this club is the temple of intoxication. If my enfeebled health could support the excitement more often, you may depend upon it I should be more often here. It requires all the sense of duty engendered by a long habit of ill-health and careful regimen, to keep me from excess in this, which is, I may say, my last dissipation. I have tried them all, sir," he went on, laying his hand on Geraldine's arm, "all without exception, and I declare to you, upon my honour, there is not one of them that has not been grossly and untruthfully overrated. People trifle with love. Now, I deny that love is a strong passion. Fear is the strong passion; it is with fear that you must trifle, if you wish to taste the intensest joys of living. Envy me—envy me, sir," he added with a chuckle, "I am a coward!"

Geraldine could scarcely repress a movement of repulsion for this deplorable wretch; but he commanded himself with an effort, and continued his inquiries.

"How, sir," he asked, "is the excitement so artfully prolonged? and where is there any element of uncertainty?"

"I must tell you how the victim for every evening is selected," returned Mr. Malthus; "and not only the victim, but another member, who is to be the instrument in the club's hands, and death's high priest for that occasion."

"Good God!" said the Colonel, "do they then kill each other?"

"The trouble of suicide is removed in that way," returned Malthus with a nod.

"Merciful Heavens!" ejaculated the Colonel, "and may you—may I—may the—my friend I mean—may any of us be pitched upon this evening as the slayer of another man's body and immortal spirit? Can such things be possible among men born of women? Oh! infamy of infamies!"

He was about to rise in his horror, when he caught the Prince's eye. It was fixed upon him from across the room with a frowning and angry stare. And in a moment Geraldine recovered his composure.

"After all," he added, "why not? And since you say the game is interesting, *vogue la galère*—I follow the club!"

Mr. Malthus had keenly enjoyed the Colonel's amazement and disgust. He had the vanity of wickedness; and it pleased him to see another man give way to a generous movement, while he felt himself, in his entire corruption, superior to such emotions.

"You now, after your first moment of surprise," said he, "are in a position to appreciate the delights of our society. You can see how it combines the excitement of a gaming table, a duel, and a Roman amphitheatre. The Pagans did well enough; I cordially admire the refinement of their minds; but it has been reserved for a Christian country to attain this extreme, this quintessence, this absolute of poignancy. You will understand how vapid are all amusements to a man who has acquired a taste for this one. The game we play," he continued, "is one of extreme simplicity. A full pack—but I perceive you are about to see the thing in progress. Will you lend me the help of your arm? I am unfortunately paralysed."

Indeed, just as Mr. Malthus was beginning his description, another pair of folding-doors was thrown open, and the whole club began to pass, not without some hurry, into the adjoining room. It was similar in every respect to the one from which it was entered, but somewhat differently furnished. The centre was occupied by a long green table, at which the President sat shuffling a pack of cards with great particularity. Even with the stick and the Colonel's arm, Mr. Malthus walked with so much difficulty that everyone was seated before this pair and the Prince, who had waited for them, entered the apartment; and, in consequence, the three took seats close together at the lower end of the board.

"It is a pack of fifty-two," whispered Mr. Malthus. "Watch for the ace of spades, which is the sign of death, and the ace of clubs, which designates the official of the night. Happy, happy young men!" he added. "You have good eyes, and can follow the game. Alas! I cannot tell an ace from a deuce across the table."

And he proceeded to equip himself with a second pair of spectacles.

"I must at least watch the faces," he explained.

The Colonel rapidly informed his friend of all that he had learned from the honorary member, and of the horrible alternative that lay before them. The Prince was conscious of a deadly chill and a contraction about his heart; he swallowed with difficulty, and looked from side to side like a man in a maze.

"One bold stroke," whispered the Colonel, "and we may still escape."

But the suggestion recalled the Prince's spirits.

"Silence!" said he. "Let me see that you can play like a gentleman for any stake, however serious."

And he looked about him, once more to all appearance at his ease, although his heart beat thickly, and he was conscious of an unpleasant heat in his bosom. The members were all very quiet and intent; everyone was pale, but none so pale as Mr. Malthus. His eyes protruded; his head kept nodding involuntarily upon his spine; his hands found their way, one after the other, to his mouth, where they made clutches at his tremulous and ashen lips. It was plain that the honorary member enjoyed his membership on very startling terms.

"Attention, gentlemen!" said the President.

And he began slowly dealing the cards about the table in the reverse direction, pausing until each man had shown his card. Nearly everyone hesitated; and sometimes you would see a player's fingers stumble more than once before he could turn over the momentous slip of pasteboard. As the Prince's turn drew nearer, he was conscious of a growing and almost suffocating excitement; but he had somewhat of the gambler's nature, and recognised almost with astonishment that there was a degree of pleasure in his sensations. The nine of clubs fell to his lot; the three of spades was dealt to Geraldine; and the queen of hearts to Mr. Malthus, who was unable to suppress a sob of relief. The young man of the cream tarts almost immediately afterwards turned over the ace of clubs, and remained frozen with horror, the card still resting on his finger; he had not come there to kill, but to be killed; and the Prince in his generous sympathy with his position almost forgot the peril that still hung over himself and his friend.

The deal was coming round again, and still Death's card had not come out. The players held their respiration, and only breathed by gasps. The Prince received another club; Geraldine had a diamond; but when Mr. Malthus turned up his card a horrible noise, like that of something breaking, issued from his mouth; and he rose from his seat and sat down again, with no sign of his paralysis. It was the ace of spades. The honorary member had trifled once too often with his terrors.

Conversation broke out again almost at once. The players relaxed their rigid attitudes, and began to rise from the table and stroll back by twos and threes into the smoking room. The President stretched his arms and yawned, like a man who has finished his day's work. But Mr. Malthus sat in his place, with his head in his hands, and his hands upon the table, drunk and motionless—a thing stricken down.

The Prince and Geraldine made their escape at once. In the cold night air their horror of what they had witnessed was redoubled.

"Alas!" cried the Prince, "to be bound by an oath in such a matter! to allow this wholesale trade in murder to be continued with profit and impunity! If I but dared to forfeit my pledge!"

"That is impossible for your Highness," replied the Colonel, "whose honour is the honour of Bohemia. But I dare, and may with propriety, forfeit mine."

"Geraldine," said the Prince, "if your honour suffers in any of the adventures into which you follow me, not only will I never pardon you, but—what I believe will much more sensibly affect you—I should never forgive myself."

"I receive your Highness's commands," replied the Colonel. "Shall we go from this accursed spot?"

"Yes," said the Prince. "Call a cab in Heaven's name, and let me try to forget in slumber the memory of this night's disgrace."

But it was notable that he carefully read the name of the court before he left it.

The next morning, as soon as the Prince was stirring, Colonel Geraldine brought him a daily newspaper, with the following paragraph marked:

"MELANCHOLY ACCIDENT—This morning, about two o'clock, Mr. Bartholomew Malthus, of 16, Chepstow Place, Westbourne Grove, on his way home from a party at a friend's house, fell over the upper parapet in Trafalgar Square, fracturing his skull and breaking a leg and an arm. Death was instantaneous. Mr. Malthus, accompanied by a friend, was engaged in looking for a cab at the time of the unfortunate occurrence. As Mr. Malthus was paralytic, it is thought that his fall may have been occasioned by another seizure. The unhappy gentleman was well known in the most respectable circles, and his loss will be widely and deeply deplored."

"If ever a soul went straight to Hell," said Geraldine solemnly, "it was that paralytic man's."

The Prince buried his face in his hands, and remained silent.

"I am almost rejoiced," continued the Colonel, "to know that he is dead. But for our young man of the cream tarts I confess my heart bleeds."

"Geraldine," said the Prince, raising his face, "that unhappy lad was last night as innocent as you and I; and this morning the guilt of blood is on his soul. When I think of the President, my heart grows sick within me. I do not know how it shall be done, but I shall have that scoundrel at my mercy as there is a God in heaven. What an experience, what a lesson, was that game of cards!"

"One," said the Colonel, "never to be repeated."

The Prince remained so long without replying, that Geraldine grew alarmed.

"You cannot mean to return," he said. "You have suffered too much and seen too much horror already. The duties of your high position forbid the repetition of the hazard."

"There is much in what you say," replied Prince Florizel, "and I am not altogether pleased with my own determination. Alas! in the clothes of the greatest potentate, what is there but a man? I never felt my weakness more acutely than now, Geraldine, but it is stronger than I. Can I cease to interest myself in the fortunes of the unhappy young man who supped with us some hours ago? Can I leave the President to follow his nefarious career unwatched? Can I begin an adventure so entrancing, and not follow it to an end? No, Geraldine: you ask of the Prince more than the man is able to perform. Tonight, once more, we take our places at the table of the Suicide Club."

Colonel Geraldine fell upon his knees.

"Will your Highness take my life?" he cried. "It is his—his freely; but do not, O do not! let him ask me to countenance so terrible a risk."

"Colonel Geraldine," replied the Prince, with some haughtiness of manner, "your life is absolutely your own. I only look for obedience; and when that is unwillingly rendered, I shall look for that no longer. I add one word: your importunity in this affair has been sufficient."

The Master of the Horse regained his feet at once.

"Your Highness," he said, "may I be excused in my attendance this afternoon? I dare not, as an honourable man, venture a second time into that fatal house until I have perfectly ordered my affairs. Your Highness shall meet, I promise him, with no more opposition from the most devoted and grateful of his servants."

"My dear Geraldine," returned Prince Florizel, "I always regret when you oblige me to remember my rank. Dispose of your day as you think fit, but be here before eleven in the same disguise."

The club, on this second evening, was not so fully attended; and when Geraldine and the Prince arrived, there were not above half-a-dozen persons in the smoking-room. His Highness took the President aside and congratulated him warmly on the demise of Mr. Malthus.

"I like," he said, "to meet with capacity, and certainly find much of it in you. Your profession is of a very delicate nature, but I see you are well qualified to conduct it with success and secresy."

The President was somewhat affected by these compliments from one of his Highness's superior bearing. He acknowledged them almost with humility.

"Poor Malthy!" he added, "I shall hardly know the club without him. The most of my patrons are boys, sir, and poetical boys, who are not much company for me. Not but what Malthy had some poetry, too; but it was of a kind that I could understand."

"I can readily imagine you should find yourself in sympathy with

Mr. Malthus," returned the Prince. "He struck me as a man of a very original disposition."

The young man of the cream tarts was in the room, but painfully depressed and silent. His late companions sought in vain to lead him into conversation.

"How bitterly I wish," he cried, "that I had never brought you to this infamous abode! Begone, while you are clean-handed. If you could have heard the old man scream as he fell, and the noise of his bones upon the pavement! Wish me, if you have any kindness to so fallen a being—wish the ace of spades for me tonight!"

A few more members dropped in as the evening went on, but the club did not muster more than the devil's dozen when they took their places at the table. The prince was again conscious of a certain joy in his alarms; but he was astonished to see Geraldine so much more self-possessed than on the night before.

"It is extraordinary," thought the Prince, "that a will, made or un-made, should so greatly influence a young man's spirit."

"Attention, gentlemen!" said the President, and he began to deal.

Three times the cards went all round the table, and neither of the marked cards had yet fallen from his hand. The excitement as he began the fourth distribution was overwhelming. There were just cards enough to go once more entirely round. The Prince, who sat second from the dealer's left, would receive, in the reverse mode of dealing practised at the club, the second last card. The third player turned up a black ace—it was the ace of clubs. The next received a diamond, the next a heart, and so on; but the ace of spades was still undelivered. At last Geraldine, who sat upon the Prince's left, turned his card; it was an ace, but the ace of hearts.

When Prince Florizel saw his fate upon the table in front of him, his heart stood still. He was a brave man, but the sweat poured off his face. There were exactly fifty chances out of a hundred that he was doomed. He reversed the card; it was the ace of spades. A loud roaring filled his brain, and the table swam before his eyes. He heard the player on his right break into a fit of laughter that sounded between mirth and dis-appointment; he saw the company rapidly dispersing, but his mind was full of other thoughts. He recognised how foolish, how criminal, had been his conduct. In perfect health, in the prime of his years, the heir to a throne, he had gambled away his future and that of a brave and loyal country. "God," he cried, "God forgive me!" And with that, the confusion of his senses passed away, and he regained his self-possession in a moment.

To his surprise Geraldine had disappeared. There was no one in the cardroom but his destined butcher consulting with the President, and the young man of the cream tarts, who slipped up to the Prince and whispered in his ear:

"I would give a million, if I had it, for your luck."

His Highness could not help reflecting, as the young man departed, that he would have sold his opportunity for a much more moderate sum.

The whispered conference now came to an end. The holder of the ace of clubs left the room with a look of intelligence, and the President, approaching the unfortunate Prince, proffered him his hand.

"I am pleased to have met you, sir," said he, "and pleased to have been in a position to do you this trifling service. At least, you cannot complain of delay. On the second evening—what a stroke of luck!"

The Prince endeavoured in vain to articulate something in response, but his mouth was dry and his tongue seemed paralysed.

"You feel a little sickish?" asked the President, with some show of solicitude. "Most gentlemen do. Will you take a little brandy?"

The Prince signified in the affirmative, and the other immediately filled some of the spirit into a tumbler.

"Poor old Malthy!" ejaculated the President, as the Prince drained the glass. "He drank near upon a pint, and little enough good it seemed to do him!"

"I am more amenable to treatment," said the Prince, a good deal revived. "I am my own man again at once, as you perceive. And so, let me ask you, what are my directions?"

"You will proceed along the Strand in the direction of the City, and on the left-hand pavement, until you meet the gentleman who has just left the room. He will continue your instructions, and him you will have the kindness to obey; the authority of the club is vested in his person for the night. And now," added the President, "I wish you a pleasant walk."

Florizel acknowledged the salutation rather awkwardly, and took his leave. He passed through the smoking room, where the bulk of the players were still consuming champagne, some of which he had himself ordered and paid for; and he was surprised to find himself cursing them in his heart. He put on his hat and greatcoat in the cabinet, and selected his umbrella from a corner. The familiarity of these acts, and the thought that he was about them for the last time, betrayed him into a fit of laughter which sounded unpleasantly in his own ears. He conceived a reluctance to leave the cabinet, and turned instead to the window. The sight of the lamps and the darkness recalled him to himself.

"Come, come, I must be a man," he thought, "and tear myself away."

At the corner of Box Court three men fell upon Prince Florizel and he was unceremoniously thrust into a carriage, which at once drove rapidly away. There was already an occupant.

"Will your Highness pardon my zeal?" said a well-known voice.

The Prince threw himself upon the Colonel's neck in a passion of relief.

"How can I ever thank you?" he cried. "And how was this effected?"

Although he had been willing to march upon his doom, he was overjoyed to yield to friendly violence, and return once more to life and hope.

"You can thank me effectually enough," replied the Colonel, "by avoiding all such dangers in the future. And as for your second question, all has been managed by the simplest means. I arranged this afternoon with a celebrated detective. Secrecy has been promised and paid for. Your own servants have been principally engaged in the affair. The house in Box Court has been surrounded since nightfall, and this, which is one of your own carriages, has been awaiting you for nearly an hour."

"And the miserable creature who was to have slain me—what of him?" inquired the Prince.

"He was pinioned as he left the club," replied the Colonel, "and now awaits your sentence at the Palace, where he will soon be joined by his accomplices."

"Geraldine," said the Prince, "you have saved me against my explicit orders, and you have done well. I owe you not only my life, but a lesson; and I should be unworthy of my rank if I did not show myself grateful to my teacher. Let it be yours to choose the manner."

There was a pause, during which the carriage continued to speed through the streets, and the two men were each buried in his own reflections. The silence was broken by Colonel Geraldine.

"Your Highness," said he, "has by this time a considerable body of prisoners. There is at least one criminal among the number to whom justice should be dealt. Our oath forbids us all recourse to law; and discretion would forbid it equally if the oath were loosened. May I inquire your Highness's intention?"

"It is decided," answered Florizel; "the President must fall in duel. It only remains to choose his adversary."

"Your Highness has permitted me to name my own recompense," said the Colonel. "Will he permit me to ask the appointment of my brother? It is an honourable post, but I dare assure your Highness that the lad will acquit himself with credit."

"You ask me an ungracious favour," said the Prince, "but I must refuse you nothing."

The Colonel kissed his hand with the greatest affection; and at that moment the carriage rolled under the archway of the Prince's splendid residence.

An hour after, Florizel in his official robes, and covered with all the orders of Bohemia, received the members of the Suicide Club.

"Foolish and wicked men," said he, "as many of you as have been driven into this strait by the lack of fortune shall receive employment and remuneration from my officers. Those who suffer under a sense of guilt must have recourse to a higher and more generous Potentate than I. I feel pity for all of you, deeper than you can imagine; tomorrow you shall tell me your stories; and as you answer more frankly, I shall be the more able to remedy your misfortunes. As for you," he added, turning to the President, "I should only offend a person of your parts by any offer of assistance; but I have instead a piece of diversion to propose to you. Here," laying his hand on the shoulder of Colonel Geraldine's young brother, "is an officer of mine who desires to make a little tour upon the Continent; and I ask you, as a favour, to accompany him on this excursion. Do you," he went on, changing his tone, "do you shoot well with the pistol? Because you may have need of that accomplishment. When two men go travelling together, it is best to be prepared for all. Let me add that, if by any chance you should lose young Mr. Geraldine upon the way, I shall always have another member of my household to place at your disposal; and I am known, Mr. President, to have long eyesight, and as long an arm."

With these words, said with much sternness, the Prince concluded his address. Next morning the members of the club were suitably provided for by his munificence, and the President set forth upon his travels, under the supervision of Mr. Geraldine, and a pair of faithful and adroit lackeys, well trained in the Prince's household. Not content with this, discreet agents were put in possession of the house in Box Court, and all letters or visitors for the Suicide Club or its officials were to be examined by Prince Florizel in person.

Here (says my Arabian author) *ends* THE STORY OF THE YOUNG MAN WITH THE CREAM TARTS, *who is now a comfortable householder in Wigmore Street, Cavendish Square. The number, for obvious reasons, I suppress. Those who care to pursue the adventures of Prince Florizel and the President of the Suicide Club, may read the* HISTORY OF THE PHYSICIAN AND THE SARATOGA TRUNK.

STORY OF THE PHYSICIAN AND THE SARATOGA TRUNK

Mr. Silas Q. Scuddamore was a young American of a simple and harmless disposition, which was the more to his credit as he came from New England—a quarter of the New World not precisely famous for those qualities. Although he was exceedingly rich, he kept a note of all his expenses in a little paper pocketbook; and he had chosen to study the attractions of Paris from the seventh story of what is called a furnished hotel, in the Latin Quarter. There was a great deal of habit in his penuriousness; and his virtue, which was very remarkable among his associates, was principally founded upon diffidence and youth.

The next room to his was inhabited by a lady, very attractive in her air and very elegant in toilette, whom, on his first arrival, he had taken for a Countess. In course of time he had learned that she was known by the name of Madame Zéphyrine, and that whatever station she occupied in life it was not that of a person of title. Madame Zéphyrine, probably in the hope of enchanting the young American, used to flaunt by him on the stairs with a civil inclination, a word of course, and a knock-down look out of her black eyes, and disappear in a rustle of silk, and with the revelation of an admirable foot and ankle. But these advances, so far from encouraging Mr. Scuddamore, plunged him into the depths of depression and bashfulness. She had come to him several times for a light, or to apologise for the imaginary depre-

Original illustration by W. J. Hennessy for
The Suicide Club and The Rajah's Diamond (LONDON, 1894).

dations of her poodle; but his mouth was closed in the presence of so superior a being, his French promptly left him, and he could only stare and stammer until she was gone. The slenderness of their intercourse did not prevent him from throwing out insinuations of a very glorious order when he was safely alone with a few males.

The room on the other side of the American's—for there were three rooms on a floor in the hotel—was tenanted by an old English physician of rather doubtful reputation. Dr. Noel, for that was his name, had been forced to leave London, where he enjoyed a large and increasing practice; and it was hinted that the police had been the instigators of this change of scene. At least he, who had made something of a figure in earlier life, now dwelt in the Latin Quarter in great simplicity and solitude, and devoted much of his time to study. Mr. Scuddamore had made his acquaintance, and the pair would now and then dine together frugally in a restaurant across the street.

Silas Q. Scuddamore had many little vices of the more respectable order, and was not restrained by delicacy from indulging them in many rather doubtful ways. Chief among his foibles stood curiosity. He was a born gossip; and life, and especially those parts of it in which he had no experience, interested him to the degree of passion. He was a pert, invincible questioner, pushing his inquiries with equal pertinacity and indiscretion; he had been observed, when he took a letter to the post, to weigh it in his hand, to turn it over and over, and to study the address with care; and when he found a flaw in the partition between his room and Madame Zéphyrine's, instead of filling it up, he enlarged and improved the opening, and made use of it as a spy-hole on his neighbour's affairs.

One day, in the end of March, his curiosity growing as it was indulged, he enlarged the hole a little further, so that he might command another corner of the room. That evening, when he went as usual to inspect Madame Zéphyrine's movements, he was astonished to find the aperture obscured in an odd manner on the other side, and still more abashed when the obstacle was suddenly withdrawn and a titter of laughter reached his ears. Some of the plaster had evidently betrayed the secret of his spy-hole, and his neighbour had been returning the compliment in kind. Mr. Scuddamore was moved to a very acute feeling of annoyance; he condemned Madame Zéphyrine unmercifully; he even blamed himself; but when he found, next day, that she had taken no means to baulk him of his favourite pastime, he continued to profit by her carelessness, and gratify his idle curiosity.

That next day Madame Zéphyrine received a long visit from a tall, loosely-built man of fifty or upwards, whom Silas had not hitherto seen. His tweed suit and coloured shirt, no less than his shaggy side whiskers, identified him as a Britisher, and his dull grey eye affected Silas with a sense of cold. He kept screwing his mouth from side to side and round and round during the whole colloquy, which was carried on in whispers. More than once it seemed to the young New Englander as if their gestures indicated his own apartment; but the only thing definite he could gather by the most scrupulous attention was this remark made by the Englishman in a somewhat higher key, as if in answer to some reluctance or opposition.

"I have studied his taste to a nicety, and I tell you again and again you are the only woman of the sort that I can lay my hands on."

In answer to this, Madame Zéphyrine sighed, and appeared by a gesture to resign herself, like one yielding to unqualified authority.

That afternoon the observatory was finally blinded, a wardrobe having been drawn in front of it upon the other side; and while Silas was still lamenting over this misfortune, which he attributed to the Britisher's malign suggestion, the concierge brought him up a letter in a female handwriting. It was conceived in French of no very rigorous orthography, bore no signature, and in the most encouraging terms invited the young American to be present in a certain part of the Bullier Ball at eleven o'clock that night. Curiosity and timidity fought a long battle in his heart; sometimes he was all virtue, sometimes all fire and daring; and the result of it was that, long before ten, Mr. Silas Q. Scuddamore presented himself in unimpeachable attire at the door of the Bullier Ball Rooms, and paid his entry money with a sense of reckless deviltry that was not without its charm.

It was Carnival time, and the Ball was very full and noisy. The lights and the crowd at first rather abashed our young adventurer, and then, mounting to his brain with a sort of intoxication, put him in possession of more than his own share of manhood. He felt ready to face the devil, and strutted in the ballroom with the swagger of a cavalier. While he was thus parading, he became aware of Madame Zéphyrine and her Britisher in conference behind a pillar. The catlike spirit of eavesdropping overcame him at once. He stole nearer and nearer on the couple from behind, until he was within earshot.

"That is the man," the Britisher was saying; "there—with the long blond hair—speaking to a girl in green."

Silas identified a very handsome young fellow of small stature, who was plainly the object of this designation.

"It is well," said Madame Zéphyrine. "I shall do my utmost. But, remember, the best of us may fail in such a matter."

"Tut!" returned her companion; "I answer for the result. Have I not chosen you from thirty? Go; but be wary of the Prince. I cannot think what cursed accident has brought him here tonight. As if there were not a dozen balls in Paris better worth his notice than this riot of students and counterjumpers! See him where he sits, more like a reigning Emperor at home than a Prince upon his holidays!"

Silas was again lucky. He observed a person of rather a full build, strikingly handsome, and of a very stately and courteous demeanour, seated at table with another handsome young man, several years his junior, who addressed him with conspicuous deference. The name of Prince struck gratefully on Silas's Republican hearing, and the aspect of the person to whom that name was applied exercised its usual charm upon his mind. He left Madame Zéphyrine and her Englishman to take care of each other, and threading his way through the assembly, approached the table which the Prince and his confidant had honoured with their choice.

"I tell you, Geraldine," the former was saying, "the action is madness. Yourself (I am glad to remember it) chose your brother for this perilous service, and you are bound in duty to have a guard upon his conduct. He has consented to delay so many days in Paris; that was already an imprudence, considering the character of the man he has to deal with; but now, when he is within eight-and-forty hours of his departure, when he is within two or three days of the decisive trial, I ask you, is this a place for him to spend his time? He should be in a gallery at practice; he should be sleeping long hours and taking moderate exercise on foot; he should be on a rigorous diet, without white wines or brandy. Does the dog imagine we are all playing comedy? The thing is deadly earnest, Geraldine."

"I know the lad too well to interfere," replied Colonel Geraldine, "and well enough not to be alarmed. He is more cautious than you fancy, and of an indomitable spirit. If it had been a woman I should not say so much, but I trust the President to him and the two valets without an instant's apprehension."

"I am gratified to hear you say so," replied the Prince; "but my mind is not at rest. These servants are well-trained spies, and already has not this miscreant succeeded three times in eluding their observation and spending several hours on end in private, and most likely dangerous affairs? An amateur might have lost him by accident, but if Rudolph and Jérome were thrown off the scent, it must have been done on purpose, and by a man who had a cogent reason and exceptional resources."

"I believe the question is now one between my brother and myself," replied Geraldine, with a shade of offence in his tone.

"I permit it to be so, Colonel Geraldine," returned Prince Florizel. "Perhaps, for that very reason, you should be all the more ready to accept my counsels. But enough. That girl in yellow dances well."

And the talk veered into the ordinary topics of a Paris ballroom in the Carnival.

Silas remembered where he was, and that the hour was already near at hand when he ought to be upon the scene of his assignation. The more he reflected the less he liked the prospect, and as at that moment an eddy in the crowd began to draw him in the direction of the door, he suffered it to carry him away without resistance. The eddy stranded him in a corner under the gallery, where his ear was immediately struck with the voice of Madame Zéphyrine. She was speaking in French with the young man of the blond locks who had been pointed out by the strange Britisher not half an hour before.

"I have a character at stake," she said, "or I would put no other condition than my heart recommends. But you have only to say so much to the porter, and he will let you go by without a word."

"But why this talk of debt?" objected her companion.

"Heavens!" said she, "do you think I do not understand my own hotel?"

And she went by, clinging affectionately to her companion's arm.

This put Silas in mind of his billet.

"Ten minutes hence," thought he, "and I may be walking with as beautiful a woman as that, and even better dressed—perhaps a real lady, possibly a woman of title."

And then he remembered the spelling, and was a little downcast.

"But it may have been written by her maid," he imagined.

The clock was only a few minutes from the hour, and this immediate proximity set his heart beating at a curious and rather disagreeable speed. He reflected with relief that he was in no way bound to put in an appearance. Virtue and cowardice were together, and he made once more for the door, but this time of his own accord, and battling against the stream of people which was now moving in a contrary direction. Perhaps this prolonged resistance wearied him, or perhaps he was in that frame of mind when merely to continue in the same determination for a certain number of minutes produces a reaction and a different purpose. Certainly, at least, he wheeled about for a third time, and did not stop until he had found a place of concealment within a few yards of the appointed place.

Here he went through an agony of spirit, in which he several times prayed to God for help, for Silas had been devoutly educated. He had now not the least inclination for the meeting; nothing kept him from flight but a silly fear lest he should be thought unmanly; but this was so powerful that it kept head against all other motives; and although it could not decide him to advance, prevented him from definitely running away. At last the clock indicated ten minutes past the hour. Young Scuddamore's spirit began to rise; he peered round the corner and saw no one at the place of meeting; doubtless his unknown correspondent had wearied and gone away. He became as bold as he had formerly been timid. It seemed to him that if he came at all to the appointment, however late, he was clear from the charge of cowardice. Nay, now he began to suspect a hoax, and actually complimented himself on his shrewdness in having suspected and outmanoeuvered his mystifiers. So very idle a thing is a boy's mind!

Armed with these reflections, he advanced boldly from his corner; but he had not taken above a couple of steps before a hand was laid upon his arm. He turned and beheld a lady cast in a very large mould and with somewhat stately features, but bearing no mark of severity in her looks.

"I see that you are a very self-confident lady-killer," said she; "for you make yourself expected. But I was determined to meet you. When a woman has once so far forgotten herself as to make the first advance, she has long ago left behind her all considerations of petty pride."

Silas was overwhelmed by the size and attractions of his correspondent and the suddenness with which she had fallen upon him. But she soon set him at his ease. She was very towardly and lenient in her behaviour; she led him on to make pleasantries, and then applauded him to the echo; and in a very short time, between blandishments and a liberal exhibition of warm brandy, she had not only induced him to fancy himself in love, but to declare his passion with the greatest vehemence.

"Alas!" she said; "I do not know whether I ought not to deplore this moment, great as is the pleasure you give me by your words. Hitherto I was alone to suffer; now, poor boy, there will be two. I am not my own mistress. I dare not ask you to visit me at my own house, for I am watched by jealous eyes. Let me see," she added; "I am older than you, although so much weaker; and while I trust in your courage and determination, I must employ my own knowledge of the world for our mutual benefit. Where do you live?"

He told her that he lodged in a furnished hotel, and named the street and number.

She seemed to reflect for some minutes, with an effort of mind.

"I see," she said at last. "You will be faithful and obedient, will you not?"

Silas assured her eagerly of his fidelity.

"Tomorrow night, then," she continued, with an encouraging smile, "you must remain at home all the evening; and if any friends should visit you, dismiss them at once on any pretext that most readily presents itself. Your door is probably shut by ten?" she asked.

"By eleven," answered Silas.

"At a quarter past eleven," pursued the lady, "leave the house. Merely cry for the door to be opened, and be sure you fall into no talk with the porter, as that might ruin everything. Go straight to the corner where the Luxembourg Gardens join the Boulevard; there you will find me waiting you. I trust you to follow my advice from point to point: and remember, if you fail me in only one particular, you will bring the sharpest trouble on a woman whose only fault is to have seen and loved you."

"I cannot see the use of all these instructions," said Silas.

"I believe you are already beginning to treat me as a master," she cried, tapping him with her fan upon the arm. "Patience, patience! that should come in time. A woman loves to be obeyed at first, although afterwards she finds her pleasure in obeying. Do as I ask you, for

Heaven's sake, or I will answer for nothing. Indeed, now I think of it," she added, with the manner of one who has just seen further into a difficulty, "I find a better plan of keeping importunate visitors away. Tell the porter to admit no one for you, except a person who may come that night to claim a debt; and speak with some feeling, as though you feared the interview, so that he may take your words in earnest."

"I think you may trust me to protect myself against intruders," he said, not without a little pique.

"That is how I should prefer the thing arranged," she answered, coldly. "I know you men; you think nothing of a woman's reputation."

Silas blushed and somewhat hung his head; for the scheme he had in view had involved a little vainglorying before his acquaintances.

"Above all," she added, "do not speak to the porter as you come out."

"And why?" said he. "Of all your instructions, that seems to me the least important."

"You at first doubted the wisdom of some of the others, which you now see to be very necessary," she replied. "Believe me, this also has its uses; in time you will see them; and what am I to think of your affection, if you refuse me such trifles at our first interview?"

Silas confounded himself in explanations and apologies; in the middle of these she looked up at the clock and clapped her hands together with a suppressed scream.

"Heavens!" she cried, "is it so late? I have not an instant to lose. Alas, we poor women, what slaves we are! What have I not risked for you already?"

And after repeating her directions, which she artfully combined with caresses and the most abandoned looks, she bade him farewell and disappeared among the crowd.

The whole of the next day Silas was filled with a sense of great importance; he was now sure she was a countess; and when evening came he minutely obeyed her orders and was at the corner of the Luxembourg Gardens by the hour appointed. No one was there. He waited nearly half an hour, looking in the face of everyone who passed or loitered near the spot; he even visited the neighbouring corners of the Boulevard and made a complete circuit of the garden railings; but there was no beautiful countess to throw herself into his arms. At last, and most reluctantly, he began to retrace his steps towards his hotel. On the way he remembered the words he had heard pass between

Madame Zéphyrine and the blond young man, and they gave him an indefinite uneasiness.

"It appears," he reflected, "that everyone has to tell lies to our porter."

He rang the bell, the door opened before him, and the porter in his bedclothes came to offer him a light.

"Has he gone?" inquired the porter.

"He? Whom do you mean?" asked Silas, somewhat sharply, for he was irritated by his disappointment.

"I did not notice him go out," continued the porter, "but I trust you paid him. We do not care, in this house, to have lodgers who cannot meet their liabilities."

"What the devil do you mean?" demanded Silas, rudely. "I cannot understand a word of this farrago."

"The short, blond young man who came for his debt," returned the other. "Him it is I mean. Who else should it be, when I had your orders to admit no one else?"

"Why, good God, of course he never came," retorted Silas.

"I believe what I believe," returned the porter, putting his tongue into his cheek with a most roguish air.

"You are an insolent scoundrel," cried Silas, and, feeling that he had made a ridiculous exhibition of asperity, and at the same time bewildered by a dozen alarms, he turned and began to run upstairs.

"Do you not want a light then?" cried the porter.

But Silas only hurried the faster, and did not pause until he had reached the seventh landing and stood in front of his own door. There he waited a moment to recover his breath, assailed by the worst forebodings and almost dreading to enter the room.

When at last he did so he was relieved to find it dark, and to all appearance, untenanted. He drew a long breath. Here he was, home again in safety, and this should be his last folly as certainly as it had been his first. The matches stood on a little table by the bed, and he began to grope his way in that direction. As he moved, his apprehensions grew upon him once more, and he was pleased, when his foot encountered an obstacle, to find it nothing more alarming than a chair. At last he touched curtains. From the position of the window, which was faintly visible, he knew he must be at the foot of the bed, and had only to feel his way along it in order to reach the table in question.

He lowered his hand, but what it touched was not simply a counterpane—it was a counterpane with something underneath it like the outline of a human leg. Silas withdrew his arm and stood a moment petrified.

"What, what," he thought, "can this betoken?"

He listened intently, but there was no sound of breathing. Once more, with a great effort, he reached out the end of his finger to the spot he had already touched; but this time he leaped back half a yard, and stood shivering and fixed with terror. There was something in his bed. What it was he knew not, but there was something there.

It was some seconds before he could move. Then, guided by an instinct, he fell straight upon the matches, and keeping his back towards the bed lighted a candle. As soon as the flame had kindled, he turned slowly round and looked for what he feared to see. Sure enough, there was the worst of his imaginations realised. The coverlid was drawn carefully up over the pillow, but it moulded the outline of a human body lying motionless; and when he dashed forward and flung aside the sheets, he beheld the blond young man whom he had seen in the Bullier Ball the night before, his eyes open and without speculation, his face swollen and blackened, and a thin stream of blood trickling from his nostrils.

Silas uttered a long, tremulous wail, dropped the candle, and fell on his knees beside the bed.

Silas was awakened from the stupor into which his terrible discovery had plunged him, by a prolonged but discreet tapping at the door. It took him some seconds to remember his position; and when he hastened to prevent anyone from entering it was already too late. Dr. Noel, in a tall nightcap, carrying a lamp which lighted up his long white countenance, sidling in his gait, and peering and cocking his head like some sort of bird, pushed the door slowly open, and advanced into the middle of the room.

"I thought I heard a cry," began the Doctor, "and fearing you might be unwell I did not hesitate to offer this intrusion."

Silas, with a flushed face and a fearful beating heart, kept between the Doctor and the bed; but he found no voice to answer.

"You are in the dark," pursued the Doctor; "and yet you have not even begun to prepare for rest. You will not easily persuade me against my own eyesight; and your face declares most eloquently that you require either a friend or a physician—which is it to be? Let me feel your pulse, for that is often a just reporter of the heart."

He advanced to Silas, who still retreated before him backwards, and sought to take him by the wrist; but the strain on the young American's nerves had become too great for endurance. He avoided the Doctor with a febrile movement, and, throwing himself upon the floor, burst into a flood of weeping.

As soon as Dr. Noel perceived the dead man in the bed his face darkened; and hurrying back to the door which he had left ajar, he hastily closed and double-locked it.

"Up!" he cried, addressing Silas in strident tones; "this is no time for weeping. What have you done? How came this body in your room? Speak freely to one who may be helpful. Do you imagine I would ruin you? Do you think this piece of dead flesh on your pillow can alter in any degree the sympathy with which you have inspired me? Credulous youth, the horror with which blind and unjust law regards an action never attaches to the doer in the eyes of those who love him; and if I saw the friend of my heart return to me out of seas of blood he would be in no way changed in my affection. Raise yourself," he said; "good and ill are a chimera; there is nought in life except destiny, and however you may be circumstanced there is one at your side who will help you to the last."

Thus encouraged, Silas gathered himself together, and in a broken voice, and helped out by the Doctor's interrogations, contrived at last to put him in possession of the facts. But the conversation between the Prince and Geraldine he altogether omitted, as he had understood little of its purport, and had no idea that it was in any way related to his own misadventure.

"Alas!" cried Dr. Noel, "I am much abused, or you have fallen innocently into the most dangerous hands in Europe. Poor boy, what a pit has been dug for your simplicity! into what a deadly peril have your unwary feet been conducted! This man," he said, "this Englishman, whom you twice saw, and whom I suspect to be the soul of the contrivance, can you describe him? Was he young or old? tall or short?"

But Silas, who, for all his curiosity, had not a seeing eye in his head, was able to supply nothing but meagre generalities, which it was impossible to recognise.

"I would have it a piece of education in all schools!" cried the Doctor angrily. "Where is the use of eyesight and articulate speech if a man cannot observe and recollect the features of his enemy? I, who know all the gangs of Europe, might have identified him, and gained new weapons for your defence. Cultivate this art in future, my poor boy; you may find it of momentous service."

"The future!" repeated Silas. "What future is there left for me except the gallows?"

"Youth is but a cowardly season," returned the Doctor; "and a man's own troubles look blacker than they are. I am old, and yet I never despair."

"Can I tell such a story to the police?" demanded Silas.

"Assuredly not," replied the Doctor. "From what I see already of the machination in which you have been involved, your case is desperate upon that side; and for the narrow eye of the authorities you are infallibly the guilty person. And remember that we only know a portion of the plot; and the same infamous contrivers have doubtless arranged many other circumstances which would be elicited by a police inquiry, and help to fix the guilt more certainly upon your innocence."

"I am then lost, indeed!" cried Silas.

"I have not said so," answered Dr. Noel, "for I am a cautious man."

"But look at this!" objected Silas, pointing to the body. "Here is this object in my bed: not to be explained, not to be disposed of, not to be regarded without horror."

"Horror?" replied the Doctor. "No. When this sort of clock has run down, it is no more to me than an ingenious piece of mechanism, to be investigated with the bistery. When blood is once cold and stagnant, it is no longer human blood; when flesh is once dead, it is no longer that flesh which we desire in our lovers and respect in our friends. The grace, the attraction, the terror, have all gone from it with the animating spirit. Accustom yourself to look upon it with composure; for if my scheme is practicable you will have to live some days in constant proximity to that which now so greatly horrifies you."

"Your scheme?" cried Silas. "What is that? Tell me speedily, Doctor; for I have scarcely courage enough to continue to exist."

Without replying, Dr. Noel turned towards the bed, and proceeded to examine the corpse.

"Quite dead," he murmured. "Yes, as I had supposed, the pockets empty. Yes, and the name cut off the shirt. Their work has been done thoroughly and well. Fortunately, he is of small stature."

Silas followed these words with an extreme anxiety. At last the Doctor, his autopsy completed, took a chair and addressed the young American with a smile.

"Since I came into your room," said he, "although my ears and my tongue have been so busy, I have not suffered my eyes to remain idle. I noted a little while ago that you have there, in the corner, one of those monstrous constructions which your fellow countrymen carry with them into all quarters of the globe—in a word, a Saratoga trunk. Until this moment I have never been able to conceive the utility of these erections; but then I began to have a glimmer. Whether it was for convenience in the slave trade, or to obviate the results of too ready an employment of the bowie knife, I cannot bring myself to decide. But one thing I see plainly—the object of such a box is to contain a human body."

"Surely," cried Silas, "surely this is not a time for jesting."

"Although I may express myself with some degree of pleasantry," replied the Doctor, "the purport of my words is entirely serious. And the first thing we have to do, my young friend, is to empty your coffer of all that it contains."

Silas, obeying the authority of Doctor Noel, put himself at his disposition. The Saratoga trunk was soon gutted of its contents, which made a considerable litter on the floor; and then—Silas taking the heels and the Doctor supporting the shoulders—the body of the murdered man was carried from the bed, and, after some difficulty, doubled up and inserted whole into the empty box. With an effort on the part of both, the lid was forced down upon this unusual baggage, and the trunk was locked and corded by the Doctor's own hand, while Silas disposed of what had been taken out between the closet and a chest of drawers.

"Now," said the Doctor, "the first step has been taken on the way to your deliverance. Tomorrow, or rather today, it must be your task to allay the suspicions of your porter, paying him all that you owe; while you may trust me to make the arrangements necessary to a safe conclusion. Meantime, follow me to my room, where I shall give you a safe and powerful opiate; for, whatever you do, you must have rest."

The next day was the longest in Silas's memory; it seemed as if it would never be done. He denied himself to his friends, and sat in a corner with his eyes fixed upon the Saratoga trunk in dismal contemplation. His own former indiscretions were now returned upon him in kind; for the observatory had been once more opened, and he was conscious of an almost continual study from Madame Zéphyrine's apartment. So distressing did this become, that he was at last obliged to block up the spy-hole from his own side; and when he was thus secured from observation he spent a considerable portion of his time in contrite tears and prayer.

Late in the evening Dr. Noel entered the room carrying in his hand a pair of sealed envelopes without address, one somewhat bulky, and the other so slim as to seem without enclosure.

"Silas," he said, seating himself at the table, "the time has now come for me to explain my plan for your salvation. Tomorrow morning, at an early hour, Prince Florizel of Bohemia returns to London, after having diverted himself for a few days with the Parisian carnival. It was my fortune, a good while ago, to do Colonel Geraldine, his Master of the Horse, one of those services, so common in my profession, which are never forgotten upon either side. I have no need to explain to you the nature of the obligation under which he was laid; suffice it to say that I knew him ready to serve me in any practicable manner. Now, it was necessary for you to gain London with your trunk unopened. To this the Custom House seemed to oppose a fatal difficulty; but I bethought me that the baggage of so considerable a person as the Prince, is, as a matter of courtesy, passed without examination by the officers of Custom. I applied to Colonel Geraldine, and succeeded in obtaining a favourable answer. Tomorrow, if you go before six to the hotel where the Prince lodges, your baggage will be passed over as a part of his, and you yourself will make the journey as a member of his suite."

"It seems to me, as you speak, that I have already seen both the Prince and Colonel Geraldine; I even overheard some of their conversation the other evening at the Bullier Ball."

"It is probable enough; for the Prince loves to mix with all societies," replied the Doctor. "Once arrived in London," he pursued, "your task is nearly ended. In this more bulky envelope I have given you a letter which I dare not address; but in the other you will find the designation of the house to which you must carry it along with your box, which will there be taken from you and not trouble you any more."

"Alas!" said Silas, "I have every wish to believe you; but how is it possible? You open up to me a bright prospect, but, I ask you, is my mind capable of receiving so unlikely a solution? Be more generous, and let me farther understand your meaning."

The Doctor seemed painfully impressed.

"Boy," he answered, "you do not know how hard a thing you ask of me. But be it so. I am now inured to humiliation; and it would be strange if I refused you this, after having granted you so much. Know, then, that although I now make so quiet an appearance—frugal, solitary, addicted to study—when I was younger, my name was once a rallying cry among the most astute and dangerous spirits of London; and while I was outwardly an object for respect and consideration, my true power resided in the most secret, terrible, and criminal relations. It is to one of the persons who then obeyed me that I now address myself to deliver you from your burden. They were men of many different nations and dexterities, all bound together by a formidable oath, and working to the same purposes; the trade of the association was in murder; and I who speak to you, innocent as I appear, was the chieftain of this redoubtable crew."

"What?" cried Silas. "A murderer? And one with whom murder was a trade? Can I take your hand? Ought I so much as to accept your services? Dark and criminal old man, would you make an accomplice of my youth and my distress?"

The Doctor bitterly laughed.

"You are difficult to please, Mr. Scuddamore," said he; "but I now offer you your choice of company between the murdered man and the murderer. If your conscience is too nice to accept my aid, say so, and I will immediately leave you. Thenceforward you can deal with your trunk and its belongings as best suits your upright conscience."

"I own myself wrong," replied Silas. "I should have remembered how generously you offered to shield me, even before I had convinced you of my innocence, and I continue to listen to your counsels with gratitude."

"That is well," returned the Doctor; "and I perceive you are beginning to learn some of the lessons of experience."

"At the same time," resumed the New Englander, "as you confess yourself accustomed to this tragical business, and the people to whom you recommend me are your own former associates and friends, could you not yourself undertake the transport of the box, and rid me at once of its detested presence?"

"Upon my word," replied the Doctor, "I admire you cordially. If you do not think I have already meddled sufficiently in your concerns, believe me, from my heart I think the contrary. Take or leave my services as I offer them; and trouble me with no more words of gratitude, for I value your consideration even more lightly than I do your intellect. A time will come, if you should be spared to see a number of years in health of mind, when you will think differently of all this, and blush for your tonight's behaviour."

So saying, the Doctor arose from his chair, repeated his directions briefly and clearly, and departed from the room without permitting Silas any time to answer.

The next morning Silas presented himself at the hotel, where he was politely received by Colonel Geraldine, and relieved, from that moment, of all immediate alarm about his trunk and its grisly contents. The journey passed over without much incident, although the young man was horrified to overhear the sailors and railway porters complaining among themselves about the unusual weight of the Prince's baggage. Silas travelled in a carriage with the valets, for Prince Florizel chose to be alone with his Master of the Horse. On board the steamer, however, Silas attracted his Highness's attention by the melancholy of his air and attitude as he stood gazing at the pile of baggage; for he was still full of disquietude about the future.

"There is a young man," observed the Prince, "who must have some cause for sorrow."

"That," replied Geraldine, "is the American for whom I obtained permission to travel with your suite."

"You remind me that I have been remiss in courtesy," said Prince Florizel, and advancing to Silas, he addressed him with the most exquisite condescension in these words:

"I was charmed, young sir, to be able to gratify the desire you made known to me through Colonel Geraldine. Remember, if you please, that I shall be glad at any future time to lay you under a more serious obligation."

And he then put some questions as to the political condition of America, which Silas answered with sense and propriety.

"You are still a young man," said the Prince; "but I observe you to be very serious for your years. Perhaps you allow your attention to be too much occupied with grave studies. But, perhaps, on the other hand, I am myself indiscreet and touch upon a painful subject."

"I have certainly cause to be the most miserable of men," said Silas; "never has a more innocent person been more dismally abused."

"I will not ask you for your confidence," returned Prince Florizel. "But do not forget that Colonel Geraldine's recommendation is an unfailing passport; and that I am not only willing, but possibly more able than many others, to do you a service."

Silas was delighted with the amiability of this great personage; but his mind soon returned upon its gloomy preoccupations; for not even the favour of a prince to a Republican can discharge a brooding spirit of its cares.

The train arrived at Charing Cross, where the officers of the Revenue respected the baggage of Prince Florizel in the usual manner. The most elegant equipages were in waiting; and Silas was driven, along with the rest, to the Prince's residence. There Colonel Geraldine sought him out, and expressed himself pleased to have been of any service to a friend of the physician's, for whom he professed a great consideration.

"I hope," he added, "that you will find none of your porcelain injured. Special orders were given along the line to deal tenderly with the Prince's effects."

And then, directing the servants to place one of the carriages at the young gentleman's disposal, and at once to charge the Saratoga trunk upon the dickey, the Colonel shook hands and excused himself on account of his occupations in the princely household.

Silas now broke the seal of the envelope containing the address, and directed the stately footman to drive him to Box Court, opening off the Strand. It seemed as if the place were not at all unknown to the man, for he looked startled and begged a repetition of the order. It was with a heart full of alarms, that Silas mounted into the luxurious vehicle, and was driven to his destination. The entrance to Box Court was too narrow for the passage of a coach; it was a mere footway between railings, with a post at either end. On one of these posts was seated a man, who at once jumped down and exchanged a friendly sign with the driver, while the footman opened the door and inquired of Silas whether he should take down the Saratoga trunk, and to what number it should be carried.

"If you please," said Silas. "To number three."

The footman and the man who had been sitting on the post, even with the aid of Silas himself, had hard work to carry in the trunk; and before it was deposited at the door of the house in question, the young American was horrified to find a score of loiterers looking on. But he knocked with as good a countenance as he could muster up, and presented the other envelope to him who opened.

"He is not at home," said he, "but if you will leave your letter and return tomorrow early, I shall be able to inform you whether and when he can receive your visit. Would you like to leave your box?" he added.

"Dearly," cried Silas; and the next moment he repented his precipitation, and declared, with equal emphasis, that he would carry the box along with him to the hotel.

The crowd jeered at his indecision and followed him to the carriage with insulting remarks; and Silas, covered with shame and terror, implored the servants to conduct him to some quiet and comfortable house of entertainment in the immediate neighbourhood.

The Prince's equipage deposited Silas at the Craven Hotel in Craven Street, and immediately drove away, leaving him alone with the servants of the inn. The only vacant room, it appeared, was a little den up four pairs of stairs, and looking towards the back. To this hermitage, with infinite trouble and complaint, a pair of stout porters carried the Saratoga trunk. It is needless to mention that Silas kept closely at their heels throughout the ascent, and had his heart in his mouth at every corner. A single false step, he reflected, and the box might go over the bannisters and land its fatal contents, plainly discovered, on the pavement of the hall.

Arrived in the room, he sat down on the edge of his bed to recover from the agony that he had just endured; but he had hardly taken his position when he was recalled to a sense of his peril by the action of the boots, who had knelt beside the trunk, and was proceeding officiously to undo its elaborate fastenings.

"Let it be!" cried Silas. "I shall want nothing from it while I stay here."

"You might have let it lie in the hall, then," growled the man; "a thing as big and heavy as a church. What you have inside, I cannot fancy. If it is all money, you are a richer man than me."

"Money?" repeated Silas, in a sudden perturbation. "What do you mean by money? I have no money, and you are speaking like a fool."

"All right, captain," retorted the boots with a wink. "There's nobody will touch your lordship's money. I'm as safe as the bank," he added; "but as the box is heavy, I shouldn't mind drinking something to your lordship's health."

Silas pressed two Napoleons upon his acceptance, apologising, at the same time, for being obliged to trouble him with foreign money, and pleading his recent arrival for excuse. And the man, grumbling with even greater fervour, and looking contemptuously from the money in his hand to the Saratoga trunk and back again from the one to the other, at last consented to withdraw.

For nearly two days the dead body had been packed into Silas's box; and as soon as he was alone the unfortunate New Englander nosed all the cracks and openings with the most passionate attention. But the weather was cool, and the trunk still managed to contain his shocking secret.

He took a chair beside it, and buried his face in his hands, and his mind in the most profound reflection. If he were not speedily relieved, no question but he must be speedily discovered. Alone in a strange city, without friends or accomplices, if the Doctor's introduction failed him, he was indubitably a lost New Englander. He reflected pathetically over his ambitious designs for the future; he should not now become the hero and spokesman of his native place of Bangor, Maine; he should not, as he had fondly anticipated, move on from office to office, from honour to honour; he might as well divest himself at once of all hope of being acclaimed President of the United States, and leaving behind him a statue, in the worst possible style of art, to adorn the Capitol at Washington. Here he was, chained to a dead Englishman doubled up inside a Saratoga trunk; whom he must get rid of, or perish from the rolls of national glory!

I should be afraid to chronicle the language employed by this young man to the Doctor, to the murdered man, to Madame Zéphyrine, to the boots of the hotel, to the Prince's servants, and, in a word, to all who had been ever so remotely connected with his horrible misfortune.

He slunk down to dinner about seven at night; but the yellow coffee room appalled him, the eyes of the other diners seemed to rest on his with suspicion, and his mind remained upstairs with the Saratoga trunk. When the waiter came to offer him cheese, his nerves were already so much on edge that he leaped halfway out of his chair and upset the remainder of a pint of ale upon the tablecloth.

The fellow offered to show him to the smoking room when he had done; and although he would have much preferred to return at once to his perilous treasure, he had not the courage to refuse, and was shown downstairs to the black, gas-lit cellar, which formed, and possibly still forms, the divan of the Craven Hotel.

Two very sad betting men were playing billiards, attended by a moist, consumptive marker; and for the moment Silas imagined that these were the only occupants of the apartment. But at the next glance his eye fell upon a person smoking in the farthest corner, with lowered eyes and a most respectable and modest aspect. He knew at once that he had seen the face before; and, in spite of the entire change of clothes, recognised the man whom he had found seated on a post at the entrance to Box Court, and who had helped him to carry the trunk to and from the carriage. The New Englander simply turned and ran, nor did he pause until he had locked and bolted himself into his bedroom.

There, all night long, a prey to the most terrible imaginations, he watched beside the fatal boxful of dead flesh. The suggestion of the boots that his trunk was full of gold inspired him with all manner of new terrors, if he so much as dared to close an eye; and the presence in the smoking room, and under an obvious disguise, of the loiterer from Box Court convinced him that he was once more the centre of obscure machinations.

Midnight had sounded some time, when, impelled by uneasy suspicions, Silas opened his bedroom door and peered into the passage. It was dimly illuminated by a single jet of gas; and some distance off he perceived a man sleeping on the floor in the costume of an hotel underservant. Silas drew near the man on tiptoe. He lay partly on his back, partly on his side, and his right forearm concealed his face from recognition. Suddenly, while the American was still bending over him, the sleeper removed his arm and opened his eyes, and Silas found himself once more face to face with the loiterer of Box Court.

"Good night, sir," said the man, pleasantly.

But Silas was too profoundly moved to find an answer, and regained his room in silence.

Towards morning, worn out by apprehension, he fell asleep on his chair, with his head forward on the trunk. In spite of so constrained an attitude and such a grisly pillow, his slumber was sound and prolonged, and he was only awakened at a late hour and by a sharp tapping at the door.

He hurried to open, and found the boots without.

"You are the gentleman who called yesterday at Box Court?" he asked.

Silas, with a quaver, admitted that he had done so.

"Then this note is for you," added the servant, proffering a sealed envelope.

Silas tore it open, and found inside the words: "Twelve o'clock."

He was punctual to the hour; the trunk was carried before him by several stout servants; and he was himself ushered into a room, where a man sat warming himself before the fire with his back towards the door. The sound of so many persons entering and leaving, and the scraping of the trunk as it was deposited upon the bare boards, were alike unable to attract the notice of the occupant; and Silas stood waiting, in an agony of fear, until he should deign to recognise his presence.

Perhaps five minutes had elapsed before the man turned leisurely about, and disclosed the features of Prince Florizel of Bohemia.

"So, sir," he said, with great severity, "this is the manner in which you abuse my politeness. You join yourselves to persons of condition, I perceive, for no other purpose than to escape the consequences of your crimes; and I can readily understand your embarrassment when I addressed myself to you yesterday."

"Indeed," cried Silas, "I am innocent of everything except misfortune."

And in a hurried voice, and with the greatest ingenuousness, he recounted to the Prince the whole history of his calamity.

"I see I have been mistaken," said his Highness, when he had heard him to an end. "You are no other than a victim, and since I am not to punish you may be sure I shall do my utmost to help. And now," he continued, "to business. Open your box at once, and let me see what it contains."

Silas changed colour.

"I almost fear to look upon it," he exclaimed.

"Nay," replied the Prince, "have you not looked at it already? This is a form of sentimentality to be resisted. The sight of a sick man, whom we can still help, should appeal more directly to the feelings than that of a dead man who is equally beyond help or harm, love or hatred. Nerve yourself, Mr. Scuddamore," and then, seeing that Silas still hesitated, "I do not desire to give another name to my request," he added.

The young American awoke as if out of a dream, and with a shiver of repugnance addressed himself to loose the straps and open the lock of the Saratoga trunk. The Prince stood by, watching with a composed countenance and his hands behind his back. The body was quite stiff, and it cost Silas a great effort, both moral and physical, to dislodge it from its position, and discover the face.

Prince Florizel started back with an exclamation of painful surprise.

"Alas!" he cried, "you little know, Mr. Scuddamore, what a cruel gift you have brought me. This is a young man of my own suite, the brother of my trusted friend; and it was upon matters of my own service that he has thus perished at the hands of violent and treacherous men. Poor Geraldine," he went on, as if to himself, "in what words am I to tell you of your brother's fate? How can I excuse myself in your eyes, or in the eyes of God, for the presumptuous schemes that led him to this bloody and unnatural death? Ah, Florizel! Florizel! when will you learn the discretion that suits mortal life, and be no longer dazzled with the image of power at your disposal? Power!" he cried; "who is more powerless? I look upon this young man whom I have sacrificed, Mr. Scuddamore, and feel how small a thing it is to be a Prince."

Silas was moved at the sight of his emotion. He tried to murmur some consolatory words, and burst into tears. The Prince, touched by his obvious intention, came up to him and took him by the hand.

"Command yourself," said he. "We have both much to learn, and we shall both be better men for today's meeting."

Silas thanked him in silence with an affectionate look.

"Write me the address of Doctor Noel on this piece of paper," continued the Prince, leading him towards the table; "and let me recommend you, when you are again in Paris, to avoid the society of that dangerous man. He has acted in this matter on a generous inspiration; that I must believe; had he been privy to young Geraldine's death he would never have despatched the body to the care of the actual criminal."

"The actual criminal!" repeated Silas in astonishment.

"Even so," returned the Prince. "This letter, which the disposition of Almighty Providence has so strangely delivered into my hands, was addressed to no less a person than the criminal himself, the infamous President of the Suicide Club. Seek to pry no farther in these perilous affairs, but content yourself with your own miraculous escape, and leave this house at once. I have pressing affairs, and must arrange at once about this poor clay, which was so lately a gallant and handsome youth."

Silas took a grateful and submissive leave of Prince Florizel, but he lingered in Box Court until he saw him depart in a splendid carriage on a visit to Colonel Henderson of the police. Republican as he was, the young American took off his hat with almost a sentiment of devotion to the retreating carriage. And the same night he started by rail on his return to Paris.

Here (observes my Arabian author) *is the end of* THE HISTORY OF THE PHYSICIAN AND THE SARATOGA TRUNK. *Omitting some reflections on the power of Providence, highly pertinent in the original, but little suited to our occidental taste, I shall only add that Mr. Scuddamore has already begun to mount the ladder of political fame, and by last advices was the Sheriff of his native town.*

THE ADVENTURE OF THE HANSOM CABS

Lieutenant Brackenbury Rich had greatly distinguished himself in one of the lesser Indian hill wars. He it was who took the chieftain prisoner with his own hand; his gallantry was universally applauded; and when he came home, prostrated by an ugly sabre cut and a protracted jungle fever, society was prepared to welcome the Lieutenant as a celebrity of minor lustre. But his was a character remarkable for unaffected modesty; adventure was dear to his heart, but he cared little for adulation; and he waited at foreign watering places and in Algiers until the fame of his exploits had run through its nine days' vitality and begun to be forgotten. He arrived in London at last, in the early season, with as little observation as he could desire; and as he was an orphan and had none but distant relatives who lived in the provinces, it was almost as a foreigner that he installed himself in the capital of the country for which he had shed his blood.

On the day following his arrival he dined alone at a military club. He shook hands with a few old comrades, and received their warm congratulations; but as one and all had some engagement for the evening, he found himself left entirely to his own resources. He was in dress, for he had entertained the notion of visiting a theatre. But the great city was new to him; he had gone from a provincial school to a military college, and thence direct to the Eastern Empire; and he promised himself a variety of delights in this world for exploration. Swinging his cane, he took his way westward. It was a mild evening, already dark, and now and then threatening rain. The succession of faces in the lamplight stirred the Lieutenant's imagination; and it seemed to him as if he could walk for ever in that stimulating city atmosphere and surrounded by the mystery of four million private lives. He glanced at the houses, and marvelled what was passing behind those warmly lighted windows; he looked into face after face, and saw them each intent upon some unknown interest, criminal or kindly.

"They talk of war," he thought, "but this is the great battlefield of mankind."

And then he began to wonder that he should walk so long in this complicated scene, and not chance upon so much as the shadow of an adventure for himself.

"All in good time," he reflected. "I am still a stranger, and perhaps wear a strange air. But I must be drawn into the eddy before long."

The night was already well advanced when a plump of cold rain fell suddenly out of the darkness. Brackenbury paused under some trees, and as he did so he caught sight of a hansom cabman making him a sign that he was disengaged. The circumstance fell in so happily to the occasion that he at once raised his cane in answer, and had soon ensconced himself in the London gondola.

"Where to, sir?" asked the driver.

"Where you please," said Brackenbury.

And immediately, at a pace of surprising swiftness, the hansom drove off through the rain into a maze of villas. One villa was so like another, each with its front garden, and there was so little to distinguish the deserted lamplit streets and crescents through which the flying hansom took its way, that Brackenbury soon lost all idea of direction. He would have been tempted to believe that the cabman was amusing himself by driving him round and round and in and out about a small quarter, but there was something businesslike in the speed which convinced him of the contrary. The man had an object in view, he was hastening towards a definite end; and Brackenbury was at once astonished at the fellow's skill in picking a way through such a labyrinth, and a little concerned to imagine what was the occasion of his hurry. He had heard tales of strangers falling ill in London. Did the driver belong to some bloody and treacherous association? and was he himself being whirled to a murderous death?

The thought had scarcely presented itself, when the cab swung sharply round a corner and pulled up before the garden gate of a villa in a long and wide road. The house was brilliantly lighted up. Another hansom had just driven away, and Brackenbury could see a gentleman being admitted at the front door and received by several liveried servants. He was surprised that the cabman should have stopped so immediately in front of a house where a reception was being held; but he did not doubt it was the result of accident, and sat placidly smoking where he was, until he heard the trap thrown open over his head.

"Here we are, sir," said the driver.

"Here!" repeated Brackenbury. "Where?"

"You told me to take you where I pleased, sir," returned the man with a chuckle, "and here we are."

It struck Brackenbury that the voice was wonderfully smooth and courteous for a man in so inferior a position; he remembered the speed at which he had been driven; and now it occurred to him that the hansom was more luxuriously appointed than the common run of public conveyances.

"I must ask you to explain," said he. "Do you mean to turn me out into the rain? My good man, I suspect the choice is mine."

"The choice is certainly yours," replied the driver; "but when I tell you all, I believe I know how a gentleman of your figure will decide. There is a gentlemen's party in this house. I do not know whether the master be a stranger to London and without acquaintances of his own;

or whether he is a man of odd notions. But certainly I was hired to kidnap single gentlemen in evening dress, as many as I pleased, but military officers by preference. You have simply to go in and say that Mr. Morris invited you."

"Are you Mr. Morris?" inquired the Lieutenant.

"Oh, no," replied the cabman. "Mr. Morris is the person of the house."

"It is not a common way of collecting guests," said Brackenbury: "but an eccentric man might very well indulge the whim without any intention to offend. And suppose that I refuse Mr. Morris's invitation," he went on, "what then?"

"My orders are to drive you back where I took you from," replied the man, "and set out to look for others up to midnight. Those who have no fancy for such an adventure, Mr. Morris said, were not the guests for him."

These words decided the Lieutenant on the spot.

"After all," he reflected, as he descended from the hansom, "I have not had long to wait for my adventure."

He had barely found footing on the sidewalk, and was still feeling in his pocket for the fare, when the cab swung about and drove off by the way it came at the former breakneck velocity. Brackenbury shouted after the man, who paid no heed, and continued to drive away; but the sound of his voice was overheard in the house, the door was again thrown open, emitting a flood of light upon the garden, and a servant ran down to meet him holding an umbrella.

"The cabman has been paid," observed the servant in a very civil tone; and he proceeded to escort Brackenbury along the path and up the steps. In the hall several other attendants relieved him of his hat, cane, and paletot, gave him a ticket with a number in return, and politely hurried him up a stair adorned with tropical flowers, to the door of an apartment on the first storey. Here a grave butler inquired his name, and announcing "Lieutenant Brackenbury Rich," ushered him into the drawing room of the house.

A young man, slender and singularly handsome, came forward and greeted him with an air at once courtly and affectionate. Hundreds of candles, of the finest wax, lit up a room that was perfumed, like the staircase, with a profusion of rare and beautiful flowering shrubs. A side table was loaded with tempting viands. Several servants went to and fro with fruits and goblets of champagne. The company was perhaps sixteen in number, all men, few beyond the prime of life, and with hardly an exception, of a dashing and capable exterior. They were divided into two groups, one about a roulette board, and the other surrounding a table at which one of their number held a bank of baccarat.

"I see," thought Brackenbury, "I am in a private gambling saloon, and the cabman was a tout."

His eye had embraced the details, and his mind formed the conclusion, while his host was still holding him by the hand; and to him his looks returned from this rapid survey. At a second view Mr. Morris surprised him still more than on the first. The easy elegance of his manners, the distinction, amiability, and courage that appeared upon his features, fitted very ill with the Lieutenant's preconceptions on the subject of the proprietor of a hell; and the tone of his conversation seemed to mark him out for a man of position and merit. Brackenbury found he had an instinctive liking for his entertainer; and though he chid himself for the weakness, he was unable to resist a sort of friendly attraction for Mr. Morris's person and character.

"I have heard of you, Lieutenant Rich," said Mr. Morris, lowering his tone; "and believe me I am gratified to make your acquaintance. Your looks accord with the reputation that has preceded you from India. And if you will forget for a while the irregularity of your presentation in my house, I shall feel it not only an honour, but a genuine pleasure besides. A man who makes a mouthful of barbarian cavaliers," he added with a laugh, "should not be appalled by a breach of etiquette, however serious."

And he led him towards the sideboard and pressed him to partake of some refreshment.

"Upon my word," the Lieutenant reflected, "this is one of the pleasantest fellows and, I do not doubt, one of the most agreeable societies in London."

He partook of some champagne, which he found excellent; and observing that many of the company were already smoking, he lit one of his own Manillas, and strolled up to the roulette board, where he sometimes made a stake and sometimes looked on smilingly on the fortune of others. It was while he was thus idling that he became aware of a sharp scrutiny to which the whole of the guests were subjected.

Mr. Morris went here and there, ostensibly busied on hospitable concerns; but he had ever a shrewd glance at disposal; not a man of the party escaped his sudden, searching looks; he took stock of the bearing of heavy losers, he valued the amount of the stakes, he paused behind couples who were deep in conversation; and, in a word, there was hardly a characteristic of anyone present but he seemed to catch and make a note of it. Brackenbury began to wonder if this were indeed a gambling hell: it had so much the air of a private inquisition. He followed Mr. Morris in all his movements; and although the man had a ready smile, he seemed to perceive, as it were under a mask, a haggard, careworn, and preoccupied spirit. The fellows around him laughed and made their game; but Brackenbury had lost interest in the guests.

"This Morris," thought he, "is no idler in the room. Some deep purpose inspires him; let it be mine to fathom it."

Now and then Mr. Morris would call one of his visitors aside; and after a brief colloquy in an anteroom, he would return alone, and the visitors in question reappeared no more. After a certain number of repetitions, this performance excited Brackenbury's curiosity to a high degree. He determined to be at the bottom of this minor mystery at once; and strolling into the anteroom, found a deep window recess concealed by curtains of the fashionable green. Here he hurriedly ensconced himself; nor had he to wait long before the sound of steps and voices drew near him from the principal apartment. Peering through the division, he saw Mr. Morris escorting a fat and ruddy personage, with somewhat the look of a commercial traveller, whom Brackenbury had already remarked for his coarse laugh and underbred behaviour at the table. The pair halted immediately before the window, so that Brackenbury lost not a word of the following discourse:

"I beg you a thousand pardons!" began Mr. Morris, with the most conciliatory manner; "and, if I appear rude, I am sure you will readily forgive me. In a place so great as London accidents must continually happen; and the best that we can hope is to remedy them with as small delay as possible. I will not deny that I fear you have made a mistake and honoured my poor house by inadvertence; for, to speak openly, I cannot at all remember your appearance. Let me put the question without unnecessary circumlocution—between gentlemen of honour a word will suffice—Under whose roof do you suppose yourself to be?"

"That of Mr. Morris," replied the other, with a prodigious display of confusion, which had been visibly growing upon him throughout the last few words.

"Mr. John or Mr. James Morris?" inquired the host.

"I really cannot tell you," returned the unfortunate guest. "I am not personally acquainted with the gentleman, any more than I am with yourself."

"I see," said Mr. Morris. "There is another person of the same name farther down the street; and I have no doubt the policeman will be able to supply you with his number. Believe me, I felicitate myself on the misunderstanding which has procured me the pleasure of your company for so long; and let me express a hope that we may meet again upon a more regular footing. Meantime, I would not for the world detain you longer from your friends. John," he added, raising his voice, "will you see that this gentleman finds his greatcoat?"

And with the most agreeable air Mr. Morris escorted his visitor as far as the anteroom door, where he left him under the conduct of the butler. As he passed the window, on his return to the drawing room, Brackenbury could hear him utter a profound sigh, as though his mind was loaded with a great anxiety, and his nerves already fatigued with the task on which he was engaged.

For perhaps an hour the hansoms kept arriving with such frequency, that Mr. Morris had to receive a new guest for every old one that he sent away, and the company preserved its number undiminished. But towards the end of that time the arrivals grew few and far between, and at length ceased entirely, while the process of elimination was continued with unimpaired activity. The drawing room began to look empty: the baccarat was discontinued for lack of a banker; more than one person said good night of his own accord, and was suffered to part without expostulation; and in the meanwhile Mr. Morris redoubled in agreeable attentions to those who stayed behind. He went from group to group and from person to person with looks of the readiest sympathy and the most pertinent and pleasing talk; he was not so much like a host as like a hostess, and there was a feminine coquetry and condescension in his manner which charmed the hearts of all.

As the guests grew thinner, Lieutenant Rich strolled for a moment out of the drawing room into the hall in quest of fresher air. But he had no sooner passed the threshold of the antechamber than he was brought to a dead halt by a discovery of the most surprising nature. The flowering shrubs had disappeared from the staircase; three large furniture waggons stood beside the garden gate; the servants were busy dismantling the house upon all sides; and some of them had already donned their greatcoats and were preparing to depart. It was like the end of a country ball, where everything has been supplied by contract. Brackenbury had indeed some matter for reflection. First, the guests, who were no real guests after all, had been dismissed; and now the servants, who could hardly be genuine servants, were actively dispersing.

"Was the whole establishment a sham?" he asked himself. "The mushroom of a single night which should disappear before morning?"

Watching a favourable opportunity, Brackenbury dashed upstairs to the higher regions of the house. It was as he had expected. He ran from room to room, and saw not a stick of furniture nor so much as a picture on the walls. Although the house had been painted and papered, it was not only uninhabited at present, but plainly had never been inhabited at all. The young officer remembered with astonishment its specious, settled, and hospitable air on his arrival. It was only at a prodigious cost that the imposture could have been carried out upon so great a scale.

Who, then, was Mr. Morris? What was his intention in thus playing the householder for a single night in the remote west of London? And why did he collect his visitors at hazard from the streets?

Brackenbury remembered that he had already delayed too long, and hastened to join the company. Many had left during his absence; and counting the Lieutenant and his host, there were not more than five persons in the drawing room—recently so thronged. Mr. Morris greeted him, as he reentered the apartment, with a smile, and immediately rose to his feet.

"It is now time, gentlemen," said he, "to explain my purpose in decoying you from your amusements. I trust you did not find the evening hang very dully on your hands; but my object, I will confess it, was not to entertain your leisure, but to help myself in an unfortunate necessity. You are all gentlemen," he continued, "your appearance does you that much justice, and I ask for no better security. Hence, I speak it without concealment, I ask you to render me a dangerous and delicate service; dangerous because you may run the hazard of your lives, and delicate because I must ask an absolute discretion upon all that you shall see or hear. From an utter stranger the request is almost comically extravagant; I am well aware of this; and I would add at once, if there be anyone present who has heard enough, if there be one among the party who recoils from a dangerous confidence and a piece of Quixotic devotion to he knows not whom—here is my hand ready, and I shall wish him good night and Godspeed with all the sincerity in the world."

A very tall, black man, with a heavy stoop, immediately responded to this appeal.

"I commend your frankness, Sir," said he; "and, for my part, I go. I make no reflections; but I cannot deny that you fill me with suspicious thoughts. I go myself, as I say; and perhaps you will think I have no right to add words to my example."

"On the contrary," replied Mr. Morris, "I am obliged to you for all you say. It would be impossible to exaggerate the gravity of my proposal."

"Well, gentlemen, what do you say?" said the tall man, addressing the others. "We have had our evening's frolic; shall we all go homeward peaceably in a body? You will think well of my suggestion in the morning, when you see the sun again in innocence and safety."

The speaker pronounced the last words with an intonation which added to their force; and his face wore a singular expression, full of gravity and significance. Another of the company rose hastily, and, with some appearance of alarm, prepared to take his leave. There were only two who held their ground, Brackenbury and an old red-nosed cavalry Major; but these two preserved a nonchalant demeanour, and, beyond a look of intelligence which they rapidly exchanged, appeared entirely foreign to the discussion that had just been terminated.

Mr. Morris conducted the deserters as far as the door, which he closed upon their heels; then he turned round, disclosing a countenance of mingled relief and animation, and addressed the two officers as follows.

"I have chosen my men like Joshua in the Bible," said Mr. Morris, "and I now believe I have the pick of London. Your appearance pleased my hansom cabmen; then it delighted me; I have watched your behaviour in a strange company, and under the most unusual circumstances: I have studied how you played and how you bore your losses; lastly, I have put you to the test of a staggering announcement, and you received it like an invitation to dinner. It is not for nothing," he cried, "that I have been for years the companion and the pupil of the bravest and wisest potentate in Europe."

"At the affair of Bunderchang," observed the Major, "I asked for twelve volunteers, and every trooper in the ranks replied to my appeal. But a gaming party is not the same thing as a regiment under fire. You may be pleased, I suppose, to have found two, and two who will not fail you at a push. As for the pair who ran away, I count them among the most pitiful hounds I ever met with. Lieutenant Rich," he added, addressing Brackenbury, "I have heard much of you of late; and I cannot doubt but you have also heard of me. I am Major O'Rooke."

And the veteran tendered his hand, which was red and tremulous, to the young Lieutenant.

"Who has not?" answered Brackenbury.

"When this little matter is settled," said Mr. Morris, "you will think I have sufficiently rewarded you; for I could offer neither a more valuable service than to make him acquainted with the other."

"And now," said Major O'Rooke, "is it a duel?"

"A duel after a fashion," replied Mr. Morris, "a duel with unknown and dangerous enemies, and, as I gravely fear, a duel to the death. I must ask you," he continued, "to call me Morris no longer; call me, if you please, Hammersmith; my real name, as well as that of another person to whom I hope to present you before long, you will gratify me by not asking and not seeking to discover for yourselves. Three days ago the person of whom I speak disappeared suddenly from home; and, until this morning, I received no hint of his situation. You will fancy my alarm when I tell you that he is engaged upon a work of private justice. Bound by an unhappy oath, too lightly sworn, he finds it necessary, without the help of law, to rid the earth of an insidious and bloody villain. Already two of our friends, and one of them my own born brother, have perished in the enterprise. He himself, or I am much deceived, is taken in the same fatal toils. But at least he still lives and still hopes, as this billet sufficiently proves."

And the speaker, no other than Colonel Geraldine, proffered a letter, thus conceived:

"Major Hammersmith,—On Wednesday, at 3 A.M., you will be admitted by the small door to the gardens of Rochester House, Regent's Park, by a man who is entirely in my interest. I must request you not to fail me by a second. Pray bring my case of swords, and, if you can find them, one or two gentlemen of conduct and discretion to whom my person is unknown. My name must not be used in this affair.

T. GODALL."

"From his wisdom alone, if he had no other title," pursued Colonel Geraldine, when the others had each satisfied his curiosity, "my friend is a man whose directions should implicitly be followed. I need not tell you, therefore, that I have not so much as visited the neighbourhood of Rochester House; and that I am still as wholly in the dark as either of yourselves as to the nature of my friend's dilemma. I betook myself, as soon as I had received this order, to a furnishing contractor, and, in a few hours, the house in which we now are had assumed its late air of festival. My scheme was at least original; and I am far from regretting an action which has procured me the services of Major O'Rooke and Lieutenant Brackenbury Rich. But the servants in the street will have a strange awakening. The house which this evening was full of lights and visitors they will find uninhabited and for sale tomorrow morning. Thus even the most serious concerns," added the Colonel, "have a merry side."

"And let us add a merry ending," said Brackenbury.

The Colonel consulted his watch.

"It is now hard on two," he said. "We have an hour before us, and a swift cab is at the door. Tell me if I may count upon your help."

"During a long life," replied Major O'Rooke, "I never took back my hand from anything, nor so much as hedged a bet."

Brackenbury signified his readiness in the most becoming terms; and after they had drunk a glass or two of wine, the Colonel gave each of them a loaded revolver, and the three mounted into the cab and drove off for the address in question.

Rochester House was a magnificent residence on the banks of the canal. The large extent of the garden isolated it in an unusual degree from the annoyances of neighbourhood. It seemed the *parc aux cerfs* of some great nobleman or millionaire. As far as could be seen from the street, there was not a glimmer of light in any of the numerous windows of the mansion; and the place had a look of neglect, as though the master had been long from home.

The cab was discharged, and the three gentlemen were not long in discovering the small door, which was a sort of postern in a lane between two garden walls. It still wanted ten or fifteen minutes of the appointed time; the rain fell heavily, and the adventurers sheltered themselves below some pendant ivy, and spoke in low tones of the approaching trial.

Suddenly Geraldine raised his finger to command silence, and all three bent their hearing to the utmost. Through the continuous noise of the rain, the steps and voices of two men became audible from the other side of the wall; and, as they drew nearer, Brackenbury, whose sense of hearing was remarkably acute, could even distinguish some fragments of their talk.

"Is the grave dug?" asked one.

"It is," replied the other; "behind the laurel hedge. When the job is done, we can cover it with a pile of stakes."

The first speaker laughed, and the sound of his merriment was shocking to the listeners on the other side.

"In an hour from now," he said.

And by the sound of the steps it was obvious that the pair had separated, and were proceeding in contrary directions.

Almost immediately after the postern door was cautiously opened, a white face was protruded into the lane, and a hand was seen beckoning to the watchers. In dead silence the three passed the door, which was immediately locked behind them, and followed their guide through several garden alleys to the kitchen entrance of the house. A single candle burned in the great paved kitchen, which was destitute of the customary furniture; and as the party proceeded to ascend from thence by a flight of winding stairs, a prodigious noise of rats testified still more plainly to the dilapidation of the house.

Their conductor preceded them, carrying the candle. He was a lean man, much bent, but still agile; and he turned from time to time and admonished silence and caution by his gestures. Colonel Geraldine followed on his heels, the case of swords under one arm, and a pistol ready in the other. Brackenbury's heart beat thickly. He perceived that they were still in time; but he judged from the alacrity of the old man that the hour of action must be near at hand; and the circumstances of this adventure were so obscure and menacing, the place seemed so well chosen for the darkest acts, that an older man than Brackenbury might have been pardoned a measure of emotion as he closed the procession up the winding stair.

At the top the guide threw open a door and ushered the three officers before him into a small apartment, lighted by a smoky lamp and the glow of a modest fire. At the chimney corner sat a man in the early prime of life, and of a stout but courtly and commanding appearance. His attitude and expression were those of the most unmoved composure; he was smoking a cheroot with much enjoyment and deliberation, and on a table by his elbow stood a long glass of some effervescing beverage which diffused an agreeable odour through the room.

"Welcome," said he, extending his hand to Colonel Geraldine. "I knew I might count on your exactitude."

"On my devotion," replied the Colonel, with a bow.

"Present me to your friends," continued the first; and, when that ceremony had been performed, "I wish, gentlemen," he added, with the most exquisite affability, "that I could offer you a more cheerful programme; it is ungracious to inaugurate an acquaintance upon serious affairs; but the compulsion of events is stronger than the obligations of good-fellowship. I hope and believe you will be able to forgive me this unpleasant evening; and for men of your stamp it will be enough to know that you are conferring a considerable favour."

"Your Highness," said the Major, "must pardon my bluntness. I am unable to hide what I know. For some time back I have suspected Major Hammersmith, but Mr. Godall is unmistakable. To seek two men in London unacquainted with Prince Florizel of Bohemia was to ask too much at Fortune's hands."

"Prince Florizel!" cried Brackenbury in amazement.

And he gazed with the deepest interest on the features of the celebrated personage before him.

"I shall not lament the loss of my incognito," remarked the Prince, "for it enables me to thank you with the more authority. You would have done as much for Mr. Godall, I feel sure, as for the Prince of Bohemia; but the latter can perhaps do more for you. The gain is mine," he added, with a courteous gesture.

And the next moment he was conversing with the two officers about the Indian army and the native troops, a subject on which, as on all others, he had a remarkable fund of information and the soundest views.

There was something so striking in this man's attitude at a moment of deadly peril that Brackenbury was overcome with respectful admiration; nor was he less sensible to the charm of his conversation or the surprising amenity of his address. Every gesture, every intonation, was not only noble in itself, but seemed to ennoble the fortunate mortal for whom it was intended; and Brackenbury confessed to himself with enthusiasm that this was a sovereign for whom a brave man might thankfully lay down his life.

Many minutes had thus passed, when the person who had introduced them into the house, and who had sat ever since in a corner, and with his watch in his hand, arose and whispered a word into the Prince's ear.

"It is well, Dr. Noel," replied Florizel, aloud; and then addressing the others, "You will excuse me, gentlemen," he added, "if I have to leave you in the dark. The moment now approaches."

Dr. Noel extinguished the lamp. A faint, gray light, premonitory of the dawn, illuminated the window, but was not sufficient to illuminate the room; and when the Prince rose to his feet, it was impossible to distinguish his features or to make a guess at the nature of the emotion which obviously affected him as he spoke. He moved towards the door, and placed himself at one side of it in an attitude of the wariest attention.

"You will have the kindness," he said, "to maintain the strictest silence, and to conceal yourselves in the densest of the shadow."

The three officers and the physician hastened to obey, and for nearly ten minutes the only sound in Rochester House was occasioned by the excursions of the rats behind the woodwork. At the end of that period, a loud creak of a hinge broke in with surprising distinctness on the silence; and shortly after, the watchers could distinguish a slow and cautious tread approaching up the kitchen stair. At every second step the intruder seemed to pause and lend an ear, and during these intervals, which seemed of an incalculable duration, a profound disquiet possessed the spirit of the listeners. Dr. Noel, accustomed as he was to dangerous emotions, suffered an almost pitiful physical prostration; his breath whistled in his lungs, his teeth grated one upon another, and his joints cracked aloud as he nervously shifted his position.

At last a hand was laid upon the door, and the bolt shot back with a slight report. There followed another pause, during which Brackenbury could see the Prince draw himself together noiselessly as if for some unusual exertion. Then the door opened, letting in a little more of the light of the morning; and the figure of a man appeared upon the threshold and stood motionless. He was tall, and carried a knife in his hand. Even in the twilight they could see his upper teeth bare and glistening, for his mouth was open like that of a hound about to leap. The man had evidently been over the head in water but a minute or two before; and even while he stood there the drops kept falling from his wet clothes and pattered on the floor.

The next moment he crossed the threshold. There was a leap, a stifled cry, an instantaneous struggle; and before Colonel Geraldine could spring to his aid, the Prince held the man, disarmed and helpless, by the shoulders.

"Dr. Noel," he said, "you will be so good as to relight the lamp."

And relinquishing the charge of his prisoner to Geraldine and Brackenbury, he crossed the room and set his back against the chimneypiece. As soon as the lamp had kindled, the party beheld an unaccustomed sternness on the Prince's features. It was no longer Florizel, the careless gentleman; it was the Prince of Bohemia, justly incensed and full of deadly purpose, who now raised his head and addressed the captive President of the Suicide Club.

"President," he said, "you have laid your last snare, and your own feet are taken in it. The day is beginning; it is your last morning. You have just swum the Regent's Canal; it is your last bathe in this world. Your old accomplice, Dr. Noel, so far from betraying me, has delivered you into my hands for judgment. And the grave you had dug for me this afternoon shall serve, in God's almighty providence, to hide your own just doom from the curiosity of mankind. Kneel and pray, sir, if you have a mind that way; for your time is short, and God is weary of your iniquities."

The President made no answer either by word or sign; but continued to hang his head and gaze sullenly on the floor, as though he were conscious of the Prince's prolonged and unsparing regard.

"Gentlemen," continued Florizel, resuming the ordinary tone of his conversation, "this is a fellow who has long eluded me, but whom, thanks to Dr. Noel, I now have tightly by the heels. To tell the story of his misdeeds would occupy more time than we can now afford; but if the canal had contained nothing but the blood of his victims, I believe the wretch would have been no drier than you see him. Even in an affair of this sort I desire to preserve the forms of honour. But I make you the judges, gentlemen—this is more an execution than a duel; and to give the rogue his choice of weapons would be to push too far a point of etiquette. I cannot afford to lose my life in such a business," he continued, unlocking the case of swords; "and as a pistol bullet travels so often on the wings of chance, and skill and courage may fall by the most trembling marksman, I have decided, and I feel sure you will approve my determination, to put this question to the touch of swords."

When Brackenbury and Major O'Rooke, to whom these remarks were particularly addressed, had each intimated his approval, "Quick, sir," added Prince Florizel to the President, "choose a blade and do not keep me waiting; I have an impatience to be done with you for ever."

For the first time since he was captured and disarmed the President raised his head, and it was plain that he began instantly to pluck up courage.

"Is it to be stand up?" he asked eagerly, "and between you and me?"

"I mean so far to honour you," replied the Prince.

"Oh, come!" cried the President. "With a fair field, who knows how things may happen? I must add that I consider it handsome behaviour on your Highness's part; and if the worst comes to the worst I shall die by one of the most gallant gentlemen in Europe."

And the President, liberated by those who had detained him, stepped up to the table and began, with minute attention, to select a sword. He was highly elated, and seemed to feel no doubt that he should issue victorious from the contest. The spectators grew alarmed in the face of so entire a confidence, and adjured Prince Florizel to reconsider his intention.

"It is but a farce," he answered; "and I think I can promise you, gentlemen, that it will not be long a-playing."

"Your Highness will be careful not to overreach," said Colonel Geraldine.

"Geraldine," returned the Prince, "did you ever know me fail in a debt of honour? I owe you this man's death, and you shall have it."

The President at last satisfied himself with one of the rapiers, and signified his readiness by a gesture that was not devoid of a rude nobility. The nearness of peril, and the sense of courage, even to this obnoxious villain, lent an air of manhood and a certain grace.

The Prince helped himself at random to a sword.

"Colonel Geraldine and Doctor Noel," he said, "will have the goodness to await me in this room. I wish no personal friend of mine to be involved in this transaction. Major O'Rooke, you are a man of some years and a settled reputation—let me recommend the President to your good graces. Lieutenant Rich will be so good as lend me his attentions: a young man cannot have too much experience in such affairs."

"Your Highness," replied Brackenbury, "it is an honour I shall prize extremely."

"It is well," returned Prince Florizel; "I shall hope to stand your friend in more important circumstances."

And so saying he led the way out of the apartment and down the kitchen stairs.

The two men who were thus left alone threw open the window and leaned out, straining every sense to catch an indication of the tragical events that were to follow. The rain was now over; day had almost come, and the birds were piping in the shrubbery and on the forest trees of the garden. The Prince and his companions were visible for a moment as they followed an alley between two flowering thickets; but at the first corner a clump of foliage intervened, and they were again concealed from view. This was all that the Colonel and the Physician had an opportunity to see, and the garden was so vast, and the place of combat evidently so remote from the house, that not even the noise of swordplay reached their ears.

"He has taken him towards the grave," said Dr. Noel, with a shudder.

"God," cried the Colonel, "God defend the right!"

And they awaited the event in silence, the Doctor shaking with fear, the Colonel in an agony of sweat. Many minutes must have elapsed, the day was sensibly broader, and the birds were singing more heartily in the garden before a sound of returning footsteps recalled their glances towards the door. It was the Prince and the two Indian officers who entered. God had defended the right.

"I am ashamed of my emotion," said Prince Florizel; "I feel it is a weakness unworthy of my station, but the continued existence of that hound of hell had begun to prey upon me like a disease, and his death has more refreshed me than a night of slumber. Look, Geraldine," he continued, throwing his sword upon the floor, "there is the blood of the man who killed your brother. It should be a welcome sight. And yet," he added, "see how strangely we men are made! my revenge is not yet five minutes old, and already I am beginning to ask myself if even revenge be attainable on this precarious stage of life. The ill he did, who can undo it? The career in which he amassed a huge fortune (for the house itself in which we stand belonged to him)—that career is now a part of the destiny of mankind for ever; and I might weary myself making thrusts in carte until the crack of judgment, and Geraldine's brother would be none the less dead, and a thousand other innocent persons would be none the less dishonoured and debauched! The existence of a man is so small a thing to take, so mighty a thing to employ! Alas!" he cried, "is there anything in life so disenchanting as attainment?"

"God's justice has been done," replied the Doctor. "So much I behold. The lesson, your Highness, has been a cruel one for me; and I await my own turn with deadly apprehension."

"What was I saying?" cried the Prince. "I have punished, and here is the man beside us who can help me to undo. Ah, Dr. Noel! you and I have before us many a day of hard and honourable toil; and perhaps, before we have done, you may have more than redeemed your early errors."

"And in the meantime," said the Doctor, "let me go and bury my oldest friend."

(And this, observes the erudite Arabian, *is the fortunate conclusion of the tale. The Prince, it is superfluous to mention, forgot none of those who served him in this great exploit; and to this day his authority and influence help them forward in their public career, while his condescending friendship adds a charm to their private life. To collect,* continues my author, *all the strange events in which this Prince has played the part of Providence were to fill the habitable globe with books. But the stories which relate to the fortunes of* THE RAJAH'S DIAMOND *are of too entertaining a description,* says he, *to be omitted. Following prudently in the footsteps of this Oriental, we shall now begin the series to which he refers with the* STORY OF THE BANDBOX.*)*

THE RAJAH'S DIAMOND

STORY OF THE BANDBOX

Up to the age of sixteen, at a private school and afterwards at one of those great institutions for which England is justly famous, Mr. Harry Hartley had received the ordinary education of a gentleman. At that period, he manifested a remarkable distaste for study; and his only surviving parent being both weak and ignorant, he was permitted thenceforward to spend his time in the attainment of petty and purely elegant accomplishments. Two years later, he was left an orphan and almost a beggar. For all active and industrious pursuits, Harry was unfitted alike by nature and training. He could sing romantic ditties, and accompany himself with discretion on the piano; he was a graceful although a timid cavalier; he had a pronounced taste for chess; and nature had sent him into the world with one of the most engaging exteriors that can well be fancied. Blond and pink, with dove's eyes and a gentle smile, he had an air of agreeable tenderness and melancholy, and the most submissive and caressing manners. But when all is said, he was not the man to lead armaments of war, or direct the councils of a State.

A fortunate chance and some influence obtained for Harry, at the time of his bereavement, the position of private secretary to Major-General Sir Thomas Vandeleur, C.B. Sir Thomas was a man of sixty, loud-spoken, boisterous, and domineering. For some reason, some service the nature of which had been often whispered and repeatedly denied, the Rajah of Kashgar had presented this officer with the sixth known diamond of the world. The gift transformed General Vandeleur from a poor into a wealthy man, from an obscure and unpopular soldier into one of the lions of London society; the possessor of the Rajah's Diamond was welcome in the most exclusive circles; and he had found a lady, young, beautiful, and well-born, who was willing to call the diamond hers even at the price of marriage with Sir Thomas Vandeleur. It was commonly said at the time that, as like draws to like, one jewel had attracted another; certainly Lady Vandeleur was not only a gem of the finest water in her own person, but she showed herself to the world in a very costly setting; and she was considered by many respectable authorities, as one among the three or four best-dressed women in England.

Harry's duty as secretary was not particularly onerous; but he had a dislike for all prolonged work; it gave him pain to ink his fingers; and the charms of Lady Vandeleur and her toilettes drew him often from the library to the boudoir. He had the prettiest ways among women, could talk fashions with enjoyment, and was never more happy than when criticising a shade of ribbon, or running on an errand to the milliner's. In short, Sir Thomas's correspondence fell into pitiful arrears, and my Lady had another lady's maid.

At last the General, who was one of the least patient of military commanders, arose from his place in a violent access of passion, and indicated to his secretary that he had no further need for his services, with one of those explanatory gestures which are most rarely employed between gentlemen. The door being unfortunately open, Mr. Hartley fell downstairs head foremost.

He arose somewhat hurt and very deeply aggrieved. The life in the General's house precisely suited him; he moved, on a more or less doubtful footing, in very genteel company, he did little, he ate of the best, and he had a lukewarm satisfaction in the presence of Lady Vandeleur, which, in his own heart, he dubbed by a more emphatic name.

Immediately after he had been outraged by the military foot, he hurried to the boudoir and recounted his sorrows.

"You know very well, my dear Harry," replied Lady Vandeleur, for she called him by name like a child or a domestic servant, "that you never by any chance do what the General tells you. No more do I, you may say. But that is different. A woman can earn her pardon for a good year of disobedience by a single adroit submission; and, besides, no one is married to his private secretary. I shall be sorry to lose you; but since you cannot stay longer in a house where you have been insulted, I shall wish you good-bye, and I promise you to make the General smart for his behaviour."

Harry's countenance fell; tears came into his eyes, and he gazed on Lady Vandeleur with a tender reproach.

"My Lady," said he, "what is an insult? I should think little indeed of anyone who could not forgive them by the score. But to leave one's friends; to tear up the bonds of affection——"

He was unable to continue, for his emotion choked him, and he began to weep.

Lady Vandeleur looked at him with a curious expression.

"This little fool," she thought, "imagines himself to be in love with me. Why should he not become my servant instead of the General's? He is good-natured, obliging, and understands dress; and besides it will keep him out of mischief. He is positively too pretty to be unattached."

That night she talked over the General, who was already somewhat ashamed of his vivacity; and Harry was transferred to the feminine department, where his life was little short of heavenly. He was always dressed with uncommon nicety, wore delicate flowers in his button-hole, and could entertain a visitor with tact and pleasantry. He took a pride in servility to a beautiful woman; received Lady Vandeleur's commands as so many marks of favour; and was pleased to exhibit himself before other men, who derided and despised him, in his character of male lady's maid and man milliner. Nor could he think enough of his existence from a moral point of view. Wickedness seemed to him an essentially male attribute, and to pass one's days with a delicate woman, and principally occupied about trimmings, was to inhabit an enchanted isle among the storms of life.

One fine morning he came into the drawing room and began to arrange some music on the top of the piano. Lady Vandeleur, at the other end of the apartment, was speaking somewhat eagerly with her brother, Charlie Pendragon, an elderly young man, much broken with dissipation, and very lame of one foot. The private secretary, to whose entrance they paid no regard, could not avoid overhearing a part of their conversation.

"Today or never," said the lady. "Once and for all, it shall be done today."

"Today, if it must be," replied the brother, with a sigh. "But it is a false step, a ruinous step, Clara; and we shall live to repent it dismally."

Lady Vandeleur looked her brother steadily and somewhat strangely in the face.

"You forget," she said; "the man must die at last."

"Upon my word, Clara," said Pendragon, "I believe you are the most heartless rascal in England."

"You men," she returned, "are so coarsely built, that you can never appreciate a shade of meaning. You are yourselves rapacious, violent, immodest, careless of distinction; and yet the least thought for the future shocks you in a woman. I have no patience with such stuff. You would despise in a common banker the imbecility that you expect to find in us."

"You are very likely right," replied her brother; "you were always cleverer than I. And, anyway, you know my motto: The family before all."

"Yes, Charlie," she returned, taking his hand in hers, "I know your motto better than you know it yourself. 'And Clara before the family!' Is not that the second part of it? Indeed, you are the best of brothers, and I love you dearly."

Mr Pendragon got up, looking a little confused by these family endearments.

"I had better not be seen," said he. "I understand my part to a miracle, and I'll keep an eye on the Tame Cat."

"Do," she replied. "He is an abject creature, and might ruin all."

She kissed the tips of her fingers to him daintily; and the brother withdrew by the boudoir and the back stair.

"Harry," said Lady Vandeleur, turning towards the secretary as soon as they were alone, "I have a commission for you this morning. But you shall take a cab; I cannot have my secretary freckled."

She spoke the last words with emphasis and a look of half-motherly pride that caused great contentment to poor Harry; and he professed himself charmed to find an opportunity of serving her.

"It is another of our great secrets," she went on, archly, "and no one must know of it but my secretary and me. Sir Thomas would make the saddest disturbance; and if you only knew how weary I am of these scenes! Oh, Harry, Harry, can you explain to me what makes you men so violent and unjust? But, indeed, I know you cannot; you are the only man in the world who knows nothing of these shameful passions; you are so good, Harry, and so kind; you, at least, can be a woman's friend; and, do you know? I think you make the others more ugly by comparison."

"It is you," said Harry, gallantly, "who are so kind to me. You treat me like——"

"Like a mother," interposed Lady Vandeleur, "I try to be a mother to you. Or, at least," she corrected herself with a smile, "almost a mother. I am afraid I am too young to be your mother really. Let us say a friend—a dear friend."

She paused long enough to let her words take effect in Harry's sentimental quarters, but not long enough to allow him a reply.

"But all this is beside our purpose," she resumed. "You will find a bandbox in the left-hand side of the oak wardrobe; it is underneath the pink slip that I wore on Wednesday with my Mechlin. You will take it immediately to this address," and she gave him a paper, "but do not, on any account, let it out of your hands until you have received a receipt written by myself. Do you understand? Answer, if you please—answer! This is extremely important, and I must ask you to pay some attention."

Harry pacified her by repeating her instructions perfectly; and she was just going to tell him more when General Vandeleur flung into the apartment, scarlet with anger, and holding a long and elaborate milliner's bill in his hand.

"Will you look at this, madam?" cried he. "Will you have the goodness to look at this document? I know well enough you married me for my money, and I hope I can make as great allowances as any other man in the service; but, as sure as God made me, I mean to put a period to this disreputable prodigality."

"Mr. Hartley," said Lady Vandeleur, "I think you understand what you have to do. May I ask you to see to it at once?"

"Stop," said the General, addressing Harry, "one word before you go." And then, turning again to Lady Vandeleur, "What is this precious fellow's errand?" he demanded. "I trust him no further than I do yourself, let me tell you. If he had as much as the rudiments of honesty, he would scorn to stay in this house; and what he does for his wages is a mystery to all the world. What is his errand, madam? and why are you hurrying him away?"

"I supposed you had something to say to me in private," replied the lady.

"You spoke about an errand," insisted the General. "Do not attempt to deceive me in my present state of temper. You certainly spoke about an errand."

"If you insist on making your servants privy to our humiliating dissensions," replied Lady Vandeleur, "perhaps I had better ask Mr. Hartley to sit down. No?" she continued; "then you may go, Mr. Hartley. I trust you may remember all that you have heard in this room; it may be useful to you."

Harry at once made his escape from the drawing room; and as he ran upstairs he could hear the General's voice upraised in declamation, and the thin tones of Lady Vandeleur planting icy repartees at every opening. How cordially he admired the wife! How skilfully she could evade an awkward question! with what secure effrontery she repeated her instructions under the very guns of the enemy! and on the other hand, how he detested the husband!

There had been nothing unfamiliar in the morning's events, for he was continually in the habit of serving Lady Vandeleur on secret missions, principally connected with millinery. There was a skeleton in the house, as he well knew. The bottomless extravagance and the unknown liabilities of the wife had long since swallowed her own fortune, and threatened day by day to engulf that of the husband. Once or twice in every year exposure and ruin seemed imminent, and Harry kept trotting round to all sorts of furnishers' shops, telling small fibs, and paying small advances on the gross amount, until another term was tided over, and the lady and her faithful secretary breathed again. For Harry, in a double capacity, was heart and soul upon that side of the war: not only did he adore Lady Vandeleur and fear and dislike her husband, but he naturally sympathised with the love of finery, and his own single extravagance was at the tailor's.

He found the bandbox where it had been described, arranged his toilette with care, and left the house. The sun shone brightly; the distance he had to travel was considerable, and he remembered with dismay that the General's sudden irruption had prevented Lady

Vandeleur from giving him money for a cab. On this sultry day there was every chance that his complexion would suffer severely; and to walk through so much of London with a bandbox on his arm was a humiliation almost insupportable to a youth of his character. He paused, and took counsel with himself. The Vandeleurs lived in Eaton Place; his destination was near Notting Hill; plainly, he might cross the Park by keeping well in the open and avoiding populous alleys; and he thanked his stars when he reflected that it was still comparatively early in the day.

Anxious to be rid of his incubus, he walked somewhat faster than his ordinary, and he was already some way through Kensington Gardens when, in a solitary spot among trees, he found himself confronted by the General.

"I beg your pardon, Sir Thomas," observed Harry, politely falling on one side; for the other stood directly in his path.

"Where are you going, sir?" asked the General.

"I am taking a little walk among the trees," replied the lad.

The general struck the bandbox with his cane.

"With that thing?" he cried; "you lie, sir, and you know you lie!"

"Indeed, Sir Thomas," returned Harry, "I am not accustomed to be questioned in so high a key."

"You do not understand your position," said the General. "You are my servant, and a servant of whom I have conceived the most serious suspicions. How do I know but that your box is full of teaspoons?"

"It contains a silk hat belonging to a friend," said Harry.

"Very well," replied General Vandeleur. "Then I want to see your friend's silk hat. I have," he added, grimly, "a singular curiosity for hats; and I believe you know me to be somewhat positive."

"I beg your pardon, Sir Thomas, I am exceedingly grieved," Harry apologised; "but indeed this is a private affair."

The General caught him roughly by the shoulder with one hand, while he raised his cane in the most menacing manner with the other. Harry gave himself up for lost; but at the same moment Heaven vouchsafed him an unexpected defender in the person of Charlie Pendragon, who now strode forward from behind the trees.

"Come, come, General, hold your hand," said he, "this is neither courteous nor manly."

"Aha!" cried the General, wheeling round upon his new antagonist, "Mr. Pendragon! And do you suppose, Mr. Pendragon, that because I have had the misfortune to marry your sister, I shall suffer myself to be dogged and thwarted by a discredited and bankrupt libertine like you? My acquaintance with Lady Vandeleur, sir, has taken away all my appetite for the other members of her family."

"And do you fancy, General Vandeleur," retorted Charlie, "that because my sister has had the misfortune to marry you, she there and then forfeited her rights and privileges as a lady? I own, sir, that by the action she did as much as anybody could to derogate from her position; but to me she is still a Pendragon. I make it my business to protect her from ungentlemanly outrage, and if you were ten times her husband I would not permit her liberty to be restrained, nor her private messengers to be violently arrested."

"How is that, Mr. Hartley?" interrogated the General. "Mr. Pendragon is of my opinion, it appears. He too suspects that Lady Vandeleur has something to do with your friend's silk hat."

Charlie saw that he had committed an unpardonable blunder, which he hastened to repair.

"How, sir?" he cried; "I suspect, do you say? I suspect nothing. Only where I find strength abused and a man brutalising his inferiors, I take the liberty to interfere."

As he said these words he made a sign to Harry, which the latter was too dull or too much troubled to understand.

"In what way am I to construe your attitude, sir?" demanded Vandeleur.

"Why, sir, as you please," returned Pendragon.

The General once more raised his cane, and made a cut for Charlie's head; but the latter, lame foot and all, evaded the blow with his umbrella, ran in, and immediately closed with his formidable adversary.

"Run, Harry, run!" he cried; "run, you dolt!"

Harry stood petrified for a moment, watching the two men sway together in this fierce embrace; then he turned and took to his heels. When he cast a glance over his shoulder he saw the General prostrate under Charlie's knee, but still making desperate efforts to reverse the situation; and the Gardens seemed to have filled with people, who were running from all directions towards the scene of fight. This spectacle lent the secretary wings; and he did not relax his pace until he had gained the Bayswater road, and plunged at random into an unfrequented bystreet.

To see two gentlemen of his acquaintance thus brutally mauling each other was deeply shocking to Harry. He desired to forget the sight; he desired, above all, to put as great a distance as possible between himself and General Vandeleur; and in his eagerness for this he forgot everything about his destination, and hurried before him headlong and trembling. When he remembered that Lady Vandeleur was the wife of one and the sister of the other of these gladiators, his heart was touched with sympathy for a woman so distressingly misplaced in life. Even his own situation in the General's household looked hardly so pleasing as usual in the light of these violent transactions.

He had walked some little distance, busied with these meditations, before a slight collision with another passenger reminded him of the bandbox on his arm.

"Heavens!" cried he, "where was my head? and whither have I wandered?"

Thereupon he consulted the envelope which Lady Vandeleur had given him. The address was there, but without a name. Harry was simply directed to ask for "the gentleman who expected a parcel from Lady Vandeleur," and if he were not at home to await his return. The gentleman, added the note, should present a receipt in the handwriting of the lady herself. All this seemed mightily mysterious, and Harry was above all astonished at the omission of the name and the formality of the receipt. He had thought little of this last when he heard it dropped in conversation; but reading it in cold blood, and taking it in connection with the other strange particulars, he became convinced that he was engaged in perilous affairs. For half a moment he had a doubt of Lady Vandeleur herself; for he found these obscure proceedings somewhat unworthy of so high a lady, and became more critical when her secrets were preserved against himself. But her empire over his spirit was too complete, he dismissed his suspicions, and blamed himself roundly for having so much as entertained them.

In one thing, however, his duty and interest, his generosity and his terrors, coincided—to get rid of the bandbox with the greatest possible despatch.

He accosted the first policeman and courteously inquired his way. It turned out that he was already not far from his destination, and a walk of a few minutes brought him to a small house in a lane, freshly painted, and kept with the most scrupulous attention. The knocker and bellpull were highly polished; flowering pot-herbs garnished the sills of the different windows; and curtains of some rich material concealed the interior from the eyes of curious passengers. The place had an air of repose and secrecy; and Harry was so far caught with this spirit that he knocked with more than usual discretion, and was more than usually careful to remove all impurity from his boots.

A servant maid of some personal attractions immediately opened the door, and seemed to regard the secretary with no unkind eyes.

"This is the parcel from Lady Vandeleur," said Harry.

"I know," replied the maid, with a nod. "But the gentleman is from home. Will you leave it with me?"

"I cannot," answered Harry. "I am directed not to part with it but upon a certain condition, and I must ask you, I am afraid, to let me wait."

"Well," said she, "I suppose I may let you wait. I am lonely enough, I can tell you, and you do not look as though you would eat a girl. But be sure and do not ask the gentleman's name, for that I am not to tell you."

"Do you say so?" cried Harry. "Why, how strange! But indeed for some time back I walk among surprises. One question I think I may surely ask without indiscretion: Is he the master of this house?"

"He is a lodger, and not eight days old at that," returned the maid. "And now a question for a question: Do you know Lady Vandeleur?"

"I am her private secretary," replied Harry with a glow of modest pride.

"She is pretty, is she not?" pursued the servant.

"Oh, beautiful!" cried Harry; "wonderfully lovely, and not less good and kind!"

"You look kind enough yourself," she retorted; "and I wager you are worth a dozen Lady Vandeleurs."

Harry was properly scandalised.

"I!" he cried. "I am only a secretary!"

"Do you mean that for me?" said the girl. "Because I am only a housemaid, if you please." And then, relenting at the sight of Harry's obvious confusion, "I know you mean nothing of the sort," she added; "and I like your looks; but I think nothing of your Lady Vandeleur. Oh, these mistresses!" she cried. "To send out a real gentleman like you—with a bandbox—in broad day!"

During this talk they had remained in their original positions—she on the doorstep, he on the sidewalk, bareheaded for the sake of coolness, and with the bandbox on his arm. But upon this last speech Harry, who was unable to support such point-blank compliments to his appearance, nor the encouraging look with which they were accompanied, began to change his attitude, and glance from left to right in perturbation. In so doing he turned his face towards the lower end of the lane, and there, to his indescribable dismay, his eyes encountered those of General Vandeleur. The General, in a prodigious fluster of heat, hurry, and indignation, had been scouring the streets in chase of his brother-in-law; but so soon as he caught a glimpse of the delinquent secretary, his purpose changed, his anger flowed into a new channel, and he turned on his heel and came tearing up the lane with truculent gestures and vociferations.

Harry made but one bolt of it into the house, driving the maid before him; and the door was slammed in his pursuer's countenance.

"Is there a bar? Will it lock?" asked Harry, while a salvo on the knocker made the house echo from wall to wall.

"Why, what is wrong with you?" asked the maid. "Is it this old gentleman?"

"If he gets hold of me," whispered Harry, "I am as good as dead. He has been pursuing me all day, carries a sword stick, and is an Indian military officer."

"These are fine manners," cried the maid. "And what, if you please, may be his name?"

"It is the General, my master," answered Harry. "He is after this bandbox."

"Did not I tell you?" cried the maid in triumph. "I told you I thought worse than nothing of your Lady Vandeleur; and if you had an eye in your head you might see what she is for yourself. An ungrateful minx, I will be bound for that!"

The General renewed his attack upon the knocker, and his passion growing with delay, began to kick and beat upon the panels of the door.

"It is lucky," observed the girl, "that I am alone in the house; your General may hammer until he is weary, and there is none to open for him. Follow me!"

So saying she led Harry into the kitchen, where she made him sit down, and stood by him herself in an affectionate attitude, with a hand upon his shoulder. The din at the door, so far from abating, continued to increase in volume, and at each blow the unhappy secretary was shaken to the heart.

"What is your name?" asked the girl.

"Harry Hartley," he replied.

"Mine," she went on, "is Prudence. Do you like it?"

"Very much," said Harry. "But hear for a moment how the General beats upon the door. He will certainly break it in, and then, in heaven's name, what have I to look for but death?"

"You put yourself very much about with no occasion," answered Prudence. "Let your General knock, he will do no more than blister his hands. Do you think I would keep you here if I were not sure to save you? Oh, no, I am a good friend to those that please me! and we have a back door upon another lane. But," she added, checking him, for he had got upon his feet immediately on this welcome news, "but I will not show where it is unless you kiss me. Will you, Harry?"

"That I will," he cried, remembering his gallantry, "not for your back door, but because you are good and pretty."

And he administered two or three cordial salutes, which were returned to him in kind.

Then Prudence led him to the back gate, and put her hand upon the key.

"Will you come and see me?" she asked.

"I will indeed," said Harry. "Do not I owe you my life?"

"And now," she added, opening the door, "run as hard as you can, for I shall let in the General."

Harry scarcely required this advice; fear had him by the forelock; and he addressed himself diligently to flight. A few steps, and he believed he would escape from his trials, and return to Lady Vandeleur in honour and safety. But these few steps had not been taken before he heard a man's voice hailing him by name with many execrations, and, looking over his shoulder, he beheld Charlie Pendragon waving him with both arms to return. The shock of this new incident was so sudden and profound, and Harry was already worked into so high a state of nervous tension, that he could think of nothing better than to accelerate his pace, and continue running. He should certainly have remembered the scene in Kensington Gardens; he should certainly have concluded that, where the General was his enemy, Charlie Pendragon could be no other than a friend. But such was the fever and perturbation of his mind that he was struck by none of these considerations, and only continued to run the faster up the lane.

Charlie, by the sound of his voice and the vile terms that he hurled after the secretary, was obviously beside himself with rage. He, too, ran his very best; but, try as he might, the physical advantages were not upon his side, and his outcries and the fall of his lame foot on the macadam began to fall farther and farther into the wake.

Harry's hopes began once more to arise. The lane was both steep and narrow, but it was exceedingly solitary, bordered on either hand by garden walls, overhung with foliage; and, for as far as the fugitive could see in front of him, there was neither a creature moving nor an open door. Providence, weary of persecution, was now offering him an open field for his escape.

Alas! as he came abreast of a garden door under a tuft of chestnuts, it was suddenly drawn back, and he could see inside, upon a garden path, the figure of a butcher's boy with his tray upon his arm. He had hardly recognised the fact before he was some steps beyond upon the other side. But the fellow had had time to observe him; he was evidently much surprised to see a gentleman go by at so unusual a pace; and he came out into the lane and began to call after Harry with shouts of ironical encouragement.

His appearance gave a new idea to Charlie Pendragon, who, although he was now sadly out of breath, once more upraised his voice.

"Stop, thief!" he cried.

And immediately the butcher's boy had taken up the cry and joined in the pursuit.

This was a bitter moment for the hunted secretary. It is true that his terror enabled him once more to improve his pace, and gain with every step on his pursuers; but he was well aware that he was near the end of his resources, and should he meet anyone coming the other way, his predicament in the narrow lane would be desperate indeed.

"I must find a place of concealment," he thought, "and that within the next few seconds, or all is over with me in this world."

Scarcely had the thought crossed his mind than the lane took a sudden turning; and he found himself hidden from his enemies. There are circumstances in which even the least energetic of mankind learn to behave with vigour and decision; and the most cautious forget their prudence and embrace foolhardy resolutions. This was one of those occasions for Harry Hartley; and those who knew him best would have been the most astonished at the lad's audacity. He stopped dead, flung the bandbox over a garden wall, and leaping upward with incredible agility and seizing the copestone with his hands, he tumbled headlong after it into the garden.

He came to himself a moment afterwards, seated in a border of small rosebushes. His hands and knees were cut and bleeding, for the wall had been protected against such an escalade by a liberal provision of old bottles; and he was conscious of a general dislocation and a painful swimming in the head. Facing him across the garden, which was in admirable order, and set with flowers of the most delicious perfume, he beheld the back of a house. It was of considerable extent, and plainly habitable; but, in odd contrast to the grounds, it was crazy, ill-kept, and of a mean appearance. On all other sides the circuit of the garden wall appeared unbroken.

He took in these features of the scene with mechanical glances, but his mind was still unable to piece together or draw a rational conclusion from what he saw. And when he heard footsteps advancing on the gravel, although he turned his eyes in that direction, it was with no thought either for defence or flight.

The new comer was a large, coarse, and very sordid personage, in gardening clothes, and with a watering pot in his left hand. One less confused would have been affected with some alarm at the sight of this man's huge proportions and black and lowering eyes. But Harry was too gravely shaken by his fall to be so much as terrified; and if he was unable to divert his glances from the gardener, he remained absolutely passive, and suffered him to draw near, to take him by the shoulder, and to plant him roughly on his feet, without a motion of resistance.

For a moment the two stared into each other's eyes, Harry fascinated, the man filled with wrath and a cruel, sneering humour.

"Who are you?" he demanded at last. "Who are you to come flying over my wall and break my *Gloire de Dijons?* What is your name?" he added, shaking him; "and what may be your business here?"

Harry could not as much as proffer a word in explanation.

But just at that moment Pendragon and the butcher's boy went clumping past, and the sound of their feet and their hoarse cries echoed loudly in the narrow lane. The gardener had received his answer; and he looked down into Harry's face with an obnoxious smile.

"A thief!" he said. "Upon my word, and a very good thing you must make of it; for I see you dressed like a gentleman from top to toe. Are you not ashamed to go about the world in such a trim, with honest folk, I dare say, glad to buy your cast-off finery secondhand? Speak up, you dog," the man went on; "you can understand English, I suppose; and I mean to have a bit of talk with you before I march you to the station."

"Indeed, sir," said Harry, "this is all a dreadful misconception; and if you will go with me to Sir Thomas Vandeleur's in Eaton Place, I can promise that all will be made plain. The most upright person, as I now perceive, can be led into suspicious positions."

"My little man," replied the gardener, "I will go with you no farther than the station-house in the next street. The inspector, no doubt, will be glad to take a stroll with you as far as Eaton Place, and have a bit of afternoon tea with your great acquaintances. Or would you prefer to go direct to the Home Secretary? Sir Thomas Vandeleur, indeed! Perhaps you think I don't know a gentleman when I see one, from a common run-the-hedge like you? Clothes or no clothes, I can read you like a book. Here is a shirt that maybe cost as much as my Sunday hat; and that coat, I take it, has never seen the inside of Rag-fair, and then your boots——"

The man, whose eyes had fallen upon the ground, stopped short in his insulting commentary, and remained for a moment looking intently upon something at his feet. When he spoke his voice was strangely altered.

"What, in God's name," said he, "is all this?"

Harry, following the direction of the man's eyes, beheld a spectacle that struck him dumb with terror and amazement. In his fall he had descended vertically upon the bandbox and burst it open from end to end; thence a great treasure of diamonds had poured forth, and now lay abroad, part trodden in the soil, part scattered on the surface in regal and glittering profusion. There was a magnificent coronet which he had often admired on Lady Vandeleur; there were rings and brooches, ear-drops and bracelets, and even unset brilliants rolling here and there among the rosebushes like drops of morning dew. A princely fortune lay between the two men upon the ground—a fortune in the most inviting, solid, and durable form, capable of being carried in an apron, beautiful in itself, and scattering the sunlight in a million rainbow flashes.

"Good God!" said Harry, "I am lost!"

His mind raced backwards into the past with the incalculable velocity of thought, and he began to comprehend his day's adventures, to conceive them as a whole, and to recognise the sad imbroglio in which his own character and fortunes had become involved. He looked round him, as if for help, but he was alone in the garden, with his scattered diamonds and his redoubtable interlocutor; and when he gave ear, there was no sound but the rustle of the leaves and the hurried pulsation of his heart. It was little wonder if the young man felt himself deserted by his spirits, and with a broken voice repeated his last ejaculation——

"I am lost!"

The gardener peered in all directions with an air of guilt; but there was no face at any of the windows, and he seemed to breathe again.

"Pick up a heart," he said, "you fool! The worst of it is done. Why could you not say at first there was enough for two? Two?" he repeated, "aye, and for two hundred! But come away from here, where we may be observed; and, for the love of wisdom, straighten out your hat and brush your clothes. You could not travel two steps the figure of fun you look just now."

While Harry mechanically adopted these suggestions, the gardener, getting upon his knees, hastily drew together the scattered jewels and returned them to the bandbox. The touch of these costly crystals sent a shiver of emotion through the man's stalwart frame; his face was transfigured, and his eyes shone with concupiscence; indeed it seemed as if he luxuriously prolonged his occupation, and dallied with every diamond that he handled. At last, however, it was done; and, concealing the bandbox in his smock, the gardener beckoned to Harry and preceded him in the direction of the house.

Near the door they were met by a young man evidently in holy orders, dark and strikingly handsome, with a look of mingled weakness and resolution, and very neatly attired after the manner of his caste. The gardener was plainly annoyed by this encounter; but he put as good a face upon it as he could, and accosted the clergyman with an obsequious and smiling air.

"Here is a fine afternoon, Mr. Rolles," said he: "a fine afternoon, as sure as God made it! And here is a young friend of mine who had a fancy to look at my roses. I took the liberty to bring him in, for I thought none of the lodgers would object."

"Speaking for myself," replied the Reverend Mr. Rolles, "I do not; nor do I fancy any of the rest of us would be more difficult upon so small a matter. The garden is your own, Mr. Raeburn; we must none of us forget that; and because you give us liberty to walk there we should be indeed ungracious if we so far presumed upon your politeness as to interfere with the convenience of your friends. But, on second thoughts," he added, "I believe that this gentleman and I have met before. Mr. Hartley, I think. I regret to observe that you have had a fall."

And he offered his hand.

A sort of maiden dignity and a desire to delay as long as possible the necessity for explanation moved Harry to refuse this chance of help, and to deny his own identity. He chose the tender mercies of the gardener, who was at least unknown to him, rather than the curiosity and perhaps the doubts of an acquaintance.

"I fear there is some mistake," said he. "My name is Thomlinson and I am a friend of Mr. Raeburn's."

"Indeed?" said Mr. Rolles. "The likeness is amazing."

Mr. Raeburn, who had been upon thorns throughout this colloquy, now felt it high time to bring it to a period.

"I wish you a pleasant saunter sir," said he.

And with that he dragged Harry after him into the house, and then into a chamber on the garden. His first care was to draw down the blind, for Mr. Rolles still remained where they had left him, in an attitude of perplexity and thought. Then he emptied the broken bandbox on the table, and stood before the treasure, thus fully displayed, with an expression of rapturous greed, and rubbing his hands upon his thighs. For Harry, the sight of the man's face under the influence of this base emotion, added another pang to those he was already suffering. It seemed incredible that, from his life of pure and delicate trifling, he should be plunged in a breath among sordid and criminal relations. He could reproach his conscience with no sinful act; and yet he was now suffering the punishment of sin in its most acute and cruel forms—the dread of punishment, the suspicions of the good, and the companionship and contamination of vile and brutal natures. He felt he could lay his life down with gladness to escape from the room and the society of Mr. Raeburn.

"And now," said the latter, after he had separated the jewels into two nearly equal parts, and drawn one of them nearer to himself; "and now," said he, "everything in this world has to be paid for, and some things sweetly. You must know, Mr. Hartley, if such be your name, that I am a man of a very easy temper, and good nature has been my stumbling block from first to last. I could pocket the whole of these pretty pebbles, if I chose, and I should like to see you dare to say a word; but I think I must have taken a liking to you; for I declare I have not the heart to shave you so close. So, do you see, in pure kind feeling, I propose that we divide; and these," indicating the two heaps, "are the proportions that seem to me just and friendly. Do you see any objection, Mr. Hartley, may I ask? I am not the man to stick upon a brooch."

"But, sir," cried Harry, "what you propose to me is impossible. The jewels are not mine, and I cannot share what is another's, no matter with whom, nor in what proportions."

"They are not yours, are they not?" returned Raeburn. "And you could not share them with anybody, couldn't you? Well now, that is what I call a pity; for here am I obliged to take you to the station. The police—think of that," he continued; "think of the disgrace for your respectable parents; think," he went on, taking Harry by the wrist; "think of the Colonies and the Day of Judgment."

"I cannot help it," wailed Harry. "It is not my fault. You will not come with me to Eaton Place."

"No," replied the man, "I will not, that is certain. And I mean to divide these playthings with you here."

And so saying he applied a sudden and severe torsion to the lad's wrist.

Harry could not suppress a scream, and the perspiration burst forth upon his face. Perhaps pain and terror quickened his intelligence, but certainly at that moment the whole business flashed across him in another light; and he saw that there was nothing for it but to accede to the ruffian's proposal, and trust to find the house and force him to disgorge, under more favourable circumstances, and when he himself was clear from all suspicion.

"I agree," he said.

"There is a lamb," sneered the gardener. "I thought you would recognise your interests at last. This bandbox," he continued, "I shall burn with my rubbish; it is a thing that curious folk might recognise; and as for you, scrape up your gaieties and put them in your pocket."

Harry proceeded to obey, Raeburn watching him, and every now and again his greed rekindled by some bright scintillation, abstracting another jewel from the secretary's share, and adding it to his own.

When this was finished, both proceeded to the front door, which Raeburn cautiously opened to observe the street. This was apparently clear of passengers; for he suddenly seized Harry by the nape of the neck, and holding his face downward so that he could see nothing but the roadway and the doorsteps of the houses, pushed him violently before him down one street and up another for the space of perhaps a minute and a half. Harry had counted three corners before the bully relaxed his grasp, and crying, "Now be off with you!" sent the lad flying headforemost with a well-directed and athletic kick.

When Harry gathered himself up, half-stunned and bleeding freely at the nose, Mr. Raeburn had entirely disappeared. For the first time, anger and pain so completely overcame the lad's spirits that he burst into a fit of tears and remained sobbing in the middle of the road.

After he had thus somewhat assuaged his emotion, he began to look about him and read the names of the streets at whose intersection he had been deserted by the gardener. He was still in an unfrequented portion of West London, among villas and large gardens; but he could see some persons at a window who had evidently witnessed his misfortune; and almost immediately after a servant came running from the house and offered him a glass of water. At the same time, a dirty rogue, who had been slouching somewhere in the neighbourhood, drew near him from the other side.

"Poor fellow," said the maid, "how vilely you have been handled, to be sure! Why, your knees are all cut, and your clothes ruined! Do you know the wretch who used you so?"

"That I do!" cried Harry, who was somewhat refreshed by the water; "and shall run him home in spite of his precautions. He shall pay dearly for this day's work, I promise you."

"You had better come into the house and have yourself washed and brushed," continued the maid. "My mistress will make you welcome, never fear. And see, I will pick up your hat. Why, love of mercy!" she screamed, "if you have not dropped diamonds all over the street!"

Such was the case; a good half of what remained to him after the depredations of Mr. Raeburn, had been shaken out of his pockets by the somersault and once more lay glittering on the ground. He blessed his fortune that the maid had been so quick of eye; "there is nothing so bad but it might be worse," thought he; and the recovery of these few seemed to him almost as great an affair as the loss of all the rest. But, alas! as he stooped to pick up his treasures, the loiterer made a rapid onslaught, overset both Harry and the maid with a movement of his arms, swept up a double handful of the diamonds, and made off along the street with an amazing swiftness.

Harry, as soon as he could get upon his feet, gave chase to the miscreant with many cries, but the latter was too fleet of foot, and probably too well acquainted with the locality; for turn where the pursuer would he could find no traces of the fugitive.

In the deepest despondency, Harry revisited the scene of his mishap, where the maid, who was still waiting, very honestly returned him his hat and the remainder of the fallen diamonds. Harry thanked her from his heart, and being now in no humour for economy, made his way to the nearest cabstand and set off for Eaton Place by coach.

The house, on his arrival, seemed in some confusion, as if a catastrophe had happened in the family; and the servants clustered together in the hall, and were unable, or perhaps not altogether anxious, to suppress their merriment at the tatterdemalion figure of the secretary. He passed them with as good an air of dignity as he could assume, and made directly for the boudoir. When he opened the door an astonishing and even menacing spectacle presented itself to his eyes; for he beheld the General and his wife and, of all people, Charlie Pendragon, closeted together and speaking with earnestness and gravity on some important subject. Harry saw at once that there was little left for him to explain—plenary confession had plainly been made to the General of the intended fraud upon his pocket, and the unfortunate miscarriage of the scheme; and they had all made common cause against a common danger.

"Thank Heaven!" cried Lady Vandeleur, "here he is! The bandbox, Harry—the bandbox!"

But Harry stood before them silent and downcast.

"Speak!" she cried. "Speak! Where is the bandbox?"

And the men, with threatening gestures, repeated the demand.

Harry drew a handful of jewels from his pocket. He was very white.

"This is all that remains," said he. "I declare before Heaven it was through no fault of mine; and if you will have patience, although some are lost, I am afraid, for ever, others, I am sure, may be still recovered."

"Alas!" cried Lady Vandeleur, "all our diamonds are gone, and I owe ninety thousand pounds for dress!"

"Madam," said the General, "you might have paved the gutter with your own trash; you might have made debts to fifty times the sum you mention; you might have robbed me of my mother's coronet and ring; and Nature might have still so far prevailed that I could have forgiven you at last. But, madam, you have taken the Rajah's Diamond—the Eye of Light, as the Orientals poetically termed it—the Pride of Kashgar! You have taken from me the Rajah's Diamond," he cried, raising his hands, "and all, madam, all is at an end between us!"

"Believe me, General Vandeleur," she replied, "that is one of the most agreeable speeches that ever I heard from your lips; and since we are to be ruined, I could almost welcome the change, if it delivers me from you. You have told me often enough that I married you for your money; let me tell you now that I always bitterly repented the bargain; and if you were still marriageable, and had a diamond bigger than your head, I should counsel even my maid against a union so uninviting and disastrous. As for you, Mr. Hartley," she continued, turning on the secretary, "you have sufficiently exhibited your valuable qualities in this house; we are now persuaded that you equally lack manhood, sense, and self-respect; and I can see only one course open for you—to withdraw instanter, and, if possible, return no more. For your wages you may rank as a creditor in my late husband's bankruptcy."

Harry had scarcely comprehended this insulting address before the General was down upon him with another.

"And in the meantime," said that personage, "follow me before the nearest Inspector of Police. You may impose upon a simple-minded soldier, sir, but the eye of the law will read your disreputable secret. If I must spend my old age in poverty through your underhand intriguing with my wife, I mean at least that you shall not remain unpunished for your pains; and God, sir, will deny me a very considerable satisfaction if you do not pick oakum from now until your dying day."

With that, the General dragged Harry from the apartment, and hurried him downstairs and along the street to the police station of the district.

Here (says my Arabian author) *ended this deplorable business of the band-box. But to the unfortunate Secretary the whole affair was the beginning of a new and manlier life. The police were easily persuaded of his innocence; and, after he had given what help he could in the subsequent investigations, he was even complimented by one of the chiefs of the detective department on the probity and simplicity of his behaviour. Several persons interested themselves in one so unfortunate; and soon after he inherited a sum of money from a maiden aunt in Worcestershire. With this he married Prudence, and set sail for Bendigo, or according to another account, for Trincomalee, exceedingly content, and with the best of prospects.*

STORY OF THE YOUNG MAN IN HOLY ORDERS

The Reverend Mr. Simon Rolles had distinguished himself in the Moral Sciences, and was more than usually proficient in the study of Divinity. His essay "On the Christian Doctrine of the Social Obligations" obtained for him, at the moment of its production, a certain celebrity in the University of Oxford; and it was understood in clerical and learned circles that young Mr. Rolles had in contemplation a considerable work—a folio, it was said—on the authority of the Fathers of the Church. These attainments, these ambitious designs, however, were far from helping him to any preferment; and he was still in quest of his first curacy when a chance ramble in that part of London, the peaceful and rich aspect of the garden, a desire for solitude and study, and the cheapness of the lodging, led him to take up his abode with Mr. Raeburn, the nurseryman of Stockdove Lane.

It was his habit every afternoon, after he had worked seven or eight hours on St. Ambrose or St. Chrysostom, to walk for a while in meditation among the roses. And this was usually one of the most productive moments of his day. But even a sincere appetite for thought, and the excitement of grave problems awaiting solution, are not always sufficient to preserve the mind of the philosopher against the petty shocks and contacts of the world. And when Mr. Rolles found General Vandeleur's secretary, ragged and bleeding, in the company of his landlord; when he saw both change colour and seek to avoid his questions; and, above all, when the former denied his own identity with the most unmoved assurance, he speedily forgot the Saints and Fathers in the vulgar interest of curiosity.

"I cannot be mistaken," thought he. "That is Mr. Hartley beyond a doubt. How comes he in such a pickle? why does he deny his name? and what can be his business with that black-looking ruffian, my landlord?"

As he was thus reflecting, another peculiar circumstance attracted his attention. The face of Mr. Raeburn appeared at a low window next the door; and, as chance directed, his eyes met those of Mr. Rolles. The nurseryman seemed disconcerted, and even alarmed; and immediately after the blind of the apartment was pulled sharply down.

"This may all be very well," reflected Mr. Rolles; "it may be all excellently well; but I confess freely that I do not think so. Suspicious, underhand, untruthful, fearful of observation—I believe upon my soul," he thought, "the pair are plotting some disgraceful action."

The detective that there is in all of us awoke and became clamant in the bosom of Mr. Rolles; and with a brisk, eager step, that bore no resemblance to his usual gait, he proceeded to make the circuit of the garden. When he came to the scene of Harry's escalade, his eye was at once arrested by a broken rosebush and marks of trampling on the mould. He looked up, and saw scratches on the brick, and a rag of trouser floating from a broken bottle. This, then, was the mode of entrance chosen by Mr. Raeburn's particular friend! It was thus that General Vandeleur's secretary came to admire a flower garden! The young clergyman whistled softly to himself as he stooped to examine the ground. He could make out where Harry had landed from his perilous leap; he recognised the flat foot of Mr. Raeburn where it had sunk deeply in the soil as he pulled up the Secretary by the collar; nay, on a closer inspection, he seemed to distinguish the marks of groping fingers, as though something had been spilt abroad and eagerly collected.

"Upon my word," he thought, "the thing grows vastly interesting."

And just then he caught sight of something almost entirely buried in the earth. In an instant he had disinterred a dainty morocco case, ornamented and clasped in gilt. It had been trodden heavily underfoot, and thus escaped the hurried search of Mr. Raeburn. Mr. Rolles opened the case, and drew a long breath of almost horrified astonishment; for there lay before him, in a cradle of green velvet, a diamond of prodigious magnitude and of the finest water. It was of the bigness of a duck's egg; beautifully shaped, and without a flaw; and as the sun shone upon it, it gave forth a lustre like that of electricity, and seemed to burn in his hand with a thousand internal fires.

He knew little of previous stones; but the Rajah's Diamond was a wonder that explained itself; a village child, if he found it, would run screaming for the nearest cottage; and a savage would prostrate himself in adoration before so imposing a fetish. The beauty of the stone flattered the young clergyman's eyes; the thought of its incalculable value overpowered his intellect. He knew that what he held in his hand was worth more than many years' purchase of an archiepiscopal see; that it would build cathedrals more stately than Ely or Cologne; that he who possessed it was set free for ever from the primal curse, and might follow his own inclinations without concern or hurry, without let or hindrance. And as he suddenly turned it, the rays leaped forth again with renewed brilliancy, and seemed to pierce his very heart.

Decisive actions are often taken in a moment and without any conscious deliverance from the rational parts of man. So it was now with Mr. Rolles. He glanced hurriedly round; beheld, like Mr. Raeburn before him, nothing but the sunlit flower garden, the tall treetops, and the house with blinded windows; and in a trice he had shut the case, thrust it into his pocket, and was hastening to his study with the speed of guilt.

The Reverend Simon Rolles had stolen the Rajah's Diamond.

Early in the afternoon the police arrived with Harry Hartley. The nurseryman, who was beside himself with terror, readily discovered his hoard; and the jewels were identified and inventoried in the presence of the Secretary. As for Mr. Rolles, he showed himself in a most obliging temper, communicated what he knew with freedom, and professed regret that he could do no more to help the officers in their duty.

"Still," he added, "I suppose your business is nearly at an end."

"By no means," replied the man from Scotland Yard; and he narrated the second robbery of which Harry had been the immediate victim, and gave the young clergyman a description of the more important jewels that were still not found, dilating particularly on the Rajah's Diamond.

"It must be worth a fortune," observed Mr. Rolles.

"Ten fortunes—twenty fortunes," cried the officer.

"The more it is worth," remarked Simon, shrewdly, "the more difficult it must be to sell. Such a thing has a physiognomy not to be disguised, and I should fancy a man might as easily negotiate St. Paul's Cathedral."

"Oh, truly!" said the officer; "but if the thief be a man of any intelligence, he will cut it into three or four, and there will be still enough to make him rich."

"Thank you," said the clergyman. "You cannot imagine how much your conversation interests me."

Whereupon the functionary admitted that they knew many strange things in his profession, and immediately after took his leave.

Mr. Rolles regained his apartment. It seemed smaller and barer than usual; the materials for his great work had never presented so little interest; and he looked upon his library with the eyes of scorn. He took down, volume by volume, several Fathers of the Church, and glanced them through; but they contained nothing to his purpose.

"These old gentlemen," thought he, "are no doubt very valuable writers, but they seem to me conspicuously ignorant of life. Here am I, with learning enough to be a Bishop, and I positively do not know how to dispose of a stolen diamond. I glean a hint from a common policeman, and, with all my folios, I cannot so much as put it into execution. This inspires me with very low ideas of University training."

Herewith he kicked over his bookshelf and, putting on his hat, hastened from the house to the club of which he was a member. In such a place of mundane resort he hoped to find some man of good counsel and a shrewd experience in life. In the reading room he saw many of the country clergy and an Archdeacon; there were three journalists and a writer upon the Higher Metaphysic, playing pool; and at dinner only the raff of ordinary club frequenters showed their commonplace and obliterated countenances. None of these, thought Mr. Rolles, would know more on dangerous topics than he knew himself; none of them were fit to give him guidance in his present strait. At length, in the smoking room, up many weary stairs, he hit upon a gentleman of somewhat portly build and dressed with conspicuous plainness. He was smoking a cigar and reading the *Fortnightly Review;* his face was singularly free from all sign of preoccupation or fatigue; and there was something in his air which seemed to invite confidence and to expect submission. The more the young clergyman scrutinised his features, the more he was convinced that he had fallen on one capable of giving pertinent advice.

"Sir," said he, "you will excuse my abruptness; but I judge you from your appearance to be preeminently a man of the world."

"I have indeed considerable claims to that distinction," replied the stranger, laying aside his magazine with a look of mingled amusement and surprise.

"I, sir," continued the Curate, "am a recluse, a student, a creature of ink bottles and patristic folios. A recent event has brought my folly vividly before my eyes, and I desire to instruct myself in life. By life," he added, "I do not mean Thackeray's novels; but the crimes and secret possibilities of our society, and the principles of wise conduct among exceptional events. I am a patient reader; can the thing be learnt in books?"

"You put me in a difficulty," said the stranger. "I confess I have no great notion of the use of books, except to amuse a railway journey; although, I believe, there are some very exact treatises on astronomy, the use of the globes, agriculture, and the art of making paper flowers. Upon the less apparent provinces of life I fear you will find nothing truthful. Yet stay," he added, "have you read Gaboriau?"

Mr. Rolles admitted he had never even heard the name.

"You may gather some notions from Gaboriau," resumed the stranger. "He is at least suggestive; and as he is an author much studied by Prince Bismarck, you will, at the worst, lose your time in good society."

"Sir," said the Curate, "I am infinitely obliged by your politeness."

"You have already more than repaid me," returned the other.

"How?" inquired Simon.

"By the novelty of your request," replied the gentleman; and with a polite gesture, as though to ask permission, he resumed the study of the *Fortnightly Review*.

On his way home Mr. Rolles purchased a work on precious stones and several of Gaboriau's novels. These last he eagerly skimmed until an advanced hour in the morning; but although they introduced him to many new ideas, he could nowhere discover what to do with a stolen diamond. He was annoyed, moreover, to find the information scattered amongst romantic storytelling, instead of soberly set forth after the manner of a manual; and he concluded that, even if the writer had thought much upon these subjects, he was totally lacking in educational method. For the character and attainments of Lecoq, however, he was unable to contain his admiration.

"He was truly a great creature," ruminated Mr. Rolles. "He knew the world as I know Paley's Evidences. There was nothing that he could not carry to a termination with his own hand, and against the largest odds. Heavens!" he broke out suddenly, "is not this the lesson? Must I not learn to cut diamonds for myself?"

It seemed to him as if he had sailed at once out of his perplexities; he remembered that he knew a jeweller, one B. Macculloch, in Edinburgh, who would be glad to put him in the way of the necessary training; a few months, perhaps a few years, of sordid toil, and he would be sufficiently expert to divide and sufficiently cunning to dispose with advantage of the Rajah's Diamond. That done, he might return to pursue his researches at leisure, a wealthy and luxurious student, envied and respected by all. Golden visions attended him through his slumber, and he awoke refreshed and lighthearted with the morning sun.

Mr. Raeburn's house was on that day to be closed by the police, and this afforded a pretext for his departure. He cheerfully prepared his baggage, transported it to King's Cross, where he left it in the cloakroom, and returned to the club to while away the afternoon and dine.

"If you dine here today, Rolles," observed an acquaintance, "you may see two of the most remarkable men in England—Prince Florizel of Bohemia, and old Jack Vandeleur."

"I have heard of the Prince," replied Mr. Rolles; "and General Vandeleur I have even met in society."

"General Vandeleur is an ass!" returned the other. "This is his brother John, the biggest adventurer, the best judge of precious stones, and one of the most acute diplomatists in Europe. Have you never heard of his duel with the Duc de Val d'Orge? of his exploits and atrocities when he was Dictator of Paraguay? of his dexterity in recovering Sir Samuel Levi's jewellery? nor of his services in the Indian Mutiny—services by which the Government profited, but which the Government dared not recognise? You make me wonder what we mean by fame, or even by infamy; for Jack Vandeleur has prodigious claims to both. Run down stairs," he continued, "take a table near them, and keep your ears open. You will hear some strange talk, or I am much misled."

"But how shall I know them?" inquired the clergyman.

"Know them!" cried his friend; "why, the Prince is the finest gentle-man in Europe, the only living creature who looks like a king; and as for Jack Vandeleur, if you can imagine Ulysses at seventy years of age, and with a sabre cut across his face, you have the man before you! Know them, indeed! Why, you could pick either of them out of a Derby day!"

Rolles eagerly hurried to the dining room. It was as his friend had asserted; it was impossible to mistake the pair in question. Old John Vandeleur was of a remarkable force of body, and obviously broken to the most difficult exercises. He had neither the carriage of a swords-man, nor of a sailor, nor yet of one much inured to the saddle; but something made up of all these, and the result and expression of many different habits and dexterities. His features were bold and aquiline; his expression arrogant and predatory; his whole appearance that of a swift, violent, unscrupulous man of action; and his copious white hair and the deep sabre cut that traversed his nose and temple added a note of savagery to a head already remarkable and menacing in itself.

In his companion, the Prince of Bohemia, Mr Rolles was astonished to recognise the gentleman who had recommended him the study of Gaboriau. Doubtless Prince Florizel, who rarely visited the club, of which, as of most others, he was an honorary member, had been wait-ing for John Vandeleur when Simon accosted him on the previous evening.

The other diners had modestly retired into the angles of the room, and left the distinguished pair in a certain isolation, but the young clergyman was unrestrained by any sentiment of awe, and, marching boldly up, took his place at the nearest table.

The conversation was, indeed, new to the student's ears. The ex-Dictator of Paraguay stated many extraordinary experiences in differ-ent quarters of the world; and the Prince supplied a commentary which, to a man of thought, was even more interesting than the events themselves. Two forms of experience were thus brought together and laid before the young clergyman; and he did not know which to ad-mire the most—the desperate actor or the skilled expert in life; the man who spoke boldly of his own deeds and perils, or the man who seemed, like a god, to know all things and to have suffered nothing. The manner of each aptly fitted with his part in the discourse. The Dictator indulged in brutalities alike of speech and gesture; his hand opened and shut and fell roughly on the table; and his voice was loud and heady. The Prince, on the other hand, seemed the very type of urbane docility and quiet; the least movement, the least inflection, had with him a weightier significance than all the shouts and pantomime of his companion; and if ever, as must frequently have been the case, he described some experience personal to himself, it was so aptly dissimulated as to pass unnoticed with the rest.

At length the talk wandered on to the late robberies and the Rajah's Diamond.

"That diamond would be better in the sea," observed Prince Florizel.

"As a Vandeleur," replied the Dictator, "your Highness may imagine my dissent."

"I speak on grounds of public policy," pursued the Prince. "Jewels so valuable should be reserved for the collection of a Prince or the treasury of a great nation. To hand them about among the common sort of men is to set a price on Virtue's head; and if the Rajah of Kashgar—a Prince, I understand, of great enlightenment—desired vengeance upon the men of Europe, he could hardly have gone more efficaciously about his purpose than by sending us this apple of discord. There is no honesty too robust for such a trial. I myself, who have many duties and many privileges of my own—I myself, Mr. Vandeleur, could scarce handle the intoxicating crystal and be safe. As for you, who are a diamond hunter by taste and profession, I do not believe there is a crime in the calendar you would not perpetrate—I do not believe you have a friend in the world whom you would not eagerly betray—I do not know if you have a family, but if you have I declare you would sacrifice your children—and all this for what? Not to be richer, nor to have more comforts or more respect, but simply to call this diamond yours for a year or two until you die, and now and again to open a safe and look at it as one looks at a picture."

"It is true," replied Vandeleur. "I have hunted most things, from men and women down to mosquitos; I have dived for coral; I have followed both whales and tigers; and a diamond is the tallest quarry of the lot. It has beauty and worth; it alone can properly reward the ardours of the chase. At this moment, as your Highness may fancy, I am upon the trail; I have a sure knack, a wide experience; I know every stone of price in my brother's collection as a shepherd knows his sheep; and I wish I may die if I do not recover them every one!"

"Sir Thomas Vandeleur will have great cause to thank you," said the Prince.

"I am not so sure," returned the Dictator, with a laugh. "One of the Vandeleurs will. Thomas or John—Peter or Paul—we are all apostles."

"I did not catch your observation," said the Prince with some disgust.

And at the same moment the waiter informed Mr. Vandeleur that his cab was at the door.

Mr. Rolles glanced at the clock, and saw that he also must be moving; and the coincidence struck him sharply and unpleasantly, for he desired to see no more of the diamond hunter.

Much study having somewhat shaken the young man's nerves, he was in the habit of travelling in the most luxurious manner; and for the present journey he had taken a sofa in the sleeping carriage.

"You will be very comfortable," said the guard; "there is no one in your compartment, and only one old gentleman in the other end."

It was close upon the hour, and the tickets were being examined, when Mr. Rolles beheld this other fellow passenger ushered by several porters into his place; certainly, there was not another man in the world whom he would not have preferred—for it was old John Vandeleur, the ex-Dictator.

The sleeping carriages on the Great Northern line were divided into three compartments—one at each end for travellers, and one in the centre fitted with the conveniences of a lavatory. A door running in grooves separated each of the others from the lavatory; but as there were neither bolts nor locks, the whole suite was practically common ground.

When Mr. Rolles had studied his position, he perceived himself without defence. If the Dictator chose to pay him a visit in the course of the night, he could do no less than receive it; he had no means of fortification, and lay open to attack as if he had been lying in the fields. This situation caused him some agony of mind. He recalled with alarm the boastful statements of his fellow traveller across the dining table, and the professions of immorality which he had heard him offering to the disgusted Prince. Some persons, he remembered to have read, are endowed with a singular quickness of perception for the neighbourhood of precious metals; through walls and even at considerable distances they are said to divine the presence of gold. Might it not be the same with diamonds? he wondered; and if so, who was more likely to enjoy this transcendental sense than the person who gloried in the appellation of the Diamond Hunter? From such a man he recognised that he had everything to fear, and longed eagerly for the arrival of the day.

In the meantime he neglected no precaution, concealed his diamond in the most internal pocket of a system of greatcoats, and devoutly recommended himself to the care of Providence.

The train pursued its usual even and rapid course; and nearly half the journey had been accomplished before slumber began to triumph over uneasiness in the breast of Mr. Rolles. For some time he resisted its influence; but it grew upon him more and more, and a little before York he was fain to stretch himself upon one of the couches and suffer his eyes to close; and almost at the same instant consciousness deserted the young clergyman. His last thought was of his terrifying neighbour.

When he awoke it was still pitch dark, except for the flicker of the veiled lamp; and the continual roaring and oscillation testified to the unrelaxed velocity of the train. He sat upright in a panic, for he had been tormented by the most uneasy dreams; it was some seconds before he recovered his self-command; and even after he had resumed a recumbent attitude sleep continued to flee him, and he lay awake with his brain in a state of violent agitation, and his eyes fixed upon the lavatory door. He pulled his clerical felt hat over his brow still farther to shield him from the light; and he adopted the usual expedients, such as counting a thousand or banishing thought, by which experienced invalids are accustomed to woo the approach of sleep. In the case of Mr. Rolles they proved one and all vain; he was harassed by a dozen different anxieties—the old man in the other end of the carriage haunted him in the most alarming shapes; and in whatever attitude he chose to lie the diamond in his pocket occasioned him a sensible physical distress. It burned, it was too large, it bruised his ribs; and there were infinitesimal fractions of a second in which he had half a mind to throw it from the window.

While he was thus lying, a strange incident took place.

The sliding door into the lavatory stirred a little, and then a little more, and was finally drawn back for the space of about twenty inches. The lamp in the lavatory was unshaded, and in the lighted aperture thus disclosed, Mr. Rolles could see the head of Mr. Vandeleur in an attitude of deep attention. He was conscious that the gaze of the Dictator rested intently on his own face; and the instinct of self-preservation moved him to hold his breath, to refrain from the least movement, and keeping his eyes lowered, to watch his visitor from underneath the lashes. After about a moment, the head was withdrawn and the door of the lavatory replaced.

The Dictator had not come to attack, but to observe; his action was not that of a man threatening another, but that of a man who was himself threatened; if Mr. Rolles was afraid of him, it appeared that he, in his turn, was not quite easy on the score of Mr. Rolles. He had come, it would seem, to make sure that his only fellow traveller was asleep; and, when satisfied on that point, he had at once withdrawn.

The clergyman leaped to his feet. The extreme of terror had given place to a reaction of foolhardy daring. He reflected that the rattle of the flying train concealed all other sounds, and determined, come what might, to return the visit he had just received. Divesting himself of his cloak, which might have interfered with the freedom of his action, he entered the lavatory and paused to listen. As he had expected, there was nothing to be heard above the roar of the train's progress; and laying his hand on the door at the farther side, he proceeded cautiously to draw it back for about six inches. Then he stopped, and could not contain an ejaculation of surprise.

John Vandeleur wore a fur travelling cap with lappets to protect his ears; and this may have combined with the sound of the express to keep him in ignorance of what was going forward. It is certain, at least, that he did not raise his head, but continued without interruption to pursue his strange employment. Between his feet stood an open hatbox; in one hand he held the sleeve of his sealskin greatcoat, in the other a formidable knife, with which he had just slit up the lining of the sleeve. Mr. Rolles had read of persons carrying money in a belt; and as he had no acquaintance with any but cricketbelts, he had never been able rightly to conceive how this was managed. But here was a stranger thing before his eyes; for John Vandeleur, it appeared, carried diamonds in the lining of his sleeve; and even as the young clergyman gazed, he could see one glittering brilliant drop after another into the hatbox.

He stood riveted to the spot, following this unusual business with his eyes. The diamonds were, for the most part, small, and not easily distinguishable either in shape or fire. Suddenly the Dictator appeared to find a difficulty; he employed both hands and stooped over his task; but it was not until after considerable manoeuvering that he extricated a large tiara of diamonds from the lining, and held it up for some seconds' examination before he placed it with the others in the hatbox. The tiara was a ray of light to Mr. Rolles; he immediately recognised it for a part of the treasure stolen from Harry Hartley by the loiterer. There was no room for mistake; it was exactly as the detective had described it; there were the ruby stars, with a great emerald in the centre; there were the interlacing crescents; and there were the pear-shaped pendants, each a single stone, which gave a special value to Lady Vandeleur's tiara.

Mr. Rolles was hugely relieved. The Dictator was as deeply in the affair as he was; neither could tell tales upon the other. In the first glow of happiness, the clergyman suffered a deep sigh to escape him; and as his bosom had become choked and his throat dry during his previous suspense, the sigh was followed by a cough.

Mr. Vandeleur looked up; his face contracted with the blackest and most deadly passion; his eyes opened widely, and his under jaw dropped in an astonishment that was upon the brink of fury. By an instinctive movement he had covered the hatbox with the coat. For half a minute the two men stared upon each other in silence. It was not a long interval, but it sufficed for Mr. Rolles; he was one of those who think swiftly on dangerous occasions; he decided on a course of action of a singularly daring nature; and although he felt he was setting his life upon the hazard, he was the first to break silence.

"I beg your pardon," said he.

The Dictator shivered slightly, and when he spoke his voice was hoarse.

"What do you want here?" he asked.

"I take a particular interest in diamonds," replied Mr. Rolles, with an air of perfect self-possession. "Two connoisseurs should be acquainted. I have here a trifle of my own which may perhaps serve for an introduction."

And so saying, he quietly took the case from his pocket, showed the Rajah's Diamond to the Dictator for an instant, and replaced it in security.

"It was once your brother's," he added.

John Vandeleur continued to regard him with a look of almost painful amazement; but he neither spoke nor moved.

"I was pleased to observe," resumed the young man, "that we have gems from the same collection."

The Dictator's surprise overpowered him.

"I beg your pardon," he said; "I begin to perceive that I am growing old! I am positively not prepared for little incidents like this. But set my mind at rest upon one point: do my eyes deceive me, or are you indeed a parson?"

"I am in holy orders," answered Mr. Rolles.

"Well," cried the other, "as long as I live I will never hear another word against the cloth!"

"You flatter me," said Mr. Rolles.

"Pardon me," replied Vandeleur; "pardon me, young man. You are no coward, but it still remains to be seen whether you are not the worst of fools. Perhaps," he continued, leaning back upon his seat, "perhaps you would oblige me with a few particulars. I must suppose you had some object in the stupefying impudence of your proceedings, and I confess I have a curiosity to know it."

"It is very simple," replied the clergyman; "it proceeds from my great inexperience of life."

"I shall be glad to be persuaded," answered Vandeleur.

Whereupon Mr. Rolles told him the whole story of his connection with the Rajah's Diamond, from the time he found it in Raeburn's garden to the time when he left London in the Flying Scotchman. He added a brief sketch of his feelings and thoughts during the journey, and concluded in these words:

"When I recognised the tiara I knew we were in the same attitude towards Society, and this inspired me with a hope, which I trust you will say was not ill-founded, that you might become in some sense my partner in the difficulties and, of course, the profits of my situation. To one of your special knowledge and obviously great experience the negotiation of the diamond would give but little trouble, while to me it was a matter of impossibility. On the other part, I judged that I might lose nearly as much by cutting the diamond, and that not improbably with an unskilful hand, as might enable me to pay you with proper generosity for your assistance. The subject was a delicate one to broach; and perhaps I fell short in delicacy. But I must ask you to remember that for me the situation was a new one, and I was entirely unacquainted with the etiquette in use. I believe without vanity that I could have married or baptised you in a very acceptable manner; but every man has his own aptitudes, and this sort of bargain was not among the list of my accomplishments."

"I do not wish to flatter you," replied Vandeleur; "but upon my word, you have an unusual disposition for a life of crime. You have more accomplishments than you imagine; and though I have encountered a number of rogues in different quarters of the world, I never met with one so unblushing as yourself. Cheer up, Mr. Rolles, you are in the right profession at last! As for helping you, you may command me as you will. I have only a day's business in Edinburgh on a little matter for my brother; and once that is concluded, I return to Paris, where I usually reside. If you please, you may accompany me thither. And before the end of a month I believe I shall have brought your little business to a satisfactory conclusion."

(At this point, contrary to all the canons of his art, our Arabian Author breaks off the STORY OF THE YOUNG MAN IN HOLY ORDERS. *I regret and condemn such practices; but I must follow my original, and refer the reader for the conclusion of Mr. Rolles' adventures to the next number of the cycle, the* STORY OF THE HOUSE WITH THE GREEN BLINDS.*)*

STORY OF THE HOUSE WITH THE GREEN BLINDS

Francis Scrymgeour, a clerk in the Bank of Scotland at Edinburgh, had attained the age of twenty-five in a sphere of quiet, creditable, and domestic life. His mother died while he was young; but his father, a man of sense and probity, had given him an excellent education at school, and brought him up at home to orderly and frugal habits. Francis, who was of a docile and affectionate disposition, profited by these advantages with zeal, and devoted himself heart and soul to his employment. A walk upon Saturday afternoon, an occasional dinner with members of his family, and a yearly tour of a fortnight in the Highlands or even on the continent of Europe, were his principal distractions, and he grew rapidly in favour with his superiors, and enjoyed already a salary of nearly two hundred pounds a year, with the prospect of an ultimate advance to almost double that amount. Few young men were more contented, few more willing and laborious than Francis Scrymgeour. Sometimes at night, when he had read the daily paper, he would play upon the flute to amuse his father, for whose qualities he entertained a great respect.

One day he received a note from a well-known firm of Writers to the Signet, requesting the favour of an immediate interview with him. The letter was marked "Private and Confidential," and had been addressed to him at the bank, instead of at home—two unusual circumstances which made him obey the summons with the more alacrity. The senior member of the firm, a man of much austerity of manner, made him gravely welcome, requested him to take a seat, and proceeded to explain the matter in hand in the picked expressions of a veteran man of business. A person, who must remain nameless, but of whom the lawyer had every reason to think well— a man, in short, of some station in the country—desired to make Francis an annual allowance of five hundred pounds. The capital was to be placed under the control of the lawyer's firm and two trustees who must also remain anonymous. There were conditions annexed to this liberality, but he was of opinion that his new client would find nothing either excessive or dishonourable in the terms; and he repeated these two words with emphasis, as though he desired to commit himself to nothing more.

Francis asked their nature.

"The conditions," said the Writer to the Signet, "are, as I have twice remarked, neither dishonourable nor excessive. At the same time I cannot conceal from you that they are most unusual. Indeed, the whole case is very much out of our way; and I should certainly have refused it had it not been for the reputation of the gentleman who entrusted it to my care, and, let me add, Mr. Scrymgeour, the interest I have been led to take in yourself by many complimentary and, I have no doubt, well-deserved reports."

Francis entreated him to be more specific.

"You cannot picture my uneasiness as to these conditions," he said.

"They are two," replied the lawyer, "only two; and the sum, as you will remember, is five hundred a year—and unburdened, I forgot to add, unburdened."

And the lawyer raised his eyebrows at him with solemn gusto.

"The first," he resumed, "is of remarkable simplicity. You must be in

Paris by the afternoon of Sunday, the 15th; there you will find, at the box office of the Comédie Française, a ticket for admission taken in your name and waiting you. You are requested to sit out the whole performance in the seat provided, and that is all."

"I should certainly have preferred a weekday," replied Francis. "But, after all, once in a way——"

"And in Paris, my dear sir," added the lawyer, soothingly. "I believe I am something of a precisian myself, but upon such a consideration, and in Paris, I should not hesitate an instant."

And the pair laughed pleasantly together.

"The other is of more importance," continued the Writer to the Signet. "It regards your marriage. My client, taking a deep interest in your welfare, desires to advise you absolutely in the choice of a wife. Absolutely, you understand," he repeated.

"Let us be more explicit, if you please," returned Francis. "Am I to marry anyone, maid or widow, black or white, whom this invisible person chooses to propose?"

"I was to assure you that suitability of age and position should be a principle with your benefactor," replied the lawyer. "As to race, I confess the difficulty had not occurred to me, and I failed to inquire; but if you like I will make a note of it at once, and advise you on the earliest opportunity."

"Sir," said Francis, "it remains to be seen whether this whole affair is not a most unworthy fraud. The circumstances are inexplicable—I had almost said incredible; and until I see a little more daylight, and some plausible motive, I confess I should be very sorry to put a hand to the transaction. I appeal to you in this difficulty for information. I must learn what is at the bottom of it all. If you do not know, cannot guess, or are not at liberty to tell me, I shall take my hat and go back to my bank as I came."

"I do not know," answered the lawyer, "but I have an excellent guess. Your father, and no one else, is at the root of this apparently unnatural business."

"My father!" cried Francis, in extreme disdain. "Worthy man, I know every thought of his mind, every penny of his fortune!"

"You misinterpret my words," said the lawyer. "I do not refer to Mr. Scrymgeour, senior; for he is not your father. When he and his wife came to Edinburgh, you were already nearly one year old, and you had not yet been three months in their care. The secret has been well kept; but such is the fact. Your father is unknown, and I say again that I believe him to be the original of the offers I am charged at present to transmit to you."

It would be impossible to exaggerate the astonishment of Francis Scrymgeour at this unexpected information. He pled this confusion to the lawyer.

"Sir," said he, "after a piece of news so startling, you must grant me some hours for thought. You shall know this evening what conclusion I have reached."

The lawyer commended his prudence; and Francis, excusing himself upon some pretext at the bank, took a long walk into the country, and fully considered the different steps and aspects of the case. A pleasant sense of his own importance rendered him the more deliberate: but the issue was from the first not doubtful. His whole carnal man leaned irresistibly towards the five hundred a year, and the strange conditions with which it was burdened; he discovered in his heart an invincible repugnance to the name of Scrymgeour, which he had never hitherto disliked; he began to despise the narrow and unromantic interests of his former life; and when once his mind was fairly made up, he walked with a new feeling of strength and freedom, and nourished himself with the gayest anticipations.

He said but a word to the lawyer, and immediately received a cheque for two quarters' arrears; for the allowance was antedated from the first of January. With this in his pocket, he walked home. The flat in Scotland Street looked mean in his eyes; his nostrils, for the first time, rebelled against the odour of broth; and he observed little defects of manner in his adoptive father which filled him with surprise and almost with disgust. The next day, he determined, should see him on his way to Paris.

In that city, where he arrived long before the appointed date, he put up at a modest hotel frequented by English and Italians, and devoted himself to improvement in the French tongue; for this purpose he had a master twice a week, entered into conversation with loiterers in the Champs Elysées, and nightly frequented the theatre. He had his whole toilette fashionably renewed; and was shaved and had his hair dressed every morning by a barber in a neighbouring street. This gave him something of a foreign air, and seemed to wipe off the reproach of his past years.

At length, on the Saturday afternoon, he betook himself to the box office of the theatre in the Rue Richelieu. No sooner had he mentioned his name than the clerk produced the order in an envelope of which the address was scarcely dry.

"It has been taken this moment," said the clerk.

"Indeed!" said Francis. "May I ask what the gentleman was like?"

"Your friend is easy to describe," replied the official. "He is old and strong and beautiful, with white hair and a sabre cut across his face. You cannot fail to recognise so marked a person."

"No, indeed," returned Francis; "and I thank you for your politeness."

"He cannot yet be far distant," added the clerk. "If you make haste you might still overtake him."

Francis did not wait to be twice told; he ran precipitately from the theatre into the middle of the street and looked in all directions. More than one white-haired man was within sight; but though he overtook each of them in succession, all wanted the sabre cut. For nearly half an hour he tried one street after another in the neighbourhood, until at length, recognising the folly of continued search, he started on a walk to compose his agitated feelings; for this proximity of an encounter with him to whom he could not doubt he owed the day had profoundly moved the young man.

It chanced that his way lay up the Rue Drouot and thence up the Rue des Martyrs; and chance, in this case, served him better than all the forethought in the world. For on the outer boulevard he saw two men in earnest colloquy upon a seat. One was dark, young, and handsome, secularly dressed, but with an indelible clerical stamp; the other answered in every particular to the description given him by the clerk. Francis felt his heart beat high in his bosom; he knew he was now about to hear the voice of his father; and making a wide circuit, he noiselessly took his place behind the couple in question, who were too much interested in their talk to observe much else. As Francis had expected, the conversation was conducted in the English language.

"Your suspicions begin to annoy me, Rolles," said the older man. "I tell you I am doing my utmost; a man cannot lay his hand on millions in a moment. Have I not taken you up, a mere stranger, out of pure goodwill? Are you not living largely on my bounty?"

"On your advances, Mr. Vandeleur," corrected the other.

"Advances, if you choose; and interest instead of goodwill, if you prefer it," returned Vandeleur, angrily. "I am not here to pick expressions. Business is business; and your business, let me remind you, is too muddy for such airs. Trust me, or leave me alone and find someone else; but let us have an end, for God's sake, of your jeremiads."

"I am beginning to learn the world," replied the other, "and I see that you have every reason to play me false, and not one to deal honestly. I am not here to pick expressions either; you wish the diamond for yourself; you know you do—you dare not deny it. Have you not already forged my name, and searched my lodging in my absence? I understand the cause of your delays; you are lying in wait; you are the diamond hunter, forsooth; and sooner or later, by fair means or foul, you'll lay your hands upon it. I tell you, it must stop; push me much further and I promise you a surprise."

"It does not become you to use threats," returned Vandeleur. "Two can play at that. My brother is here in Paris; the police are on the alert; and if you persist in wearying me with your caterwauling, I will arrange a little astonishment for you, Mr. Rolles. But mine shall be once and for all. Do you understand, or would you prefer me to tell it you in Hebrew? There is an end to all things, and you have come to the end of my patience. Tuesday, at seven; not a day, not an hour sooner, not the least part of a second, if it were to save your life. And if you do not choose to wait, you may go to the bottomless pit for me, and welcome."

And so saying, the Dictator arose from the bench, and marched off in the direction of Montmartre, shaking his head and swinging his cane with a most furious air; while his companion remained where he was, in an attitude of great dejection.

Francis was at the pitch of surprise and horror; his sentiments had been shocked to the last degree; the hopeful tenderness with which he had taken his place upon the bench was transformed into repulsion and despair; old Mr. Scrymgeour, he reflected, was a far more kindly and creditable parent than this dangerous and violent intriguer; but he retained his presence of mind, and suffered not a moment to elapse before he was on the trail of the Dictator.

That gentleman's fury carried him forward at a brisk pace, and he was so completely occupied in his angry thoughts that he never so much as cast a look behind him till he reached his own door.

His house stood high up in the Rue Lepic, commanding a view of all Paris and enjoying the pure air of the heights. It was two stories high, with green blinds and shutters; and all the windows looking on the street were hermetically closed. Tops of trees showed over the high garden wall, and the wall was protected by *chevaux-de-frise*. The Dictator paused a moment while he searched his pocket for a key; and then, opening a gate, disappeared within the enclosure.

Francis looked about him; the neighbourhood was very lonely; the house isolated in its garden. It seemed as if his observation must here come to an abrupt end. A second glance, however, showed him a tall house next door presenting a gable to the garden, and in this gable a single window. He passed to the front and saw a ticket offering unfurnished lodgings by the month; and, on inquiry, the room which commanded the Dictator's garden proved to be one of those to let. Francis did not hesitate a moment; he took the room, paid an advance upon the rent, and returned to his hotel to seek his baggage.

The old man with the sabre cut might or might not be his father; he might or he might not be upon the true scent; but he was certainly on the edge of an exciting mystery, and he promised himself that he would not relax his observation until he had got to the bottom of the secret.

From the window of his new apartment Francis Scrymgeour commanded a complete view into the garden of the house with the green blinds. Immediately below him a very comely chestnut with wide boughs sheltered a pair of rustic tables where people might dine in the height of summer. On all sides save one a dense vegetation concealed the soil; but there, between the tables and the house, he saw a patch of gravel walk leading from the verandah to the garden gate. Studying the place from between the boards of the Venetian shutters, which he durst not open for fear of attracting attention, Francis observed but little to indicate the manners of the inhabitants, and that little argued no more than a close reserve and a taste for solitude. The garden was conventual, the house had the air of a prison. The green blinds were all drawn down upon the outside; the door into the verandah was closed; the garden, as far as he could see it, was left entirely to itself in the evening sunshine. A modest curl of smoke from a single chimney alone testified to the presence of living people.

In order that he might not be entirely idle, and to give a certain colour to his way of life, Francis had purchased Euclid's Geometry in French, which he set himself to copy and translate on the top of his portmanteau and seated on the floor against the wall; for he was equally without chair or table. From time to time he would rise and cast a glance into the enclosure of the house with the green blinds; but the windows remained obstinately closed and the garden empty.

Only late in the evening did anything occur to reward his continued attention. Between nine and ten the sharp tinkle of a bell aroused him from a fit of dozing; and he sprang to his observatory in time to hear an important noise of locks being opened and bars removed, and to see Mr. Vandeleur, carrying a lantern and clothed in a flowing robe of black velvet with a skullcap to match, issue from under the verandah and proceed leisurely towards the garden gate. The sound of bolts and bars was then repeated; and a moment after Francis perceived the Dictator escorting into the house, in the mobile light of the lantern, an individual of the lowest and most despicable appearance.

Half an hour afterwards the visitor was reconducted to the street; and Mr. Vandeleur, setting his light upon one of the rustic tables, finished a cigar with great deliberation under the foliage of the chestnut. Francis, peering through a clear space among the leaves, was able to follow his gestures as he threw away the ash or enjoyed a copious inhalation; and beheld a cloud upon the old man's brow and a forcible action of the lips, which testified to some deep and probably painful train of thought. The cigar was already almost at an end, when the voice of a young girl was heard suddenly crying the hour from the interior of the house.

"In a moment," replied John Vandeleur.

And, with that, he threw away the stump and, taking up the lantern, sailed away under the verandah for the night. As soon as the door was closed, absolute darkness fell upon the house; Francis might try his eyesight as much as he pleased, he could not detect so much as a single chink of light below a blind; and he concluded, with great good sense, that the bedchambers were all upon the other side.

Early the next morning (for he was early awake after an uncomfortable night upon the floor), he saw cause to adopt a different explanation. The blinds rose, one after another, by means of a spring in the interior, and disclosed steel shutters such as we see on the front of shops; these in their turn were rolled up by a similar contrivance; and for the space of about an hour, the chambers were left open to the morning air. At the end of that time, Mr. Vandeleur, with his own hand, once more closed the shutters and replaced the blinds from within.

While Francis was still marvelling at these precautions, the door opened and a young girl came forth to look about her in the garden. It was not two minutes before she reentered the house, but even in that short time he saw enough to convince him that she possessed the most unusual attractions. His curiosity was not only highly excited by this incident, but his spirits were improved to a still more notable degree. The alarming manners and more than equivocal life of his father ceased from that moment to prey upon his mind; from that moment he embraced his new family with ardour; and whether the young lady should prove his sister or his wife, he felt convinced she was an angel in disguise. So much was this the case that he was seized with a sudden horror when he reflected how little he really knew, and how possible it was that he had followed the wrong person when he followed Mr. Vandeleur.

The porter, whom he consulted, could afford him little information; but, such as it was, it had a mysterious and questionable sound. The person next door was an English gentleman of extraordinary wealth, and proportionately eccentric in his tastes and habits. He possessed great collections, which he kept in the house beside him; and it was to protect these that he had fitted the place with steel shutters, elaborate fastenings, and *chevaux-de-frise* along the garden wall. He lived much alone, in spite of some strange visitors with whom, it seemed, he had business to transact; and there was no one else in the house, except Mademoiselle and an old woman servant.

"Is Mademoiselle his daughter?" inquired Francis.

"Certainly," replied the porter. "Mademoiselle is the daughter of the house; and strange it is to see how she is made to work. For all his riches, it is she who goes to market; and every day in the week you may see her going by with a basket on her arm."

"And the collections?" asked the other.

"Sir," said the man, "they are immensely valuable. More I cannot tell you. Since M. de Vandeleur's arrival no one in the quarter has so much as passed the door."

"Suppose not," returned Francis, "you must surely have some notion what these famous galleries contain. Is it pictures, silks, statues, jewels, or what?"

"My faith, sir," said the fellow with a shrug, "it might be carrots, and still I could not tell you. How should I know? The house is kept like a garrison, as you perceive."

And then as Francis was returning disappointed to his room, the porter called him back.

"I have just remembered, sir," said he. "M. de Vandeleur has been in all parts of the world, and I once heard the old woman declare that he had brought many diamonds back with him. If that be the truth, there must be a fine show behind those shutters."

By an early hour on Sunday Francis was in his place at the theatre. The seat which had been taken for him was only two or three numbers from the left-hand side, and directly opposite one of the lower boxes. As the seat had been specially chosen there was doubtless something to be learned from its position; and he judged by an instinct that the box upon his right was, in some way or other, to be connected with the drama in which he ignorantly played a part. Indeed it was so situated that its occupants could safely observe him from beginning to end of the piece, if they were so minded; while, profiting by the depth, they could screen themselves sufficiently well from any counterexamination on his side. He promised himself not to leave it for a moment out of sight; and whilst he scanned the rest of the theatre, or made a show of attending to the business of the stage, he always kept a corner of an eye upon the empty box.

The second act had been some time in progress, and was even drawing towards a close, when the door opened and two persons entered and ensconced themselves in the darkest of the shade. Francis could hardly control his emotion. It was Mr. Vandeleur and his daughter. The blood came and went in his arteries and veins with stunning activity; his ears sang; his head turned. He dared not look lest he should awake suspicion; his playbill, which he kept reading from end to end and over and over again, turned from white to red before his eyes; and when he cast a glance upon the stage, it seemed incalculably far away, and he found the voices and gestures of the actors to the last degree impertinent and absurd.

From time to time he risked a momentary look in the direction which principally interested him; and once at least he felt certain that his eyes encountered those of the young girl. A shock passed over his body, and he saw all the colours of the rainbow. What would he not have given to overhear what passed between the Vandeleurs? What would he not have given for the courage to take up his opera glass and steadily inspect their attitude and expression? There, for aught he knew, his whole life was being decided—and he not able to interfere, not able even to follow the debate, but condemned to sit and suffer where he was, in impotent anxiety.

At last the act came to an end. The curtain fell, and the people around him began to leave their places for the interval. It was only natural that he should follow their example; and if he did so, it was not only natural but necessary that he should pass immediately in front of the box in question. Summoning all his courage, but keeping his eyes lowered, Francis drew near the spot. His progress was slow, for the old gentleman before him moved with incredible deliberation, wheezing as he went. What was he to do? Should he address the Vandeleurs by name as he went by? Should he take the flower from his buttonhole and throw it into the box? Should he raise his face and direct one long and affectionate look upon the lady who was either his sister or his betrothed? As he found himself thus struggling among so many alternatives, he had a vision of his old equable existence in the bank, and was assailed by a thought of regret for the past.

By this time he had arrived directly opposite the box; and although he was still undetermined what to do or whether to do anything, he turned his head and lifted his eyes. No sooner had he done so than he uttered a cry of disappointment and remained rooted to the spot. The box was empty. During his slow advance Mr. Vandeleur and his daughter had quietly slipped away.

A polite person in his rear reminded him that he was stopping the path; and he moved on again with mechanical footsteps, and suffered the crowd to carry him unresisting out of the theatre. Once in the street, the pressure ceasing, he came to a halt, and the cool night air speedily restored him to the possession of his faculties. He was surprised to find that his head ached violently, and that he remembered not one word of the two acts which he had witnessed. As the excitement wore away, it was succeeded by an overweening appetite for sleep, and he hailed a cab and drove to his lodging in a state of extreme exhaustion and some disgust of life.

Next morning he lay in wait for Miss Vandeleur on her road to market, and by eight o'clock beheld her stepping down a lane. She was simply, and even poorly, attired; but in the carriage of her head and body there was something flexible and noble that would have lent distinction to the meanest toilette. Even her basket, so aptly did she carry it, became her like an ornament. It seemed to Francis, as he slipped into a doorway, that the sunshine followed and the shadows fled before her as she walked; and he was conscious, for the first time, of a bird singing in a cage above the lane.

He suffered her to pass the doorway, and then, coming forth once more, addressed her by name from behind.

"Miss Vandeleur," said he.

She turned and, when she saw who he was, became deadly pale.

"Pardon me," he continued; "Heaven knows I had no will to startle you; and, indeed, there should be nothing startling in the presence of one who wishes you so well as I do. And, believe me, I am acting rather from necessity than choice. We have many things in common, and I am sadly in the dark. There is much that I should be doing, and my hands are tied. I do not know even what to feel, nor who are my friends and enemies."

She found her voice with an effort.

"I do not know who you are," she said.

"Ah, yes! Miss Vandeleur, you do," returned Francis; "better than I do myself. Indeed it is on that, above all, that I seek light. Tell me what you know," he pleaded. "Tell me who I am, who you are, and how our destinies are intermixed. Give me a little help with my life, Miss Vandeleur—only a word or two to guide me, only the name of my father, if you will—and I shall be grateful and content."

"I will not attempt to deceive you," she replied. "I know who you are, but I am not at liberty to say."

"Tell me, at least, that you have forgiven my presumption, and I shall wait with all the patience I have," he said. "If I am not to know, I must do without. It is cruel, but I can bear more upon a push. Only do not add to my troubles the thought that I have made an enemy of you."

"You did only what was natural," she said, "and I have nothing to forgive you. Farewell."

"Is it to be *farewell?*" he asked.

"Nay, that I do not know myself," she answered. "Farewell for the present, if you like."

And with these words she was gone.

Francis returned to his lodging in a state of considerable commotion of mind. He made the most trifling progress with his Euclid for that forenoon, and was more often at the window than at his improvised writing table. But beyond seeing the return of Miss Vandeleur, and the meeting between her and her father, who was smoking a Trichinopoli cigar in the verandah, there was nothing notable in the neighbourhood of the house with the green blinds before the time of the midday meal. The young man hastily allayed his appetite in a neighbouring restaurant, and returned with the speed of unallayed curiosity to the house in the Rue Lepic. A mounted servant was leading a saddle horse to and fro before the garden wall; and the porter of Francis's lodging was smoking a pipe against the doorpost, absorbed in contemplation of the livery and the steeds.

"Look!" he cried to the young man, "what fine cattle! what an elegant costume! They belong to the brother of M. de Vandeleur, who is now within upon a visit. He is a great man, a general, in your country; and you doubtless know him well by reputation."

"I confess," returned Francis, "that I have never heard of General Vandeleur before. We have many officers of that grade, and my pursuits have been exclusively civil."

"It is he," replied the porter, "who lost the great diamond of the Indies. Of that at least you must have read often in the papers."

As soon as Francis could disengage himself from the porter he ran upstairs and hurried to the window. Immediately below the clear space in the chestnut leaves, the two gentlemen were seated in conversation over a cigar. The General, a red, military-looking man, offered some traces of a family resemblance to his brother; he had something of the same features, something, although very little, of the same free and powerful carriage; but he was older, smaller, and more common in air; his likeness was that of a caricature, and he seemed altogether a poor and debile being by the side of the Dictator.

They spoke in tones so low, leaning over the table with every appearance of interest, that Francis could catch no more than a word or two on an occasion. For as little as he heard, he was convinced that the conversation turned upon himself and his own career; several times the name of Scrymgeour reached his ear, for it was easy to distinguish, and still more frequently he fancied he could distinguish the name Francis.

At length the General, as if in a hot anger, broke forth into several violent exclamations.

"Francis Vandeleur!" he cried, accentuating the last word. "Francis Vandeleur, I tell you."

The Dictator made a movement of his whole body, half affirmative, half contemptuous, but his answer was inaudible to the young man.

Was he the Francis Vandeleur in question? he wondered. Were they discussing the name under which he was to be married? Or was the whole affair a dream and a delusion of his own conceit and self-absorption?

After another interval of inaudible talk, dissension seemed again to arise between the couple underneath the chestnut, and again the General raised his voice angrily so as to be audible to Francis.

"My wife?" he cried. "I have done with my wife for good. I will not hear her name. I am sick of her very name."

And he swore aloud and beat the table with his fist.

The Dictator appeared, by his gestures, to pacify him after a paternal fashion; and a little after he conducted him to the garden gate. The pair shook hands affectionately enough; but as soon as the door had closed behind his visitor, John Vandeleur fell into a fit of laughter which sounded unkindly and even devilish in the ears of Francis Scrymgeour.

So another day had passed, and little more learnt. But the young man remembered that the morrow was Tuesday, and promised himself some curious discoveries; all might be well, or all might be ill; he was sure, at least, to glean some curious information, and, perhaps, by good luck, get at the heart of the mystery which surrounded his father and his family.

As the hour of the dinner drew near many preparations were made in the garden of the house with the green blinds. That table which was partly visible to Francis through the chestnut leaves was destined to serve as a sideboard, and carried relays of plates and the materials for salad: the other, which was almost entirely concealed, had been set apart for the diners, and Francis could catch glimpses of white cloth and silver plate.

Mr. Rolles arrived, punctual to the minute; he looked like a man upon his guard, and spoke low and sparingly. The Dictator, on the other hand, appeared to enjoy an unusual flow of spirits; his laugh, which was youthful and pleasant to hear, sounded frequently from the garden; by the modulation and the changes of his voice it was obvious that he told many droll stories and imitated the accents of a variety of different nations; and before he and the young clergyman had finished their vermouth all feeling of distrust was at an end, and they were talking together like a pair of school companions.

At length Miss Vandeleur made her appearance, carrying the soup tureen. Mr. Rolles ran to offer her assistance which she laughingly refused; and there was an interchange of pleasantries among the trio which seemed to have reference to this primitive manner of waiting by one of the company.

"One is more at one's ease," Mr. Vandeleur was heard to declare.

Next moment they were all three in their places, and Francis could see as little as he could hear of what passed. But the dinner seemed to go merrily; there was a perpetual babble of voices and sound of knives and forks below the chestnut; and Francis, who had no more than a roll to gnaw, was affected with envy by the comfort and deliberation of the meal. The party lingered over one dish after another, and then over a delicate dessert, with a bottle of old wine carefully uncorked by the hand of the Dictator himself. As it began to grow dark a lamp was set upon the table and a couple of candles on the sideboard; for the night was perfectly pure, starry, and windless. Light overflowed besides from the door and window in the verandah, so that the garden was fairly illuminated and the leaves twinkled in the darkness.

For perhaps the tenth time Miss Vandeleur entered the house; and on this occasion she returned with the coffee tray, which she placed upon the sideboard. At the same moment her father rose from his seat.

"The coffee is my province," Francis heard him say.

And next moment he saw his supposed father standing by the sideboard in the light of the candles.

Talking over his shoulder all the while, Mr. Vandeleur poured out two cups of the brown stimulant, and then, by a rapid act of prestidigitation, emptied the contents of a tiny phial into the smaller of the two. The thing was so swiftly done that even Francis, who looked straight into his face, had hardly time to perceive the movement before it was completed. And next instant, and still laughing, Mr. Vandeleur had turned again towards the table with a cup in either hand.

"Ere we have done with this," said he, "we may expect our famous Hebrew."

It would be impossible to depict the confusion and distress of Francis Scrymgeour. He saw foul play going forward before his eyes, and he felt bound to interfere, but knew not how. It might be a mere pleasantry, and then how should he look if he were to offer an unnecessary warning? Or again, if it were serious, the criminal might be his own father, and then how should he not lament if he were to bring ruin on the author of his days? For the first time he became conscious of his own position as a spy. To wait inactive at such a juncture and with such a conflict of sentiments in his bosom was to suffer the most acute torture; he clung to the bars of the shutters, his heart beat fast and with irregularity, and he felt a strong sweat break forth upon his body.

Several minutes passed.

He seemed to perceive the conversation die away and grow less and less in vivacity and volume; but still no sign of any alarming or even notable event.

Suddenly the ring of a glass breaking was followed by a faint and dull sound, as of a person who should have fallen forward with his head upon the table. At the same moment a piercing scream rose from the garden.

"What have you done?" cried Miss Vandeleur. "He is dead!"

The Dictator replied in a violent whisper, so strong and sibilant that every word was audible to the watcher at the window.

"Silence!" said Mr. Vandeleur; "the man is as well as I am. Take him by the heels whilst I carry him by the shoulders."

Francis heard Miss Vandeleur break forth into a passion of tears.

"Do you hear what I say?" resumed the Dictator, in the same tones. "Or do you wish to quarrel with me? I give you your choice, Miss Vandeleur."

There was another pause, and the Dictator spoke again.

"Take that man by the heels," he said. "I must have him brought into the house. If I were a little younger, I could help myself against the world. But now that years and dangers are upon me and my hands are weakened, I must turn to you for aid."

"It is a crime," replied the girl.

"I am your father," said Mr. Vandeleur.

This appeal seemed to produce its effect. A scuffling noise followed upon the gravel, a chair was overset, and then Francis saw the father and daughter stagger across the walk and disappear under the verandah, bearing the inanimate body of Mr. Rolles embraced about the knees and shoulders. The young clergyman was limp and pallid, and his head rolled upon his shoulders at every step.

Was he alive or dead? Francis, in spite of the Dictator's declaration, inclined to the latter view. A great crime had been committed; a great calamity had fallen upon the inhabitants of the house with the green blinds. To his surprise, Francis found all horror for the deed swallowed up in sorrow for a girl and an old man whom he judged to be in the height of peril. A tide of generous feeling swept into his heart; he, too, would help his father against man and mankind, against fate and justice; and casting open the shutters he closed his eyes and threw himself with outstretched arms into the foliage of the chestnut.

Branch after branch slipped from his grasp or broke under his weight; then he caught a stalwart bough under his armpit, and hung suspended for a second; and then he let himself drop and fell heavily against the table. A cry of alarm from the house warned him that his entrance had not been effected unobserved. He recovered himself with a stagger, and in three bounds crossed the intervening space and stood before the door in the verandah.

In a small apartment, carpeted with matting and surrounded by glazed cabinets full of rare and costly curios, Mr. Vandeleur was stooping over the body of Mr. Rolles. He raised himself as Francis entered, and there was an instantaneous passage of hands. It was the business of a second; as fast as an eye can wink the thing was done; the young man had not the time to be sure, but it seemed to him as if the Dictator had taken something from the curate's breast, looked at it for the least fraction of time as it lay in his hand, and then suddenly and swiftly passed it to his daughter.

All this was over while Francis had still one foot upon the threshold, and the other raised in air. The next instant he was on his knees to Mr. Vandeleur.

"Father!" he cried. "Let me too help you. I will do what you wish and ask no questions; I will obey you with my life; treat me as a son, and you will find I have a son's devotion."

A deplorable explosion of oaths was the Dictator's first reply.

"Son and father?" he cried. "Father and son? What d—d unnatural comedy is all this? How do you come in my garden? What do you want? And who, in God's name, are you?"

Francis, with a stunned and shamefaced aspect, got upon his feet again, and stood in silence.

Then a light seemed to break upon Mr. Vandeleur, and he laughed aloud.

"I see," cried he. "It is the Scrymgeour. Very well, Mr. Scrymgeour. Let me tell you in a few words how you stand. You have entered my private residence by force, or perhaps by fraud, but certainly with no encouragement from me; and you come at a moment of some annoyance, a guest having fainted at my table, to besiege me with your protestations. You are no son of mine. You are my brother's bastard by a fishwife, if you want to know. I regard you with an indifference closely bordering on aversion; and from what I now see of your conduct, I judge your mind to be exactly suitable to your exterior. I recommend you these mortifying reflections for your leisure; and, in the meantime, let me beseech you to rid us of your presence. If I were not occupied," added the Dictator, with a terrifying oath, "I should give you the unholiest drubbing ere you went!"

Francis listened in profound humiliation. He would have fled had it been possible; but as he had no means of leaving the residence into which he had so unfortunately penetrated, he could do no more than stand foolishly where he was.

It was Miss Vandeleur who broke the silence.

"Father," she said, "you speak in anger. Mr. Scrymgeour may have been mistaken, but he meant well and kindly."

"Thank you for speaking," returned the Dictator. "You remind me of some other observations which I hold it a point of honour to make to Mr. Scrymgeour. My brother," he continued, addressing the young man, "has been foolish enough to give you an allowance; he was foolish enough and presumptuous enough to propose a match between you and this young lady. You were exhibited to her two nights ago; and I rejoice to tell you that she rejected the idea with disgust. Let me add that I have considerable influence with your father; and it shall not be my fault if you are not beggared of your allowance and sent back to your scrivening ere the week be out."

The tones of the old man's voice were, if possible, more wounding than his language; Francis felt himself exposed to the most cruel, blighting, and unbearable contempt; his head turned, and he covered his face with his hands, uttering at the same time a tearless sob of agony. But Miss Vandeleur once again interfered in his behalf.

"Mr. Scrymgeour," she said, speaking in clear and even tones, "you must not be concerned at my father's harsh expressions. I felt no disgust for you; on the contrary, I asked an opportunity to make your better acquaintance. As for what has passed tonight, believe me it has filled my mind with both pity and esteem."

Just then Mr. Rolles made a convulsive movement with his arm, which convinced Francis that he was only drugged, and was beginning to throw off the influence of the opiate. Mr. Vandeleur stooped over him and examined his face for an instant.

"Come, come!" cried he, raising his head. "Let there be an end of this. And since you are so pleased with his conduct, Miss Vandeleur, take a candle and show the bastard out."

The young lady hastened to obey.

"Thank you," said Francis, as soon as he was alone with her in the garden. "I thank you from my soul. This has been the bitterest evening of my life, but it will have always one pleasant recollection."

"I spoke as I felt," she replied, "and in justice to you. It made my heart sorry that you should be so unkindly used."

By this time they had reached the garden gate; and Miss Vandeleur, having set the candle on the ground, was already unfastening the bolts.

"One word more," said Francis. "This is not for the last time—I shall see you again, shall I not?"

"Alas!" she answered. "You have heard my father. What can I do but obey?"

"Tell me at least that it is not with your consent," returned Francis; "tell me that you have no wish to see the last of me."

"Indeed," replied she, "I have none. You seem to me both brave and honest."

"Then," said Francis, "give me a keepsake."

She paused for a moment, with her hand upon the key; for the various bars and bolts were all undone, and there was nothing left but to open the lock.

"If I agree," she said, "will you promise to do as I tell you from point to point?"

"Can you ask?" replied Francis. "I would do so willingly on your bare word."

She turned the key and threw open the door.

"Be it so," said she. "You do not know what you ask, but be it so. Whatever you hear," she continued, "whatever happens, do not return to this house; hurry fast until you reach the lighted and populous quarters of the city; even there be upon your guard. You are in a greater danger than you fancy. Promise me you will not so much as look at my keepsake until you are in a place of safety."

"I promise," replied Frances.

She put something loosely wrapped in a handkerchief into the young man's hand; and at the same time, with more strength than he could have anticipated, she pushed him into the street.

"Now, run!" she cried.

He heard the door close behind him, and the noise of the bolts being replaced.

"My faith," said he, "since I have promised!"

And he took to his heels down the lane that leads into the Rue Ravignan.

He was not fifty paces from the house with the green blinds when the most diabolical outcry suddenly arose out of the stillness of the night. Mechanically he stood still; another passenger followed his example; in the neighbouring floors he saw people crowding to the windows; a conflagration could not have produced more disturbance in this empty quarter. And yet it seemed to be all the work of a single man, roaring between grief and rage, like a lioness robbed of her whelps; and Francis was surprised and alarmed to hear his own name shouted with English imprecations to the wind.

His first movement was to return to the house; his second, as he remembered Miss Vandeleur's advice, to continue his flight with greater expedition than before; and he was in the act of turning to put his thought in action, when the Dictator, bareheaded, bawling aloud, his white hair blowing about his head, shot past him like a ball out of the cannon's mouth, and went careering down the street.

"That was a close shave," thought Francis to himself. "What he wants with me, and why he should be so disturbed, I cannot think; but he is plainly not good company for the moment, and I cannot do better than follow Miss Vandeleur's advice."

So saying, he turned to retrace his steps, thinking to double and descend by the Rue Lepic itself while his pursuer should continue to follow after him on the other line of street. The plan was ill-devised: as a matter of fact, he should have taken his seat in the nearest café, and waited there until the first heat of the pursuit was over. But besides that Francis had no experience and little natural aptitude for the small war of private life, he was so unconscious of any evil on his part, that he saw nothing to fear beyond a disagreeable interview. And to disagreeable interviews he felt he had already served his apprenticeship that evening; nor could he suppose that Miss Vandeleur had left anything unsaid. Indeed, the young man was sore both in body and mind—the one was all bruised, the other was full of smarting arrows; and he owned to himself that Mr. Vandeleur was master of a very deadly tongue.

The thought of his bruises reminded him that he had not only come without a hat, but that his clothes had considerably suffered in his descent through the chestnut. At the first magazine he purchased a cheap wideawake, and had the disorder of his toilet summarily repaired. The keepsake, still rolled in the handkerchief, he thrust in the meanwhile into his trousers pocket.

Not many steps beyond the shop he was conscious of a sudden shock, a hand upon his throat, an infuriated face close to his own, and an open mouth bawling curses in his ear. The Dictator, having found no trace of his quarry, was returning by the other way. Francis was a stalwart young fellow; but he was no match for his adversary whether in strength or skill; and after a few ineffectual struggles he resigned himself entirely to his captor.

"What do you want with me?" said he.

"We will talk of that at home," returned the Dictator, grimly.

And he continued to march the young man up hill in the direction of the house with the green blinds.

But Francis, although he no longer struggled, was only waiting an opportunity to make a bold push for freedom. With a sudden jerk he left the collar of his coat in the hands of Mr. Vandeleur, and once more made off at his best speed in the direction of the Boulevards.

The tables were now turned. If the Dictator was the stronger, Francis, in the top of his youth, was the more fleet of foot, and he had soon effected his escape among the crowds. Relieved for a moment, but with a growing sentiment of alarm and wonder in his mind, he walked briskly until he debouched upon the Place de l'Opéra, lit up like day with electric lamps.

"This, at least," thought he, "should satisfy Miss Vandeleur."

And turning to his right along the Boulevards, he entered the Café Américain and ordered some beer. It was both late and early for the majority of the frequenters of the establishment. Only two or three persons, all men, were dotted here and there at separate tables in the hall; and Francis was too much occupied by his own thoughts to observe their presence.

He drew the handkerchief from his pocket. The object wrapped in it proved to be a morocco case, clasped and ornamented in gilt, which opened by means of a spring, and disclosed to the horrified young man a diamond of monstrous bigness and extraordinary brilliancy. The circumstance was so inexplicable, the value of the stone was plainly so enormous, that Francis sat staring into the open casket without movement, without conscious thought, like a man stricken suddenly with idiocy.

A hand was laid upon his shoulder, lightly but firmly, and a quiet voice, which yet had in it the ring of command, uttered these words in his ear—

"Close the casket, and compose your face."

Looking up, he beheld a man, still young, of an urbane and tranquil presence, and dressed with rich simplicity. This personage had risen from a neighbouring table, and, bringing his glass with him, had taken a seat beside Francis.

"Close the casket," repeated the stranger, "and put it quietly back into your pocket, where I feel persuaded it should never have been. Try, if you please, to throw off your bewildered air, and act as though I were one of your acquaintances whom you had met by chance. So! Touch glasses with me. That is better. I fear, sir, you must be an amateur."

And the stranger pronounced these last words with a smile of peculiar meaning, leaned back in his seat and enjoyed a deep inhalation of tobacco.

"For God's sake," said Francis, "tell me who you are and what this means? Why I should obey your most unusual suggestions I am sure I know not; but the truth is, I have fallen this evening into so many perplexing adventures, and all I meet conduct themselves so strangely, that I think I must either have gone mad or wandered into another planet. Your face inspires me with confidence; you seem wise, good, and experienced; tell me, for heaven's sake, why you accost me in so odd a fashion?"

"All in due time," replied the stranger. "But I have the first hand, and you must begin by telling me how the Rajah's Diamond is in your possession."

"The Rajah's Diamond!" echoed Francis.

"I would not speak so loud, if I were you," returned the other. "But most certainly you have the Rajah's Diamond in your pocket. I have seen and handled it a score of times in Sir Thomas Vandeleur's collection."

"Sir Thomas Vandeleur! The General! My father!" cried Francis.

"Your father?" repeated the stranger. "I was not aware the General had any family."

"I am illegitimate, sir," replied Francis, with a flush.

The other bowed with gravity. It was a respectful bow, as of a man silently apologising to his equal; and Francis felt relieved and comforted, he scarce knew why. The society of this person did him good; he seemed to touch firm ground; a strong feeling of respect grew up in his bosom, and mechanically he removed his wideawake as though in the presence of a superior.

"I perceive," said the stranger, "that your adventures have not all been peaceful. Your collar is torn, your face is scratched, you have a cut upon your temple; you will, perhaps, pardon my curiosity when I ask you to explain how you came by these injuries, and how you happen to have stolen property to an enormous value in your pocket."

"I must differ from you!" returned Francis, hotly. "I possess no stolen property. And if you refer to the diamond, it was given to me not an hour ago by Miss Vandeleur in the Rue Lepic."

"By Miss Vandeleur of the Rue Lepic!" repeated the other. "You interest me more than you suppose. Pray continue."

"Heavens!" cried Francis.

His memory had made a sudden bound. He had seen Mr. Vandeleur take an article from the breast of his drugged visitor, and that article, he was now persuaded, was a morocco case.

"You have a light?" inquired the stranger.

"Listen," replied Francis. "I know not who you are, but I believe you to be worthy of confidence and helpful; I find myself in strange waters; I must have counsel and support, and since you invite me I shall tell you all."

And he briefly recounted his experiences since the day when he was summoned from the bank by his lawyer.

"Yours is indeed a remarkable history," said the stranger, after the young man had made an end of his narrative; "and your position is full of difficulty and peril. Many would counsel you to seek out your father, and give the diamond to him; but I have other views. Waiter!" he cried.

The waiter drew near.

"Will you ask the manager to speak with me a moment?" said he; and Francis observed once more, both in his tone and manner, the evidence of a habit of command.

The waiter withdrew, and returned in a moment with the manager, who bowed with obsequious respect.

"What," said he, "can I do to serve you?"

"Have the goodness," replied the stranger, indicating Francis, "to tell this gentleman my name."

"You have the honour, sir," said the functionary, addressing young Scrymgeour, "to occupy the same table with His Highness Prince Florizel of Bohemia."

Francis rose with precipitation, and made a grateful reverence to the Prince, who bade him resume his seat.

"I thank you," said Florizel, once more addressing the functionary; "I am sorry to have deranged you for so small a matter."

And he dismissed him with a movement of his hand.

"And now," added the Prince, turning to Francis, "give me the diamond."

Without a word the casket was handed over.

"You have done right," said Florizel; "your sentiments have properly inspired you, and you will live to be grateful for the misfortunes of tonight. A man, Mr. Scrymgeour, may fall into a thousand perplexities, but if his heart be upright and his intelligence unclouded, he will issue from them all without dishonour. Let your mind be at rest; your affairs are in my hand; and with the aid of heaven I am strong enough to bring them to a good end. Follow me, if you please, to my carriage."

So saying the Prince arose and, having left a piece of gold for the waiter, conducted the young man from the café and along the Boulevard to where an unpretentious brougham and a couple of servants out of livery awaited his arrival.

"This carriage," said he, "is at your disposal; collect your baggage as rapidly as you can make it convenient, and my servants will conduct you to a villa in the neighbourhood of Paris where you can wait in some degree of comfort until I have had time to arrange your situation. You will find there a pleasant garden, a library of good authors, a cook, a cellar, and some good cigars, which I recommend to your attention. Jérome," he added, turning to one of the servants, "you have heard what I say; I leave Mr. Scrymgeour in your charge; you will, I know, be careful of my friend."

Francis uttered some broken phrases of gratitude.

"It will be time enough to thank me," said the Prince, "when you are acknowledged by your father and married to Miss Vandeleur."

And with that the Prince turned away and strolled leisurely in the direction of Montmartre. He hailed the first passing cab, gave an address, and a quarter of an hour afterwards, having discharged the driver some distance lower, he was knocking at Mr. Vandeleur's garden gate.

It was opened with singular precautions by the Dictator in person.

"Who are you?" he demanded.

"You must pardon me this late visit, Mr. Vandeleur," replied the Prince.

"Your Highness is always welcome," returned Mr. Vandeleur, stepping back.

The Prince profited by the open space, and without waiting for his host walked right into the house and opened the door of the *salon*. Two people were seated there; one was Miss Vandeleur, who bore the marks of weeping about her eyes, and was still shaken from time to time by a sob; in the other the Prince recognised the young man who had consulted him on literary matters about a month before, in a club smoking room.

"Good evening, Miss Vandeleur," said Florizel; "you look fatigued. Mr. Rolles, I believe? I hope you have profited by the study of Gaboriau, Mr. Rolles."

But the young clergyman's temper was too much embittered for speech; and he contented himself with bowing stiffly, and continued to gnaw his lip.

"To what good wind," said Mr. Vandeleur, following his guest, "am I to attribute the honour of your Highness's presence?"

"I am come on business," returned the Prince; "on business with you; as soon as that is settled I shall request Mr. Rolles to accompany me for a walk. Mr. Rolles," he added, with severity, "let me remind you that I have not yet sat down."

The clergyman sprang to his feet with an apology; whereupon the Prince took an armchair beside the table, handed his hat to Mr. Vandeleur, his cane to Mr. Rolles, and, leaving them standing and thus menially employed upon his service, spoke as follows:

"I have come here, as I said, upon business; but, had I come looking for pleasure, I could not have been more displeased with my reception nor more dissatisfied with my company. You, sir," addressing Mr. Rolles, "you have treated your superior in station with discourtesy; you, Vandeleur, receive me with a smile, but you know right well that your hands are not yet cleansed from misconduct. I do not desire to be interrupted, sir," he added, imperiously; "I am here to speak, and not to listen; and I have to ask you to hear me with respect, and to obey punctiliously. At the earliest possible date your daughter shall be married at the Embassy to my friend, Francis Scrymgeour, your brother's acknowledged son. You will oblige me by offering not less than ten thousand pounds dowry. For yourself, I will indicate to you in writing a mission of some importance in Siam which I destine to your care. And now, sir, you will answer me in two words whether or not you agree to these conditions."

"Your Highness will pardon me," said Mr. Vandeleur, "and permit me, with all respect, to submit to him two queries?"

"The permission is granted," replied the Prince.

"Your Highness," resumed the Dictator, "has called Mr. Scrymgeour his friend. Believe me, had I known he was thus honoured, I should have treated him with proportional respect."

"You interrogate adroitly," said the Prince; "but it will not serve your turn. You have my commands; if I had never seen that gentleman before tonight, it would not render them less absolute."

"Your Highness interprets my meaning with his usual subtlety," returned Vandeleur. "Once more: I have, unfortunately, put the police upon the track of Mr. Scrymgeour on a charge of theft; am I to withdraw or to uphold the accusation?"

"You will please yourself," replied Florizel. "The question is one between your conscience and the laws of this land. Give me my hat; and you, Mr. Rolles, give me my cane and follow me. Miss Vandeleur, I wish you good evening. I judge," he added to Vandeleur, "that your silence means unqualified assent."

"If I can do no better," replied the old man, "I shall submit; but I warn you openly it shall not be without a struggle."

"You are old," said the Prince; "but years are disgraceful to the wicked. Your age is more unwise than the youth of others. Do not provoke me, or you may find me harder than you dream. This is the first time that I have fallen across your path in anger; take care that it be the last."

With these words, motioning the clergyman to follow, Florizel left the apartment and directed his steps towards the garden gate; and the Dictator, following with a candle, gave them light, and once more undid the elaborate fastenings with which he sought to protect himself from intrusion.

"Your daughter is no longer present," said the Prince, turning on the threshold. "Let me tell you that I understand your threats; and you have only to lift your hand to bring upon yourself sudden and irremediable ruin."

The Dictator made no reply; but as the Prince turned his back upon him in the lamplight he made a gesture full of menace and insane fury; and the next moment, slipping round a corner, he was running at full speed for the nearest cabstand.

(Here, says my Arabian, *the thread of events is finally diverted from* The House with the Green Blinds. *One more adventure,* he adds, *and we*

have done with THE RAJAH'S DIAMOND. *That last link in the chain is known among the inhabitants of Bagdad by the name of* THE ADVENTURE OF PRINCE FLORIZEL AND A DETECTIVE.*)*

THE ADVENTURE OF PRINCE FLORIZEL AND A DETECTIVE

Prince Florizel walked with Mr. Rolles to the door of a small hotel where the latter resided. They spoke much together, and the clergyman was more than once affected to tears by the mingled severity and tenderness of Florizel's reproaches.

"I have made ruin of my life," he said at last. "Help me; tell me what I am to do; I have, alas! neither the virtues of a priest nor the dexterity of a rogue."

"Now that you are humbled," said the Prince, "I command no longer; the repentant have to do with God and not with princes. But if you will let me advise you, go to Australia as a colonist, seek menial labour in the open air, and try to forget that you have ever been a clergyman, or that you ever set eyes on that accursed stone."

"Accurst indeed!" replied Mr. Rolles. "Where is it now? What further hurt is it not working for mankind?"

"It will do no more evil," returned the Prince. "It is here in my pocket. And this," he added, kindly, "will show that I place some faith in your penitence, young as it is."

"Suffer me to touch your hand," pleaded Mr. Rolles.

"No," replied Prince Florizel, "not yet."

The tone in which he uttered these last words was eloquent in the ears of the young clergyman; and for some minutes after the Prince had turned away he stood on the threshold following with his eyes the retreating figure and invoking the blessing of heaven upon a man so excellent in counsel.

For several hours the Prince walked alone in unfrequented streets. His mind was full of concern; what to do with the diamond, whether to return it to its owner, whom he judged unworthy of this rare possession, or to take some sweeping and courageous measure and put it out of the reach of all mankind at once and for ever, was a problem too grave to be decided in a moment. The manner in which it had come into his hands appeared manifestly providential; and as he took out the jewel and looked at it under the streetlamps, its size and surprising brilliancy inclined him more and more to think of it as of an unmixed and dangerous evil for the world.

"God help me!" he thought; "if I look at it much oftener I shall begin to grow covetous myself."

At last, though still uncertain in his mind, he turned his steps towards the small but elegant mansion on the riverside which had belonged for centuries to his royal family. The arms of Bohemia are deeply graved over the door and upon the tall chimneys; passengers have a look into a green court set with the most costly flowers, and a stork, the only one in Paris, perches on the gable all day long and keeps a crowd before the house. Grave servants are seen passing to and fro within; and from time to time the great gate is thrown open and a carriage rolls below the arch. For many reasons this residence was especially dear to the heart of Prince Florizel; he never drew near to it without enjoying that sentiment of homecoming so rare in the lives of the great; and on the present evening he beheld its tall roof and mildly illuminated windows with unfeigned relief and satisfaction.

As he was approaching the postern door by which he always entered when alone, a man stepped forth from the shadow and presented himself with an obeisance in the Prince's path.

"I have the honour of addressing Prince Florizel of Bohemia?" said he.

"Such is my title," replied the Prince. "What do you want with me?"

"I am," said the man, "a detective, and I have to present your Highness with this billet from the Prefect of Police."

The Prince took the letter and glanced it through by the light of the streetlamp. It was highly apologetic, but requested him to follow the bearer to the Prefecture without delay.

"In short," said Florizel, "I am arrested."

"Your Highness," replied the officer, "nothing, I am certain, could be further from the intention of the Prefect. You will observe that he has not granted a warrant. It is mere formality, or call it, if you prefer, an obligation that your Highness lays on the authorities."

"At the same time," asked the Prince, "if I were to refuse to follow you?"

"I will not conceal from your Highness that a considerable discretion has been granted me," replied the detective with a bow.

"Upon my word," cried Florizel, "your effrontery astounds me! Yourself, as an agent, I must pardon; but your superiors shall dearly smart for their misconduct. What, have you any idea, is the cause of this impolitic and unconstitutional act? You will observe that I have as yet neither refused nor consented, and much may depend on your prompt and ingenuous answer. Let me remind you, officer, that this is an affair of some gravity."

"Your Highness," said the detective humbly, "General Vandeleur and his brother have had the incredible presumption to accuse you of theft. The famous diamond, they declare, is in your hands. A word from you in denial will most amply satisfy the Prefect; nay, I go farther: if your Highness would so far honour a subaltern as to declare his ignorance of the matter even to myself, I should ask permission to retire upon the spot."

Florizel, up to the last moment, had regarded his adventure in the light of a trifle, only serious upon international considerations. At the name of Vandeleur the horrible truth broke upon him in a moment; he was not only arrested, but he was guilty. This was not only an annoying incident—it was a peril to his honour. What was he to say? What was he to do? The Rajah's Diamond was indeed an accursed stone; and it seemed as if he were to be the last victim to its influence.

One thing was certain. He could not give the required assurance to the detective. He must gain time.

His hesitation had not lasted a second.

"Be it so," said he, "let us walk together to the Prefecture."

The man once more bowed, and proceeded to follow Florizel at a respectful distance in the rear.

"Approach," said the Prince. "I am in a humour to talk, and, if I mistake not, now I look at you again, this is not the first time that we have met."

"I count it an honour," replied the officer, "that your Highness should recollect my face. It is eight years since I had the pleasure of an interview."

"To remember faces," returned Florizel, "is as much a part of my profession as it is of yours. Indeed, rightly looked upon, a Prince and a detective serve in the same corps. We are both combatants against crime; only mine is the more lucrative and yours the more dangerous rank, and there is a sense in which both may be made equally honourable to a good man. I had rather, strange as you may think it, be a detective of character and parts than a weak and ignoble sovereign."

The officer was overwhelmed.

"Your Highness returns good for evil," said he. "To an act of presumption he replies by the most amiable condescension."

"How do you know," replied Florizel, "that I am not seeking to corrupt you?"

"Heaven preserve me from the temptation!" cried the detective.

"I applaud your answer," returned the Prince. "It is that of a wise and honest man. The world is a great place and stocked with wealth and beauty, and there is no limit to the rewards that may be offered. Such an one who would refuse a million of money may sell his honour for an empire or the love of a woman; and I myself, who speak to you, have seen occasions so tempting, provocations so irresistible to the strength of human virtue, that I have been glad to tread in your steps and recommend myself to the grace of God. It is thus, thanks to that modest and becoming habit alone," he added, "that you and I can walk this town together with untarnished hearts."

"I had always heard that you were brave," replied the officer, "but I was not aware that you were wise and pious. You speak the truth, and you speak it with an accent that moves me to the heart. This world is indeed a place of trial."

"We are now," said Florizel, "in the middle of the bridge. Lean your elbows on the parapet and look over. As the water rushing below, so the passions and complications of life carry away the honesty of weak men. Let me tell you a story."

"I receive your Highness's commands," replied the man.

And, imitating the Prince, he leaned against the parapet, and disposed himself to listen. The city was already sunk in slumber; had it not been for the infinity of lights and the outline of buildings on the starry sky, they might have been alone beside some country river.

"An officer," began Prince Florizel, "a man of courage and conduct, who had already risen by merit to an eminent rank, and won not only admiration but respect, visited, in an unfortunate hour for his peace of mind, the collections of an Indian Prince. Here he beheld a diamond so extraordinary for size and beauty that from that instant he had only one desire in life: honour, reputation, friendship, the love of country, he was ready to sacrifice all for this lump of sparkling crystal. For three years he served this semi-barbarian potentate as Jacob served Laban; he falsified frontiers, he connived at murders, he unjustly condemned and executed a brother officer who had the misfortune to displease the Rajah by some honest freedoms; lastly, at a time of great danger to his native land, he betrayed a body of his fellow soldiers, and suffered them to be defeated and massacred by thousands. In the end, he had amassed a magnificent fortune, and brought home with him the coveted diamond.

"Years passed," continued the Prince, "and at length the diamond is accidentally lost. It falls into the hands of a simple and laborious youth, a student, a minister of God, just entering on a career of usefulness and even distinction. Upon him also the spell is cast; he deserts everything, his holy calling, his studies, and flees with the gem into a foreign country. The officer has a brother, an astute, daring, unscrupulous man, who learns the clergyman's secret. What does he do? Tell his brother, inform the police? No; upon this man also the Satanic charm has fallen; he must have the stone for himself. At the risk of murder, he drugs the young priest and seizes the prey. And now, by an accident which is not important to my moral, the jewel passes out of his custody into that of another, who, terrified at what he sees, gives it into the keeping of a man in high station and above reproach.

"The officer's name is Thomas Vandeleur," continued Florizel. "The stone is called the Rajah's Diamond. And"—suddenly opening his hand—"you behold it here before your eyes."

The officer started back with a cry.

"We have spoken of corruption," said the Prince. "To me this nugget of bright crystal is as loathsome as though it were crawling with the worms of death; it is as shocking as though it were compacted out of innocent blood. I see it here in my hand, and I know it is shining with hellfire. I have told you but a hundredth part of its story; what passed in former ages, to what crimes and treacheries it incited men of yore, the imagination trembles to conceive; for years and years it has faithfully served the powers of hell; enough, I say, of blood, enough of disgrace, enough of broken lives and friendships; all things come to an end, the evil like the good; pestilence as well as beautiful music; and as for this diamond, God forgive me if I do wrong, but its empire ends tonight."

The Prince made a sudden movement with his hand, and the jewel, describing an arc of light, dived with a splash into the flowing river.

"Amen," said Florizel, with gravity. "I have slain a cockatrice!"

"God pardon me!" cried the detective. "What have you done? I am a ruined man."

"I think," returned the Prince with a smile, "that many well-to-do people in this city might envy you your ruin."

"Alas! your Highness!" said the officer, "and you corrupt me after all?"

"It seems there was no help for it," replied Florizel. "And now let us go forward to the Prefecture."

———

Not long after, the marriage of Francis Scrymgeour and Miss Vandeleur was celebrated in great privacy; and the Prince acted on that occasion as groom's man. The two Vandeleurs surprised some rumour of what had happened to the diamond; and their vast diving operations on the River Seine are the wonder and amusement of the idle. It is true that through some miscalculation they have chosen the wrong branch of the river. As for the Prince, that sublime person, having now served his turn, may go, along with the *Arabian Author,* topsy-turvy into space. But if the reader insists on more specific information, I am happy to say that a recent revolution hurled him from the throne of Bohemia, in consequence of his continued absence and edifying neglect of public business; and that his Highness now keeps a cigar store in Rupert Street, much frequented by other foreign refugees. I go there from time to time to smoke and have a chat, and find him as great a creature as in the days of his prosperity; he has an Olympian air behind the counter; and although a sedentary life is beginning to tell upon his waistcoat, he is probably, take him for all in all, the handsomest tobacconist in London.

THE PAVILION ON THE LINKS

Inscribed to D.A.S. in memory of days near Fidra

CHAPTER ONE

Tells how I camped in Graden Sea-Wood, and beheld a light in the pavilion

I was a great solitary when I was young. I made it my pride to keep
aloof and suffice for my own entertainment; and I may say that I had
neither friends nor acquaintances until I met that friend who became
my wife and the mother of my children. With one man only was I on
private terms; this was R. Northmour, Esquire, of Graden Easter, in
Scotland. We had met at college; and though there was not much liking between us, nor even much intimacy, we were so nearly of a humour that we could associate with ease to both. Misanthropes, we
believed ourselves to be; but I have thought since that we were only
sulky fellows. It was scarcely a companionship, but a coexistence in
unsociability. Northmour's exceptional violence of temper made it no
easy affair for him to keep the peace with anyone but me; and as he respected my silent ways, and let me come and go as I pleased, I could
tolerate his presence without concern. I think we called each other
friends.

When Northmour took his degree and I decided to leave the university without one, he invited me on a long visit to Graden Easter;
and it was thus that I first became acquainted with the scene of my ad-

ventures. The mansion house of Graden stood in a bleak stretch of country some three miles from the shore of the German Ocean. It was as large as a barrack; and as it had been built of a soft stone, liable to consume in the eager air of the seaside, it was damp and draughty within and half ruinous without. It was impossible for two young men to lodge with comfort in such a dwelling. But there stood in the northern part of the estate, in a wilderness of links and blowing sandhills, and between a plantation and the sea, a small Pavilion or Belvidere, of modern design, which was exactly suited to our wants; and in this hermitage, speaking little, reading much, and rarely associating except at meals, Northmour and I spent four tempestuous winter months. I might have stayed longer; but one March night there sprang up between us a dispute, which rendered my departure necessary. Northmour spoke hotly, I remember, and I suppose I must have made some tart rejoinder. He leaped from his chair and grappled me; I had to fight, without exaggeration, for my life; and it was only with a great effort that I mastered him, for he was near as strong in body as myself, and seemed filled with the devil. The next morning, we met on our usual terms; but I judged it more delicate to withdraw; nor did he attempt to dissuade me.

It was nine years before I revisited the neighbourhood. I travelled at that time with a tilt cart, a tent, and a cooking stove, tramping all day beside the waggon, and at night, whenever it was possible, gipsying in a cove of the hills, or by the side of a wood. I believe I visited in this manner most of the wild and desolate regions both in England and Scotland; and, as I had neither friends nor relations, I was troubled with no correspondence, and had nothing in the nature of headquarters, unless it was the office of my solicitors, from whom I drew my income twice a year. It was a life in which I delighted; and I fully thought to have grown old upon the march, and at last died in a ditch.

It was my whole business to find desolate corners, where I could camp without the fear of interruption; and hence, being in another part of the same shire, I bethought me suddenly of the Pavilion on the Links. No thoroughfare passed within three miles of it. The nearest town, and that was but a fisher village, was at a distance of six or seven. For ten miles of length, and from a depth varying from three miles to half a mile, this belt of barren country lay along the sea. The beach, which was the natural approach, was full of quicksands. Indeed I may say there is hardly a better place of concealment in the United Kingdom. I determined to pass a week in the Sea-Wood of Graden-Easter, and making a long stage, reached it about sundown on a wild September day.

The country, I have said, was mixed sandhill and links; *links* being a Scottish name for sand which has ceased drifting and become more or less solidly covered with turf. The pavilion stood on an even space; a little behind it, the wood began in a hedge of elders huddled together by the wind; in front, a few tumbled sandhills stood between it and the sea. An outcropping of rock had formed a bastion for the sand, so that there was here a promontory in the coastline between two shallow bays; and just beyond the tides, the rock again cropped out and formed an islet of small dimensions but strikingly designed. The quicksands were of great extent at low water, and had an infamous reputation in the country. Close in shore, between the islet and the promontory, it was said they would swallow a man in four minutes and a half; but there may have been little ground for this precision. The district was alive with rabbits, and haunted by gulls which made a continual piping about the pavilion. On summer days the outlook was bright and even gladsome; but at sundown in September, with a high wind, and a heavy surf rolling in close along the links, the place told of nothing but dead mariners and sea disaster. A ship beating to windward on the horizon, and a huge truncheon of wreck half buried in the sands at my feet, completed the innuendo of the scene.

The pavilion—it had been built by the last proprietor, Northmour's uncle, a silly and prodigal virtuoso—presented little signs of age. It was two stories in height, Italian in design, surrounded by a patch of garden in which nothing had prospered but a few coarse flowers; and looked, with its shuttered windows, not like a house that had been deserted, but like one that had never been tenanted by man. Northmour was plainly from home; whether, as usual, sulking in the cabin of his yacht, or in one of his fitful and extravagant appearances in the world of society, I had, of course, no means of guessing. The place had an air of solitude that daunted even a solitary like myself; the wind cried in the chimneys with a strange and wailing note; and it was with a sense of escape, as if I were going indoors, that I turned away and, driving my cart before me, entered the skirts of the wood.

The Sea-Wood of Graden had been planted to shelter the cultivated fields behind, and check the encroachments of the blowing sand. As you advanced into it from coastward, elders were succeeded by other hardy shrubs; but the timber was all stunted and bushy; it led a life of conflict; the trees were accustomed to swing there all night long in fierce winter tempests; and even in early spring, the leaves were already flying, and autumn was beginning, in this exposed plantation. Inland the ground rose into a little hill, which, along with the islet, served as a sailing mark for seamen. When the hill was open of the islet to the north, vessels must bear well to the eastward to clear Graden Ness and the Graden Bullers. In the lower ground, a streamlet ran among the trees, and, being dammed with dead leaves and clay of its own carrying, spread out every here and there, and lay in stagnant pools. One or two ruined cottages were dotted about the wood; and, according to Northmour, these were ecclesiastical foundations, and in their time had sheltered pious hermits.

I found a den, or small hollow, where there was a spring of pure water; and there, clearing away the brambles, I pitched the tent, and made a fire to cook my supper. My horse I picketed farther in the wood where there was a patch of sward. The banks of the den not only concealed the light of my fire, but sheltered me from the wind, which was cold as well as high.

The life I was leading made me both hardy and frugal. I never drank but water and rarely ate anything more costly than oatmeal; and I required so little sleep, that, although I rose with the peep of day, I would often lie long awake in the dark or starry watches of the night. Thus in Graden Sea-Wood, although I fell thankfully asleep by eight in the evening I was awake again before eleven with a full possession of my faculties, and no sense of drowsiness or fatigue. I rose and sat by the fire, watching the trees and clouds tumultuously tossing and fleeing overhead, and hearkening to the wind and the rollers along the shore; till at length, growing weary of inaction, I quitted the den, and strolled towards the borders of the wood. A young moon, buried in mist, gave a faint illumination to my steps; and the light grew brighter as I walked forth into the links. At the same moment, the wind, smelling salt of the open ocean and carrying particles of sand, struck me with its full force, so that I had to bow my head.

When I raised it again to look about me, I was aware of a light in the pavilion. It was not stationary; but passed from one window to another, as though someone were reviewing the different apartments with a lamp or candle. I watched it for some seconds in great surprise. When I had arrived in the afternoon the house had been plainly deserted; now it was as plainly occupied. It was my first idea that a gang of thieves might have broken in and be now ransacking Northmour's cupboards, which were many and not ill supplied. But what should bring thieves to Graden Easter? And, again, all the shutters had been thrown open, and it would have been more in the character of such gentry to close them. I dismissed the notion, and fell back upon another. Northmour himself must have arrived, and was now airing and inspecting the pavilion.

I have said that there was no real affection between this man and me; but, had I loved him like a brother, I was then so much more in love with solitude that I should none the less have shunned his company. As it was, I turned and ran for it; and it was with genuine satisfaction that I found myself safely back beside the fire. I had escaped an acquaintance; I should have one more night in comfort. In the morning, I might either slip away before Northmour was abroad, or pay him as short a visit as I chose.

But when morning came, I thought the situation so diverting that I forgot my shyness. Northmour was at my mercy; I arranged a good practical jest, though I knew well that my neighbour was not the man to jest with in security; and, chuckling beforehand over its success, took my place among the elders at the edge of the wood, whence I could command the door of the pavilion. The shutters were all once more closed, which I remember thinking odd; and the house, with its white walls and green venetians, looked spruce and habitable in the morning light. Hour after hour passed, and still no sign of Northmour. I knew him for a sluggard in the morning; but, as it drew on towards noon, I lost my patience. To say the truth, I had promised myself to break my fast in the pavilion, and hunger began to prick me sharply. It was a pity to let the opportunity go by without some cause for mirth; but the grosser appetite prevailed, and I relinquished my jest with regret, and sallied from the wood.

The appearance of the house affected me, as I drew near, with disquietude. It seemed unchanged since last evening; and I had expected it, I scarce knew why, to wear some external signs of habitation. But no: the windows were all closely shuttered, the chimneys breathed no smoke, and the front door itself was closely padlocked. Northmour, therefore, had entered by the back; this was the natural, and indeed, the necessary conclusion; and you may judge of my surprise when, on turning the house, I found the back door similarly secured.

My mind at once reverted to the original theory of thieves; and I blamed myself sharply for my last night's inaction. I examined all the windows on the lower story, but none of them had been tampered with; I tried the padlocks, but they were both secure. It thus became a problem how the thieves, if thieves they were, had managed to enter the house. They must have got, I reasoned, upon the roof of the out-house where Northmour used to keep his photographic battery; and from thence, either by the window of the study or that of my old bed-room, completed their burglarious entry.

I followed what I supposed was their example; and, getting on the roof, tried the shutters of each room. Both were secure; but I was not to be beaten; and, with a little force, one of them flew open, grazing, as it did so, the back of my hand. I remember, I put the wound to my mouth, and stood for perhaps half a minute licking it like a dog, and mechanically gazing behind me over the waste links and the sea; and, in that space of time, my eye made note of a large schooner yacht some miles to the northeast. Then I threw up the window and climbed in.

I went over the house, and nothing can express my mystification. There was no sign of disorder, but, on the contrary, the rooms were unusually clean and pleasant. I found fires laid, ready for lighting; three bedrooms prepared with a luxury quite foreign to Northmour's habits, and with water in the ewers and the beds turned down; a table set for three in the dining room; and an ample supply of cold meats, game, and vegetables on the pantry shelves. There were guests expected, that was plain; but why guests, when Northmour hated society? And, above all, why was the house thus stealthily prepared at dead of night? and why were the shutters closed and the doors padlocked?

I effaced all traces of my visit, and came forth from the window feeling sobered and concerned.

The schooner yacht was still in the same place; and it flashed for a moment through my mind that this might be the *Red Earl* bringing the owner of the pavilion and his guests. But the vessel's head was set the other way.

CHAPTER TWO

Tells of the nocturnal landing from the yacht

I returned to the den to cook myself a meal, of which I stood in great need, as well as to care for my horse, whom I had somewhat neglected in the morning. From time to time I went down to the edge of the wood; but there was no change in the pavilion, and not a human creature was seen all day upon the links. The schooner in the offing was the one touch of life within my range of vision. She, apparently with no set object, stood off and on or lay to, hour after hour; but as the evening deepened, she drew steadily nearer. I became more convinced that she carried Northmour and his friends, and that they would probably come ashore after dark; not only because that was of a piece with the secrecy of the preparations, but because the tide would not have flowed sufficiently before eleven to cover Graden Floe and the other sea quags that fortified the shore against invaders.

All day the wind had been going down, and the sea along with it; but there was a return towards sunset of the heavy weather of the day before. The night set in pitch dark. The wind came off the sea in squalls, like the firing of a battery of cannon; now and then there was a flaw of rain, and the surf rolled heavier with the rising tide. I was down at my observatory among the elders, when a light was run up to the masthead of the schooner, and showed she was closer in than when I had last seen her by the dying daylight. I concluded that this must be a signal to Northmour's associates on shore; and, stepping forth into the links, looked around me for something in response.

A small footpath ran along the margin of the wood, and formed the most direct communication between the pavilion and the mansion house; and, as I cast my eyes to that side, I saw a spark of light, not a quarter of a mile away, and rapidly approaching. From its uneven course it appeared to be the light of a lantern carried by a person who followed the windings of the path, and was often staggered and taken aback by the more violent squalls. I concealed myself once more among the elders, and waited eagerly for the newcomer's advance. It proved to be a woman; and, as she passed within half a rod of my ambush, I was able to recognise the features. The deaf and silent old dame, who had nursed Northmour in his childhood, was his associate in this underhand affair.

I followed her at a little distance, taking advantage of the innumerable heights and hollows, concealed by the darkness, and favoured not only by the nurse's deafness, but by the uproar of the wind and surf. She entered the pavilion, and, going at once to the upper story, opened and set a light in one of the windows that looked towards the sea. Immediately afterwards the light at the schooner's masthead was run down and extinguished. Its purpose had been attained, and those on board were sure that they were expected. The old woman resumed her preparations; although the other shutters remained closed, I could see a glimmer going to and fro about the house; and a gush of sparks from one chimney after another soon told me that the fires were being kindled.

Northmour and his guests, I was now persuaded, would come ashore as soon there was water on the floe. It was a wild night for boat service; and I felt some alarm mingle with my curiosity as I reflected on the danger of the landing. My old acquaintance, it was true, was the most eccentric of men; but the present eccentricity was both disquieting and lugubrious to consider. A variety of feelings thus led me towards the beach, where I lay flat on my face in a hollow within six feet of the track that led to the pavilion. Thence, I should have the satisfaction of recognising the arrivals, and, if they should prove to be acquaintances, greeting them as soon as they had landed.

Some time before eleven, while the tide was still dangerously low, a boat's lantern appeared close in shore; and, my attention being thus awakened, I could perceive another still far to seaward, violently tossed, and sometimes hidden by the billows. The weather, which was getting dirtier as the night went on, and the perilous situation of the yacht upon a leeshore, had probably driven them to attempt a landing at the earliest possible moment.

A little afterwards, four yachtsmen carrying a very heavy chest, and guided by a fifth with a lantern, passed close in front of me as I lay, and were admitted to the pavilion by the nurse. They returned to the beach, and passed me a third time with another chest, larger but apparently not so heavy as the first. A third time they made the transit; and on this occasion one of the yachtsmen carried a leather portmanteau, and the others a lady's trunk and carriage bag. My curiosity was sharply excited. If a woman were among the guests of Northmour, it would show a change in his habits and an apostasy from his pet theories of life, well calculated to fill me with surprise. When he and I dwelt there together, the pavilion had been a temple of misogyny. And now, one of the detested sex was to be installed under its roof. I remembered one or two particulars, a few notes of daintiness and almost of coquetry which had struck me the day before as I surveyed the preparations in the house; their purpose was now clear, and I thought myself dull not to have perceived it from the first.

While I was thus reflecting, a second lantern drew near me from the beach. It was carried by a yachtsman whom I had not yet seen, and who was conducting two other persons to the pavilion. These two persons were unquestionably the guests for whom the house was made ready; and, straining eye and ear, I set myself to watch them as they passed One was an unusually tall man, in a travelling hat slouched over his eyes, and a highland cape closely buttoned and turned up so as to conceal his face. You could make out no more of him than that he was, as I have said, unusually tall, and walked feebly with a heavy stoop. By his side, and either clinging to him or giving him support—I could not make out which—was a young, tall, and slender figure of a woman. She was extremely pale; but in the light of the lantern her face was so marred by strong and changing shadows, that she might equally well have been as ugly as sin or as beautiful as I afterwards found her to be.

When they were just abreast of me, the girl made some remark which was drowned by the noise of the wind.

"Hush!" said her companion; and there was something in the tone with which the word was uttered that thrilled and rather shook my spirits. It seemed to breathe from a bosom labouring under the deadliest terror; I have never heard another syllable so expressive; and I still hear it again when I am feverish at night, and my mind runs upon old times. The man turned towards the girl as he spoke; I had a glimpse of much red beard and a nose which seemed to have been broken in youth; and his light eyes seemed shining in his face with some strong and unpleasant emotion.

But these two passed on and were admitted in their turn to the pavilion.

One by one, or in groups, the seamen returned to the beach. The wind brought me the sound of a rough voice crying, "Shove off!" Then, after a pause, another lantern drew near. It was Northmour alone.

My wife and I, a man and a woman, have often agreed to wonder how a person could be, at the same time, so handsome and so repulsive as Northmour. He had the appearance of a finished gentleman; his face bore every mark of intelligence and courage; but you had only to look at him, even in his most amiable moment, to see that he had the temper of a slaver captain. I never knew a character that was both explosive and revengeful to the same degree; he combined the vivacity of the south with the sustained and deadly hatreds of the north; and both traits were plainly written on his face, which was a sort of danger signal. In person, he was tall, strong, and active; his hair and complexion very dark; his features handsomely designed, but spoiled by a menacing expression.

At that moment he was somewhat paler than by nature; he wore a heavy frown; and his lips worked, and he looked sharply round him as he walked, like a man besieged with apprehensions. And yet I thought he had a look of triumph underlying all, as though he had already done much, and was near the end of an achievement.

Partly from a scruple of delicacy—which I daresay came too late—partly from the pleasure of startling an acquaintance, I desired to make my presence known to him without delay.

I got suddenly to my feet, and stepped forward.

"Northmour!" said I.

I have never had so shocking a surprise in all my days. He leaped on me without a word; something shone in his hand; and he struck for my heart with a dagger. At the same moment I knocked him head over heels. Whether it was my quickness, or his own uncertainty, I know not; but the blade only grazed my shoulder, while the hilt and his fist struck me violently on the mouth.

I fled, but not far. I had often and often observed the capabilities of the sandhills for protracted ambush or stealthy advances and retreats; and, not ten yards from the scene of the scuffle, plumped down again upon the grass. The lantern had fallen and gone out. But what was my astonishment to see Northmour slip at a bound into the pavilion, and hear him bar the door behind him with a clang of iron!

He had not pursued me. He had run away. Northmour, whom I knew for the most implacable and daring of men, had run away! I could scarce believe my reason; and yet in this strange business, where all was incredible, there was nothing to make a work about in an incredibility more or less. For why was the pavilion secretly prepared? Why had Northmour landed with his guests at dead of night, in half a gale of wind, and with the floe scarce covered? Why had he sought to kill me? Had he not recognised my voice? I wondered. And, above all, how had he come to have a dagger ready in his hand? A dagger, or even a sharp knife, seemed out of keeping with the age in which we lived; and a gentleman landing from his yacht on the shore of his own estate, even although it was at night and with some mysterious circumstances, does not usually, as a matter of fact, walk thus prepared for deadly onslaught. The more I reflected, the further I felt at sea. I recapitulated the elements of mystery, counting them on my fingers: the pavilion secretly prepared for guests; the guests landed at the risk of their lives and to the imminent peril of the yacht; the guests, or at least one of them, in undisguised and seemingly causeless terror; Northmour with a naked weapon; Northmour stabbing his most intimate acquaintance at a word; last, and not least strange, Northmour fleeing from the man whom he had sought to murder, and barricading himself, like a hunted creature, behind the door of the pavilion. Here were at least six separate causes for extreme surprise; each part and parcel with the others, and forming all together one consistent story. I felt almost ashamed to believe my own senses.

As I thus stood, transfixed with wonder, I began to grow painfully conscious of the injuries I had received in the scuffle; skulked round among the sandhills; and, by a devious path, regained the shelter of the wood. On the way, the old nurse passed again within several yards of me, still carrying her lantern, on the return journey to the mansion house of Graden. This made a seventh suspicious feature in the case. Northmour and his guests, it appeared, were to cook and do the cleaning for themselves, while the old woman continued to inhabit the big empty barrack among the policies. There must surely be great cause for secrecy, when so many inconveniences were confronted to preserve it.

So thinking, I made my way to the den. For greater security, I trod out the embers of the fire, and lit my lantern to examine the wound upon my shoulder. It was a trifling hurt, although it bled somewhat freely, and I dressed it as well as I could (for its position made it difficult to reach) with some rag and cold water from the spring. While I was thus busied, I mentally declared war against Northmour and his mystery. I am not an angry man by nature, and I believe there was more curiosity than resentment in my heart. But war I certainly declared; and, by way of preparation, I got out my revolver, and, having drawn the charges, cleaned and reloaded it with scrupulous care. Next I became preoccupied about my horse. It might break loose, or fall to neighing, and so betray my camp in the Sea-Wood. I determined to rid myself of its neighbourhood; and long before dawn I was leading it over the links in the direction of the fisher village.

CHAPTER THREE

Tells how I became acquainted with my wife

For two days I skulked round the pavilion, profiting by the uneven surface of the links. I became an adept in the necessary tactics. These low hillocks and shallow dells, running one into another, became a kind of cloak of darkness for my enthralling, but perhaps dishonourable, pursuit. Yet, in spite of this advantage, I could learn but little of Northmour or his guests.

Fresh provisions were brought under cover of darkness by the old woman from the mansion house. Northmour, and the young lady, sometimes together, but more often singly, would walk for an hour or two at a time on the beach beside the quicksand. I could not but conclude that this promenade was chosen with an eye to secrecy; for the spot was open only to the seaward. But it suited me not less excellently; the highest and most accidented of the sandhills immediately adjoined; and from these, lying flat in a hollow, I could overlook Northmour or the young lady as they walked.

The tall man seemed to have disappeared. Not only did he never cross the threshold, but he never so much as showed face at a window; or, at least, not so far as I could see; for I dared not creep forward beyond a certain distance in the day, since the upper floor commanded the bottoms of the links; and at night, when I could venture farther, the lower windows were barricaded as if to stand a siege. Sometimes I thought the tall man must be confined to bed, for I remembered the feebleness of his gait; and sometimes I thought he must have gone clear away, and that Northmour and the young lady remained alone together in the pavilion. The idea, even then, displeased me.

Whether or not this pair were man and wife, I had seen abundant reason to doubt the friendliness of their relation. Although I could hear nothing of what they said, and rarely so much as glean a decided expression on the face of either, there was a distance, almost a stiffness, in their bearing which showed them to be either unfamiliar or at enmity. The girl walked faster when she was with Northmour than when she was alone; and I conceived that any inclination between a man and a woman would rather delay than accelerate the step. Moreover, she kept a good yard free of him, and trailed her umbrella, as if it were a barrier, on the side between them. Northmour kept sidling closer; and, as the girl retired from his advance, their course lay at a sort of diagonal across the beach, and would have landed them in the surf had it been long enough continued. But, when this was imminent, the girl would unostentatiously change sides and put Northmour between her and the sea. I watched these manoeuvers, for my part, with high enjoyment and approval, and chuckled to myself at every move.

On the morning of the third day, she walked alone for some time, and I perceived, to my great concern, that she was more than once in tears. You will see that my heart was already interested more than I supposed. She had a firm yet airy motion of the body, and carried her head with unimaginable grace; every step was a thing to look at, and she seemed in my eyes to breathe sweetness and distinction.

The day was so agreeable, being calm and sunshiny, with a tranquil sea, and yet with a healthful piquancy and vigour in the air, that, contrary to custom, she was tempted forth a second time to walk. On this occasion she was accompanied by Northmour, and they had been but a short while on the beach, when I saw him take forcible possession of her hand. She struggled, and uttered a cry that was almost a scream. I sprang to my feet, unmindful of my strange position; but, ere I had taken a step, I saw Northmour bareheaded and bowing very low, as if to apologise; and dropped again at once into my ambush. A few words were interchanged; and then, with another bow, he left the beach to return to the pavilion. He passed not far from me, and I could see him, flushed and lowering, and cutting savagely with his cane among the grass. It was not without satisfaction that I recognised my own handi-work in a great cut under his right eye, and a considerable discolouration round the socket.

For some time the girl remained where he had left her, looking out past the islet and over the bright sea. Then with a start, as one who throws off preoccupation and puts energy again upon its mettle, she broke into a rapid and decisive walk. She also was much incensed by what had passed. She had forgotten where she was. And I beheld her walk straight into the borders of the quicksand where it is most abrupt and dangerous. Two or three steps farther and her life would have been in serious jeopardy, when I slid down the face of the sand-hill, which is there precipitous, and, running halfway forward, called to her to stop.

She did so, and turned round. There was not a tremor of fear in her behaviour, and she marched directly up to me like a queen. I was bare-foot, and clad like a common sailor, save for an Egyptian scarf round my waist; and she probably took me at first for some one from the fisher village, straying after bait. As for her, when I thus saw her face to face, her eyes set steadily and imperiously upon mine, I was filled with admiration and astonishment, and thought her even more beautiful than I had looked to find her. Nor could I think enough of one who, acting with so much boldness, yet preserved a maidenly air that was both quaint and engaging; for my wife kept an old-fashioned preci-sion of manner through all her admirable life—an excellent thing in woman, since it sets another value on her sweet familiarities.

"What does this mean?" she asked.

"You were walking," I told her, "directly into Graden Floe."

"You do not belong to these parts," she said again. "You speak like an educated man."

"I believe I have right to that name," said I, "although in this disguise."

But her woman's eye had already detected the sash.

"Oh!" she said; "your sash betrays you."

"You have said the word *betray*," I resumed. "May I ask you not to betray me? I was obliged to disclose myself in your interest; but if Northmour learned my presence it might be worse than disagreeable for me."

"Do you know," she asked, "to whom you are speaking?"

"Not to Mr. Northmour's wife?" I asked, by way of answer.

She shook her head. All this while she was studying my face with an embarrassing intentness. Then she broke out—

"You have an honest face. Be honest like your face, sir, and tell me what you want and what you are afraid of. Do you think I could hurt you? I believe you have far more power to injure me! And yet you do not look unkind. What do you mean—you, a gentleman—by skulking like a spy about this desolate place? Tell me," she said, "who is it you hate?"

"I hate no one," I answered; "and I fear no one face to face. My name is Cassilis—Frank Cassilis. I lead the life of a vagabond for my own good pleasure. I am one of Northmour's oldest friends; and three nights ago, when I addressed him on these links, he stabbed me in the shoulder with a knife."

"It was you!" she said.

"Why he did so," I continued, disregarding the interruption, "is more than I can guess, and more than I care to know. I have not many friends, nor am I very susceptible to friendship; but no man shall drive me from a place by terror. I had camped in Graden Sea-Wood ere he came; I camp in it still. If you think I mean harm to you or yours, madam, the remedy is in your hand. Tell him that my camp is in the Hemlock Den, and tonight he can stab me in safety while I sleep."

With this I doffed my cap to her, and scrambled up once more among the sandhills. I do not know why, but I felt a prodigious sense of injustice, and felt like a hero and a martyr; while, as a matter of fact, I had not a word to say in my defence, nor so much as one plausible reason to offer for my conduct. I had stayed at Graden out of a curiosity natural enough, but undignified; and though there was another motive growing in along with the first, it was not one which, at that period, I could have properly explained to the lady of my heart.

Certainly, that night, I thought of no one else; and, though her whole conduct and position seemed suspicious, I could not find it in my heart to entertain a doubt of her integrity. I could have staked my life that she was clear of blame, and, though all was dark at the present, that the explanation of the mystery would show her part in these events to be both right and needful. It was true, let me cudgel my imagination as I pleased, that I could invent no theory of her relations to Northmour; but I felt none the less sure of my conclusion because it was founded on instinct in place of reason, and, as I may say, went to sleep that night with the thought of her under my pillow.

Next day she came out about the same hour alone, and, as soon as the sandhills concealed her from the pavilion, drew nearer to the edge, and called me by name in guarded tones. I was astonished to observe that she was deadly pale, and seemingly under the influence of strong emotion.

"Mr. Cassilis!" she cried; "Mr. Cassilis!"

I appeared at once, and leaped down upon the beach. A remarkable air of relief overspread her countenance as soon as she saw me.

"Oh!" she cried, with a hoarse sound, like one whose bosom has been lightened of a weight. And then, "Thank God you are still safe!" she added; "I knew, if you were, you would be here." (Was not this strange? So swiftly and wisely does Nature prepare our hearts for these great lifelong intimacies, that both my wife and I had been given a presentiment on this the second day of our acquaintance. I had even then hoped that she would seek me; she had felt sure that she would find me.) "Do not," she went on swiftly, "do not stay in this place. Promise me that you will sleep no longer in that wood. You do not know how I suffer; all last night I could not sleep for thinking of your peril."

"Peril?" I repeated. "Peril from whom? From Northmour?"

"Not so," she said. "Did you think I would tell him after what you said?"

"Not from Northmour?" I repeated. "Then how? From whom? I see none to be afraid of."

"You must not ask me," was her reply, "for I am not free to tell you. Only believe me, and go hence—believe me, and go away quickly, quickly, for your life!"

An appeal to his alarm is never a good plan to rid oneself of a spirited young man. My obstinacy was but increased by what she said, and I made it a point of honour to remain. And her solicitude for my safety still more confirmed me in the resolve.

"You must not think me inquisitive, madam," I replied; "but, if Graden is so dangerous a place, you yourself perhaps remain here at some risk."

She only looked at me reproachfully.

"You and your father——" I resumed; but she interrupted me almost with a gasp.

"My father! How do you know that?" she cried.

"I saw you together when you landed," was my answer; and I do not know why, but it seemed satisfactory to both of us, as indeed it was the truth. "But," I continued, "you need have no fear from me. I see you have some reason to be secret, and, you may believe me, your secret is as safe with me as if I were in Graden Floe. I have scarce spoken to anyone for years; my horse is my only companion, and even he, poor beast, is not beside me. You see, then, you may count on me for silence. So tell me the truth, my dear young lady, are you not in danger?"

"Mr. Northmour says you are an honourable man," she returned, "and I believe it when I see you. I will tell you so much; you are right; we are in dreadful, dreadful danger, and you share it by remaining where you are."

"Ah!" said I; "you have heard of me from Northmour? And he gives me a good character?"

"I asked him about you last night," was her reply. "I pretended," she hesitated, "I pretended to have met you long ago, and spoken to you of him. It was not true; but I could not help myself without betraying you, and you had put me in a difficulty. He praised you highly."

"And—you may permit me one question—does this danger come from Northmour?" I asked.

"From Mr. Northmour?" she cried. "Oh, no; he stays with us to share it."

"While you propose that I should run away?" I said. "You do not rate me very high."

"Why should you stay?" she asked. "You are no friend of ours."

I know not what came over me, for I had not been conscious of a similar weakness since I was a child, but I was so mortified by this retort that my eyes pricked and filled with tears, as I continued to gaze upon her face.

"No, no," she said, in a changed voice; "I did not mean the words unkindly."

"It was I who offended," I said; and I held out my hand with a look of appeal that somehow touched her, for she gave me hers at once, and even eagerly. I held it for awhile in mine, and gazed into her eyes. It was she who first tore her hand away, and, forgetting all about her request and the promise she had sought to extort, ran at the top of her speed, and without turning, till she was out of sight. And then I knew that I loved her, and thought in my glad heart that she—she herself—was not indifferent to my suit. Many a time she has denied it in after days, but it was with a smiling and not a serious denial. For my part, I am sure our hands would not have lain so closely in each other if she had not begun to melt to me already. And, when all is said, it is no great contention, since, by her own avowal, she began to love me on the morrow.

And yet on the morrow very little took place. She came and called me down as on the day before, upbraided me for lingering at Graden, and, when she found I was still obdurate, began to ask me more particularly as to my arrival. I told her by what series of accidents I had come to witness their disembarkation, and how I had determined to remain, partly from the interest which had been wakened in me by North-mour's guests, and partly because of his own murderous attack. As to the former, I fear I was disingenuous, and led her to regard herself as having been an attraction to me from the first moment that I saw her on the links. It relieves my heart to make this confession even now, when my wife is with God, and already knows all things, and the honesty of my purpose even in this; for while she lived, although it often pricked my conscience, I had never the hardihood to undeceive her. Even a little secret, in such a married life as ours, is like the rose leaf which kept the Princess from her sleep.

From this the talk branched into other subjects, and I told her much about my lonely and wandering existence; she, for her part, giving ear, and saying little. Although we spoke very naturally, and latterly on topics that might seem indifferent, we were both sweetly agitated. Too soon it was time for her to go; and we separated, as if by mutual consent, without shaking hands, for both knew that, between us, it was no idle ceremony.

The next, and that was the fourth day of our acquaintance, we met in the same spot, but early in the morning, with much familiarity and yet much timidity on either side. When she had once more spoken about my danger—and that, I understood, was her excuse for coming—I, who had prepared a great deal of talk during the night, began to tell her how highly I valued her kind interest, and how no one had ever cared to hear about my life, nor had I ever cared to relate it, before yesterday. Suddenly she interrupted me, saying with vehemence—

"And yet, if you knew who I was, you would not so much as speak to me!"

I told her such a thought was madness, and, little as we had met, I counted her already a dear friend; but my protestations seemed only to make her more desperate.

"My father is in hiding!" she cried.

"My dear," I said, forgetting for the first time to add "young lady," "what do I care? If he were in hiding twenty times over, would it make one thought of change in you?"

"Ah, but the cause!" she cried, "the cause! It is——" she faltered for a second——"it is disgraceful to us!"

CHAPTER FOUR

*Tells in what a startling manner I learned that I was not alone
in Graden Sea-Wood*

This was my wife's story, as I drew it from her among tears and sobs. Her name was Clara Huddlestone: it sounded very beautiful in my ears; but not so beautiful as that other name of Clara Cassilis, which she wore during the longer and, I thank God, the happier portion of her life. Her father, Bernard Huddlestone, had been a private banker in a very large way of business. Many years before, his affairs becoming disordered, he had been led to try dangerous, and at last criminal, expedients to retrieve himself from ruin. All was in vain; he became more and more cruelly involved, and found his honour lost at the same moment with his fortune. About this period, Northmour had been courting his daughter with great assiduity, though with small encouragement; and to him, knowing him thus disposed in his favour, Bernard Huddlestone turned for help in his extremity. It was not merely ruin and dishonour, nor merely a legal condemnation, that the unhappy man had brought upon his head. It seems he could have gone to prison with a light heart. What he feared, what kept him awake at night or recalled him from slumber into frenzy, was some secret, sudden, and unlawful attempt upon his life. Hence, he desired to bury his existence and escape to one of the islands in the South Pacific, and it was in Northmour's yacht, the *Red Earl,* that he designed to go. The yacht picked them up clandestinely upon the coast of Wales, and had once more deposited them at Graden, till she could be refitted and provisioned for the longer voyage. Nor could Clara doubt that her hand had been stipulated as the price of passage. For, although Northmour was neither unkind nor even discourteous, he had shown himself in several instances somewhat overbold in speech and manner.

I listened, I need not say, with fixed attention, and put many questions as to the more mysterious part. It was in vain. She had no clear idea of what the blow was, nor of how it was expected to fall. Her father's alarm was unfeigned and physically prostrating, and he had thought more than once of making an unconditional surrender to the police. But the scheme was finally abandoned, for he was convinced that not even the strength of our English prisons could shelter him from his pursuers. He had had many affairs with Italy, and with Italians resident in London, in the later years of his business; and these last, as Clara fancied, were somehow connected with the doom that threatened him. He had shown great terror at the presence of an Italian seaman on board the *Red Earl,* and had bitterly and repeatedly accused Northmour in consequence. The latter had protested that Beppo (that was the seaman's name) was a capital fellow, and could be trusted to the death; but Mr. Huddlestone had continued ever since to declare that all was lost, that it was only a question of days, and that Beppo would be the ruin of him yet.

I regarded the whole story as the hallucination of a mind shaken by calamity. He had suffered heavy loss by his Italian transactions; and hence the sight of an Italian was hateful to him, and the principal part in his nightmare would naturally enough be played by one of that nation.

"What your father wants," I said, "is a good doctor and some calming medicine."

"But Mr. Northmour?" objected your mother. "He is untroubled by losses, and yet he shares in this terror."

I could not help laughing at what I considered her simplicity.

"My dear," said I, "you have told me yourself what reward he has to look for. All is fair in love, you must remember; and if Northmour foments your father's terrors, it is not at all because he is afraid of any

Italian man, but simply because he is infatuated with a charming English woman."

She reminded me of his attack upon myself on the night of the disembarkation, and this I was unable to explain. In short, and from one thing to another, it was agreed between us, that I should set out at once for the fisher village, Graden Wester, as it was called, look up all the newspapers I could find, and see for myself if there seemed any basis of fact for these continued alarms. The next morning, at the same hour and place, I was to make my report to Clara. She said no more on that occasion about my departure; nor, indeed, did she make it a secret that she clung to the thought of my proximity as something helpful and pleasant; and, for my part, I could not have left her, if she had gone upon her knees to ask it.

I reached Graden Wester before ten in the forenoon; for in those days I was an excellent pedestrian, and the distance, as I think I have said, was little over seven miles; fine walking all the way upon the springy turf. The village is one of the bleakest on that coast, which is saying much: there is a church in a hollow; a miserable haven in the rocks, where many boats have been lost as they returned from fishing; two or three score of stone houses arranged along the beach and in two streets, one leading from the harbour, and another striking out from it at right angles; and, at the corner of these two, a very dark and cheerless tavern, by way of principal hotel.

I had dressed myself somewhat more suitably to my station in life, and at once called upon the minister in his little manse beside the graveyard. He knew me, although it was more than nine years since we had met; and when I told him that I had been long upon a walking tour, and was behind with the news, readily lent me an armful of newspapers, dating from a month back to the day before. With these I sought the tavern, and, ordering some breakfast, sat down to study the "Huddlestone Failure."

It had been, it appeared, a very flagrant case. Thousands of persons were reduced to poverty; and one in particular had blown out his brains as soon as payment was suspended. It was strange to myself that, while I read these details, I continued rather to sympathise with Mr. Huddlestone than with his victims; so complete already was the empire of my love for my wife. A price was naturally set upon the banker's head; and, as the case was inexcusable and the public indignation thoroughly aroused, the unusual figure of 750*l.* was offered for his capture. He was reported to have large sums of money in his possession. One day, he had been heard of in Spain; the next, there was sure intelligence that he was still lurking between Manchester and Liverpool, or along the border of Wales; and the day after, a telegram would announce his arrival in Cuba or Yucatan. But in all this there was no word of an Italian, nor any sign of mystery.

In the very last paper, however, there was one item not so clear. The accountants who were charged to verify the failure had, it seemed, come upon the traces of a very large number of thousands, which figured for some time in the transactions of the house of Huddlestone; but which came from nowhere, and disappeared in the same mysterious fashion. It was only once referred to by name, and then under the initials "X. X."; but it had plainly been floated for the first time into the business at a period of great depression some six years ago. The name of a distinguished Royal personage had been mentioned by rumour in connection with this sum. "The cowardly desperado"—such, I remember, was the editorial expression—was supposed to have escaped with a large part of this mysterious fund still in his possession.

I was still brooding over the fact, and trying to torture it into some connection with Mr. Huddlestone's danger, when a man entered the tavern and asked for some bread and cheese with a decided foreign accent.

"*Siete Italiano?*" said I.

"*Sì signor,*" was his reply.

I said it was unusually far north to find one of his compatriots; at which he shrugged his shoulders, and replied that a man would go anywhere to find work. What work he could hope to find at Graden Wester, I was totally unable to conceive; and the incident struck so unpleasantly upon my mind, that I asked the landlord, while he was counting me some change, whether he had ever before seen an Italian in the village. He said he had once seen some Norwegians, who had been shipwrecked on the other side of Graden Ness and rescued by the lifeboat from Cauld-haven.

"No!" said I; "but an Italian, like the man who has just had bread and cheese."

"What?" cried he, "yon black-avised fellow wi' the teeth? Was he an

I-talian? Weel, yon's the first that ever I saw, an' I dare say he's like to be the last."

Even as he was speaking, I raised my eyes, and, casting a glance into the street, beheld three men in earnest conversation together, and not thirty yards away. One of them was my recent companion in the tavern parlour; the other two, by their handsome, sallow features and soft hats, should evidently belong to the same race. A crowd of village children stood around them, gesticulating and talking gibberish in imitation. The trio looked singularly foreign to the bleak dirty street in which they were standing, and the dark grey heaven that overspread them; and I confess my incredulity received at that moment a shock from which it never recovered. I might reason with myself as I pleased, but I could not argue down the effect of what I had seen, and I began to share in the Italian terror.

It was already drawing towards the close of the day before I had returned the newspapers at the manse, and got well forward on to the links on my way home. I shall never forget that walk. It grew very cold and boisterous; the wind sang in the short grass about my feet; thin rain showers came running on the gusts; and an immense mountain range of clouds began to arise out of the bosom of the sea. It would be hard to imagine a more dismal evening; and whether it was from these external influences, or because my nerves were already affected by what I had heard and seen, my thoughts were as gloomy as the weather.

The upper windows of the pavilion commanded a considerable spread of links in the direction of Graden Wester. To avoid observation, it was necessary to hug the beach until I had gained cover from the higher sandhills on the little headland, when I might strike across, through the hollows, for the margin of the wood. The sun was about setting; the tide was low, and all the quicksands uncovered; and I was moving along, lost in unpleasant thought, when I was suddenly thunderstruck to perceive the prints of human feet. They ran parallel to my own course, but low down upon the beach instead of along the border of the turf; and, when I examined them, I saw at once, by the size and coarseness of the impression, that it was a stranger to me and to those in the pavilion who had recently passed that way. Not only so; but from the recklessness of the course which he had followed, steering near to the most formidable portions of the sand, he was as evidently a stranger to the country and to the ill-repute of Graden beach.

Step by step I followed the prints; until, a quarter of a mile farther, I beheld them die away into the southeastern boundary of Graden Floe. There, whoever he was, the miserable man had perished. One or two gulls, who had, perhaps, seen him disappear, wheeled over his sepulchre with their usual melancholy piping. The sun had broken through the clouds by a last effort, and coloured the wide level of quicksands with a dusky purple. I stood for some time gazing at the spot, chilled and disheartened by my own reflections, and with a strong and commanding consciousness of death. I remember wondering how long the tragedy had taken, and whether his screams had been audible at the pavilion. And then, making a strong resolution, I was about to tear myself away, when a gust fiercer than usual fell upon this quarter of the beach, and I saw now, whirling high in air, now skimming lightly across the surface of the sands, a soft, black, felt hat, somewhat conical in shape, such as I had remarked already on the heads of the Italians.

I believe, but I am not sure, that I uttered a cry. The wind was driving the hat shoreward, and I ran round the border of the floe to be ready against its arrival. The gust fell, dropping the hat for a while upon the quicksand, and then, once more freshening, landed it a few yards from where I stood. I seized it with the interest you may imagine. It had seen some service; indeed, it was rustier than either of those I had seen that day upon the street. The lining was red, stamped with the name of the maker, which I have forgotten, and that of the place of manufacture, *Venedig*. This (it is not yet forgotten) was the name given by the Austrians to the beautiful city of Venice, then, and for long after, a part of their dominions.

The shock was complete. I saw imaginary Italians upon every side; and for the first, and, I may say, for the last time in my experience, became overpowered by what is called a panic terror. I knew nothing, that is, to be afraid of, and yet I admit that I was heartily afraid; and it was with a sensible reluctance that I returned to my exposed and solitary camp in the Sea-Wood.

There I ate some cold porridge which had been left over from the

night before, for I was disinclined to make a fire; and, feeling strengthened and reassured, dismissed all these fanciful terrors from my mind,
and lay down to sleep with composure.

How long I may have slept it is impossible for me to guess; but I was
awakened at last by a sudden, blinding flash of light into my face. It
woke me like a blow. In an instant I was upon my knees. But the light
had gone as suddenly as it came. The darkness was intense. And, as it
was blowing great guns from the sea and pouring with rain, the noises
of the storm effectually concealed all others.

It was, I dare say, half a minute before I regained my self-possession.
But for two circumstances, I should have thought I had been awakened
by some new and vivid form of nightmare. First, the flap of my tent,
which I had shut carefully when I retired, was now unfastened; and,
second, I could still perceive, with a sharpness that excluded any theory of hallucination, the smell of hot metal and of burning oil. The
conclusion was obvious. I had been wakened by someone flashing a
bull's-eye lantern in my face. It had been but a flash, and away He had
seen my face, and then gone. I asked myself the object of so strange a
proceeding, and the answer came pat. The man, whoever he was, had
thought to recognise me, and he had not. There was yet another question unresolved; and to this, I may say, I feared to give an answer; if he
had recognised me, what would he have done?

My fears were immediately diverted from myself, for I saw that I
had been visited in a mistake; and I became persuaded that some
dreadful danger threatened the pavilion. It required some nerve to
issue forth into the black and intricate thicket which surrounded and
overhung the den; but I groped my way to the links, drenched with
rain, beaten upon and deafened by the gusts, and fearing at every step
to lay my hand upon some lurking adversary. The darkness was so
complete that I might have been surrounded by an army and yet none
the wiser, and the uproar of the gale so loud that my hearing was as
useless as my sight.

For the rest of that night, which seemed interminably long, I pa-
trolled the vicinity of the pavilion, without seeing a living creature or
hearing any noise but the concert of the wind, the sea, and the rain. A
light in the upper story filtered through a cranny of the shutter, and
kept me company till the approach of dawn.

CHAPTER FIVE

Tells of an interview between Northmour, Clara, and myself

With the first peep of day, I retired from the open to my old lair among the sandhills, there to await the coming of my wife. The morning was grey, wild, and melancholy; the wind moderated before sunrise, and then went about, and blew in puffs from the shore; the sea began to go down, but the rain still fell without mercy. Over all the wilderness of links there was not a creature to be seen. Yet I felt sure the neighbourhood was alive with skulking foes. The light had been so suddenly and surprisingly flashed upon my face as I lay sleeping, and the hat that had been blown ashore by the wind from over Graden Floe, were two speaking signals of the peril that environed Clara and the party in the pavilion.

It was, perhaps, half past seven, or nearer eight, before I saw the door open, and that dear figure come towards me in the rain. I was waiting for her on the beach before she had crossed the sandhills.

"I have had such trouble to come!" she cried. "They did not wish me to go walking in the rain."

"Clara," I said, "you are not frightened!"

"No," said she, with a simplicity that filled my heart with confidence. For my wife was the bravest as well as the best of women; in my experience, I have not found the two go always together, but with her they did; and she combined the extreme of fortitude with the most endearing and beautiful virtues.

I told her what had happened; and, though her cheek grew visibly paler, she retained perfect control over her senses.

"You see now that I am safe," said I, in conclusion. "They do not mean to harm me; for, had they chosen, I was a dead man last night."

She laid her hand upon my arm.

"And I had no presentiment!" she cried.

Her accent thrilled me with delight. I put my arm about her, and strained her to my side; and, before either of us was aware, her hands were on my shoulders and my lips upon her mouth. Yet up to that moment no word of love had passed between us. To this day I remember the touch of her cheek, which was wet and cold with the rain; and many a time since, when she has been washing her face, I have kissed it again for the sake of that morning on the beach. Now that she is taken from me, and I finish my pilgrimage alone, I recall our old loving-kindnesses and the deep honesty and affection which united us, and my present loss seems but a trifle in comparison.

We may have thus stood for some seconds—for time passes quickly with lovers—before we were startled by a peal of laughter close at hand. It was not natural mirth, but seemed to be affected in order to conceal an angrier feeling. We both turned, though I still kept my left arm about Clara's waist; nor did she seek to withdraw herself; and there, a few paces off upon the beach, stood Northmour, his head lowered, his hands behind his back, his nostrils white with passion.

"Ah! Cassilis!" he said, as I disclosed my face.

"That same," said I; for I was not at all put about.

"And so, Miss Huddlestone," he continued slowly but savagely, "this is how you keep your faith to your father and to me? This is the value you set upon your father's life? And you are so infatuated with this young gentleman that you must brave ruin, and decency, and common human caution——"

"Miss Huddlestone——" I was beginning to interrupt him, when he, in his turn, cut in brutally——

"You hold your tongue," said he; "I am speaking to that girl."

"That girl, as you call her, is my wife," said I; and my wife only leaned a little nearer, so that I knew she had affirmed my words.

"Your what?" he cried. "You lie!"

"Northmour," I said, "we all know you have a bad temper, and I am the last man to be irritated by words. For all that, I propose that you speak lower, for I am convinced that we are not alone."

He looked round him, and it was plain my remark had in some degree sobered his passion. "What do you mean?" he asked.

I only said one word: "Italians."

He swore a round oath, and looked at us, from one to the other.

"Mr. Cassilis knows all that I know," said my wife.

"What I want to know," he broke out, "is where the devil Mr. Cassilis comes from, and what the devil Mr. Cassilis is doing here. You say you are married; that I do not believe. If you were, Graden Floe would soon divorce you; four minutes and a half, Cassilis. I keep my private cemetery for my friends."

"It took somewhat longer," said I, "for that Italian."

He looked at me for a moment half daunted, and then, almost civilly, asked me to tell my story. "You have too much the advantage of me, Cassilis," he added. I complied of course; and he listened, with several ejaculations, while I told him how I had come to Graden: that it was I whom he had tried to murder on the night of landing; and what I had subsequently seen and heard of the Italians.

"Well," said he, when I had done, "it is here at last; there is no mistake about that. And what, may I ask, do you propose to do?"

"I propose to stay with you and lend a hand," said I.

"You are a brave man," he returned, with a peculiar intonation.

"I am not afraid," said I.

"And so," he continued, "I am to understand that you two are married? And you stand up to it before my face, Miss Huddlestone?"

"We are not yet married," said Clara; "but we shall be as soon as we can."

"Bravo!" cried Northmour. "And the bargain? D—n it, you're not a fool, young woman; I may call a spade a spade with you. How about the bargain? You know as well as I do what your father's life depends upon. I have only to put my hands under my coattails and walk away, and his throat would be cut before the evening."

"Yes, Mr. Northmour," returned Clara, with great spirit; "but that is what you will never do. You made a bargain that was unworthy of a gentleman; but you are gentleman for all that, and you will never desert a man whom you have begun to help."

"Aha!" said he. "You think I will give my yacht for nothing? You think I will risk my life and liberty for love of the old gentleman; and then, I suppose, be best man at the wedding, to wind up? Well," he added, with an odd smile, "perhaps you are not altogether wrong. But ask Cassilis here. *He* knows me. Am I a man to trust? Am I safe and scrupulous? Am I kind?"

"I know you talk a great deal, and sometimes, I think, very foolishly," replied Clara, "but I know you are a gentleman, and I am not the least afraid."

He looked at her with a peculiar approval and admiration; then, turning to me, "Do you think I would give her up without a struggle, Frank?" said he. "I tell you plainly, you look out. The next time we come to blows——"

"Will make the third," I interrupted, smiling.

"Aye, true; so it will," he said. "I had forgotten. Well, the third time's lucky."

"The third time, you mean, you will have the crew of the *Red Earl* to help," I said.

"Do you hear him?" he asked, turning to my wife.

"I hear two men speaking like cowards," said she. "I should despise myself either to think or speak like that. And neither of you believe one word that you are saying, which makes it the more wicked and silly."

"She's a trump!" cried Northmour. "But she's not yet Mrs. Cassilis. I say no more. The present is not for me."

Then my wife surprised me.

"I leave you here," she said suddenly. "My father has been too long alone. But remember this: you are to be friends, for you are both good friends to me."

She has since told me her reason for this step. As long as she remained, she declares that we two would have continued to quarrel; and I suppose that she was right, for when she was gone we fell at once into a sort of confidentiality.

Northmour stared after her as she went away over the sandhill.

"She is the only woman in the world!" he exclaimed with an oath. "Look at her action."

I, for my part, leaped at this opportunity for a little further light.

"See here, Northmour," said I; "we are all in a tight place, are we not?"

"I believe you, my boy," he answered, looking me in the eyes, and with great emphasis. "We have all hell upon us, that's the truth. You may believe me or not, but I'm afraid of my life."

"Tell me one thing," said I. "What are they after, these Italians? What do they want with Mr. Huddlestone?"

"Don't you know?" he cried. "The black old scamp had *carbonaro* funds on a deposit—two hundred and eighty thousand; and of course he gambled it away on stocks. There was to have been a revolution in the Tridentino, or Parma; but the revolution is off, and the whole wasp's nest is after Huddlestone. We shall all be lucky if we can save our skins."

"The *carbonari!*" I exclaimed; "God help him indeed!"

"Amen!" said Northmour. "And now, look here: I have said that we are in a fix; and, frankly, I shall be glad of your help. If I can't save

Huddlestone, I want at least to save the girl. Come and stay in the pavilion; and, there's my hand on it, I shall act as your friend until the old man is either clear or dead. But," he added, "once that is settled, you become my rival once again, and I warn you—mind yourself."

"Done!" said I; and we shook hands.

"And now let us go directly to the fort," said Northmour; and he began to lead the way through the rain.

CHAPTER SIX

Tells of my introduction to the tall man

We were admitted to the pavilion by Clara, and I was surprised by the completeness and security of the defences. A barricade of great strength, and yet easy to displace, supported the door against any violence from without; and the shutters of the dining room, into which I was led directly, and which was feebly illuminated by a lamp, were even more elaborately fortified. The panels were strengthened by bars and crossbars; and these, in their turn, were kept in position by a system of braces and struts, some abutting on the floor, some on the roof, and others, in fine, against the opposite wall of the apartment. It was at once a solid and well-designed piece of carpentry; and I did not seek to conceal my admiration.

"I am the engineer," said Northmour. "You remember the planks in the garden? Behold them!"

"I did not know you had so many talents," said I.

"Are you armed?" he continued, pointing to an array of guns and pistols, all in admirable order, which stood in line against the wall or were displayed upon the sideboard.

"Thank you," I returned; "I have gone armed since our last encounter. But, to tell you the truth, I have had nothing to eat since early yesterday evening."

Northmour produced some cold meat, to which I eagerly set myself, and a bottle of good Burgundy, by which, wet as I was, I did not scruple to profit. I have always been an extreme temperance man on principle; but it is useless to push principle to excess, and on this occasion I believe that I finished three-quarters of the bottle. As I ate, I still continued to admire the preparations for defence.

"We could stand a siege," I said at length.

"Ye—es," drawled Northmour; "a very little one, per—haps. It is not so much the strength of the pavilion I misdoubt; it is the double danger that kills me. If we get to shooting, wild as the country is some one is sure to hear it, and then—why then it's the same thing, only different, as they say: caged by law, or killed by *carbonari*. There's the choice. It is a devilish bad thing to have the law against you in this world, and so I tell the old gentleman upstairs. He is quite of my way of thinking."

"Speaking of that," said I, "what kind of person is he?"

"Oh, he!" cried the other; "he's a rancid fellow, as far as he goes. I should like to have his neck wrung tomorrow by all the devils in Italy. I am not in this affair for him. You take me? I made a bargain for Missy's hand and I mean to have it too."

"That, by the way," said I. "I understand. But how will Mr. Huddlestone take my intrusion?"

"Leave that to Clara," returned Northmour.

I could have struck him in the face for this coarse familiarity; but I respected the truce, as, I am bound to say, did Northmour, and so long as the danger continued not a cloud arose in our relation. I bear him this testimony with the most unfeigned satisfaction; nor am I without pride when I look back upon my own behaviour. For surely no two men were ever left in a position so invidious and irritating.

As soon as I had done eating, we proceeded to inspect the lower floor. Window by window we tried the different supports, now and then making an inconsiderable change; and the strokes of the hammer sounded with startling loudness through the house. I proposed, I remember, to make loopholes; but he told me they were already made in the windows of the upper story. It was an anxious business this inspection, and left me downhearted. There were two doors and five windows to protect, and, counting Clara, only four of us to defend them against an unknown number of foes. I communicated my doubts to Northmour, who assured me, with unmoved composure, that he entirely shared them.

"Before morning," said he, "we shall all be butchered and buried in Graden Floe. For me, that is written."

I could not help shuddering at the mention of the quicksand, but reminded Northmour that our enemies had spared me in the wood.

"Do not flatter yourself," said he. "Then you were not in the same boat with the old gentleman; now you are. It's the floe for all of us, mark my words."

I trembled for Clara; and just then her dear voice was heard calling us to come upstairs. Northmour showed me the way, and, when he had reached the landing, knocked at the door of what used to be called *My Uncle's Bedroom*, as the founder of the pavilion had designed it especially for himself.

"Come in, Northmour; come in, dear Mr. Cassilis," said a voice from within.

Pushing open the door, Northmour admitted me before him into the apartment. As I came in I could see the daughter slipping out by the side door into the study, which had been prepared as her bedroom. In the bed, which was drawn back against the wall, instead of standing, as I had last seen it, boldly across the window, sat Bernard Huddlestone, the defaulting banker. Little as I had seen of him by the shifting light of the lantern on the links, I had no difficulty in recognising him for the same. He had a long and sallow countenance, surrounded by a long red beard and side-whiskers. His broken nose and high cheekbones gave him somewhat the air of a Kalmuck, and his light eyes shone with the excitement of a high fever. He wore a skullcap of black silk; a huge Bible lay open before him on the bed, with a pair of gold spectacles in the place, and a pile of other books lay on the stand by his side. The green curtains lent a cadaverous shade to his cheek; and, as he sat propped on pillows, his great stature was painfully hunched, and his head protruded till it overhung his knees. I believe if he had not died otherwise, he must have fallen a victim to consumption in the course of but a very few weeks.

He held out to me a hand, long, thin, and disagreeably hairy.

"Come in, come in, Mr. Cassilis," said he. "Another protector—ahem!—another protector. Always welcome as a friend of my daughter's, Mr. Cassilis. How they have rallied about me, my daughter's friends! May God in heaven bless and reward them for it!"

I gave him my hand, of course, because I could not help it; but the sympathy I had been prepared to feel for Clara's father was immediately soured by his appearance, and the wheedling, unreal tones in which he spoke.

"Cassilis is a good man," said Northmour; "worth ten."

"So I hear," cried Mr. Huddlestone eagerly; "so my girl tells me. Ah, Mr. Cassilis, my sin has found me out, you see! I am very low, very low; but I hope equally penitent. We must all come to the throne of grace at last, Mr. Cassilis. For my part, I come late indeed; but with unfeigned humility, I trust."

"Fiddle-de-dee!" said Northmour roughly.

"No, no, dear Northmour!" cried the banker. "You must not say that; you must not try to shake me. You forget, my dear, good boy, you forget I may be called this very night before my Maker."

His excitement was pitiful to behold; and I felt myself grow indignant with Northmour, whose infidel opinions I well knew, and heartily derided, as he continued to taunt the poor sinner out of his humour of repentance.

"Pooh, my dear Huddlestone!" said he. "You do yourself injustice. You are a man of the world inside and out, and were up to all kinds of mischief before I was born. Your conscience is tanned like South American leather—only you forgot to tan your liver, and that, if you will believe me, is the seat of the annoyance."

"Rogue, rogue! bad boy!" said Mr. Huddlestone, shaking his finger. "I am no precisian, if you come to that; I always hated a precisian; but I never lost hold of something better through it all. I have been a bad boy, Mr. Cassilis; I do not seek to deny that; but it was after my wife's death, and you know, with a widower, it's a different thing: sinful—I won't say no; but there is a gradation, we shall hope. And talking of that——Hark!" he broke out suddenly, his hand raised, his fingers spread, his face racked with interest and terror. "Only the rain, bless God!" he added, after a pause, and with indescribable relief.

For some seconds he lay back among the pillows like a man near to fainting; then he gathered himself together, and, in somewhat tremulous tones, began once more to thank me for the share I was prepared to take in his defence.

"One question, sir," said I, when he had paused. "Is it true that you have money with you?"

He seemed annoyed by the question, but admitted with reluctance that he had a little.

"Well," I continued, "it is their money they are after, is it not? Why not give it up to them?"

"Ah!" replied he, shaking his head, "I have tried that already, Mr. Cassilis; and alas! that it should be so, but it is blood they want."

"Huddlestone, that's a little less than fair," said Northmour. "You should mention that what you offered them was upwards of two hundred thousand short. The deficit is worth a reference; it is for what they call a cool sum, Frank. Then, you see, the fellows reason in their clear Italian way; and it seems to them, as indeed it seems to me, that they may just as well have both while they're about it—money and blood together, by George, and no more trouble for the extra pleasure."

"Is it in the pavilion?" I asked.

"It is; and I wish it were in the bottom of the sea instead," said Northmour; and then suddenly—"What are you making faces at me for?" he cried to Mr. Huddlestone, on whom I had unconsciously turned my back. "Do you think Cassilis would sell you?"

Mr. Huddlestone protested that nothing had been further from his mind.

"It is a good thing," retorted Northmour in his ugliest manner. "You might end by wearying us. What were you going to say?" he added, turning to me.

"I was going to propose an occupation for the afternoon," said I. "Let us carry that money out, piece by piece, and lay it down before the pavilion door. If the *carbonari* come, why, it's theirs at any rate."

"No, no," cried Mr. Huddlestone; "it does not, it cannot belong to them! It should be distributed *pro rata* among all my creditors."

"Come now, Huddlestone," said Northmour, "none of that."

"Well, but my daughter," moaned the wretched man.

"Your daughter will do well enough. Here are two suitors, Cassilis and I, neither of us beggars, between whom she has to choose. And as for yourself, to make an end of arguments, you have no right to a farthing, and, unless I'm much mistaken, you are going to die."

It was certainly very cruelly said; but Mr. Huddlestone was a man who attracted little sympathy; and, although I saw him wince and shudder, I mentally endorsed the rebuke; nay, I added a contribution of my own.

"Northmour and I," I said, "are willing enough to help you to save your life, but not to escape with stolen property."

He struggled for a while with himself, as though he were on the point of giving way to anger, but prudence had the best of the controversy.

"My dear boys," he said, "do with me or my money what you will. I leave all in your hands. Let me compose myself."

And so we left him, gladly enough I am sure. The last that I saw, he had once more taken up his great Bible, and with tremulous hands was adjusting his spectacles to read.

Chapter Seven

Tells how a word was cried through the pavilion window

The recollection of that afternoon will always be graven on my mind. Northmour and I were persuaded that an attack was imminent; and if it had been in our power to alter in any way the order of events, that power would have been used to precipitate rather than delay the critical moment. The worst was to be anticipated; yet we could conceive no extremity so miserable as the suspense we were now suffering. I have never been an eager, though always a great, reader; but I never knew books so insipid as those which I took up and cast aside that afternoon in the pavilion. Even talk became impossible, as the hours went on. One or other was always listening for some sound, or peering from an upstairs window over the links. And yet not a sign indicated the presence of our foes.

We debated over and over again my proposal with regard to the money; and had we been in complete possession of our faculties, I am sure we should have condemned it as unwise; but we were flustered with alarm, grasped at a straw, and determined, although it was as much as advertising Mr. Huddlestone's presence in the pavilion, to carry my proposal into effect.

The sum was part in specie, part in bank paper, and part in circular notes payable to the name of James Gregory. We took it out, counted it, enclosed it once more in a dispatch box belonging to Northmour, and prepared a letter in Italian which he tied to the handle. It was signed by both of us under oath, and declared that this was all the money which had escaped the failure of the house of Huddlestone. This was, perhaps, the maddest action ever perpetrated by two persons professing to be sane. Had the dispatch box fallen into other hands than those for which it was intended, we stood criminally convicted on our own written testimony; but, as I have said, we were neither of us in a condition to judge soberly, and had a thirst for action that drove us to do something, right or wrong, rather than endure the agony of waiting. Moreover, as we were both convinced that the hollows of the links were alive with hidden spies upon our movements, we hoped that our appearance with the box might lead to a parley, and, perhaps, a compromise.

It was nearly three when we issued from the pavilion. The rain had taken off; the sun shone quite cheerfully. I have never seen the gulls fly so close about the house or approach so fearlessly to human beings. On the very doorstep one flapped heavily past our heads, and uttered its wild cry in my very ear.

"There is an omen for you," said Northmour, who like all free-thinkers was much under the influence of superstition. "They think we are already dead."

I made some light rejoinder, but it was with half my heart; for the circumstance had impressed me.

A yard or two before the gate, on a patch of smooth turf, we set down the dispatch box; and Northmour waved a white handkerchief over his head. Nothing replied. We raised our voices, and cried aloud in Italian that we were there as ambassadors to arrange the quarrel; but the stillness remained unbroken save by the seagulls and the surf. I had a weight at my heart when we desisted; and I saw that even Northmour was unusually pale. He looked over his shoulder nervously, as though he feared that someone had crept between him and the pavilion door.

"By God," he said in a whisper, "this is too much for me!"

I replied in the same key: "Suppose there should be none, after all!"

"Look there," he returned, nodding with his head, as though he had been afraid to point.

I glanced in the direction indicated; and there, from the northern quarter of the Sea-Wood, beheld a thin column of smoke rising steadily against the now cloudless sky.

"Northmour," I said (we still continued to talk in whispers), "it is not possible to endure this suspense. I prefer death fifty times over. Stay you here to watch the pavilion; I will go forward and make sure, if I have to walk right into their camp."

He looked once again all round him with puckered eyes, and then nodded assentingly to my proposal.

My heart beat like a sledgehammer as I set out walking rapidly in the direction of the smoke; and, though up to that moment I had felt chill and shivering, I was suddenly conscious of a glow of heat over all my body. The ground in this direction was very uneven; a hundred men might have lain hidden in as many square yards about my path. But I had not practised the business in vain, chose such routes as cut at the very root of concealment, and, by keeping along the most convenient ridges, commanded several hollows at a time. It was not long before I was rewarded for my caution. Coming suddenly on to a mound somewhat more elevated than the surrounding hummocks, I saw, not thirty yards away, a man bent almost double, and running as fast as his attitude permitted, along the bottom of a gully. I had dislodged one of the spies from his ambush. As soon as I sighted him, I called loudly both in English and Italian; and he, seeing concealment was no longer possible, straightened himself out, leaped from the gully, and made off as straight as an arrow for the borders of the wood.

It was none of my business to pursue; I had learned what I wanted—that we were beleaguered and watched in the pavilion; and I returned at once, and walking as nearly as possible in my old footsteps, to where Northmour awaited me beside the dispatch box. He was even paler than when I had left him, and his voice shook a little.

"Could you see what he was like?" he asked.

"He kept his back turned," I replied.

"Let us get into the house, Frank. I don't think I'm a coward, but I can stand no more of this," he whispered.

All was still and sunshiny about the pavilion, as we turned to reenter it; even the gulls had flown in a wider circuit, and were seen flickering along the beach and sandhills; and this loneliness terrified me more than a regiment under arms. It was not until the door was barricaded that I could draw a full inspiration and relieve the weight that lay upon my bosom. Northmour and I exchanged a steady glance; and I suppose each made his own reflections on the white and startled aspect of the other.

"You were right," I said. "All is over. Shake hands, old man, for the last time."

"Yes," replied he, "I will shake hands; for, as sure as I am here, I bear no malice. But, remember, if, by some impossible accident, we should give the slip to these blackguards, I'll take the upper hand of you by fair or foul."

"Oh," said I, "you weary me!"

He seemed hurt, and walked away in silence to the foot of the stairs, where he paused.

"You do not understand," said he. "I am not a swindler, and I guard myself; that is all. It may weary you or not, Mr. Cassilis, I do not care a rush; I speak for my own satisfaction, and not for your amusement. You had better go upstairs and court the girl; for my part, I stay here."

"And I stay with you," I returned. "Do you think I would steal a march, even with your permission?"

"Frank," he said, smiling, "it's a pity you are an ass, for you have the makings of a man. I think I must be *fey* today; you cannot irritate me even when you try. Do you know," he continued softly, "I think we are the two most miserable men in England, you and I? we have got on to thirty without wife or child, or so much as a shop to look after—poor, pitiful, lost devils, both! And now we clash about a girl! As if there were not several millions in the United Kingdom! Ah, Frank, Frank, the one who loses this throw, be it you or me, he has my pity! It were better for him—how does the Bible say?—that a millstone were hanged about his neck and he were cast into the depth of the sea. Let us take a drink," he concluded suddenly, but without any levity of tone.

I was touched by his words, and consented. He sat down on the table in the dining room, and held up the glass of sherry to his eye.

"If you beat me, Frank," he said, "I shall take to drink. What will you do, if it goes the other way?"

"God knows," I returned.

"Well," said he, "here is a toast in the meantime: '*Italia irredenta!*'"

The remainder of the day was passed in the same dreadful tedium and suspense. I laid the table for dinner, while Northmour and Clara prepared the meal together in the kitchen. I could hear their talk as I went to and fro, and was surprised to find it ran all the time upon myself. Northmour again bracketed us together, and rallied Clara on a choice of husbands; but he continued to speak of me with some feeling, and uttered nothing to my prejudice unless he included himself in the condemnation. This awakened a sense of gratitude in my heart, which combined with the immediateness of our peril to fill my eyes with tears. After all, I thought—and perhaps the thought was laughably vain—we were here three very noble human beings to perish in defence of a thieving banker.

Before we sat down to table, I looked forth from an upstairs window. The day was beginning to decline; the links were utterly deserted; the dispatch box still lay untouched where we had left it hours before.

Mr. Huddlestone, in a long yellow dressing gown, took one end of the table, Clara the other; while Northmour and I faced each other from the sides. The lamp was brightly trimmed; the wine was good; the viands, although mostly cold, excellent of their sort. We seemed to have agreed tacitly; all reference to the impending catastrophe was carefully avoided; and, considering our tragic circumstances, we made a merrier party than could have been expected. From time to time, it is true, Northmour or I would rise from table and make a round of the defences; and, on each of these occasions, Mr. Huddlestone was recalled to a sense of his tragic predicament, glanced up with ghastly eyes, and bore for an instant on his countenance the stamp of terror. But he hastened to empty his glass, wiped his forehead with his handkerchief, and joined again in the conversation.

I was astonished at the wit and information he displayed. Mr. Huddlestone's was certainly no ordinary character; he had read and observed for himself; his gifts were sound; and, though I could never have learned to love the man, I began to understand his success in business, and the great respect in which he had been held before his failure. He had, above all, the talent of society; and though I never heard him speak but on this one and most unfavourable occasion, I set him down among the most brilliant conversationalists I ever met.

He was relating with great gusto, and seemingly no feeling of shame, the manoeuvers of a scoundrelly commission merchant whom he had known and studied in his youth, and we were all listening with an odd mixture of mirth and embarrassment, when our little party was brought abruptly to an end in the most startling manner.

A noise like that of a wet finger on the windowpane interrupted Mr. Huddlestone's tale; and in an instant we were all four as white as paper, and sat tongue-tied and motionless round the table.

"A snail," I said at last; for I had heard that these animals make a noise somewhat similar in character.

"Snail be d—d!" said Northmour. "Hush!"

The same sound was repeated twice at regular intervals; and then a formidable voice shouted through the shutters the Italian word *"Traditore!"*

Mr. Huddlestone threw his head in the air; his eyelids quivered; next moment he fell insensible below the table. Northmour and I had each run to the armoury and seized a gun. Clara was on her feet with her hand at her throat.

So we stood waiting, for we thought the hour of attack was certainly come; but second passed after second, and all but the surf remained silent in the neighbourhood of the pavilion.

"Quick," said Northmour; "upstairs with him before they come."

CHAPTER EIGHT

Tells the last of the tall man

Somehow or other, by hook and crook, and between the three of us, we got Bernard Huddlestone bundled upstairs and laid upon the bed in *My Uncle's Room*. During the whole process, which was rough enough, he gave no sign of consciousness, and he remained, as we had thrown him, without changing the position of a finger. His daughter opened his shirt and began to wet his head and bosom; while Northmour and I ran to the window. The weather continued clear; the moon, which was now about full, had risen and shed a very clear light upon the links; yet, strain our eyes as we might, we could distinguish nothing moving. A few dark spots, more or less, on the uneven expanse were not to be identified; they might be crouching men, they might be shadows; it was impossible to be sure.

"Thank God," said Northmour, "Aggie is not coming tonight."

Aggie was the name of the old nurse; he had not thought of her till now; but that he should think of her at all, was a trait that surprised me in the man.

We were again reduced to waiting. Northmour went to the fireplace and spread his hands before the red embers, as if he were cold. I followed him mechanically with my eyes, and in so doing turned my back upon the window. At that moment a very faint report was audible from without, and a ball shivered a pane of glass, and buried itself in the shutter two inches from my head. I heard Clara scream; and though I whipped instantly out of range and into a corner, she was there, so to speak, before me, beseeching to know if I were hurt. I felt that I could stand to be shot at every day and all day long, with such marks of solicitude for a reward; and I continued to reassure her, with the tenderest caresses and in complete forgetfulness of our situation, till the voice of Northmour recalled me to myself.

"An air gun," he said. "They wish to make no noise."

I put Clara aside, and looked at him. He was standing with his back to the fire and his hands clasped behind him; and I knew by the black look on his face, that passion was boiling within. I had seen just such a look before he attacked me, that March night, in the adjoining chamber; and, though I could make every allowance for his anger, I confess I trembled for the consequences. He gazed straight before him; but he could see us with the tail of his eye, and his temper kept rising like a gale of wind. With regular battle awaiting us outside, this prospect of an internecine strife within the walls began to daunt me.

Suddenly, as I was thus closely watching his expression and prepared against the worst, I saw a change, a flash, a look of relief, upon his face. He took up the lamp which stood beside him on the table, and turned to us with an air of some excitement.

"There is one point that we must know," said he. "Are they going to butcher the lot of us, or only Huddlestone? Did they take you for him, or fire at you for your own *beaux yeux?*"

"They took me for him, for certain," I replied. "I am near as tall, and my head is fair."

"I am going to make sure," returned Northmour; and he stepped up to the window, holding the lamp above his head, and stood there, quietly affronting death, for half a minute.

Clara sought to rush forward and pull him from the place of danger; but I had the pardonable selfishness to hold her back by force.

"Yes," said Northmour, turning coolly from the window; "it's only Huddlestone they want."

"Oh, Mr. Northmour!" cried Clara; but found no more to add; the temerity she had just witnessed seeming beyond the reach of words.

He, on his part, looked at me, cocking his head, with a fire of triumph in his eyes; and I understood at once that he had thus hazarded his life, merely to attract Clara's notice, and depose me from my position as the hero of the hour. He snapped his fingers.

"The fire is only beginning," said he. "When they warm up to their work, they won't be so particular."

A voice was now heard hailing us from the entrance. From the window we could see the figure of a man in the moonlight; he stood motionless, his face uplifted to ours, and a rag of something white on his extended arm; and as we looked right down upon him, though he was a good many yards distant on the links, we could see the moonlight glitter on his eyes.

He opened his lips again, and spoke for some minutes on end, in a key so loud that he might have been heard in every corner of the pavilion, and as far away as the borders of the wood. It was the same voice that had already shouted *"Traditore!"* through the shutters of the dining room; this time it made a complete and clear statement. If the traitor "Oddlestone" were given up, all others should be spared; if not, no one should escape to tell the tale.

"Well, Huddlestone, what do you say to that?" asked Northmour, turning to the bed.

Up to that moment the banker had given no sign of life, and I, at least, had supposed him to be still lying in a faint; but he replied at once, and in such tones as I have never heard elsewhere, save from a delirious patient, adjured and besought us not to desert him. It was the most hideous and abject performance that my imagination can conceive.

"Enough," cried Northmour; and then he threw open the window, leaned out into the night, and in a tone of exultation, and with a total forgetfulness of what was due to the presence of a lady, poured out upon the ambassador a string of the most abominable raillery both in English and Italian, and bade him be gone where he had come from. I believe that nothing so delighted Northmour at that moment as the thought that we must all infallibly perish before the night was out.

Meantime the Italian put his flag of truce into his pocket, and disappeared, at a leisurely pace, among the sandhills.

"They make honourable war," said Northmour. "They are all gentlemen and soldiers. For the credit of the thing, I wish we could change sides—you and I, Frank, and you too, Missy my darling—and leave that being on the bed to someone else. Tut! Don't look shocked! We are all going post to what they call eternity, and may as well be aboveboard while there's time. As far as I'm concerned, if I could first strangle Huddlestone and then get Clara in my arms, I could die with some pride and satisfaction. And as it is, by God, I'll have a kiss!"

Before I could do anything to interfere, he had rudely embraced and repeatedly kissed the resisting girl. Next moment I had pulled him away with fury, and flung him heavily against the wall. He laughed loud and long, and I feared his wits had given way under the strain; for even in the best of days he had been a sparing and a quiet laugher.

"Now, Frank," said he, when his mirth was somewhat appeased, "it's your turn. Here's my hand. Good-bye; farewell!" Then, seeing me stand rigid and indignant, and holding Clara to my side—"Man!" he broke out, "are you angry? Did you think we were going to die with all the airs and graces of society? I took a kiss; I'm glad I had it; and now you can take another if you like, and square accounts."

I turned from him with a feeling of contempt which I did not seek to dissemble.

"As you please," said he. "You've been a prig in life; a prig you'll die."

And with that he sat down in a chair, a rifle over his knee, and amused himself with snapping the lock; but I could see that his ebullition of light spirits (the only one I ever knew him to display) had already come to an end, and was succeeded by a sullen, scowling humour.

All this time our assailants might have been entering the house, and we been none the wiser; we had in truth almost forgotten the danger that so imminently overhung our days. But just then Mr. Huddlestone uttered a cry, and leaped from the bed.

I asked him what was wrong.

"Fire!" he cried. "They have set the house on fire!"

Northmour was on his feet in an instant, and he and I ran through the door of communication with the study. The room was illuminated by a red and angry light. Almost at the moment of our entrance, a tower of flame arose in front of the window, and, with a tingling report, a pane fell inwards on the carpet. They had set fire to the lean-to outhouse, where Northmour used to nurse his negatives.

"Hot work," said Northmour. "Let us try in your old room."

We ran thither in a breath, threw up the casement, and looked forth. Along the whole back wall of the pavilion piles of fuel had been arranged and kindled; and it is probable they had been drenched with mineral oil, for, in spite of the morning's rain, they all burned bravely. The fire had taken a firm hold already on the outhouse, which blazed higher and higher every moment; the back door was in the centre of a red-hot bonfire; the eaves we could see, as we looked upward, were already smouldering, for the roof overhung, and was supported by considerable beams of wood. At the same time, hot, pungent, and choking volumes of smoke began to fill the house. There was not a human being to be seen to right or left.

"Ah, well!" said Northmour, "here's the end, thank God."

And we returned to *My Uncle's Room.* Mr. Huddlestone was putting on his boots, still violently trembling, but with an air of determination such as I had not hitherto observed. Clara stood close by him, with her cloak in both hands ready to throw about her shoulders, and a strange look in her eyes, as if she were half hopeful, half doubtful of her father.

"Well, boys and girls," said Northmour, "how about a sally? The oven is heating; it is not good to stay here and be baked; and, for my part, I want to come to my hands with them, and be done."

"There is nothing else left," I replied.

And both Clara and Mr. Huddlestone, though with a very different intonation, added, "Nothing."

As we went downstairs the heat was excessive, and the roaring of the fire filled our ears; and we had scarce reached the passage before the stairs window fell in, a branch of flame shot brandishing through the aperture, and the interior of the pavilion became lit up with that dreadful and fluctuating glare. At the same moment we heard the fall of something heavy and inelastic in the upper story. The whole pavilion, it was plain, had gone alight like a box of matches, and now not only flamed sky-high to land and sea, but threatened with every moment to crumble and fall in about our ears.

Northmour and I cocked our revolvers. Mr. Huddlestone, who had already refused a firearm, put us behind him with a manner of command.

"Let Clara open the door," said he. "So, if they fire a volley, she will be protected. And in the meantime stand behind me. I am the scapegoat; my sins have found me out."

I heard him, as I stood breathless by his shoulder, with my pistol ready, pattering off prayers in a tremulous, rapid whisper; and I confess, horrid as the thought may seem, I despised him for thinking of supplications in a moment so critical and thrilling. In the meantime, Clara, who was dead white but still possessed her faculties, had displaced the barricade from the front door. Another moment, and she had pulled it open. Firelight and moonlight illuminated the links with confused and changeful lustre, and far away against the sky we could see a long trail of glowing smoke.

Mr. Huddlestone, filled for the moment with a strength greater than his own, struck Northmour and myself a backhander in the chest; and while we were thus for the moment incapacitated from action, lifting his arms above his head like one about to dive, he ran straight forward out of the pavilion.

"Here am I!" he cried—"Huddlestone! Kill me, and spare the others!"

His sudden appearance daunted, I suppose, our hidden enemies; for Northmour and I had time to recover, to seize Clara between us, one by each arm, and to rush forth to his assistance, ere anything further had taken place. But scarce had we passed the threshold when there came near a dozen reports and flashes from every direction among the hollows of the links. Mr. Huddlestone staggered, uttered a weird and freezing cry, threw up his arms over his head, and fell backward on the turf.

"Traditore! Traditore!" cried the invisible avengers.

And just then, a part of the roof of the pavilion fell in, so rapid was the progress of the fire. A loud, vague, and horrible noise accompanied the collapse, and a vast volume of flame went soaring up to heaven. It must have been visible at that moment from twenty miles out at sea, from the shore at Graden Wester, and far inland from the peak of Graystiel, the most eastern summit of the Caulder Hills. Bernard Huddlestone, although God knows what were his obsequies, had a fine pyre at the moment of his death.

Chapter Nine

Tells how Northmour carried out his threat

I should have the greatest difficulty to tell you what followed next after this tragic circumstance. It is all to me, as I look back upon it, mixed, strenuous, and ineffectual, like the struggles of a sleeper in a nightmare. Clara, I remember, uttered a broken sigh and would have fallen forward to earth, had not Northmour and I supported her insensible body. I do not think we were attacked; I do not remember even to have seen an assailant; and I believe we deserted Mr. Huddlestone without a glance. I only remember running like a man in a panic, now carrying Clara altogether in my own arms, now sharing her weight with North-mour, now scuffling confusedly for the possession of that dear burden. Why we should have made for my camp in the Hemlock Den, or how we reached it, are points lost for ever to my recollection. The first moment at which I became definitely sure, Clara had been suffered to fall against the outside of my little tent, Northmour and I were tumbling together on the ground, and he, with contained ferocity, was striking for my head with the butt of his revolver. He had already twice wounded me on the scalp; and it is to the consequent loss of blood that I am tempted to attribute the sudden clearness of my mind.

I caught him by the wrist.

"Northmour," I remember saying, "you can kill me afterwards. Let us first attend to Clara."

He was at the moment uppermost. Scarcely had the words passed my lips, when he had leaped to his feet and ran towards the tent; and the next moment, he was straining Clara to his heart and covering her unconscious hands and face with his caresses.

"Shame!" I cried. "Shame to you, Northmour!"

And, giddy though I still was, I struck him repeatedly upon the head and shoulders.

He relinquished his grasp, and faced me in the broken moonlight.

"I had you under, and I let you go," said he; "and now you strike me! Coward!"

"You are the coward," I retorted. "Did she wish your kisses while she was still sensible of what she wanted? Not she! And now she may be dying; and you waste this precious time, and abuse her helplessness. Stand aside, and let me help her."

He confronted me for a moment, white and menacing; then suddenly he stepped aside.

"Help her then," said he.

I threw myself on my knees beside her, and loosened, as well as I was able, her dress and corset; but while I was thus engaged, a grasp descended on my shoulder.

"Keep your hands off her," said Northmour fiercely. "Do you think I have no blood in my veins?"

"Northmour," I cried, "if you will neither help her yourself, nor let me do so, do you know that I shall have to kill you?"

"That is better!" he cried. "Let her die also, where's the harm? Step aside from that girl! and stand up to fight."

"You will observe," said I, half rising, "that I have not kissed her yet."

"I dare you to," he cried.

I do not know what possessed me; it was one of the things I am most ashamed of in my life, though, as my wife used to say, I knew that my kisses would be always welcome were she dead or living; down I fell again upon my knees, parted the hair from her forehead, and, with the dearest respect, laid my lips for a moment on that cold brow. It was such a caress as a father might have given; it was such a one as was not unbecoming from a man soon to die to a woman already dead.

"And now," said I, "I am at your service, Mr. Northmour."

But I saw, to my surprise, that he had turned his back upon me.

"Do you hear?" I asked.

"Yes," said he, "I do. If you wish to fight, I am ready. If not, go on and save Clara. All is one to me."

I did not wait to be twice bidden; but, stooping again over Clara, continued my efforts to revive her. She still lay white and lifeless; I began to fear that her sweet spirit had indeed fled beyond recall, and horror and a sense of utter desolation seized upon my heart. I called her by name with the most endearing inflections; I chafed and beat her hands; now I laid her head low, now supported it against my knee; but all seemed to be in vain, and the lids still lay heavy on her eyes.

"Northmour," I said, "there is my hat. For God's sake bring some water from the spring."

Almost in a moment he was by my side with the water.

"I have brought it in my own," he said. "You do not grudge me the privilege?"

"Northmour," I was beginning to say, as I laved her head and breast; but he interrupted me savagely.

"Oh, you hush up!" he said. "The best thing you can do is to say nothing."

I had certainly no desire to talk, my mind being swallowed up in concern for my dear love and her condition; so I continued in silence to do my best towards her recovery, and, when the hat was empty, returned it to him, with one word—"More." He had, perhaps, gone several times upon this errand, when Clara reopened her eyes.

"Now," said he, "since she is better, you can spare me, can you not? I wish you a good night, Mr. Cassilis."

And with that he was gone among the thicket. I made a fire, for I had now no fear of the Italians, who had even spared all the little possessions left in my encampment; and, broken as she was by the excitement and the hideous catastrophe of the evening, I managed, in one way or another—by persuasion, encouragement, warmth, and such simple remedies as I could lay my hand on—to bring her back to some composure of mind and strength of body.

Day had already come, when a sharp "Hist!" sounded from the thicket. I started from the ground; but the voice of Northmour was heard adding, in the most tranquil tones: "Come here, Cassilis, and alone; I want to show you something."

I consulted Clara with my eyes, and, receiving her tacit permission, left her alone, and clambered out of the den. At some distance off I saw Northmour leaning against an elder; and, as soon as he perceived me, he began walking seaward. I had almost overtaken him as he reached the outskirts of the wood.

"Look," said he, pausing.

A couple of steps more brought me out of the foliage. The light of the morning lay cold and clear over that well-known scene. The pavilion was but a blackened wreck; the roof had fallen in, one of the gables had fallen out; and, far and near, the face of the links was cicatrised with little patches of burnt furze. Thick smoke still went straight upwards in the windless air of the morning, and a great pile of ardent cinders filled the bare walls of the house, like coals in an open grate. Close by the islet a schooner yacht lay to, and a well-manned boat was pulling vigorously for the shore.

"The *Red Earl!*" I cried. "The *Red Earl* twelve hours too late!"

"Feel in your pocket, Frank. Are you armed?" asked Northmour.

I obeyed him, and I think I must have become deadly pale. My revolver had been taken from me.

"You see I have you in my power," he continued. "I disarmed you last night while you were nursing Clara; but this morning—here—take your pistol. No thanks!" he cried, holding up his hand. "I do not like them; that is the only way you can annoy me now."

He began to walk forward across the links to meet the boat, and I followed a step or two behind. In front of the pavilion I paused to see where Mr. Huddlestone had fallen; but there was no sign of him, nor so much as a trace of blood.

"Graden Floe," said Northmour.

He continued to advance till we had come to the head of the beach.

"No farther, please," said he. "Would you like to take her to Graden House?"

"Thank you," replied I; "I shall try to get her to the minister's at Graden Wester."

The prow of the boat here grated on the beach, and a sailor jumped ashore with a line in his hand.

"Wait a minute, lads!" cried Northmour; and then lower and to my private ear: "You had better say nothing of all this to her," he added.

"On the contrary!" I broke out, "she shall know everything that I can tell."

"You do not understand," he returned, with an air of great dignity. "It will be nothing to her; she expects it of me. Good-bye!" he added, with a nod.

I offered him my hand.

"Excuse me," said he. "It's small, I know; but I can't push things quite so far as that. I don't wish any sentimental business, to sit by your hearth a white-haired wanderer, and all that. Quite the contrary: I hope to God I shall never again clap eyes on either one of you."

"Well, God bless you, Northmour!" I said heartily.

"Oh, yes," he returned.

He walked down the beach; and the man who was ashore gave him an arm on board, and then shoved off and leaped into the bows himself. Northmour took the tiller; the boat rose to the waves, and the oars between the tholepins sounded crisp and measured in the morning air.

They were not yet half way to the *Red Earl,* and I was still watching their progress, when the sun rose out of the sea.

One word more, and my story is done. Years after, Northmour was killed fighting under the colours of Garibaldi for the liberation of the Tyrol.

A Lodging for the Night

It was late in November 1456. The snow fell over Paris with rigorous, relentless persistence; sometimes the wind made a sally and scattered it in flying vortices; sometimes there was a lull, and flake after flake descended out of the black night air, silent, circuitous, interminable. To poor people, looking up under moist eyebrows, it seemed a wonder where it all came from. Master Francis Villon had propounded an alternative that afternoon, at a tavern window: was it only Pagan Jupiter plucking geese upon Olympus? or were the holy angels moulting? He was only a poor Master of Arts, he went on; and as the question somewhat touched upon divinity, he durst not venture to conclude. A silly old priest from Montargis, who was among the company, treated the young rascal to a bottle of wine in honour of the jest and the grimaces with which it was accompanied, and swore on his own white beard that he had been just such another irreverent dog when he was Villon's age.

The air was raw and pointed, but not far below freezing; and the flakes were large, damp, and adhesive. The whole city was sheeted up. An army might have marched from end to end and not a footfall given the alarm. If there were any belated birds in heaven, they saw the island like a large white patch, and the bridges like slim white spars, on the black ground of the river. High up overhead the snow settled among the tracery of the cathedral towers. Many a niche was drifted full; many a statue wore a long white bonnet on its grotesque or sainted head. The gargoyles had been transformed into great false noses, drooping towards the point. The crockets were like upright pillows swollen on one side. In the intervals of the wind, there was a dull sound of dripping about the precincts of the church.

The cemetery of St. John had taken its own share of the snow. All the graves were decently covered; tall white housetops stood around in grave array; worthy burghers were long ago in bed, benightcapped like their domiciles; there was no light in all the neighbourhood but a little peep from a lamp that hung swinging in the church choir, and tossed the shadows to and fro in time to its oscillations. The clock was hard on ten when the patrol went by with halberds and a lantern, beating their hands; and they saw nothing suspicious about the cemetery of St. John.

Yet there was a small house, backed up against the cemetery wall, which was still awake, and awake to evil purpose, in that snoring district. There was not much to betray it from without; only a stream of warm vapour from the chimney top, a patch where the snow melted on the roof, and a few half-obliterated footprints at the door. But within, behind the shuttered windows, Master Francis Villon the poet, and some of the thievish crew with whom he consorted, were keeping the night alive and passing round the bottle.

A great pile of living embers diffused a strong and ruddy glow from the arched chimney. Before this straddled Dom Nicolas, the Picardy monk, with his skirts picked up and his fat legs bared to the comfortable warmth. His dilated shadow cut the room in half; and the firelight only escaped on either side of his broad person, and in a little pool between his outspread feet. His face had the beery, bruised appearance of the continual drinker's; it was covered with a network of congested veins, purple in ordinary circumstances, but now pale violet, for even with his back to the fire the cold pinched him on the other side. His cowl had half fallen back, and made a strange excrescence on either side of his bull neck. So he straddled, grumbling, and cut the room in half with the shadow of his portly frame.

On the right, Villon and Guy Tabary were huddled together over a scrap of parchment; Villon making a ballade which he was to call the "Ballade of Roast Fish," and Tabary spluttering admiration at his shoulder. The poet was a rag of a man, dark, little, and lean, with hollow cheeks and thin black locks. He carried his four-and-twenty years with feverish animation. Greed had made folds about his eyes, evil smiles had puckered his mouth. The wolf and pig struggled together in his face. It was an eloquent, sharp, ugly, earthly countenance. His hands were small and prehensile, with fingers knotted like a cord; and they were continually flickering in front of him in violent and expressive pantomime. As for Tabary, a broad, complacent, admiring imbecility breathed from his squash nose and slobbering lips: he had become a thief, just as he might have become the most decent of burgesses, by the imperious chance that rules the lives of human geese and human donkeys.

At the monk's other hand, Montigny and Thevenin Pensete played a game of chance. About the first there clung some flavour of good birth and training, as about a fallen angel; something long, lithe, and courtly in the person; something aquiline and darkling in the face. Thevenin, poor soul, was in great feather: he had done a good stroke of knavery that afternoon in the Faubourg St. Jacques, and all night he had been gaining from Montigny. A flat smile illuminated his face; his bald head shone rosily in a garland of red curls; his little protuberant stomach shook with silent chucklings as he swept in his gains.

"Doubles or quits?" said Thevenin.

Montigny nodded grimly.

"Some may prefer to dine in state," wrote Villon, *"On bread and cheese on silver plate.* Or—or—help me out, Guido!"

Tabary giggled.

"Or parsley on a golden dish," scribbled the poet.

The wind was freshening without; it drove the snow before it, and sometimes raised its voice in a victorious whoop, and made sepulchral grumblings in the chimney. The cold was growing sharper as the night went on. Villon, protruding his lips, imitated the gust with something between a whistle and a groan. It was an eerie, uncomfortable talent of the poet's, much detested by the Picardy monk.

"Can't you hear it rattle in the gibbet?" said Villon. "They are all dancing the devil's jig on nothing, up there. You may dance, my gallants, you'll be none the warmer! Whew! what a gust! Down went somebody just now! A medlar the fewer on the three-legged medlar tree!—I say, Dom Nicolas, it'll be cold tonight on the St. Denis Road?" he asked.

Dom Nicolas winked both his big eyes, and seemed to choke upon his Adam's apple. Montfaucon, the great grisly Paris gibbet, stood hard by the St. Denis Road, and the pleasantry touched him on the raw. As for Tabary, he laughed immoderately over the medlars; he had never heard anything more lighthearted; and he held his sides and crowed. Villon fetched him a fillip on the nose, which turned his mirth into an attack of coughing.

"Oh, stop that row," said Villon, "and think of rhymes to 'fish.' "

"Doubles or quits," said Montigny doggedly.

"With all my heart," quoth Thevenin.

"Is there any more in that bottle?" asked the monk.

"Open another," said Villon. "How do you ever hope to fill that big hogshead, your body, with little things like bottles? And how do you expect to get to heaven? How many angels, do you fancy, can be spared to carry up a single monk from Picardy? Or do you think yourself another Elias—and they'll send the coach for you?"

"Hominibus impossibile," replied the monk, as he filled his glass.

Tabary was in ecstasies.

Villon filliped his nose again.

"Laugh at my jokes, if you like," he said.

"It was very good," objected Tabary.

Villon made a face at him. "Think of rhymes to 'fish,' " he said. "What have you to do with Latin? You'll wish you knew none of it at the great assizes, when the devil calls for Guido Tabary, clericus—the devil with the humpback and red-hot fingernails. Talking of the devil," he added in a whisper, "look at Montigny!"

All three peered covertly at the gamester. He did not seem to be enjoying his luck. His mouth was a little to a side; one nostril nearly shut, and the other much inflated. The black dog was on his back, as people say, in terrifying nursery metaphor; and he breathed hard under the gruesome burden.

"He looks as if he could knife him," whispered Tabary, with round eyes.

The monk shuddered, and turned his face and spread his open hands to the red embers. It was the cold that thus affected Dom Nicolas, and not any excess of moral sensibility.

"Come now," said Villon—"about this ballade. How does it run so far?" And beating time with his hand, he read it aloud to Tabary.

They were interrupted at the fourth rhyme by a brief and fatal movement among the gamesters. The round was completed, and

Thevenin was just opening his mouth to claim another victory, when Montigny leaped up, swift as an adder, and stabbed him to the heart. The blow took effect before he had time to utter a cry, before he had time to move. A tremor or two convulsed his frame; his hands opened and shut, his heels rattled on the floor; then his head rolled backward over one shoulder with the eyes wide open; and Thevenin Pensete's spirit had returned to Him who made it.

Everyone sprang to his feet; but the business was over in two twos. The four living fellows looked at each other in rather a ghastly fashion; the dead man contemplating a corner of the roof with a singular and ugly leer.

"My God!" said Tabary; and he began to pray in Latin.

Villon broke out into hysterical laughter. He came a step forward and ducked a ridiculous bow at Thevenin, and laughed still louder. Then he sat down suddenly, all of a heap, upon a stool, and continued laughing bitterly as though he would shake himself to pieces.

Montigny recovered his composure first.

"Let's see what he has about him," he remarked; and he picked the dead man's pockets with a practised hand, and divided the money into four equal portions on the table. "There's for you," he said.

The monk received his share with a deep sigh, and a single stealthy glance at the dead Thevenin, who was beginning to sink into himself and topple sideways off the chair.

"We're all in for it," cried Villon, swallowing his mirth. "It's a hanging job for every man jack of us that's here—not to speak of those who aren't." He made a shocking gesture in the air with his raised right hand, and put out his tongue and threw his head on one side, so as to counterfeit the appearance of one who has been hanged. Then he pocketed his share of the spoil, and executed a shuffle with his feet as if to restore the circulation.

Tabary was the last to help himself; he made a dash at the money, and retired to the other end of the apartment.

Montigny stuck Thevenin upright in the chair, and drew out the dagger, which was followed by a jet of blood.

"You fellows had better be moving," he said, as he wiped the blade on his victim's doublet.

"I think we had," returned Villon with a gulp. "Damn his fat head!" he broke out. "It sticks in my throat like phlegm. What right has a man to have red hair when he is dead?" And he fell all of a heap again upon the stool, and fairly covered his face with his hands.

Montigny and Dom Nicolas laughed aloud, even Tabary feebly chiming in.

"Cry baby," said the monk.

"I always said he was a woman," added Montigny with a sneer. "Sit up, can't you?" he went on, giving another shake to the murdered body. "Tread out that fire, Nick!"

But Nick was better employed; he was quietly taking Villon's purse, as the poet sat, limp and trembling, on the stool where he had been making a ballade not three minutes before. Montigny and Tabary dumbly demanded a share of the booty, which the monk silently promised as he passed the little bag into the bosom of his gown. In many ways an artistic nature unfits a man for practical existence.

No sooner had the theft been accomplished than Villon shook himself, jumped to his feet, and began helping to scatter and extinguish the embers. Meanwhile Montigny opened the door and cautiously peered into the street. The coast was clear; there was no meddlesome patrol in sight. Still it was judged wiser to slip out severally; and as Villon was himself in a hurry to escape from the neighbourhood of the dead Thevenin, and the rest were in a still greater hurry to get rid of him before he should discover the loss of his money, he was the first by general consent to issue forth into the street.

The wind had triumphed and swept all the clouds from heaven. Only a few vapours, as thin as moonlight, fleeted rapidly across the stars. It was bitter cold; and by a common optical effect, things seemed almost more definite than in the broadest daylight. The sleeping city was absolutely still: a company of white hoods, a field full of little Alps, below the twinkling stars. Villon cursed his fortune. Would it were still snowing! Now, wherever he went, he left an indelible trail behind him on the glittering streets; wherever he went he was still tethered to the house by the cemetery of St. John; wherever he went he must weave, with his own plodding feet, the rope that bound him to the crime and would bind him to the gallows. The leer of the dead man came back to him with a new significance. He snapped his fingers as if to pluck up his own spirits, and choosing a street at random, stepped boldly forward in the snow.

Two things preoccupied him as he went: the aspect of the gallows at

Montfaucon in this bright windy phase of the night's existence, for one; and for another, the look of the dead man with his bald head and garland of red curls. Both struck cold upon his heart, and he kept quickening his pace as if he could escape from unpleasant thoughts by mere fleetness of foot. Sometimes, he looked back over his shoulder with a sudden nervous jerk; but he was the only moving thing in the white streets, except when the wind swooped round a corner and threw up the snow, which was beginning to freeze, in spouts of glittering dust.

Suddenly he saw, a long way before him, a black clump and a couple of lanterns. The clump was in motion, and the lanterns swung as though carried by men walking. It was a patrol. And though it was merely crossing his line of march, he judged it wiser to get out of eyeshot as speedily as he could. He was not in the humour to be challenged, and he was conscious of making a very conspicuous mark upon the snow. Just on his left hand there stood a great hotel, with some turrets and a large porch before the door; it was half-ruinous, he remembered, and had long stood empty; and so he made three steps of it and jumped into the shelter of the porch. It was pretty dark inside, after the glimmer of the snowy streets, and he was groping forward with outspread hands, when he stumbled over some substance which offered an indescribable mixture of resistances, hard and soft, firm and loose. His heart gave a leap, and he sprang two steps back and stared dreadfully at the obstacle. Then he gave a little laugh of relief. It was only a woman, and she dead. He knelt beside her to make sure upon this latter point. She was freezing cold, and rigid like a stick. A little ragged finery fluttered in the wind about her hair, and her cheeks had been heavily rouged that same afternoon. Her pockets were quite empty; but in her stocking, underneath the garter, Villon found two of the small coins that went by the name of whites. It was little enough; but it was always something; and the poet was moved with a deep sense of pathos that she should have died before she had spent her money. That seemed to him a dark and pitiable mystery; and he looked from the coins in his hand to the dead woman, and back again to the coins, shaking his head over the riddle of man's life. Henry V. of England, dying at Vincennes just after he had conquered France, and this poor jade cut off by a cold draught in a great man's doorway, before she had time to spend her couple of whites—it seemed a cruel way to carry on the world. Two whites would have taken such a little while to squander; and yet it would have been one more good taste in the mouth, one more smack of the lips, before the devil got the soul, and the body was left to birds and vermin. He would like to use all his tallow before the light was blown out and the lantern broken.

While these thoughts were passing through his mind, he was feeling, half mechanically, for his purse. Suddenly his heart stopped beating; a feeling of cold scales passed up the back of his legs, and a cold blow seemed to fall upon his scalp. He stood petrified for a moment; then he felt again with one feverish movement; and then his loss burst upon him, and he was covered at once with perspiration. To spendthrifts money is so living and actual—it is such a thin veil between them and their pleasures! There is only one limit to their fortune—that of time; and a spendthrift with only a few crowns is the Emperor of Rome until they are spent. For such a person to lose his money is to suffer the most shocking reverse, and fall from heaven to hell, from all to nothing, in a breath. And all the more if he has put his head in the halter for it; if he may be hanged tomorrow for that same purse, so dearly earned, so foolishly departed! Villon stood and cursed; he threw the two whites into the street; he shook his fist at heaven; he stamped, and was not horrified to find himself trampling the poor corpse. Then he began rapidly to retrace his steps towards the house beside the cemetery. He had forgotten all fear of the patrol, which was long gone by at any rate, and had no idea but that of his lost purse. It was in vain that he looked right and left upon the snow: nothing was to be seen. He had not dropped it in the streets. Had it fallen in the house? He would have liked dearly to go in and see; but the idea of the grisly occupant unmanned him. And he saw besides, as he drew near, that their efforts to put out the fire had been unsuccessful; on the contrary, it had broken into a blaze, and a changeful light played in the chinks of door and window, and revived his terror for the authorities and Paris gibbet.

He returned to the hotel with the porch, and groped about upon the snow for the money he had thrown away in his childish passion. But he could only find one white; the other had probably struck sideways and sunk deeply in. With a single white in his pocket, all his projects for a rousing night in some wild tavern vanished utterly away. And it was not only pleasure that fled laughing from his grasp; positive discomfort, positive pain, attacked him as he stood ruefully before the porch. His perspiration had dried upon him; and though the wind had now fallen, a binding frost was setting in stronger with every hour, and he felt benumbed and sick at heart. What was to be done? Late as was the hour, improbable as was success, he would try the house of his adopted father, the chaplain of St. Benoît.

He ran there all the way, and knocked timidly. There was no answer. He knocked again and again, taking heart with every stroke; and at last steps were heard approaching from within. A barred wicket fell open in the iron-studded door, and emitted a gush of yellow light.

"Hold up your face to the wicket," said the chaplain from within.

"It's only me," whimpered Villon.

"Oh, it's only you, is it?" returned the chaplain; and he cursed him with foul unpriestly oaths for disturbing him at such an hour, and bade him be off to hell, where he came from.

"My hands are blue to the wrist," pleaded Villon; "my feet are dead and full of twinges; my nose aches with the sharp air; the cold lies at my heart. I may be dead before morning. Only this once, father, and before God I will never ask again!"

"You should have come earlier," said the ecclesiastic coolly. "Young men require a lesson now and then." He shut the wicket and retired deliberately into the interior of the house.

Villon was beside himself; he beat upon the door with his hands and feet, and shouted hoarsely after the chaplain.

"Wormy old fox!" he cried. "If I had my hand under your twist, I would send you flying headlong into the bottomless pit."

A door shut in the interior, faintly audible to the poet down long passages. He passed his hand over his mouth with an oath. And then the humour of the situation struck him, and he laughed and looked lightly up to heaven, where the stars seemed to be winking over his discomfiture.

What was to be done? It looked very like a night in the frosty streets. The idea of the dead woman popped into his imagination, and gave him a hearty fright; what had happened to her in the early night might very well happen to him before morning. And he so young! and with such immense possibilities of disorderly amusement before him! He felt quite pathetic over the notion of his own fate, as if it had been someone else's, and made a little imaginative vignette of the scene in the morning when they should find his body.

He passed all his chances under review, turning the white between his thumb and forefinger. Unfortunately he was on bad terms with some old friends who would once have taken pity on him in such a plight. He had lampooned them in verses, he had beaten and cheated them; and yet now, when he was in so close a pinch, he thought there was at least one who might perhaps relent. It was a chance. It was worth trying at least, and he would go and see.

On the way, two little accidents happened to him which coloured his musings in a very different manner. For, first, he fell in with the track of a patrol, and walked in it for some hundred yards, although it lay out of his direction. And this spirited him up; at least he had confused his trail; for he was still possessed with the idea of people tracking him all about Paris over the snow, and collaring him next morning before he was awake. The other matter affected him very differently. He passed a street corner, where, not so long before, a woman and her child had been devoured by wolves. This was just the kind of weather, he reflected, when wolves might take it into their heads to enter Paris again; and a lone man in these deserted streets would run the chance of something worse than a mere scare. He stopped and looked upon the place with an unpleasant interest—it was a centre where several lanes intersected each other; and he looked down them all one after another, and held his breath to listen, lest he should detect some galloping black things on the snow or hear the sound of howling between him and the river. He remembered his mother telling him the story and pointing out the spot, while he was yet a child. His mother! If he only knew where she lived, he might make sure at least of shelter. He determined he would inquire upon the morrow; nay, he would go and see her too, poor old girl! So thinking, he arrived at his destination—his last hope for the night.

The house was quite dark, like its neighbours; and yet after a few taps, he heard a movement overhead, a door opening, and a cautious voice asking who was there. The poet named himself in a loud whisper, and waited, not without some trepidation, the result. Nor had he to wait long. A window was suddenly opened, and a pailful of slops splashed down upon the doorstep. Villon had not been unprepared for something of the sort, and had put himself as much in shelter as the nature of the porch admitted; but for all that, he was deplorably drenched below the waist. His hose began to freeze almost at once.

Death from cold and exposure stared him in the face; he remembered he was of phthisical tendency, and began coughing tentatively. But the gravity of the danger steadied his nerves. He stopped a few hundred yards from the door where he had been so rudely used, and reflected with his finger to his nose. He could only see one way of getting a lodging, and that was to take it. He had noticed a house not far away, which looked as if it might be easily broken into, and thither he betook himself promptly, entertaining himself on the way with the idea of a room still hot, with a table still loaded with the remains of supper, where he might pass the rest of the black hours, and whence he should issue, on the morrow, with an armful of valuable plate. He even considered on what viands and what wines he should prefer; and as he was calling the roll of his favourite dainties, roast fish presented itself to his mind with an odd mixture of amusement and horror.

"I shall never finish that ballade," he thought to himself; and then, with another shudder at the recollection, "Oh, damn his fat head!" he repeated fervently, and spat upon the snow.

The house in question looked dark at first sight; but as Villon made a preliminary inspection in search of the handiest point of attack, a little twinkle of light caught his eye from behind a curtained window.

"The devil!" he thought. "People awake! Some student or some saint, confound the crew! Can't they get drunk and lie in bed snoring like their neighbours! What's the good of curfew, and poor devils of bell-ringers jumping at a rope's end in bell-towers? What's the use of day, if people sit up all night? The gripes to them!" He grinned as he saw where his logic was leading him. "Every man to his business, after all," added he, "and if they're awake, by the lord, I may come by a supper honestly for this once, and cheat the devil."

He went boldly to the door and knocked with an assured hand. On both previous occasions, he had knocked timidly and with some dread of attracting notice; but now when he had just discarded the thought of a burglarious entry, knocking at a door seemed a mighty simple and innocent proceeding. The sound of his blows echoed through the house with thin, phantasmal reverberations, as though it were quite empty; but these had scarcely died away before a measured tread drew near, a couple of bolts were withdrawn, and one wing was opened broadly, as though no guile or fear of guile were known to those within. A tall figure of a man, muscular and spare, but a little bent, confronted Villon. The head was massive in bulk, but finely sculptured; the nose blunt at the bottom, but refining upward to where it joined a pair of strong and honest eyebrows; the mouth and eyes surrounded with delicate markings, and the whole face based upon a thick white beard, boldly and squarely trimmed. Seen as it was by the light of a flickering handlamp, it looked perhaps nobler than it had a right to do; but it was a fine face, honourable rather than intelligent, strong, simple, and righteous.

"You knock late, sir," said the old man in resonant, courteous tones.

Villon cringed, and brought up many servile words of apology; at a crisis of this sort, the beggar was uppermost in him, and the man of genius hid his head with confusion.

"You are cold," repeated the old man, "and hungry? Well, step in." And he ordered him into the house with a noble enough gesture.

"Some great seigneur," thought Villon, as his host, setting down the lamp on the flagged pavement of the entry, shot the bolts once more into their places.

"You will pardon me if I go in front," he said, when this was done; and he preceded the poet upstairs into a large apartment, warmed with a pan of charcoal and lit by a great lamp hanging from the roof. It was very bare of furniture: only some gold plate on a sideboard; some folios; and a stand of armour between the windows. Some smart tapestry hung upon the walls, representing the crucifixion of our Lord in one piece, and in another a scene of shepherds and shepherdesses by a running stream. Over the chimney was a shield of arms.

"Will you seat yourself," said the old man, "and forgive me if I leave you? I am alone in my house tonight, and if you are to eat I must forage for you myself."

No sooner was his host gone than Villon leaped from the chair on which he had just seated himself, and began examining the room, with the stealth and passion of a cat. He weighed the gold flagons in his hand, opened all the folios, and investigated the arms upon the shield, and the stuff with which the seats were lined. He raised the window curtains, and saw that the windows were set with rich stained glass in figures, so far as he could see, of martial import. Then he stood in the middle of the room, drew a long breath, and retaining it with puffed cheeks, looked round and round him, turning on his heels, as if to impress every feature of the apartment on his memory.

"Seven pieces of plate," he said. "If there had been ten, I would have risked it. A fine house, and a fine old master, so help me all the saints!"

And just then, hearing the old man's tread returning along the corridor, he stole back to his chair, and began humbly toasting his wet legs before the charcoal pan.

His entertainer had a plate of meat in one hand and a jug of wine in the other. He set down the plate upon the table, motioning Villon to draw in his chair, and going to the sideboard, brought back two goblets, which he filled.

"I drink to your better fortune," he said, gravely touching Villon's cup with his own.

"To our better acquaintance," said the poet, growing bold. A mere man of the people would have been awed by the courtesy of the old seigneur, but Villon was hardened in that matter; he had made mirth for great lords before now, and found them as black rascals as himself. And so he devoted himself to the viands with a ravenous gusto, while the old man, leaning backward, watched him with steady, curious eyes.

"You have blood on your shoulder, my man," he said.

Montigny must have laid his wet right hand upon him as he left the house. He cursed Montigny in his heart.

"It was none of my shedding," he stammered.

"I had not supposed so," returned his host quietly. "A brawl?"

"Well, something of that sort," Villon admitted with a quaver.

"Perhaps a fellow murdered?"

"Oh, no, not murdered," said the poet, more and more confused. "It was all fair play—murdered by accident. I had no hand in it, God strike me dead!" he added fervently.

"One rogue the fewer, I dare say," observed the master of the house.

"You may dare to say that," agreed Villon, infinitely relieved. "As big a rogue as there is between here and Jerusalem. He turned up his toes like a lamb. But it was a nasty thing to look at. I dare say you've seen dead men in your time, my lord?" he added, glancing at the armour.

"Many," said the old man. "I have followed the wars, as you imagine."

Villon laid down his knife and fork, which he had just taken up again.

"Were any of them bald?" he asked.

"Oh yes, and with hair as white as mine."

"I don't think I should mind the white so much," said Villon. "His was red." And he had a return of his shuddering and tendency to laughter, which he drowned with a great draught of wine. "I'm a little put out when I think of it," he went on. "I knew him—damn him! And then the cold gives a man fancies—or the fancies give a man cold, I don't know which."

"Have you any money?" asked the old man.

"I have one white," returned the poet, laughing. "I got it out of a dead jade's stocking in a porch. She was as dead as Caesar, poor wench, and as cold as a church, with bits of ribbon sticking in her hair. This is a hard world in winter for wolves and wenches and poor rogues like me."

"I," said the old man, "am Enguerrand de la Feuillée, seigneur de Brisetout, bailly du Patatrac. Who and what may you be?"

Villon rose and made a suitable reverence. "I am called Francis Villon," he said, "a poor Master of Arts of this university. I know some Latin, and a deal of vice. I can make chansons, ballades, lais, virelais, and roundels, and I am very fond of wine. I was born in a garret, and I shall not improbably die upon the gallows. I may add, my lord, that from this night forward I am your lordship's very obsequious servant to command."

"No servant of mine," said the knight; "my guest for this evening, and no more."

"A very grateful guest," said Villon politely; and he drank in dumb show to his entertainer.

"You are shrewd," began the old man, tapping his forehead, "very shrewd; you have learning; you are a clerk; and yet you take a small piece of money off a dead woman in the street. Is it not a kind of theft?"

"It is a kind of theft much practised in the wars, my lord."

"The wars are the field of honour," returned the old man proudly. "There a man plays his life upon the cast; he fights in the name of his lord the king, his Lord God, and all their lordships the holy saints and angels."

"Put it," said Villon, "that I were really a thief, should I not play my life also, and against heavier odds?"

"For gain, but not for honour."

"Gain?" repeated Villon with a shrug. "Gain! The poor fellow wants supper, and takes it. So does the soldier in a campaign. Why, what are all these requisitions we hear so much about? If they are not gain to those who take them, they are loss enough to the others. The men-at-arms drink by a good fire, while the burgher bites his nails to buy them wine and wood. I have seen a good many ploughmen swinging on trees about the country; ay, I have seen thirty on one elm, and a very poor figure they made; and when I asked someone how all these came to be hanged, I was told it was because they could not scrape together enough crowns to satisfy the men-at-arms."

"These things are a necessity of war, which the low-born must endure with constancy. It is true that some captains drive overhard; there are spirits in every rank not easily moved by pity; and indeed many follow arms who are no better than brigands."

"You see," said the poet, "you cannot separate the soldier from the brigand; and what is a thief but an isolated brigand with circumspect manners? I steal a couple of mutton chops, without so much as disturbing people's sleep; the farmer grumbles a bit, but sups none the less wholesomely on what remains. You come up blowing gloriously on a trumpet, take away the whole sheep, and beat the farmer pitifully into the bargain. I have no trumpet; I am only Tom, Dick, or Harry; I am a rogue and a dog, and hanging's too good for me—with all my heart; but just you ask the farmer which of us he prefers, just find out which of us he lies awake to curse on cold nights."

"Look at us two," said his lordship. "I am old, strong, and honoured. If I were turned from my house tomorrow, hundreds would be proud to shelter me. Poor people would go out and pass the night in the streets with their children, if I merely hinted that I wished to be alone. And I find you up, wandering homeless, and picking farthings off dead women by the wayside! I fear no man and nothing; I have seen you tremble and lose countenance at a word. I wait God's summons contentedly in my own house, or, if it please the king to call me out again, upon the field of battle. You look for the gallows; a rough, swift death, without hope or honour. Is there no difference between these two?"

"As far as to the moon," Villon acquiesced. "But if I had been born lord of Brisetout, and you had been the poor scholar Francis, would the difference have been any the less? Should not I have been warming my knees at this charcoal pan, and would not you have been groping for farthings in the snow? Should not I have been the soldier, and you the thief?"

"A thief!" cried the old man. "I a thief! If you understood your words, you would repent them."

Villon turned out his hands with a gesture of inimitable impudence. "If your lordship had done me the honour to follow my argument!" he said.

"I do you too much honour in submitting to your presence," said the knight. "Learn to curb your tongue when you speak with old and honourable men, or some one hastier than I may reprove you in a sharper fashion." And he rose and paced the lower end of the apartment, struggling with anger and antipathy. Villon surreptitiously refilled his cup, and settled himself more comfortably in the chair, crossing his knees and leaning his head upon one hand and the elbow against the back of the chair. He was now replete and warm; and he was in nowise frightened for his host, having gauged him as justly as was possible between two such different characters. The night was far spent, and in a very comfortable fashion after all; and he felt morally certain of a safe departure on the morrow.

"Tell me one thing," said the old man, pausing in his walk. "Are you really a thief?"

"I claim the sacred rights of hospitality," returned the poet. "My lord, I am."

"You are very young," the knight continued.

"I should never have been so old," replied Villon, showing his fingers, "if I had not helped myself with these ten talents. They have been my nursing mothers and my nursing fathers."

"You may still repent and change."

"I repent daily," said the poet. "There are few people more given to repentance than poor Francis. As for change, let somebody change my circumstances. A man must continue to eat, if it were only that he may continue to repent."

"The change must begin in the heart," returned the old man solemnly.

"My dear lord," answered Villon, "do you really fancy that I steal for pleasure? I hate stealing, like any other piece of work or of danger. My teeth chatter when I see a gallows. But I must eat, I must drink, I must mix in society of some sort. What the devil! Man is not a solitary animal—*Cui Deus faeminam tradit*. Make me king's pantler—make me abbot of St. Denis; make me bailly of the Patatrac; and then I shall be changed indeed. But as long as you leave me the poor scholar Francis Villon, without a farthing, why, of course, I remain the same."

"The grace of God is all-powerful."

"I should be a heretic to question it," said Francis. "It has made you lord of Brisetout and bailly of the Patatrac; it has given me nothing but the quick wits under my hat and these ten toes upon my hands. May I help myself to wine? I thank you respectfully. By God's grace, you have a very superior vintage."

The lord of Brisetout walked to and fro with his hands behind his back. Perhaps he was not yet quite settled in his mind about the parallel between thieves and soldiers; perhaps Villon had interested him by some cross-thread of sympathy; perhaps his wits were simply muddled by so much unfamiliar reasoning; but whatever the cause, he somehow yearned to convert the young man to a better way of thinking, and could not make up his mind to drive him forth again into the street.

"There is something more than I can understand in this," he said at length. "Your mouth is full of subtleties, and the devil has led you very far astray; but the devil is only a very weak spirit before God's truth, and all his subtleties vanish at a word of true honour, like darkness at morning. Listen to me once more. I learned long ago that a gentleman should live chivalrously and lovingly to God, and the king, and his lady; and though I have seen many strange things done, I have still striven to command my ways upon that rule. It is not only written in all noble histories, but in every man's heart, if he will take care to read. You speak of food and wine, and I know very well that hunger is a difficult trial to endure; but you do not speak of other wants; you say nothing of honour, of faith to God and other men, of courtesy, of love without reproach. It may be that I am not very wise—and yet I think I am—but you seem to me like one who has lost his way and made a great error in life. You are attending to the little wants, and you have totally forgotten the great and only real ones, like a man who should be doctoring a toothache on the Judgment Day. For such things as honour and love and faith are not only nobler than food and drink, but indeed I think that we desire them more, and suffer more sharply for their absence. I speak to you as I think you will most easily understand me. Are you not, while careful to fill your belly, disregarding another appetite in your heart, which spoils the pleasure of your life and keeps you continually wretched?"

Villon was sensibly nettled under all this sermonising. "You think I have no sense of honour!" he cried. "I'm poor enough, God knows! It's hard to see rich people with their gloves, and you blowing in your hands. An empty belly is a bitter thing, although you speak so lightly of it. If you had had as many as I, perhaps you would change your tune. Anyway I'm a thief—make the most of that—but I'm not a devil from hell, God strike me dead. I would have you to know I've an honour of my own, as good as yours, though I don't prate about it all day long, as if it was a God's miracle to have any. It seems quite natural to me; I keep it in its box till it's wanted. Why now, look you here, how long have I been in this room with you? Did you not tell me you were alone in the house? Look at your gold plate! You're strong, if you like, but you're old and unarmed, and I have my knife. What did I want but a jerk of the elbow and here would have been you with the cold steel in your bowels, and there would have been me, linking in the streets, with an armful of gold cups! Did you suppose I hadn't wit enough to see that? And I scorned the action. There are your damned goblets, as safe as in a church; there are you, with your heart ticking as good as new; and here am I, ready to go out again as poor as I came in, with my one white that you threw in my teeth! And you think I have no sense of honour—God strike me dead!"

The old man stretched out his right arm. "I will tell you what you are," he said. "You are a rogue, my man, an impudent and a black-hearted rogue and vagabond. I have passed an hour with you. Oh! believe me, I feel myself disgraced! And you have eaten and drunk at my table. But now I am sick at your presence; the day has come, and the night bird should be off to his roost. Will you go before, or after?"

"Which you please," returned the poet, rising. "I believe you to be strictly honourable." He thoughtfully emptied his cup. "I wish I could add you were intelligent," he went on, knocking on his head with his knuckles. "Age, age! the brains stiff and rheumatic."

The old man preceded him from a point of self-respect; Villon followed, whistling, with his thumbs in his girdle.

"God pity you," said the lord of Brisetout at the door.

"Good-bye, papa," returned Villon with a yawn. "Many thanks for the cold mutton."

The door closed behind him. The dawn was breaking over the white roofs. A chill, uncomfortable morning ushered in the day. Villon stood and heartily stretched himself in the middle of the road.

"A very dull old gentleman," he thought. "I wonder what his goblets may be worth."

The Sire de Malétroit's Door

Denis de Beaulieu was not yet two-and-twenty, but he counted himself a grown man, and a very accomplished cavalier into the bargain. Lads were early formed in that rough, warfaring epoch; and when one has been in a pitched battle and a dozen raids, has killed one's man in an honourable fashion, and knows a thing or two of strategy and mankind, a certain swagger in the gait is surely to be pardoned. He had put up his horse with due care, and supped with due deliberation; and then, in a very agreeable frame of mind, went out to pay a visit in the grey of the evening. It was not a very wise proceeding on the young man's part. He would have done better to remain beside the fire or go decently to bed. For the town was full of the troops of Burgundy and England under a mixed command; and though Denis was there on safe-conduct, his safe-conduct was like to serve him little on a chance encounter.

It was September 1429; the weather had fallen sharp; a flighty piping wind, laden with showers, beat about the township; and the dead leaves ran riot along the streets. Here and there a window was already lighted up; and the noise of men-at-arms making merry over supper within, came forth in fits and was swallowed up and carried away by the wind. The night fell swiftly; the flag of England, fluttering on the spire-top, grew ever fainter and fainter against the flying clouds—a black speck like a swallow in the tumultuous, leaden chaos of the sky.

As the night fell the wind rose, and began to hoot under archways and roar amid the treetops in the valley below the town.

Denis de Beaulieu walked fast and was soon knocking at his friend's door; but though he promised himself to stay only a little while and make an early return, his welcome was so pleasant, and he found so much to delay him, that it was already long past midnight before he said good-bye upon the threshold. The wind had fallen again in the meanwhile; the night was as black as the grave; not a star, nor a glimmer of moonshine, slipped through the canopy of cloud. Denis was ill-acquainted with the intricate lanes of Chateau Landon; even by daylight he had found some trouble in picking his way; and in this absolute darkness he soon lost it altogether. He was certain of one thing only—to keep mounting the hill; for his friend's house lay at the lower end, or tail, of Chateau Landon, while the inn was up at the head, under the great church spire. With this clue to go upon he stumbled and groped forward, now breathing more freely in open places where there was a good slice of sky overhead, now feeling along the wall in stifling closes. It is an eerie and mysterious position to be thus submerged in opaque blackness in an almost unknown town. The silence is terrifying in its possibilities. The touch of cold window bars to the exploring hand startles the man like the touch of a toad; the inequalities of the pavement shake his heart into his mouth; a piece of denser darkness threatens an ambuscade or a chasm in the pathway; and where the air is brighter, the houses put on strange and bewildering appearances, as if to lead him farther from his way. For Denis, who had to regain his inn without attracting notice, there was real danger as well as mere discomfort in the walk; and he went warily and boldly at once, and at every corner paused to make an observation.

He had been for some time threading a lane so narrow that he could touch a wall with either hand when it began to open out and go sharply downward. Plainly this lay no longer in the direction of his inn; but the hope of a little more light tempted him forward to reconnoitre. The lane ended in a terrace with a bartizan wall, which gave an outlook between high houses, as out of an embrasure, into the valley lying dark and formless several hundred feet below. Denis looked down, and could discern a few treetops waving and a single speck of brightness where the river ran across a weir. The weather was clearing up, and the sky had lightened, so as to show the outline of the heavier clouds and the dark margin of the hills. By the uncertain glimmer, the house on his left hand should be a place of some pretensions; it was surmounted by several pinnacles and turret-tops; the round stern of a chapel, with a fringe of flying buttresses, projected boldly from the main block; and the door was sheltered under a deep porch carved with figures and overhung by two long gargoyles. The windows of the chapel gleamed through their intricate tracery with a light as of many tapers, and threw out the buttresses and the peaked roof in a more intense blackness against the sky. It was plainly the hotel of some great family of the neighbourhood; and as it reminded Denis of a town house of his own at Bourges, he stood for some time gazing up at it and mentally gauging the skill of the architects and the consideration of the two families.

There seemed to be no issue to the terrace but the lane by which he had reached it; he could only retrace his steps, but he had gained some notion of his whereabouts, and hoped by this means to hit the main thoroughfare and speedily regain the inn. He was reckoning without that chapter of accidents which was to make this night memorable above all others in his career; for he had not gone back above a hundred yards before he saw a light coming to meet him, and heard loud voices speaking together in the echoing narrows of the lane. It was a party of men-at-arms going the night round with torches. Denis assured himself that they had all been making free with the wine-bowl, and were in no mood to be particular about safe-conducts or the niceties of chivalrous war. It was as like as not that they would kill him like a dog and leave him where he fell. The situation was inspiriting but nervous. Their own torches would conceal him from sight, he reflected; and he hoped that they would drown the noise of his footsteps with their own empty voices. If he were but fleet and silent, he might evade their notice altogether.

Unfortunately, as he turned to beat a retreat, his foot rolled upon a pebble; he fell against the wall with an ejaculation, and his sword rang loudly on the stones. Two or three voices demanded who went there—some in French, some in English; but Denis made no reply, and ran the faster down the lane. Once upon the terrace, he paused to look back. They still kept calling after him, and just then began to double the pace in pursuit, with a considerable clank of armour, and great tossing of the torchlight to and fro in the narrow jaws of the passage.

Denis cast a look around and darted into the porch. There he might escape observation, or—if that were too much to expect—was in a capital posture whether for parley or defence. So thinking, he drew his sword and tried to set his back against the door. To his surprise, it yielded behind his weight; and though he turned in a moment, continued to swing back on oiled and noiseless hinges, until it stood wide open on a black interior. When things fall out opportunely for the person concerned, he is not apt to be critical about the how or why, his own immediate personal convenience seeming a sufficient reason for the strangest oddities and revolutions in our sublunary things; and so Denis, without a moment's hesitation, stepped within and partly closed the door behind him to conceal his place of refuge. Nothing was further from his thoughts than to close it altogether; but for some inexplicable reason—perhaps by a spring or a weight—the ponderous mass of oak whipped itself out of his fingers and clanked to, with a formidable rumble and a noise like the falling of an automatic bar.

The round, at that very moment, debouched upon the terrace and proceeded to summon him with shouts and curses. He heard them ferreting in the dark corners; the stock of a lance even rattled along the outer surface of the door behind which he stood; but these gentlemen were in too high a humour to be long delayed, and soon made off down a corkscrew pathway which had escaped Denis's observation, and passed out of sight and hearing along the battlements of the town.

Denis breathed again. He gave them a few minutes' grace for fear of accidents, and then groped about for some means of opening the door and slipping forth again. The inner surface was quite smooth, not a handle, not a moulding, not a projection of any sort. He got his fingernails round the edges and pulled, but the mass was immovable. He shook it, it was as firm as a rock. Denis de Beaulieu frowned and gave vent to a little noiseless whistle. What ailed the door? he wondered. Why was it open? How came it to shut so easily and so effectually after him? There was something obscure and underhand about all this, that was little to the young man's fancy. It looked like a snare; and yet who could suppose a snare in such a quiet bystreet and in a house of so prosperous and even noble an exterior? And yet—snare or no snare, intentionally or unintentionally—here he was, prettily trapped; and for the life of him he could see no way out of it again. The darkness began to weigh upon him. He gave ear; all was silent without, but within and close by he seemed to catch a faint sighing, a faint sobbing rustle, a little stealthy creak—as though many persons were at his side, holding themselves quite still, and governing even their respiration with the extreme of slyness. The idea went to his vitals with a shock, and he faced about suddenly as if to defend his life. Then, for the first time, he became aware of a light about the level of his eyes and at some distance in the interior of the house—a vertical thread of light, widening towards the bottom, such as might escape between two wings of arras over a doorway. To see anything was a relief to Denis; it was like a piece of solid ground to a man labouring in a morass; his mind seized upon it with avidity; and he stood staring at it and trying to piece together some logical conception of his surroundings. Plainly there was a flight of steps ascending from his own level to that of this illuminated doorway; and indeed he thought he could make out another thread of light, as fine as a needle and as faint as phosphorescence, which might very well be reflected along the polished wood of a handrail. Since he had begun to suspect that he was not alone, his heart had continued to beat with smothering violence, and an intolerable desire for action of any sort had possessed itself of his spirit. He was in deadly peril, he believed. What could be more natural than to mount the staircase, lift the curtain, and confront his difficulty at once? At least he would be dealing with something tangible; at least he would be no longer in the dark. He stepped slowly forward with outstretched hands, until his foot struck the bottom step; then he rapidly scaled the stairs, stood for a moment to compose his expression, lifted the arras and went in.

He found himself in a large apartment of polished stone. There were three doors; one on each of three sides; all similarly curtained with tapestry. The fourth side was occupied by two large windows and a great stone chimney piece, carved with the arms of the Malétroits. Denis recognised the bearings, and was gratified to find himself in such good hands. The room was strongly illuminated; but it contained little furniture except a heavy table and a chair or two, the hearth was innocent of fire, and the pavement was but sparsely strewn with rushes clearly many days old.

On a high chair beside the chimney, and directly facing Denis as he entered, sat a little old gentleman in a fur tippet. He sat with his legs crossed and his hands folded, and a cup of spiced wine stood by his elbow on a bracket on the wall. His countenance had a strongly masculine cast; not properly human, but such as we see in the bull, the goat, or the domestic boar; something equivocal and wheedling, something greedy, brutal, and dangerous. The upper lip was inordinately full, as though swollen by a blow or a toothache; and the smile, the peaked eyebrows, and the small, strong eyes were quaintly and almost comically evil in expression. Beautiful white hair hung straight all round his head, like a saint's, and fell in a single curl upon the tippet. His beard and moustache were the pink of venerable sweetness. Age, probably in consequence of inordinate precautions, had left no mark upon his hands; and the Malétroit hand was famous. It would be difficult to imagine anything at once so fleshy and so delicate in design; the taper, sensual fingers were like those of one of Leonardo's women; the fork of the thumb made a dimpled protuberance when closed; the nails were perfectly shaped, and of a dead, surprising whiteness. It rendered his aspect tenfold more redoubtable, that a man with hands like these should keep them devoutly folded in his lap like a virgin martyr—that a man with so intense and startling an expression of face should sit patiently on his seat and contemplate people with an unwinking stare, like a god, or a god's statue. His quiescence seemed ironical and treacherous, it fitted so poorly with his looks.

Such was Alain, Sire de Malétroit.

Denis and he looked silently at each other for a second or two.

"Pray step in," said the Sire de Malétroit. "I have been expecting you all the evening."

He had not risen, but he accompanied his words with a smile and a slight but courteous inclination of the head. Partly from the smile, partly from the strange musical murmur with which the Sire prefaced his observation, Denis felt a strong shudder of disgust go through his marrow. And what with disgust and honest confusion of mind, he could scarcely get words together in reply.

"I fear," he said, "that this is a double accident. I am not the person you suppose me. It seems you were looking for a visit; but for my part, nothing was further from my thoughts—nothing could be more contrary to my wishes—than this intrusion."

"Well, well," replied the old gentleman indulgently, "here you are, which is the main point. Seat yourself, my friend, and put yourself entirely at your ease. We shall arrange our little affairs presently."

Denis perceived that the matter was still complicated with some misconception, and he hastened to continue his explanations.

"Your door...." he began.

"About my door?" asked the other, raising his peaked eyebrows. "A little piece of ingenuity." And he shrugged his shoulders. "A hospitable fancy! By your own account, you were not desirous of making my acquaintance. We old people look for such reluctance now and then; and when it touches our honour, we cast about until we find some way of overcoming it. You arrive uninvited, but believe me, very welcome."

"You persist in error, sir," said Denis. "There can be no question between you and me. I am a stranger in this countryside. My name is Denis, damoiseau de Beaulieu. If you see me in your house, it is only——"

"My young friend," interrupted the other, "you will permit me to have my own ideas on that subject. They probably differ from yours at the present moment," he added with a leer, "but time will show which of us is in the right."

Denis was convinced he had to do with a lunatic. He seated himself with a shrug, content to wait the upshot; and a pause ensued, during which he thought he could distinguish a hurried gabbling as of prayer from behind the arras immediately opposite him. Sometimes there seemed to be but one person engaged, sometimes two; and the vehemence of the voice, low as it was, seemed to indicate either great haste or an agony of spirit. It occurred to him that this piece of tapestry covered the entrance to the chapel he had noticed from without.

The old gentleman meanwhile surveyed Denis from head to foot with a smile, and from time to time emitted little noises like a bird or a mouse, which seemed to indicate a high degree of satisfaction. This state of matters became rapidly insupportable; and Denis, to put an end to it, remarked politely that the wind had gone down.

The old gentleman fell into a fit of silent laughter, so prolonged and violent that he became quite red in the face. Denis got upon his feet at once, and put on his hat with a flourish.

"Sir," he said, "if you are in your wits, you have affronted me grossly. If you are out of them, I flatter myself I can find better employment for my brains than to talk with lunatics. My conscience is clear; you have made a fool of me from the first moment; you have refused to hear my explanations; and now there is no power under God will make me stay here any longer; and if I cannot make my way out in a more decent fashion, I will hack your door in pieces with my sword."

The Sire de Malétroit raised his right hand and wagged it at Denis with the fore and little fingers extended.

"My dear nephew," he said, "sit down."

"Nephew!" retorted Denis, "you lie in your throat;" and he snapped his fingers in his face.

"Sit down, you rogue!" cried the old gentleman, in a sudden, harsh voice, like the barking of a dog. "Do you fancy," he went on, "that when I had made my little contrivance for the door I had stopped short with that? If you prefer to be bound hand and foot till your bones ache, rise and try to go away. If you choose to remain a free young buck, agreeably conversing with an old gentleman—why, sit where you are in peace, and God be with you."

"Do you mean I am a prisoner?" demanded Denis.

"I state the facts," replied the other. "I would rather leave the conclusion to yourself."

Denis sat down again. Externally he managed to keep pretty calm; but within, he was now boiling with anger, now chilled with apprehension. He no longer felt convinced that he was dealing with a madman. And if the old gentleman was sane, what, in God's name, had he to look for? What absurd or tragical adventure had befallen him? What countenance was he to assume?

While he was thus unpleasantly reflecting, the arras that overhung the chapel door was raised, and a tall priest in his robes came forth and, giving a long, keen stare at Denis, said something in an undertone to Sire de Malétroit.

"She is in a better frame of spirit?" asked the latter.

"She is more resigned, messire," replied the priest.

"Now the Lord help her, she is hard to please!" sneered the old gentleman. "A likely stripling—not ill-born—and of her own choosing, too? Why, what more would the jade have?"

"The situation is not usual for a young damsel," said the other, "and somewhat trying to her blushes."

"She should have thought of that before she began the dance? It was none of my choosing, God knows that: but since she is in it, by our lady, she shall carry it to the end." And then addressing Denis, "Monsieur de Beaulieu," he asked, "may I present you to my niece? She has been waiting your arrival, I may say, with even greater impatience than myself."

Denis had resigned himself with a good grace—all he desired was to know the worst of it as speedily as possible; so he rose at once, and bowed in acquiescence. The Sire de Malétroit followed his example and limped, with the assistance of the chaplain's arm, towards the chapel door. The priest pulled aside the arras, and all three entered. The building had considerable architectural pretensions. A light groining sprang from six stout columns, and hung down in two rich pendants from the centre of the vault. The place terminated behind the altar in a round end, embossed and honeycombed with a super-fluity of ornament in relief, and pierced by many little windows shaped like stars, trefoils, or wheels. These windows were imperfectly glazed, so that the night air circulated freely in the chapel. The tapers, of which there must have been half a hundred burning on the altar, were unmercifully blown about; and the light went through many different phases of brilliancy and semi-eclipse. On the steps in front of the altar knelt a young girl richly attired as a bride. A chill settled over Denis as he observed her costume; he fought with desperate energy against the conclusion that was being thrust upon his mind; it could not—it should not—be as he feared.

"Blanche," said the Sire, in his most flute-like tones, "I have brought a friend to see you, my little girl; turn round and give him your pretty hand. It is good to be devout; but it is necessary to be polite, my niece."

The girl rose to her feet and turned towards the new comers. She moved all of a piece; and shame and exhaustion were expressed in every line of her fresh young body; and she held her head down and kept her eyes upon the pavement, as she came slowly forward. In the course of her advance, her eyes fell upon Denis de Beaulieu's feet—feet of which he was justly vain, be it remarked, and wore in the most elegant accoutrement even while travelling. She paused—started, as if his yellow boots had conveyed some shocking meaning—and glanced suddenly up into the wearer's countenance. Their eyes met; shame gave place to horror and terror in her looks; the blood left her lips; with a piercing scream she covered her face with her hands and sank upon the chapel floor.

"That is not the man!" she cried. "My uncle, that is not the man!"

The Sire de Malétroit chirped agreeably. "Of course not," he said, "I expected as much. It was so unfortunate you could not remember his name."

"Indeed," she cried, "indeed, I have never seen this person till this moment—I have never so much as set eyes upon him—I never wish to see him again. Sir," she said, turning to Denis, "if you are a gentleman, you will bear me out. Have I ever seen you—have you ever seen me— before this accursed hour?"

"To speak for myself, I have never had that pleasure," answered the young man. "This is the first time, messire, that I have met with your engaging niece."

The old gentleman shrugged his shoulders.

"I am distressed to hear it," he said. "But it is never too late to begin. I had little more acquaintance with my own late lady ere I married her; which proves," he added with a grimace, "that these impromptu marriages may often produce an excellent understanding in the long run. As the bridegroom is to have a voice in the matter, I will give him two hours to make up for lost time before we proceed with the ceremony." And he turned towards the door, followed by the clergyman.

The girl was on her feet in a moment. "My uncle, you cannot be in earnest," she said. "I declare before God I will stab myself rather than be forced on that young man. The heart rises at it; God forbids such marriages; you dishonour your white hair. Oh, my uncle, pity me! There is not a woman in all the world but would prefer death to such a nuptial. Is it possible," she added, faltering—"is it possible that you do not believe me—that you still think this"—and she pointed at Denis with a tremor of anger and contempt—"that you still think *this* to be the man?"

"Frankly," said the old gentleman, pausing on the threshold, "I do. But let me explain to you once for all, Blanche de Malétroit, my way of thinking about this affair. When you took it into your head to dishonour my family and the name that I have borne, in peace and war, for more than threescore years, you forfeited, not only the right to question my designs, but that of looking me in the face. If your father had been alive, he would have spat on you and turned you out of doors. His was the hand of iron. You may bless your God you have only to deal with the hand of velvet, mademoiselle. It was my duty to get you married without delay. Out of pure goodwill, I have tried to find your own gallant for you. And I believe I have succeeded. But before God and all the holy angels, Blanche de Malétroit, if I have not, I care not one jackstraw. So let me recommend you to be polite to our young friend; for upon my word, your next groom may be less appetising."

And with that he went out, with the chaplain at his heels; and the arras fell behind the pair.

The girl turned upon Denis with flashing eyes.

"And what, sir," she demanded, "may be the meaning of all this?"

"God knows," returned Denis gloomily. "I am a prisoner in this house, which seems full of mad people. More I know not; and nothing do I understand."

"And pray how came you here?" she asked.

He told her as briefly as he could. "For the rest," he added, "perhaps you will follow my example, and tell me the answer to all these riddles, and what, in God's name, is like to be the end of it."

She stood silent for a little, and he could see her lips tremble and her tearless eyes burn with a feverish lustre. Then she pressed her forehead in both hands.

"Alas, how my head aches!" she said wearily—"to say nothing of my poor heart! But it is due to you to know my story, unmaidenly as it must seem. I am called Blanche de Malétroit; I have been without father or mother for—oh! for as long as I can recollect, and indeed I have been most unhappy all my life. Three months ago a young captain began to stand near me every day in church. I could see that I pleased him; I am much to blame, but I was so glad that anyone should love me; and when he passed me a letter, I took it home with me and read it with great pleasure. Since that time he has written many. He was so anxious to speak with me, poor fellow! and kept asking me to leave the door open some evening that we might have two words upon the stair. For he knew how much my uncle trusted me." She gave something like a sob at that, and it was a moment before she could go on. "My uncle is a hard man, but he is very shrewd," she said at last. "He has performed many feats in war, and was a great person at court, and much trusted by Queen Isabeau in old days. How he came to suspect me I cannot tell; but it is hard to keep anything from his knowledge; and this morning, as we came from mass, he took my hand in his, forced it open, and read my little billet, walking by my side all the while. When he had finished, he gave it back to me with great politeness. It contained another request to have the door left open; and this has been the ruin of us all.

My uncle kept me strictly in my room until evening, and then ordered me to dress myself as you see me—a hard mockery for a young girl, do you not think so? I suppose, when he could not prevail with me to tell him the young captain's name, he must have laid a trap for him: into which, alas! you have fallen in the anger of God. I looked for much confusion; for how could I tell whether he was willing to take me for his wife on these sharp terms? He might have been trifling with me from the first; or I might have made myself too cheap in his eyes. But truly I had not looked for such a shameful punishment as this! I could not think that God would let a girl be so disgraced before a young man. And now I have told you all; and I can scarcely hope that you will not despise me."

Denis made her a respectful inclination.

"Madam," he said, "you have honoured me by your confidence. It remains for me to prove that I am not unworthy of the honour. Is Messire de Malétroit at hand?"

"I believe he is writing in the salle without," she answered.

"May I lead you thither, madam?" asked Denis, offering his hand with his most courtly bearing.

She accepted it; and the pair passed out of the chapel, Blanche in a very drooping and shamefast condition, but Denis strutting and ruffling in the consciousness of a mission, and the boyish certainty of accomplishing it with honour.

The Sire de Malétroit rose to meet them with an ironical obeisance.

"Sir," said Denis, with the grandest possible air, "I believe I am to have some say in the matter of this marriage; and let me tell you at once, I will be no party to forcing the inclination of this young lady. Had it been freely offered to me, I should have been proud to accept her hand, for I perceive she is as good as she is beautiful; but as things are, I have now the honour, messire, of refusing."

Blanche looked at him with gratitude in her eyes; but the old gentleman only smiled and smiled, until his smile grew positively sickening to Denis.

"I am afraid," he said, "Monsieur de Beaulieu, that you do not perfectly understand the choice I have to offer you. Follow me, I beseech you, to this window." And he led the way to one of the large windows which stood open on the night. "You observe," he went on, "there is an iron ring in the upper masonry, and reeved through that, a very efficacious rope. Now, mark my words: if you should find your disinclination to my niece's person insurmountable, I shall have you hanged out of this window before sunrise. I shall only proceed to such an extremity with the greatest regret, you may believe me. For it is not at all your death that I desire, but my niece's establishment in life. At the same time, it must come to that if you prove obstinate. Your family, Monsieur de Beaulieu, is very well in its way; but if you sprang from Charlemagne, you should not refuse the hand of a Malétroit with impunity—not if she had been as common as the Paris road—not if she were as hideous as the gargoyle over my door. Neither my niece nor you, nor my own private feelings, move me at all in this matter. The honour of my house has been compromised; I believe you to be the guilty person; at least you are now in the secret; and you can hardly wonder if I request you to wipe out the stain. If you will not, your blood be on your own head! It will be no great satisfaction to me to have your interesting relics kicking their heels in the breeze below my windows but half a loaf is better than no bread, and if I cannot cure the dishonour, I shall at least stop the scandal."

There was a pause.

"I believe there are other ways of settling such imbroglios among gentlemen," said Denis. "You wear a sword, and I hear you have used it with distinction."

The Sire de Malétroit made a signal to the chaplain, who crossed the room with long silent strides and raised the arras over the third of the three doors. It was only a moment before he let it fall again; but Denis had time to see a dusky passage full of armed men.

"When I was a little younger, I should have been delighted to honour you, Monsieur de Beaulieu," said Sire Alain; "but I am now too old. Faithful retainers are the sinews of age, and I must employ the strength I have. This is one of the hardest things to swallow as a man grows up in years; but with a little patience, even this becomes habitual. You and the lady seem to prefer the salle for what remains of your two hours; and as I have no desire to cross your preference, I shall resign it to your use with all the pleasure in the world. No haste!" he added, holding up his hand, as he saw a dangerous look come into Denis de Beaulieu's face. "If your mind revolts against hanging, it will be time enough two hours hence to throw yourself out of the window or upon the pikes of my retainers. Two hours of life are always two hours. A great many things may turn up in even as little a while as that. And, besides, if I understand her appearance, my niece has still something to say to you. You will not disfigure your last hours by a want of politeness to a lady?"

Denis looked at Blanche, and she made him an imploring gesture.

It is likely that the old gentleman was hugely pleased at this symptom of an understanding; for he smiled on both, and added sweetly: "If you will give me your word of honour, Monsieur de Beaulieu, to await my return at the end of the two hours before attempting anything desperate, I shall withdraw my retainers, and let you speak in greater privacy with mademoiselle."

Denis again glanced at the girl, who seemed to beseech him to agree.

"I give you my word of honour," he said.

Messire de Malétroit bowed, and proceeded to limp about the apartment, clearing his throat the while with that odd musical chirp which had already grown so irritating in the ears of Denis de Beaulieu. He first possessed himself of some papers which lay upon the table; then he went to the mouth of the passage and appeared to give an order to the men behind the arras; and lastly he hobbled out through the door by which Denis had come in, turning upon the threshold to address a last smiling bow to the young couple, and followed by the chaplain with a hand lamp.

No sooner were they alone than Blanche advanced towards Denis with her hands extended. Her face was flushed and excited, and her eyes shone with tears.

"You shall not die!" she cried, "you shall marry me after all."

"You seem to think, madam," replied Denis, "that I stand much in fear of death."

"Oh, no, no," she said, "I see you are no poltroon. It is for my own sake—I could not bear to have you slain for such a scruple."

"I am afraid," returned Denis, "that you underrate the difficulty, madam. What you may be too generous to refuse, I may be too proud to accept. In a moment of noble feeling towards me, you forgot what you perhaps owe to others."

He had the decency to keep his eyes upon the floor as he said this, and after he had finished, so as not to spy upon her confusion. She stood silent for a moment, then walked suddenly away, and falling on her uncle's chair, fairly burst out sobbing. Denis was in the acme of embarrassment. He looked round, as if to seek for inspiration, and seeing a stool, plumped down upon it for something to do. There he sat, playing with the guard of his rapier, and wishing himself dead a thousand times over, and buried in the nastiest kitchen-heap in France. His eyes wandered round the apartment, but found nothing to arrest them. There were such wide spaces between the furniture, the light fell so baldly and cheerlessly over all, the dark outside air looked in so coldly through the windows, that he thought he had never seen a church so vast, nor a tomb so melancholy. The regular sobs of Blanche de Malétroit measured out the time like the ticking of a clock. He read the device upon the shield over and over again, until his eyes became obscured; he stared into shadowy corners until he imagined they were swarming with horrible animals; and every now and again he awoke with a start, to remember that his last two hours were running, and death was on the march.

Oftener and oftener, as the time went on, did his glance settle on the girl herself. Her face was bowed forward and covered with her hands, and she was shaken at intervals by the convulsive hiccup of grief. Even thus she was not an unpleasant object to dwell upon, so plump and yet so fine, with a warm brown skin, and the most beautiful hair, Denis thought, in the whole world of womankind. Her hands were like her uncle's; but they were more in place at the end of her young arms, and looked infinitely soft and caressing. He remembered how her blue eyes had shone upon him, full of anger, pity, and innocence. And the more he dwelt on her perfections, the uglier death looked, and the more deeply was he smitten with penitence at her continued tears. Now he felt that no man could have the courage to leave a world which contained so beautiful a creature; and now he would have given forty minutes of his last hour to have unsaid his cruel speech.

Suddenly a hoarse and ragged peal of cockcrow rose to their ears from the dark valley below the windows. And this shattering noise in the silence of all around was like a light in a dark place, and shook them both out of their reflections.

"Alas, can I do nothing to help you?" she said, looking up.

"Madam," replied Denis, with a fine irrelevancy, "if I have said anything to wound you, believe me, it was for your own sake and not for mine."

She thanked him with a tearful look.

"I feel your position cruelly," he went on. "The world has been bitter hard on you. Your uncle is a disgrace to mankind. Believe me, madam, there is no young gentleman in all France but would be glad of my opportunity, to die in doing you a momentary service."

"I know already that you can be very brave and generous," she answered. "What I *want* to know is whether I can serve you—now or afterwards," she added, with a quaver.

"Most certainly," he answered with a smile. "Let me sit beside you as if I were a friend, instead of a foolish intruder; try to forget how awkwardly we are placed to one another; make my last moments go pleasantly; and you will do me the chief service possible."

"You are very gallant," she added, with a yet deeper sadness.... "very gallant.... and it somehow pains me. But draw nearer, if you please; and if you find anything to say to me, you will at least make certain of a very friendly listener. Ah! Monsieur de Beaulieu," she broke forth—"ah! Monsieur de Beaulieu, how can I look you in the face?" And she fell to weeping again with a renewed effusion.

"Madam," said Denis, taking her hand in both of his, "reflect on the little time I have before me, and the great bitterness into which I am cast by the sight of your distress. Spare me, in my last moments, the spectacle of what I cannot cure even with the sacrifice of my life."

"I am very selfish," answered Blanche. "I will be braver, Monsieur de Beaulieu, for your sake. But think if I can do you no kindness in the future—if you have no friends to whom I could carry your adieux. Charge me as heavily as you can; every burden will lighten, by so little, the invaluable gratitude I owe you. Put it in my power to do something more for you than weep."

"My mother is married again, and has a young family to care for. My brother Guichard will inherit my fiefs; and if I am not in error, that will content him amply for my death. Life is a little vapour that passeth away, as we are told by those in holy orders. When a man is in a fair way and sees all life open in front of him, he seems to himself to make a very important figure in the world. His horse whinnies to him; the trumpets blow and the girls look out of window as he rides into town before his company; he receives many assurances of trust and regard—sometimes by express in a letter—sometimes face to face, with persons of great consequence falling on his neck. It is not wonderful if his head is turned for a time. But once he is dead, were he as brave as Hercules or as wise as Solomon, he is soon forgotten. It is not ten years since my father fell, with many other knights around him, in a very fierce encounter, and I do not think that any one of them, nor so much as the name of the fight is now remembered. No, no, madam, the nearer you come to it, you see that death is a dark and dusty corner, where a man gets into his tomb and has the door shut after him till the judgment day. I have few friends just now, and once I am dead I shall have none."

"Ah, Monsieur de Beaulieu!" she exclaimed, "you forget Blanche de Malétroit."

"You have a sweet nature, madam, and you are pleased to estimate a little service far beyond its worth."

"It is not that," she answered. "You mistake me if you think I am so easily touched by my own concerns. I say so, because you are the noblest man I have ever met; because I recognise in you a spirit that would have made even a common person famous in the land."

"And yet here I die in a mousetrap—with no more noise about it than my own squeaking," answered he.

A look of pain crossed her face, and she was silent for a little while. Then a light came into her eyes, and with a smile she spoke again.

"I cannot have my champion think meanly of himself. Anyone who gives his life for another will be met in Paradise by all the heralds and angels of the Lord God. And you have no such cause to hang your head. For.... Pray, do you think me beautiful?" she asked, with a deep flush.

"Indeed, madam, I do," he said.

"I am glad of that," she answered heartily. "Do you think there are many men in France who have been asked in marriage by a beautiful maiden—with her own lips—and who have refused her to her face? I know you men would half despise such a triumph; but believe me, we women know more of what is precious in love. There is nothing that should set a person higher in his own esteem; and we women would prize nothing more dearly."

"You are very good," he said; "but you cannot make me forget that I was asked in pity and not for love."

"I am not so sure of that," she replied, holding down her head. "Hear me to an end, Monsieur de Beaulieu. I know how you must despise me; I feel you are right to do so; I am too poor a creature to occupy one thought of your mind, although, alas! you must die for me this morning. But when I asked you to marry me, indeed, and indeed, it was because I respected and admired you, and loved you with my whole soul, from the very moment that you took my part against my uncle. If you had seen yourself, and how noble you looked, you would pity rather than despise me. And now," she went on, hurriedly checking him with her hand, "although I have laid aside all reserve and told you so much, remember that I know your sentiments towards me already. I would not, believe me, being nobly born, weary you with importunities into consent. I too have a pride of my own: and I declare before the holy mother of God, if you should now go back from your word already given, I would no more marry you than I would marry my uncle's groom."

Denis smiled a little bitterly.

"It is a small love," he said, "that shies at a little pride."

She made no answer, although she probably had her own thoughts.

"Come hither to the window," he said, with a sigh. "Here is the dawn."

And indeed the dawn was already beginning. The hollow of the sky was full of essential daylight, colourless and clean; and the valley underneath was flooded with a grey reflection. A few thin vapours clung in the coves of the forest or lay along the winding course of the river. The scene disengaged a surprising effect of stillness, which was hardly interrupted when the cocks began once more to crow among the steadings. Perhaps the same fellow who had made so horrid a clangour in the darkness not half an hour before, now sent up the merriest cheer to greet the coming day. A little wind went bustling and eddying among the treetops underneath the windows. And still the daylight kept flooding insensibly out of the east, which was soon to grow incandescent and cast up that red-hot cannonball, the rising sun.

Denis looked out over all this with a bit of a shiver. He had taken her hand, and retained it in his almost unconsciously.

"Has the day begun already?" she said; and then, illogically enough: "the night has been so long! Alas! what shall we say to my uncle when he returns?"

"What you will," said Denis, and he pressed her fingers in his.

She was silent.

"Blanche," he said, with a swift, uncertain, passionate utterance, "you have seen whether I fear death. You must know well enough that I would as gladly leap out of that window into the empty air as lay a finger on you without your free and full consent. But if you care for me at all do not let me lose my life in a misapprehension; for I love you better than the whole world; and though I will die for you blithely, it would be like all the joys of Paradise to live on and spend my life in your service."

As he stopped speaking, a bell began to ring loudly in the interior of the house; and a clatter of armour in the corridor showed that the retainers were returning to their post, and the two hours were at an end.

"After all that you have heard?" she whispered, leaning towards him with her lips and eyes.

"I have heard nothing," he replied.

"The captain's name was Florimond de Champdivers," she said in his ear.

"I did not hear it," he answered, taking her supple body in his arms and covered her wet face with kisses.

A melodious chirping was audible behind, followed by a beautiful chuckle, and the voice of Messire de Malétroit wished his new nephew a good morning.

PROVIDENCE AND THE GUITAR

CHAPTER I

Monsieur Léon Berthelini had a great care of his appearance, and sedulously suited his deportment to the costume of the hour. He affected something Spanish in his air, and something of the bandit, with a flavour of Rembrandt at home. In person he was decidedly small and inclined to be stout; his face was the picture of good humour; his dark eyes, which were very expressive, told of a kind heart, a brisk, merry nature, and the most indefatigable spirits. If he had worn the clothes of the period you would have set him down for a hitherto undiscovered hybrid between the barber, the innkeeper, and the affable dispensing chemist. But in the outrageous bravery of velvet jacket and flapped hat, with trousers that were more accurately described as fleshings, a white handkerchief cavalierly knotted at his neck, a shock of Olympian curls upon his brow, and his feet shod through all weathers in the slenderest of Molière shoes—you had but to look at him and you knew you were in the presence of a Great Creature. When he wore an overcoat he scorned to pass the sleeves; a single button held it round his shoulders; it was tossed backwards after the manner of a cloak, and carried with the gait and presence of an Almaviva. I am of opinion that M. Berthelini was nearing forty. But he had a boy's heart, gloried in his finery, and walked through life like a child in a perpetual dramatic performance. If he were not Almaviva after all, it was not for lack of making believe. And he enjoyed the artist's compensation. If he were not really Almaviva, he was sometimes just as happy as though he were.

I have seen him, at moments when he has fancied himself alone with his Maker, adopt so gay and chivalrous a bearing, and represent his own part with so much warmth and conscience, that the illusion became catching, and I believed implicitly in the Great Creature's pose.

But, alas! life cannot be entirely conducted on these principles; man cannot live by Almavivery alone; and the Great Creature, having failed upon several theatres, was obliged to step down every evening from his heights, and sing from half-a-dozen to a dozen comic songs, twang a guitar, keep a country audience in good humour, and preside finally over the mysteries of a tombola.

Madame Berthelini, who was art and part with him in these undignified labours, had perhaps a higher position in the scale of beings, and enjoyed a natural dignity of her own. But her heart was not any more rightly placed, for that would have been impossible; and she had acquired a little air of melancholy, attractive enough in its way, but not good to see like the wholesome, skyscraping, boyish spirits of her lord.

He, indeed, swam like a kite on a fair wind, high above earthly troubles. Detonations of temper were not unfrequent in the zones he travelled; but sulky fogs and tearful depressions were there alike unknown. A well-delivered blow upon a table, or a noble attitude, imitated from Mélingue or Frederic, relieved his irritation like a vengeance. Though the heaven had fallen, if he had played his part with propriety, Berthelini had been content! And the man's atmosphere, if not his example, reacted on his wife; for the couple doated on each other, and although you would have thought they walked in different worlds, yet continued to walk hand in hand.

It chanced one day that Monsieur and Madame Berthelini descended with two boxes and a guitar in a fat case at the station of the little town of Castel-le-Gâchis, and the omnibus carried them with their effects to the Hotel of the Black Head. This was a dismal, conventual building in a narrow street, capable of standing siege when once the gates were shut, and smelling strangely in the interior of straw and chocolate and old feminine apparel. Berthelini paused upon the threshold with a painful premonition. In some former state, it seemed to him, he had visited a hostelry that smelt not otherwise, and been ill received.

The landlord, a tragic person in a large felt hat, rose from a business table under the key-rack, and came forward, removing his hat with both hands as he did so.

"Sir, I salute you. May I inquire what is your charge for artists?" inquired Berthelini, with a courtesy at once splendid and insinuating.

"For artists?" said the landlord. His countenance fell and the smile of welcome disappeared. "Oh, artists!" he added brutally; "four francs a day." And he turned his back upon these inconsiderable customers.

A commercial traveller is received, he also, upon a reduction—yet is he welcome, yet can he command the fatted calf; but an artist, had he the manners of an Almaviva, were he dressed like Solomon in all his glory, is received like a dog and served like a timid lady travelling alone.

Accustomed as he was to the rubs of his profession, Berthelini was unpleasantly affected by the landlord's manner.

"Elvira," said he to his wife, "mark my words: Castel-le-Gâchis is a tragic folly."

"Wait till we see what we take," replied Elvira.

"We shall take nothing," returned Berthelini; "we shall feed upon insults. I have an eye, Elvira; I have a spirit of divination; and this place is accursed. The landlord has been discourteous, the Commissary will be brutal, the audience will be sordid and uproarious, and you will take a cold upon your throat. We have been besotted enough to come; the die is cast—it will be a second Sédan."

Sédan was a town hateful to the Berthelinis, not only from patriotism (for they were French, and answered after the flesh to the somewhat homely name of Duval), but because it had been the scene of their most sad reverses. In that place they had lain three weeks in pawn for their hotel bill, and had it not been for a surprising stroke of fortune they might have been lying there in pawn until this day. To mention the name of Sédan was for the Berthelinis to dip the brush in earthquake and eclipse. Count Almaviva slouched his hat with a gesture expressive of despair, and even Elvira felt as if ill-fortune had been personally invoked.

"Let us ask for breakfast," said she, with a woman's tact.

The Commissary of Police of Castel-le-Gâchis was a large red Commissary, pimpled, and subject to a strong cutaneous transpiration. I have repeated the name of his office because he was so very much more a Commissary than a man. The spirit of his dignity had entered into him. He carried his corporation as if it were something official. Whenever he insulted a common citizen it seemed to him as if he were adroitly flattering the Government by a side wind; in default of dignity he was brutal from an overweening sense of duty. His office was a den, whence passersby could hear rude accents laying down, not the law, but the good pleasure of the Commissary.

Six several times in the course of the day did M. Berthelini hurry thither in quest of the requisite permission for his evening's entertainment; six several times he found the official was abroad. Léon Berthelini began to grow quite a familiar figure in the streets of Castel-le-Gâchis; he became a local celebrity, and was pointed out as "the man who was looking for the Commissary." Idle children attached themselves to his footsteps, and trotted after him back and forward between the hotel and the office. Léon might try as he liked; he might roll cigarettes, he might straddle, he might cock his hat at a dozen different jaunty inclinations—the part of Almaviva was, under the circumstances, difficult to play.

As he passed the marketplace upon the seventh excursion the Commissary was pointed out to him, where he stood, with his waistcoat unbuttoned and his hands behind his back, to superintend the sale and measurement of butter. Berthelini threaded his way through the market stalls and baskets, and accosted the dignitary with a bow which was a triumph of the histrionic art.

"I have the honour," he asked, "of meeting M. le Commissaire?"

The Commissary was affected by the nobility of his address. He excelled Léon in the depth if not in the airy grace of his salutation.

"The honour," said he, "is mine!"

"I am," continued the strolling player, "I am, sir, an artist, and I have permitted myself to interrupt you on an affair of business. Tonight I give a trifling musical entertainment at the Café of the Triumphs of the Plough—permit me to offer you this little programme—and I have come to ask you for the necessary authorisation."

At the word "artist," the Commissary had replaced his hat with the

air of a person who, having condescended too far, should suddenly remember the duties of his rank.

"Go, go," said he, "I am busy—I am measuring butter."

"Heathen Jew!" thought Léon. "Permit me, sir," he resumed, aloud.
"I have gone six times already—"

"Put up your bills if you choose," interrupted the Commissary. "In
an hour or so I will examine your papers at the office. But now go; I am
busy."

"Measuring butter!" thought Berthelini. "Oh, France, and it is for
this that we made '93!"

The preparations were soon made; the bills posted, programmes
laid on the dinner table of every hotel in the town, and a stage erected
at one end of the Café of the Triumphs of the Plough; but when Léon
returned to the office, the Commissary was once more abroad.

"He is like Madame Benoîton," thought Léon, "Fichu Commissaire!"

And just then he met the man face to face.

"Here, sir," said he, "are my papers. Will you be pleased to verify?"

But the Commissary was now intent upon dinner.

"No use," he replied, "no use; I am busy; I am quite satisfied. Give
your entertainment."

And he hurried on.

"Fichu Commissaire!" thought Léon.

Chapter II

The audience was pretty large; and the proprietor of the café made a
good thing of it in beer. But the Berthelinis exerted themselves in vain.

Léon was radiant in velveteen; he had a rakish way of smoking a
cigarette between his songs that was worth money in itself; he under-
lined his comic points, so that the dullest numskull in Castel-le-
Gâchis had a notion when to laugh; and he handled his guitar in a
manner worthy of himself. Indeed his play with that instrument was as
good as a whole romantic drama; it was so dashing, so florid, and so
cavalier.

Elvira, on the other hand, sang her patriotic and romantic songs
with more than usual expression; her voice had charm and plangency;
and as Léon looked at her, in her low-bodied maroon dress, with her
arms bare to the shoulder, and a red flower set provocatively in her

corset, he repeated to himself for the many hundredth time that she was one of the loveliest creatures in the world of women.

Alas! when she went round with the tambourine, the golden youth of Castel-le-Gâchis turned from her coldly. Here and there a single halfpenny was forthcoming; the net result of a collection never exceeded half a franc; and the Maire himself, after seven different applications, had contributed exactly twopence. A certain chill began to settle upon the artists themselves; it seemed as if they were singing to slugs; Apollo himself might have lost heart with such an audience. The Berthelinis struggled against the impression; they put their back into their work, they sang loud and louder, the guitar twanged like a living thing; and at last Léon arose in his might, and burst with inimitable conviction into his great song, "Y a des honnêtes gens partout!" Never had he given more proof of his artistic mastery; it was his intimate, indefeasible conviction that Castel-le-Gâchis formed an exception to the law he was now lyrically proclaiming, and was peopled exclusively by thieves and bullies; and yet, as I say, he flung it down like a challenge, he trolled it forth like an article of faith; and his face so beamed the while that you would have thought he must make converts of the benches.

He was at the top of his register, with his head thrown back and his mouth open, when the door was thrown violently open, and a pair of newcomers marched noisily into the café. It was the Commissary, followed by the Garde Champêtre.

The undaunted Berthelini still continued to proclaim, "Y a des honnêtes gens partout!" But now the sentiment produced an audible titter among the audience. Berthelini wondered why; he did not know the antecedents of the Garde Champêtre; he had never heard of a little story about postage stamps. But the public knew all about the postage stamps and enjoyed the coincidence hugely.

The Commissary planted himself upon a vacant chair with somewhat the air of Cromwell visiting the Rump, and spoke in occasional whispers to the Garde Champêtre, who remained respectfully standing at his back. The eyes of both were directed upon Berthelini, who persisted in his statement.

"Y a des honnêtes gens partout," he was just chanting for the twentieth time; when up got the Commissary upon his feet and waved brutally to the singer with his cane.

"Is it me you want?" inquired Léon, stopping in his song.

"It is you," replied the potentate.

"Fichu Commissaire!" thought Léon, and he descended from the stage and made his way to the functionary.

"How does it happen, sir," said the Commissary, swelling in person, "that I find you mountebanking in a public café without my permission?"

"Without?" cried the indignant Léon. "Permit me to remind you——"

"Come, come sir!" said the Commissary, "I desire no explanations."

"I care nothing about what you desire," returned the singer. "I choose to give them, and I will not be gagged. I am an artist, sir, a distinction that you cannot comprehend. I received your permission and stand here upon the strength of it; interfere with me who dare."

"You have not got my signature, I tell you," cried the Commissary. "Show me my signature! Where is my signature?"

That was just the question; where was his signature? Léon recognised that he was in a hole; but his spirit rose with the occasion, and he blustered nobly, tossing back his curls. The Commissary played up to him in the character of tyrant; and as the one leaned farther forward, the other leaned farther back—majesty confronting fury. The audience had transferred their attention to this new performance, and listened with that silent gravity common to all Frenchmen in the neighbourhood of the Police. Elvira had sat down, she was used to these distractions, and it was rather melancholy than fear that now oppressed her.

"Another word," cried the Commissary, "and I arrest you."

"Arrest me?" shouted Léon. "I defy you!"

"I am the Commissary of Police," said the official.

Léon commanded his feelings, and replied, with great delicacy of innuendo—

"So it would appear."

The point was too refined for Castel-le-Gâchis; it did not raise a smile; and as for the Commissary, he simply bade the singer follow him to his office, and directed his proud footsteps towards the door. There was nothing for it but to obey. Léon did so with a proper pantomime of indifference, but it was a leek to eat, and there was no denying it.

The Maire had slipped out and was already waiting at the Commissary's door. Now the Maire, in France, is the refuge of the oppressed.

He stands between his people and the boisterous rigours of the Police. He can sometimes understand what is said to him; he is not always puffed up beyond measure by his dignity. 'Tis a thing worth the knowledge of travellers. When all seems over, and a man has made up his mind to injustice, he has still, like the heroes of romance, a little bugle at his belt whereon to blow; and the Maire, a comfortable *deus ex machina,* may still descend to deliver him from the minions of the law. The Maire of Castel-le-Gâchis, although inaccessible to the charms of music as retailed by the Berthelinis, had no hesitation whatever as to the rights of the matter. He instantly fell foul of the Commissary in very high terms, and the Commissary, pricked by this humiliation, accepted battle on the point of fact. The argument lasted some little while with varying success, until at length victory inclined so plainly to the Commissary's side that the Maire was fain to re-assert himself by an exercise of authority. He had been out-argued, but he was still the Maire. And so, turning from his interlocutor, he briefly but kindly recommended Léon to get back instanter to his concert.

"It is already growing late," he added.

Léon did not wait to be told twice. He returned to the Café of the Triumphs of the Plough with all expedition. Alas! the audience had melted away during his absence; Elvira was sitting in a very disconsolate attitude on the guitar-box; she had watched the company dispersing by twos and threes, and the prolonged spectacle had somewhat overwhelmed her spirits. Each man, she reflected, retired with a certain proportion of her earnings in his pocket, and she saw tonight's board and tomorrow's railway expenses, and finally even tomorrow's dinner, walk one after another out of the café door and disappear into the night.

"What was it?" she asked, languidly.

But Léon did not answer. He was looking round him on the scene of defeat. Scarce a score of listeners remained, and these of the least promising sort. The minute hand of the clock was already climbing upward towards eleven.

"It's a lost battle," said he, and then taking up the money box, he turned it out. "Three francs seventy-five!" he cried, "as against four of board and six of railway fares; and no time for the tombola! Elvira, this is Waterloo." And he sat down and passed both hands desperately among his curls. "O Fichu Commissaire!" he cried, "Fichu Commissaire!"

"Let us get the things together and be off," returned Elvira. "We might try another song, but there is not six halfpence in the room."

"Six halfpence?" cried Léon, "six hundred thousand devils! There is not a human creature in the town—nothing but pigs and dogs and commissaries! Pray heaven, we get safe to bed."

"Don't imagine things!" exclaimed Elvira, with a shudder.

And with that they set to work on their preparations. The tobacco jar, the cigarette holder, the three papers of shirt-studs, which were to have been the prizes of the tombola had the tombola come off, were made into a bundle with the music; the guitar was stowed into the fat guitar case; and Elvira having thrown a thin shawl about her neck and shoulders, the pair issued from the café and set off for the Black Head.

As they crossed the marketplace the church bell rang out eleven. It was a dark, mild night, and there was no one in the streets.

"It is all very fine," said Léon: "but I have a presentiment. The night is not yet done."

CHAPTER III

The "Black Head" presented not a single chink of light upon the street, and the carriage gate was closed.

"This is unprecedented," observed Léon. "An inn closed by five minutes after eleven! And there were several commercial travellers in the café up to a late hour. Elvira, my heart misgives me. Let us ring the bell."

The bell had a potent note; and being swung under the arch it filled the house from top to bottom with surly, clanging reverberations. The sound accentuated the conventual appearance of the building; a wintry sentiment, a thought of prayer and mortification, took hold upon Elvira's mind; and, as for Léon, he seemed to be reading the stage directions for a lugubrious fifth act.

"This is your fault," said Elvira: "this is what comes of fancying things!"

Again Léon pulled the bell rope; again the solemn tocsin awoke the echoes of the inn; and ere they had died away, a light glimmered in the carriage entrance, and a powerful voice was heard upraised and tremulous with wrath.

"What's all this?" cried the tragic host through the spars of the gate. "Hard upon twelve, and you come clamouring like Prussians at the door of a respectable hotel? Oh!" he cried, "I know you now! Common singers! People in trouble with the police! And you present yourselves at midnight like lords and ladies? Be off with you!"

"You will permit me to remind you," replied Léon, in thrilling tones, "that I am a guest in your house, that I am properly inscribed, and that I have deposited baggage to the value of four hundred francs."

"You cannot get in at this hour," returned the man. "This is no thieves' tavern, for mohocks and night rakes and organ-grinders."

"Brute!" cried Elvira, for the organ-grinders touched her home.

"Then I demand my baggage," said Léon, with unabated dignity.

"I know nothing of your baggage," replied the landlord.

"You detain my baggage? You dare to detain my baggage?" cried the singer.

"Who are you?" returned the landlord. "It is dark—I cannot recognise you."

"Very well, then—you detain my baggage," concluded Léon. "You shall smart for this. I will weary out your life with persecutions; I will drag you from court to court; if there is justice to be had in France, it shall be rendered between you and me. And I will make you a by-word—I will put you in a song—a scurrilous song—an indecent song—a popular song—which the boys shall sing to you in the street, and come and howl through these spars at midnight!"

He had gone on raising his voice at every phrase, for all the while the landlord was very placidly retiring; and now, when the last glimmer of light had vanished from the arch, and the last footstep died away in the interior, Léon turned to his wife with a heroic countenance.

"Elvira," said he, "I have now a duty in life. I shall destroy that man as Eugène Sue destroyed the concierge. Let us come at once to the Gendarmerie and begin our vengeance."

He picked up the guitar case, which had been propped against the wall, and they set forth through the silent and ill-lighted town with burning hearts.

The Gendarmerie was concealed beside the telegraph office at the bottom of a vast court, which was partly laid out in gardens; and here all the shepherds of the public lay locked in grateful sleep. It took a deal of knocking to waken one; and he, when he came at last to the door, could find no other remark but that "it was none of his business." Léon reasoned with him, threatened him, besought him; "here," he said, "was Madame Berthelini in evening dress—a delicate woman—in an interesting condition"—the last was thrown in, I fancy, for effect; and to all this the man-at-arms made the same answer:

"It is none of my business," said he.

"Very well," said Léon, "then we shall go to the Commissary." Thither they went; the office was closed and dark; but the house was close by, and Léon was soon swinging the bell like a madman. The Commissary's wife appeared at a window. She was a thread-paper creature, and informed them that the Commissary had not yet come home.

"Is he at the Maire's?" demanded Léon.

She thought that was not unlikely.

"Where is the Maire's house?" he asked.

And she gave him some rather vague information on that point.

"Stay you here, Elvira," said Léon, "lest I should miss him by the way. If, when I return, I find you here no longer, I shall follow at once to the Black Head."

And he set out to find the Maire's. It took him some ten minutes wandering among blind lanes, and when he arrived it was already half an hour past midnight. A long white garden wall overhung by some thick chestnuts, a door with a letter box, and an iron bellpull, that was all that could be seen of the Maire's domicile. Léon took the bellpull in both hands, and danced furiously upon the sidewalk. The bell itself was just upon the other side of the wall, it responded to his activity, and scattered an alarming clangour far and wide into the night.

A window was thrown open in a house across the street, and a voice inquired the cause of this untimely uproar.

"I wish the Maire," said Léon.

"He has been in bed this hour," returned the voice.

"He must get up again," retorted Léon, and he was for tackling the bellpull once more.

"You will never make him hear," responded the voice. "The garden is of great extent, the house is at the farther end, and both the Maire and his housekeeper are deaf."

"Aha!" said Léon, pausing. "The Maire is deaf, is he? That explains." And he thought of the evening's concert with a momentary feeling of relief. "Ah!" he continued, "and so the Maire is deaf, and the garden vast, and the house at the far end?"

"And you might ring all night," added the voice, "and be none the better for it. You would only keep me awake."

"Thank you, neighbour," replied the singer. "You shall sleep."

And he made off again at his best pace for the Commissary's. Elvira was still walking to and fro before the door.

"He has not come?" asked Léon.

"Not he," she replied.

"Good," returned Léon. "I am sure our man's inside. Let me see the guitar case. I shall lay this siege in form, Elvira; I am angry; I am indignant; I am truculently inclined; but I thank my Maker I have still a sense of fun. The unjust judge shall be importuned in a serenade, Elvira. Set him up—and set him up."

He had the case opened by this time, struck a few chords, and fell into an attitude which was irresistibly Spanish.

"Now," he continued, "feel your voice. Are you ready? Follow me!"

The guitar twanged, and the two voices upraised, in harmony and with a startling loudness, the chorus of a song of old Béranger's:—

"Commissaire! Commissaire!
Colin bat sa ménagère."

The stones of Castel-le-Gâchis thrilled at this audacious innovation. Hitherto had the night been sacred to repose and nightcaps; and now what was this? Window after window was opened; matches scratched, and candles began to flicker; swollen sleepy faces peered forth into the starlight. There were the two figures before the Commissary's house, each bolt upright, with head thrown back and eyes interrogating the starry heavens; the guitar wailed, shouted, and reverberated like half an orchestra; and the voices, with a crisp and spirited delivery, hurled the appropriate burden at the Commissary's window. All the echoes repeated the functionary's name. It was more like an entr'acte in a farce of Molière's than a passage of real life in Castel-le-Gâchis.

The Commissary, if he was not the first, was not the last of the neighbours to yield to the influence of music, and furiously throw open the window of his bedroom. He was beside himself with rage. He leaned far over the windowsill, raving and gesticulating; the tassel of his white nightcap danced like a thing of life: he opened his mouth to dimensions hitherto unprecedented, and yet his voice, instead of escaping from it in a roar, came forth shrill and choked and tottering. A little more serenading, and it was clear he would be better acquainted with the apoplexy.

I scorn to reproduce his language; he touched upon too many serious topics by the way for a quiet storyteller. Although he was known for a man who was prompt with his tongue, and had a power of strong expression at command, he excelled himself so remarkably this night that one maiden lady, who had got out of bed like the rest to hear the serenade, was obliged to shut her window at the second clause. Even what she had heard disquieted her conscience; and next day she said she scarcely reckoned as a maiden lady any longer.

Léon tried to explain his predicament, but he received nothing but threats of arrest by way of answer.

"If I come down to you!" cried the Commissary.

"Aye," said Léon, "do!"

"I will not!" cried the Commissary.

"You dare not!" answered Léon.

At that the Commissary closed his window.

"All is over," said the singer. "The serenade was perhaps ill-judged. These boors have no sense of humour."

"Let us get away from here," said Elvira, with a shiver. "All these people looking—it is so rude and so brutal." And then giving way once more to passion—"Brutes!" she cried aloud to the candlelit spectators—"brutes! brutes! brutes!"

"Sauve qui peut," said Léon. "You have done it now!"

And taking the guitar in one hand and the case in the other, he led the way with something too precipitate to be merely called precipitation from the scene of this absurd adventure.

CHAPTER IV

To the west of Castel-le-Gâchis four rows of venerable lime trees formed, in this starry night, a twilit avenue with two side aisles of pitch darkness. Here and there stone benches were disposed between the trunks. There was not a breath of wind; a heavy atmosphere of perfume hung about the alleys; and every leaf stood stock-still upon its twig. Hither, after vainly knocking at an inn or two, the Berthelinis came at length to pass the night. After an amiable contention, Léon insisted on giving his coat to Elvira, and they sat down together on the first bench in silence. Léon made a cigarette, which he smoked to an end, looking up into the trees, and, beyond them, at the constellations, of which he tried vainly to recall the names. The silence was broken by the church bell; it rang the four quarters on a light and tinkling measure; then followed a single deep stroke that died slowly away with a thrill; and stillness resumed its empire.

"One," said Léon. "Four hours till daylight. It is warm; it is starry; I have matches and tobacco. Do not let us exaggerate, Elvira—the experience is positively charming. I feel a glow within me; I am born again. This is the poetry of life. Think of Cooper's novels, my dear."

"Léon," she said, fiercely, "how can you talk such wicked, infamous nonsense? To pass all night out of doors—it is like a nightmare! We shall die."

"You suffer yourself to be led away," he replied, soothingly. "It is not unpleasant here; only you brood. Come, now, let us repeat a scene. Shall we try Alceste and Célimène? No? Or a passage from the 'Two Orphans'? Come, now, it will occupy your mind; I will play up to you as I never have played before; I feel art moving in my bones."

"Hold your tongue," she cried, "or you will drive me mad! Will nothing solemnise you—not even this hideous situation?"

"Oh, hideous!" objected Léon. "Hideous is not the word. Why, where would you be? 'Dites, la jeune belle, où voulez-vous aller?'" he carolled. "Well, now," he went on, opening the guitar case, "there's another idea for you—sing. Sing 'Dites, la jeune belle'! It will compose your spirits, Elvira, I am sure."

And without waiting an answer he began to strum the symphony. The first chords awoke a young man who was lying asleep upon a neighbouring bench.

"Hullo!" cried the young man, "who are you?"

"Under which king, Bezonian?" declaimed the artist. "Speak or die!"

Or if it was not exactly that, it was something to much the same purpose from a French tragedy.

The young man drew near in the twilight. He was a tall, powerful, gentlemanly fellow, with a somewhat puffy face, dressed in a grey tweed suit, with a deerstalker hat of the same material; and as he now came forward he carried a knapsack slung upon one arm.

"Are you camping out here too?" he asked, with a strong English accent. "I'm not sorry for company."

Léon explained their misadventure; and the other told them that he was a Cambridge undergraduate on a walking tour, that he had run short of money, could no longer pay for his night's lodging, had already been camping out for two nights, and feared he should require to continue the same manœuvre for at least two nights more.

"Luckily, it's jolly weather," he concluded.

"You hear that, Elvira," said Léon. "Madame Berthelini," he went on, "is ridiculously affected by this trifling occurrence. For my part, I find it romantic and far from uncomfortable; or at least," he added, shifting on the stone bench, "not quite so uncomfortable as might have been expected. But pray be seated."

"Yes," returned the undergraduate, sitting down, "it's rather nice than otherwise when once you're used to it; only it's devilish difficult to get washed. I like the fresh air and these stars and things."

"Aha!" said Léon, "Monsieur is an artist."

"An artist?" returned the other, with a blank stare. "Not if I know it!"

"Pardon me," said the actor. "What you said this moment about the orbs of heaven——"

"Oh, nonsense!" cried the Englishman. "A fellow may admire the stars and be anything he likes."

"You have an artist's nature, however, Mr.—— I beg your pardon; may I, without indiscretion, inquire your name?" asked Léon.

"My name is Stubbs," replied the Englishman.

"I thank you," returned Léon. "Mine is Berthelini—Léon Berthelini, ex-artist of the theatres of Montrouge, Belleville, and Montmartre. Humble as you see me, I have created with applause more than one important *rôle*. The Press were unanimous in praise of my Howling Devil of the Mountains, in the piece of the same name. Madame, whom I now present to you, is herself an artist, and I must not omit to state, a better artist than her husband. She also is a creator; she created nearly twenty successful songs at one of the principal Parisian music-halls. But, to continue, I was saying you had an artist's nature, Monsieur Stubbs, and you must permit me to be a judge in such a question. I trust you will not falsify your instincts; let me beseech you to follow the career of an artist."

"Thank you," returned Stubbs, with a chuckle. "I'm going to be a banker."

"No," said Léon, "do not say so. Not that. A man with such a nature as yours should not derogate so far. What are a few privations here and there, so long as you are working for a high and noble goal?"

"This fellow's mad," thought Stubbs; "but the woman's rather pretty, and he's not bad fun himself, if you come to that." What he said was different. "I thought you said you were an actor?"

"I certainly did so," replied Léon. "I am one, or, alas! I was."

"And so you want me to be an actor, do you?" continued the undergraduate. "Why, man, I could never so much as learn the stuff; my memory's like a sieve; and as for acting, I've no more idea than a cat."

"The stage is not the only course," said Léon. "Be a sculptor, be a dancer, be a poet or a novelist; follow your heart, in short, and do some thorough work before you die."

"And do you call all these things *art?*" inquired Stubbs.

"Why, certainly!" returned Léon. "Are they not all branches?"

"Oh! I didn't know," replied the Englishman. "I thought an artist meant a fellow who painted."

The singer stared at him in some surprise.

"It is the difference of language," he said at last. "This Tower of Babel, when shall we have paid for it? If I could speak English you would follow me more readily."

"Between you and me, I don't believe I should," replied the other. "You seem to have thought a devil of a lot about this business. For my part, I admire the stars, and like to have them shining—it's so cheery—but hang me if I had an idea it had anything to do with art! It's not in my line, you see. I'm not intellectual; I have no end of trouble to scrape through my exams., I can tell you! But I'm not a bad sort at bottom," he added, seeing his interlocutor looked distressed even in the dim starshine, "and I rather like the play, and music, and guitars, and things."

Léon had a perception that the understanding was incomplete. He changed the subject.

"And so you travel on foot?" he continued. "How romantic! How courageous! And how are you pleased with my land? How does the scenery affect you among these wild hills of ours?"

"Well, the fact is," began Stubbs—he was about to say that he didn't care for scenery, which was not at all true, being, on the contrary, only an athletic undergraduate pretension; but he had begun to suspect that Berthelini liked a different sort of meat, and substituted something else—"The fact is, I think it jolly. They told me it was no good up here; even the guidebook said so; but I don't know what they meant. I think it is deuced pretty—upon my word, I do."

At this moment, in the most unexpected manner, Elvira burst into tears.

"My voice!" she cried. "Léon, if I stay here longer I shall lose my voice!"

"You shall not stay another moment," cried the actor. "If I have to beat in a door, if I have to burn the town, I shall find you shelter."

With that, he replaced the guitar, and comforting her with some caresses, drew her arm through his.

"Monsieur Stubbs," said he, taking off his hat, "the reception I offer you is rather problematical; but let me beseech you to give us the pleasure of your society. You are a little embarrassed for the moment; you must, indeed, permit me to advance what may be necessary. I ask it as a favour; we must not part so soon after having met so strangely."

"Oh, come, you know," said Stubbs, "I can't let a fellow like you——" And there he paused, feeling somehow or other on a wrong tack.

"I do not wish to employ menaces," continued Léon, with a smile; "but if you refuse, indeed I shall not take it kindly."

"I don't quite see my way out of it," thought the undergraduate; and then, after a pause, he said, aloud and ungraciously enough, "All right. I—I'm very much obliged, of course." And he proceeded to follow them, thinking in his heart, "But it's bad form, all the same, to force an obligation on a fellow."

Chapter V

Léon strode ahead as if he knew exactly where he was going; the sobs of Madame were still faintly audible, and no one uttered a word. A dog barked furiously in a courtyard as they went by; then the church clock struck two, and many domestic clocks followed or preceded it in piping tones. And just then Berthelini spied a light. It burned in a small house on the outskirts of the town, and thither the party now directed their steps.

"It is always a chance," said Léon.

The house in question stood back from the street behind an open space, part garden, part turnip field; and several outhouses stood forward from either wing at right angles to the front. One of these had recently undergone some change. An enormous window, looking towards the north, had been effected in the wall and roof, and Léon began to hope it was a studio.

"If it's only a painter," he said, with a chuckle, "ten to one we get as good a welcome as we want."

"I thought painters were principally poor," said Stubbs.

"Ah!" cried Léon, "you do not know the world as I do. The poorer the better for us!"

And the trio advanced into the turnip field.

The light was in the ground floor; as one window was brightly illuminated and two others more faintly, it might be supposed that there was a single lamp in one corner of a large apartment; and a certain tremulousness and temporary dwindling showed that a live fire contributed to the effect. The sound of a voice now became audible; and the trespassers paused to listen. It was pitched in a high, angry key, but had still a good, full, and masculine note in it. The utterance was voluble, too voluble even to be quite distinct; a stream of words, rising and falling, with ever and again a phrase thrown out by itself, as if the speaker reckoned on its virtue.

Suddenly another voice joined in. This time it was a woman's; and if the man were angry, the woman was incensed to the degree of fury. There was that absolutely blank composure known to suffering males; that colourless unnatural speech which shows a spirit accurately balanced between homicide and hysterics; the tone in which the best of women sometimes utter words worse than death to those most dear to them. If Abstract Bones-and-Sepulchre were to be endowed with the gift of speech, thus, and not otherwise, would it discourse. Léon was a brave man, and I fear he was somewhat sceptically given (he had been educated in a Papistical country), but the habit of childhood prevailed, and he crossed himself devoutly. He had met several women in his career. It was obvious that his instinct had not deceived him, for the male voice broke forth instantly in a towering passion.

The undergraduate, who had not understood the significance of the woman's contribution, pricked up his ears at the change upon the man.

"There's going to be a free fight," he opined.

There was another retort from the woman, still calm but a little higher.

"Hysterics?" asked Léon of his wife. "Is that the stage direction?"

"How should I know?" returned Elvira, somewhat tartly.

"Oh, woman, woman!" said Léon, beginning to open the guitar case. "It is one of the burdens of my life, Monsieur Stubbs; they support each other; they always pretend there is no system; they say it's nature. Even Madame Berthelini, who is a dramatic artist!"

"You are heartless, Léon," said Elvira; "that woman is in trouble."

"And the man, my angel?" inquired Berthelini, passing the ribbon of his guitar. "And the man, *m'amour?*"

"He is a man," she answered.

"You hear that?" said Léon to Stubbs. "It is not too late for you. Mark the intonation. And now," he continued, "what are we to give them?"

"Are you going to sing?" asked Stubbs.

"I am a troubadour," replied Léon. "I claim a welcome by and for my art. If I were a banker could I do as much?"

"Well, you wouldn't need, you know," answered the undergraduate.

"Egad," said Léon, "but that's true. Elvira, that is true."

"Of course it is," she replied. "Did you not know it?"

"My dear," answered Léon, impressively, "I know nothing but what is agreeable. Even my knowledge of life is a work of art superiorly composed. But what are we to give them? It should be something appropriate."

Visions of "Let dogs delight" passed through the undergraduate's mind; but it occurred to him that the poetry was English and that he did not know the air. Hence he contributed no suggestion.

"Something about our houselessness," said Elvira.

"I have it," cried Léon. And he broke forth into a song of Pierre Dupont's:—

Savez-vous où gite
Mai, ce joli mois?

Elvira joined in; so did Stubbs, with a good ear and voice, but an imperfect acquaintance with the music. Léon and the guitar were equal to the situation. The actor dispensed his throat-notes with prodigality and enthusiasm; and, as he looked up to heaven in his heroic way, tossing the black ringlets, it seemed to him that the very stars contributed a dumb applause to his efforts, and the universe lent him its silence for a chorus. That is one of the best features of the heavenly bodies, that they belong to everybody in particular; and a man like Léon, a chronic Endymion who managed to get along without encouragement, is always the world's centre for himself.

He alone—and it is to be noted, he was the worst singer of the three—took the music seriously to heart, and judged the serenade from a high artistic point of view. Elvira, on the other hand, was preoccupied about their reception; and, as for Stubbs, he considered the whole affair in the light of a broad joke.

"Know you the lair of May, the lovely month?" went the three voices in the turnip field.

The inhabitants were plainly fluttered; the light moved to and fro, strengthening in one window, paling in another; and then the door was thrown open, and a man in a blouse appeared on the threshold carrying a lamp. He was a powerful young fellow, with bewildered hair and beard, wearing his neck open; his blouse was stained with oil colours in a harlequinesque disorder; and there was something rural in the droop and bagginess of his belted trousers.

From immediately behind him, and indeed over his shoulder, a woman's face looked out into the darkness; it was pale and a little weary, although still young; it wore a dwindling, disappearing prettiness, soon to be quite gone, and the expression was both gentle and sour, and reminded one faintly of the taste of certain drugs. For all that, it was not a face to dislike; when the prettiness had vanished, it seemed as if a certain pale beauty might step in to take its place; and as both the mildness and the asperity were characters of youth, it might be hoped that, with years, both would merge into a constant, brave, and not unkindly temper.

"What is all this?" cried the man.

CHAPTER VI

Léon had his hat in his hand at once. He came forward with his customary grace; it was a moment which would have earned him a round of cheering on the stage. Elvira and Stubbs advanced behind him, like a couple of Admetus's sheep following the god Apollo.

"Sir," said Léon, "the hour is unpardonably late, and our little serenade has the air of an impertinence. Believe me, sir, it is an appeal. Monsieur is an artist, I perceive. We are here three artists benighted and without shelter, one a woman—a delicate woman—in evening dress—in an interesting situation. This will not fail to touch the woman's heart of Madame, whom I perceive indistinctly behind Monsieur her husband, and whose face speaks eloquently of a well-regulated mind. Ah! Monsieur, Madame—one generous movement, and you make three people happy! Two or three hours beside your fire—I ask it of Monsieur in the name of Art—I ask it of Madame by the sanctity of womanhood."

The two, as by a tacit consent, drew back from the door.

"Come in," said the man.

"Entrez, Madame," said the woman.

The door opened directly upon the kitchen of the house, which was to all appearance the only sitting room. The furniture was both plain and scanty; but there were one or two landscapes on the wall handsomely framed, as if they had already visited the committee rooms of an exhibition and been thence extruded. Léon walked up to the pictures and represented the part of a connoisseur before each in turn, with his usual dramatic insight and force. The master of the house, as if irresistibly attracted, followed him from canvas to canvas with the lamp. Elvira was led directly to the fire, where she proceeded to warm herself, while Stubbs stood in the middle of the floor and followed the proceedings of Léon with mild astonishment in his eyes.

"You should see them by daylight," said the artist.

"I promise myself that pleasure," said Léon. "You possess, sir, if you will permit me an observation, the art of composition to a T."

"You are very good," returned the other. "But should you not draw nearer to the fire?"

"With all my heart," said Léon.

And the whole party was soon gathered at the table over a hasty and not an elegant cold supper, washed down with the least of small wines.

Nobody liked the meal, but nobody complained; they put a good face upon it, one and all, and made a great clattering of knives and forks. To see Léon eating a single cold sausage was to see a triumph; by the time he had done he had got through as much pantomime as would have sufficed for a baron of beef, and he had the relaxed expression of the overeaten.

As Elvira had naturally taken a place by the side of Léon, and Stubbs as naturally, although I believe unconsciously, by the side of Elvira, the host and hostess were left together. Yet it was to be noted that they never addressed a word to each other, nor so much as suffered their eyes to meet. The interrupted skirmish still survived in ill-feeling; and the instant the guests departed it would break forth again as bitterly as ever. The talk wandered from this to that subject—for with one accord the party had declared it was too late to go to bed; but those two never relaxed towards each other; Goneril and Regan in a sisterly tiff were not more bent on enmity.

It chanced that Elvira was so much tired by all the little excitements of the night, that for once she laid aside her company manners, which were both easy and correct, and in the most natural manner in the world leaned her head on Léon's shoulder. At the same time, fatigue suggesting tenderness, she locked the fingers of her right hand into those of her husband's left; and, half-closing her eyes, dozed off into a golden borderland between sleep and waking. But all the time she was not aware of what was passing, and saw the painter's wife studying her with looks between contempt and envy.

It occurred to Léon that his constitution demanded the use of some tobacco; and he undid his fingers from Elvira's in order to roll a cigarette. It was gently done, and he took care that his indulgence should in no other way disturb his wife's position. But it seemed to catch the eye of the painter's wife with a special significancy. She looked straight before her for an instant, and then, with a swift and stealthy movement, took hold of her husband's hand below the table. Alas! she might have spared herself the dexterity. For the poor fellow was so overcome by this caress that he stopped with his mouth open in the middle of a word, and by the expression of his face plainly declared to all the company that his thoughts had been diverted into softer channels.

If it had not been rather amiable, it would have been absurdly droll. His wife at once withdrew her touch; but it was plain she had to exert some force. Thereupon the young man coloured and looked for a moment beautiful.

Léon and Elvira both observed the byplay, and a shock passed from one to the other; for they were inveterate matchmakers, especially between those who were already married.

"I beg your pardon," said Léon, suddenly. "I see no use in pretending. Before we came in here we heard sounds indicating—if I may so express myself—an imperfect harmony."

"Sir——" began the man.

But the woman was beforehand.

"It is quite true," she said. "I see no cause to be ashamed. If my husband is mad I shall at least do my utmost to prevent the consequences. Picture to yourself, Monsieur and Madame," she went on, for she passed Stubbs over, "that this wretched person—a dauber, an incompetent, not fit to be a sign painter—receives this morning an admirable offer from an uncle—an uncle of my own, my mother's brother, and tenderly beloved—of a clerkship with nearly a hundred and fifty pounds a year, and that he—picture to yourself!—he refuses it! Why? For the sake of Art, he says. Look at his art, I say—look at it! Is it fit to be seen? Ask him—is it fit to be sold? And it is for this, Monsieur and Madame, that he condemns me to the most deplorable existence, without luxuries, without comforts, in a vile suburb of a country town. O non!" she cried, "non—je ne me tairai pas—c'est plus fort que moi! I take these gentlemen and this lady for judges—is this kind? is it decent? is it manly? Do I not deserve better at his hands after having married him and"—(a visible hitch)—"done everything in the world to please him."

I doubt if there were ever a more embarrassed company at a table; everyone looked like a fool; and the husband like the biggest.

"The art of Monsieur, however," said Elvira, breaking the silence, "is not wanting in distinction."

"It has this distinction," said the wife, "that nobody will buy it."

"I should have supposed a clerkship——" began Stubbs.

"Art is Art," swept in Léon. "I salute Art. It is the beautiful, the divine; it is the spirit of the world, and the pride of life. But——" And the actor paused.

"A clerkship——" began Stubbs.

"I'll tell you what it is," said the painter. "I am an artist, and as this gentleman says, Art is this and the other; but of course, if my wife is going to make my life a piece of perdition all day long, I prefer to go and drown myself out of hand."

"Go!" said his wife. "I should like to see you!"

"I was going to say," resumed Stubbs, "that a fellow may be a clerk and paint almost as much as he likes. I know a fellow in a bank who makes capital watercolour sketches; he even sold one for seven-and-six."

To both the women this seemed a plank of safety; each hopefully interrogated the countenance of her lord; even Elvira, an artist herself!—but indeed there must be something permanently mercantile in the female nature. The two men exchanged a glance; it was tragic; not otherwise might two philosophers salute, as at the end of a laborious life each recognised that he was still a mystery to his disciples.

Léon arose.

"Art is Art," he repeated, sadly. "It is not watercolour sketches, nor practising on a piano. It is a life to be lived."

"And in the meantime people starve!" observed the woman of the house. "If that's a life, it is not one for me."

"I'll tell you what," burst forth Léon; "you, Madame, go into another room and talk it over with my wife; and I'll stay here and talk it over with your husband. It may come to nothing, but let's try."

"I am very willing," replied the young woman; and she proceeded to light a candle. "This way if you please." And she led Elvira upstairs into a bedroom. "The fact is," said she, sitting down, "that my husband cannot paint."

"No more can mine act," replied Elvira.

"I should have thought he could," returned the other; "he seems clever."

"He is so, and the best of men besides," said Elvira; "but he cannot act."

"At least he is not a sheer humbug like mine; he can at least sing."

"You mistake Léon," returned his wife, warmly. "He does not even pretend to sing; he has too fine a taste; he does so for a living. And, believe me, neither of the men are humbugs. They are people with a mission—which they cannot carry out."

"Humbug or not," replied the other, "you came very near passing the night in the fields; and, for my part, I live in terror of starvation. I should think it was a man's mission to think twice about his wife. But it appears not. Nothing is their mission but to play the fool. Oh!" she broke out, "is it not something dreary to think of that man of mine? If he could only do it, who would care? But no—not he—no more than I can!"

"Have you any children?" asked Elvira.

"No; but then I may."

"Children change so much," said Elvira, with a sigh.

And just then from the room below there flew up a sudden snapping chord on the guitar; one followed after another; then the voice of Léon joined in; and there was an air being played and sung that stopped the speech of the two women. The wife of the painter stood like a person transfixed; Elvira, looking into her eyes, could see all manner of beautiful memories and kind thoughts that were passing in and out of her soul with every note; it was a piece of her youth that went before her; a green French plain, the smell of apple flowers, the far and shining ringlets of a river, and the words and presence of love.

"Léon has hit the nail," thought Elvira to herself. "I wonder how."

The how was plain enough. Léon had asked the painter if there were no air connected with courtship and pleasant times; and having learnt what he wished, and allowed an interval to pass, he had soared forth into

> O mon amante,
> O mon désir,
> Sachons cueillir
> L'heure charmante!

"Pardon me, Madame," said the painter's wife, "your husband sings admirably well."

"He sings that with some feeling," replied Elvira, critically, although she was a little moved herself, for the song cut both ways in the upper chamber; "but it is as an actor and not as a musician."

"Life is very sad," said the other; "it so wastes away under one's fingers."

"I have not found it so," replied Elvira. "I think the good parts of it last and grow greater every day."

"Frankly, how would you advise me?"

"Frankly, I would let my husband do what he wished. He is obviously a very loving painter; you have not yet tried him as a clerk. And you know—if it were only as the possible father of your children—it is as well to keep him at his best."

"He is an excellent fellow," said the wife.

———

They kept it up till sunrise with music and all manner of good fellow-ship; and at sunrise, while the sky was still temperate and clear, they separated on the threshold with a thousand excellent wishes for each other's welfare. Castel-le-Gâchis was beginning to send up its smoke against the golden East; and the church bell was ringing six.

"My guitar is a familiar spirit," said Léon, as he and Elvira took the nearest way towards the inn; "it resuscitated a Commissary, created an English tourist, and reconciled a man and wife."

Stubbs, on his part, went off into the morning with reflections of his own.

"They are all mad," thought he, "all mad—but wonderfully decent."

STRANGE CASE OF DR. JEKYLL AND MR. HYDE

Contents

STORY OF THE DOOR

Mr. Utterson the lawyer was a man of a rugged countenance, that was never lighted by a smile; cold, scanty and embarrassed in discourse; backward in sentiment; lean, long, dusty, dreary and yet somehow lovable. At friendly meetings, and when the wine was to his taste, something eminently human beaconed from his eye; something indeed which never found its way into his talk, but which spoke not only in these silent symbols of the after-dinner face, but more often and loudly in the acts of his life. He was austere with himself; drank gin when he was alone, to mortify a taste for vintages; and though he enjoyed the theatre, had not crossed the doors of one for twenty years. But he had an approved tolerance for others; sometimes wondering, almost with envy, at the high pressure of spirits involved in their misdeeds; and in any extremity inclined to help rather than to reprove. "I incline to Cain's heresy," he used to say quaintly: "I let my brother go to the devil in his own way." In this character, it was frequently his fortune to be the last reputable acquaintance and the last good influence in the lives of down-going men. And to such as these, so long as they came about his chambers, he never marked a shade of change in his demeanour.

No doubt the feat was easy to Mr. Utterson; for he was undemonstrative at the best, and even his friendships seemed to be founded in a similar catholicity of good-nature. It is the mark of a modest man to accept his friendly circle readymade from the hands of opportunity; and that was the lawyer's way. His friends were those of his own blood or those whom he had known the longest; his affections, like ivy, were the growth of time, they implied no aptness in the object. Hence, no doubt, the bond that united him to Mr. Richard Enfield, his distant kinsman, the well-known man about town. It was a nut to crack for many, what these two could see in each other or what subject they could find in common. It was reported by those who encountered them in their Sunday walks, that they said nothing, looked singularly dull, and would hail with obvious relief the appearance of a friend. For all that, the two men put the greatest store by these excursions, counted them the chief jewel of each week, and not only set aside occasions of pleasure, but even resisted the calls of business, that they might enjoy them uninterrupted.

It chanced on one of these rambles that their way led them down a by-street in a busy quarter of London. The street was small and what is called quiet, but it drove a thriving trade on the week-days. The inhabitants were all doing well, it seemed, and all emulously hoping to do better still, and laying out the surplus of their gains in coquetry; so that the shop fronts stood along that thoroughfare with an air of invitation, like rows of smiling saleswomen. Even on Sunday, when it veiled its more florid charms and lay comparatively empty of passage, the street shone out in contrast to its dingy neighbourhood, like a fire in a forest; and with its freshly painted shutters, well-polished brasses, and general cleanliness and gaiety of note, instantly caught and pleased the eye of the passenger.

Two doors from one corner, on the left hand going east, the line was broken by the entry of a court; and just at that point, a certain sinister block of building thrust forward its gable on the street. It was two storeys high; showed no window, nothing but a door on the lower storey and a blind forehead of discoloured wall on the upper; and bore in every feature, the marks of prolonged and sordid negligence. The door, which was equipped with neither bell nor knocker, was blistered and distained. Tramps slouched into the recess and struck matches on the panels; children kept shop upon the steps; the schoolboy had tried his knife on the mouldings; and for close on a generation, no one had appeared to drive away these random visitors or to repair their ravages.

Mr. Enfield and the lawyer were on the other side of the by-street;

but when they came abreast of the entry, the former lifted up his cane and pointed.

"Did you ever remark that door?" he asked; and when his companion had replied in the affirmative, "It is connected in my mind," added he, "with a very odd story."

"Indeed?" said Mr. Utterson, with a slight change of voice, "and what was that?"

"Well, it was this way," returned Mr. Enfield: "I was coming home from some place at the end of the world, about three o'clock of a black winter morning, and my way lay through a part of town where there was literally nothing to be seen but lamps. Street after street, and all the folks asleep—street after street, all lighted up as if for a procession and all as empty as a church—till at last I got into that state of mind when a man listens and listens and begins to long for the sight of a policeman. All at once, I saw two figures: one a little man who was stumping along eastward at a good walk, and the other a girl of maybe eight or ten who was running as hard as she was able down a cross street. Well, sir, the two ran into one another naturally enough at the corner; and then came the horrible part of the thing; for the man trampled calmly over the child's body and left her screaming on the ground. It sounds nothing to hear, but it was hellish to see. It wasn't like a man; it was like some damned Juggernaut. I gave a view halloa, took to my heels, collared my gentleman, and brought him back to where there was already quite a group about the screaming child. He was perfectly cool and made no resistance, but gave me one look, so ugly that it brought out the sweat on me like running. The people who had turned out were the girl's own family; and pretty soon, the doctor, for whom she had been sent, put in his appearance. Well, the child was not much the worse, more frightened, according to the Sawbones; and there you might have supposed would be an end to it. But there was one curious circumstance. I had taken a loathing to my gentleman at first sight. So had the child's family, which was only natural. But the doctor's case was what struck me. He was the usual cut and dry apothecary, of no particular age and colour, with a strong Edinburgh accent, and about as emotional as a bagpipe. Well, sir, he was like the rest of us; every time he looked at my prisoner, I saw that Sawbones turn sick and white with the desire to kill him. I knew what was in his mind, just as he knew what was in mine; and killing being out of the question, we did the next best. We told the man we could and would make such a scandal out of this, as should make his name stink from one end of London to the other. If he had any friends or any credit, we undertook that he should lose them. And all the time, as we were pitching it in red hot, we were keeping the women off him as best we could, for they were as wild as harpies. I never saw a circle of such hateful faces; and there was the man in the middle, with a kind of black, sneering coolness—frightened too, I could see that—but carrying it off, sir, really like Satan. 'If you choose to make capital out of this accident,' said he, 'I am naturally helpless. No gentleman but wishes to avoid a scene,' says he. 'Name your figure.' Well, we screwed him up to a hundred pounds for the child's family; he would have clearly liked to stick out; but there was something about the lot of us that meant mischief, and at last he struck. The next thing was to get the money; and where do you think he carried us but to that place with the door?—whipped out a key, went in, and presently came back with the matter of ten pounds in gold and a cheque for the balance on Coutts's, drawn payable to bearer and signed with a name that I can't mention, though it's one of the points of my story, but it was a name at least very well known and often printed. The figure was stiff; but the signature was good for more than that, if it was only genuine. I took the liberty of pointing out to my gentleman that the whole business looked apocryphal, and that a man does not, in real life, walk into a cellar door at four in the morning and come out of it with another man's cheque for close upon a hundred pounds. But he was quite easy and sneering. 'Set your mind at rest,' says he, 'I will stay with you till the banks open and cash the cheque myself.' So we all set off, the doctor, and the child's father, and our friend and myself, and passed the rest of the night in my chambers; and next day, when we had breakfasted, went in a body to the bank. I gave in the cheque myself, and said I had every reason to believe it was a forgery. Not a bit of it. The cheque was genuine."

"Tut-tut," said Mr. Utterson.

"I see you feel as I do," said Mr. Enfield. "Yes, it's a bad story. For my man was a fellow that nobody could have to do with, a really damnable man; and the person that drew the cheque is the very pink of the proprieties, celebrated too, and (what makes it worse) one of your fellows who do what they call good. Black mail, I suppose; an honest man paying through the nose for some of the capers of his youth. Black mail

House is what I call that place with the door, in consequence. Though even that, you know, is far from explaining all," he added, and with the words fell into a vein of musing.

From this he was recalled by Mr. Utterson asking rather suddenly: "And you don't know if the drawer of the cheque lives there?"

"A likely place isn't it?" returned Mr. Enfield. "But I happen to have noticed his address; he lives in some square or other."

"And you never asked about—the place with the door?" said Mr. Utterson.

"No, sir: I had a delicacy," was the reply. "I feel very strongly about putting questions; it partakes too much of the style of the day of judgment. You start a question, and it's like starting a stone. You sit quietly on the top of a hill; and away the stone goes, starting others; and presently some bland old bird (the last you would have thought of) is knocked on the head in his own back garden and the family have to change their name. No, sir, I make it a rule of mine: the more it looks like Queer Street, the less I ask."

"A very good rule, too," said the lawyer.

"But I have studied the place for myself," continued Mr. Enfield. "It seems scarcely a house. There is no other door, and nobody goes in or out of that one but, once in a great while, the gentleman of my adventure. There are three windows looking on the court on the first floor; none below; the windows are always shut but they're clean. And then there is a chimney which is generally smoking; so somebody must live there. And yet it's not so sure; for the buildings are so packed together about that court, that it's hard to say where one ends and another begins."

The pair walked on again for a while in silence; and then "Enfield," said Mr. Utterson, "that's a good rule of yours."

"Yes, I think it is," returned Enfield.

"But for all that," continued the lawyer, "there's one point I want to ask: I want to ask the name of that man who walked over the child."

"Well," said Mr. Enfield, "I can't see what harm it would do. It was a man of the name of Hyde."

"Hm," said Mr. Utterson. "What sort of a man is he to see?"

"He is not easy to describe. There is something wrong with his appearance; something displeasing, something downright detestable. I never saw a man I so disliked, and yet I scarce know why. He must be deformed somewhere; he gives a strong feeling of deformity, although I couldn't specify the point. He's an extraordinary looking man, and yet I really can name nothing out of the way. No, sir; I can make no hand of it; I can't describe him. And it's not want of memory; for I declare I can see him this moment."

Mr. Utterson again walked some way in silence and obviously under a weight of consideration. "You are sure he used a key?" he inquired at last.

"My dear sir..." began Enfield, surprised out of himself.

"Yes, I know," said Utterson; "I know it must seem strange. The fact is, if I do not ask you the name of the other party, it is because I know it already. You see, Richard, your tale has gone home. If you have been inexact in any point, you had better correct it."

"I think you might have warned me," returned the other with a touch of sullenness. "But I have been pedantically exact, as you call it. The fellow had a key; and what's more, he has it still. I saw him use it, not a week ago."

Mr. Utterson sighed deeply but said never a word; and the young man presently resumed. "Here is another lesson to say nothing," said he. "I am ashamed of my long tongue. Let us make a bargain never to refer to this again."

"With all my heart," said the lawyer. "I shake hands on that, Richard."

SEARCH FOR MR. HYDE

That evening, Mr. Utterson came home to his bachelor house in sombre spirits and sat down to dinner without relish. It was his custom of
a Sunday, when this meal was over, to sit close by the fire, a volume of
some dry divinity on his reading desk, until the clock of the neighbouring church rang out the hour of twelve, when he would go soberly
and gratefully to bed. On this night, however, as soon as the cloth was
taken away, he took up a candle and went into his business room.
There he opened his safe, took from the most private part of it a document endorsed on the envelope as Dr. Jekyll's Will, and sat down with
a clouded brow to study its contents. The will was holograph, for Mr.
Utterson, though he took charge of it now that it was made, had refused to lend the least assistance in the making of it; it provided not
only that, in case of the decease of Henry Jekyll, M.D., D.C.L., LL.D.,
F.R.S., &c., all his possessions were to pass into the hands of his "friend
and benefactor Edward Hyde," but that in case of Dr. Jekyll's "disappearance or unexplained absence for any period exceeding three calendar months," the said Edward Hyde should step into the said Henry
Jekyll's shoes without further delay and free from any burthen or
obligation, beyond the payment of a few small sums to the members of
the doctor's household. This document had long been the lawyer's
eyesore. It offended him both as a lawyer and as a lover of the sane and
customary sides of life, to whom the fanciful was the immodest. And

hitherto it was his ignorance of Mr. Hyde that had swelled his indignation; now, by a sudden turn, it was his knowledge. It was already bad enough when the name was but a name of which he could learn no more. It was worse when it began to be clothed upon with detestable attributes; and out of the shifting, insubstantial mists that had so long baffled his eye, there leaped up the sudden, definite presentment of a fiend.

"I thought it was madness," he said, as he replaced the obnoxious paper in the safe, "and now I begin to fear it is disgrace."

With that he blew out his candle, put on a great coat and set forth in the direction of Cavendish Square, that citadel of medicine, where his friend, the great Dr. Lanyon, had his house and received his crowding patients. "If anyone knows, it will be Lanyon," he had thought.

The solemn butler knew and welcomed him; he was subjected to no stage of delay, but ushered direct from the door to the dining room where Dr. Lanyon sat alone over his wine. This was a hearty, healthy, dapper, red-faced gentleman, with a shock of hair prematurely white, and a boisterous and decided manner. At sight of Mr. Utterson, he sprang up from his chair and welcomed him with both hands. The geniality, as was the way of the man, was somewhat theatrical to the eye; but it reposed on genuine feeling. For these two were old friends, old mates both at school and college, both thorough respecters of themselves and of each other, and, what does not always follow, men who thoroughly enjoyed each other's company.

After a little rambling talk, the lawyer led up to the subject which so disagreeably preoccupied his mind.

"I suppose, Lanyon," said he, "you and I must be the two oldest friends that Henry Jekyll has?"

"I wish the friends were younger," chuckled Dr. Lanyon. "But I suppose we are. And what of that? I see little of him now."

"Indeed?" said Utterson. "I thought you had a bond of common interest."

"We had," was the reply. "But it is more than ten years since Henry Jekyll became too fanciful for me. He began to go wrong, wrong in mind; and though of course I continue to take an interest in him for old sake's sake as they say, I see and I have seen devilish little of the man. Such unscientific balderdash," added the doctor, flushing suddenly purple, "would have estranged Damon and Pythias."

This little spirt of temper was somewhat of a relief to Mr. Utterson. "They have only differed on some point of science," he thought; and being a man of no scientific passions (except in the matter of conveyancing) he even added: "It is nothing worse than that!" He gave his friend a few seconds to recover his composure, and then approached the question he had come to put. "Did you ever come across a protégé of his—one Hyde?" he asked.

"Hyde?" repeated Lanyon. "No. Never heard of him. Since my time."

That was the amount of information that the lawyer carried back with him to the great, dark bed on which he tossed to and fro, until the small hours of the morning began to grow large. It was a night of little ease to his toiling mind, toiling in mere darkness and besieged by questions.

Six o'clock struck on the bells of the church that was so conveniently near to Mr. Utterson's dwelling, and still he was digging at the problem. Hitherto it had touched him on the intellectual side alone; but now his imagination also was engaged or rather enslaved; and as he lay and tossed in the gross darkness of the night and the curtained room, Mr. Enfield's tale went by before his mind in a scroll of lighted pictures. He would be aware of the great field of lamps of a nocturnal city; then of the figure of a man walking swiftly; then of a child running from the doctor's; and then these met, and that human Juggernaut trod the child down and passed on regardless of her screams. Or else he would see a room in a rich house, where his friend lay asleep, dreaming and smiling at his dreams; and then the door of that room would be opened, the curtains of the bed plucked apart, the sleeper recalled, and lo! there would stand by his side a figure to whom power was given, and even at that dead hour, he must rise and do its bidding. The figure in these two phases haunted the lawyer all night; and if at any time he dozed over, it was but to see it glide more stealthily through sleeping houses, or move the more swiftly and still the more swiftly, even to dizziness, through wider labyrinths of lamplighted city, and at every street corner crush a child and leave her screaming. And still the figure had no face by which he might know it; even in his dreams, it had no face, or one that baffled him and melted before his eyes; and thus it was that there sprang up and grew apace in the lawyer's mind a singularly strong, almost an inordinate, curiosity to behold the features of the real Mr. Hyde. If he could but once set eyes on him, he thought the mystery would lighten and perhaps roll altogether away, as was the habit of mysterious things when well examined. He might see a reason for his friend's strange preference or bondage (call it which you please) and even for the startling clauses of the will. And at least it would be a face worth seeing: the face of a man who was without bowels of mercy: a face which had but to show itself to raise up, in the mind of the unimpressionable Enfield, a spirit of enduring hatred.

From that time forward, Mr. Utterson began to haunt the door in the bystreet of shops. In the morning before office hours, at noon when business was plenty and time scarce, at night under the face of the fogged city moon, by all lights and at all hours of solitude or concourse, the lawyer was to be found on his chosen post.

"If he be Mr. Hyde," he had thought, "I shall be Mr. Seek."

And at last his patience was rewarded. It was a fine dry night; frost in the air; the streets as clean as a ballroom floor; the lamps, unshaken by any wind, drawing a regular pattern of light and shadow. By ten o'clock, when the shops were closed, the bystreet was very solitary and, in spite of the low growl of London from all round, very silent. Small sounds carried far; domestic sounds out of the houses were clearly audible on either side of the roadway; and the rumour of the approach of any passenger preceded him by a long time. Mr. Utterson had been some minutes at his post, when he was aware of an odd, light footstep drawing near. In the course of his nightly patrols, he had long grown accustomed to the quaint effect with which the footfalls of a single person, while he is still a great way off, suddenly spring out distinct from the vast hum and clatter of the city. Yet his attention had never before been so sharply and decisively arrested; and it was with a strong, superstitious prevision of success that he withdrew into the entry of the court.

The steps drew swiftly nearer, and swelled out suddenly louder as they turned the end of the street. The lawyer, looking forth from the entry, could soon see what manner of man he had to deal with. He was small and very plainly dressed, and the look of him, even at that distance, went somehow strongly against the watcher's inclination. But he made straight for the door, crossing the roadway to save time; and as he came, he drew a key from his pocket like one approaching home.

Mr. Utterson stepped out and touched him on the shoulder as he passed. "Mr. Hyde, I think?"

Mr. Hyde shrank back with a hissing intake of the breath. But his fear was only momentary; and though he did not look the lawyer in the face, he answered coolly enough: "That is my name. What do you want?"

"I see you are going in," returned the lawyer. "I am an old friend of Dr. Jekyll's—Mr. Utterson of Gaunt Street—you must have heard my name; and meeting you so conveniently, I thought you might admit me."

"You will not find Dr. Jekyll; he is from home," replied Mr. Hyde, blowing in the key. And then suddenly, but still without looking up, "How did you know me?" he asked.

"On your side," said Mr. Utterson, "will you do me a favour?"

"With pleasure," replied the other. "What shall it be?"

"Will you let me see your face?" asked the lawyer.

Mr. Hyde appeared to hesitate, and then, as if upon some sudden reflection, fronted about with an air of defiance; and the pair stared at each other pretty fixedly for a few seconds. "Now I shall know you again," said Mr. Utterson. "It may be useful."

"Yes," returned Mr. Hyde, "it is as well we have met; and *à propos*, you should have my address." And he gave a number of a street in Soho.

"Good God!" thought Mr. Utterson, "can he too have been thinking of the will?" But he kept his feelings to himself and only grunted in acknowledgement of the address.

"And now," said the other, "how did you know me?"

"By description," was the reply.

"Whose description?"

"We have common friends," said Mr. Utterson.

"Common friends?" echoed Mr. Hyde, a little hoarsely. "Who are they?"

"Jekyll, for instance," said the lawyer.

"He never told you," cried Mr. Hyde, with a flush of anger. "I did not think you would have lied."

"Come," said Mr. Utterson, "that is not fitting language."

The other snarled aloud into a savage laugh; and the next moment, with extraordinary quickness, he had unlocked the door and disappeared into the house.

The lawyer stood awhile when Mr. Hyde had left him, the picture of disquietude. Then he began slowly to mount the street, pausing every step or two and putting his hand to his brow like a man in mental perplexity. The problem he was thus debating as he walked, was one of a class that is rarely solved. Mr. Hyde was pale and dwarfish, he gave an impression of deformity without any nameable malformation, he had a displeasing smile, he had borne himself to the lawyer with a sort of murderous mixture of timidity and boldness, and he spoke with a husky, whispering and somewhat broken voice; all these were points against him, but not all of these together could explain the hitherto unknown disgust, loathing and fear with which Mr. Utterson regarded him. "There must be something else," said the perplexed gentleman. "There *is* something more, if I could find a name for it. God bless me, the man seems hardly human! Something troglodytic, shall we say? or can it be the old story of Dr. Fell? or is it the mere radiance of a foul soul that thus transpires through, and transfigures, its clay continent? The last, I think; for O my poor old Harry Jekyll, if ever I read Satan's signature upon a face, it is on that of your new friend."

Round the corner from the bystreet, there was a square of ancient, handsome houses, now for the most part decayed from their high estate and let in flats and chambers to all sorts and conditions of men: map-engravers, architects, shady lawyers and the agents of obscure enterprises. One house, however, second from the corner, was still occupied entire; and at the door of this, which wore a great air of wealth and comfort, though it was now plunged in darkness except for the fan-light, Mr. Utterson stopped and knocked. A well-dressed, elderly servant opened the door.

"Is Dr. Jekyll at home, Poole?" asked the lawyer.

"I will see, Mr. Utterson," said Poole, admitting the visitor, as he spoke, into a large, low-roofed, comfortable hall, paved with flags, warmed (after the fashion of a country house) by a bright, open fire, and furnished with costly cabinets of oak. "Will you wait here by the fire, sir? or shall I give you a light in the dining room?"

"Here, thank you," said the lawyer, and he drew near and leaned on the tall fender. This hall, in which he was now left alone, was a pet fancy of his friend the doctor's; and Utterson himself was wont to speak of it as the pleasantest room in London. But tonight there was a shudder in his blood; the face of Hyde sat heavy on his memory; he felt (what was rare with him) a nausea and distaste of life; and in the gloom of his spirits, he seemed to read a menace in the flickering of the firelight on the polished cabinets and the uneasy starting of the shadow on the roof. He was ashamed of his relief, when Poole presently returned to announce that Dr. Jekyll was gone out.

"I saw Mr. Hyde go in by the old dissecting room door, Poole," he said. "Is that right, when Dr. Jekyll is from home?"

"Quite right, Mr. Utterson, sir," replied the servant. "Mr. Hyde has a key."

"Your master seems to repose a great deal of trust in that young man, Poole," resumed the other musingly.

"Yes, sir, he do indeed," said Poole. "We have all orders to obey him."

"I do not think I ever met Mr. Hyde?" asked Utterson.

"O, dear no, sir. He never *dines* here," replied the butler. "Indeed we see very little of him on this side of the house; he mostly comes and goes by the laboratory."

"Well, good night, Poole."

"Good night, Mr. Utterson."

And the lawyer set out homeward with a very heavy heart. "Poor Harry Jekyll," he thought, "my mind misgives me he is in deep waters! He was wild when he was young; a long while ago to be sure; but in the law of God, there is no statute of limitations. Ay, it must be that; the ghost of some old sin, the cancer of some concealed disgrace: punishment coming, *pede claudo*, years after memory has forgotten and self-love condoned the fault." And the lawyer, scared by the thought, brooded awhile on his own past, groping in all the corners of memory, lest by chance some Jack-in-the-Box of an old iniquity should leap to light there. His past was fairly blameless; few men could read the rolls of their life with less apprehension; yet he was humbled to the dust by the many ill things he had done, and raised up again into a sober and fearful gratitude by the many that he had come so near to doing, yet avoided. And then by a return on his former subject, he conceived a spark of hope. "This Master Hyde, if he were studied," thought he, "must have secrets of his own: black secrets, by the look of him; secrets compared to which poor Jekyll's worst would be like sunshine. Things cannot continue as they are. It turns me cold to think of this creature stealing like a thief to Harry's bedside; poor Harry, what a wakening! And the danger of it; for if this Hyde suspects the existence of the will, he may grow impatient to inherit. Ay, I must put my shoulder to the wheel—if Jekyll will but let me," he added, "if Jekyll will only let me." For once more he saw before his mind's eye, as clear as a transparency, the strange clauses of the will.

Dr. Jekyll Was Quite at Ease

A fortnight later, by excellent good fortune, the doctor gave one of his pleasant dinners to some five or six old cronies, all intelligent, reputable men and all judges of good wine; and Mr. Utterson so contrived that he remained behind after the others had departed. This was no new arrangement, but a thing that had befallen many scores of times. Where Utterson was liked, he was liked well. Hosts loved to detain the dry lawyer, when the light-hearted and the loose-tongued had already their foot on the threshold; they liked to sit awhile in his unobtrusive company, practising for solitude, sobering their minds in the man's rich silence after the expense and strain of gaiety. To this rule, Dr. Jekyll was no exception; and as he now sat on the opposite side of the fire—a large, well-made, smooth-faced man of fifty, with something of a slyish cast perhaps, but every mark of capacity and kindness—you could see by his looks that he cherished for Mr. Utterson a sincere and warm affection.

"I have been wanting to speak to you, Jekyll," began the latter. "You know that will of yours?"

A close observer might have gathered that the topic was distasteful; but the doctor carried it off gaily. "My poor Utterson," said he, "you are unfortunate in such a client. I never saw a man so distressed as you were by my will; unless it were that hide-bound pedant, Lanyon, at what he called my scientific heresies. O, I know he's a good fellow—

you needn't frown—an excellent fellow, and I always mean to see more of him; but a hide-bound pedant for all that; an ignorant, blatant pedant. I was never more disappointed in any man than Lanyon."

"You know I never approved of it," pursued Utterson, ruthlessly disregarding the fresh topic.

"My will? Yes, certainly, I know that," said the doctor, a trifle sharply. "You have told me so."

"Well, I tell you so again," continued the lawyer. "I have been learning something of young Hyde."

The large handsome face of Dr. Jekyll grew pale to the very lips, and there came a blackness about his eyes. "I do not care to hear more," said he. "This is a matter I thought we had agreed to drop."

"What I heard was abominable," said Utterson.

"It can make no change. You do not understand my position," returned the doctor, with a certain incoherency of manner. "I am painfully situated, Utterson; my position is a very strange—a very strange one. It is one of those affairs that cannot be mended by talking."

"Jekyll," said Utterson, "you know me: I am a man to be trusted. Make a clean breast of this in confidence; and I make no doubt I can get you out of it."

"My good Utterson," said the doctor, "this is very good of you, this is downright good of you, and I cannot find words to thank you in. I believe you fully; I would trust you before any man alive, ay, before myself, if I could make the choice; but indeed it isn't what you fancy; it is not so bad as that; and just to put your good heart at rest, I will tell you one thing: the moment I choose, I can be rid of Mr. Hyde. I give you my hand upon that; and I thank you again and again; and I will just add one little word, Utterson, that I'm sure you'll take in good part: this is a private matter, and I beg of you to let it sleep."

Utterson reflected a little looking in the fire.

"I have no doubt you are perfectly right," he said at last, getting to his feet.

"Well, but since we have touched upon this business, and for the last time I hope," continued the doctor, "there is one point I should like you to understand. I have really a very great interest in poor Hyde. I know you have seen him; he told me so; and I fear he was rude. But I do sincerely take a great, a very great interest in that young man; and if I am taken away, Utterson, I wish you to promise me that you will bear with him and get his rights for him. I think you would, if you knew all; and it would be a weight off my mind if you would promise."

"I can't pretend that I shall ever like him," said the lawyer.

"I don't ask that," pleaded Jekyll, laying his hand upon the other's arm; "I only ask for justice; I only ask you to help him for my sake, when I am no longer here."

Utterson heaved an irrepressible sigh. "Well," said he. "I promise."

THE CAREW MURDER CASE

Nearly a year later, in the month of October 18—, London was startled by a crime of singular ferocity and rendered all the more notable by the high position of the victim. The details were few and startling. A maid servant living alone in a house not far from the river, had gone upstairs to bed about eleven. Although a fog rolled over the city in the small hours, the early part of the night was cloudless, and the lane, which the maid's window overlooked, was brilliantly lit by the full moon. It seems she was romantically given, for she sat down upon her box, which stood immediately under the window, and fell into a dream of musing. Never (she used to say, with streaming tears, when she narrated that experience) never had she felt more at peace with all men or thought more kindly of the world. And as she so sat she became aware of an aged and beautiful gentleman with white hair, drawing near along the lane; and advancing to meet him, another and very small gentleman, to whom at first she paid less attention. When they had come within speech (which was just under the maid's eyes) the older man bowed and accosted the other with a very pretty manner of politeness. It did not seem as if the subject of his address were of great importance; indeed, from his pointing, it sometimes appeared as if he were only inquiring his way; but the moon shone on his face as he spoke, and the girl was pleased to watch it, it seemed to breathe such an innocent and old-world kindness of disposition, yet with something high too, as of a well-founded self-content. Presently her eye wandered to the other, and she was surprised to recognise in him a certain Mr. Hyde, who had once visited her master and for whom she had conceived a dislike. He had in his hand a heavy cane, with which he was trifling; but he answered never a word, and seemed to listen with an ill-contained impatience. And then all of a sudden he broke out in a great flame of anger, stamping with his foot, brandishing the cane, and carrying on (as the maid described it) like a madman. The old gentleman took a step back, with the air of one very much surprised and a trifle hurt; and at that Mr. Hyde broke out of all bounds and clubbed him to the earth. And next moment, with ape-like fury, he was trampling his victim under foot, and hailing down a storm of blows, under which the bones were audibly shattered and the body jumped upon the roadway. At the horror of these sights and sounds, the maid fainted.

It was two o'clock when she came to herself and called for the police. The murderer was gone long ago; but there lay his victim in the middle of the lane, incredibly mangled. The stick with which the deed had been done, although it was of some rare and very tough and heavy wood, had broken in the middle under the stress of this insensate cruelty; and one splintered half had rolled in the neighbouring gutter— the other, without doubt, had been carried away by the murderer. A purse and a gold watch were found upon the victim; but no cards or papers, except a sealed and stamped envelope, which he had been probably carrying to the post, and which bore the name and address of Mr. Utterson.

This was brought to the lawyer the next morning, before he was out of bed; and he had no sooner seen it, and been told the circumstances, than he shot out a solemn lip. "I shall say nothing till I have seen the body," said he; "this may be very serious. Have the kindness to wait while I dress." And with the same grave countenance he hurried through his breakfast and drove to the police station, whither the body had been carried. As soon as he came into the cell, he nodded.

"Yes," said he, "I recognise him. I am sorry to say that this is Sir Danvers Carew."

"Good God, sir," exclaimed the officer, "is it possible?" And the next moment his eye lighted up with professional ambition. "This will make a deal of noise," he said. "And perhaps you can help us to the man." And he briefly narrated what the maid had seen, and showed the broken stick.

Mr. Utterson had already quailed at the name of Hyde; but when the stick was laid before him, he could doubt no longer: broken and battered as it was, he recognised it for one that he had himself presented many years before to Henry Jekyll.

"Is this Mr. Hyde a person of small stature?" he inquired.

"Particularly small and particularly wicked-looking, is what the maid calls him," said the officer.

Mr. Utterson reflected; and then, raising his head, "If you will come with me in my cab," he said, "I think I can take you to his house."

It was by this time about nine in the morning, and the first fog of the season. A great chocolate-coloured pall lowered over heaven, but the wind was continually charging and routing these embattled vapours; so that as the cab crawled from street to street, Mr. Utterson beheld a marvellous number of degrees and hues of twilight; for here it would be dark like the back-end of evening; and there would be a glow of a rich, lurid brown, like the light of some strange conflagration; and here, for a moment, the fog would be quite broken up, and a haggard shaft of daylight would glance in between the swirling wreaths. The dismal quarter of Soho seen under these changing glimpses, with its muddy ways, and slatternly passengers, and its lamps, which had never been extinguished or had been kindled afresh to combat this mournful reïnvasion of darkness, seemed, in the lawyer's eyes, like a district of some city in a nightmare. The thoughts of his mind, besides, were of the gloomiest dye; and when he glanced at the companion of his drive, he was conscious of some touch of that terror of the law and the law's officers, which may at times assail the most honest.

As the cab drew up before the address indicated, the fog lifted a little and showed him a dingy street, a gin palace, a low French eating house, a shop for the retail of penny numbers and twopenny salads, many ragged children huddled in the doorways, and many women of many different nationalities passing out, key in hand, to have a morning glass; and the next moment the fog settled down again upon that part, as brown as umber, and cut him off from his blackguardly surroundings. This was the home of Henry Jekyll's favourite; of a man who was heir to quarter of a million sterling.

An ivory-faced and silvery-haired old woman opened the door. She had an evil face, smoothed by hypocrisy; but her manners were excellent. Yes, she said, this was Mr. Hyde's, but he was not at home; he had been in that night very late, but had gone away again in less than an hour; there was nothing strange in that; his habits were very irregular, and he was often absent; for instance, it was nearly two months since she had seen him till yesterday.

"Very well then, we wish to see his rooms," said the lawyer; and when the woman began to declare it was impossible, "I had better tell you who this person is," he added. "This is Inspector Newcomen of Scotland Yard."

A flash of odious joy appeared upon the woman's face. "Ah!" said she, "he is in trouble! What has he done?"

Mr. Utterson and the inspector exchanged glances. "He don't seem a very popular character," observed the latter. "And now, my good woman, just let me and this gentleman have a look about us."

In the whole extent of the house, which but for the old woman remained otherwise empty, Mr. Hyde had only used a couple of rooms; but these were furnished with luxury and good taste. A closet was filled with wine; the plate was of silver, the napery elegant; a good picture hung upon the walls, a gift (as Utterson supposed) from Henry Jekyll, who was much of a connoisseur; and the carpets were of many plies and agreeable in colour. At this moment, however, the rooms bore every mark of having been recently and hurriedly ransacked; clothes lay about the floor, with their pockets inside out; lockfast drawers stood open; and on the hearth there lay a pile of gray ashes, as though many papers had been burned. From these embers the inspector disinterred the butt end of a green cheque book, which had resisted the action of the fire; the other half of the stick was found behind the door; and as this clinched his suspicions, the officer declared himself delighted. A visit to the bank, where several thousand pounds were found to be lying to the murderer's credit, completed his gratification.

"You may depend upon it, sir," he told Mr. Utterson: "I have him in my hand. He must have lost his head, or he never would have left the stick or, above all, burned the cheque book. Why, money's life to the man. We have nothing to do but wait for him at the bank, and get out the handbills."

This last, however, was not so easy of accomplishment; for Mr.

Hyde had numbered few familiars—even the master of the servant maid had only seen him twice; his family could nowhere be traced; he had never been photographed; and the few who could describe him differed widely, as common observers will. Only on one point, were they agreed; and that was the haunting sense of unexpressed deformity with which the fugitive impressed his beholders.

INCIDENT OF THE LETTER

It was late in the afternoon, when Mr. Utterson found his way to Dr. Jekyll's door, where he was at once admitted by Poole, and carried down by the kitchen offices and across a yard which had once been a garden, to the building which was indifferently known as the laboratory or the dissecting rooms. The doctor had bought the house from the heirs of a celebrated surgeon; and his own tastes being rather chemical than anatomical, had changed the destination of the block at the bottom of the garden. It was the first time that the lawyer had been received in that part of his friend's quarters; and he eyed the dingy windowless structure with curiosity, and gazed round with a distasteful sense of strangeness as he crossed the theatre, once crowded with eager students and now lying gaunt and silent, the tables laden with chemical apparatus, the floor strewn with crates and littered with packing straw, and the light falling dimly through the foggy cupola. At the further end, a flight of stairs mounted to a door covered with red baize; and through this, Mr. Utterson was at last received into the doctor's cabinet. It was a large room, fitted round with glass presses, furnished, among other things, with a cheval-glass and a business table, and looking out upon the court by three dusty windows barred with iron. The fire burned in the grate; a lamp was set lighted on the chimney shelf, for even in the houses the fog began to lie thickly; and there, close up to the warmth, sat Dr. Jekyll, looking deadly sick. He did not rise to meet his visitor, but held out a cold hand and bade him welcome in a changed voice.

"And now," said Mr. Utterson, as soon as Poole had left them, "you have heard the news?"

The doctor shuddered. "They were crying it in the square," he said. "I heard them in my dining room."

"One word," said the lawyer. "Carew was my client, but so are you, and I want to know what I am doing. You have not been mad enough to hide this fellow?"

"Utterson, I swear to God," cried the doctor, "I swear to God I will never set eyes on him again. I bind my honour to you that I am done with him in this world. It is all at an end. And indeed he does not want my help; you do not know him as I do; he is safe, he is quite safe; mark my words, he will never more be heard of."

The lawyer listened gloomily; he did not like his friend's feverish manner. "You seem pretty sure of him," said he; "and for your sake, I hope you may be right. If it came to a trial, your name might appear."

"I am quite sure of him," replied Jekyll; "I have grounds for certainty that I cannot share with anyone. But there is one thing on which you may advise me. I have—I have received a letter; and I am at a loss whether I should show it to the police. I should like to leave it in your hands, Utterson; you would judge wisely I am sure; I have so great a trust in you."

"You fear, I suppose, that it might lead to his detection?" asked the lawyer.

"No," said the other. "I cannot say that I care what becomes of Hyde; I am quite done with him. I was thinking of my own character, which this hateful business has rather exposed."

Utterson ruminated awhile; he was surprised at his friend's selfishness, and yet relieved by it. "Well," said he, at last, "let me see the letter."

The letter was written in an odd, upright hand and signed "Edward Hyde": and it signified, briefly enough, that the writer's benefactor, Dr. Jekyll, whom he had long so unworthily repaid for a thousand generosities, need labour under no alarm for his safety as he had means of escape on which he placed a sure dependence. The lawyer liked this letter well enough; it put a better colour on the intimacy than he had looked for; and he blamed himself for some of his past suspicions.

"Have you the envelope?" he asked.

"I burned it," replied Jekyll, "before I thought what I was about. But it bore no postmark. The note was handed in."

"Shall I keep this and sleep upon it?" asked Utterson.

"I wish you to judge for me entirely," was the reply. "I have lost confidence in myself."

"Well, I shall consider," returned the lawyer. "And now one word more: it was Hyde who dictated the terms in your will about that disappearance?"

The doctor seemed seized with a qualm of faintness; he shut his mouth tight and nodded.

"I knew it," said Utterson. "He meant to murder you. You have had a fine escape."

"I have had what is far more to the purpose," returned the doctor solemnly: "I have had a lesson—O God, Utterson, what a lesson I have had!" And he covered his face for a moment with his hands.

On his way out, the lawyer stopped and had a word or two with Poole. "By the by," said he, "there was a letter handed in today: what was the messenger like?" But Poole was positive nothing had come except by post; "and only circulars by that," he added.

This news sent off the visitor with his fears renewed. Plainly the letter had come by the laboratory door; possibly, indeed, it had been written in the cabinet; and if that were so, it must be differently judged, and handled with the more caution. The newsboys, as he went, were crying themselves hoarse along the footways: "Special edition. Shocking murder of an M.P." That was the funeral oration of one friend and client; and he could not help a certain apprehension lest the good name of another should be sucked down in the eddy of the scandal. It was, at least, a ticklish decision that he had to make; and self-reliant as he was by habit, he began to cherish a longing for advice. It was not to be had directly; but perhaps, he thought, it might be fished for.

Presently after, he sat on one side of his own hearth, with Mr. Guest, his head clerk, upon the other, and midway between, at a nicely calculated distance from the fire, a bottle of a particular old wine that had long dwelt unsunned in the foundations of his house. The fog still slept on the wing above the drowned city, where the lamps glimmered like carbuncles; and through the muffle and smother of these fallen clouds, the procession of the town's life was still rolling in through the great arteries with a sound as of a mighty wind. But the room was gay with firelight. In the bottle the acids were long ago resolved; the imperial dye had softened with time, as the colour grows richer in stained windows; and the glow of hot autumn afternoons on hillside vineyards, was ready to be set free and to disperse the fogs of London. Insensibly the lawyer melted. There was no man from whom he kept fewer secrets than Mr. Guest; and he was not always sure that he kept as many as he meant. Guest had often been on business to the doctor's; he knew Poole; he could scarce have failed to hear of Mr. Hyde's familiarity about the house; he might draw conclusions: was it not as well, then, that he should see a letter which put that mystery to rights? and above all since Guest, being a great student and critic of handwriting, would consider the step natural and obliging? The clerk, besides, was a man of counsel; he would scarce read so strange a document without dropping a remark; and by that remark Mr. Utterson might shape his future course.

"This is a sad business about Sir Danvers," he said.

"Yes, sir, indeed. It has elicited a great deal of public feeling," returned Guest. "The man, of course, was mad."

"I should like to hear your views on that," replied Utterson. "I have a document here in his handwriting; it is between ourselves, for I scarce know what to do about it; it is an ugly business at the best. But there it is; quite in your way: a murderer's autograph."

Guest's eyes brightened, and he sat down at once and studied it with passion. "No, sir," he said; "not mad; but it is an odd hand."

"And by all accounts a very odd writer," added the lawyer.

Just then the servant entered with a note.

"Is that from Doctor Jekyll, sir?" inquired the clerk. "I thought I knew the writing. Anything private, Mr. Utterson?"

"Only an invitation to dinner. Why? do you want to see it?"

"One moment. I thank you, sir;" and the clerk laid the two sheets of paper alongside and sedulously compared their contents. "Thank you, sir," he said at last, returning both; "it's a very interesting autograph."

There was a pause, during which Mr. Utterson struggled with himself. "Why did you compare them, Guest?" he inquired suddenly.

"Well, sir," returned the clerk, "there's a rather singular resemblance; the two hands are in many points identical: only differently sloped."

"Rather quaint," said Utterson.

"It is, as you say, rather quaint," returned Guest.

"I wouldn't speak of this note, you know," said the master.

"No, sir," said the clerk. "I understand."

But no sooner was Mr. Utterson alone that night, than he locked the note into his safe where it reposed from that time forward. "What!" he thought. "Henry Jekyll forge for a murderer!" And his blood ran cold in his veins.

Remarkable Incident
of Doctor Lanyon

Time ran on; thousands of pounds were offered in reward, for the death of Sir Danvers was resented as a public injury; but Mr. Hyde had disappeared out of the ken of the police as though he had never existed. Much of his past was unearthed, indeed, and all disreputable: tales came out of the man's cruelty, at once so callous and violent, of his vile life, of his strange associates, of the hatred that seemed to have surrounded his career; but of his present whereabouts, not a whisper. From the time he had left the house in Soho on the morning of the murder, he was simply blotted out; and gradually, as time drew on, Mr. Utterson began to recover from the hotness of his alarm, and to grow more at quiet with himself. The death of Sir Danvers was, to his way of thinking, more than paid for by the disappearance of Mr. Hyde. Now that that evil influence had been withdrawn, a new life began for Dr. Jekyll. He came out of his seclusion, renewed relations with his friends, became once more their familiar guest and entertainer; and whilst he had always been known for charities, he was now no less distinguished for religion. He was busy, he was much in the open air, he did good; his face seemed to open and brighten, as if with an inward consciousness of service; and for more than two months, the doctor was at peace.

On the 8th of January Utterson had dined at the doctor's with a small party; Lanyon had been there; and the face of the host had looked from one to the other as in the old days when the trio were inseparable friends. On the 12th, and again on the 14th, the door was shut against the lawyer. "The doctor was confined to the house," Poole said, "and saw no one." On the 15th, he tried again, and was again refused; and having now been used for the last two months to see his friend almost daily, he found this return of solitude to weigh upon his spirits. The fifth night, he had in Guest to dine with him; and the sixth he betook himself to Doctor Lanyon's.

There at least he was not denied admittance; but when he came in, he was shocked at the change which had taken place in the doctor's appearance. He had his death-warrant written legibly upon his face. The rosy man had grown pale; his flesh had fallen away; he was visibly balder and older; and yet it was not so much these tokens of a swift physical decay that arrested the lawyer's notice, as a look in the eye and quality of manner that seemed to testify to some deep-seated terror of the mind. It was unlikely that the doctor should fear death; and yet that was what Utterson was tempted to suspect. "Yes," he thought; "he is a doctor, he must know his own state and that his days are counted; and the knowledge is more than he can bear." And yet when Utterson remarked on his ill-looks, it was with an air of great firmness that Lanyon declared himself a doomed man.

"I have had a shock," he said, "and I shall never recover. It is a question of weeks. Well, life has been pleasant; I liked it; yes, sir, I used to like it. I sometimes think if we knew all, we should be more glad to get away."

"Jekyll is ill, too," observed Utterson. "Have you seen him?"

But Lanyon's face changed, and he held up a trembling hand. "I wish to see or hear no more of Doctor Jekyll," he said in a loud, unsteady voice. "I am quite done with that person; and I beg that you will spare me any allusion to one whom I regard as dead."

"Tut-tut," said Mr. Utterson; and then after a considerable pause, "Can't I do anything?" he inquired. "We are three very old friends, Lanyon; we shall not live to make others."

"Nothing can be done," returned Lanyon; "ask himself."

"He will not see me," said the lawyer.

"I am not surprised at that," was the reply. "Some day, Utterson, after I am dead, you may perhaps come to learn the right and wrong of this. I cannot tell you. And in the meantime, if you can sit and talk with me of other things, for God's sake, stay and do so; but if you cannot keep clear of this accursed topic, then, in God's name, go, for I cannot bear it."

As soon as he got home, Utterson sat down and wrote to Jekyll, complaining of his exclusion from the house, and asking the cause of this unhappy break with Lanyon; and the next day brought him a long answer, often very pathetically worded, and sometimes darkly mysterious in drift. The quarrel with Lanyon was incurable. "I do not blame our old friend," Jekyll wrote, "but I share his view that we must never meet. I mean from henceforth to lead a life of extreme seclusion; you must not be surprised, nor must you doubt my friendship, if my door is often shut even to you. You must suffer me to go my own dark way. I have brought on myself a punishment and a danger that I cannot name. If I am the chief of sinners, I am the chief of sufferers also. I could not think that this earth contained a place for sufferings and terrors so unmanning; and you can do but one thing, Utterson, to lighten this destiny, and that is to respect my silence." Utterson was amazed; the dark influence of Hyde had been withdrawn, the doctor had returned to his old tasks and amities; a week ago, the prospect had smiled with every promise of a cheerful and an honoured age; and now in a moment, friendship, and peace of mind and the whole tenor of his life were wrecked. So great and unprepared a change pointed to madness; but in view of Lanyon's manner and words, there must lie for it some deeper ground.

A week afterwards Dr. Lanyon took to his bed, and in something less than a fortnight he was dead. The night after the funeral, at which he had been sadly affected, Utterson locked the door of his business room, and sitting there by the light of a melancholy candle, drew out and set before him an envelope addressed by the hand and sealed with the seal of his dead friend. "PRIVATE: for the hands of J. G. Utterson ALONE and in case of his predecease *to be destroyed unread*," so it was emphatically superscribed; and the lawyer dreaded to behold the contents. "I have buried one friend today," he thought: "what if this should cost me another?" And then he condemned the fear as a disloyalty, and broke the seal. Within there was another enclosure, likewise sealed, and marked upon the cover as "not to be opened till the death or disappearance of Dr. Henry Jekyll." Utterson could not trust his eyes. Yes, it was disappearance; here again, as in the mad will which he had long ago restored to its author, here again were the idea of a disappearance and the name of Henry Jekyll bracketed. But in the will, that idea had sprung from the sinister suggestion of the man Hyde; it was set there with a purpose all too plain and horrible. Written by the hand of Lanyon, what should it mean? A great curiosity came on the trustee, to disregard the prohibition and dive at once to the bottom of these mysteries; but professional honour and faith to his dead friend were stringent obligations; and the packet slept in the inmost corner of his private safe.

It is one thing to mortify curiosity, another to conquer it; and it may be doubted if, from that day forth, Utterson desired the society of his surviving friend with the same eagerness. He thought of him kindly; but his thoughts were disquieted and fearful. He went to call indeed; but he was perhaps relieved to be denied admittance; perhaps, in his heart, he preferred to speak with Poole upon the doorstep and surrounded by the air and sounds of the open city, rather than to be admitted into that house of voluntary bondage, and to sit and speak with its inscrutable recluse. Poole had, indeed, no very pleasant news to communicate. The doctor, it appeared, now more than ever confined himself to the cabinet over the laboratory, where he would sometimes even sleep; he was out of spirits, he had grown very silent, he did not read; it seemed as if he had something on his mind. Utterson became so used to the unvarying character of these reports, that he fell off little by little in the frequency of his visits.

Incident at the Window

It chanced on Sunday, when Mr. Utterson was on his usual walk with Mr. Enfield, that their way lay once again through the bystreet; and that when they came in front of the door, both stopped to gaze on it.

"Well," said Enfield, "that story's at an end at least. We shall never see more of Mr. Hyde."

"I hope not," said Utterson. "Did I ever tell you that I once saw him, and shared your feeling of repulsion?"

"It was impossible to do the one without the other," returned Enfield. "And by the way what an ass you must have thought me, not to know that this was a back way to Dr. Jekyll's! It was partly your own fault that I found it out, even when I did."

"So you found it out, did you?" said Utterson. "But if that be so, we may step into the court and take a look at the windows. To tell you the truth, I am uneasy about poor Jekyll; and even outside, I feel as if the presence of a friend might do him good."

The court was very cool and a little damp, and full of premature twilight, although the sky, high up overhead, was still bright with sunset. The middle one of the three windows was half way open; and sitting close beside it, taking the air with an infinite sadness of mien, like some disconsolate prisoner, Utterson saw Dr. Jekyll.

"What! Jekyll!" he cried. "I trust you are better."

"I am very low, Utterson," replied the doctor drearily, "very low. It will not last long, thank God."

"You stay too much indoors," said the lawyer. "You should be out, whipping up the circulation like Mr. Enfield and me. (This is my cousin—Mr. Enfield—Dr. Jekyll.) Come now; get your hat and take a quick turn with us."

"You are very good," sighed the other. "I should like to very much; but no, no, no, it is quite impossible; I dare not. But indeed, Utterson, I am very glad to see you; this is really a great pleasure; I would ask you and Mr. Enfield up, but the place is really not fit."

"Why then," said the lawyer, good-naturedly, "the best thing we can do is to stay down here and speak with you from where we are."

"That is just what I was about to venture to propose," returned the doctor with a smile. But the words were hardly uttered, before the smile was struck out of his face and succeeded by an expression of such abject terror and despair, as froze the very blood of the two gentlemen below. They saw it but for a glimpse, for the window was instantly thrust down; but that glimpse had been sufficient, and they turned and left the court without a word. In silence, too, they traversed the bystreet; and it was not until they had come into a neighbouring thoroughfare, where even upon a Sunday there were still some stirrings of life, that Mr. Utterson at last turned and looked at his companion. They were both pale; and there was an answering horror in their eyes.

"God forgive us, God forgive us," said Mr. Utterson.

But Mr. Enfield only nodded his head very seriously, and walked on once more in silence.

THE LAST NIGHT

Mr. Utterson was sitting by his fireside one evening after dinner, when he was surprised to receive a visit from Poole.

"Bless me, Poole, what brings you here?" he cried; and then taking a second look at him, "What ails you?" he added, "is the doctor ill?"

"Mr. Utterson," said the man, "there is something wrong."

"Take a seat, and here is a glass of wine for you," said the lawyer. "Now, take your time, and tell me plainly what you want."

"You know the doctor's ways, sir," replied Poole, "and how he shuts himself up. Well, he's shut up again in the cabinet; and I don't like it, sir—I wish I may die if I like it. Mr. Utterson, sir, I'm afraid."

"Now, my good man," said the lawyer, "be explicit. What are you afraid of?"

"I've been afraid for about a week," returned Poole, doggedly disregarding the question, "and I can bear it no more."

The man's appearance amply bore out his words; his manner was altered for the worse; and except for the moment when he had first announced his terror, he had not once looked the lawyer in the face. Even now, he sat with the glass of wine untasted on his knee, and his eyes directed to a corner of the floor. "I can bear it no more," he repeated.

"Come," said the lawyer, "I see you have some good reason, Poole; I see there is something seriously amiss. Try to tell me what it is."

"I think there's been foul play," said Poole, hoarsely.

"Foul play!" cried the lawyer, a good deal frightened and rather inclined to be irritated in consequence. "What foul play? What does the man mean?"

"I daren't say, sir," was the answer; "but will you come along with me and see for yourself?"

Mr. Utterson's only answer was to rise and get his hat and great coat; but he observed with wonder the greatness of the relief that appeared upon the butler's face, and perhaps with no less, that the wine was still untasted when he set it down to follow.

It was a wild, cold, seasonable night of March, with a pale moon, lying on her back as though the wind had tilted her, and a flying wrack of the most diaphanous and lawny texture. The wind made talking difficult, and flecked the blood into the face. It seemed to have swept the streets unusually bare of passengers, besides; for Mr. Utterson thought he had never seen that part of London so deserted. He could have wished it otherwise; never in his life had he been conscious of so sharp a wish to see and touch his fellow-creatures; for struggle as he might, there was borne in upon his mind a crushing anticipation of calamity. The square, when they got there, was all full of wind and dust, and the thin trees in the garden were lashing themselves along the railing. Poole, who had kept all the way a pace or two ahead, now pulled up in the middle of the pavement, and in spite of the biting weather, took off his hat and mopped his brow with a red pocket-handkerchief. But for all the hurry of his coming, these were not the dews of exertion that he wiped away, but the moisture of some strangling anguish; for his face was white and his voice, when he spoke, harsh and broken.

"Well, sir," he said, "here we are, and God grant there be nothing wrong."

"Amen, Poole," said the lawyer.

Thereupon the servant knocked in a very guarded manner; the door was opened on the chain; and a voice asked from within, "Is that you, Poole?"

"It's all right," said Poole. "Open the door."

The hall, when they entered it, was brightly lighted up; the fire was built high; and about the hearth the whole of the servants, men and women, stood huddled together like a flock of sheep. At the sight of

Mr. Utterson, the housemaid broke into hysterical whimpering; and the cook, crying out "Bless God! it's Mr. Utterson," ran forward as if to take him in her arms.

"What, what? Are you all here?" said the lawyer peevishly. "Very irregular, very unseemly; your master would be far from pleased."

"They're all afraid," said Poole.

Blank silence followed, no one protesting; only the maid lifted up her voice and now wept loudly.

"Hold your tongue!" Poole said to her, with a ferocity of accent that testified to his own jangled nerves; and indeed, when the girl had so suddenly raised the note of her lamentation, they had all started and turned towards the inner door with faces of dreadful expectation. "And now," continued the butler, addressing the knife-boy, "reach me a candle, and we'll get this through hands at once." And then he begged Mr. Utterson to follow him, and led the way to the back garden.

"Now, sir," said he, "you come as gently as you can. I want you to hear, and I don't want you to be heard. And see here, sir, if by any chance he was to ask you in, don't go."

Mr. Utterson's nerves, at this unlooked-for termination, gave a jerk that nearly threw him from his balance; but he recollected his courage and followed the butler into the laboratory building and through the surgical theatre, with its lumber of crates and bottles, to the foot of the stair. Here Poole motioned him to stand on one side and listen; while he himself, setting down the candle and making a great and obvious call on his resolution, mounted the steps and knocked with a somewhat uncertain hand on the red baize of the cabinet door.

"Mr. Utterson, sir, asking to see you," he called; and even as he did so, once more violently signed to the lawyer to give ear.

A voice answered from within: "Tell him I cannot see anyone," it said complainingly.

"Thank you, sir," said Poole, with a note of something like triumph in his voice; and taking up his candle, he led Mr. Utterson back across the yard and into the great kitchen, where the fire was out and the beetles were leaping on the floor.

"Sir," he said, looking Mr. Utterson in the eyes, "was that my master's voice?"

"It seems much changed," replied the lawyer, very pale, but giving look for look.

"Changed? Well, yes, I think so," said the butler. "Have I been twenty years in this man's house, to be deceived about his voice? No, sir; master's made away with; he was made away with, eight days ago, when we heard him cry out upon the name of God; and *who's* in there instead of him, and *why* it stays there, is a thing that cries to Heaven, Mr. Utterson!"

"This is a very strange tale, Poole; this is rather a wild tale, my man," said Mr. Utterson, biting his finger. "Suppose it were as you suppose, supposing Dr. Jekyll to have been—well, murdered, what could induce the murderer to stay? That won't hold water; it doesn't commend itself to reason."

"Well, Mr. Utterson, you are a hard man to satisfy, but I'll do it yet," said Poole. "All this last week (you must know) him, or it, or whatever it is that lives in that cabinet, has been crying night and day for some sort of medicine and cannot get it to his mind. It was sometimes his way—the master's, that is—to write his orders on a sheet of paper and throw it on the stair. We've had nothing else this week back; nothing but papers, and a closed door, and the very meals left there to be smuggled in when nobody was looking. Well, sir, every day, ay, and twice and thrice in the same day, there have been orders and complaints, and I have been sent flying to all the wholesale chemists in town. Every time I brought the stuff back, there would be another paper telling me to return it, because it was not pure, and another order to a different firm. This drug is wanted bitter bad, sir, whatever for."

"Have you any of these papers?" asked Mr. Utterson.

Poole felt in his pocket and handed out a crumpled note, which the lawyer, bending nearer to the candle, carefully examined. Its contents ran thus: "Dr. Jekyll presents his compliments to Messrs. Maw. He assures them that their last sample is impure and quite useless for his present purpose. In the year 18——, Dr. J. purchased a somewhat large quantity from Messrs. M. He now begs them to search with the most sedulous care, and should any of the same quality be left, to forward it to him at once. Expense is no consideration. The importance of this to Dr. J. can hardly be exaggerated." So far the letter had run composedly enough, but here with a sudden splutter of the pen, the writer's emotion had broken loose. "For God's sake," he had added, "find me some of the old."

"This is a strange note," said Mr. Utterson; and then sharply, "How do you come to have it open?"

"The man at Maw's was main angry, sir, and he threw it back to me like so much dirt," returned Poole.

"This is unquestionably the doctor's hand, do you know?" resumed the lawyer.

"I thought it looked like it," said the servant rather sulkily; and then, with another voice, "But what matters hand of write," he said. "I've seen him!"

"Seen him?" repeated Mr. Utterson. "Well?"

"That's it!" said Poole. "It was this way. I came suddenly into the theatre from the garden. It seems he had slipped out to look for this drug or whatever it is; for the cabinet door was open, and there he was at the far end of the room digging among the crates. He looked up when I came in, gave a kind of cry, and whipped upstairs into the cabinet. It was but for one minute that I saw him, but the hair stood upon my head like quills. Sir, if that was my master, why had he a mask upon his face? If it was my master, why did he cry out like a rat, and run from me? I have served him long enough. And then..." the man paused and passed his hand over his face.

"These are all very strange circumstances," said Mr. Utterson, "but I think I begin to see daylight. Your master, Poole, is plainly seized with one of those maladies that both torture and deform the sufferer; hence, for aught I know, the alteration of his voice; hence the mask and his avoidance of his friends; hence his eagerness to find this drug, by means of which the poor soul retains some hope of ultimate recovery—God grant that he be not deceived! There is my explanation; it is sad enough, Poole, ay, and appalling to consider; but it is plain and natural, hangs well together and delivers us from all exorbitant alarms."

"Sir," said the butler, turning to a sort of mottled pallor, "that thing was not my master, and there's the truth. My master"—here he looked round him and began to whisper—"is a tall fine build of a man, and this was more of a dwarf." Utterson attempted to protest. "O, sir," cried Poole, "do you think I do not know my master after twenty years? do you think I do not know where his head comes to in the cabinet door, where I saw him every morning of my life? No, sir, that thing in the mask was never Doctor Jekyll—God knows what it was, but it was never Doctor Jekyll; and it is the belief of my heart that there was murder done."

"Poole," replied the lawyer, "if you say that, it will become my duty to make certain. Much as I desire to spare your master's feelings, much as I am puzzled by this note which seems to prove him to be still alive, I shall consider it my duty to break in that door."

"Ah, Mr. Utterson, that's talking!" cried the butler.

"And now comes the second question," resumed Utterson: "Who is going to do it?"

"Why, you and me, sir," was the undaunted reply.

"That is very well said," returned the lawyer; "and whatever comes of it, I shall make it my business to see you are no loser."

"There is an axe in the theatre," continued Poole; "and you might take the kitchen poker for yourself."

The lawyer took that rude but weighty instrument into his hand, and balanced it. "Do you know Poole," he said, looking up, "that you and I are about to place ourselves in a position of some peril?"

"You may say so, sir, indeed," returned the butler.

"It is well, then, that we should be frank," said the other. "We both think more than we have said; let us make a clean breast. This masked figure that you saw, did you recognise it?"

"Well, sir, it went so quick, and the creature was so doubled up, that I could hardly swear to that," was the answer. "But if you mean, was it Mr. Hyde?—why, yes, I think it was! You see, it was much of the same bigness; and it had the same quick light way with it; and then who else could have got in by the laboratory door? You have not forgot, sir, that at the time of the murder he had still the key with him? But that's not all. I don't know, Mr. Utterson, if ever you met this Mr. Hyde?"

"Yes," said the lawyer, "I once spoke with him."

"Then you must know as well as the rest of us that there was something queer about that gentleman—something that gave a man a turn—I don't know rightly how to say it, sir, beyond this: that you felt it in your marrow kind of cold and thin."

"I own I felt something of what you describe," said Mr. Utterson.

"Quite so, sir," returned Poole. "Well, when that masked thing like a monkey jumped from among the chemicals and whipped into the cabinet, it went down my spine like ice. O, I know it's not evidence, Mr.

Utterson; I'm book-learned enough for that; but a man has his feelings, and I give you my bible-word it was Mr. Hyde!"

"Ay, ay," said the lawyer. "My fears incline to the same point. Evil, I fear, founded—evil was sure to come—of that connection. Ay, truly, I believe you; I believe poor Harry is killed; and I believe his murderer (for what purpose, God alone can tell) is still lurking in his victim's room. Well, let our name be vengeance. Call Bradshaw."

The footman came at the summons, very white and nervous.

"Pull yourself together, Bradshaw," said the lawyer. "This suspense, I know, is telling upon all of you; but it is now our intention to make an end of it. Poole, here, and I are going to force our way into the cabinet. If all is well, my shoulders are broad enough to bear the blame. Meanwhile, lest anything should really be amiss, or any malefactor seek to escape by the back, you and the boy must go round the corner with a pair of good sticks, and take your post at the laboratory door. We give you ten minutes, to get to your stations."

As Bradshaw left, the lawyer looked at his watch. "And now, Poole, let us get to ours," he said; and taking the poker under his arm, he led the way into the yard. The scud had banked over the moon, and it was now quite dark. The wind, which only broke in puffs and draughts into that deep well of building, tossed the light of the candle to and fro about their steps, until they came into the shelter of the theatre, where they sat down silently to wait. London hummed solemnly all around; but nearer at hand, the stillness was only broken by the sound of a footfall moving to and fro along the cabinet floor.

"So it will walk all day, sir," whispered Poole; "ay, and the better part of the night. Only when a new sample comes from the chemist, there's a bit of a break. Ah, it's an ill-conscience that's such an enemy to rest! Ah, sir, there's blood foully shed in every step of it! But hark again, a little closer—put your heart in your ears Mr. Utterson, and tell me, is that the doctor's foot?"

The steps fell lightly and oddly, with a certain swing, for all they went so slowly; it was different indeed from the heavy creaking tread of Henry Jekyll. Utterson sighed. "Is there never anything else?" he asked.

Poole nodded. "Once," he said. "Once I heard it weeping!"

"Weeping? how that?" said the lawyer, conscious of a sudden chill of horror.

"Weeping like a woman or a lost soul," said the butler. "I came away with that upon my heart, that I could have wept too."

But now the ten minutes drew to an end. Poole disinterred the axe from under a stack of packing straw; the candle was set upon the nearest table to light them to the attack; and they drew near with bated breath to where that patient foot was still going up and down, up and down, in the quiet of the night.

"Jekyll," cried Utterson, with a loud voice, "I demand to see you." He paused a moment, but there came no reply. "I give you fair warning, our suspicions are aroused, and I must and shall see you," he resumed; "if not by fair means, then by foul—if not of your consent, then by brute force!"

"Utterson," said the voice, "for God's sake, have mercy!"

"Ah, that's not Jekyll's voice—it's Hyde's!" cried Utterson. "Down with the door, Poole."

Poole swung the axe over his shoulder; the blow shook the building, and the red baize door leaped against the lock and hinges. A dismal screech, as of mere animal terror, rang from the cabinet. Up went the axe again, and again the panels crashed and the frame bounded; four times the blow fell; but the wood was tough and the fittings were of excellent workmanship; and it was not until the fifth, that the lock burst in sunder and the wreck of the door fell inwards on the carpet.

The besiegers, appalled by their own riot and the stillness that had succeeded, stood back a little and peered in. There lay the cabinet before their eyes in the quiet lamplight, a good fire glowing and chattering on the hearth, the kettle singing its thin strain, a drawer or two open, papers neatly set forth on the business table, and nearer the fire, the things laid out for tea: the quietest room, you would have said, and, but for the glazed presses full of chemicals, the most commonplace that night in London.

Right in the midst there lay the body of a man sorely contorted and still twitching. They drew near on tiptoe, turned it on its back and beheld the face of Edward Hyde. He was dressed in clothes far too large for him, clothes of the doctor's bigness; the cords of his face still moved with a semblance of life, but life was quite gone; and by the crushed phial in the hand and the strong smell of kernels that hung upon the air, Utterson knew that he was looking on the body of a self-destroyer.

"We have come too late," he said sternly, "whether to save or punish. Hyde is gone to his account; and it only remains for us to find the body of your master."

The far greater proportion of the building was occupied by the theatre, which filled almost the whole ground story and was lighted from above, and by the cabinet, which formed an upper story at one end and looked upon the court. A corridor joined the theatre to the door on the bystreet; and with this, the cabinet communicated separately by a second flight of stairs. There were besides a few dark closets and a spacious cellar. All these they now thoroughly examined. Each closet needed but a glance, for all were empty and all, by the dust that fell from their doors, had stood long unopened. The cellar, indeed, was filled with crazy lumber, mostly dating from the times of the surgeon who was Jekyll's predecessor; but even as they opened the door, they were advertised of the uselessness of further search, by the fall of a perfect mat of cobweb which had for years sealed up the entrance. Nowhere was there any trace of Henry Jekyll, dead or alive.

Poole stamped on the flags of the corridor. "He must be buried here," he said, hearkening to the sound.

"Or he may have fled," said Utterson, and he turned to examine the door in the bystreet. It was locked; and lying nearby on the flags, they found the key, already stained with rust.

"This does not look like use," observed the lawyer.

"Use!" echoed Poole. "Do you not see, sir, it is broken? much as if a man had stamped on it."

"Ay," continued Utterson, "and the fractures, too, are rusty." The two men looked at each other with a scare. "This is beyond me, Poole," said the lawyer. "Let us go back to the cabinet."

They mounted the stair in silence, and still with an occasional awestruck glance at the dead body, proceeded more thoroughly to examine the contents of the cabinet. At one table, there were traces of chemical work, various measured heaps of some white salt being laid on glass saucers, as though for an experiment in which the unhappy man had been prevented.

"That is the same drug that I was always bringing him," said Poole; and even as he spoke, the kettle with a startling noise boiled over.

This brought them to the fireside, where the easy chair was drawn cosily up, and the tea things stood ready to the sitter's elbow, the very sugar in the cup. There were several books on a shelf; one lay beside the tea things open, and Utterson was amazed to find it a copy of a pious work, for which Jekyll had several times expressed a great esteem, annotated, in his own hand, with startling blasphemies.

Next, in the course of their review of the chamber, the searchers came to the cheval glass, into whose depths they looked with an involuntary horror. But it was so turned as to show them nothing but the rosy glow playing on the roof, the fire sparkling in a hundred repetitions along the glazed front of the presses, and their own pale and fearful countenances stooping to look in.

"This glass have seen some strange things, sir," whispered Poole.

"And surely none stranger than itself," echoed the lawyer in the same tones. "For what did Jekyll"—he caught himself up at the word with a start, and then conquering the weakness: "what could Jekyll want with it?" he said.

"You may say that!" said Poole.

Next they turned to the business table. On the desk among the neat array of papers, a large envelope was uppermost, and bore, in the doctor's hand, the name of Mr. Utterson. The lawyer unsealed it, and several enclosures fell to the floor. The first was a will, drawn in the same eccentric terms as the one which he had returned six months before, to serve as a testament in case of death and as a deed of gift in case of disappearance; but in place of the name of Edward Hyde, the lawyer, with indescribable amazement, read the name of Gabriel John Utterson. He looked at Poole, and then back at the paper, and last of all at the dead malefactor stretched upon the carpet.

"My head goes round," he said. "He has been all these days in possession; he had no cause to like me; he must have raged to see himself displaced; and he has not destroyed this document."

He caught up the next paper; it was a brief note in the doctor's hand and dated at the top. "O Poole!" the lawyer cried, "he was alive and here this day. He cannot have been disposed of in so short a space, he must be still alive, he must have fled! And then, why fled? and how? and in that case, can we venture to declare this suicide? O, we must be careful. I foresee that we may yet involve your master in some dire catastrophe."

"Why don't you read it, sir?" asked Poole.

"Because I fear," replied the lawyer solemnly. "God grant I have no cause for it!" And with that he brought the paper to his eyes and read as follows.

"My dear Utterson,—When this shall fall into your hands, I shall have disappeared, under what circumstances I have not the penetration to foresee, but my instinct and all the circumstances of my nameless situation tell me that the end is sure and must be early. Go then, and first read the narrative which Lanyon warned me he was to place in your hands; and if you care to hear more, turn to the confession of

"Your unworthy and unhappy friend,

"HENRY JEKYLL."

"There was a third enclosure?" asked Utterson.

"Here, sir," said Poole, and gave into his hands a considerable packet sealed in several places.

The lawyer put it in his pocket. "I would say nothing of this paper. If your master has fled or is dead, we may at least save his credit. It is now ten; I must go home and read these documents in quiet; but I shall be back before midnight, when we shall send for the police."

They went out, locking the door of the theatre behind them; and Utterson, once more leaving the servants gathered about the fire in the hall, trudged back to his office to read the two narratives in which this mystery was now to be explained.

DOCTOR LANYON'S NARRATIVE

On the ninth of January, now four days ago, I received by the evening delivery a registered envelope, addressed in the hand of my colleague and old school-companion, Henry Jekyll. I was a good deal surprised by this; for we were by no means in the habit of correspondence; I had seen the man, dined with him, indeed, the night before; and I could imagine nothing in our intercourse that should justify the formality of registration. The contents increased my wonder; for this is how the letter ran:

"10TH DECEMBER, 18—

"Dear Lanyon,—You are one of my oldest friends; and although we may have differed at times on scientific questions, I cannot remember, at least on my side, any break in our affection. There was never a day when, if you had said to me, 'Jekyll, my life, my honour, my reason, depend upon you,' I would not have sacrificed my fortune or my left hand to help you. Lanyon, my life, my honour, my reason, are all at your mercy; if you fail me tonight, I am lost. You might suppose, after this preface, that I am going to ask you for something dishonourable to grant. Judge for yourself.

"I want you to postpone all other engagements for tonight—ay, even if you were summoned to the bedside of an emperor; to take a cab, unless your carriage should be actually at the door; and with this letter in your hand for consultation, to drive straight to my house. Poole, my butler, has his orders; you will find him waiting your arrival with a locksmith. The door of my cabinet is then to be forced; and you are to go in alone; to open the glazed press (letter E) on the left hand, breaking the lock if it be shut; and to draw out, *with all its contents as they stand*, the fourth drawer from the top or (which is the same thing) the third from the bottom. In my extreme distress of mind, I have a morbid fear of misdirecting you; but even if I am in error, you may know the right drawer by its contents: some powders, a phial and a paper book. This drawer I beg of you to carry back with you to Cavendish Square exactly as it stands.

"That is the first part of the service: now for the second. You should be back, if you set out at once on the receipt of this, long before midnight; but I will leave you that amount of margin, not only in the fear of one of those obstacles that can neither be prevented nor foreseen, but because an hour when your servants are in bed is to be preferred for what will then remain to do. At midnight, then, I have to ask you to be alone in your consulting room, to admit with your own hand into the house a man who will present himself in my name, and to place in his hands the drawer that you will have brought with you from my cabinet. Then you will have played your part and earned my gratitude completely. Five minutes, afterwards, if you insist upon an explanation, you will have understood that these arrangements are of capital importance; and that by the neglect of one of them, fantastic as they must appear, you might have charged your conscience with my death or the shipwreck of my reason.

"Confident as I am that you will not trifle with this appeal, my heart sinks and my hand trembles at the bare thought of such a possibility. Think of me at this hour, in a strange place, labouring under a blackness of distress that no fancy can exaggerate, and yet well aware that, if you will but punctually serve me, my troubles will roll away like a story that is told. Serve me, my dear Lanyon, and save

"Your friend,

"H. J.

"P.S. I had already sealed this up when a fresh terror struck upon my soul. It is possible that the post office may fail me, and this letter not come into your hands until tomorrow morning. In that case, dear Lanyon, do my errand when it shall be most convenient for you in the course of the day; and once more expect my messenger at midnight. It may then already be too late; and if that night passes without event, you will know that you have seen the last of Henry Jekyll."

Upon the reading of this letter, I made sure my colleague was insane; but till that was proved beyond the possibility of doubt, I felt bound to do as he requested. The less I understood of this farrago, the less I was in a position to judge of its importance; and an appeal so worded could not be set aside without a grave responsibility. I rose accordingly from table, got into a hansom, and drove straight to Jekyll's house. The butler was awaiting my arrival; he had received by the same post as mine a registered letter of instruction, and had sent at once for a locksmith and a carpenter. The tradesmen came while we were yet speaking; and we moved in a body to old Dr. Denman's surgical theatre, from which (as you are doubtless aware) Jekyll's private cabinet is most conveniently entered. The door was very strong, the lock excellent; the carpenter avowed he would have great trouble and have to do much damage, if force were to be used; and the locksmith was near despair. But this last was a handy fellow, and after two hours' work, the door stood open. The press marked E was unlocked; and I took out the drawer, had it filled up with straw and tied in a sheet, and returned with it to Cavendish Square.

Here I proceeded to examine its contents. The powders were neatly enough made up, but not with the nicety of the dispensing chemist; so that it was plain they were of Jekyll's private manufacture; and when I opened one of the wrappers, I found what seemed to me a simple, crystalline salt of a white colour. The phial, to which I next turned my attention, might have been about half-full of a blood-red liquor, which was highly pungent to the sense of smell and seemed to me to contain phosphorus and some volatile ether. At the other ingredients, I could make no guess. The book was an ordinary version book and contained little but a series of dates. These covered a period of many years, but I observed that the entries ceased nearly a year ago and quite abruptly. Here and there a brief remark was appended to a date, usually no more than a single word: "double" occurring perhaps six times in a total of several hundred entries; and once very early in the list and followed by several marks of exclamation, "total failure!!!" All this, though it whetted my curiosity, told me little that was definite. Here were a phial of some tincture, a paper of some salt, and the record of a series of experiments that had led (like too many of Jekyll's investigations) to no end of practical usefulness. How could the presence of these articles in my house affect either the honour, the sanity, or the life of my flighty colleague? If his messenger could go to one place, why could he not go to another? And even granting some impediment, why was this gentleman to be received by me in secret? The more I reflected, the more convinced I grew that I was dealing with a case of cerebral disease; and though I dismissed my servants to bed, I loaded an old revolver that I might be found in some posture of self-defence.

Twelve o'clock had scarce rung out over London, ere the knocker sounded very gently on the door. I went myself at the summons, and found a small man crouching against the pillars of the portico.

"Are you come from Dr. Jekyll?" I asked.

He told me "yes" by a constrained gesture; and when I had bidden him enter, he did not obey me without a searching backward glance into the darkness of the square. There was a policeman not far off, advancing with his bull's eye open; and at the sight, I thought my visitor started and made greater haste.

These particulars struck me, I confess, disagreeably; and as I followed him into the bright light of the consulting room, I kept my hand ready on my weapon. Here, at last, I had a chance of clearly seeing him. I had never set eyes on him before, so much was certain. He was small, as I have said; I was struck besides with the shocking expression of his face, with his remarkable combination of great muscular activity and great apparent debility of constitution, and—last but not least—with the odd, subjective disturbance caused by his neighbourhood. This bore some resemblance to incipient rigor, and was accompanied by a marked sinking of the pulse. At the time, I set it down to some idiosyncratic, personal distaste, and merely wondered at the acuteness of the symptoms; but I have since had reason to believe the cause to lie much deeper in the nature of man, and to turn on some nobler hinge than the principle of hatred.

This person (who had thus, from the first moment of his entrance, struck in me what I can only describe as a disgustful curiosity) was dressed in a fashion that would have made an ordinary person laughable: his clothes, that is to say, although they were of rich and sober fabric, were enormously too large for him in every measurement—the trousers hanging on his legs and rolled up to keep them from the ground, the waist of the coat below his haunches, and the collar sprawling wide upon his shoulders. Strange to relate, this ludicrous accoutrement was far from moving me to laughter. Rather, as there was something abnormal and misbegotten in the very essence of the creature that now faced me—something seizing, surprising and revolting—this fresh disparity seemed but to fit in with and to reïnforce it, so that to my interest in the man's nature and character, there was added a curiosity as to his origin, his life, his fortune and status in the world.

These observations, though they have taken so great a space to be set down in, were yet the work of a few seconds. My visitor was, indeed, on fire with sombre excitement.

"Have you got it?" he cried. "Have you got it?" And so lively was his impatience that he even laid his hand upon my arm and sought to shake me.

I put him back, conscious at his touch of a certain icy pang along my blood. "Come, sir," said I. "You forget that I have not yet the pleasure of your acquaintance. Be seated, if you please." And I showed him an example, and sat down myself in my customary seat and with as fair an imitation of my ordinary manner to a patient, as the lateness of the hour, the nature of my preöccupations, and the horror I had of my visitor, would suffer me to muster.

"I beg your pardon, Dr. Lanyon," he replied civilly enough. "What you say is very well founded; and my impatience has shown its heels to my politeness. I come here at the instance of your colleague, Dr. Henry Jekyll, on a piece of business of some moment; and I understood..." he paused and put his hand to his throat, and I could see, in spite of his collected manner, that he was wrestling against the approaches of the hysteria—"I understood, a drawer..."

But here I took pity on my visitor's suspense, and some perhaps on my own growing curiosity.

"There it is, sir," said I, pointing to the drawer, where it lay on the floor behind a table and still covered with the sheet.

He sprang to it, and then paused, and laid his hand upon his heart; I could hear his teeth grate with the convulsive action of his jaws; and his face was so ghastly to see that I grew alarmed both for his life and reason.

"Compose yourself," said I.

He turned a dreadful smile to me, and as if with the decision of despair, plucked away the sheet. At sight of the contents, he uttered one loud sob of such immense relief that I sat petrified. And the next moment, in a voice that was already fairly well under control, "Have you a graduated glass?" he asked.

I rose from my place with something of an effort and gave him what he asked.

He thanked me with a smiling nod, measured out a few minims of the red tincture and added one of the powders. The mixture, which was at first of a reddish hue, began, in proportion as the crystals melted, to brighten in colour, to effervesce audibly, and to throw off small fumes of vapour. Suddenly and at the same moment, the ebullition ceased and the compound changed to a dark purple, which faded again more slowly to a watery green. My visitor, who had watched these metamorphoses with a keen eye, smiled, set down the glass upon the table, and then turned and looked upon me with an air of scrutiny.

"And now," said he, "to settle what remains. Will you be wise? will you be guided? will you suffer me to take this glass in my hand and to go forth from your house without further parley? or has the greed of curiosity too much command of you? Think before you answer, for it shall be done as you decide. As you decide, you shall be left as you were before, and neither richer nor wiser, unless the sense of service rendered to a man in mortal distress may be counted as a kind of riches of the soul. Or, if you shall so prefer to choose, a new province of knowledge and new avenues to fame and power shall be laid open to you, here, in this room, upon the instant; and your sight shall be blasted by a prodigy to stagger the unbelief of Satan."

"Sir," said I, affecting a coolness that I was far from truly possessing, "you speak enigmas, and you will perhaps not wonder that I hear you with no very strong impression of belief. But I have gone too far in the way of inexplicable services to pause before I see the end."

"It is well," replied my visitor. "Lanyon, you remember your vows: what follows is under the seal of our profession. And now, you who have so long been bound to the most narrow and material views, you who have denied the virtue of transcendental medicine, you who have derided your superiors—behold!"

He put the glass to his lips and drank at one gulp. A cry followed; he reeled, staggered, clutched at the table and held on, staring with injected eyes, gasping with open mouth; and as I looked there came, I thought, a change—he seemed to swell—his face became suddenly black and the features seemed to melt and alter—and the next moment, I had sprung to my feet and leaped back against the wall, my arm raised to shield me from that prodigy, my mind submerged in terror.

"O God!" I screamed, and "O God!" again and again; for there before my eyes—pale and shaken, and half fainting, and groping before him with his hands, like a man restored from death—there stood Henry Jekyll!

What he told me in the next hour, I cannot bring my mind to set on paper. I saw what I saw, I heard what I heard, and my soul sickened at it; and yet now when that sight has faded from my eyes, I ask myself if I believe it, and I cannot answer. My life is shaken to its roots; sleep has left me; the deadliest terror sits by me at all hours of the day and night; I feel that my days are numbered, and that I must die; and yet I shall die incredulous. As for the moral turpitude that man unveiled to me, even with tears of penitence, I cannot, even in memory, dwell on it without a start of horror. I will say but one thing, Utterson, and that (if you can bring your mind to credit it) will be more than enough. The creature who crept into my house that night was, on Jekyll's own confession, known by the name of Hyde and hunted for in every corner of the land as the murderer of Carew.

HASTIE LANYON

Henry Jekyll's Full Statement
of the Case

I was born in the year 18— to a large fortune, endowed besides with excellent parts, inclined by nature to industry, fond of the respect of the wise and good among my fellow-men, and thus, as might have been supposed, with every guarantee of an honourable and distinguished future. And indeed the worst of my faults was a certain impatient gaiety of disposition, such as has made the happiness of many, but such as I found it hard to reconcile with my imperious desire to carry my head high, and wear a more than commonly grave countenance before the public. Hence it came about that I concealed my pleasures; and that when I reached years of reflection, and began to look round me and take stock of my progress and position in the world, I stood already committed to a profound duplicity of life. Many a man would have even blazoned such irregularities as I was guilty of; but from the high views that I had set before me, I regarded and hid them with an almost morbid sense of shame. It was thus rather the exacting nature of my aspirations than any particular degradation in my faults, that made me what I was and, with even a deeper trench than in the majority of men, severed in me those provinces of good and ill which divide and compound man's dual nature. In this case, I was driven to reflect deeply and inveterately on that hard law of life, which lies at the root of religion and is one of the most plentiful springs of distress. Though so profound a double-dealer, I was in no sense a hypocrite; both sides of me were in dead earnest; I was no more myself when I laid aside restraint and plunged in shame, than when I laboured, in the eye of day, at the furtherance of knowledge or the relief of sorrow and suffering. And it chanced that the direction of my scientific studies, which led wholly towards the mystic and the transcendental, rëacted and shed a strong light on this consciousness of the perennial war among my members. With every day, and from both sides of my intelligence, the moral and the intellectual, I thus drew steadily nearer to that truth, by whose partial discovery I have been doomed to such a dreadful shipwreck: that man is not truly one, but truly two. I say two, because the state of my own knowledge does not pass beyond that point. Others will follow, others will outstrip me on the same lines; and I hazard the guess that man will be ultimately known for a mere polity of multifarious, incongruous and independent denizens. I for my part, from the nature of my life, advanced infallibly in one direction and in one direction only. It was on the moral side, and in my own person, that I learned to recognise the thorough and primitive duality of man; I saw that, of the two natures that contended in the field of my consciousness, even if I could rightly be said to be either, it was only because I was radically both; and from an early date, even before the course of my scientific discoveries had begun to suggest the most naked possibility of such a miracle, I had learned to dwell with pleasure, as a beloved daydream, on the thought of the separation of these elements. If each, I told myself, could but be housed in separate identities, life would be relieved of all that was unbearable; the unjust might go his way, delivered from the aspirations and remorse of his more upright twin; and the just could walk steadfastly and securely on his upward path, doing the good things in which he found his pleasure, and no longer exposed to disgrace and penitence by the hands of this extraneous evil. It was the curse of mankind that these incongruous faggots were thus bound together—that in the agonised womb of consciousness, these polar twins should be continuously struggling. How, then, were they dissociated?

I was so far in my reflections when, as I have said, a side light began to shine upon the subject from the laboratory table. I began to perceive more deeply than it has ever yet been stated, the trembling immateriality, the mist-like transience, of this seemingly so solid body in which we walk attired. Certain agents I found to have the power to shake and to pluck back that fleshly vestment, even as a wind might toss the curtains of a pavilion. For two good reasons, I will not enter deeply into this scientific branch of my confession. First, because I have been made to learn that the doom and burthen of our life is bound forever on man's shoulders, and when the attempt is made to cast it off, it but returns upon us with more unfamiliar and more awful pressure. Second, because as my narrative will make alas! too evident, my discoveries were incomplete. Enough, then, that I not only recognised my natural body for the mere aura and effulgence of certain of the powers that made up my spirit, but managed to compound a drug by which these powers should be dethroned from their supremacy, and a second form and countenance substituted, none the less natural to me because they were the expression, and bore the stamp, of lower elements in my soul.

I hesitated long before I put this theory to the test of practice. I knew well that I risked death; for any drug that so potently controlled and shook the very fortress of identity, might by the least scruple of an overdose or at the least inopportunity in the moment of exhibition, utterly blot out that immaterial tabernacle which I looked to it to change. But the temptation of a discovery so singular and profound, at last overcame the suggestions of alarm. I had long since prepared my tincture; I purchased at once, from a firm of wholesale chemists, a large quantity of a particular salt which I knew, from my experiments, to be the last ingredient required; and late one accursed night, I compounded the elements, watched them boil and smoke together in the glass, and when the ebullition had subsided, with a strong glow of courage, drank off the potion.

The most racking pangs succeeded: a grinding in the bones, deadly nausea, and a horror of the spirit that cannot be exceeded at the hour of birth or death. Then these agonies began swiftly to subside, and I came to myself as if out of a great sickness. There was something strange in my sensations, something indescribably new and, from its very novelty, incredibly sweet. I felt younger, lighter, happier in body; within I was conscious of a heady recklessness, a current of disordered sensual images running like a mill race in my fancy, a solution of the bonds of obligation, an unknown but not an innocent freedom of the soul. I knew myself, at the first breath of this new life, to be more wicked, tenfold more wicked, sold a slave to my original evil; and the thought, in that moment, braced and delighted me like wine. I stretched out my hands, exulting in the freshness of these sensations; and in the act, I was suddenly aware that I had lost in stature.

There was no mirror, at that date, in my room; that which stands beside me as I write, was brought there later on and for the very purpose of these transformations. The night, however, was far gone into the morning—the morning, black as it was, was nearly ripe for the conception of the day—the inmates of my house were locked in the most rigorous hours of slumber; and I determined, flushed as I was with hope and triumph, to venture in my new shape as far as to my bedroom. I crossed the yard, wherein the constellations looked down upon me, I could have thought, with wonder, the first creature of that sort that their unsleeping vigilance had yet disclosed to them; I stole through the corridors, a stranger in my own house; and coming to my room, I saw for the first time the appearance of Edward Hyde.

I must here speak by theory alone, saying not that which I know, but that which I suppose to be most probable. The evil side of my nature, to which I had now transferred the stamping efficacy, was less robust and less developed than the good which I had just deposed. Again, in the course of my life, which had been, after all, nine tenths a life of effort, virtue and control, it had been much less exercised and much less exhausted. And hence, as I think, it came about that Edward Hyde was so much smaller, slighter and younger than Henry Jekyll. Even as good shone upon the countenance of the one, evil was written broadly and plainly on the face of the other. Evil besides (which I must still believe to be the lethal side of man) had left on that body an imprint of deformity and decay. And yet when I looked upon that ugly idol in the glass, I was conscious of no repugnance, rather of a leap of welcome. This, too, was myself. It seemed natural and human. In my eyes it bore a livelier image of the spirit, it seemed more express and single, than the imperfect and divided countenance, I had been hitherto accustomed to call mine. And in so far I was doubtless right. I have observed that when I wore the semblance of Edward Hyde, none could come near to me at first without a visible misgiving of the flesh. This, as I take it, was because all human beings, as we meet them, are commingled out of good and evil: and Edward Hyde, alone in the ranks of mankind, was pure evil.

I lingered but a moment at the mirror: the second and conclusive experiment had yet to be attempted; it yet remained to be seen if I had lost my identity beyond redemption and must flee before daylight from a house that was no longer mine; and hurrying back to my cabinet, I once more prepared and drank the cup, once more suffered the pangs of dissolution, and came to myself once more with the character, the stature and the face of Henry Jekyll.

That night I had come to the fatal cross roads. Had I approached my discovery in a more noble spirit, had I risked the experiment while under the empire of generous or pious aspirations, all must have been otherwise, and from these agonies of death and birth, I had come forth an angel instead of a fiend. The drug had no discriminating action; it was neither diabolical nor divine; it but shook the doors of the prison-house of my disposition; and like the captives of Philippi, that which stood within ran forth. At that time my virtue slumbered; my evil, kept awake by ambition, was alert and swift to seize the occasion; and the thing that was projected was Edward Hyde. Hence, although I had now two characters as well as two appearances, one was wholly evil, and the other was still the old Henry Jekyll, that incongruous compound of whose reformation and improvement I had already learned to despair. The movement was thus wholly toward the worse.

Even at that time, I had not yet conquered my aversion to the dryness of a life of study. I would still be merrily disposed at times; and as my pleasures were (to say the least) undignified, and I was not only well known and highly considered, but growing towards the elderly man, this incoherency of my life was daily growing more unwelcome. It was on this side that my new power tempted me until I fell in slavery. I had but to drink the cup, to doff at once the body of the noted professor, and to assume, like a thick cloak, that of Edward Hyde. I smiled at the notion; it seemed to me at the time to be humorous; and I made my preparations with the most studious care. I took and furnished that house in Soho, to which Hyde was tracked by the police; and engaged as housekeeper a creature whom I well knew to be silent and unscrupulous. On the other side, I announced to my servants that a Mr. Hyde (whom I described) was to have full liberty and power about my house in the square; and to parry mishaps, I even called and made myself a familiar object, in my second character. I next drew up that will to which you so much objected; so that if anything befell me in the person of Doctor Jekyll, I could enter on that of Edward Hyde without pecuniary loss. And thus fortified, as I supposed, on every side, I began to profit by the strange immunities of my position.

Men have before hired bravos to transact their crimes, while their own person and reputation sat under shelter. I was the first that ever did so for his pleasures. I was the first that could thus plod in the public eye with a load of genial respectability, and in a moment, like a schoolboy, strip off these lendings and spring headlong into the sea of liberty. But for me, in my impenetrable mantle, the safety was complete. Think of it—I did not even exist! Let me but escape into my laboratory door, give me but a second or two to mix and swallow the draught that I had always standing ready; and whatever he had done, Edward Hyde would pass away like the stain of breath upon a mirror; and there in his stead, quietly at home, trimming the midnight lamp in his study, a man who could afford to laugh at suspicion, would be Henry Jekyll.

The pleasures which I made haste to seek in my disguise were, as I have said, undignified; I would scarce use a harder term. But in the hands of Edward Hyde, they soon began to turn towards the monstrous. When I would come back from these excursions, I was often plunged into a kind of wonder at my vicarious depravity. This familiar that I called out of my own soul, and sent forth alone to do his good pleasure, was a being inherently malign and villainous; his every act and thought centered on self; drinking pleasure with bestial avidity from any degree of torture to another; relentless like a man of stone. Henry Jekyll stood at times aghast before the acts of Edward Hyde; but the situation was apart from ordinary laws, and insidiously relaxed the grasp of conscience. It was Hyde, after all, and Hyde alone, that was guilty. Jekyll was no worse; he woke again to his good qualities seemingly unimpaired; he would even make haste, where it was possible, to undo the evil done by Hyde. And thus his conscience slumbered.

Into the details of the infamy at which I thus connived (for even now I can scarce grant that I committed it) I have no design of entering I mean but to point out the warnings and the successive steps with which my chastisement approached. I met with one accident which, as it brought on no consequence, I shall no more than mention. An act of cruelty to a child aroused against me the anger of a passer by, whom I recognised the other day in the person of your kinsman; the doctor and the child's family joined him; there were moments when I feared for my life; and at last, in order to pacify their too just resentment, Edward Hyde had to bring them to the door, and pay them in a cheque drawn in the name, of Henry Jekyll. But this danger was easily eliminated from the future, by opening an account at another bank in the name of Edward Hyde himself; and when, by sloping my own hand backward, I had supplied my double with a signature, I thought I sat beyond the reach of fate.

Some two months before the murder of Sir Danvers, I had been out for one of my adventures, had returned at a late hour, and woke the next day in bed with somewhat odd sensations. It was in vain I looked about me; in vain I saw the decent furniture and tall proportions of my room in the square; in vain that I recognised the pattern of the bed curtains and the design of the mahogany frame; something still kept insisting that I was not where I was, that I had not wakened where I seemed to be, but in the little room in Soho where I was accustomed to sleep in the body of Edward Hyde. I smiled to myself, and, in my psychological way, began lazily to inquire into the elements of this illusion, occasionally, even as I did so, dropping back into a comfortable morning doze. I was still so engaged when, in one of my more wakeful moments, my eye fell upon my hand. Now the hand of Henry Jekyll (as you have often remarked) was professional in shape and size: it was large, firm, white and comely. But the hand which I now saw, clearly enough, in the yellow light of a mid-London morning, lying half shut on the bed clothes, was lean, corded, knuckly, of a dusky pallor and thickly shaded with a swart growth of hair. It was the hand of Edward Hyde.

I must have stared upon it for near half a minute, sunk as I was in the mere stupidity of wonder, before terror woke up in my breast as sudden and startling as the crash of cymbals; and bounding from my bed, I rushed to the mirror. At the sight that met my eyes, my blood was changed into something exquisitely thin and icy. Yes, I had gone to bed Henry Jekyll, I had awakened Edward Hyde. How was this to be explained? I asked myself; and then, with another bound of terror— how was it to be remedied? It was well on in the morning; the servants were up; all my drugs were in the cabinet—a long journey, down two pair of stairs, through the back passage, across the open court and through the anatomical theatre, from where I was then standing horror-struck. It might indeed be possible to cover my face; but of what use was that, when I was unable to conceal the alteration in my stature? And then with an overpowering sweetness of relief, it came back upon my mind that the servants were already used to the coming and going of my second self. I had soon dressed, as well as I was able, in clothes of my own size: had soon passed through the house, where Bradshaw stared and drew back at seeing Mr. Hyde at such an hour and in such a strange array; and ten minutes later, Dr. Jekyll had returned to his own shape and was sitting down, with a darkened brow, to make a feint of breakfasting.

Small indeed was my appetite. This inexplicable incident, this reversal of my previous experience, seemed, like the Babylonian finger on the wall, to be spelling out the letters of my judgment; and I began to reflect more seriously than ever before on the issues and possibilities of my double existence. That part of me which I had the power of projecting, had lately been much exercised and nourished; it had seemed to me of late as though the body of Edward Hyde had grown in stature, as though (when I wore that form) I were conscious of a more generous tide of blood; and I began to spy a danger that, if this were much prolonged, the balance of my nature might be permanently overthrown, the power of voluntary change be forfeited, and the character of Edward Hyde become irrevocably mine. The power of the drug had not been always equally displayed. Once, very early in my career, it had totally failed me; since then I had been obliged on more than one occasion to double, and once, with infinite risk of death, to treble the amount; and these rare uncertainties had cast hitherto the sole shadow on my contentment. Now, however, and in the light of that morning's accident, I was led to remark that whereas, in the beginning, the difficulty had been to throw off the body of Jekyll, it had of late, gradually but decidedly transferred itself to the other side. All things therefore seemed to point to this: that I was slowly losing hold of my original and better self, and becoming slowly incorporated with my second and worse.

Between these two, I now felt I had to choose. My two natures had memory in common, but all other faculties were most unequally shared between them. Jekyll (who was composite) now with the most sensitive apprehensions, now with a greedy gusto, projected and shared in the pleasures and adventures of Hyde; but Hyde was indifferent to Jekyll, or but remembered him as the mountain bandit remembers the cavern in which he conceals himself from pursuit. Jekyll had more than a father's interest; Hyde had more than a son's indifference. To cast in my lot with Jekyll, was to die to those appetites which I had long secretly indulged and had of late begun to pamper. To cast it in with Hyde, was to die to a thousand interests and aspirations, and to become, at a blow and forever, despised and friendless. The bargain might appear unequal; but there was still another consideration in the scales; for while Jekyll would suffer smartingly in the fires of abstinence, Hyde would be not even conscious of all that he had lost. Strange as my circumstances were, the terms of this debate are as old and commonplace as man; much the same inducements and alarms cast the die for any tempted and trembling sinner; and it fell out with me, as it falls with so vast a majority of my fellows, that I chose the better part and was found wanting in the strength to keep to it.

Yes, I preferred the elderly and discontented doctor, surrounded by friends and cherishing honest hopes; and bade a resolute farewell to the liberty, the comparative youth, the light step, leaping pulses and secret pleasures, that I had enjoyed in the disguise of Hyde. I made this choice perhaps with some unconscious reservation, for I neither gave up the house in Soho, nor destroyed the clothes of Edward Hyde, which still lay ready in my cabinet. For two months, however, I was true to my determination; for two months, I led a life of such severity as I had never before attained to, and enjoyed the compensations of an approving conscience. But time began at last to obliterate the freshness of my alarm; the praises of conscience began to grow into a thing of course; I began to be tortured with throes and longings, as of Hyde struggling after freedom; and at last, in an hour of moral weakness, I once again compounded and swallowed the transforming draught.

I do not suppose that, when a drunkard reasons with himself upon his vice, he is once out of five hundred times affected by the dangers that he runs through his brutish, physical insensibility; neither had I, long as I had considered my position, made enough allowance for the complete moral insensibility and insensate readiness to evil, which were the leading characters of Edward Hyde. Yet it was by these that I was punished. My devil had been long caged, he came out roaring. I was conscious, even when I took the draught, of a more unbridled, a more furious propensity to ill. It must have been this, I suppose, that stirred in my soul that tempest of impatience with which I listened to the civilities of my unhappy victim; I declare at least, before God, no man morally sane could have been guilty of that crime upon so pitiful a provocation; and that I struck in no more reasonable spirit than that in which a sick child may break a plaything. But I had voluntarily stripped myself of all those balancing instincts, by which even the worst of us continues to walk with some degree of steadiness among temptations; and in my case, to be tempted, however slightly, was to fall.

Instantly the spirit of hell awoke in me and raged. With a transport of glee, I mauled the unresisting body, tasting delight from every blow; and it was not till weariness had begun to succeed, that I was suddenly, in the top fit of my delirium, struck through the heart by a cold thrill of terror. A mist dispersed; I saw my life to be forfeit; and fled from the scene of these excesses, at once glorying and trembling, my lust of evil gratified and stimulated, my love of life screwed to the topmost peg. I ran to the house in Soho, and (to make assurance doubly sure) destroyed my papers; thence I set out through the lamplit streets, in the same divided ecstasy of mind, gloating on my crime, light-headedly devising others in the future, and yet still hastening and still hearkening in my wake for the steps of the avenger. Hyde had a song upon his lips as he compounded the draught, and as he drank it, pledged the dead man. The pangs of transformation had not done tearing him, before Henry Jekyll, with streaming tears of gratitude and remorse, had fallen upon his knees and lifted his clasped hands to God. The veil of self-indulgence was rent from head to foot, I saw my life as a whole: I followed it up from the days of childhood, when I had walked with my father's hand, and through the self-denying toils of my professional life, to arrive again and again, with the same sense of unreality, at the damned horrors of the evening. I could have screamed aloud; I sought with tears and prayers to smother down the crowd of hideous images and sounds with which my memory swarmed against me; and still, between the petitions, the ugly face of my iniquity stared into my soul. As the acuteness of this remorse began to die away, it was succeeded by a sense of joy. The problem of my conduct was solved. Hyde was thenceforth impossible; whether I would or not, I was now confined to the better part of my existence; and O, how I rejoiced to think it! with what willing humility, I embraced anew the restrictions of natural life! with what sincere renunciation, I locked the door by which I had so often gone and come, and ground the key under my heel!

The next day, came the news that the murder had been overlooked, that the guilt of Hyde was patent to the world, and that the victim was a man high in public estimation. It was not only a crime, it had been a tragic folly. I think I was glad to know it; I think I was glad to have my better impulses thus buttressed and guarded by the terrors of the scaffold. Jekyll was now my city of refuge; let but Hyde peep out an instant, and the hands of all men would be raised to take and slay him.

I resolved in my future conduct to redeem the past; and I can say with honesty that my resolve was fruitful of some good. You know yourself how earnestly in the last months of last year, I laboured to relieve suffering; you know that much was done for others, and that the days passed quietly, almost happily for myself. Nor can I truly say that I wearied of this beneficent and innocent life; I think instead that I daily enjoyed it more completely; but I was still cursed with my duality of purpose; and as the first edge of my penitence wore off, the lower side of me, so long indulged, so recently chained down, began to growl for license. Not that I dreamed of resuscitating Hyde; the bare idea of that would startle me to frenzy: no, it was in my own person, that I was once more tempted to trifle with my conscience; and it was as an ordinary secret sinner, that I at last fell before the assaults of temptation.

There comes an end to all things; the most capacious measure is filled at last; and this brief condescension to my evil finally destroyed the balance of my soul. And yet I was not alarmed; the fall seemed natural, like a return to the old days before I had made my discovery. It was a fine, clear, January day, wet under foot where the frost had melted, but cloudless overhead; and the Regent's park was full of winter chirruppings and sweet with Spring odours. I sat in the sun on a bench; the animal within me licking the chops of memory; the spiritual side a little drowsed, promising subsequent penitence, but not yet moved to begin. After all, I reflected I was like my neighbours; and then I smiled, comparing myself with other men, comparing my active goodwill with the lazy cruelty of their neglect. And at the very moment of that vainglorious thought, a qualm came over me, a horrid nausea and the most deadly shuddering. These passed away, and left me faint; and then as in its turn the faintness subsided, I began to be aware of a change in the temper of my thoughts, a greater boldness, a contempt of danger, a solution of the bonds of obligation. I looked down; my clothes hung formlessly on my shrunken limbs; the hand that lay on my knee was corded and hairy. I was once more Edward Hyde. A moment before I had been safe of all men's respect, wealthy, beloved—the cloth laying for me in the dining room at home; and now I was the common quarry of mankind, hunted, houseless, a known murderer, thrall to the gallows.

My reason wavered, but it did not fail me utterly. I have more than once observed that, in my second character, my faculties seemed sharpened to a point and my spirits more tensely elastic; thus it came about that, where Jekyll perhaps might have succumbed, Hyde rose to the importance of the moment. My drugs were in one of the presses of my cabinet; how was I to reach them? That was the problem that (crushing my temples in my hands) I set myself to solve. The laboratory door I had closed. If I sought to enter by the house, my own servants would consign me to the gallows. I saw I must employ another hand, and thought of Lanyon. How was he to be reached? how persuaded? Supposing that I escaped capture in the streets, how was I to make my way into his presence? and how should I, an unknown and displeasing visitor, prevail on the famous physician to rifle the study of his colleague, Dr. Jekyll? Then I remembered that of my original character, one part remained to me: I could write my own hand; and once I had conceived that kindling spark, the way that I must follow became lighted up from end to end.

Thereupon, I arranged my clothes as best I could, and summoning a passing hansom; drove to an hotel in Portland street, the name of which I chanced to remember. At my appearance (which was indeed comical enough, however tragic a fate these garments covered) the driver could not conceal his mirth. I gnashed my teeth upon him with a gust of devilish fury; and the smile withered from his face—happily for him—yet more happily for myself, for in another instant I had certainly dragged him from his perch. At the inn, as I entered, I looked about me with so black a countenance as made the attendants tremble; not a look did they exchange in my presence; but obsequiously took my orders, led me to a private room, and brought me wherewithal to write. Hyde in danger of his life was a creature new to me: shaken with inordinate anger, strung to the pitch of murder, lusting to inflict pain. Yet the creature was astute; mastered his fury with a great effort of the will; composed his two important letters, one to Lanyon and one to

Poole; and that he might receive actual evidence of their being posted, sent them out with directions that they should be registered.

Thenceforward, he sat all day over the fire in the private room, gnawing his nails; there he dined, sitting alone with his fears, the waiter visibly quailing before his eye; and thence, when the night was fully come, he set forth in the corner of a closed cab, and was driven to and fro about the streets of the city. He, I say—I cannot say, I. That child of Hell had nothing human; nothing lived in him but fear and hatred. And when at last, thinking the driver had begun to grow suspicious, he discharged the cab and ventured on foot, attired in his misfitting clothes, an object marked out for observation, into the midst of the nocturnal passengers, these two base passions raged within him like a tempest. He walked fast, hunted by his fears, chattering to himself, skulking through the less frequented thoroughfares, counting the minutes that still divided him from midnight. Once a woman spoke to him, offering, I think, a box of lights. He smote her in the face, and she fled.

When I came to myself at Lanyon's, the horror of my old friend perhaps affected me somewhat: I do not know; it was at least but a drop in the sea to the abhorrence with which I looked back upon these hours. A change had come over me. It was no longer the fear of the gallows, it was the horror of being Hyde that racked me. I received Lanyon's condemnation partly in a dream; it was partly in a dream that I came home to my own house and got into bed. I slept after the prostration of the day, with a stringent and profound slumber which not even the nightmares that wrung me could avail to break. I awoke in the morning shaken, weakened, but refreshed. I still hated and feared the thought of the brute that slept within me, and I had not of course forgotten the appalling dangers of the day before; but I was once more at home, in my own house and close to my drugs; and gratitude for my escape shone so strong in my soul that it almost rivalled the brightness of hope.

I was stepping leisurely across the court after breakfast, drinking the chill of the air with pleasure, when I was seized again with those indescribable sensations that heralded the change; and I had but the time to gain the shelter of my cabinet, before I was once again raging and freezing with the passions of Hyde. It took on this occasion a double dose to recall me to myself; and alas, six hours after, as I sat looking sadly in the fire, the pangs returned, and the drug had to be re-administered. In short, from that day forth it seemed only by a great effort as of gymnastics, and only under the immediate stimulation of the drug, that I was able to wear the countenance of Jekyll. At all hours of the day and night, I would be taken with the premonitory shudder; above all, if I slept, or even dozed for a moment in my chair, it was always as Hyde that I awakened. Under the strain of this continually impending doom and by the sleeplessness to which I now condemned myself, ay, even beyond what I had thought possible to man, I became, in my own person, a creature eaten up and emptied by fever, languidly weak both in body and mind, and solely occupied by one thought: the horror of my other self. But when I slept, or when the virtue of the medicine wore off, I would leap almost without transition (for the pangs of transformation grew daily less marked) into the possession of a fancy brimming with images of terror, a soul boiling with causeless hatreds, and a body that seemed not strong enough to contain the raging energies of life. The powers of Hyde seemed to have grown with the sickliness of Jekyll. And certainly the hate that now divided them was equal on each side. With Jekyll, it was a thing of vital instinct. He had now seen the full deformity of that creature that shared with him some of the phenomena of consciousness, and was co-heir with him to death: and beyond these links of community, which in themselves made the most poignant part of his distress, he thought of Hyde, for all his energy of life, as of something not only hellish but inorganic. This was the shocking thing; that the slime of the pit seemed to utter cries and voices; that the amorphous dust gesticulated and sinned; that what was dead, and had no shape, should usurp the offices of life. And this again, that that insurgent horror was knit to him closer than a wife, closer than an eye; lay caged in his flesh, where he heard it mutter and felt it struggle to be born; and at every hour of weakness, and in the confidence of slumber, prevailed against him, and deposed him out of life. The hatred of Hyde for Jekyll, was of a different order. His terror of the gallows drove him continually to commit temporary suicide, and return to his subordinate station of a part instead of a person; but he loathed the necessity, he loathed the despondency into which Jekyll was now fallen, and he resented the dislike with which he was himself regarded. Hence the apelike tricks that he would play me, scrawling in my own hand blasphemies on the pages of my books, burning the letters and destroying the portrait of my father; and indeed, had it not been for his fear of death, he would long ago have ruined himself in order to involve me in the ruin. But his love of life is wonderful; I go further: I, who sicken and freeze at the mere thought of him, when I recall the abjection and passion of this attachment, and when I know how he fears my power to cut him off by suicide, I find it in my heart to pity him.

It is useless, and the time awfully fails me, to prolong this description; no one has ever suffered such torments, let that suffice; and yet even to these, habit brought—no, not alleviation—but a certain callousness of soul, a certain acquiescence of despair; and my punishment might have gone on for years, but for the last calamity which has now fallen, and which has finally severed me from my own face and nature. My provision of the salt, which had never been renewed since the date of the first experiment, began to run low. I sent out for a fresh supply, and mixed the draught; the ebullition followed, and the first change of colour, not the second; I drank it and it was without efficiency. You will learn from Poole how I have had London ransacked; it was in vain; and I am now persuaded that my first supply was impure, and that it was that unknown impurity which lent efficacy to the draught.

About a week has passed, and I am now finishing this statement under the influence of the last of the old powders. This, then, is the last time, short of a miracle, that Henry Jekyll can think his own thoughts or see his own face (now how sadly altered!) in the glass. Nor must I delay too long to bring my writing to an end; for if my narrative has hitherto escaped destruction, it has been by a combination of great prudence and great good luck. Should the throes of change take me in the act of writing it, Hyde will tear it in pieces; but if some time shall have elapsed after I have laid it by, his wonderful selfishness and circumscription to the moment will probably save it once again from the action of his apelike spite. And indeed the doom that is closing on us both, has already changed and crushed him. Half an hour from now, when I shall again and forever reindue that hated personality, I know how I shall sit shuddering and weeping in my chair, or continue, with the most strained and fearstruck ecstasy of listening, to pace up and down this room (my last earthly refuge) and give ear to every sound of menace. Will Hyde die upon the scaffold? or will he find the courage to release himself at the last moment? God knows; I am careless; this is my true hour of death, and what is to follow concerns another than myself. Here then, as I lay down the pen and proceed to seal up my confession, I bring the life of that unhappy Henry Jekyll to an end.

Binding for the English edition of
The Merry Men and Other Tales and Fables (LONDON, 1887).

THE MERRY MEN
AND
OTHER TALES AND FABLES

THE MERRY MEN

CHAPTER ONE

Eilean Aros

It was a beautiful morning in the late July when I set forth on foot for the last time for Aros. A boat had put me ashore the night before at Grisapol; I had such breakfast as the little inn afforded, and leaving all my baggage till I had an occasion to come round for it by sea, struck right across the promontory with a cheerful heart.

I was far from being a native of these parts, springing, as I did, from an unmixed lowland stock. But an uncle of mine, Gordon Darnaway, after a poor, rough youth, and some years at sea, had married a young wife in the islands; Mary Maclean she was called, the last of her family; and when she died in giving birth to a daughter, Aros, the sea-girt farm, had remained in his possession. It brought him in nothing but the means of life, as I was well aware; but he was a man whom ill-fortune had pursued; he feared, cumbered as he was with the young child, to make a fresh adventure upon life; and remained in Aros, biting his nails at destiny. Years passed over his head in that isolation, and brought neither help nor contentment. Meantime our family was dying out in the lowlands; there is little luck for any of that race; and perhaps my father was the luckiest of all, for not only was he one of the last to die, but he left a son to his name and a little money to support it. I was a student of Edinburgh University, living well enough at my own charges, but without kith or kin; when some news of me found its way to Uncle Gordon on the Ross of Grisapol; and he, as he was a man who held blood thicker than water, wrote to me the day he heard of my existence, and taught me to count Aros as my home. Thus it was that I came to spend my vacations in that part of the country, so far from all society and comfort, between the codfish and the moorcocks; and thus it was that now, when I had done with my classes, I was returning thither with so light a heart that July day.

The Ross, as we call it, is a promontory neither wide nor high, but as rough as God made it to this day; the deep sea on either hand of it, full of rugged isles and reefs most perilous to seamen—all overlooked from the eastward by some very high cliffs and the great peak of Ben Kyaw. *The Mountain of the Mist,* they say the words signify in the Gaelic tongue; and it is well named. For that hilltop, which is more than three thousand feet in height, catches all the clouds that come blowing from the seaward; and indeed, I used often to think that it must make them for itself; since when all heaven was clear to the sea level, there would ever be a streamer on Ben Kyaw. It brought water, too, and was mossy* to the top in consequence. I have seen us sitting in broad sunshine on the Ross, and the rain falling black like crape upon the mountain. But the wetness of it made it often appear more beautiful to my eyes; for when the sun struck upon the hillsides, there were many wet rocks and watercourses that shone like jewels even as far as Aros, fifteen miles away.

The road that I followed was a cattle track. It twisted so as nearly to double the length of my journey; it went over rough boulders so that a man had to leap from one to another, and through soft bottoms where the moss came nearly to the knee. There was no cultivation anywhere, and not one house in the ten miles from Grisapol to Aros. Houses of course there were—three at least; but they lay so far on the one side or the other that no stranger could have found them from the track. A large part of the Ross is covered with big granite rocks, some of them larger than a two-roomed house, one beside another, with fern and deep heather in between them where the vipers

*Boggy. [R.L.S.]

breed. Any way the wind was, it was always sea air, as salt as on a ship; the gulls were as free as moorfowl over all the Ross; and whenever the way rose a little, your eye would kindle with the brightness of the sea. From the very midst of the land, on a day of wind and a high spring, I have heard the Roost roaring like a battle where it runs by Aros, and the great and fearful voices of the breakers that we call the Merry Men.

Aros itself—Aros Jay, I have heard the natives call it, and they say it means *the House of God*—Aros itself was not properly a piece of the Ross, nor was it quite an islet. It formed the southwest corner of the land, fitted close to it, and was in one place only separated from the coast by a little gut of the sea, not forty feet across the narrowest. When the tide was full, this was clear and still, like a pool on a land river; only there was a difference in the weeds and fishes, and the water itself was green instead of brown; but when the tide went out, in the bottom of the ebb, there was a day or two in every month when you could pass dryshod from Aros to the mainland. There was some good pasture, where my uncle fed the sheep he lived on; perhaps the feed was better because the ground rose higher on the islet than the main level of the Ross, but this I am not skilled enough to settle. The house was a good one for that country, two storeys high. It looked westward over a bay, with a pier hard by for a boat, and from the door you could watch the vapours blowing on Ben Kyaw.

On all this part of the coast, and especially near Aros, these great granite rocks that I have spoken of go down together in troops into the sea, like cattle on a summer's day. There they stand, for all the world like their neighbours ashore; only the salt water sobbing between them instead of the quiet earth, and clots of sea pink blooming on their sides instead of heather; and the great sea conger to wreathe about the base of them instead of the poisonous viper of the land. On calm days you can go wandering between them in a boat for hours, echoes following you about the labyrinth; but when the sea is up, Heaven help the man that hears that cauldron boiling.

Off the southwest end of Aros these blocks are very many, and much greater in size. Indeed, they must grow monstrously bigger out to sea, for there must be ten sea miles of open water sown with them as thick as a country place with houses, some standing thirty feet above the tides, some covered, but all perilous to ships; so that on a clear, westerly blowing day, I have counted, from the top of Aros, the great rollers breaking white and heavy over as many as six-and-forty buried reefs. But it is nearer in shore that the danger is worst; for the tide, here running like a mill race, makes a long belt of broken water—a *Roost* we call it—at the tail of the land. I have often been out there in a dead calm at the slack of the tide; and a strange place it is, with the sea swirling and combing up and boiling like the cauldrons of a linn, and now and again a little dancing mutter of sound as though the Roost were talking to itself. But when the tide begins to run again, and above all in heavy weather, there is no man could take a boat within half a mile of it, nor a ship afloat that could either steer or live in such a place. You can hear the roaring of it six miles away. At the seaward end there comes the strongest of the bubble; and it's here that these big breakers dance together—the dance of death, it may be called—that have got the name, in these parts, of the Merry Men. I have heard it said that they run fifty feet high; but that must be the green water only, for the spray runs twice as high as that. Whether they got the name from their movements, which are swift and antic, or from the shouting they make about the turn of the tide, so that all Aros shakes with it, is more than I can tell.

The truth is, that in a southwesterly wind, that part of our archipelago is no better than a trap. If a ship got through the reefs, and weathered the Merry Men, it would be to come ashore on the south coast of Aros, in Sandag Bay, where so many dismal things befell our family, as I propose to tell. The thought of all these dangers, in the place I knew so long, makes me particularly welcome the works now going forward to set lights upon the headlands and buoys along the channels of our ironbound, inhospitable islands.

The country people had many a story about Aros, as I used to hear from my uncle's man, Rorie, an old servant of the Macleans, who had transferred his services without afterthought on the occasion of the marriage. There was some tale of an unlucky creature, a sea-kelpie, that dwelt and did business in some fearful manner of his own among the boiling breakers of the Roost. A mermaid had once met a piper on Sandag beach, and there sang to him a long, bright midsummer's night, so that in the morning he was found stricken crazy, and from thenceforward, till the day he died, said only one form of words; what they were in the original Gaelic I cannot tell, but they were thus translated:

"Ah, the sweet singing out of the sea." Seals that haunted on that coast have been known to speak to man in his own tongue, presaging great disasters. It was here that a certain saint first landed on his voyage out of Ireland to convert the Hebrideans. And, indeed, I think he had some claim to be called saint; for, with the boats of that past age, to make so rough a passage, and land on such a ticklish coast, was surely not far short of the miraculous. It was to him, or to some of his monkish underlings who had a cell there, that the islet owes its holy and beautiful name, the House of God.

Among these old wives' stories there was one which I was inclined to hear with more credulity. As I was told, in that tempest which scattered the ships of the Invincible Armada over all the north and west of Scotland, one great vessel came ashore on Aros, and before the eyes of some solitary people on a hilltop, went down in a moment with all hands, her colours flying even as she sank. There was some likelihood in this tale; for another of that fleet lay sunk on the north side, twenty miles from Grisapol. It was told, I thought, with more detail and gravity than its companion stories, and there was one particularity which went far to convince me of its truth: the name, that is, of the ship was still remembered, and sounded, in my ears, Spanishly. The *Espirito Santo* they called it, a great ship of many decks of guns, laden with treasure and grandees of Spain, and fierce soldadoes, that now lay fathom deep to all eternity, done with her wars and voyages, in Sandag Bay, upon the west of Aros. No more salvos of ordnance for that tall ship, the "Holy Spirit," no more fair winds or happy ventures; only to rot there deep in the sea tangle and hear the shoutings of the Merry Men as the tide ran high about the island. It was a strange thought to me first and last, and only grew stranger as I learned the more of Spain, from which she had set sail with so proud a company, and King Philip, the wealthy king, that sent her on that voyage.

And now I must tell you, as I walked from Grisapol that day, the *Espirito Santo* was very much in my reflections. I had been favourably remarked by our then Principal in Edinburgh College, that famous writer, Dr. Robertson, and by him had been set to work on some papers of an ancient date to rearrange and sift of what was worthless; and in one of these, to my great wonder, I found a note of this very ship, the *Espirito Santo,* with her captain's name, and how she carried a great part of the Spaniard's treasure, and had been lost upon the Ross of Grisapol; but in what particular spot, the wild tribes of that place and pe-riod would give no information to the king's inquiries. Putting one thing with another, and taking our island tradition together with this note of old King Jamie's perquisitions after wealth, it had come strongly on my mind that the spot for which he sought in vain could be no other than the small bay of Sandag on my uncle's land; and being a fellow of a mechanical turn, I had ever since been plotting how to weigh that good ship up again with all her ingots, ounces, and dou-bloons, and bring back our house of Darnaway to its long-forgotten dignity and wealth.

This was a design of which I soon had reason to repent. My mind was sharply turned on different reflections; and since I became the witness of a strange judgment of God's, the thought of dead men's treasures has been intolerable to my conscience. But even at that time I must acquit myself of sordid greed; for if I desired riches, it was not for their own sake, but for the sake of a person who was dear to my heart—my uncle's daughter, Mary Ellen. She had been educated well, and had been a time to school upon the mainland; which, poor girl, she would have been happier without. For Aros was no place for her, with old Rorie the servant, and her father, who was one of the unhappiest men in Scotland, plainly bred up in a country place among Cameroni-ans, long a skipper sailing out of the Clyde about the islands, and now, with infinite discontent, managing his sheep and a little 'long shore fishing for the necessary bread. If it was sometimes weariful to me, who was there but a month or two, you may fancy what it was to her who dwelt in that same desert all the year round, with the sheep and flying sea gulls, and the Merry Men singing and dancing in the Roost!

CHAPTER TWO

What the wreck had brought to Aros

It was half-flood when I got the length of Aros; and there was nothing for it but to stand on the far shore and whistle for Rorie with the boat. I had no need to repeat the signal. At the first sound, Mary was at the door flying a handkerchief by way of answer, and the old long-legged servingman was shambling down the gravel to the pier. For all his hurry, it took him a long while to pull across the bay; and I observed him several times to pause, go into the stern, and look over curiously into the wake. As he came nearer, he seemed to me aged and haggard, and I thought he avoided my eye. The coble had been repaired, with two new thwarts and several patches of some rare and beautiful foreign wood, the name of it unknown to me.

"Why, Rorie," said I, as we began the return voyage, "this is fine wood. How came you by that?"

"It will be hard to cheesel," Rorie opined reluctantly; and just then, dropping the oars, he made another of those dives into the stern which I had remarked as he came across to fetch me, and, leaning his hand on my shoulder, stared with an awful look into the waters of the bay.

"What is wrong?" I asked, a good deal startled.

"It will be a great feesh," said the old man, returning to his oars; and nothing more could I get out of him, but strange glances and an ominous nodding of the head. In spite of myself, I was infected with a measure of uneasiness; I turned also, and studied the wake. The water was still and transparent, but, out here in the middle of the bay, exceeding deep. For some time I could see naught; but at last it did seem to me as if something dark—a great fish, or perhaps only a shadow— followed studiously in the track of the moving coble. And then I remembered one of Rorie's superstitions: how in a ferry in Morven, in some great, exterminating feud among the clans, a fish, the like of it unknown in all our waters, followed for some years the passage of the ferryboat, until no man dared to make the crossing

"He will be waiting for the right man," said Rorie.

Mary met me on the beach, and led me up the brae and into the house of Aros. Outside and inside there were many changes. The garden was fenced with the same wood that I had noted in the boat; there were chairs in the kitchen covered with strange brocade; curtains of brocade hung from the window; a clock stood silent on the dresser; a lamp of brass was swinging from the roof; the table was set for dinner with the finest of linen and silver; and all these new riches were displayed in the plain old kitchen that I knew so well, with the high-backed settle, and the stools, and the closet bed for Rorie; with the wide chimney the sun shone into, 'and the clear-smouldering peats; with the pipes on the mantelshelf and the three-cornered spittoons, filled with seashells instead of sand, on the floor; with the bare stone walls and the bare wooden floor, and the three patchwork rugs that were of yore its sole adornment—poor man's patchwork, the like of it unknown in cities, woven with homespun, and Sunday black, and sea cloth polished on the bench of rowing. The room, like the house, had been a sort of wonder in that countryside, it was so neat and habitable; and to see it now, shamed by these incongruous additions, filled me with indignation and a kind of anger. In view of the errand I had come upon to Aros, the feeling was baseless and unjust; but it burned high, at the first moment, in my heart.

"Mary, girl," said I, "this is the place I had learned to call my home, and I do not know it."

"It is my home by nature, not by the learning," she replied; "the place I was born and the place I'm like to die in; and I neither like these changes, nor the way they came, nor that which came with them. I would have liked better, under God's pleasure, they had gone down into the sea, and the Merry Men were dancing on them now."

Mary was always serious; it was perhaps the only trait that she shared with her father; but the tone with which she uttered these words was even graver than of custom.

"Ay," said I, "I feared it came by wreck, and that's by death; yet when my father died, I took his goods without remorse."

"Your father died a clean strae death, as the folk say," said Mary.

"True," I returned; "and a wreck is like a judgment. What was she called?"

"They ca'd her the *Christ-Anna*," said a voice behind me; and, turning round, I saw my uncle standing in the doorway.

He was a sour, small, bilious man, with a long face and very dark eyes; fifty-six years old, sound and active in body, and with an air somewhat between that of a shepherd and that of a man following the sea. He never laughed, that I heard; read long at the Bible; prayed much, like the Cameronians he had been brought up among; and indeed, in many ways, used to remind me of one of the hill-preachers in the killing times before the Revolution. But he never got much comfort, nor even, as I used to think, much guidance, by his piety. He had his black fits when he was afraid of hell; but he had led a rough life, to which he would look back with envy, and was still a rough, cold, gloomy man.

As he came in at the door out of the sunlight, with his bonnet on his head and a pipe hanging in his buttonhole, he seemed, like Rorie, to have grown older and paler, the lines were deeplier ploughed upon his face, and the whites of his eyes were yellow, like old stained ivory, or the bones of the dead.

"Ay," he repeated, dwelling upon the first part of the word, "the *Christ-Anna*. It's an awfu' name."

I made him my salutations, and complimented him upon his look of health; for I feared he had perhaps been ill.

"I'm in the body," he replied, ungraciously enough; "aye in the body and the sins of the body, like yoursel'. Denner," he said abruptly to Mary, and then ran on to me: "They're grand braws, thir that we hae gotten, are they no? Yon's a bonny knock,* but it'll no gang; and the napery's by ordnar. Bonny, bairnly braws; it's for the like o' them folk sells the peace of God that passeth understanding; it's for the like o' them, an' maybe no even sae muckle worth, folk daunton God to His face and burn in muckle hell; and it's for that reason the Scripture ca's them, as I read the passage, the accursed thing. Mary, ye girzie," he interrupted himself to cry with some asperity, "what for hae ye no put out the twa candlesticks?"

"Why should we need them at high noon?" she asked.

But my uncle was not to be turned from his idea. "We'll bruik† them while we may," he said; and so two massive candlesticks of wrought silver were added to the table equipage, already so unsuited to that rough seaside farm.

"She cam' ashore Februar' 10, about ten at nicht," he went on to me. "There was nae wind, and a sair run o' sea; and she was in the sook o' the Roost, as I jaloose. We had seen her a' day, Rorie and me, beating to the wind. She wasnae a handy craft, I'm thinking, that *Christ-Anna;* for she would neither steer nor stey wi' them. A sair day they had of it; their hands was never aff the sheets, and it perishin' cauld—ower cauld to snaw; and aye they would get a bit nip o' wind, and awa' again, to put the emp'y hope into them. Eh, man! but they had a sair day for the last o't! He would have had a prood, prood heart that won ashore upon the back o' that."

*Clock. [R.L.S.]
†Enjoy. [R.L.S.]

"And were all lost?" I cried. "God help them!"

"Wheesht!" he said sternly. "Nane shall pray for the deid on my hearth-stane."

I disclaimed a Popish sense for my ejaculation; and he seemed to accept my disclaimer with unusual facility, and ran on once more upon what had evidently become a favourite subject.

"We fand her in Sandag Bay, Rorie an' me, and a' thae braws in the inside of her. There's a kittle bit, ye see, about Sandag; whiles the sook rins strong for the Merry Men; an' whiles again, when the tide's makin' hard an' ye can hear the Roost blawin' at the far-end of Aros, there comes a back-spang of current straucht into Sandag Bay. Weel, there's the thing that got the grip on the *Christ-Anna*. She but to have come in ram-stam an' stern forrit; for the bows of her are aften under, and the back-side of her is clear at hie-water o' neaps. But, man! the dunt that she cam doon wi' when she struck! Lord save us a'! but it's an unco life to be a sailor—a cauld, wanchancy life. Mony's the gliff I got mysel' in the great deep; and why the Lord should hae made yon unco water is mair than ever I could win to understand. He made the vales and the pastures, the bonny green yaird, the halesome, canty land—

> And now they shout and sing to Thee,
> For Thou hast made them glad,

as the Psalms say in the metrical version. No that I would preen my faith to that clink neither; but it's bonny, and easier to mind. 'Who go to sea in ships,' they hae't again—

> And in
> Great waters trading be,
> Within the deep these men God's works
> And His great wonders see.

Weel, it's easy sayin' sae. Maybe Dauvit wasnae very weel acquant wi' the sea. But, troth, if it wasnae prentit in the Bible, I wad whiles be temp'it to think it wasnae the Lord, but the muckle, black deil that made the sea. There's naething good comes oot o't but the fish; an' the spentacle o' God riding on the tempest, to be shüre, whilk would be what Dauvit was likely ettling at. But, man, they were sair wonders that God showed to the *Christ-Anna*—wonders, do I ca' them? Judgments, rather: judgments in the mirk nicht among the draygons o' the deep. And their souls—to think o' that—their souls, man, maybe no prepared! The sea—a muckle yett to hell!"

I observed, as my uncle spoke, that his voice was unnaturally moved and his manner unwontedly demonstrative. He leaned forward at these last words, for example, and touched me on the knee with his spread fingers, looking up into my face with a certain pallor, and I could see that his eyes shone with a deep-seated fire, and that the lines about his mouth were drawn and tremulous.

Even the entrance of Rorie, and the beginning of our meal, did not detach him from his train of thought beyond a moment. He condescended, indeed, to ask me some questions as to my success at college, but I thought it was with half his mind; and even in his extempore grace, which was, as usual, long and wandering, I could find the trace of his preoccupation, praying, as he did, that God would "remember in mercy fower puir, feckless, fiddling, sinful creatures here by their lee-lane beside the great and dowie waters."

Soon there came an interchange of speeches between him and Rorie.

"Was it there?" asked my uncle.

"Ou, ay!" said Rorie.

I observed that they both spoke in a manner of aside, and with some show of embarrassment, and that Mary herself appeared to colour, and looked down on her plate. Partly to show my knowledge, and so relieve the party from an awkward strain, partly because I was curious, I pursued the subject.

"You mean the fish?" I asked.

"Whatten fish?" cried my uncle. "Fish, quo' he! Fish! Your een are fu' o' fatness, man; your heid dozened wi' carnal leir. Fish! it's a bogle!"

He spoke with great vehemence, as though angry; and perhaps I was not very willing to be put down so shortly, for young men are disputatious. At least I remember I retorted hotly, crying out upon childish superstitions.

"And ye come frae the College!" sneered Uncle Gordon. "Gude kens what they learn folk there; it's no muckle service onyway. Do ye think, man, that there's naething in a' yon saut wilderness o' a world oot wast there, wi' the sea grasses growin', an' the sea beasts fechtin', an' the sun glintin' down into it, day by day? Na; the sea's like the land, but fearsomer. If there's folk ashore, there's folk in the sea—deid they may be, but they're folk whatever; and as for deils, there's nane that's like the sea deils. There's no sae muckle harm in the land deils, when a's said and done. Lang syne, when I was a callant in the south country, I mind there was an auld, bald bogle in the Peewie Moss. I got a glisk o' him mysel', sittin' on his hunkers in a hag, as gray's a tombstane. An', troth, he was a fearsome-like taed. But he steered naebody. Nae doobt, if ane that was a reprobate, ane the Lord hated, had gane by there wi' his sin still upon his stamach, nae doobt the creature would hae lowped upo' the likes o' him. But there's deils in the deep sea would yoke on a communicant! Eh, sirs, if ye had gane doon wi' the puir lads in the *Christ-Anna*, ye would ken by now the mercy o' the seas. If ye had sailed it for as lang as me, ye would hate the thocht of it as I do. If ye had but used the een God gave ye, ye would hae learned the wickedness o' that fause, saut, cauld, bullering creature, and of a' that's in it by the Lord's permission: labsters an' partans, an' sic like, howking in the deid; muckle, gutsy, blawing whales; an' fish—the hale clan o' them—cauld-wamed, blind-eed uncanny ferlies. O, sirs," he cried, "the horror—the horror o' the sea!"

We were all somewhat staggered by this outburst; and the speaker himself, after that last hoarse apostrophe, appeared to sink gloomily into his own thoughts. But Rorie, who was greedy of superstitious lore, recalled him to the subject by a question.

"You will not ever have seen a teevil of the sea?" he asked.

"No clearly," replied the other. "I misdoobt if a mere man could see ane clearly and conteenue in the body. I hae sailed wi' a lad—they ca'd him Sandy Gabart; he saw ane, shüre eneuch, an' shüre eneuch it was the end of him. We were seeven days oot frae the Clyde—a sair wark we had had—gaun north wi' seeds an' braws an' things for the Macleod. We had got in ower near under the Cutchull'ns, an' had just gane about by Soa, an' were off on a lang tack, we thocht would maybe hauld as far's Copnahow. I mind the nicht weel; a mune smoored wi' mist; a fine gaun breeze upon the water, but no steedy; an'—what nane o' us likit to hear—anither wund gurlin' owerheid, amang thae fearsome, auld stane craigs o' the Cutchull'ns. Weel, Sandy was forrit wi' the jib sheet; we couldnae see him for the mains'l, that had just begude to draw, when a' at ance he gied a skirl. I luffed for my life, for I thocht we were ower near Soa; but na, it wasnae that, it was puir Sandy Gabart's deid skreigh, or near hand, for he was deid in half an hour. A't he could tell was that a sea deil, or sea bogle, or sea spenster, or sic-like, had clum up by the bowsprit, an' gi'en him ae cauld, uncanny look. An', or the life was oot o' Sandy's body, we kent weel what the thing betokened, and why the wund gurled in the taps o' the Cutchull'ns; for doon it cam'—a wund do I ca' it! it was the wund o' the Lord's anger—an' a' that nicht we foucht like men dementit, and the niest that we kenned we were ashore in Loch Uskevagh, an' the cocks were crawin' in Benbecula."

"It will have been a merman," Rorie said.

"A merman!" screamed my uncle with immeasurable scorn. "Auld wives' clavers! There's nae sic things as mermen."

"But what was the creature like?" I asked.

"What like was it? Gude forbid that we suld ken what like it was! It had a kind ot a heid upon it—man could say nae mair."

Then Rorie, smarting under the affront, told several tales of mermen, mermaids, and sea-horses that had come ashore upon the islands and attacked the crews of boats upon the sea; and my uncle, in spite of his incredulity, listened with uneasy interest.

"Aweel, aweel," he said, "it may be sae; I may be wrang; but I find nae word o' mermen in the Scriptures."

"And you will find nae word of Aros Roost, maybe," objected Rorie, and his argument appeared to carry weight.

When dinner was over, my uncle carried me forth with him to a bank behind the house. It was a very hot and quiet afternoon; scarce a ripple anywhere upon the sea, nor any voice but the familiar voice of sheep and gulls; and perhaps in consequence of this repose in nature, my kinsman showed himself more rational and tranquil than before. He spoke evenly and almost cheerfully of my career, with every now and then a reference to the lost ship or the treasures it had brought to Aros. For my part, I listened to him in a sort of trance, gazing with all my heart on that remembered scene, and drinking gladly the sea air and the smoke of peats that had been lit by Mary.

Perhaps an hour had passed when my uncle, who had all the while been covertly gazing on the surface of the little bay, rose to his feet and bade me follow his example. Now I should say that the great run of tide at the southwest end of Aros exercises a perturbing influence round all the coast. In Sandag Bay, to the south, a strong current runs at certain periods of the flood and ebb respectively; but in this northern bay—Aros Bay, as it is called—where the house stands and on which my uncle was now gazing, the only sign of disturbance is towards the end of the ebb, and even then it is too slight to be remarkable. When there is any swell, nothing can be seen at all; but when it is calm, as it often is, there appear certain strange, undecipherable marks—sea-runes, as we may name them—on the glassy surface of the bay. The like is common in a thousand places on the coast; and many a boy must have amused himself as I did, seeking to read in them some reference to himself or those he loved. It was to these marks that my uncle now directed my attention, struggling, as he did so, with an evident reluctance.

"Do ye see yon scart upo' the water?" he inquired; "yon ane wast the gray stane? Ay? Weel, it'll no be like a letter, wull it?"

"Certainly it is," I replied. "I have often remarked it. It is like a C."

He heaved a sigh as if heavily disappointed with my answer, and then added below his breath: "Ay, for the *Christ-Anna*."

"I used to suppose, sir, it was for myself," said I; "for my name is Charles."

"And so ye saw't afore?" he ran on, not heeding my remark. "Weel, weel, but that's unco strange. Maybe, it's been there waitin', as a man wad say, through a' the weary ages. Man, but that's awfu'." And then, breaking off: "Ye'll no see anither, will ye?" he asked.

"Yes," said I. "I see another very plainly, near the Ross side, where the road comes down—an M."

"An M," he repeated very low; and then, again after another pause: "An' what wad ye make o' that?" he inquired.

"I had always thought it to mean Mary, sir," I answered, growing somewhat red, convinced as I was in my own mind that I was on the threshold of a decisive explanation.

But we were each following his own train of thought to the exclusion of the other's. My uncle once more paid no attention to my words; only hung his head and held his peace; and I might have been led to fancy that he had not heard me, if his next speech had not contained a kind of echo from my own.

"I would say naething o' thae clavers to Mary," he observed, and began to walk forward.

There is a belt of turf along the side of Aros Bay where walking is easy; and it was along this that I silently followed my silent kinsman. I was perhaps a little disappointed at having lost so good an opportunity to declare my love; but I was at the same time far more deeply exercised at the change that had befallen my uncle. He was never an ordinary, never, in the strict sense, an amiable, man; but there was nothing in even the worst that I had known of him before, to prepare me for so strange a transformation. It was impossible to close the eyes against one fact; that he had, as the saying goes, something on his mind; and as I mentally ran over the different words which might be represented by the letter M—misery, mercy, marriage, money, and the like—I was arrested with a sort of start by the word murder. I was still considering the ugly sound and fatal meaning of the word, when the direction of our walk brought us to a point from which a view was to be had to either side, back towards Aros Bay and homestead, and forward on the ocean, dotted to the north with isles, and lying to the southward blue and open to the sky. There my guide came to a halt, and stood staring for awhile on that expanse. Then he turned to me and laid a hand on my arm.

"Ye think there's naething there?" he said, pointing with his pipe; and then cried out aloud, with a kind of exultation. "I'll tell ye, man! The deid are down there—thick like rattons!"

He turned at once, and, without another word, we retraced our steps to the house of Aros.

I was eager to be alone with Mary; yet it was not till after supper, and then but for a short while, that I could have a word with her. I lost no time beating about the bush, but spoke out plainly what was on my mind.

"Mary," I said, "I have not come to Aros without a hope. If that should prove well founded, we may all leave and go somewhere else, secure of daily bread and comfort; secure, perhaps, of something far beyond that, which it would seem extravagant in me to promise. But there's a hope that lies nearer to my heart than money." And at that I paused. "You can guess fine what that is, Mary," I said. She looked away from me in silence, and that was small encouragement, but I was not to be put off. "All my days I have thought the world of you," I continued; "the time goes on and I think always the more of you; I could not think to be happy or hearty in my life without you: you are the apple of my eye." Still she looked away, and said never a word; but I thought I saw that her hands shook. "Mary," I cried in fear, "do ye no like me?"

"O, Charlie man," she said, "is this a time to speak of it? Let me be, a while; let me be the way I am; it'll not be you that loses by the waiting!"

I made out by her voice that she was nearly weeping, and this put me out of any thought but to compose her. "Mary Ellen," I said, "say no more; I did not come to trouble you: your way shall be mine, and your time too; and you have told me all I wanted. Only just this one thing more: what ails you?"

She owned it was her father, but would enter into no particulars, only shook her head, and said he was not well and not like himself, and it was a great pity. She knew nothing of the wreck. "I havenae been near it," said she. "What for would I go near it, Charlie lad? The poor souls are gone to their account long syne; and I would just have wished they had ta'en their gear with them—poor souls!"

This was scarcely any great encouragement for me to tell her of the *Espirito Santo;* yet I did so, and at the very first word she cried out in surprise. "There was a man at Grisapol," she said, "in the month of May—a little, yellow, black-avised body, they tell me, with gold rings upon his fingers, and a beard; and he was speiring high and low for that same ship."

It was towards the end of April that I had been given these papers to sort out by Dr. Robertson: and it came suddenly back upon my mind that they were thus prepared for a Spanish historian, or a man calling himself such, who had come with high recommendations to the Principal, on a mission of inquiry as to the dispersion of the great Armada. Putting one thing with another, I fancied that the visitor "with the gold rings upon his fingers" might be the same with Dr. Robertson's historian from Madrid. If that were so, he would be more likely after treasure for himself than information for a learned society. I made up my mind, I should lose no time over my undertaking; and if the ship lay sunk in Sandag Bay, as perhaps both he and I supposed, it should not be for the advantage of this ringed adventurer, but for Mary and myself, and for the good, old, honest, kindly family of the Darnaways.

Chapter Three
Land and sea in Sandag Bay

I was early afoot next morning; and as soon as I had a bite to eat, set forth upon a tour of exploration. Something in my heart distinctly told me that I should find the ship of the Armada; and although I did not give way entirely to such hopeful thoughts, I was still very light in spirits and walked upon air. Aros is a very rough islet, its surface strewn with great rocks and shaggy with fern and heather; and my way lay almost north and south across the highest knoll; and though the whole distance was inside of two miles, it took more time and exertion than four upon a level road. Upon the summit, I paused. Although not very high—not three hundred feet, as I think—it yet outtops all the neighbouring lowlands of the Ross, and commands a great view of sea and islands. The sun, which had been up some time, was already hot upon my neck; the air was listless and thundery, although purely clear; away over the northwest, where the isles lie thickliest congregated, some half-a-dozen small and ragged clouds hung together in a covey; and the head of Ben Kyaw wore, not merely a few streamers, but a solid hood of vapour. There was a threat in the weather. The sea, it is true, was smooth like glass: even the Roost was but a seam on that wide mirror, and the Merry Men no more than caps of foam; but to my eye and ear, so long familiar with these places, the sea also seemed to lie uneasily; a sound of it, like a long sigh, mounted to me where I stood; and, quiet as it was, the Roost itself appeared to be revolving mischief. For I ought to say that all we dwellers in these parts attributed, if not prescience, at least a quality of warning, to that strange and dangerous creature of the tides.

I hurried on, then, with the greater speed, and had soon descended the slope of Aros to the part that we call Sandag Bay. It is a pretty large piece of water compared with the size of the isle; well sheltered from all but the prevailing wind; sandy and shoal and bounded by low sandhills to the west, but to the eastward lying several fathoms deep along a ledge of rocks. It is upon that side that, at a certain time each flood, the current mentioned by my uncle sets so strong into the bay; a little later, when the Roost begins to work higher, an undertow runs still more strongly in the reverse direction; and it is the action of this last, as I suppose, that has scoured that part so deep. Nothing is to be seen out of Sandag Bay but one small segment of the horizon and, in heavy weather, the breakers flying high over a deep sea reef.

From halfway down the hill, I had perceived the wreck of February last, a brig of considerable tonnage, lying, with her back broken, high and dry on the east corner of the sands; and I was making directly towards it, and already almost on the margin of the turf, when my eyes were suddenly arrested by a spot, cleared of fern and heather, and marked by one of those long, low, and almost human-looking mounds that we see so commonly in graveyards. I stopped like a man shot. Nothing had been said to me of any dead man or interment on the island; Rorie, Mary, and my uncle had all equally held their peace; of her at least, I was certain that she must be ignorant; and yet here, before my eyes, was proof indubitable of the fact. Here was a grave; and I had to ask myself, with a chill, what manner of man lay there in his last sleep, awaiting the signal of the Lord in that solitary, sea-beat resting-place? My mind supplied no answer but what I feared to entertain. Shipwrecked, at least, he must have been; perhaps, like the old Armada mariners, from some far and rich land oversea; or perhaps one of my own race, perishing within eyesight of the smoke of home. I stood awhile uncovered by his side, and I could have desired that it had lain in our religion to put up some prayer for that unhappy stranger, or, in the old classic way, outwardly to honour his misfortune. I knew, although his bones lay there, a part of Aros, till the trumpet sounded, his imperishable soul was forth and far away, among the raptures of the everlasting Sabbath or the pangs of hell; and yet my mind misgave me even with a fear, that perhaps he was near me where I stood, guarding his sepulchre, and lingering on the scene of his unhappy fate.

Certainly it was with a spirit somewhat overshadowed that I turned away from the grave to the hardly less melancholy spectacle of the wreck. Her stem was above the first arc of the flood; she was broken in two a little abaft the foremast—though indeed she had none, both masts having broken short in her disaster; and as the pitch of the beach was very sharp and sudden, and the bows lay many feet below the stern, the fracture gaped widely open, and you could see right through her poor hull upon the farther side. Her name was much defaced, and I could not make out clearly whether she was called *Christiania,* after the Norwegian city, or *Christiana,* after the good woman, Christian's wife, in that old book the "Pilgrim's Progress." By her build she was a foreign ship, but I was not certain of her nationality. She had been painted green, but the colour was faded and weathered, and the paint peeling off in strips. The wreck of the mainmast lay alongside, half-buried in sand. She was a forlorn sight, indeed, and I could not look without emotion at the bits of rope that still hung about her, so often handled of yore by shouting seamen; or the little scuttle where they had passed up and down to their affairs; or that poor noseless angel of a figurehead that had dipped into so many running billows.

I do not know whether it came most from the ship or from the grave, but I fell into some melancholy scruples, as I stood there, leaning with one hand against the battered timbers. The homelessness of men and even of inanimate vessels, cast away upon strange shores, came strongly in upon my mind. To make a profit of such pitiful mis-adventures seemed an unmanly and a sordid act; and I began to think of my then quest as of something sacrilegious in its nature. But when I remembered Mary, I took heart again. My uncle would never consent to an imprudent marriage, nor would she, as I was persuaded, wed without his full approval. It behoved me, then, to be up and doing for my wife; and I thought with a laugh how long it was since that great sea-castle, the *Espirito Santo,* had left her bones in Sandag Bay, and how weak it would be to consider rights so long extinguished and misfortunes so long forgotten in the process of time.

I had my theory of where to seek for her remains. The set of the current and the soundings both pointed to the east side of the bay under the ledge of rocks. If she had been lost in Sandag Bay, and if, after these centuries, any portion of her held together, it was there that I should find it. The water deepens, as I have said, with great rapidity, and even close alongside the rocks several fathoms may be found. As I walked upon the edge I could see far and wide over the sandy bottom of the bay; the sun shone clear and green and steady in the deeps; the bay seemed rather like a great transparent crystal, as one sees them in a lapidary's shop; there was naught to show that it was water but an internal trembling, a hovering within of sun-glints and netted shadows, and now and then a faint lap and a dying bubble round the edge. The shadows of the rocks lay out for some distance at their feet, so that my own shadow, moving, pausing, and stooping on the top of that, reached sometimes half across the bay. It was above all in this belt of shadows that I hunted for the *Espirito Santo;* since it was there the undertow ran strongest, whether in or out. Cool as the whole water seemed this broiling day, it looked, in that part, yet cooler, and had a mysterious invitation for the eyes. Peer as I pleased, however, I could see nothing but a few fishes or a bush of sea tangle, and here and there a lump of rock that had fallen from above and now lay separate on the sandy floor. Twice did I pass from one end to the other of the rocks, and in the whole distance I could see nothing of the wreck, nor any place but one where it was possible for it to be. This was a large terrace in five fathoms of water, raised off the surface of the sand to a considerable height, and looking from above like a mere outgrowth of the rocks on which I walked. It was one mass of great sea tangles like a grove, which prevented me judging of its nature, but in shape and size it bore some likeness to a vessel's hull. At least it was my best chance. If the *Espirito Santo* lay not there under the tangles, it lay nowhere at all in Sandag Bay; and I prepared to put the question to the proof, once and for all, and either go back to Aros a rich man or cured for ever of my dreams of wealth.

I stripped to the skin, and stood on the extreme margin with my hands clasped, irresolute. The bay at that time was utterly quiet; there was no sound but from a school of porpoises somewhere out of sight behind the point; yet a certain fear withheld me on the threshold of my venture. Sad sea-feelings, scraps of my uncle's superstitions, thoughts of the dead, of the grave, of the old broken ships, drifted through my mind. But the strong sun upon my shoulders warmed me to the heart, and I stooped forward and plunged into the sea.

It was all that I could do to catch a trail of the sea-tangle that grew so thickly on the terrace; but once so far anchored I secured myself by grasping a whole armful of these thick and slimy stalks, and, planting my feet against the edge, I looked around me. On all sides the clear sand stretched forth unbroken; it came to the foot of the rocks, scoured into the likeness of an alley in a garden by the action of the tides; and before me, for as far as I could see, nothing was visible but the same many-folded sand upon the sun-bright bottom of the bay. Yet the terrace to which I was then holding was as thick with strong sea-growths as a tuft of heather, and the cliff from which it bulged hung draped below the waterline with brown lianas. In this complexity of forms, all swaying together in the current, things were hard to be distinguished; and I was still uncertain whether my feet were pressed upon the natural rock or upon the timbers of the Armada treasure ship, when the whole tuft of tangle came away in my hand, and in an instant I was on the surface, and the shores of the bay and the bright water swam before my eyes in a glory of crimson.

I clambered back upon the rocks, and threw the plant of tangle at my feet. Something at the same moment rang sharply, like a falling coin. I stooped, and there, sure enough, crusted with the red rust, there lay an iron shoe-buckle. The sight of this poor human relic thrilled me to the heart, but not with hope nor fear, only with a desolate melancholy. I held it in my hand, and the thought of its owner appeared before me like the presence of an actual man. His weather-beaten face, his sailor's hands, his sea-voice hoarse with singing at the capstan, the very foot that had once worn that buckle and trod so much along the swerving decks—the whole human fact of him, as a creature like myself, with hair and blood and seeing eyes, haunted me in that sunny, solitary place, not like a spectre, but like some friend whom I had basely injured. Was the great treasure ship indeed below there, with her guns and chain and treasure, as she had sailed from Spain; her decks a garden for the seaweed, her cabin a breeding place for fish, soundless but for the dredging water, motionless but for the waving of the tangle upon her battlements—that old, populous, sea-riding castle, now a reef in Sandag Bay? Or, as I thought it likelier, was this a waif from the disaster of the foreign brig—was this shoe-buckle bought but the other day and worn by a man of my own period in the world's history, hearing the same news from day to day, thinking the same thoughts, praying, perhaps, in the same temple with myself? However it was, I was assailed with dreary thoughts; my uncle's words, "the dead are down there," echoed in my ears; and though I determined to dive once more, it was with a strong repugnance that I stepped forward to the margins of the rocks.

A great change passed at that moment over the appearance of the bay. It was no more that clear, visible interior, like a house roofed with glass, where the green, submarine sunshine slept so stilly. A breeze, I suppose, had flawed the surface, and a sort of trouble and blackness filled its bosom, where flashes of light and clouds of shadow tossed confusedly together. Even the terrace below obscurely rocked and quivered. It seemed a graver thing to venture on this place of ambushes; and when I leaped into the sea the second time it was with a quaking in my soul.

I secured myself as at first, and groped among the waving tangle. All that met my touch was cold and soft and gluey. The thicket was alive with crabs and lobsters, trundling to and fro lopsidedly, and I had to harden my heart against the horror of their carrion neighbourhood. On all sides I could feel the grain and the clefts of hard, living stone; no planks, no iron, not a sign of any wreck; the *Espirito Santo* was not there. I remember I had almost a sense of relief in my disappointment, and I was about ready to leave go, when something happened that sent me to the surface with my heart in my mouth. I had already stayed somewhat late over my explorations; the current was freshening with the change of the tide, and Sandag Bay was no longer a safe place for a single swimmer. Well, just at the last moment there came a sudden flush of current, dredging through the tangles like a wave. I lost one hold, was flung sprawling on my side, and, instinctively grasping for a fresh support, my fingers closed on something hard and cold. I think I knew at that moment what it was. At least I instantly left hold of the tangle, leaped for the surface, and clambered out next moment on the friendly rocks with the bone of a man's leg in my grasp.

Mankind is a material creature, slow to think and dull to perceive connections. The grave, the wreck of the brig, and the rusty shoe-buckle were surely plain advertisements. A child might have read their dismal story, and yet it was not until I touched that actual piece of mankind that the full horror of the charnel ocean burst upon my spirit. I laid the bone beside the buckle, picked up my clothes, and ran as I was along the rocks towards the human shore. I could not be far enough from the spot; no fortune was vast enough to tempt me back again. The bones of the drowned dead should henceforth roll undisturbed by me, whether on tangle or minted gold. But as soon as I trod the good earth again, and had covered my nakedness against the sun, I knelt down over against the ruins of the brig, and out of the fulness of my heart prayed long and passionately for all poor souls upon the sea. A generous prayer is never presented in vain; the petition may be refused, but the petitioner is always, I believe, rewarded by some gracious visitation. The horror, at least, was lifted from my mind; I could look with calm of spirit on that great bright creature, God's ocean; and as I set off homeward up the rough sides of Aros, nothing remained of my concern beyond a deep determination to meddle no more with the spoils of wrecked vessels or the treasures of the dead.

I was already some way up the hill before I paused to breathe and look behind me. The sight that met my eyes was doubly strange.

For, first, the storm that I had foreseen was now advancing with almost tropical rapidity. The whole surface of the sea had been dulled from its conspicuous brightness to an ugly hue of corrugated lead; already in the distance the white waves, the "skipper's daughters," had begun to flee before a breeze that was still insensible on Aros; and already along the curve of Sandag Bay there was a splashing run of sea that I could hear from where I stood. The change upon the sky was even more remarkable. There had begun to arise out of the southwest a huge and solid continent of scowling cloud; here and there, through rents in its contexture, the sun still poured a sheaf of spreading rays; and here and there, from all its edges, vast inky streamers lay forth along the yet unclouded sky. The menace was express and imminent. Even as I gazed, the sun was blotted out. At any moment the tempest might fall upon Aros in its might.

The suddenness of this change of weather so fixed my eyes on heaven that it was some seconds before they alighted on the bay, mapped out below my feet, and robbed a moment later of the sun. The knoll which I had just surmounted overflanked a little amphitheatre of lower hillocks sloping towards the sea, and beyond that the yellow arc of beach and the whole extent of Sandag Bay. It was a scene on which I had often looked down, but where I had never before beheld a human figure. I had but just turned my back upon it and left it empty, and my wonder may be fancied when I saw a boat and several men in that deserted spot. The boat was lying by the rocks. A pair of fellows, bareheaded, with their sleeves rolled up, and one with a boathook, kept her with difficulty to her moorings, for the current was growing brisker every moment. A little way off upon the ledge two men in black clothes, whom I judged to be superior in rank, laid their heads together over some task which at first I did not understand, but a second after I had made it out—they were taking bearings with the compass; and just then I saw one of them unroll a sheet of paper and lay his finger down, as though identifying features in a map. Meanwhile a third was walking to and fro, poking among the rocks and peering over the edge into the water. While I was still watching them with the stupefaction of surprise, my mind hardly yet able to work on what my eyes reported, this third person suddenly stooped and summoned his companions with a cry so loud that it reached my ears upon the hill. The others ran to him, even dropping the compass in their hurry, and I could see the bone and the shoe-buckle going from hand to hand, causing the most unusual gesticulations of surprise and interest. Just then I could hear the seamen crying from the boat, and saw them point westward to that cloud continent which was ever the more rapidly unfurling its blackness over heaven. The others seemed to consult; but the danger was too pressing to be braved, and they bundled into the boat carrying my relics with them, and set forth out of the bay with all speed of oars.

I made no more ado about the matter, but turned and ran for the house. Whoever these men were, it was fit my uncle should be instantly informed. It was not then altogether too late in the day for a descent of the Jacobites; and maybe Prince Charlie, whom I knew my uncle to detest, was one of the three superiors whom I had seen upon the rock. Yet as I ran, leaping from rock to rock, and turned the matter loosely in my mind, this theory grew ever the longer the less welcome to my reason. The compass, the map, the interest awakened by the buckle, and the conduct of that one among the strangers who had looked so often below him in the water, all seemed to point to a different explanation of their presence on that outlying, obscure islet of the western sea. The Madrid historian, the search instituted by Dr. Robertson, the bearded stranger with the rings, my own fruitless search that very morning in the deep water of Sandag Bay, ran together, piece by piece, in my memory, and I made sure that these strangers must be Spaniards in quest of ancient treasure and the lost ship of the Armada. But the people living in outlying islands, such as Aros, are answerable for their own security; there is none nearby to protect or even to help them; and the presence in such a spot of a crew of foreign adventurers—poor, greedy, and most likely lawless—filled me with apprehensions for my uncle's money, and even for the safety of his daughter. I was still wondering how we were to get rid of them when I came, all breathless, to the top of Aros. The whole world was shadowed over; only in the extreme east, on a hill of the mainland, one last gleam of sunshine lingered like a jewel; rain had begun to fall, not heavily, but in great drops; the sea was rising with each moment, and already a band of white encircled Aros and the nearer coasts of Grisapol. The boat was still pulling seaward, but I now became aware of what had been hidden from me lower down—a large, heavily sparred, handsome schooner, lying to at the south end of Aros. Since I had not seen her in the morning when I had looked around so closely at the signs of the weather, and upon these lone waters where a sail was rarely visible, it was clear she must have lain last night behind the uninhabited Eilean Gour, and this proved conclusively that she was manned by strangers to our coast, for that anchorage, though good enough to look at, is little better than a trap for ships. With such ignorant sailors upon so wild a coast, the coming gale was not unlikely to bring death upon its wings.

CHAPTER FOUR

The gale

I found my uncle at the gable end, watching the signs of the weather, with a pipe in his fingers.

"Uncle," said I, "there were men ashore at Sandag Bay——"

I had no time to go further; indeed, I not only forgot my words, but even my weariness, so strange was the effect on Uncle Gordon. He dropped his pipe and fell back against the end of the house with his jaw fallen, his eyes staring, and his long face as white as paper. We must have looked at one another silently for a quarter of a minute, before he made answer in this extraordinary fashion: "Had he a hair kep on?"

I knew as well as if I had been there that the man who now lay buried at Sandag had worn a hairy cap, and that he had come ashore alive. For the first and only time I lost toleration for the man who was my benefactor and the father of the woman I hoped to call my wife.

"These were living men," said I, "perhaps Jacobites, perhaps the French, perhaps pirates, perhaps adventurers come here to seek the Spanish treasure ship; but, whatever they may be, dangerous at least to your daughter and my cousin. As for your own guilty terrors, man, the dead sleeps well where you have laid him. I stood this morning by his grave; he will not wake before the trump of doom."

My kinsman looked upon me, blinking, while I spoke; then he fixed his eyes for a little on the ground, and pulled his fingers foolishly; but it was plain that he was past the power of speech.

"Come," said I. "You must think for others. You must come up the hill with me, and see this ship."

He obeyed without a word or a look, following slowly after my impatient strides. The spring seemed to have gone out of his body, and he scrambled heavily up and down the rocks, instead of leaping, as he was wont, from one to another. Nor could I, for all my cries, induce him to make better haste. Only once he replied to me complainingly, and like one in bodily pain: "Ay, ay, man, I'm coming." Long before we had reached the top, I had no other thought for him but pity. If the crime had been monstrous, the punishment was in proportion.

At last we emerged above the skyline of the hill, and could see around us. All was black and stormy to the eye; the last gleam of sun had vanished; a wind had sprung up, not yet high, but gusty and unsteady to the point; the rain, on the other hand, had ceased. Short as was the interval, the sea already ran vastly higher than when I had stood there last; already it had begun to break over some of the outward reefs, and already it moaned aloud in the sea-caves of Aros. I looked, at first, in vain for the schooner.

"There she is," I said at last. But her new position, and the course she was now lying, puzzled me. "They cannot mean to beat to sea," I cried.

"That's what they mean," said my uncle, with something like joy; and just then the schooner went about and stood upon another tack, which put the question beyond the reach of doubt. These strangers, seeing a gale on hand, had thought first of sea room. With the wind that threatened, in these reef-sown waters and contending against so violent a stream of tide, their course was certain death.

"Good God!" said I, "they are all lost."

"Ay," returned my uncle, "a'—a' lost. They hadnae a chance but to rin for Kyle Dona. The gate they're gaun the noo, they couldnae win through an the muckle deil were there to pilot them. Eh, man," he continued, touching me on the sleeve, "it's a braw nicht for a shipwreck! Twa in ae twalmonth! Eh, but the Merry Men'll dance bonny!"

I looked at him, and it was then that I began to fancy him no longer in his right mind. He was peering up to me, as if for sympathy, a timid joy in his eyes. All that had passed between us was already forgotten in the prospect of this fresh disaster.

"If it were not too late," I cried with indignation, "I would take the coble and go out to warn them."

"Na, na," he protested, "ye maunnae interfere; ye maunnae meddle wi' the like o' that. It's His"—doffing his bonnet—"His wull. And, eh, man! but it's a braw nicht for't!"

Something like fear began to creep into my soul; and, reminding him that I had not yet dined, I proposed we should return to the house. But no; nothing would tear him from his place of outlook.

"I maun see the hail thing, man, Cherlie," he explained; and then as the schooner went about a second time, "Eh, but they han'le her bonny!" he cried. "The *Christ-Anna* was naething to this."

Already the men on board the schooner must have begun to realise some part, but not yet the twentieth, of the dangers that environed their doomed ship. At every lull of the capricious wind they must have seen how fast the current swept them back. Each tack was made shorter, as they saw how little it prevailed. Every moment the rising swell began to boom and foam upon another sunken reef; and ever and again a breaker would fall in sounding ruin under the very bows of her, and the brown reef and streaming tangle appear in the hollow of the wave. I tell you, they had to stand to their tackle: there was no idle man aboard that ship, God knows. It was upon the progress of a scene so horrible to any human-hearted man that my misguided uncle now pored and gloated like a connoisseur. As I turned to go down the hill, he was lying on his belly on the summit, with his hands stretched forth and clutching in the heather. He seemed rejuvenated, mind and body.

When I got back to the house already dismally affected, I was still more sadly downcast at the sight of Mary. She had her sleeves rolled up over her strong arms, and was quietly making bread. I got a bannock from the dresser and sat down to eat it in silence.

"Are ye wearied, lad?" she asked after a while.

"I am not so much wearied, Mary," I replied, getting on my feet, "as I am weary of delay, and perhaps of Aros too. You know me well enough to judge me fairly, say what I like. Well, Mary, you may be sure of this: you had better be anywhere but here."

"I'll be sure of one thing," she returned: "I'll be where my duty is."

"You forget, you have a duty to yourself," I said.

"Ay, man?" she replied, pounding at the dough; "will you have found that in the Bible, now?"

"Mary," I said solemnly, "you must not laugh at me just now. God knows I am in no heart for laughing. If we could get your father with us, it would be best; but with him or without him, I want you far away from here, my girl; for your own sake, and for mine, ay, and for your father's too, I want you far—far away from here. I came with other thoughts; I came here as a man comes home; now it is all changed, and I have no desire nor hope but to flee—for that's the word—flee, like a bird out of the fowler's snare, from this accursed island."

She had stopped her work by this time.

"And do you think, now," said she, "do you think, now, I have neither eyes nor ears? Do ye think I havenae broken my heart to have these braws (as he calls them, God forgive him!) thrown into the sea? Do ye think I have lived with him, day in, day out, and not seen what you saw in an hour or two? No," she said, "I know there's wrong in it; what wrong, I neither know nor want to know. There was never an ill thing made better by meddling, that I could hear of. But, my lad, you must never ask me to leave my father. While the breath is in his body, I'll be with him. And he's not long for here, either: that I can tell you, Charlie—he's not long for here. The mark is on his brow; and better so—maybe better so."

I was a while silent, not knowing what to say; and when I roused my head at last to speak, she got before me.

"Charlie," she said, "what's right for me, neednae be right for you. There's sin upon this house and trouble; you are a stranger; take your things upon your back and go your ways to better places and to better folk, and if you were ever minded to come back, though it were twenty years syne, you would find me aye waiting."

"Mary Ellen," I said, "I asked you to be my wife, and you said as good as yes. That's done for good. Wherever you are, I am; as I shall answer to my God."

As I said the words, the wind suddenly burst out raving, and then seemed to stand still and shudder round the house of Aros. It was the first squall, or prologue, of the coming tempest, and as we started and looked about us, we found that a gloom, like the approach of evening, had settled round the house.

"God pity all poor folks at sea!" she said. "We'll see no more of my father till the morrow's morning."

And then she told me, as we sat by the fire and hearkened to the rising gusts, of how this change had fallen upon my uncle. All last winter he had been dark and fitful in his mind. Whenever the Roost ran high, or, as Mary said, whenever the Merry Men were dancing, he would lie out for hours together on the Head, if it were at night, or on the top of Aros by day, watching the tumult of the sea, and sweeping the horizon for a sail. After February the tenth, when the wealth-bringing wreck was cast ashore at Sandag, he had been at first unnaturally gay, and his excitement had never fallen in degree, but only changed in kind from dark to darker. He neglected his work, and kept Rorie idle. The two would speak together by the hour at the gable end, in guarded tones and with an air of secrecy and almost of guilt; and if she questioned either, as at first she sometimes did, her inquiries were put aside with confusion. Since Rorie had first remarked the fish that hung about the ferry, his master had never set foot but once upon the mainland of the Ross. That once—it was in the height of the springs—he had passed dryshod while the tide was out; but, having lingered overlong on the far side, found himself cut off from Aros by the returning waters. It was with a shriek of agony that he had leaped across the gut, and he had reached home thereafter in a fever-fit of fear. A fear of the sea, a constant haunting thought of the sea, appeared in his talk and devotions, and even in his looks when he was silent.

Rorie alone came in to supper; but a little later my uncle appeared, took a bottle under his arm, put some bread in his pocket, and set forth again to his outlook, followed this time by Rorie. I heard that the schooner was losing ground, but the crew were still fighting every inch with hopeless ingenuity and courage; and the news filled my mind with blackness.

A little after sundown the full fury of the gale broke forth, such a gale as I have never seen in summer, nor, seeing how swiftly it had come, even in winter. Mary and I sat in silence, the house quaking overhead, the tempest howling without, the fire between us sputtering with raindrops. Our thoughts were far away with the poor fellows on the schooner, or my not less unhappy uncle, houseless on the promontory; and yet ever and again we were startled back to ourselves, when the wind would rise and strike the gable like a solid body, or suddenly fall and draw away, so that the fire leaped into flame and our hearts bounded in our sides. Now the storm in its might would seize and shake the four corners of the roof, roaring like Leviathan in anger. Anon, in a lull, cold eddies of tempest moved shudderingly in the room, lifting the hair upon our heads and passing between us as we sat. And again the wind would break forth in a chorus of melancholy sounds, hooting low in the chimney, wailing with flutelike softness round the house.

It was perhaps eight o'clock when Rorie came in and pulled me mysteriously to the door. My uncle, it appeared, had frightened even his constant comrade; and Rorie, uneasy at his extravagance, prayed me to come out and share the watch. I hastened to do as I was asked; the more readily as, what with fear and horror, and the electrical tension of the night, I was myself restless and disposed for action. I told Mary to be under no alarm, for I should be a safeguard on her father; and wrapping myself warmly in a plaid, I followed Rorie into the open air.

The night, though we were so little past midsummer, was as dark as January. Intervals of a groping twilight alternated with spells of utter blackness; and it was impossible to trace the reason of these changes in the flying horror of the sky. The wind blew the breath out of a man's nostrils; all heaven seemed to thunder overhead like one huge sail; and when there fell a momentary lull on Aros, we could hear the gusts dismally sweeping in the distance. Over all the lowlands of the Ross, the wind must have blown as fierce as on the open sea; and God only knows the uproar that was raging around the head of Ben Kyaw. Sheets of mingled spray and rain were driven in our faces. All round the isle of Aros the surf, with an incessant, hammering thunder, beat upon the reefs and beaches. Now louder in one place, now lower in another, like the combinations of orchestral music, the constant mass of sound was hardly varied for a moment. And loud above all this hurly-burly I could hear the changeful voices of the Roost and the intermittent roaring of the Merry Men. At that hour, there flashed into my mind the reason of the name that they were called. For the noise of them seemed almost mirthful, as it outtopped the other noises of the night; or if not mirthful, yet instinct with a portentous joviality. Nay, and it seemed even human. As when savage men have drunk away their reason, and, discarding speech, bawl together in their madness by the hour; so, to my ears, these deadly breakers shouted by Aros in the night.

Arm in arm, and staggering against the wind, Rorie and I won every yard of ground with conscious effort. We slipped on the wet sod, we fell together sprawling on the rocks. Bruised, drenched, beaten, and breathless, it must have taken us near half an hour to get from the house down to the Head that overlooks the Roost. There, it seemed, was my uncle's favourite observatory. Right in the face of it, where the cliff is highest and most sheer, a hump of earth, like a parapet, makes a place of shelter from the common winds, where a man may sit in quiet and see the tide and the mad billows contending at his feet. As he might look down from the window of a house upon some street disturbance, so, from this post, he looks down upon the tumbling of the Merry Men. On such a night, of course, he peers upon a world of blackness, where the waters wheel and boil, where the waves joust together with the noise of an explosion, and the foam towers and vanishes in the twinkling of an eye. Never before had I seen the Merry Men thus violent. The fury, height, and transiency of their spoutings was a thing to be seen and not recounted. High over our heads on the cliff rose their white columns in the darkness; and the same instant, like phantoms, they were gone. Sometimes three at a time would thus aspire and vanish; sometimes a gust took them, and the spray would fall about us, heavy as a wave. And yet the spectacle was rather maddening in its levity than impressive by its force. Thought was beaten down by the confounding uproar; a gleeful vacancy possessed the brains of men, a state akin to madness; and I found myself at times following the dance of the Merry Men as it were a tune upon a jigging instrument.

I first caught sight of my uncle when we were still some yards away in one of the flying glimpses of twilight that chequered the pitch darkness of the night. He was standing up behind the parapet, his head thrown back and the bottle to his mouth. As he put it down, he saw and recognised us with a toss of one hand fleeringly above his head.

"Has he been drinking?" shouted I to Rorie.

"He will aye be drunk when the wind blaws," returned Rorie in the same high key, and it was all that I could do to hear him.

"Then—was he so—in February?" I inquired.

Rorie's "Ay" was a cause of joy to me. The murder, then, had not sprung in cold blood from calculation; it was an act of madness no more to be condemned than to be pardoned. My uncle was a dangerous madman, if you will, but he was not cruel and base as I had feared. Yet what a scene for a carouse, what an incredible vice, was this that the poor man had chosen! I have always thought drunkenness a wild and almost fearful pleasure, rather demoniacal than human; but drunkenness, out here in the roaring blackness, on the edge of a cliff above that hell of waters, the man's head spinning like the Roost, his foot tottering on the edge of death, his ear watching for the signs of shipwreck, surely that, if it were credible in anyone, was morally impossible in a man like my uncle, whose mind was set upon a damnatory creed and haunted by the darkest superstitions. Yet so it was; and, as we reached the bight of shelter and could breathe again, I saw the man's eyes shining in the night with an unholy glimmer.

"Eh, Charlie, man, it's grand!" he cried. "See to them!" he continued, dragging me to the edge of the abyss from whence arose that deafening clamour and those clouds of spray; "see to them dancin', man! Is that no wicked?"

He pronounced the word with gusto, and I thought it suited with the scene.

"They're yowlin' for thon schooner," he went on, his thin, insane voice clearly audible in the shelter of the bank, "an' she's comin' aye nearer, aye nearer, aye nearer an' nearer an' nearer; an' they ken't, the folk kens it, they ken weel it's by wi' them. Charlie, lad, they're a' drunk in yon schooner, a' dozened wi' drink. They were a' drunk in the *Christ-Anna*, at the hinder end. There's nane could droon at sea wantin' the brandy. Hoot awa, what do you ken?" with a sudden blast of anger. "I tell ye, it cannae be; they daurnae droon withoot it. Ha'e," holding out the bottle, "tak' a sowp."

I was about to refuse, but Rorie touched me as if in warning; and indeed I had already thought better of the movement. I took the bottle, therefore, and not only drank freely myself, but contrived to spill even more as I was doing so. It was pure spirit, and almost strangled me to swallow. My kinsman did not observe the loss, but, once more throwing back his head, drained the remainder to the dregs. Then, with a loud laugh, he cast the bottle forth among the Merry Men, who seemed to leap up, shouting to receive it.

"Ha'e, bairns!" he cried, "there's your han'sel. Ye'll get bonnier nor that, or morning."

Suddenly, out in the black night before us, and not two hundred yards away, we heard, at a moment when the wind was silent, the clear note of a human voice. Instantly the wind swept howling down upon the Head, and the Roost bellowed, and churned, and danced with a new fury. But we had heard the sound, and we knew, with agony, that this was the doomed ship now close on ruin, and that what we had heard was the voice of her master issuing his last command. Crouching together on the edge, we waited, straining every sense, for the inevitable end. It was long, however, and to us it seemed like ages, ere the schooner suddenly appeared for one brief instant, relieved against a tower of glimmering foam. I still see her reefed mainsail flapping loose, as the boom fell heavily across the deck; I still see the black outline of the hull, and still think I can distinguish the figure of a man stretched upon the tiller. Yet the whole sight we had of her passed swifter than lightning; the very wave that disclosed her fell burying her for ever; the mingled cry of many voices at the point of death rose and was quenched in the roaring of the Merry Men. And with that the tragedy was at an end. The strong ship, with all her gear, and the lamp perhaps still burning in the cabin, the lives of so many men, precious surely to others, dear, at least, as heaven to themselves, had all, in that one moment, gone down into the surging waters. They were gone like a dream. And the wind still ran and shouted, and the senseless waters in the Roost still leaped and tumbled as before.

How long we lay there together, we three, speechless and motionless, is more than I can tell, but it must have been for long. At length, one by one, and almost mechanically, we crawled back into the shelter of the bank. As I lay against the parapet, wholly wretched and not entirely master of my mind, I could hear my kinsman maundering to himself in an altered and melancholy mood. Now he would repeat to himself with maudlin iteration, "Sic a fecht as they had—sic a sair fecht as they had, puir lads, puir lads!" and anon he would bewail that "a' the gear was as gude's tint," because the ship had gone down among the Merry Men instead of stranding on the shore; and throughout, the name—the *Christ-Anna*—would come and go in his divagations, pronounced with shuddering awe. The storm all this time was rapidly abating. In half an hour the wind had fallen to a breeze, and the change was accompanied or caused by a heavy, cold, and plumping rain. I must then have fallen asleep, and when I came to myself, drenched, stiff, and unrefreshed, day had already broken, grey, wet, discomfortable day; the wind blew in faint and shifting capfuls, the tide was out, the Roost was at its lowest, and only the strong beating surf round all the coasts of Aros remained to witness of the furies of the night.

CHAPTER FIVE

A man out of the sea

Rorie set out for the house in search of warmth and breakfast; but my uncle was bent upon examining the shores of Aros, and I felt it a part of duty to accompany him throughout. He was now docile and quiet, but tremulous and weak in mind and body; and it was with the eagerness of a child that he pursued his exploration. He climbed far down upon the rocks; on the beaches, he pursued the retreating breakers. The merest broken plank or rag of cordage was a treasure in his eyes to be secured at the peril of his life. To see him, with weak and stumbling footsteps, expose himself to the pursuit of the surf, or the snares and pitfalls of the weedy rock, kept me in a perpetual terror. My arm was ready to support him, my hand clutched him by the skirt, I helped him to draw his pitiful discoveries beyond the reach of the returning wave; a nurse accompanying a child of seven would have had no different experience.

Yet, weakened as he was by the reaction from his madness of the night before, the passions that smouldered in his nature were those of a strong man. His terror of the sea, although conquered for the moment, was still undiminished; had the sea been a lake of living flames, he could not have shrunk more panically from its touch; and once, when his foot slipped and he plunged to the midleg into a pool of water, the shriek that came up out of his soul was like the cry of death. He sat still for a while, panting like a dog, after that; but his desire for the spoils of shipwreck triumphed once more over his fears; once more he tottered among the curded foam; once more he crawled upon the rocks among the bursting bubbles; once more his whole heart seemed to be set on driftwood, fit, if it was fit for anything, to throw upon the fire. Pleased as he was with what he found, he still incessantly grumbled at his ill-fortune.

"Aros," he said, "is no a place for wrecks ava'—no ava'. A' the years I've dwalt here, this ane maks the second; and the best o' the gear clean tint!"

"Uncle," said I, for we were now on a stretch of open sand, where there was nothing to divert his mind, "I saw you last night, as I never thought to see you—you were drunk."

"Na, na," he said, "no as bad as that. I had been drinking, though. And to tell ye the God's truth, it's a thing I cannae mend. There's nae soberer man than me in my ordnar; but when I hear the wind blaw in my lug, it's my belief that I gang gyte."

"You are a religious man," I replied, "and this is sin."

"Oh," he returned, "if it wasnae sin, I dinnae ken that I would care for't. Ye see, man, it's defiance. There's a sair spang o' the auld sin o' the warld in yon sea; it's an unchristian business at the best o't; an' whiles when it gets up, an' the wind skreighs—the wind an' her are a kind of sib, I'm thinkin'—an' thae Merry Men, the daft callants, blawin' and lauchin', and puir souls in the deid thraws warstlin' the leelang nicht wi' their bit ships—weel, it comes ower me like a glamour. I'm a deil, I ken't. But I think naething o' the puir sailor lads; I'm wi' the sea, I'm just like ane o' her ain Merry Men."

I thought I should touch him in a joint of his harness. I turned me towards the sea; the surf was running gaily, wave after wave, with their manes blowing behind them, riding one after another up the beach, towering, curving, falling one upon another on the trampled sand. Without, the salt air, the scared gulls, the widespread army of the seachargers, neighing to each other, as they gathered together to the assault of Aros; and close before us, that line on the flat sands that, with all their number and their fury, they might never pass.

"Thus far shalt thou go," said I, "and no farther." And then I quoted as solemnly as I was able a verse that I had often before fitted to the chorus of the breakers:

> But yet the Lord that is on high,
> Is more of might by far,
> Than noise of many waters is,
> As great sea billows are.

"Ay," said my kinsman, "at the hinder end, the Lord will triumph; I dinnae misdoobt that. But here on earth, even silly menfolk daur Him to His face. It is nae wise; I am nae sayin' that it's wise; but it's the pride of the eye, and it's the lust o' life, an' it's the wale o' pleesures."

I said no more, for we had now begun to cross a neck of land that lay between us and Sandag; and I withheld my last appeal to the man's better reason till we should stand upon the spot associated with his crime. Nor did he pursue the subject; but he walked beside me with a firmer step. The call that I had made upon his mind acted like a stimulant, and I could see that he had forgotten his search for worthless jetsam, in a profound, gloomy, and yet stirring train of thought. In three or four minutes we had topped the brae and begun to go down upon Sandag. The wreck had been roughly handled by the sea; the stem had been spun round and dragged a little lower down; and perhaps the stern had been forced a little higher, for the two parts now lay entirely separate on the beach. When we came to the grave I stopped, uncovered my head in the thick rain, and, looking my kinsman in the face, addressed him.

"A man," said I, "was in God's providence suffered to escape from mortal dangers; he was poor, he was naked, he was wet, he was weary, he was a stranger; he had every claim upon the bowels of your compassion; it may be that he was the salt of the earth, holy, helpful, and kind; it may be he was a man laden with iniquities to whom death was the beginning of torment. I ask you in the sight of heaven: Gordon Darnaway, where is the man for whom Christ died?"

He started visibly at the last words; but there came no answer, and his face expressed no feeling but a vague alarm.

"You were my father's brother," I continued; "you have taught me to count your house as if it were my father's house; and we are both sinful men walking before the Lord among the sins and dangers of this life. It is by our evil that God leads us into good; we sin, I dare not say by His temptation, but I must say with His consent; and to any but the brutish man his sins are the beginning of wisdom. God has warned you by this crime; He warns you still by the bloody grave between our feet; and if there shall follow no repentance, no improvement, no return to Him, what can we look for but the following of some memorable judgment?"

Even as I spoke the words, the eyes of my uncle wandered from my face. A change fell upon his looks that cannot be described; his features seemed to dwindle in size, the colour faded from his cheeks, one hand rose waveringly and pointed over my shoulder into the distance, and the oft-repeated name fell once more from his lips: "The *Christ-Anna!*"

I turned; and if I was not appalled to the same degree, as I return thanks to Heaven that I had not the cause, I was still startled by the sight that met my eyes. The form of a man stood upright on the cabin-hutch of the wrecked ship; his back was towards us; he appeared to be scanning the offing with shaded eyes, and his figure was relieved to its full height, which was plainly very great, against the sea and sky. I have said a thousand times that I am not superstitious; but at that moment, with my mind running upon death and sin, the unexplained appearance of a stranger on that sea-girt, solitary island filled me with a surprise that bordered close on terror. It seemed scarce possible that any human soul should have come ashore alive in such a sea as had raged last night along the coasts of Aros; and the only vessel within miles had gone down before our eyes among the Merry Men. I was assailed with doubts that made suspense unbearable, and, to put the matter to the touch at once, stepped forward and hailed the figure like a ship.

He turned about, and I thought he started to behold us. At this my courage instantly revived, and I called and signed to him to draw near, and he, on his part, dropped immediately to the sands, and began slowly to approach, with many stops and hesitations. At each repeated mark of the man's uneasiness I grew the more confident myself; and I advanced another step, encouraging him as I did so with my head and hand. It was plain the castaway had heard indifferent accounts of our island hospitality; and indeed, about this time, the people farther north had a sorry reputation.

"Why," I said, "the man is black!"

And just at that moment, in a voice that I could scarce have recognised, my kinsman began swearing and praying in a mingled stream. I looked at him; he had fallen on his knees, his face was agonised; at each step of the castaway's the pitch of his voice rose, the volubility of his utterance and the fervour of his language redoubled. I call it prayer, for it was addressed to God; but surely no such ranting incongruities were ever before addressed to the Creator by a creature: surely if prayer can be a sin, this mad harangue was sinful. I ran to my kinsman, I seized him by the shoulders, I dragged him to his feet.

"Silence, man," said I, "respect your God in words, if not in action. Here, on the very scene of your transgressions, He sends you an occasion of atonement. Forward and embrace it; welcome like a father yon creature who comes trembling to your mercy."

With that, I tried to force him towards the black; but he felled me to the ground, burst from my grasp, leaving the shoulder of his jacket, and fled up the hillside towards the top of Aros like a deer. I staggered to my feet again, bruised and somewhat stunned; the negro had paused in surprise, perhaps in terror, some halfway between me and the wreck; my uncle was already far away, bounding from rock to rock; and I thus found myself torn for a time between two duties. But I judged, and I pray Heaven that I judged rightly, in favour of the poor wretch upon the sands; his misfortune was at least not plainly of his own creation; it was one, besides, that I could certainly relieve; and I had begun by that time to regard my uncle as an incurable and dismal lunatic. I advanced accordingly towards the black, who now awaited my approach with folded arms, like one prepared for either destiny. As I came nearer, he reached forth his hand with a great gesture, such as I had seen from the pulpit, and spoke to me in something of a pulpit voice, but not a word was comprehensible. I tried him first in English, then in Gaelic, both in vain; so that it was clear we must rely upon the tongue of looks and gestures. Thereupon I signed to him to follow me, which he did readily and with a grave obeisance like a fallen king; all the while there had come no shade of alteration in his face, neither of anxiety while he was still waiting, nor of relief now that he was reassured; if he were a slave, as I supposed, I could not but judge he must have fallen from some high place in his own country, and fallen as he was, I could not but admire his bearing. As we passed the grave, I paused and raised my hands and eyes to heaven in token of respect and sorrow for the dead; and he, as if in answer, bowed low and spread his hands abroad; it was a strange motion, but done like a thing of common custom; and I supposed it was ceremonial in the land from which he came. At the same time he pointed to my uncle, whom we could just see perched upon a knoll, and touched his head to indicate that he was mad.

We took the long way round the shore, for I feared to excite my uncle if we struck across the island; and as we walked, I had time enough to mature the little dramatic exhibition by which I hoped to satisfy my doubts. Accordingly, pausing on a rock, I proceeded to imitate before the negro the action of the man whom I had seen the day before taking bearings with the compass at Sandag. He understood me at once, and, taking the imitation out of my hands, showed me where the boat was, pointed out seaward as if to indicate the position of the schooner, and then down along the edge of the rock with the words "Espirito Santo," strangely pronounced, but clear enough for recognition. I had thus been right in my conjecture; the pretended historical inquiry had been but a cloak for treasure hunting; the man who had played on Dr. Robertson was the same as the foreigner who visited Grisapol in spring, and now, with many others, lay dead under the Roost of Aros: there had their greed brought them, there should their bones be tossed for evermore. In the meantime the black continued his imitation of the scene, now looking up skyward as though watching the approach of the storm; now, in the character of a seaman, waving the rest to come aboard; now as an officer, running along the rock and entering the boat; and anon bending over imaginary oars with the air of a hurried boatman; but all with the same solemnity of manner, so that I was never even moved to smile. Lastly, he indicated to me, by a pantomime not to be described in words, how he himself had gone up to examine the stranded wreck, and, to his grief and indignation, had been deserted by his comrades; and thereupon folded his arms once more, and stooped his head, like one accepting fate.

The mystery of his presence being thus solved for me, I explained to him by means of a sketch the fate of the vessel and of all aboard her. He showed no surprise nor sorrow, and, with a sudden lifting of his open hand, seemed to dismiss his former friends or masters (whichever they had been) into God's pleasure. Respect came upon me and grew stronger, the more I observed him; I saw he had a powerful mind and a sober and severe character, such as I loved to commune with; and before we reached the house of Aros I had almost forgotten, and wholly forgiven him, his uncanny colour.

To Mary I told all that had passed without suppression, though I own my heart failed me; but I did wrong to doubt her sense of justice.

"You did the right," she said. "God's will be done." And she set out meat for us at once.

As soon as I was satisfied, I bade Rorie keep an eye upon the castaway, who was still eating, and set forth again myself to find my uncle. I had not gone far before I saw him sitting in the same place, upon the very topmost knoll, and seemingly in the same attitude as when I had last observed him. From that point, as I have said, the most of Aros and the neighbouring Ross would be spread below him like a map; and it was plain that he kept a bright lookout in all directions, for my head had scarcely risen above the summit of the first ascent before he had leaped to his feet and turned as if to face me. I hailed him at once, as well as I was able, in the same tones and words as I had often used before, when I had come to summon him to dinner. He made not so much as a movement in reply. I passed on a little farther, and again tried parley, with the same result. But when I began a second time to advance, his insane fears blazed up again, and still in dead silence, but with incredible speed, he began to flee from before me along the rocky summit of the hill. An hour before, he had been dead weary, and I had been comparatively active. But now his strength was recruited by the fervour of insanity, and it would have been vain for me to dream of pursuit. Nay, the very attempt, I thought, might have inflamed his terrors, and thus increased the miseries of our position. And I had nothing left but to turn homeward and make my sad report to Mary.

She heard it, as she had heard the first, with a concerned composure, and, bidding me lie down and take that rest of which I stood so much in need, set forth herself in quest of her misguided father. At that age it would have been a strange thing that put me from either meat or sleep; I slept long and deep; and it was already long past noon before I awoke and came downstairs into the kitchen. Mary, Rorie, and the black castaway were seated about the fire in silence; and I could see that Mary had been weeping. There was cause enough, as I soon learned, for tears. First she, and then Rorie, had been forth to seek my uncle; each in turn had found him perched upon the hilltop, and from each in turn he had silently and swiftly fled. Rorie had tried to chase him, but in vain; madness lent a new vigour to his bounds; he sprang from rock to rock over the widest gullies; he scoured like the wind along the hilltops; he doubled and twisted like a hare before the dogs; and Rorie at length gave in; and the last that he saw, my uncle was seated as before upon the crest of Aros. Even during the hottest excitement of the chase, even when the fleet-footed servant had come, for a moment, very near to capture him, the poor lunatic had uttered not a sound. He fled, and he was silent, like a beast; and this silence had terrified his pursuer.

There was something heartbreaking in the situation. How to capture the madman, how to feed him in the meanwhile, and what to do with him when he was captured, were the three difficulties that we had to solve.

"The black," said I, "is the cause of this attack. It may even be his presence in the house that keeps my uncle on the hill. We have done the fair thing; he has been fed and warmed under this roof; now I propose that Rorie put him across the bay in the coble, and take him through the Ross as far as Grisapol."

In this proposal Mary heartily concurred; and bidding the black follow us, we all three descended to the pier. Certainly, Heaven's will was declared against Gordon Darnaway; a thing had happened, never paralleled before in Aros; during the storm, the coble had broken loose, and, striking on the rough splinters of the pier, now lay in four feet of water with one side stove in. Three days of work at least would be required to make her float. But I was not to be beaten. I led the whole party round to where the gut was narrowest, swam to the other side, and called to the black to follow me. He signed, with the same clearness and quiet as before, that he knew not the art; and there was truth apparent in his signals, it would have occurred to none of us to doubt his truth; and that hope being over, we must all go back even as we came to the house of Aros, the negro walking in our midst without embarrassment.

All we could do that day was to make one more attempt to communicate with the unhappy madman. Again he was visible on his perch; again he fled in silence. But food and a great cloak were at least left for his comfort; the rain, besides, had cleared away, and the night promised to be even warm. We might compose ourselves, we thought, until the morrow; rest was the chief requisite, that we might be strengthened for unusual exertions; and as none cared to talk, we separated at an early hour.

I lay long awake, planning a campaign for the morrow. I was to place the black on the side of Sandag, whence he should head my uncle towards the house; Rorie in the west, I on the east, were to complete the cordon, as best we might. It seemed to me, the more I recalled the configuration of the island, that it should be possible, though hard, to force him down upon the low ground along Aros Bay; and once there, even with the strength of his madness, ultimate escape was hardly to be feared. It was on his terror of the black that I relied; for I made sure, however he might run, it would not be in the direction of the man whom he supposed to have returned from the dead, and thus one point of the compass at least would be secure.

When at length I fell asleep, it was to be awakened shortly after by a dream of wrecks, black men, and submarine adventure; and I found myself so shaken and fevered that I arose, descended the stair, and stepped out before the house. Within, Rorie and the black were asleep together in the kitchen; outside was a wonderful clear night of stars, with here and there a cloud still hanging, last stragglers of the tempest. It was near the top of the flood, and the Merry Men were roaring in the windless quiet of the night. Never, not even in the height of the tempest, had I heard their song with greater awe. Now, when the winds were gathered home, when the deep was dandling itself back into its summer slumber, and when the stars rained their gentle light over land and sea, the voice of these tide-breakers was still raised for havoc. They seemed, indeed, to be a part of the world's evil and the tragic side of life. Nor were their meaningless vociferations the only sounds that broke the silence of the night. For I could hear, now shrill and thrilling and now almost drowned, the note of a human voice that accompanied the uproar of the Roost. I knew it for my kinsman's; and a great fear fell upon me of God's judgments, and the evil in the world. I went back again into the darkness of the house as into a place of shelter, and lay long upon my bed, pondering these mysteries.

It was late when I again woke, and I leaped into my clothes and hurried to the kitchen. No one was there; Rorie and the black had both stealthily departed long before; and my heart stood still at the discovery. I could rely on Rorie's heart, but I placed no trust in his discretion. If he had thus set out without a word, he was plainly bent upon some service to my uncle. But what service could he hope to render even alone, far less in the company of the man in whom my uncle found his fears incarnated? Even if I were not already too late to prevent some deadly mischief, it was plain I must delay no longer. With the thought I was out of the house; and often as I have run on the rough sides of Aros, I never ran as I did that fatal morning. I do not believe I put twelve minutes to the whole ascent.

My uncle was gone from his perch. The basket had indeed been torn open and the meat scattered on the turf; but, as we found afterwards, no mouthful had been tasted; and there was not another trace of human existence in that wide field of view. Day had already filled the clear heavens; the sun already lighted in a rosy bloom upon the crest of Ben Kyaw; but all below me the rude knolls of Aros and the shield of sea lay steeped in the clear darkling twilight of the dawn.

"Rorie!" I cried; and again "Rorie!" My voice died in the silence, but there came no answer back. If there were indeed an enterprise afoot to catch my uncle, it was plainly not in fleetness of foot, but in dexterity of stalking, that the hunters placed their trust. I ran on farther, keeping the higher spurs, and looking right and left, nor did I pause again till I was on the mount above Sandag. I could see the wreck, the uncovered belt of sand, the waves idly beating, the long ledge of rocks, and on either hand the tumbled knolls, boulders, and gullies of the island. But still no human thing.

At a stride the sunshine fell on Aros, and the shadows and colours leaped into being. Not half a moment later, below me to the west, sheep began to scatter as in a panic. There came a cry. I saw my uncle running. I saw the black jump up in hot pursuit; and before I had time to understand, Rorie also had appeared, calling directions in Gaelic as to a dog herding sheep.

I took to my heels to interfere, and perhaps I had done better to have waited where I was, for I was the means of cutting off the madman's last escape. There was nothing before him from that moment but the grave, the wreck, and the sea in Sandag Bay. And yet Heaven knows that what I did was for the best.

My uncle Gordon saw in what direction, horrible to him, the chase was driving him. He doubled, darting to the right and left; but high as the fever ran in his veins, the black was still the swifter. Turn where he would, he was still forestalled, still driven toward the scene of his crime. Suddenly he began to shriek aloud, so that the coast re-echoed; and now both I and Rorie were calling on the black to stop. But all was vain, for it was written otherwise. The pursuer still ran, the chase still sped before him screaming; they avoided the grave, and skimmed close past the timbers of the wreck; in a breath they had cleared the sand; and still my kinsman did not pause, but dashed straight into the surf; and the black, now almost within reach, still followed swiftly behind him. Rorie and I both stopped, for the thing was now beyond the hands of men, and these were the decrees of God that came to pass before our eyes. There was never a sharper ending. On that steep beach they were beyond their depth at a bound; neither could swim; the black rose once for a moment with a throttling cry; but the current had them, racing seaward; and if ever they came up again, which God alone can tell, it would be ten minutes after, at the far end of Aros Roost, where the seabirds hover fishing.

WILL O' THE MILL

THE PLAIN AND THE STARS

The Mill where Will lived with his adopted parents stood in a falling valley between pinewoods and great mountains. Above, hill after hill, soared upwards until they soared out of the depth of the hardiest timber, and stood naked against the sky. Some way up, a long grey village lay like a seam or a rag of vapour on a wooded hillside; and when the wind was favourable, the sound of the church bells would drop down, thin and silvery, to Will. Below, the valley grew ever steeper and steeper, and at the same time widened out on either hand; and from an eminence beside the mill it was possible to see its whole length and away beyond it over a wide plain, where the river turned and shone, and moved on from city to city on its voyage towards the sea. It chanced that over this valley there lay a pass into a neighbouring kingdom; so that, quiet and rural as it was, the road that ran along beside the river was a high thoroughfare between two splendid and powerful societies. All through the summer, travelling carriages came crawling up, or went plunging briskly downwards past the mill; and as it happened that the other side was very much easier of ascent, the path was not much frequented, except by people going in one direction; and of all the carriages that Will saw go by, five-sixths were plunging briskly downwards and only one-sixth crawling up. Much more was this the case with foot-passengers. All the light-footed tourists, all the pedlars laden with strange wares, were tending downward like the river that accompanied their path. Nor was this all; for when Will was yet a child a disastrous war arose over a great part of the world. The newspapers were full of defeats and victories, the earth rang with cavalry hoofs, and often for days together and for miles around the coil of battle terrified good people from their labours in the field. Of all this, nothing was heard for a long time in the valley; but at last one of the commanders pushed an army over the pass by forced marches, and for three days horse and foot, cannon and tumbril, drum and standard, kept pouring downward past the mill. All day the child stood and watched them on their passage—the rhythmical stride, the pale, unshaven faces tanned about the eyes, the discoloured regimentals and the tattered flags, filled him with a sense of weariness, pity, and wonder; and all night long, after he was in bed, he could hear the cannon pounding and the feet trampling, and the great armament sweeping onward and downward past the mill. No one in the valley ever heard the fate of the expedition, for they lay out of the way of gossip in those troublous times; but Will saw one thing plainly, that not a man returned. Whither had they all gone? Whither went all the tourists and pedlars with strange wares? whither all the brisk barouches with servant in the dicky? whither the water of the stream, ever coursing downward and ever renewed from above? Even the wind blew oftener down the valley, and carried the dead leaves along with it in the fall. It seemed like a great conspiracy of things animate and inanimate; they all went downward, fleetly and gaily downward, and only he, it seemed, remained behind, like a stock upon the wayside. It sometimes made him glad when he noticed how the fishes kept their heads up stream. They, at least, stood faithfully by him, while all else were posting downward to the unknown world.

One evening he asked the miller where the river went.

"It goes down the valley," answered he, "and turns a power of mills—six score mills, they say, from here to Unterdeck—and it none the wearier after all. And then it goes out into the lowlands, and waters the great corn country, and runs through a sight of fine cities (so they say) where kings live all alone in great palaces, with a sentry walking up and down before the door. And it goes under bridges with stone men upon them, looking down and smiling so curious at the water, and living folks leaning their elbows on the wall and looking over too. And then it goes on and on, and down through marshes and sands, until at last it falls into the sea, where the ships are that bring parrots and tobacco from the Indies. Ay, it has a long trot before it as it goes singing over our weir, bless its heart!"

"And what is the sea?" asked Will.

"The sea!" cried the miller. "Lord help us all, it is the greatest thing God made! That is where all the water in the world runs down into a great salt lake. There it lies, as flat as my hand and as innocent-like as a child; but they do say when the wind blows it gets up into water-mountains bigger than any of ours, and swallows down great ships bigger than our mill, and makes such a roaring that you can hear it miles away upon the land. There are great fish in it five times bigger than a bull, and one old serpent as long as our river and as old as all the world, with whiskers like a man, and a crown of silver on her head."

Will thought he had never heard anything like this, and he kept on asking question after question about the world that lay away down the river, with all its perils and marvels, until the old miller became quite interested himself, and at last took him by the hand and led him to the hilltop that overlooks the valley and the plain. The sun was near setting, and hung low down in a cloudless sky. Everything was defined and glorified in golden light. Will had never seen so great an expanse of country in his life; he stood and gazed with all his eyes. He could see the cities, and the woods and fields, and the bright curves of the river, and far away to where the rim of the plain trenched along the shining heavens. An overmastering emotion seized upon the boy, soul and body; his heart beat so thickly that he could not breathe; the scene swam before his eyes; the sun seemed to wheel round and round, and throw off, as it turned, strange shapes which disappeared with the rapidity of thought, and were succeeded by others. Will covered his face with his hands, and burst into a violent fit of tears; and the poor miller, sadly disappointed and perplexed, saw nothing better for it than to take him up in his arms and carry him home in silence.

From that day forward Will was full of new hopes and longings. Something kept tugging at his heartstrings; the running water carried his desires along with it as he dreamed over its fleeting surface; the wind, as it ran over innumerable treetops, hailed him with encouraging words; branches beckoned downward; the open road, as it shouldered round the angles and went turning and vanishing fast and faster down the valley, tortured him with its solicitations. He spent long whiles on the eminence, looking down the rivershed and abroad on the fat lowlands, and watched the clouds that travelled forth upon the sluggish wind and trailed their purple shadows on the plain; or he would linger by the wayside, and follow the carriages with his eyes as they rattled downward by the river. It did not matter what it was; everything that went that way, were it cloud or carriage, bird or brown water in the stream, he felt his heart flow out after it in an ecstasy of longing.

We are told by men of science that all the ventures of mariners on the sea, all that countermarching of tribes and races that confounds old history with its dust and rumour, sprang from nothing more abstruse than the laws of supply and demand, and a certain natural instinct for cheap rations. To any one thinking deeply, this will seem a dull and pitiful explanation. The tribes that came swarming out of the North and East, if they were indeed pressed onward from behind by others, were drawn at the same time by the magnetic influence of the South and West. The fame of other lands had reached them; the name of the eternal city rang in their ears; they were not colonists, but pilgrims; they travelled towards wine and gold and sunshine, but their hearts were set on something higher. That divine unrest, that old stinging trouble of humanity that makes all high achievements and all miserable failure, the same that spread wings with Icarus, the same that sent Columbus into the desolate Atlantic, inspired and supported these barbarians on their perilous march. There is one legend which profoundly represents their spirit, of how a flying party of these wanderers encountered a very old man shod with iron. The old man asked them whither they were going; and they answered with one voice: "To the Eternal City!" He looked upon them gravely. "I have sought it," he said, "over the most part of the world. Three such pairs as I now carry on my feet have I worn out upon this pilgrimage, and now the fourth is growing slender underneath my steps. And all this while I have not found the city." And he turned and went his own way alone, leaving them astonished.

And yet this would scarcely parallel the intensity of Will's feeling for the plain. If he could only go far enough out there, he felt as if his eyesight would be purged and clarified, as if his hearing would grow more delicate, and his very breath would come and go with luxury. He was transplanted and withering where he was; he lay in a strange country and was sick for home. Bit by bit, he pieced together broken notions of the world below: of the river, ever moving and growing until it sailed forth into the majestic ocean; of the cities, full of brisk and beautiful people, playing fountains, bands of music and marble palaces, and lighted up at night from end to end with artificial stars of gold; of the great churches, wise universities, brave armies, and untold money lying stored in vaults; of the high-flying vice that moved in the sunshine, and the stealth and swiftness of midnight murder. I have said he was sick as if for home: the figure halts. He was like some one lying in twilit, formless pre-existence, and stretching out his hands lovingly towards many-coloured, many-sounding life. It was no wonder he was unhappy, he would go and tell the fish: they were made for their life, wished for no more than worms and running water, and a hole below a falling bank; but he was differently designed, full of desires and aspirations, itching at the fingers, lusting with the eyes, whom the whole variegated world could not satisfy with aspects. The true life, the true bright sunshine, lay far out upon the plain. And O! to see this sunlight once before he died! to move with a jocund spirit in a golden land! to hear the trained singers and sweet church bells, and see the holiday gardens! "And O fish!" he would cry, "if you would only turn your noses down stream, you could swim so easily into the fabled waters and see the vast ships passing over your head like clouds, and hear the great waterhills making music over you all day long!" But the fish kept looking patiently in their own direction, until Will hardly knew whether to laugh or cry.

Hitherto the traffic on the road had passed by Will, like something seen in a picture; he had perhaps exchanged salutations with a tourist, or caught sight of an old gentleman in a travelling cap at a carriage window; but for the most part it had been a mere symbol, which he contemplated from apart and with something of a superstitious feeling. A time came at last when this was to be changed. The miller, who was a greedy man in his way, and never forewent an opportunity of honest profit, turned the millhouse into a little wayside inn, and, several pieces of good fortune falling in opportunely, built stables and got the position of post master on the road. It now became Will's duty to wait upon people, as they sat to break their fasts in the little arbour at the top of the mill garden; and you may be sure that he kept his ears open, and learned many new things about the outside world as he brought the omelette or the wine. Nay, he would often get into conversation with single guests, and by adroit questions and polite attention, not only gratify his own curiosity, but win the goodwill of the travellers. Many complimented the old couple on their serving-boy; and a professor was eager to take him away with him, and have him properly educated in the plain. The miller and his wife were mightily astonished and even more pleased. They thought it a very good thing that they should have opened their inn. "You see," the old man would remark, "he has a kind of talent for a publican; he never would have made anything else!" And so life wagged on in the valley, with high satisfaction to all concerned but Will. Every carriage that left the inn door seemed to take a part of him away with it; and when people jestingly offered him a lift, he could with difficulty command his emotion. Night after night he would dream that he was awakened by flustered servants, and that a splendid equipage waited at the door to carry him down into the plain; night after night; until the dream, which had seemed all jollity to him at first, began to take on a colour of gravity, and the nocturnal summons and waiting equipage occupied a place in his mind as something to be both feared and hoped for.

One day, when Will was about sixteen, a fat young man arrived at sunset to pass the night. He was a contented-looking fellow, with a jolly eye, and carried a knapsack. While dinner was preparing, he sat in the arbour to read a book; but as soon as he had begun to observe Will, the book was laid aside; he was plainly one of those who prefer living people to people made of ink and paper. Will, on his part, although he had not been much interested in the stranger at first sight, soon began to take a great deal of pleasure in his talk, which was full of good nature and good sense, and at last conceived a great respect for his character and wisdom. They sat far into the night; and about two in the morning Will opened his heart to the young man, and told him how he longed to leave the valley and what bright hopes he had connected with the cities of the plain. The young man whistled, and then broke into a smile.

"My young friend," he remarked, "you are a very curious little fellow to be sure, and wish a great many things which you will never get. Why, you would feel quite ashamed if you knew how the little fellows in these fairy cities of yours are all after the same sort of nonsense, and keep breaking their hearts to get up into the mountains. And let me tell you, those who go down into the plains are a very short while there before they wish themselves heartily back again. The air is not so light nor so pure; nor is the sun any brighter. As for the beautiful men and women, you would see many of them in rags and many of them deformed with horrible disorders; and a city is so hard a place for people who are poor and sensitive that many choose to die by their own hand."

"You must think me very simple," answered Will. "Although I have never been out of this valley, believe me, I have used my eyes. I know how one thing lives on another; for instance, how the fish hangs in the eddy to catch his fellows; and the shepherd, who makes so pretty a picture carrying home the lamb, is only carrying it home for dinner. I do not expect to find all things right in your cities. That is not what troubles me; it might have been that once upon a time; but although I live here always, I have asked many questions and learned a great deal in these last years, and certainly enough to cure me of my old fancies. But you would not have me die like a dog and not see all that is to be seen, and do all that a man can do, let it be good or evil? you would not have me spend all my days between this road here and the river, and not so much as make a motion to be up and live my life?—I would rather die out of hand," he cried, "than linger on as I am doing."

"Thousands of people," said the young man, "live and die like you, and are none the less happy."

"Ah!" said Will, "if there are thousands who would like, why should not one of them have my place?"

It was quite dark; there was a hanging lamp in the arbour which lit up the table and the faces of the speakers; and along the arch, the leaves upon the trellis stood out illuminated against the night sky, a pattern of transparent green upon a dusky purple. The fat young man rose, and, taking Will by the arm, led him out under the open heavens.

"Did you ever look at the stars?" he asked, pointing upwards.

"Often and often," answered Will.

"And do you know what they are?"

"I have fancied many things."

"They are worlds like ours," said the young man. "Some of them less; many of them a million times greater; and some of the least sparkles that you see are not only worlds, but whole clusters of worlds turning about each other in the midst of space. We do not know what there may be in any of them; perhaps the answer to all our difficulties or the cure of all our sufferings: and yet we can never reach them; not all the skill of the craftiest of men can fit out a ship for the nearest of these our neighbours, nor would the life of the most aged suffice for such a journey. When a great battle has been lost or a dear friend is dead, when we are hipped or in high spirits, there they are unweariedly shining overhead. We may stand down here, a whole army of us together, and shout until we break our hearts, and not a whisper reaches them. We may climb the highest mountain, and we are no nearer them. All we can do is to stand down here in the garden and take off our hats; the starshine lights upon our heads, and where mine is a little bald, I dare say you can see it glisten in the darkness. The mountain and the mouse. That is like to be all we shall ever have to do with Arcturus or Aldebaran. Can you apply a parable?" he added, laying his hand upon Will's shoulder. "It is not the same thing as a reason, but usually vastly more convincing."

Will hung his head a little, and then raised it once more to heaven. The stars seemed to expand and emit a sharper brilliancy; and as he kept turning his eyes higher and higher, they seemed to increase in multitude under his gaze.

"I see," he said, turning to the young man. "We are in a rattrap."

"Something of that size. Did you ever see a squirrel turning in a cage? and another squirrel sitting philosophically over his nuts? I needn't ask you which of them looked more of a fool."

THE PARSON'S MARJORY

After some years the old people died, both in one winter, very carefully tended by their adopted son, and very quietly mourned when they were gone. People who had heard of his roving fancies supposed he would hasten to sell the property, and go down the river to push his fortunes. But there was never any sign of such an intention on the part of Will. On the contrary, he had the inn set on a better footing, and hired a couple of servants to assist him in carrying it on; and there he settled down, a kind, talkative, inscrutable young man, six feet three in his stockings, with an iron constitution and a friendly voice. He soon began to take rank in the district as a bit of an oddity: it was not much to be wondered at from the first, for he was always full of notions, and kept calling the plainest common sense in question; but what most raised the report upon him was the odd circumstance of his courtship with the parson's Marjory.

The parson's Marjory was a lass about nineteen, when Will would be about thirty; well enough looking, and much better educated than any other girl in that part of the country, as became her parentage. She held her head very high, and had already refused several offers of marriage with a grand air, which had got her hard names among the neighbours. For all that she was a good girl, and one that would have made any man well contented.

Will had never seen much of her; for although the church and parsonage were only two miles from his own door, he was never known to go there but on Sundays. It chanced, however, that the parsonage fell into disrepair, and had to be dismantled; and the parson and his daughter took lodgings for a month or so, on very much reduced terms, at Will's inn. Now, what with the inn, and the mill, and the old miller's savings, our friend was a man of substance; and besides that, he had a name for good temper and shrewdness, which make a capital portion in marriage; and so it was currently gossiped, among their ill-wishers, that the parson and his daughter had not chosen their temporary lodging with their eyes shut. Will was about the last man in the world to be cajoled or frightened into marriage. You had only to look into his eyes, limpid and still like pools of water, and yet with a sort of clear light that seemed to come from within, and you would understand at once that here was one who knew his own mind, and would stand to it immovably. Marjory herself was no weakling by her looks, with strong, steady eyes and a resolute and quiet bearing. It might be a question whether she was not Will's match in stedfastness, after all, or which of them would rule the roast in marriage. But Marjory had never given it a thought, and accompanied her father with the most unshaken innocence and unconcern.

The season was still so early that Will's customers were few and far between; but the lilacs were already flowering, and the weather was so mild that the party took dinner under the trellice, with the noise of the river in their ears and the woods ringing about them with the songs of birds. Will soon began to take a particular pleasure in these dinners.

The parson was rather a dull companion, with a habit of dozing at table; but nothing rude or cruel ever fell from his lips. And as for the parson's daughter, she suited her surroundings with the best grace imaginable; and whatever she said seemed so pat and pretty that Will conceived a great idea of her talents. He could see her face, as she leaned forward, against a background of rising pinewoods; her eyes shone peaceably; the light lay around her hair like a kerchief; something that was hardly a smile rippled her pale cheeks, an Will could not contain himself from gazing on her in an agreeable dismay. She looked, even in her quietest moments, so complete in herself, and so quick with life down to her finger tips and the very skirts of her dress, that the remainder of created things became no more than a blot by comparison; and if Will glanced away from her to her surroundings, the trees looked inanimate and senseless, the clouds hung in heaven like dead things, and even the mountain tops were disenchanted. The whole valley could not compare in looks with this one girl.

Will was always observant in the society of his fellow creatures; but his observation became almost painfully eager in the case of Marjory. He listened to all she uttered, and read her eyes, at the same time, for the unspoken commentary. Many kind, simple, and sincere speeches found an echo in his heart. He became conscious of a soul beautifully poised upon itself, nothing doubting, nothing desiring, clothed in peace. It was not possible to separate her thoughts from her appearance. The turn of her wrist, the still sound of her voice, the light in her eyes, the lines of her body, fell in tune with her grave and gentle words, like the accompaniment that sustains and harmonises the voice of the singer. Her influence was one thing, not to be divided or discussed, only to be felt with gratitude and joy. To Will, her presence recalled something of his childhood, and the thought of her took its place in his mind beside that of dawn, of running water, and of the earliest violets and lilacs. It is the property of things seen for the first time, or for the first time after long, like the flowers in spring, to reawaken in us the sharp edge of sense and that impression of mystic strangeness which otherwise passes out of life with the coming of years; but the sight of a loved face is what renews a man's character from the fountain upwards.

One day after dinner Will took a stroll among the firs; a grave beatitude possessed him from top to toe, and he kept smiling to himself and the landscape as he went. The river ran between the stepping-stones with a pretty wimple; a bird sang loudly in the wood; the hill-tops looked immeasurably high, and as he glanced at them from time to time seemed to contemplate his movements with a beneficent but awful curiosity. His way took him to the eminence which overlooked the plain; and there he sat down upon a stone, and fell into deep and pleasant thought. The plain lay abroad with its cities and silver river; everything was asleep, except a great eddy of birds which kept rising and falling and going round and round in the blue air. He repeated Marjory's name aloud, and the sound of it gratified his ear. He shut his eyes, and her image sprang up before him, quietly luminous and attended with good thoughts. The river might run for ever; the birds fly higher and higher till they touched the stars. He saw it was empty bustle after all; for here, without stirring a foot, waiting patiently in his own narrow valley, he also had attained the better sunlight.

The next day Will made a sort of declaration across the dinner table, while the parson was filling his pipe.

"Miss Marjory," he said, "I never knew any one I liked so well as you. I am mostly a cold, unkindly sort of man; not from want of heart, but out of strangeness in my way of thinking; and people seem far away from me. 'Tis as if there were a circle round me, which kept every one out but you; I can hear the others talking and laughing; but you come quite close. Maybe, this is disagreeable to you?" he asked.

Marjory made no answer.

"Speak up, girl," said the parson.

"Nay, now," returned Will, "I wouldn't press her, parson. I feel tongue-tied myself, who am not used to it; and she's a woman, and little more than a child, when all is said. But for my part, as far as I can understand what people mean by it, I fancy I must be what they call in love. I do not wish to be held as committing myself; for I may be wrong; but that is how I believe things are with me. And if Miss Marjory should feel any otherwise on her part, mayhap she would be so kind as shake her head."

Marjory was silent, and gave no sign that she had heard.

"How is that, parson?" asked Will.

"The girl must speak," replied the parson, laying down his pipe. "Here's our neighbour who says he loves you, Madge. Do you love him, ay or no?"

"I think I do," said Marjory, faintly.

"Well then, that's all that could be wished!" cried Will, heartily. And he took her hand across the table, and held it a moment in both of his with great satisfaction.

"You must marry," observed the parson, replacing his pipe in his mouth.

"Is that the right thing to do, think you?" demanded Will.

"It is indispensable," said the parson.

"Very well," replied the wooer.

Two or three days passed away with great delight to Will, although a bystander might scarce have found it out. He continued to take his meals opposite Marjory, and to talk with her and gaze upon her in her father's presence; but he made no attempt to see her alone, nor in any other way changed his conduct towards her from what it had been since the beginning. Perhaps the girl was a little disappointed, and perhaps not unjustly; and yet if it had been enough to be always in the thoughts of another person, and so pervade and alter his whole life, she might have been thoroughly contented. For she was never out of Will's mind for an instant. He sat over the stream, and watched the dust of the eddy, and the poised fish, and straining weeds; he wandered out alone into the purple even, with all the blackbirds piping round him in the wood; he rose early in the morning, and saw the sky turn from grey to gold, and the light leap upon the hilltops; and all the while he kept wondering if he had never seen such things before, or how it was that they should look so different now. The sound of his own mill wheel, or of the wind among the trees, confounded and charmed his heart. The most enchanting thoughts presented themselves unbidden in his mind. He was so happy that he could not sleep at night, and so restless that he could hardly sit still out of her company. And yet it seemed as if he avoided her rather than sought her out.

One day, as he was coming home from a ramble, Will found Marjory in the garden picking flowers, and as he came up with her, slackened his pace and continued walking by her side.

"You like flowers?" he said.

"Indeed I love them dearly," she replied. "Do you?"

"Why, no," said he, "not so much. They are a very small affair, when all is done. I can fancy people caring for them greatly, but not doing as you are just now."

"How?" she asked, pausing and looking up at him.

"Plucking them," said he. "They are a deal better off where they are, and look a deal prettier, if you go to that."

"I wish to have them for my own," she answered, "to carry them near my heart, and keep them in my room. They tempt me when they grow here; they seem to say, 'Come and do something with us;' but once I have cut them and put them by, the charm is laid, and I can look at them with quite an easy heart."

"You wish to possess them," replied Will, "in order to think no more about them. It's a bit like killing the goose with the golden eggs. It's a bit like what I wished to do when I was a boy. Because I had a fancy for looking out over the plain, I wished to go down there—where I couldn't look out over it any longer. Was not that fine reasoning? Dear, dear, if they only thought of it, all the world would do like me; and you would let your flowers alone, just as I stay up here in the mountains." Suddenly he broke off sharp. "By the Lord!" he cried. And when she asked him what was wrong, he turned the question off, and walked away into the house with rather a humorous expression of face.

He was silent at table; and after the night had fallen and the stars had come out overhead, he walked up and down for hours in the court-yard and garden with an uneven pace. There was still a light in the window of Marjory's room: one little oblong patch of orange in a world of dark blue hills and silver starlight. Will's mind ran a great deal on the window; but his thoughts were not very lover-like. "There she is in her room," he thought, "and there are the stars overhead:—a blessing upon both!" Both were good influences in his life; both soothed and braced him in his profound contentment with the world. And what more should he desire with either? The fat young man and his councils were so present to his mind, that he threw back his head, and, putting his hands before his mouth, shouted aloud to the popu-lous heavens. Whether from the position of his head or the sudden strain of the exertion, he seemed to see a momentary shock among the stars, and a diffusion of frosty light pass from one to another along the sky. At the same instant, a corner of the blind was lifted and lowered again at once. He laughed a loud ho-ho! "One and another!" thought Will. "The stars tremble, and the blind goes up. Why, before Heaven, what a great magician I must be! Now if I were only a fool, should not I be in a pretty way?" And he went off to bed, chuckling to himself: "If I were only a fool!"

The next morning, pretty early, he saw her once more in the garden, and sought her out.

"I have been thinking about getting married," he began abruptly; "and after having turned it all over, I have made up my mind it's not worth while."

She turned upon him for a single moment; but his radiant, kindly appearance would, under the circumstances, have disconcerted an angel, and she looked down again upon the ground in silence. He could see her tremble.

"I hope you don't mind," he went on, a little taken aback. "You ought not. I have turned it all over, and upon my soul there's nothing in it. We should never be one whit nearer than we are just now, and, if I am a wise man, nothing like so happy."

"It is unnecessary to go round about with me," she said. "I very well remember that you refused to commit yourself; and now that I see you were mistaken, and in reality have never cared for me, I can only feel sad that I have been so far misled."

"I ask your pardon," said Will stoutly; "you do not understand my meaning. As to whether I have ever loved you or not, I must leave that to others. But for one thing, my feeling is not changed; and for another, you may make it your boast that you have made my whole life and character something different from what they were. I mean what I say; no less. I do not think getting married is worth while. I would rather you went on living with your father, so that I could walk over and see you once, or maybe twice a week, as people go to church, and then we should both be all the happier between whiles. That's my notion. But I'll marry you if you will," he added.

"Do you know that you are insulting me?" she broke out.

"Not I, Marjory," said he; "if there is anything in a clear conscience, not I. I offer all my heart's best affection; you can take it or want it, though I suspect it's beyond either your power or mine to change what has once been done, and set me fancy-free. I'll marry you, if you like; but I tell you again and again, it's not worth while, and we had best stay friends. Though I am a quiet man I have noticed a heap of things in my life. Trust in me, and take things as I propose; or, if you don't like that, say the word, and I'll marry you out of hand."

There was a considerable pause, and Will, who began to feel uneasy, began to grow angry in consequence.

"It seems you are too proud to say your mind," he said. "Believe me that's a pity. A clean shrift makes simple living. Can a man be more downright or honourable to a woman than I have been? I have said my say, and given you your choice. Do you want me to marry you? or will you take my friendship, as I think best? or have you had enough of me for good? Speak out for the dear God's sake! You know your father told you a girl should speak her mind in these affairs."

She seemed to recover herself at that, turned without a word, walked rapidly through the garden, and disappeared into the house, leaving Will in some confusion as to the result. He walked up and down the garden, whistling softly to himself. Sometimes he stopped and contemplated the sky and hilltops; sometimes he went down to the tail of the weir and sat there, looking foolishly in the water. All this dubiety and perturbation was so foreign to his nature and the life which he had resolutely chosen for himself, that he began to regret Marjory's arrival. "After all," he thought, "I was as happy as a man need be. I could come down here and watch my fishes all day long if I wanted; I was as settled and contented as my old mill."

Marjory came down to dinner, looking very trim and quiet; and no sooner were all three at table than she made her father a speech, with her eyes fixed upon her plate, but showing no other sign of embarrassment or distress.

"Father," she began, "Mr. Will and I have been talking things over. We see that we have each made a mistake about our feelings, and he has agreed, at my request, to give up all idea of marriage, and be no more than my very good friend, as in the past. You see, there is no shadow of a quarrel, and indeed I hope we shall see a great deal of him in the future, for his visits will always be welcome in our house. Of course, father, you will know best, but perhaps we should do better to leave Mr. Will's house for the present. I believe, after what has passed, we should hardly be agreeable inmates for some days."

Will, who had commanded himself with difficulty from the first, broke out upon this into an inarticulate noise, and raised one hand with an appearance of real dismay, as if he were about to interfere and contradict. But she checked him at once, looking up at him with a swift glance and an angry flush upon her cheek.

"You will perhaps have the good grace," she said, "to let me explain these matters for myself."

Will was put entirely out of countenance by her expression and the ring of her voice. He held his peace, concluding that there were some things about this girl beyond his comprehension, in which he was exactly right.

The poor parson was quite crestfallen. He tried to prove that this was no more than a true lovers' tiff, which would pass off before night; and when he was dislodged from that position, he went on to argue that where there was no quarrel there could be no call for a separation; for the good man liked both his entertainment and his host. It was curious to see how the girl managed them, saying little all the time, and that very quietly, and yet twisting them round her finger and insensibly leading them wherever she would by feminine tact and generalship. It scarcely seemed to have been her doing—it seemed as if things had merely so fallen out—that she and her father took their departure that same afternoon in a farmcart, and went farther down the valley, to wait, until their own house was ready for them, in another hamlet. But Will had been observing closely, and was well aware of her dexterity and resolution. When he found himself alone he had a great many curious matters to turn over in his mind. He was very sad and solitary, to begin with. All the interest had gone out of his life, and he might look up at the stars as long as he pleased, he somehow failed to find support or consolation. And then he was in such a turmoil of spirit about Marjory. He had been puzzled and irritated at her behaviour, and yet he could not keep himself from admiring it. He thought he recognised a fine, perverse angel in that still soul which he had never hitherto suspected; and though he saw it was an influence that would fit but ill with his own life of artificial calm, he could not keep himself from ardently desiring to possess it. Like a man who has lived among shadows and now meets the sun, he was both pained and delighted.

As the days went forward he passed from one extreme to another; now pluming himself on the strength of his determination, now despising his timid and silly caution. The former was, perhaps, the true thought of his heart, and represented the regular tenor of the man's reflections; but the latter burst forth from time to time with an unruly violence, and then he would forget all consideration, and go up and down his house and garden or walk among the firwoods like one who is beside himself with remorse. To equable, steady-minded Will this state of matters was intolerable; and he determined, at whatever cost, to bring it to an end. So, one warm summer afternoon he put on his best clothes, took a thorn switch in his hand, and set out down the valley by the river. As soon as he had taken his determination, he had regained at a bound his customary peace of heart, and he enjoyed the bright weather and the variety of the scene without any admixture of alarm or unpleasant eagerness. It was nearly the same to him how the matter turned out. If she accepted him he would have to marry her this time, which perhaps was all for the best. If she refused him, he would have done his utmost, and might follow his own way in the future with an untroubled conscience. He hoped, on the whole, she would refuse him; and then, again, as he saw the brown roof which sheltered her, peeping through some willows at an angle of the stream, he was half inclined to reverse the wish, and more than half ashamed of himself for this infirmity of purpose.

Marjory seemed glad to see him, and gave him her hand without affectation or delay.

"I have been thinking about this marriage," he began.

"So have I," she answered. "And I respect you more and more for a very wise man. You understood me better than I understood myself; and I am now quite certain that things are all for the best as they are."

"At the same time——," ventured Will.

"You must be tired," she interrupted. "Take a seat and let me fetch you a glass of wine. The afternoon is so warm; and I wish you not to be displeased with your visit. You must come quite often; once a week, if you can spare the time; I am always so glad to see my friends."

"O, very well," thought Will to himself. "It appears I was right after all." And he paid a very agreeable visit, walked home again in capital spirits, and gave himself no further concern about the matter.

For nearly three years Will and Marjory continued on these terms, seeing each other once or twice a week without any word of love between them; and for all that time I believe Will was nearly as happy as a man can be. He rather stinted himself the pleasure of seeing her; and he would often walk halfway over to the parsonage, and then back again, as if to whet his appetite. Indeed there was one corner of the road, whence he could see the churchspire wedged into a crevice of the valley between sloping firwoods, with a triangular snatch of plain by way of background, which he greatly affected as a place to sit and moralise in before returning homewards; and the peasants got so much into the habit of finding him there in the twilight that they gave it the name of "Will o' the Mill's Corner."

At the end of the three years Marjory played him a sad trick by suddenly marrying somebody else. Will kept his countenance bravely, and merely remarked that, for as little as he knew of women, he had acted very prudently in not marrying her himself three years before. She plainly knew very little of her own mind, and, in spite of a deceptive manner, was as fickle and flighty as the rest of them. He had to congratulate himself on an escape, he said, and would take a higher opinion of his own wisdom in consequence. But at heart, he was reasonably displeased, moped a good deal for a month or two, and fell away in flesh, to the astonishment of his serving-lads.

It was perhaps a year after this marriage that Will was awakened late one night by the sound of a horse galloping on the road, followed by precipitate knocking at the inn door. He opened his window and saw a farm servant, mounted and holding a led horse by the bridle, who told him to make what haste he could and go along with him; for Marjory was dying, and had sent urgently to fetch him to her bedside. Will was no horseman, and made so little speed upon the way that the poor young wife was very near her end before he arrived. But they had some minutes' talk in private, and he was present and wept very bitterly while she breathed her last.

DEATH

Year after year went away into nothing, with great explosions and outcries in the cities on the plain: red revolt springing up and being suppressed in blood, battle swaying hither and thither, patient astronomers in observatory towers picking out and christening new stars, plays being performed in lighted theatres, people being carried into hospital on stretchers, and all the usual turmoil and agitation of men's lives in crowded centres. Up in Will's valley only the winds and seasons made an epoch; the fish hung in the swift stream, the birds circled overhead, the pinetops rustled underneath the stars, the tall hills stood over all; and Will went to and fro, minding his wayside inn, until the snow began to thicken on his head. His heart was young and vigorous; and if his pulses kept a sober time, they still beat strong and steady in his wrists. He carried a ruddy stain on either cheek, like a ripe apple; he stooped a little, but his step was still firm; and his sinewy hands were reached out to all men with a friendly pressure. His face was covered with those wrinkles which are got in open air, and which, rightly looked at, are no more than a sort of permanent sunburning; such wrinkles heighten the stupidity of stupid faces; but to a person like Will, with his clear eyes and smiling mouth, only give another charm by testifying to a simple and easy life. His talk was full of wise sayings. He had a taste for other people; and other people had a taste for him. When the valley was full of tourists in the season, there were merry nights in Will's arbour; and his views, which seemed whimsical to his neighbours, were often enough admired by learned people out of towns and colleges. Indeed, he had a very noble old age, and grew daily better known; so that his fame was heard of in the cities of the plain; and young men who had been summer travellers spoke together in *cafés* of Will o' the Mill and his rough philosophy. Many and many an invitation, you may be sure, he had; but nothing could tempt him from his upland valley. He would shake his head and smile over his tobacco pipe with a deal of meaning. "You come too late," he would answer. "I am a dead man now: I have lived and died already. Fifty years ago you would have brought my heart into my mouth; and now you do not even tempt me. But that is the object of long living, that man should cease to care about life." And again: "There is only one difference between a long life and a good dinner: that, in the dinner, the sweets come last." Or once more: "When I was a boy, I was a bit puzzled, and hardly knew whether it was myself or the world that was curious and worth looking into. Now, I know it is myself, and stick to that."

He never showed any symptom of frailty, but kept stalwart and firm to the last; but they say he grew less talkative towards the end, and would listen to other people by the hour in an amused and sympathetic silence. Only, when he did speak, it was more to the point and more charged with old experience. He drank a bottle of wine gladly; above all, at sunset on the hilltop or quite late at night under the stars in the arbour. The sight of something attractive and unattainable seasoned his enjoyment, he would say; and he professed he had lived long enough to admire a candle all the more when he could compare it with a planet.

One night, in his seventy-second year, he awoke in bed in such uneasiness of body and mind that he arose and dressed himself and went out to meditate in the arbour. It was pitch dark, without a star; the river was swollen, and the wet woods and meadows loaded the air with perfume. It had thundered during the day, and it promised more thunder for the morrow. A murky, stifling night for a man of seventy-two! Whether it was the weather or the wakefulness, or some little touch of fever in his old limbs, Will's mind was besieged by tumultuous and crying memories. His boyhood, the night with the fat young man, the death of his adopted parents, the summer days with Marjory, and many of those small circumstances, which seem nothing to another, and are yet the very gist of a man's own life to himself—things seen, words heard, looks misconstrued—arose from their forgotten corners and usurped his attention. The dead themselves were with him, not merely taking part in this thin show of memory that defiled before his brain, but revisiting his bodily senses as they do in profound and vivid dreams. The fat young man leaned his elbows on the table opposite; Marjory came and went with an apronful of flowers between the garden and the arbour; he could hear the old parson knocking out his pipe or blowing his resonant nose. The tide of his consciousness ebbed and flowed: he was sometimes half-asleep and drowned in his recollections of the past; and sometimes he was broad awake, wondering at himself. But about the middle of the night he was startled by the voice of the dead miller calling to him out of the house as he used to do on the arrival of custom. The hallucination was so perfect that Will sprang from his seat and stood listening for the summons to be repeated; and as he listened he became conscious of another noise besides the brawling of the river and the ringing in his feverish ears. It was like the stir of horses and the creaking of harness, as though a carriage with an impatient team had been brought up upon the road before the courtyard gate. At such an hour, upon this rough and dangerous pass, the supposition was no better than absurd; and Will dismissed it from his mind, and resumed his seat upon the arbour chair; and sleep closed over him again like running water. He was once again awakened by the dead miller's call, thinner and more spectral than before; and once again he heard the noise of an equipage upon the road. And so thrice and four times, the same dream, or the same fancy, presented itself to his senses: until at length, smiling to himself as when one humours a nervous child, he proceeded towards the gate to set his uncertainty at rest.

From the arbour to the gate was no great distance, and yet it took Will some time; it seemed as if the dead thickened around him in the court, and crossed his path at every step. For, first, he was suddenly surprised by an overpowering sweetness of heliotropes; it was as if his garden had been planted with this flower from end to end, and the hot, damp night had drawn forth all their perfumes in a breath. Now the heliotrope had been Marjory's favourite flower, and since her death not one of them had ever been planted in Will's ground.

"I must be going crazy," he thought. "Poor Marjory and her heliotropes!"

And with that he raised his eyes towards the window that had once been hers. If he had been bewildered before, he was now almost terrified; for there was a light in the room; the window was an orange oblong as of yore; and the corner of the blind was lifted and let fall as on the night when he stood and shouted to the stars in his perplexity. The illusion only endured an instant; but it left him somewhat unmanned, rubbing his eyes and staring at the outline of the house and the black night behind it. While he thus stood, and it seemed as if he must have stood there quite a long time, there came a renewal of the noises on the road: and he turned in time to meet a stranger, who was advancing to meet him across the court. There was something like the outline of a great carriage discernible on the road behind the stranger, and, above that, a few black pine-tops, like so many plumes.

"Master Will?" asked the newcomer, in brief military fashion.

"That same, sir," answered Will. "Can I do anything to serve you?"

"I have heard you much spoken of, Master Will," returned the other; "much spoken of, and well. And though I have both hands full of business, I wish to drink a bottle of wine with you in your arbour. Before I go, I shall introduce myself."

Will led the way to the trellis, and got a lamp lighted and a bottle uncorked. He was not altogether unused to such complimentary interviews, and hoped little enough from this one, being schooled by many disappointments. A sort of cloud had settled on his wits and prevented him from remembering the strangeness of the hour. He moved like a person in his sleep; and it seemed as if the lamp caught fire and the bottle came uncorked with the facility of thought. Still, he had some curiosity about the appearance of his visitor, and tried in vain to turn the light into his face; either he handled the lamp clumsily, or there was a dimness over his eyes; but he could make out little more than a shadow at table with him. He stared and stared at this shadow, as he wiped out the glasses, and began to feel cold and strange about the heart. The silence weighed upon him, for he could hear nothing now, not even the river, but the drumming of his own arteries in his ears.

"Here's to you," said the stranger, roughly.

"Here is my service, sir," replied Will, sipping his wine, which somehow tasted oddly.

"I understand you are a very positive fellow," pursued the stranger.

Will made answer with a smile of some satisfaction and a little nod.

"So am I," continued the other; "and it is the delight of my heart to tramp on people's corns. I will have nobody positive but myself; not one. I have crossed the whims, in my time, of kings and generals and great artists. And what would you say," he went on, "if I had come up here on purpose to cross yours?"

Will had it on his tongue to make a sharp rejoinder; but the politeness of an old innkeeper prevailed; and he held his peace and made answer with a civil gesture of the hand.

"I have," said the stranger. "And if I did not hold you in a particular esteem, I should make no words about the matter. It appears you pride yourself on staying where you are. You mean to stick by your inn. Now I mean you shall come for a turn with me in my barouche; and before this bottle's empty, so you shall."

"That would be an odd thing, to be sure," replied Will, with a chuckle. "Why, sir, I have grown here like an old oak tree; the Devil himself could hardly root me up: and for all I perceive you are a very entertaining old gentleman, I would wager you another bottle you lose your pains with me."

The dimness of Will's eyesight had been increasing all this while; but he was somehow conscious of a sharp and chilling scrutiny which irritated and yet overmastered him.

"You need not think," he broke out suddenly, in an explosive, febrile manner that startled and alarmed himself, "that I am a stay-at-home, because I fear anything under God. God knows I am tired enough of it all; and when the time comes for a longer journey than ever you dream of, I reckon I shall find myself prepared."

The stranger emptied his glass and pushed it away from him. He looked down for a little, and then, leaning over the table, tapped Will three times upon the forearm with a single finger. "The time has come!" he said solemnly.

An ugly thrill spread from the spot he touched. The tones of his voice were dull and startling, and echoed strangely in Will's heart.

"I beg your pardon," he said, with some discomposure. "What do you mean?"

"Look at me, and you will find your eyesight swim. Raise your hand; it is dead-heavy. This is your last bottle of wine, Master Will, and your last night upon the earth."

"You are a doctor?" quavered Will.

"The best that ever was," replied the other; "for I cure both mind and body with the same prescription. I take away all pain and I forgive all sins; and where my patients have gone wrong in life, I smooth out all complications and set them free again upon their feet."

"I have no need of you," said Will.

"A time comes for all men, Master Will," replied the doctor, "when the helm is taken out of their hands. For you, because you were prudent and quiet, it has been long of coming, and you have had long to discipline yourself for its reception. You have seen what is to be seen about your mill; you have sat close all your days like a hare in its form; but now that is at an end; and," added the doctor, getting on his feet, "you must arise and come with me."

"You are a strange physician," said Will, looking steadfastly upon his guest.

"I am a natural law," he replied, "and people call me Death."

"Why did you not tell me so at first?" cried Will. "I have been waiting for you these many years. Give me your hand, and welcome."

"Lean upon my arm," said the stranger, "for already your strength abates. Lean on me as heavily as you need; for though I am old, I am very strong. It is but three steps to my carriage, and there all your trouble ends. Why, Will," he added, "I have been yearning for you as if you were my own son; and of all the men that ever I came for in my long days, I have come for you most gladly. I am caustic, and sometimes offend people at first sight; but I am a good friend at heart to such as you."

"Since Marjory was taken," returned Will, "I declare before God you were the only friend I had to look for."

So the pair went arm-in-arm across the courtyard.

One of the servants awoke about this time and heard the noise of horses pawing before he dropped asleep again; all down the valley that night there was a rushing as of a smooth and steady wind descending towards the plain; and when the world rose next morning, sure enough Will o' the Mill had gone at last upon his travels.

Markheim

Yes," said the dealer, "our windfalls are of various kinds. Some customers are ignorant, and then I touch a dividend on my superior knowledge. Some are dishonest," and here he held up the candle, so that the light fell strongly on his visitor, "and in that case," he continued, "I profit by my virtue."

Markheim had but just entered from the daylight streets, and his eyes had not yet grown familiar with the mingled shine and darkness in the shop. At these pointed words, and before the near presence of the flame, he blinked painfully and looked aside.

The dealer chuckled. "You come to me on Christmas Day," he resumed, "when you know that I am alone in my house, put up my shutters, and make a point of refusing business. Well, you will have to pay for that; you will have to pay for my derangement, when I should be balancing my books; you will have to pay, besides, for a kind of manner that I remark in you today very strongly. I am the essence of discretion, and ask no awkward question; but when a customer cannot look me in the eye, he has to pay for it." The dealer once more chuckled; and then, changing to his usual business voice though still with a note of irony: "You can give, as usual, a clear account of how you came into the possession of the object?" he continued. "Still your uncle's cabinet? A remarkable collector, sir!"

Original illustration from *Unwin's Annual, 1886* (LONDON, 1886). (Used by permission of the Huntington Library, San Marino, California.)

And the little, pale, round-shouldered dealer, stood almost on tip-toe, looking over the top of his gold spectacles, and nodding his head with every mark of disbelief. Markheim returned his gaze with one of infinite pity, and a touch of horror.

"This time," said he, "you are in error. I have not come to sell, but to buy. I have no curios to dispose of; my uncle's cabinet is bare to the wainscot; even were it still intact, I have done well on the stock exchange, and should more likely add to it than otherwise; and my errand today is simplicity itself. I seek a Christmas present for a lady," he continued waxing more fluent as he struck into the speech he had prepared; "and certainly I owe you every excuse for thus disturbing you upon so small a matter. But the thing was neglected yesterday; I must produce my little compliment at dinner; and as you very well know, a rich marriage is not a thing to be neglected."

There followed a pause during which the dealer seemed to weigh this statement incredulously. The ticking of many clocks among the curious lumber of the shop, and the faint rushing of the cabs in a near thoroughfare, filled up the interval of silence.

"Well, sir," said the dealer, "be it so. You are an old customer after all; and if, as you say you have the chance of a good marriage, far be it from me to be an obstacle. Here is a nice thing for a lady now," he went on, "this hand glass: fifteenth century, warranted; comes from a good collection, too; but I reserve the name in the interests of my customer, who was just like yourself, my dear sir, the nephew and sole heir of a remarkable collector.

The dealer, while he thus ran on in his dry and biting voice, had stooped to take the object from its place; and as he had done so, a shock had passed through Markheim, a start both of hand and foot, a sudden leap of many tumultuous passions to the face. It passed as swiftly as it came, and left no trace beyond a certain tremulousness in the hand that now received the glass.

"A glass?" he said, hoarsely, and then paused, and repeated it more clearly. "A glass? For Christmas? Surely not?"

"And why not?" cried the dealer. "Why not a glass?"

Markheim was looking upon him with an indefinable expression. "You ask me why not?" he said. "Why, look here—look in it—look at yourself! Do you like to see it? No! nor I—nor any man."

The little man had jumped back when Markheim had so suddenly confronted him with the mirror; but now, perceiving there was nothing worse on hand, he chuckled. "Your future lady, sir, must be pretty hard favoured," said he.

"No," said Markheim, with great conviction. "But about you: I ask you for a Christmas present and you give me this—this damned reminder of years and sins and follies, this hand-conscience! Did you mean it? Had you a thought in your mind? Tell me. It will be better for you if you do. Come, tell me about yourself. I hazard a guess now, that you are in secret a very charitable man?"

The dealer looked closely at his companion; it was very odd, Markheim did not appear to be laughing; there was something in his face like an eager sparkle of hope, but nothing of mirth.

"What are you driving at?" the dealer asked.

"Not charitable?" returned the other, gloomily. "Not charitable; not pious; not scrupulous; unloving, unbeloved; a hand to get money, a safe to keep it. Is that all? dear God, man, is that all?"

"I will tell you what it is," began the dealer, with some sharpness, and then broke off again into a chuckle. "But I see this is a love match of yours, and you have been drinking the lady's health."

"Ah!" cried Markheim, with a strange curiosity. "Ah, have you been in love? Tell me about that."

"I?" cried the dealer. "I in love! I never had the time, nor have I the time today for all this nonsense. Will you take the glass?"

"Where is the hurry?" returned Markheim. "It is very pleasant to stand here talking; and life is so short and insecure that I would not hurry away from any pleasure—no, not even from so mild a one as this. We should rather cling, cling to what little we can get, like a man at a cliff's edge. Every second is a cliff, if you think upon it: a cliff a mile high, high enough, if we fall, to dash us out of every feature of humanity. Hence it is best to talk pleasantly. Let us talk of each other; why should we wear this mask? Let us be confidential. Who knows, we might become friends?"

"I have just one word to say to you," said the dealer: "Either make your purchase, or walk out of my shop!"

"True, true," said Markheim. "Enough fooling. To business. Show me something else."

The dealer stooped once more, this time to replace the glass upon the shelf, his thin, blond hair falling over his eyes as he did so. Markheim moved a little nearer, with one hand in the pocket of his greatcoat; he drew himself up and filled his lungs; at the same time many different emotions were depicted together on his face—terror, horror, and resolve, fascination and a physical repulsion; and through a haggard lift of his upper lip his teeth looked out.

"This perhaps may suit," observed the dealer; and then, as he began to re-arise, Markheim bounded from behind upon his victim. The long, skewerlike dagger flashed and fell. The dealer struggled like a hen, striking his temple on the shelf, and then tumbled on the floor in a heap.

Time had some score of small voices in that shop, some stately and slow as was becoming to their great age; others garrulous and hurried. All these told out the seconds in an intricate chorus of tickings. Then the passage of a lad's feet, heavily running on the pavement, broke in upon these smaller noises and startled Markheim into the consciousness of his surroundings. He looked about him awfully. The candle stood on the counter, its flame solemnly wagging in a draught; and by that inconsiderable movement, the whole room was filled with noiseless bustle, and kept heaving like a sea: the tall shadows nodding, the gross blots of darkness swelling and dwindling as with respiration, the faces of the portraits and the China gods changing and wavering like images in water. The inner door stood ajar, and peered into that leaguer of shadows with a long slit of daylight like a pointing finger.

From these fear-stricken rovings, Markheim's eyes returned to the body of his victim, where it lay both humped and sprawling, incredibly small, and strangely meaner than in life. In these poor miserly clothes, in that ungainly attitude, the dealer lay like so much sawdust. Markheim had feared to see it, and lo! it was nothing. And yet as he gazed, this bundle of old clothes and pool of blood began to find eloquent voices. There it must lie; there was none to work the cunning hinges or direct the miracle of locomotion—there it must lie till it was found. Found? ay, and then? Then would this dead flesh lift up a cry that would echo over England, and fill the world with the echoes of pursuit. Ay, dead or not, this was still the enemy. "Time was that when the brains were out," he thought; and the first word struck into his mind. Time, now that the deed was accomplished—time, which had closed for the victim, had become instant and momentous for the slayer.

The thought was yet in his mind, when first one and then another, with every variety of pace and voice, one deep as the bell from a cathedral turret, another ringing on its treble notes the prelude of a waltz, the clocks began to strike the hour of three in the afternoon.

The sudden outbreak of so many tongues in that dumb chamber staggered him. He began to bestir himself, going to and fro with the candle, beleaguered by moving shadows, and startled to the soul by chance reflections. In many rich mirrors, some of home design, some from Venice or Amsterdam, he saw his face repeated and repeated, as it were an army of spies; his own eyes met and detected him; and the sound of his own steps, lightly as they fell, vexed the surrounding quiet. And still as he continued to fill his pockets, his mind accused him with a sickening iteration of the thousand faults of his design. He should have chosen a more quiet hour; he should have prepared an alibi; he should not have used a knife; he should have been more cautious, and only bound and gagged the dealer, and not killed him; he should have been more bold, and killed the servant also; he should have done all things otherwise: poignant regrets, weary, incessant toiling of the mind to change what was unchangeable, to plan what was now useless, to be the architect of the irrevocable past. Meanwhile, and behind all this activity, brute terrors, like the scurrying of rats in a deserted attic, filled the more remote chambers of his brain with riot: the hand of the constable would fall heavy on his shoulder, and his nerves would jerk like a hooked fish; or he beheld, in galloping defile, the dock, the prison, the gallows and the black coffin.

Terror of the people in the street sat down before his mind like a besieging army. It was impossible, he thought, but that some rumour of the struggle must have reached their ears and set on edge their curiosity; and now in all the neighbouring houses, he divined them sitting motionless and with uplifted ear: solitary people, condemned to spend Christmas dwelling alone on memories of the past, and now startingly recalled from that tender exercise; happy, family parties struck into silence round the table, the mother still with raised finger: every degree and age and humour, but all, by their own hearths, prying and hearkening and weaving the rope that was to hang him. Sometimes it seemed to him he could not move too softly; the clink of the tall Bohemian goblets rang out loudly like a bell; and alarmed by the bigness of the ticking, he was tempted to stop the clocks. And then again, with a swift transition of his terrors, the very silence of the house appeared a source of peril, and a thing to strike and freeze the passer-by; and he would step more boldly, and bustle aloud among the contents of the shop, and imitate, with elaborate bravado, the movements of a busy man at ease in his own house.

But he was now so pulled about by different alarms, that while one portion of his mind was still alert and cunning, another trembled on the brink of lunacy. One hallucination, in particular took a strong hold on his credulity. The neighbour hearkening with white face beside his window, the passer-by arrested by a horrible surmise on the pavement—these could at worst suspect, they could not know; through the brick walls and shuttered windows, only sounds could penetrate. But here, within the house, was he alone? He knew he was; he had watched the servant set forth sweethearting, in her poor best, "out for the day" written in every ribbon and smile. Yes, he was alone of course; and yet in the bulk of empty house above him, he could surely hear a stir of delicate footing—he was surely conscious, inexplicably conscious of some presence. Ay, surely: to every room and corner of the house his imagination followed it; and now it was a faceless thing, that yet had eyes to see with; and again it was a shadow of himself; and yet again, and behold the image of the dead dealer reinspired with cunning and hatred.

At times, with a strong effort, he would glance at the open door which still seemed to repel his eyes. The house was tall, the skylight small and dirty, the day blind with fog; and the light that filtered down to the ground story was exceeding faint and showed dimly on the threshold of the shop. And yet, in that strip of doubtful brightness, did there not hang wavering a shadow?

Suddenly from the street outside, a very jovial gentleman began to beat with a staff on the shop door, accompanying his blows with shouts and railleries in which the dealer was continually called upon by name. Markheim, smitten into ice, glanced at the dead man. But no; he lay quite still; he was fled away far beyond earshot of these blows and shoutings; he was sunk beneath seas of silence; and his name, which would once have caught his notice above the howling of a storm, had become an empty sound. And presently the jovial gentleman desisted from his knocking and departed.

Here was a broad hint to hurry what remained to be done, to get forth from this accusing neighbourhood, to plunge into a bath of London multitudes, and to reach, on the other side of day, that haven of safety and apparent innocence—his bed. One visitor had come; at any moment another might follow and be more obstinate. To have done the deed, and yet not to reap the profit, would be too abhorred a failure. The money, that was now Markheim's concern; and as a means to that, the keys.

He glanced over his shoulder at the open door, where the shadow was still lingering and shivering; and with no conscious repugnance of the mind, yet with a tremor of the belly, he drew near the body of his victim. The human character had quite departed; like a suit half-stuffed with bran, the limbs lay scattered, the trunk doubled, on the floor; and yet the thing repelled him. Although so dingy and inconsiderable to the eye, he feared it might have more significance to the touch. He took the body by the shoulders and turned it on its back. It was strangely light and supple, and the limbs, as if they had been broken, fell into the oddest postures. The face was robbed of all expression; but it was as pale as wax and shockingly smeared with blood about one temple. That was, for Markheim, the one displeasing circumstance. It carried him back upon the instant to a certain fair-day in a fishers' village: a gray day, a piping wind, a crowd upon the street, the blare of brasses, the booming of drums, the nasal voice of a ballad singer; and a boy going to and fro, buried over head in the crowd and divided between interest and fear, until, coming out upon the chief place of concourse, he beheld a booth and a great screen with pictures, dismally designed, garishly coloured: Brownrigg with her apprentice, the Mannings with their murdered guest, Weare in the death-grip of Thurtell, and a score besides of famous crimes. The thing was as clear as an illusion; he had shrunk back into that little boy; he was looking once again, and with the same sense of physical revolt, at these vile pictures; he was still stunned by the thumping of the drums. A bar of that day's music returned upon his memory; and at that, for the first time, a qualm came over him, a breath of nausea, a sudden weakness of the joints, which he must instantly resist and conquer.

He judged it more prudent to confront than to flee from these considerations; looking the more hardily in the dead face, bending his mind to realise the nature and greatness of his crime. So little a while ago that face had moved with every change of sentiment, that pale mouth had spoken, that body had been all on fire with governable energies; and now, and by his act, that piece of life had been arrested, as the horologist, with interjected finger, arrests the beating of the clock. So he reasoned in vain; he could rise to no remorseful consciousness; the same heart which had shuddered before these painted effigies of crime, looked on its reality unmoved. At best, he felt a gleam of pity, for one who had been endowed in vain with all those faculties that can make the world a garden of enchantment, one who had never lived and who was now dead. But of penitence, no, not a tremor.

With that, shaking himself clear of these considerations, he found the keys and advanced towards the open door of the shop. Outside, it had begun to rain smartly; and the sound of the shower upon the roof had banished silence. Like some dropping cavern, the chambers of the house were haunted by a faint, incessant echoing, which filled the ear and mingled with the ticking of the clocks. And as Markheim approached the door he seemed to hear, in answer to his own cautious tread, the steps of another foot withdrawing up the stair. The shadow still palpitated loosely on the threshold. He threw a ton's weight of resolve upon his muscles, and drew back the door.

The faint, foggy daylight glimmered dimly on the bare floor and stairs; on the bright suit of armour posted, halbert in hand, upon the landing; and on the dark wood carvings and framed pictures that hung against the yellow panels of the wainscot. So loud was the beating of the rain through all the house that, in Markheim's ears, it began to be distinguished into many different sounds. Footsteps and sighs, the tread of regiments marching in the distance, the chink of money in the counting, and the creaking of doors held stealthily ajar, appeared to mingle with the patter of the drops upon the cupola and the gushing of the water in the pipes. The sense that he was not alone grew upon him to the verge of madness. On every side he was hunted and begirt by presences. He heard them moving stealthily in the upper chambers; from the shop, he heard the dead man getting to his legs; and as he began with a great effort to mount the stairs, feet fled quietly before him and followed guardedly behind. If he were but deaf, he thought, how tranquilly he would possess his soul! And then again, and hearkening with ever fresh attention, he blessed himself for that unresting sense which held the outposts and stood a trusty sentinel upon his life. His head turned continually on his neck; his eyes, which seemed starting from their orbits, scouted on every side, and on every side were half-rewarded as with the tail of something nameless vanishing. The four and twenty steps to the first floor were four and twenty agonies.

On that first story, the doors stood ajar, three of them like three ambushes, shaking his nerves like the throats of cannon. He could never again, he felt, be sufficiently immured and fortified from men's observing eyes; the sole joy for which he longed was to be home, girt in by walls, buried among bed clothes, and invisible to all but God. And at the thought he wondered a little, recollecting tales of other murderers and the fear they were said to entertain of heavenly avengers. It was not so, at least, with him. He feared the laws of nature lest, in their callous and immutable procedure, they should preserve some damning evidence of his crime. He feared tenfold more, with a slavish, superstitious terror, some scission in the continuity of man's experience, some wilful illegality of nature. He played a game of skill, depending on the rules, calculating consequence from cause; and what if nature, as the defeated tyrant overthrew the chessboard, should break the mould of their succession? The like had befallen Napoleon (so writers said) when the winter changed the time of its appearance. The like might befall Markheim: the solid walls might become transparent and reveal his doings like those of bees in a glass hive; the stout planks might yield under his foot like quicksands and detain him in their clutch; ay, and there were soberer accidents that might destroy him, if, for instance, the house should fall and imprison him beside the body of his victim; or the house next door should fly on fire, and the firemen invade him from all sides. These things he feared; and in a sense these things might be called the hands of God reached forth against sin. But about God himself he was at ease; his act was doubtless exceptional, but so were his excuses, which God knew; it was there, and not among men, that he felt sure of justice.

When he had got safe into the drawing room and shut the door behind him, he was aware of a respite from alarms. The room was quite dismantled, uncarpeted besides, and strewn with packing cases and incongruous furniture; several great pier-glasses, in which he beheld himself at various angles, like an actor on a theatre; many pictures, framed and unframed, standing with their faces to the wall; a fine Sheraton sideboard, a cabinet of marquetry, and a great old bed with tapestry hangings. The windows opened to the floor; but by great good fortune the lower part of the shutters had been closed, and this concealed him from the neighbours. Here then Markheim drew in a packing case before the cabinet, and began to search among the keys. It was a long business, for there were many; and it was irksome, besides; for after all there might be nothing in the cabinet, and time was on the wing. But the closeness of the occupation sobered him. With the tail of his eye he saw the door; even glanced at it, from time to time directly, like a besieged commander pleased to verify the good estate of his defences. But in truth he was at peace. The rain falling in the street sounded natural and pleasant. Presently, on the other side, the notes of a piano were wakened to the music of a hymn, and the voices of many children took up the air and words. How stately, how comfortable was the melody! how fresh the youthful voices! Markheim gave ear to it smilingly, as he sorted out the keys; and his mind was thronged with answerable ideas and images; churchgoing children and the pealing of the high organ; children afield, bathers by the brookside, ramblers on the brambly common, kite-flyers in the windy and cloud-navigated sky; and then, at another cadence of the hymn, back again to church, and the somnolence of summer Sundays, and the high genteel voice of the parson (which he smiled a little to recall) and the painted Jacobean tombs, and the dim lettering of the ten commandments in the chancel.

And as he sat thus, at once busy and absent, he was startled to his feet. A flash of ice, a flash of fire, a bursting gush of blood, went over him, and then he stood transfixed and thrilling. A step mounted the stair slowly and steadily; and presently a hand was laid upon the knob, and the lock clicked, and the door opened. Fear held Markheim in a vice; what to expect he knew not, whether the dead man walking, or the official ministers of human justice, or some chance witness blindly stumbling in to consign him to the gallows. But when a face was thrust into the aperture, glanced round the room, looked at him, nodded and smiled as if in friendly recognition, and then withdrew again, and the door closed behind it—his fear broke loose from his control in a hoarse cry. At the sound of this, the visitant returned.

"Did you call me?" he asked pleasantly, and with that he entered the room, and closed the door behind him.

But Markheim stood and gazed at him with all his eyes. Perhaps there was a film upon his sight, but the outlines of the newcomer seemed to change and waver like those of the idols in the wavering candlelight of the shop; and at times, he thought he knew him; and at times he thought he bore a likeness to himself; and always, like a lump of living terror, there lay in his bosom the conviction, that this thing was not of the earth and not of God.

And yet the creature had a strange air of the commonplace, as he stepped in and stood looking on Markheim with a smile; and when he added: "You are looking for the money, I believe?" it was in the tones of everyday politeness.

Markheim made no answer.

"I should warn you," resumed the other, "that the maid has left her sweetheart earlier than usual, and will soon be here. If Mr. Markheim be found in this house, I need not describe to him the consequences."

"You know me?" cried the murderer.

The visitor smiled. "You have long been a favourite of mine," he said; "and I have long observed and often sought to help you."

"What are you?" cried Markheim. "The devil?"

"What I may be," returned the other, "cannot affect the service I propose to render you."

"It can," cried Markheim. "It does! Be helped by you? no, never! not by you! You do not know me yet—thank God, you do not know me!"

"Know you?" replied the visitant, with a sort of kind severity or rather firmness, "I know you to the soul."

"Know me?" cried Markheim. "Who can do so? My life is but a travesty and slander on myself. I have lived to belie my nature. All men do; all men are better than this disguise that grows about and stifles them. You see each dragged away by life, like one whom bravos have seized and muffled in a cloak; if they had their own control—if you could see their faces, they would be altogether different, they would shine out for heroes and saints! I am worse than most; myself is more overlaid; my excuse is known to me and God. But had I the time, I could disclose myself."

"To me?" inquired the visitor.

"To you before all," returned the murderer. "I supposed you were intelligent; I thought—since you exist—you would prove a reader of the heart. And yet you would propose to judge me by my acts—think of it—my acts! I was born and I have lived in a land of giants; giants have dragged me by the wrists since I was born out of my mother—the giants of circumstance. And you would judge me by my acts! But can you not look within? Can you not understand that evil is hateful to me? Can you not see within me the clear writing of conscience, never blurred by any wilful sophistry, although too often disregarded? Can you not read me for a thing that surely must be common as humanity—the unwilling sinner?"

"All this is very feelingly expressed," was the reply, "but it regards me not. These points of casuistry are beyond my province; and I care not in the least by what compulsion you may have been dragged away, so as you are but carried in the right direction. But time flies; the servant delays, looking in the faces of the crowd and at the pictures on the hoardings; but still she keeps moving nearer; and remember, it is as if the gallows itself was walking towards you through the Christmas streets! Shall I help you—I, who know all? shall I tell you where to find the money?"

"For what price?" asked Markheim.

"I offer you the service for a Christmas gift," returned the other.

Markheim could not refrain from smiling with a kind of bitter triumph. "No," said he, "I will take nothing at your hands; if I were dying of thirst, and it was your hand that put the pitcher to my lips, I should find the courage to refuse it. It may be credulous, but I will do nothing to commit myself to evil."

"I have no objection to a deathbed repentance," observed the visitant.

"Because you disbelieve their efficacy!" Markheim cried.

"I do not say so," returned the other; "but I look on these things from a different side; and when the life is done, my interest falls. The man has lived to serve me, to spread black looks under colour of religion, or to sow tares in the wheatfield, as you do, in a course of weak compliance with desire. Now that he draws so near to his deliverance, he can add but one act of service—to repent, to die smiling, and thus to build up in confidence and hope the more timorous of my surviving followers. I am not so hard a master. Try me. Accept my help; please yourself in life as you have done hitherto; please yourself more amply, spread your elbows at the board; and when the night begins to fall and the curtains to be drawn, I tell you, for your greater comfort, that you will find it even easy to compound your quarrel with your conscience and to make a truckling peace with God. I came but now from such a deathbed; and the room was full of sincere mourners, listening to the man's last words; and when I looked into that face, which had been set as a flint against mercy, I found it smiling with hope."

"And do you then suppose me such a creature?" asked Markheim. "Do you think I have no more generous aspiration than to sin and sin and sin, and, at the last, sneak into heaven? My heart rises at the thought! Is this, then, your experience of mankind? or is it because you find me with red hands that you presume such baseness? and is this crime of murder indeed so impious as to dry up the very springs of good?"

"Murder is to me no special category," replied the other. "All sins are murder, even as all life is war. I behold your race, like starving mariners on a raft, plucking crusts out of the hands of famine and feeding on each other's lives. I follow sins beyond the moment of their acting; I find in all that the last consequence is death; and to my eyes, the pretty maid who thwarts her mother with such taking graces on a question of a ball, drips no less visibly with human gore than such a murderer as yourself. Do I say that I follow sins? I follow virtues also; they differ not by the thickness of a nail; they are both scythes for the reaping angel of death. Evil, for which I live, consists not in action but in character; the bad man is dear to me, not the bad act, whose fruits, if we could follow them far enough down the hurtling cataract of the ages, might yet be found more blessed than those of the rarest virtues; and it is not because you have killed a dealer, but because your name is Markheim, that I offer to forward your escape."

"I will lay my heart open to you," answered Markheim. "This crime on which you find me is my last. On my way to it, I have learned many lessons; itself is a lesson, a momentous lesson. Hitherto I have been driven with revolt to what I would not; I was a bondslave to poverty, driven and scourged. There are robust virtues that can stand in these temptations; mine was not so, I had a thirst of pleasure. But today, and out of this deed, I pluck both warning and riches—both the power and a fresh resolve to be myself. I become in all things a free actor in the world; and I begin to see myself all changed, these hands the agents of good, this heart at peace. Something comes over me out of the past; something of what I have dreamed on sabbath evenings to the sound of the church-organ, of what I forecast when I shed tears over noble books or talked, an innocent child, with my mother. There lies my life; I have wandered a few years, but now I see once more my city of destination."

"You are to use this money on the stock exchange, I think?" remarked the visitor. "And there, if I mistake not, you have already lost some thousands."

"Ah," said Markheim, "but this time I have a sure thing."

"This time again, you will lose," replied the visitor quietly.

"Ah, but I keep back the half!" cried Markheim.

"That also you will lose," said the other.

The sweat started upon Markheim's brow. "Well, then, what matter?" he exclaimed. "Say it be lost, say I am plunged again in poverty, shall one part of me, and that the worse, continue until the end to override the better? Evil and good run strong in me, haling me both ways. I do not love the one thing, I love all. I can conceive great deeds, renunciations, martyrdoms; and though I be fallen to such a crime as murder, pity is not stranger to my thoughts. I pity the poor—who knows their trials better than myself? I pity and help them; I prize love, I love honest laughter; there is no good thing nor true thing on earth, but I love it from my heart. And are my vices only to direct my life, and my virtues to lie without effect, like some passive lumber of the mind? Not so; good, also, is a spring of acts."

But the visitant raised his finger. "For six-and-thirty years that you have been in this world," said he, "through many changes of fortune and varieties of humour, I have watched you steadily fall. Fifteen years ago, you would have started at a theft. Three years back, you would have blenched at the name of murder. Is there any crime, is there any cruelty or meanness, from which you still recoil? Five years from now, I shall detect you in the fact! Downward, downward, lies your way; nor can anything but death avail to stop you."

"It is true," he said huskily. "I have in some degree complied with evil. But it is so with all: the very saints, in the mere exercise of living, grow less dainty and take on the tone of their surroundings."

"I will propound to you one simple question," said the other, "and as you answer, I shall read to you your moral horoscope. You have grown in many things more lax; possibly you do right to be so; and at any account, it is the same with all men. But granting that, are you in any one particular, however trifling, more difficult to please with your own conduct? Or do you go in all things with a looser rein?"

"In any one?" repeated Markheim, with an anguish of consideration. "No," he added, with despair, "in none! I have gone down in all."

"Then," said the visitor, "content yourself with what you are, for you will never change; and the words of your part on this stage are irrevocably written down."

Markheim stood for a long while silent, and indeed it was the visitor who first broke the silence. "That being so," he said, "shall I show you the money?"

"And grace?" cried Markheim.

"Have you not tried it?" returned the other. "Two or three years ago, did I not see you on the platform of revival meetings, and was not your voice the loudest in the hymn?"

"It is true," said Markheim, "and I see clearly what remains for me by way of duty. I thank you for these lessons from my soul; my eyes are opened and I behold myself at last for what I am."

At this moment, the sharp note of the door bell rang through the house; and the visitant, as though this were some concerted signal for which he had been waiting, sprang instantly upon his feet.

"The maid!" he cried. "She has returned, as I forewarned you, and there is now before you one more difficult passage. Her master, you must say, is ill; you must let her in, with an assured but rather serious countenance—no smiles, no overacting, and I promise you success! Once the girl within and the door closed, the same dexterity that has already rid you of the dealer will relieve you of this last danger in your path. Thenceforward, you have the whole evening—the whole night, if needful—to ransack the treasures of the house and to make good your safety. This is help that comes to you with the mask of danger. Up!" he cried; "up, friend; your life hangs trembling in the scales; up, and act!"

Markheim steadily regarded his counsellor. "If I be condemned to evil acts," he said, "there is still one door of freedom open: I can cease from action. If my life be an ill thing, I can lay it down. Though I be, as you say truly, at the beck of every small temptation, I can yet, by one decisive gesture, place myself beyond their reach. My love of good is damned to barrenness; it may, and let it be! But I have still my hatred of evil; and from that, to your galling disappointment, you shall see that I can draw both energy and courage."

The features of the visitor began to undergo a wonderful and lovely change: they brightened and softened with a tender triumph, and even as they brightened, faded and dislimned. But Markheim did not pause to watch or understand the transformation. He opened the door and went downstairs very slowly, thinking to himself. His past went soberly before him; he beheld it as it was, ugly and strenuous like a dream, random as chance-medley; a scene of defeat. Life, as he thus reviewed it, tempted him no longer; but on the farther side he perceived a quiet haven for his bark.

He paused in the passage, and looked into the shop where the candle still burned by the dead body. It was strangely silent. Thoughts of the dealer swarmed into his mind, as he stood gazing. And then the bell once more broke out into impatient clamour.

He confronted the maid upon the threshold with something like a smile.

"You had better go for the police," said he: "I have killed your master."

THRAWN JANET

The Reverend Murdoch Soulis was long minister of the moorland parish of Balweary, in the vale of Dule. A severe, bleak-faced old man, dreadful to his hearers, he dwelt in the last years of his life, without relative or servant or any human company, in the small and lonely manse under the Hanging Shaw. In spite of the iron composure of his features, his eye was wild, scared, and uncertain; and when he dwelt, in private admonitions, on the future of the impenitent, it seemed as if his eye pierced through the storms of time to the terrors of eternity. Many young persons, coming to prepare themselves against the season of the Holy Communion, were dreadfully affected by his talk. He had a sermon on 1st Peter, v. and 8th, "The devil as a roaring lion," on the Sunday after every seventeenth of August, and he was accustomed to surpass himself upon that text both by the appalling nature of the matter and the terror of his bearing in the pulpit. The children were frightened into fits, and the old looked more than usually oracular, and were, all that day, full of those hints that Hamlet deprecated. The manse itself, where it stood by the water of Dule among some thick trees, with the Shaw overhanging it on the one side, and on the other many cold, moorish hilltops rising towards the sky, had begun, at a very early period of Mr. Soulis's ministry, to be avoided in the dusk hours by all who valued themselves upon their prudence; and guidmen sitting at the clachan alehouse shook their heads together at the thought of passing late by that uncanny neighbourhood. There was one spot, to be more particular, which was regarded with especial awe. The manse stood between the high road and the water of Dule, with a gable to each; its back was towards the kirktown of Balweary, nearly half a mile away; in front of it, a bare garden, hedged with thorn, occupied the land between the river and the road. The house was two stories high, with two large rooms on each. It opened not directly on the garden, but on a causewayed path, or passage, giving on the road on the one hand, and closed on the other by the tall willows and elders that bordered on the stream. And it was this strip of causeway that enjoyed among the young parishioners of Balweary so infamous a reputation. The minister walked there often after dark, sometimes groaning aloud in the instancy of his unspoken prayers; and when he was from home, and the manse door was locked, the more daring schoolboys ventured, with beating hearts, to "follow my leader" across that legendary spot.

This atmosphere of terror, surrounding, as it did, a man of God of spotless character and orthodoxy, was a common cause of wonder and subject of inquiry among the few strangers who were led by chance or business into that unknown, outlying country. But many even of the people of the parish were ignorant of the strange events which had marked the first year of Mr. Soulis's ministrations; and among those who were better informed, some were naturally reticent, and others shy of that particular topic. Now and again, only, one of the older folk would warm into courage over his third tumbler, and recount the cause of the minister's strange looks and solitary life.

———

Fifty years syne, when Mr. Soulis cam first into Ba'weary, he was still a young man—a callant, the folk said—fu' o' book learnin' and grand at the exposition, but, as was natural in sae young a man, wi' nae leevin' experience in religion. The younger sort were greatly taken wi' his gifts and his gab; but auld, concerned, serious men and women were moved even to prayer for the young man, whom they took to be a self-deceiver, and the parish that was like to be sae ill-supplied. It was before the days o' the moderates—weary fa' them; but ill things are like guid—they baith come bit by bit, a pickle at a time; and there were folk even then that said the Lord had left the college professors to their ain devices, an' the lads that went to study wi' them wad hae done mair and better sittin' in a peat-bog, like their forbears of the persecution, wi' a Bible under their oxter and a speerit o' prayer in their heart. There was nae doubt, onyway, but that Mr. Soulis had been ower lang at the college. He was careful and troubled for mony things besides the ae thing needful. He had a feck o' books wi' him—mair than had ever been seen before in a' that presbytery; and a sair wark the carrier had wi' them, for they were a' like to have smoored in the Deil's Hag between this and Kilmackerlie. They were books o' divinity, to be sure, or so they ca'd them; but the serious were o' opinion there was little service for sae mony, when the hail o' God's Word would gang in the neuk of a plaid. Then he wad sit half the day and half the nicht forbye, which was scant decent—writin', nae less; and first, they were feared he was read his sermons; and syne it proved he was writin' a book himsel', which was surely no fittin' for ane of his years an' sma' experience.

Onyway it behoved him to get an auld, decent wife to keep the manse for him an' see to his bit denners; and he was recommended to an auld limmer—Janet M'Clour, they ca'd her—and sae far left to himsel' as to be ower persuaded. There was mony advised him to the contrar, for Janet was mair than suspeckit by the best folk in Ba'weary. Lang or that, she had had a wean to a dragoon; she hadnae come forrit* for maybe thretty year; and bairns had seen her mumblin' to hersel' up on Key's Loan in the gloamin', whilk was an unco time an' place for a God-fearin' woman. Howsoever, it was the laird himsel' that had first tauld the minister o' Janet; and in thae days he wad have gane a far gate to pleesure the laird. When folk tauld him that Janet was sib to the deil, it was a' superstition by his way of it; an' when they cast up the Bible to him an' the witch of Endor, he wad threep it doun their thrapples that thir days were a' gane by, and the deil was mercifully restrained.

Weel, when it got about the clachan that Janet M'Clour was to be servant at the manse, the folk were fair mad wi' her an' him thegether; and some o' the guidwives had nae better to dae than get round her door cheeks and chairge her wi' a' that was ken't again her, frae the sodger's bairn to John Tamson's twa kye. She was nae great speaker; folk usually let her gang her ain gate, an' she let them gang theirs, wi'

---

*To come forrit—to offer oneself as a communicant. [R.L.S.]

neither Fair-guid-een nor Fair-guid-day; but when she buckled to, she had a tongue to deave the miller. Up she got, an' there wasnae an auld story in Ba'weary but she gart somebody lowp for it that day; they couldnae say ae thing but she could say twa to it; till, at the hinder end, the guidwives up and claught haud of her, and clawed the coats aff her back, and pu'd her doun the clachan to the water o' Dule, to see if she were a witch or no, soum or droun. The carline skirled till ye could hear her at the Hangin' Shaw, and she focht like ten; there was mony a guidwife bure the mark of her neist day an' mony a lang day after; and just in the hettest o' the collieshangie, wha suld come up (for his sins) but the new minister.

"Women," said he (and he had a grand voice), "I charge you in the Lord's name to let her go."

Janet ran to him—she was fair wud wi' terror—an' clang to him, an' prayed him, for Christ's sake, save her frae the cummers; an' they, for their pairt, tauld him a' that was ken't, and maybe mair.

"Woman," says he to Janet, "is this true?"

"As the Lord sees me," says she, "as the Lord made me, no a word o't. Forbye the bairn," says she, "I've been a decent woman a' my days."

"Will you," says Mr. Soulis, "in the name of God, and before me, His unworthy minister, renounce the devil and his works?"

Weel, it wad appear that when he askit that, she gave a girn that fairly frichtit them that saw her, an' they could hear her teeth play dirl thegether in her chafts; but there was naething for it but the ae way or the ither; an' Janet lifted up her hand and renounced the deil before them a'.

"And now," says Mr. Soulis to the guidwives, "home with ye, one and all, and pray to God for His forgiveness."

And he gied Janet his arm, though she had little on her but a sark, and took her up the clachan to her ain door like a leddy of the land; an' her scrieghin' and laughin' as was a scandal to be heard.

There were mony grave folk lang ower their prayers that nicht; but when the morn cam' there was sic a fear fell upon a' Ba'weary that the bairns hid theirsels, and even the men folk stood and keekit frae their doors. For there was Janet comin' doun the clachan—her or her like-ness, nane could tell—wi' her neck thrawn, and her heid on ae side, like a body that has been hangit, and a girn on her face like an unstreakit corp. By an' by they got used wi' it, and even speered at her to ken what was wrang; but frae that day forth she couldnae speak like a Christian woman, but slavered and played click wi' her teeth like a pair o' shears; and frae that day forth the name o' God cam never on her lips. Whiles she wad try to say it, but it michtnae be. Them that kenned best said least; but they never gied that Thing the name o' Janet M'Clour; for the auld Janet, by their way o't, was in muckle hell that day. But the minister was neither to haud nor to bind; he preached about naething but the folk's cruelty that had gi'en her a stroke of the palsy; he skelpt the bairns that meddled her; and he had her up to the manse that same nicht, and dwalled there a' his lane wi' her under the Hangin' Shaw.

Weel, time gaed by: and the idler sort commenced to think mair lichtly o' that black business. The minister was weel thocht o'; he was aye late at the writing, folk wad see his can'le doon by the Dule water after twal' at e'en; and he seemed pleased wi' himsel' and upsitten as at first, though a' body could see that he was dwining. As for Janet she cam an' she gaed; if she didnae speak muckle afore, it was reason she should speak less then; she meddled naebody; but she was an eldritch thing to see, an' nane wad hae mistrysted wi' her for Ba'weary glebe.

About the end o' July there cam' a spell o' weather, the like o't never was in that country side; it was lown an' het an' heartless; the herds couldnae win up the Black Hill, the bairns were ower weariet to play; an' yet it was gousty too, wi' claps o' het wund that rumm'led in the glens, and bits o' shouers that slockened naething. We aye thocht it but to thun'er on the morn; but the morn cam, an' the morn's morning, and it was aye the same uncanny weather, sair on folks and bestial. Of a' that were the waur, nane suffered like Mr. Soulis; he could neither sleep nor eat, he tauld his elders; an' when he wasnae writin' at his weary book, he wad be stravaguin' ower a' the countryside like a man possessed, when a' body else was blythe to keep caller ben the house.

Abune Hangin' Shaw, in the bield o' the Black Hill, there's a bit enclosed grund wi' an iron yett; and it seems, in the auld days, that was the kirkyaird o' Ba'weary, and consecrated by the Papists before the blessed licht shone upon the kingdom. It was a great howff o' Mr. Soulis's, onyway; there he would sit an' consider his sermons; and indeed it's a bieldy bit. Weel, as he cam ower the wast end o' the Black

Hill, ae day, he saw first twa, an syne fower, an' syne seeven corbie craws fleein' round an' round abune the auld kirkyaird. They flew laigh and heavy, an' squawked to ither as they gaed; and it was clear to Mr. Soulis that something had put them frae their ordinar. He wasnae easy fleyed, an' gaed straucht up to the wa's; an' what suld he find there but a man, or the appearance of a man, sittin' in the inside upon a grave. He was of a great stature, an' black as hell, and his e'en were singular to see.* Mr. Soulis had heard tell o' black men, mony's the time; but there was something unco about this black man that daunted him. Het as he was, he took a kind o' cauld grue in the marrow o' his banes; but up he spak for a' that; an' says he: "My friend, are you a stranger in this place?" The black man answered never a word; he got upon his feet, an' begude to hirsle to the wa' on the far side; but he aye lookit at the minister; an' the minister stood an' lookit back; till a' in a meenute the black man was ower the wa' an' rinnin' for the bield o' the trees. Mr. Soulis, he hardly kenned why, ran after him; but he was sair forjaskit wi' his walk an' the het, unhalesome weather; and rin as he likit, he got nae mair than a glisk o' the black man amang the birks, till he won doun to the foot o' the hillside, an' there he saw him ance mair, gaun, hap, step, an' lowp, ower Dule water to the manse.

Mr. Soulis wasnae weel pleased that this fearsome gangrel suld mak' sae free wi' Ba'weary manse; an' he ran the harder, an', wet shoon, ower the burn, an' up the walk; but the deil a black man was there to see. He stepped out upon the road, but there was naebody there; he gaed a' ower the gairden, but na, nae black man. At the hinder end, and a bit feared as was but natural, he lifted the hasp and into the manse; and there was Janet M'Clour before his een, wi' her thrawn craig, and nane sae pleased to see him. And he aye minded sinsyne, when first he set his een upon her, he had the same cauld and deidly grue.

"Janet," says he, "have you seen a black man?"

"A black man?" quo' she. "Save us a'! Ye're no wise, minister. There's nae black man in a' Ba'weary."

But she didnae speak plain, ye maun understand; but yam-yammered, like a powney wi' the bit in its moo.

---

*It was a common belief in Scotland that the devil appeared as a black man. This appears in several witch trials and I think in Law's *Memorials,* that delightful storehouse of the quaint and grisly. [R.L.S.]

"Weel," says he, "Janet, if there was nae black man, I have spoken with the Accuser of the Brethren."

And he sat down like ane wi' a fever, an' his teeth chittered in his heid.

"Hoots," says she, "think shame to yoursel', minister"; an' gied him a drap brandy that she keepit aye by her.

Syne Mr. Soulis gaed into his study amang a' his books. It's a lang, laigh, mirk chalmer, perishin' cauld in winter, an' no very dry even in the tap o' the simmer, for the manse stands near the burn. Sae doun he sat, and thocht of a' that had come an' gane since he was in Ba'weary, an' his hame, an' the days when he was a bairn an' ran daffin' on the braes; and that black man aye ran in his heid like the owercome of a sang. Aye the mair he thocht, the mair he thocht o' the black man. He tried the prayer, an' the words wouldnae come to him; an' he tried, they say, to write at his book, but he could nae mak' nae mair o' that. There was whiles he thocht the black man was at his oxter, an' the swat stood upon him cauld as well-water; and there was other whiles, when he cam to himsel' like a christened bairn and minded naething.

The upshot was that he gaed to the window an' stood glowrin' at Dule water. The trees are unco thick, an' the water lies deep an' black under the manse; an' there was Janet washin' the cla'es wi' her coats kilted. She had her back to the minister, an' he, for his pairt, hardly kenned what he was lookin' at. Syne she turned round, an' shawed her face; Mr. Soulis had the same cauld grue as twice that day afore, an' it was borne in upon him what folk said, that Janet was deid lang syne, an' this was a bogle in the clay-cauld flesh. He drew back a pickle and he scanned her narrowly. She was tramp-trampin' in the cla'es, croonin' to hersel'; and eh! Gude guide us, but it was a fearsome face. Whiles she sang louder, but there was nae man born o' woman that could tell the words o' her sang; an' whiles she lookit side-lang doun, but there was naething there for her to look at. There gaed a scunner through the flesh upon his banes; and that was Heeven's advertisement. But Mr. Soulis just blamed himsel', he said, to think sae ill of a puir, auld afflicted wife that hadnae a freend forbye himsel'; an' he put up a bit prayer for him and her, an' drank a little caller water—for his heart rose again the meat—an' gaed up to his naked bed in the gloaming.

That was a nicht that has never been forgotten in Ba'weary, the nicht o' the seeventeenth of August, seventeen hun'er' an' twal'. It had been het afore, as I hae said, but that nicht it was hetter than ever. The sun gaed doun amang unco-lookin' clouds; it fell as mirk as the pit; no a star, no a breath o' wund; ye couldnae see your han' afore your face, and even the auld folk cuist the covers frae their beds and lay pechin' for their breath. Wi' a' that he had upon his mind, it was gey and unlikely Mr. Soulis wad get muckle sleep. He lay an' he tummled; the gude, caller bed that he got into brunt his very banes; whiles he slept, and whiles he waukened; whiles he heard the time o' nicht, and whiles a tyke yowlin' up the muir, as if somebody was deid; whiles he thocht he heard bogles claverin' in his lug, an' whiles he saw spunkies in the room. He behoved, he judged, to be sick; an' sick he was—little he jaloosed the sickness.

At the hinder end, he got a clearness in his mind, sat up in his sark on the bedside, and fell thinkin' ance mair o' the black man an' Janet. He couldnae weel tell how—maybe it was the cauld to his feet—but it cam' in upon him wi' a spate that there was some connection between thir twa, an' that either or baith o' them were bogles. And just at that moment, in Janet's room, which was neist to his, there cam' a stramp o' feet as if men were wars'lin', an' then a loud bang; an' then a wund gaed reishling round the fower quarters of the house; an' then a' was aince mair as seelent as the grave.

Mr. Soulis was feared for neither man nor deevil. He got his tinder-box, an' lit a can'le, an' made three steps o't ower to Janet's door. It was on the hasp, an' he pushed it open, an' keeked bauldly in. It was a big room, as big as the minister's ain, an' plenished wi' grand, auld, solid gear, for he had naething else. There was a fower-posted bed wi' auld tapestry; and a braw cabinet of aik, that was fu' o' the minister's divinity books, an' put there to be out o' the gate; an' a wheen duds o' Janet's lying here and there about the floor. But nae Janet could Mr. Soulis see; nor ony sign of a contention. In he gaed (an' there's few that wad ha'e followed him) an' lookit a' round, an' listened. But there was naethin' to be heard, neither inside the manse nor in a' Ba'weary parish, an' naethin' to be seen but the muckle shadows turnin' round the can'le. An' then a' at aince, the minister's heart played dunt an' stood stock-still; an' a cauld wund blew amang the hairs o' his heid. Whaten a weary sicht was that for the puir man's een! For there was Janet hangin' frae a nail beside the auld aik cabinet: her heid aye lay on her shoother, her een were steeked, the tongue projekit frae her mouth, and her heels were twa feet clear abune the floor.

"God forgive us all!" thocht Mr. Soulis; "poor Janet's dead."

He cam' a step nearer to the corp; an' then his heart fair whammled in his inside. For by what cantrip it wad ill-beseem a man to judge, she was hingin' frae a single nail an' by a single wursted thread for darnin' hose.

It's an awfu' thing to be your lane at nicht wi' siccan prodigies o' darkness; but Mr. Soulis was strong in the Lord. He turned an' gaed his ways oot o' that room, and lockit the door ahint him; and step by step, doon the stairs, as heavy as leed; and set doon the can'le on the table at the stairfoot. He couldnae pray, he couldnae think, he was dreepin' wi' caul' swat, an' naething could he hear but the dunt-dunt-duntin' o' his ain heart. He micht maybe have stood there an hour, or maybe twa, he minded sae little; when a' o' a sudden, he heard a laigh, uncanny steer upstairs; a foot gaed to an' fro in the cha'mer whaur the corp was hingin'; syne the door was opened, though he minded weel that he had lockit it; an' syne there was a step upon the landin', an' it seemed to him as if the corp was lookin' ower the rail and doun upon him whaur he stood.

He took up the can'le again (for he couldnae want the licht), and as saftly as ever he could, gaed straucht out o' the manse an' to the far end o' the causeway. It was aye pit-mirk; the flame o' the can'le, when he set it on the grund, brunt steedy and clear as in a room; naething moved, but the Dule water seepin' and sabbin' doon the glen, an' yon unhaly footstep that cam' ploddin doon the stairs inside the manse. He kenned the foot over weel, for it was Janet's; and at ilka step that cam' a wee thing nearer, the cauld got deeper in his vitals. He commended his soul to Him that made an' keepit him; "and O Lord," said he, "give me strength this night to war against the powers of evil."

By this time the foot was comin' through the passage for the door; he could hear a hand skirt alang the wa', as if the fearsome thing was feelin' for its way. The saughs tossed an' maned thegether, a lang sigh cam' ower the hills, the flame o' the can'le was blawn aboot; an' there stood the corp of Thrawn Janet, wi' her grogram goun an' her black mutch, wi' the heid aye upon the shouther, an' the girn still upon the face o't—leevin', ye wad hae said—deid, as Mr. Soulis weel kenned—upon the threshold o' the manse.

It's a strange thing that the saul of man should be that thirled into his perishable body; but the minister saw that, an' his heart didnae break.

She didnae stand there lang; she began to move again an' cam' slowly towards Mr. Soulis whaur he stood under the saughs. A' the life o' his body, a' the strength o' his speerit, were glowerin' frae his een. It seemed she was gaun to speak, but wanted words, an' made a sign wi' the left hand. There cam' a clap o' wund, like a cat's fuff; oot gaed the can'le, the saughs skrieghed like folk; an' Mr. Soulis kenned that, live or die, this was the end o't.

"Witch, beldame, devil!" he cried, "I charge you, by the power of God, begone—if you be dead, to the grave—if you be damned, to hell."

An' at that moment the Lord's ain hand out o' the Heevens struck the Horror whaur it stood; the auld, deid, desecrated corp o' the witch-wife, sae lang keepit frae the grave and hirsled round by deils, lowed up like a brunstane spunk and fell in ashes to the grund; the thunder followed, peal on dirling peal, the rairing rain upon the back o' that; and Mr. Soulis lowped through the garden hedge, and ran, wi' skelloch upon skelloch, for the clachan.

That same mornin', John Christie saw the Black Man pass the Muckle Cairn as it was chappin' six; before eicht, he gaed by the change house at Knockdow; an' no lang after, Sandy M'Lellan saw him gaun linkin' doun the braes frae Kilmackerlie. There's little doubt but it was him that dwalled sae lang in Janet's body; but he was awa' at last; and sinsyne the deil has never fashed us in Ba'weary.

But it was a sair dispensation for the minister; lang, lang he lay ravin' in his bed; and frae that hour to this, he was the man ye ken the day.

OLALLA

"Now," said the doctor, "my part is done, and, I may say, with some vanity, well done. It remains only to get you out of this cold and poisonous city, and to give you two months of a pure air and an easy conscience. The last is your affair. To the first I think I can help you. It falls indeed rather oddly; it was but the other day the Padre came in from the country; and as he and I are old friends, although of contrary professions, he applied to me in a matter of distress among some of his parishioners. This was a family—but you are ignorant of Spain, and even the names of our grandees are hardly known to you; suffice it, then, that they were once great people, and are now fallen to the brink of destitution. Nothing now belongs to them but the residencia, and certain leagues of desert mountain, in the greater part of which not even a goat could support life. But the house is a fine old place, and stands at a great height among the hills, and most salubriously; and I had no sooner heard my friend's tale, than I remembered you. I told him I had a wounded officer, wounded in the good cause, who was now able to make a change; and I proposed that his friends should take you for a lodger. Instantly the Padre's face grew dark, as I had maliciously foreseen it would. It was out of the question, he said. Then let them starve, said I, for I have no sympathy with tatterdemalion pride. Thereupon we separated, not very content with one another; but yesterday, to my wonder, the Padre returned and made a submission: the difficulty, he said, he had found upon enquiry to be less than he had feared; or, in other words, these proud people had put their pride in their pocket. I closed with the offer; and, subject to your approval, I have taken rooms for you in the residencia. The air of these mountains will renew your blood; and the quiet in which you will there live is worth all the medicines in the world."

"Doctor," said I, "you have been throughout my good angel, and your advice is a command. But tell me, if you please, something of the family with which I am to reside."

"I am coming to that," replied my friend; "and, indeed, there is a difficulty in the way. These beggars are, as I have said, of very high descent and swollen with the most baseless vanity; they have lived for some generations in a growing isolation, drawing away, on either hand, from the rich who had now become too high for them, and from the poor, whom they still regarded as too low; and even today, when poverty forces them to unfasten their door to a guest, they cannot do so without a most ungracious stipulation. You are to remain, they say, a stranger; they will give you attendance, but they refuse from the first the idea of the smallest intimacy."

I will not deny that I was piqued, and perhaps the feeling strengthened my desire to go, for I was confident that I could break down that barrier if I desired. "There is nothing offensive in such a stipulation," said I; "and I even sympathise with the feeling that inspired it."

"It is true they have never seen you," returned the doctor politely; "and if they knew you were the handsomest and the most pleasant man that ever came from England (where I am told that handsome men are common, but pleasant ones not so much so), they would doubtless make you welcome with a better grace. But since you take the thing so well, it matters not. To me, indeed, it seems discourteous. But you will find yourself the gainer. The family will not much tempt you. A mother, a son, and a daughter; an old woman said to be halfwitted, a country lout, and a country girl, who stands very high with her confessor, and is, therefore," chuckled the physician, "most likely plain; there is not much in that to attract the fancy of a dashing officer."

"And yet you say they are high-born," I objected.

"Well, as to that, I should distinguish," returned the doctor. "The mother is; not so the children. The mother was the last representative of a princely stock, degenerate both in parts and fortune. Her father was not only poor, he was mad: and the girl ran wild about the residencia till his death. Then, much of the fortune having died with him, and the family being quite extinct, the girl ran wilder than ever, until at last she married, Heaven knows whom, a muleteer some say, others a smuggler; while there are some who uphold there was no marriage at all, and that Felipe and Olalla are bastards. The union, such as it was, was tragically dissolved some years ago; but they live in such seclusion, and the country at that time was in so much disorder, that the precise manner of the man's end is known only to the priest—if even to him."

"I begin to think I shall have strange experiences," said I.

"I would not romance, if I were you," replied the doctor; "you will find, I fear, a very grovelling and commonplace reality. Felipe, for instance, I have seen. And what am I to say? He is very rustic, very cunning, very loutish, and, I should say, an innocent; the others are probably to match. No, no, señor commandante, you must seek congenial society among the great sights of our mountains; and in these at least, if you are at all a lover of the works of nature, I promise you will not be disappointed."

The next day Felipe came for me in a rough country cart, drawn by a mule; and a little before the stroke of noon, after I had said farewell to the doctor, the innkeeper, and different good souls who had befriended me during my sickness, we set forth out of the city by the Eastern gate, and began to ascend into the Sierra. I had been so long a prisoner, since I was left behind for dying after the loss of the convoy, that the mere smell of the earth set me smiling. The country through which we went was wild and rocky, partially covered with rough woods, now of the cork tree, and now of the great Spanish chestnut, and frequently intersected by the beds of mountain torrents. The sun shone, the wind rustled joyously; and we had advanced some miles, and the city had already shrunk into an inconsiderable knoll upon the plain behind us, before my attention began to be diverted to the companion of my drive. To the eye, he seemed but a diminutive, loutish, well-made country lad, such as the doctor had described, mighty quick and active, but devoid of any culture; and this first impression was with most observers final. What began to strike me was his familiar, chattering talk; so strangely inconsistent with the terms on which I was to be received; and partly from his imperfect enunciation, partly from the sprightly incoherence of the matter, so very difficult to follow clearly without an effort of the mind. It is true I had before talked with persons of a similar mental constitution; persons who seemed to live (as he did) by the senses, taken and possessed by the visual object of the moment and unable to discharge their minds of that impression. His seemed to me (as I sat, distantly giving ear) a kind of conversation proper to drivers, who pass much of their time in a great vacancy of the intellect and threading the sights of a familiar country. But this was not the case of Felipe; by his own account, he was a home-keeper; "I wish I was there now," he said; and then, spying a tree by the wayside, he broke off to tell me that he had once seen a crow among its branches.

"A crow?" I repeated, struck by the ineptitude of the remark, and thinking I had heard imperfectly.

But by this time he was already filled with a new idea; hearkening with a rapt intentness, his head on one side, his face puckered; and he struck me rudely, to make me hold my peace. Then he smiled and shook his head.

"What did you hear?" I asked.

"O, it is all right," he said; and began encouraging his mule with cries that echoed unhumanly up the mountain walls.

I looked at him more closely. He was superlatively well-built, light, and lithe and strong; he was well-featured; his yellow eyes were very large, though, perhaps, not very expressive; take him altogether, he was a pleasant-looking lad, and I had no fault to find with him, beyond that he was of a dusky hue, and inclined to hairyness; two characteristics that I disliked. It was his mind that puzzled, and yet attracted me. The doctor's phrase—an innocent—came back to me; and I was wondering if that were, after all, the true description, when the road began to go down into the narrow and naked chasm of a torrent. The waters thundered tumultuously in the bottom; and the ravine was filled full of the sound, the thin spray, and the claps of wind, that accompanied their descent. The scene was certainly impressive; but the road was in that part very securely walled in; the mule went steadily forward; and I was astonished to perceive the paleness of terror in the face of my companion. The voice of that wild river was inconstant, now sinking lower as if in weariness, now doubling its hoarse tones; momentary freshets seemed to swell its volume, sweeping down the gorge, raving and booming against the barrier walls; and I observed it was at each of these accessions to the clamour, that my driver more particularly winced and blanched. Some thoughts of Scottish superstition and the river Kelpie passed across my mind; I wondered if perchance the like were prevalent in that part of Spain; and turning to Felipe, sought to draw him out.

"What is the matter?" I asked.

"O, I am afraid," he replied.

"Of what are you afraid?" I returned. "This seems one of the safest places on this very dangerous road."

"It makes a noise," he said, with a simplicity of awe that set my doubts at rest.

The lad was but a child in intellect; his mind was like his body, active and swift, but stunted in development; and I began from that time forth to regard him with a measure of pity, and to listen at first with indulgence, and at last even with pleasure, to his disjointed babble.

By about four in the afternoon we had crossed the summit of the mountain line, said farewell to the western sunshine, and began to go down upon the other side, skirting the edge of many ravines and moving through the shadow of dusky woods. There rose upon all sides the voice of falling water, not condensed and formidable as in the gorge of the river, but scattered and sounding gaily and musically from glen to glen. Here, too, the spirits of my driver mended, and he began to sing aloud in a falsetto voice, and with a singular bluntness of musical perception, never true either to melody or key, but wandering at will, and yet somehow with an effect that was natural and pleasing, like that of the song of birds. As the dusk increased, I fell more and more under the spell of this artless warbling, listening and waiting for some articulate air, and still disappointed; and when at last I asked him what it was he sang—"O," cried he, "I am just singing!" Above all, I was taken with a trick he had of unweariedly repeating the same note at little intervals; it was not so monotonous as you would think, or, at least, not disagreeable; and it seemed to breathe a wonderful contentment with what is, such as we love to fancy in the attitude of trees, or the quiescence of a pool.

Night had fallen dark before we came out upon a plateau, and drew up a little after, before a certain lump of superior blackness which I could only conjecture to be the residencia. Here, my guide, getting down from the cart, hooted and whistled for a long time in vain; until at last an old peasant man came towards us from somewhere in the surrounding dark, carrying a candle in his hand. By the light of this I was able to perceive a great arched doorway of a Moorish character: it was closed by iron-studded gates, in one of the leaves of which Felipe opened a wicket. The peasant carried off the cart to some outbuilding; but my guide and I passed through the wicket, which was closed again behind us; and by the glimmer of the candle, passed through a court, up a stone stair, along a section of an open gallery, and up more stairs again, until we came at last to the door of a great and somewhat bare apartment. This room, which I understood was to be mine, was pierced by three windows, lined with some lustrous wood disposed in panels, and carpeted with the skins of many savage animals. A bright fire burned in the chimney, and shed abroad a changeful flicker; close up to the blaze there was drawn a table, laid for supper; and in the far end a bed stood ready. I was pleased by these preparations, and said so to Felipe; and he, with the same simplicity of disposition that I had already remarked in him, warmly re-echoed my praises. "A fine room," he said, "a very fine room. And fire, too; fire is good; it melts out the pleasure in your bones. And the bed," he continued, carrying over the candle in that direction—"see what fine sheets—how soft, how smooth, smooth"; and he passed his hand again and again over their texture, and then laid down his head and rubbed his cheeks among them with a grossness of content that somehow offended me. I took the candle from his hand (for I feared he would set the bed on fire) and walked back to the supper table, where, perceiving a measure of wine, I poured out a cup and called to him to come and drink of it. He started to his feet at once and ran to me with a strong expression of hope; but when he saw the wine, he visibly shuddered.

"Oh, no," he said, "not that; that is for you. I hate it."

"Very well, Señor," said I; "then I will drink to your good health, and to the prosperity of your house and family. Speaking of which," I added, after I had drunk, "shall I not have the pleasure of laying my salutations in person at the feet of the Señora, your mother?"

But at these words all the childishness passed out of his face, and was succeeded by a look of indescribable cunning and secrecy. He backed away from me at the same time, as though I were an animal about to leap or some dangerous fellow with a weapon, and when he had got near the door, glowered at me sullenly with contracted pupils.

"No," he said at last, and the next moment was gone noiselessly out of the room; and I heard his footing die away downstairs as light as rainfall, and silence closed over the house.

After I had supped I drew up the table nearer to the bed and began to prepare for rest; but in the new position of the light, I was struck by a picture on the wall. It represented a woman, still young. To judge by her costume and the mellow unity which reigned over the canvas, she had long been dead; to judge by the vivacity of the attitude, the eyes and the features, I might have been beholding in a mirror the image of life. Her figure was very slim and strong, and of a just proportion; red tresses lay like a crown over her brow; her eyes, of a very golden brown, held mine with a look; and her face, which was perfectly shaped, was yet marred by a cruel, sullen, and sensual expression. Something in both face and figure, something exquisitely intangible, like the echo of an echo, suggested the features and bearing of my guide; and I stood awhile, unpleasantly attracted and wondering at the oddity of the resemblance. The common, carnal stock of that race, which had been originally designed for such high dames as the one now looking on me from the canvas, had fallen to baser uses, wearing country clothes, sitting on the shaft and holding the reins of a mule cart, to bring home a lodger. Perhaps an actual link subsisted; perhaps some scruple of the delicate flesh that was once clothed upon with the satin and brocade of the dead lady, now winced at the rude contact of Felipe's frieze.

The first light of the morning shone full upon the portrait, and, as I lay awake, my eyes continued to dwell upon it with growing complacency; its beauty crept about my heart insidiously, silencing my scruples one after another; and while I knew that to love such a woman were to sign and seal one's own sentence of degeneration, I still knew that, if she were alive, I should love her. Day after day the double knowledge of her wickedness and of my weakness grew clearer. She came to be the heroine of many daydreams, in which her eyes led on to, and sufficiently rewarded, crimes. She cast a dark shadow on my fancy; and when I was out in the free air of heaven, taking vigorous exercise and healthily renewing the current of my blood, it was often a glad thought to me that my enchantress was safe in the grave, her wand of beauty broken, her lips closed in silence, her philtre spilt. And yet I had a half-lingering terror that she might not be dead after all, but re-arisen in the body of some descendant.

Felipe served my meals in my own apartment; and his resemblance to the portrait haunted me. At times it was not; at times, upon some change of attitude or flash of expression, it would leap out upon me like a ghost. It was above all in his ill tempers that the likeness triumphed. He certainly liked me; he was proud of my notice, which he sought to engage by many simple and childlike devices; he loved to sit close before my fire, talking his broken talk or singing his odd, endless, wordless songs, and sometimes drawing his hand over my clothes with an affectionate manner of caressing that never failed to cause in me an embarrassment of which I was ashamed. But for all that, he was capable of flashes of causeless anger and fits of sturdy sullenness. At a word of reproof, I have seen him upset the dish of which I was about to eat, and this not surreptitiously, but with defiance; and similarly at a hint of inquisition. I was not unnaturally curious, being in a strange place and surrounded by strange people; but at the shadow of a question, he shrank back, lowering and dangerous. Then it was that, for a fraction of a second, this rough lad might have been the brother of the lady in the frame. But these humours were swift to pass; and the resemblance died along with them.

In these first days I saw nothing of any one but Felipe, unless the portrait is to be counted; and since the lad was plainly of weak mind, and had moments of passion, it may be wondered that I bore his dangerous neighbourhood with equanimity. As a matter of fact, it was for some time irksome; but it happened before long that I obtained over him so complete a mastery as set my disquietude at rest.

It fell in this way. He was by nature slothful, and much of a vagabond, and yet he kept by the house, and not only waited upon my wants, but laboured every day in the garden or small farm to the south of the residencia. Here he would be joined by the peasant whom I had seen on the night of my arrival, and who dwelt at the far end of the en-closure, about half a mile away, in a rude outhouse; but it was plain to me that, of these two, it was Felipe who did most; and though I would sometimes see him throw down his spade and go to sleep among the very plants he had been digging, his constancy and energy were admirable in themselves, and still more so since I was well assured they were foreign to his disposition and the fruit of an ungrateful effort. But while I admired, I wondered what had called forth in a lad so shuttle-witted this enduring sense of duty. How was it sustained? I asked my-self, and to what length did it prevail over his instincts? The priest was possibly his inspirer; but the priest came one day to the residencia. I saw him both come and go after an interval of close upon an hour, from a knoll where I was sketching, and all that time Felipe continued to labour undisturbed in the garden.

At last, in a very unworthy spirit, I determined to debauch the lad from his good resolutions, and, waylaying him at the gate, easily per-suaded him to join me in a ramble. It was a fine day, and the woods to which I led him were green and pleasant and sweet-smelling and alive with the hum of insects. Here he discovered himself in a fresh charac-ter, mounting up to heights of gaiety that abashed me, and displaying an energy and grace of movement that delighted the eye. He leaped, he ran round me in mere glee; he would stop, and look and listen, and seem to drink in the world like a cordial; and then he would suddenly spring into a tree with one bound, and hang and gambol there like one at home. Little as he said to me, and that of not much import, I have rarely enjoyed more stirring company; the sight of his delight was a continual feast; the speed and accuracy of his movements pleased me to the heart; and I might have been so thoughtlessly unkind as to make a habit of these walks, had not chance prepared a very rude conclusion to my pleasure. By some swiftness or dexterity the lad captured a squirrel in a treetop. He was then some way ahead of me, but I saw him drop to the ground and crouch there, crying aloud for pleasure like a child. The sound stirred my sympathies, it was so fresh and in-nocent; but as I bettered my pace to draw near, the cry of the squirrel knocked upon my heart. I have heard and seen much of the cruelty of lads, and above all of peasants; but what I now beheld struck me into a passion of anger. I thrust the fellow aside, plucked the poor brute out of his hands, and with swift mercy killed it. Then I turned upon the torturer, spoke to him long out of the heat of my indignation, calling him names at which he seemed to wither; and at length, pointing to-ward the residencia, bade him begone and leave me, for I chose to walk with men, not with vermin. He fell upon his knees, and, the words coming to him with more clearness than usual, poured out a stream of the most touching supplications, begging me in mercy to forgive him, to forget what he had done, to look to the future. "O, I try so hard," he said. "O, commandante, bear with Felipe this once; he will never be a brute again!" Thereupon, much more affected than I cared to show, I suffered myself to be persuaded, and at last shook hands with him and made it up. But the squirrel, by way of penance, I made him bury; speaking of the poor thing's beauty, telling him what pains it had suffered, and how base a thing was the abuse of strength. "See, Felipe," said I, "you are strong indeed; but in my hands you are as helpless as that poor thing of the trees. Give me your hand in mine. You cannot remove it. Now suppose that I were cruel like you, and took a pleasure in pain. I only tighten my hold, and see how you suffer." He screamed aloud, his face stricken ashy and dotted with needle points of sweat; and when I set him free, he fell to the earth and nursed his hand and moaned over it like a baby. But he took the lesson in good part; and whether from that, or from what I had said to him, or the higher notion he now had of my bodily strength, his original affection was changed into a doglike, adoring fidelity.

Meanwhile I gained rapidly in health. The residencia stood on the crown of a stony plateau; on every side the mountains hemmed it about; only from the roof, where was a bartizan, there might be seen between two peaks, a small segment of plain, blue with extreme distance. The air in these altitudes moved freely and largely; great clouds congregated there, and were broken up by the wind and left in tatters on the hilltops; a hoarse, and yet faint rumbling of torrents rose from all round; and one could there study all the ruder and more ancient characters of nature in something of their pristine force. I delighted from the first in the vigorous scenery and changeful weather; nor less in the antique and dilapidated mansion where I dwelt. This was a large oblong, flanked at two opposite corners by bastion-like projections, one of which commanded the door, while both were loopholed for musketry. The lower storey was, besides, naked of windows, so that the building, if garrisoned, could not be carried without artillery. It enclosed an open court planted with pomegranate trees. From this a broad flight of marble stairs ascended to an open gallery, running all round and resting, towards the court, on slender pillars. Thence again, several enclosed stairs led to the upper storeys of the house, which were thus broken up into distinct divisions. The windows, both within and without, were closely shuttered; some of the stonework in the upper parts had fallen; the roof, in one place, had been wrecked in one of the flurries of wind which were common in these mountains; and the whole house, in the strong, beating sunlight, and standing out above a grove of stunted cork trees, thickly laden and discoloured with dust, looked like the sleeping palace of the legend. The court, in particular, seemed the very home of slumber. A hoarse cooing of doves haunted about the eaves; the winds were excluded, but when they blew outside, the mountain dust fell here as thick as rain, and veiled the red bloom of the pomegranates; shuttered windows and the closed doors of numerous cellars, and the vacant arches of the gallery, enclosed it; and all day long the sun made broken profiles on the four sides, and paraded the shadow of the pillars on the gallery floor. At the ground level there was, however, a certain pillared recess, which bore the marks of human habitation. Though it was open in front upon the court, it was yet provided with a chimney, where a wood fire would be always prettily blazing; and the tile floor was littered with the skins of animals.

It was in this place that I first saw my hostess. She had drawn one of the skins forward and sat in the sun, leaning against a pillar. It was her dress that struck me first of all, for it was rich and brightly coloured, and shone out in that dusty courtyard with something of the same relief as the flowers of the pomegranates. At a second look it was her beauty of person that took hold of me. As she sat back—watching me, I thought, though with invisible eyes—and wearing at the same time an expression of almost imbecile good-humour and contentment, she showed a perfectness of feature and a quiet nobility of attitude that were beyond a statue's. I took off my hat to her in passing, and her face puckered with suspicion as swiftly and lightly as a pool ruffles in the breeze; but she paid no heed to my courtesy. I went forth on my customary walk a trifle daunted, her idol-like impassivity haunting me; and when I returned, although she was still in much the same posture, I was half surprised to see that she had moved as far as the next pillar, following the sunshine. This time, however, she addressed me with some trivial salutation, civilly enough conceived, and uttered in the same deep-chested, and yet indistinct and lisping tones, that had already baffled the utmost niceness of my hearing from her son. I answered rather at a venture; for not only did I fail to take her meaning with precision, but the sudden disclosure of her eyes disturbed me. They were unusually large, the iris golden like Felipe's, but the pupil at that moment so distended that they seemed almost black; and what affected me was not so much their size as (what was perhaps its consequence) the singular insignificance of their regard. A look more blankly stupid I have never met. My eyes dropped before it even as I spoke, and I went on my way upstairs to my own room, at once baffled and embarrassed. Yet, when I came there and saw the face of the portrait, I was again reminded of the miracle of family descent. My hostess was, indeed, both older and fuller in person; her eyes were of a different colour; her face, besides, was not only free from the ill-significance that offended and attracted me in the painting; it was devoid of either good or bad—a moral blank expressing literally naught. And yet there was a likeness, not so much speaking as immanent, not so much in any particular feature as upon the whole. It should seem, I thought, as if when the master set his signature to that grave canvas, he had not only caught the image of one smiling and false-eyed woman, but stamped the essential quality of a race.

From that day forth, whether I came or went, I was sure to find the Señora seated in the sun against a pillar, or stretched on a rug before the fire; only at times she would shift her station to the top round of the stone staircase, where she lay with the same nonchalance right across my path. In all these days, I never knew her to display the least spark of energy beyond what she expended in brushing and re-brushing her copious copper-coloured hair, or in lisping out, in the rich and broken hoarseness of her voice, her customary idle salutations to myself. These, I think, were her two chief pleasures, beyond that of mere quiescence. She seemed always proud of her remarks, as though they had been witticisms: and, indeed, though they were empty enough, like the conversation of many respectable persons, and turned on a very narrow range of subjects, they were never meaningless or incoherent; nay, they had a certain beauty of their own, breathing, as they did, of her entire contentment. Now she would speak of the warmth, in which (like her son) she greatly delighted; now of the flowers of the pomegranate trees, and now of the white doves and long-winged swallows that fanned the air of the court. The birds excited her. As they raked the eaves in their swift flight, or skimmed sidelong past her with a rush of wind, she would sometimes stir, and sit a little up, and seem to awaken from her doze of satisfaction. But for the rest of her days she lay luxuriously folded on herself and sunk in sloth and pleasure. Her invincible content at first annoyed me, but I came gradually to find repose in the spectacle, until at last it grew to be my habit to sit down beside her four times in the day, both coming and going, and to talk with her sleepily, I scarce knew of what. I had come to like her dull, almost animal neighbourhood; her beauty and her stupidity soothed and amused me. I began to find a kind of transcendental good sense in her remarks, and her unfathomable good nature moved me to admiration and envy. The liking was returned; she enjoyed my presence half-unconsciously, as a man in deep meditation may enjoy the babbling of a brook. I can scarce say she brightened when I came, for satisfaction was written on her face eternally, as on some foolish statue's; but I was made conscious of her pleasure by some more intimate communication than the sight. And one day, as I sat within reach of her on the marble step, she suddenly shot forth one of her hands and patted mine. The thing was done, and she was back in her accustomed attitude, before my mind had received intelligence of the caress; and when I turned to look her in the face I could perceive no answerable sentiment. It was plain she attached no moment to the act, and I blamed myself for my own more uneasy consciousness.

The sight and (if I may so call it) the acquaintance of the mother confirmed the view I had already taken of the son. The family blood had been impoverished, perhaps by long inbreeding, which I knew to be a common error among the proud and the exclusive. No decline, indeed, was to be traced in the body, which had been handed down unimpaired in shapeliness and strength; and the faces of today were struck as sharply from the mint, as the face of two centuries ago that smiled upon me from the portrait. But the intelligence (that more precious heirloom) was degenerate; the treasure of ancestral memory ran low; and it had required the potent, plebeian crossing of a muleteer or mountain contrabandista to raise, what approached hebetude in the mother, into the active oddity of the son. Yet of the two, it was the mother I preferred. Of Felipe, vengeful and placable, full of starts and shyings, inconstant as a hare, I could even conceive as a creature possibly noxious. Of the mother I had no thoughts but those of kindness. And indeed, as spectators are apt ignorantly to take sides, I grew something of a partisan in the enmity which I perceived to smoulder between them. True, it seemed mostly on the mother's part. She would sometimes draw in her breath as he came near, and the pupils of her vacant eyes would contract as if with horror or fear. Her emotions, such as they were, were much upon the surface and readily shared; and this latent repulsion occupied my mind, and kept me wondering on what grounds it rested, and whether the son was certainly in fault.

I had been about ten days in the residencia, when there sprang up a high and harsh wind, carrying clouds of dust. It came out of malarious lowlands, and over several snowy sierras. The nerves of those on whom it blew were strung and jangled; their eyes smarted with the dust; their legs ached under the burthen of their body; and the touch of one hand upon another grew to be odious. The wind, besides, came down the gullies of the hills and stormed about the house with a great, hollow buzzing and whistling that was wearisome to the ear and dismally depressing to the mind. It did not so much blow in gusts as with the steady sweep of a waterfall, so that there was no remission of discomfort while it blew. But higher upon the mountain, it was probably of a more variable strength, with accesses of fury; for there came down at times a far-off wailing, infinitely grievous to hear; and at times, on one of the high shelves or terraces, there would start up, and then disperse, a tower of dust, like the smoke of an explosion.

I no sooner awoke in bed than I was conscious of the nervous tension and depression of the weather, and the effect grew stronger as the day proceeded. It was in vain that I resisted; in vain that I set forth upon my customary morning's walk; the irrational, unchanging fury of the storm had soon beat down my strength and wrecked my temper; and I returned to the residencia, glowing with dry heat, and foul and gritty with dust. The court had a forlorn appearance; now and then a glimmer of sun fled over it; now and then the wind swooped down upon the pomegranates, and scattered the blossoms, and set the window shutters clapping on the wall. In the recess the Señora was pacing to and fro with a flushed countenance and bright eyes; I thought, too, she was speaking to herself, like one in anger. But when I addressed her with my customary salutation, she only replied by a sharp gesture and continued her walk. The weather had distempered even this impassive creature; and as I went on upstairs I was the less ashamed of my own discomposure.

All day the wind continued; and I sat in my room and made a feint of reading, or walked up and down, and listened to the riot overhead. Night fell, and I had not so much as a candle. I began to long for some society, and stole down to the court. It was now plunged in the blue of the first darkness; but the recess was redly lighted by the fire. The wood had been piled high, and was crowned by a shock of flames, which the draught of the chimney brandished to and fro. In this strong and shaken brightness the Señora continued pacing from wall to wall with disconnected gestures, clasping her hands, stretching forth her arms, throwing back her head as in appeal to heaven. In these disordered movements the beauty and grace of the woman showed more clearly; but there was a light in her eye that struck on me unpleasantly; and when I had looked on awhile in silence, and seemingly unobserved, I turned tail as I had come, and groped my way back again to my own chamber.

By the time Felipe brought my supper and lights, my nerve was utterly gone; and, had the lad been such as I was used to seeing him, I should have kept him (even by force had that been necessary) to take off the edge from my distasteful solitude. But on Felipe, also, the wind had exercised its influence. He had been feverish all day; now that the night had come he was fallen into a low and tremulous humour that reacted on my own. The sight of his scared face, his starts and pallors and sudden harkenings, unstrung me; and when he dropped and broke a dish, I fairly leaped out of my seat.

"I think we are all mad today," said I, affecting to laugh.

"It is the black wind," he replied dolefully. "You feel as if you must do something, and you don't know what it is."

I noted the aptness of the description; but, indeed, Felipe had sometimes a strange felicity in rendering into words the sensations of the body. "And your mother, too," said I; "she seems to feel this weather much. Do you not fear she may be unwell?"

He stared at me a little, and then said, "No," almost defiantly; and the next moment, carrying his hand to his brow, cried out lamentably on the wind and the noise that made his head go round like a millwheel. "Who can be well?" he cried; and, indeed, I could only echo his question, for I was disturbed enough myself.

I went to bed early, wearied with day-long restlessness; but the poisonous nature of the wind, and its ungodly and unintermittent uproar, would not suffer me to sleep. I lay there and tossed, my nerves and senses on the stretch. At times I would doze, dream horribly, and wake again; and these snatches of oblivion confused me as to time. But it must have been late on in the night, when I was suddenly startled by an outbreak of pitiable and hateful cries. I leaped from my bed, supposing I had dreamed; but the cries still continued to fill the house, cries of pain, I thought, but certainly of rage also, and so savage and discordant that they shocked the heart. It was no illusion; some living thing, some lunatic or some wild animal, was being foully tortured. The thought of Felipe and the squirrel flashed into my mind, and I ran to the door, but it had been locked from the outside; and I might shake it as I pleased, I was a fast prisoner. Still the cries continued. Now they would dwindle down into a moaning that seemed to be articulate, and at these times I made sure they must be human; and again they would break forth and fill the house with ravings worthy of hell. I stood at the door and gave ear to them, till at last they died away. Long after that, I still lingered and still continued to hear them mingle in fancy with the storming of the wind; and when at last I crept to my bed, it was with a deadly sickness and a blackness of horror on my heart.

It was little wonder if I slept no more. Why had I been locked in? What had passed? Who was the author of these indescribable and shocking cries? A human being? It was inconceivable. A beast? The cries were scarce quite bestial; and what animal, short of a lion or a tiger, could thus shake the solid walls of the residencia? And while I was thus turning over the elements of the mystery, it came into my mind that I had not yet set eyes upon the daughter of the house. What was more probable than that the daughter of the Señora, and the sister of Felipe, should be herself insane? Or, what more likely than that these ignorant and half-witted people should seek to manage an afflicted kinswoman by violence? Here was a solution; and yet when I called to mind the cries (which I never did without a shuddering chill) it seemed altogether insufficient: not even cruelty could wring such cries from madness. But of one thing I was sure: I could not live in a house where such a thing was half conceivable, and not probe the matter home and, if necessary, interfere.

The next day came, the wind had blown itself out, and there was nothing to remind me of the business of the night. Felipe came to my bedside with obvious cheerfulness; as I passed through the court, the Señora was sunning herself with her accustomed immobility; and when I issued from the gateway, I found the whole face of nature austerely smiling, the heavens of a cold blue, and sown with great cloud islands, and the mountainsides mapped forth into provinces of light and shadow. A short walk restored me to myself, and renewed within me the resolve to plumb this mystery; and when, from the vantage of my knoll, I had seen Felipe pass forth to his labours in the garden, I returned at once to the residencia to put my design in practice. The Señora appeared plunged in slumber; I stood awhile and marked her, but she did not stir; even if my design were indiscreet, I had little to fear from such a guardian; and turning away, I mounted to the gallery and began my exploration of the house.

All morning I went from one door to another, and entered spacious and faded chambers, some rudely shuttered, some receiving their full charge of daylight, all empty and unhomely. It was a rich house, on which Time had breathed his tarnish and dust had scattered disillusion. The spider swung there; the bloated tarantula scampered on the cornices; ants had their crowded highways on the floor of halls of audience; the big and foul fly, that lives on carrion and is often the messenger of death, had set up his nest in the rotten woodwork, and buzzed heavily about the rooms. Here and there a stool or two, a couch, a bed, or a great carved chair remained behind, like islets on the bare floors, to testify of man's bygone habitation; and everywhere the walls were set with the portraits of the dead. I could judge, by these decaying effigies, in the house of what a great and what a handsome race I was then wandering. Many of the men wore orders on their breasts and had the port of noble offices; the women were all richly attired; the canvases most of them by famous hands. But it was not so much these evidences of greatness that took hold upon my mind, even contrasted, as they were, with the present depopulation and decay of that great house. It was rather the parable of family life that I read in this succession of fair faces and shapely bodies. Never before had I so realised the miracle of the continued race, the creation and recreation, the weaving and changing and handing down of fleshly elements. That a child should be born of its mother, that it should grow and clothe itself (we know not how) with humanity, and put on inherited looks, and turn its head with the manner of one ascendant, and offer its hand with the gesture of another, are wonders dulled for us by repetition. But in the singular unity of look, in the common features and common bearing, of all these painted generations on the walls of the residencia, the miracle started out and looked me in the face. And an ancient mirror falling opportunely in my way, I stood and read my own features a long while, tracing out on either hand the filaments of descent and the bonds that knit me with my family.

At last, in the course of these investigations, I opened the door of a chamber that bore the marks of habitation. It was of large proportions and faced to the north, where the mountains were most wildly figured. The embers of a fire smouldered and smoked upon the hearth, to which a chair had been drawn close. And yet the aspect of the chamber was ascetic to the degree of sternness; the chair was uncushioned; the floor and walls were naked; and beyond the books which lay here and there in some confusion, there was no instrument of either work or pleasure. The sight of books in the house of such a family exceedingly amazed me; and I began with a great hurry, and in momentary fear of interruption, to go from one to another and hastily inspect their character. They were of all sorts, devotional, historical, and scientific, but mostly of a great age and in the Latin tongue. Some I could see to bear the marks of constant study; others had been torn across and tossed aside as if in petulance or disapproval. Lastly, as I cruised about that empty chamber, I espied some papers written upon with pencil on a table near the window. An unthinking curiosity led me to take one up. It bore a copy of verses, very roughly metred in the original Spanish, and which I may render somewhat thus —

> Pleasure approached with pain and shame,
> Grief with a wreath of lilies came.
> Pleasure showed the lovely sun;
> Jesu dear, how sweet it shone!
> Grief with her worn hand pointed on,
> Jesu dear, to thee!

Shame and confusion at once fell on me; and, laying down the paper, I beat an immediate retreat from the apartment. Neither Felipe nor his mother could have read the books nor written these rough but feeling verses. It was plain I had stumbled with sacrilegious feet into the room of the daughter of the house. God knows, my own heart most sharply punished me for my indiscretion. The thought that I had thus secretly pushed my way into the confidence of a girl so strangely situated, and the fear that she might somehow come to hear of it, oppressed me like guilt. I blamed myself besides for my suspicions of the night before; wondered that I should ever have attributed those shocking cries to one of whom I now conceived as of a saint, spectral of mien, wasted with maceration, bound up in the practices of a mechanical devotion, and dwelling in a great isolation of soul with her incongruous relatives; and as I leaned on the balustrade of the gallery and looked down into the bright close of pomegranates and at the gaily dressed and somnolent woman, who just then stretched herself and delicately licked her lips as in the very sensuality of sloth, my mind swiftly compared the scene with the cold chamber looking northward on the mountains, where the daughter dwelt.

That same afternoon, as I sat upon my knoll, I saw the Padre enter the gates of the residencia. The revelation of the daughter's character had struck home to my fancy, and almost blotted out the horrors of the night before; but at sight of this worthy man the memory revived. I descended, then, from the knoll, and making a circuit among the woods, posted myself by the wayside to await his passage. As soon as he appeared I stepped forth and introduced myself as the lodger of the residencia. He had a very strong, honest countenance, on which it was easy to read the mingled emotions with which he regarded me, as a foreigner, a heretic, and yet one who had been wounded for the good cause. Of the family at the residencia he spoke with reserve, and yet with respect. I mentioned that I had not yet seen the daughter, whereupon he remarked that that was as it should be, and looked at me a little askance. Lastly, I plucked up courage to refer to the cries that had disturbed me in the night. He heard me out in silence, and then stopped and partly turned about, as though to mark beyond doubt that he was dismissing me.

"Do you take tobacco powder?" said he, offering his snuffbox; and then, when I had refused, "I am an old man," he added, "and I may be allowed to remind you that you are a guest."

"I have, then, your authority," I returned, firmly enough, although I flushed at the implied reproof, "to let things take their course, and not to interfere?"

He said "yes," and with a somewhat uneasy salute turned and left me where I was. But he had done two things: he had set my conscience at rest, and he had awakened my delicacy. I made a great effort, once more dismissed the recollections of the night, and fell once more to brooding on my saintly poetess. At the same time, I could not quite forget that I had been locked in, and that night when Felipe brought me my supper I attacked him warily on both points of interest.

"I never see your sister," said I casually.

"Oh, no," said he; "she is a good, good girl," and his mind instantly veered to something else.

"Your sister is pious, I suppose?" I asked in the next pause.

"Oh!" he cried, joining his hands with extreme fervour, "a saint; it is she that keeps me up."

"You are very fortunate," said I, "for the most of us, I am afraid, and myself among the number, are better at going down."

"Señor," said Felipe earnestly, "I would not say that. You should not tempt your angel. If one goes down, where is he to stop?"

"Why, Felipe," said I, "I had no guess you were a preacher, and I may say a good one; but I suppose that is your sister's doing?"

He nodded at me with round eyes.

"Well, then," I continued, "she has doubtless reproved you for your sin of cruelty?"

"Twelve times!" he cried; for this was the phrase by which the odd creature expressed the sense of frequency. "And I told her you had done so—I remembered that," he added proudly—"and she was pleased."

"Then, Felipe," said I, "what were those cries that I heard last night? for surely they were cries of some creature in suffering."

"The wind," returned Felipe, looking in the fire.

I took his hand in mine, at which, thinking it to be a caress, he smiled with a brightness of pleasure that came near disarming my resolve. But I trod the weakness down. "The wind," I repeated; "and yet I think it was this hand," holding it up, "that had first locked me in." The lad shook visibly, but answered never a word. "Well," said I, "I am a stranger and a guest. It is not my part either to meddle or to judge in your affairs; in these you shall take your sister's counsel, which I cannot doubt to be excellent. But in so far as concerns my own I will be no man's prisoner, and I demand that key." Half an hour later my door was suddenly thrown open, and the key tossed ringing on the floor.

A day or two after I came in from a walk a little before the point of noon. The Señora was lying lapped in slumber on the threshold of the recess; the pigeons dozed below the eaves like snowdrifts; the house was under a deep spell of noontide quiet; and only a wandering and gentle wind from the mountain stole round the galleries, rustled among the pomegranates, and pleasantly stirred the shadows. Something in the stillness moved me to imitation, and I went very lightly across the court and up the marble staircase. My foot was on the topmost round, when a door opened, and I found myself face to face with Olalla. Surprise transfixed me; her loveliness struck to my heart; she glowed in the deep shadow of the gallery, a gem of colour; her eyes took hold upon mine and clung there, and bound us together like the joining of hands; and the moments we thus stood face to face, drinking each other in, were sacramental and the wedding of souls. I know not how long it was before I awoke out of a deep trance, and, hastily bowing, passed on into the upper stair. She did not move, but followed me with her great, thirsting eyes; and as I passed out of sight it seemed to me as if she paled and faded.

In my own room, I opened the window and looked out, and could not think what change had come upon that austere field of mountains that it should thus sing and shine under the lofty heaven. I had seen her—Olalla! And the stone crags answered, Olalla! and the dumb, unfathomable azure answered, Olalla! The pale saint of my dreams had vanished for ever; and in her place I beheld this maiden on whom God had lavished the richest colours and the most exuberant energies of life, whom he had made active as a deer, slender as a reed, and in whose great eyes he had lighted the torches of the soul. The thrill of her young life, strung like a wild animal's, had entered into me; the force of soul that had looked out from her eyes and conquered mine, mantled about my heart and sprang to my lips in singing. She passed through my veins: she was one with me.

I will not say that this enthusiasm declined; rather my soul held out in its ecstasy as in a strong castle, and was there besieged by cold and sorrowful considerations. I could not doubt but that I loved her at first sight, and already with a quivering ardour that was strange to my experience. What then was to follow? She was the child of an afflicted house, the Señora's daughter, the sister of Felipe; she bore it even in her beauty. She had the lightness and swiftness of the one, swift as an arrow, light as dew; like the other, she shone on the pale background of the world with the brilliancy of flowers. I could not call by the name of brother that half-witted lad, nor by the name of mother that immovable and lovely thing of flesh, whose silly eyes and perpetual simper now recurred to my mind like something hateful. And if I could not marry, what then? She was helplessly unprotected; her eyes, in that single and long glance which had been all our intercourse, had confessed a weakness equal to my own; but in my heart I knew her for the student of the cold northern chamber, and the writer of the sorrowful lines; and this was a knowledge to disarm a brute. To flee was more than I could find courage for; but I registered a vow of unsleeping circumspection.

As I turned from the window, my eyes alighted on the portrait. It had fallen dead, like a candle after sunrise; it followed me with eyes of paint. I knew it to be like, and marvelled at the tenacity of type in that declining race; but the likeness was swallowed up in difference. I remembered how it had seemed to me a thing unapproachable in the life, a creature rather of the painter's craft than of the modesty of nature, and I marvelled at the thought, and exulted in the image of Olalla. Beauty I had seen before, and not been charmed, and I had been often drawn to women, who were not beautiful except to me; but in Olalla all that I desired and had not dared to imagine was united.

I did not see her the next day, and my heart ached and my eyes longed for her, as men long for morning. But the day after, when I returned, about my usual hour, she was once more on the gallery, and our looks once more met and embraced. I would have spoken, I would have drawn near to her; but strongly as she plucked at my heart, drawing me like a magnet, something yet more imperious withheld me; and I could only bow and pass by; and she, leaving my salutation unanswered, only followed me with her noble eyes.

I had now her image by rote, and as I conned the traits in memory it seemed as if I read her very heart. She was dressed with something of her mother's coquetry, and love of positive colour. Her robe, which I knew she must have made with her own hands, clung about her with a cunning grace. After the fashion of that country, besides, her bodice stood open in the middle, in a long slit, and here, in spite of the poverty of the house, a gold coin, hanging by a ribbon, lay on her brown bosom. These were proofs, had any been needed, of her inborn delight in life and her own loveliness. On the other hand, in her eyes that hung upon mine, I could read depth beyond depth of passion and sadness, lights of poetry and hope, blacknesses of despair, and thoughts that were above the earth. It was a lovely body, but the inmate, the soul, was more than worthy of that lodging. Should I leave this incomparable flower to wither unseen on these rough mountains? Should I despise the great gift offered me in the eloquent silence of her eyes? Here was a soul immured; should I not burst its prison? All side considerations fell off from me; were she the child of Herod I swore I should make her mine; and that very evening I set myself, with a mingled sense of treachery and disgrace, to captivate the brother. Perhaps I read him with more favourable eyes, perhaps the thought of his sister always summoned up the better qualities of that imperfect soul; but he had never seemed to me so amiable, and his very likeness to Olalla, while it annoyed, yet softened me.

A third day passed in vain—an empty desert of hours. I would not lose a chance, and loitered all afternoon in the court where (to give myself a countenance) I spoke more than usual with the Señora. God knows it was with a most tender and sincere interest that I now studied her; and even as for Felipe, so now for the mother, I was conscious of a growing warmth of toleration. And yet I wondered. Even while I spoke with her, she would doze off into a little sleep, and presently awake again without embarrassment; and this composure staggered me. And again, as I marked her make infinitesimal changes in her posture, savouring and lingering on the bodily pleasure of the movement, I was driven to wonder at this depth of passive sensuality. She lived in her body; and her consciousness was all sunk into and disseminated through her members, where it luxuriously dwelt. Lastly, I could not grow accustomed to her eyes. Each time she turned on me these great beautiful and meaningless orbs, wide open to the day, but closed against human inquiry—each time I had occasion to observe the lively changes of her pupils which expanded and contracted in a breath—I know not what it was came over me, I can find no name for the mingled feeling of disappointment, annoyance, and distaste that jarred along my nerves. I tried her on a variety of subjects, equally in vain; and at last led the talk to her daughter. But even there she proved indifferent; said she was pretty, which (as with children) was her highest word of commendation, but was plainly incapable of any higher thought; and when I remarked that Olalla seemed silent, merely yawned in my face and replied that speech was of no great use when you had nothing to say. "People speak much, very much," she added, looking at me with expanded pupils; and then again yawned, and again showed me a mouth that was as dainty as a toy. This time I took the hint, and, leaving her to her repose, went up into my own chamber to sit by the open window, looking on the hills and not beholding them, sunk in lustrous and deep dreams, and hearkening in fancy to the note of a voice that I had never heard.

I awoke on the fifth morning with a brightness of anticipation that seemed to challenge fate. I was sure of myself, light of heart and foot, and resolved to put my love incontinently to the touch of knowledge. It should lie no longer under the bonds of silence, a dumb thing, living by the eye only, like the love of beasts; but should now put on the spirit, and enter upon the joys of the complete human intimacy. I thought of it with wild hopes, like a voyager to El Dorado; into that unknown and lovely country of her soul, I no longer trembled to adventure. Yet when I did indeed encounter her, the same force of passion descended on me and at once submerged my mind; speech seemed to drop away from me like a childish habit; and I but drew near to her as the giddy man draws near to the margin of a gulf. She drew back from me a little as I came; but her eyes did not waver from mine, and these lured me forward. At last, when I was already within reach of her, I stopped. Words were denied me; if I advanced I could but clasp her to my heart in silence; and all that was sane in me, all that was still unconquered, revolted against the thought of such an accost. So we stood for a second, all our life in our eyes, exchanging salvos of attraction and yet each resisting; and then, with a great effort of the will, and conscious at the same time of a sudden bitterness of disappointment, I turned and went away in the same silence.

What power lay upon me that I could not speak? And she, why was she also silent? Why did she draw away before me dumbly, with fascinated eyes? Was this love? or was it a mere brute attraction, mindless and inevitable, like that of the magnet for the steel? We had never spoken, we were wholly strangers; and yet an influence, strong as the grasp of a giant, swept us silently together. On my side, it filled me with impatience; and yet I was sure that she was worthy; I had seen her books, read her verses, and thus, in a sense, divined the soul of my mistress. But on her side, it struck me almost cold. Of me, she knew nothing but my bodily favour; she was drawn to me as stones fall to the earth; the laws that rule the earth conducted her, unconsenting, to my arms; and

I drew back at the thought of such a bridal, and began to be jealous for myself. It was not thus that I desired to be loved. And then I began to fall into a great pity for the girl herself. I thought how sharp must be her mortification, that she, the student, the recluse, Felipe's saintly monitress, should have thus confessed an overweening weakness for a man with whom she had never exchanged a word. And at the coming of pity, all other thoughts were swallowed up; and I longed only to find and console and reassure her; to tell her how wholly her love was returned on my side, and how her choice, even if blindly made, was not unworthy.

The next day it was glorious weather; depth upon depth of blue over-canopied the mountains; the sun shone wide; and the wind in the trees and the many falling torrents in the mountains filled the air with delicate and haunting music. Yet I was prostrated with sadness. My heart wept for the sight of Olalla, as a child weeps for its mother. I sat down on a boulder on the verge of the low cliffs that bound the plateau to the north. Thence I looked down into the wooded valley of a stream, where no foot came. In the mood I was in, it was even touching to behold the place untenanted; it lacked Olalla; and I thought of the delight and glory of a life passed wholly with her in that strong air, and among these rugged and lovely surroundings, at first with a whimpering sentiment, and then again with such a fiery joy that I seemed to grow in strength and stature, like a Samson.

And then suddenly I was aware of Olalla drawing near. She appeared out of a grove of cork trees, and came straight towards me; and I stood up and waited. She seemed in her walking a creature of such life and fire and lightness as amazed me; yet she came quietly and slowly. Her energy was in the slowness; but for inimitable strength, I felt she would have run, she would have flown to me. Still, as she approached, she kept her eyes lowered to the ground; and when she had drawn quite near, it was without one glance that she addressed me. At the first note of her voice I started. It was for this I had been waiting; this was the last test of my love. And lo, her enunciation was precise and clear, not lisping and incomplete like that of her family; and the voice, though deeper than usual with women, was still both youthful and womanly. She spoke in a rich chord; golden contralto strains mingled with hoarseness, as the red threads were mingled with the brown among her tresses. It was not only a voice that spoke to my heart directly; but it spoke to me of her. And yet her words immediately plunged me back upon despair.

"You will go away," she said, "today."

Her example broke the bonds of my speech; I felt as lightened of a weight, or as if a spell had been dissolved. I know not in what words I answered; but, standing before her on the cliffs, I poured out the whole ardour of my love, telling her that I lived upon the thought of her, slept only to dream of her loveliness, and would gladly forswear my country, my language, and my friends, to live for ever by her side. And then, strongly commanding myself, I changed the note; I reassured, I comforted her; I told her I had divined in her a pious and heroic spirit, with which I was worthy to sympathise, and which I longed to share and lighten. "Nature," I told her, "was the voice of God, which men disobey at peril; and if we were thus dumbly drawn together, ay, even as by a miracle of love, it must imply a divine fitness in our souls; we must be made," I said—"made for one another. We should be mad rebels," I cried out—"mad rebels against God, not to obey this instinct."

She shook her head. "You will go today," she repeated, and then with a gesture, and in a sudden, sharp note—"no, not today," she cried, "tomorrow!"

But at this sign of relenting, power came in upon me in a tide. I stretched out my arms and called upon her name; and she leaped to me and clung to me. The hills rocked about us, the earth quailed; a shock as of a blow went through me and left me blind and dizzy. And the next moment she had thrust me back, broken rudely from my arms, and fled with the speed of a deer among the cork trees.

I stood and shouted to the mountains; I turned and went back towards the residencia, walking upon air. She sent me away, and yet I had but to call upon her name and she came to me. These were but the weaknesses of girls, from which even she, the strangest of her sex, was not exempted. Go? Not I, Olalla—O, not I, Olalla, my Olalla! A bird sang near by; and in that season, birds were rare. It bade me be of good cheer. And once more the whole countenance of nature, from the ponderous and stable mountains down to the lightest leaf and the smallest darting fly in the shadow of the groves, began to stir before me and to put on the lineaments of life and wear a face of awful joy. The sunshine struck upon the hills, strong as a hammer on the anvil, and the hills shook; the earth, under that vigorous insolation, yielded up heady scents; the woods smouldered in the blaze. I felt the thrill of travail and delight run through the earth. Something elemental, something rude, violent, and savage, in the love that sang in my heart, was like a key to nature's secrets; and the very stones that rattled under my feet appeared alive and friendly. Olalla! Her touch had quickened, and renewed, and strung me up to the old pitch of concert with the rugged earth, to a swelling of the soul that men learn to forget in their polite assemblies. Love burned in me like rage; tenderness waxed fierce; I hated, I adored, I pitied, I revered her with ecstasy. She seemed the link that bound me in with dead things on the one hand, and with our pure and pitying God upon the other: a thing brutal and divine, and akin at once to the innocence and to the unbridled forces of the earth.

My head thus reeling, I came into the courtyard of the residencia, and the sight of the mother struck me like a revelation. She sat there, all sloth and contentment, blinking under the strong sunshine, branded with a passive enjoyment, a creature set quite apart, before whom my ardour fell away like a thing ashamed. I stopped a moment, and, commanding such shaken tones as I was able, said a word or two. She looked at me with her unfathomable kindness; her voice in reply sounded vaguely out of the realm of peace in which she slumbered, and there fell on my mind, for the first time, a sense of respect for one so uniformly innocent and happy, and I passed on in a kind of wonder at myself, that I should be so much disquieted.

On my table there lay a piece of the same yellow paper I had seen in the north room; it was written on with pencil in the same hand, Olalla's hand, and I picked it up with a sudden sinking of alarm, and read, "If you have any kindness for Olalla, if you have any chivalry for a creature sorely wrought, go from here today; in pity, in honour, for the sake of Him who died, I supplicate that you shall go." I looked at this awhile in mere stupidity, then I began to awaken to a weariness and horror of life; the sunshine darkened outside on the bare hills, and I began to shake like a man in terror. The vacancy thus suddenly opened in my life unmanned me like a physical void. It was not my heart, it was not my happiness, it was life itself that was involved. I could not lose her. I said so, and stood repeating it. And then, like one in a dream, I moved to the window, put forth my hand to open the casement, and thrust it through the pane. The blood spurted from my wrist; and with an instantaneous quietude and command of myself, I pressed my thumb on the little leaping fountain, and reflected what to do. In that empty room there was nothing to my purpose; I felt, besides, that I required assistance. There shot into my mind a hope that Olalla herself might be my helper, and I turned and went down stairs, still keeping my thumb upon the wound.

There was no sign of either Olalla or Felipe, and I addressed myself to the recess, whither the Señora had now drawn quite back and sat dozing close before the fire, for no degree of heat appeared too much for her.

"Pardon me," said I, "if I disturb you, but I must apply to you for help."

She looked up sleepily and asked me what it was, and with the very words I thought she drew in her breath with a widening of the nostrils and seemed to come suddenly and fully alive.

"I have cut myself," I said, "and rather badly. See!" And I held out my two hands from which the blood was oozing and dripping.

Her great eyes opened wide, the pupils shrank into points; a veil seemed to fall from her face, and leave it sharply expressive and yet inscrutable. And as I still stood, marvelling a little at her disturbance, she came swiftly up to me, and stooped and caught me by the hand; and the next moment my hand was at her mouth, and she had bitten me to the bone. The pang of the bite, the sudden spurting of blood, and the monstrous horror of the act, flashed through me all in one, and I beat her back; and she sprang at me again and again, with bestial cries, cries that I recognised, such cries as had awakened me on the night of the high wind. Her strength was like that of madness; mine was rapidly ebbing with the loss of blood; my mind besides was whirling with the abhorrent strangeness of the onslaught, and I was already forced against the wall, when Olalla ran betwixt us, and Felipe, following at a bound, pinned down his mother on the floor.

A trance-like weakness fell upon me; I saw, heard, and felt, but I was incapable of movement. I heard the struggle roll to and fro upon the floor, the yells of that catamount ringing up to Heaven as she strove to reach me. I felt Olalla clasp me in her arms, her hair falling on my face, and, with the strength of a man, raise and half drag, half carry me upstairs into my own room, where she cast me down upon the bed. Then I saw her hasten to the door and lock it, and stand an instant listening to the savage cries that shook the residencia. And then, swift and light as a thought, she was again beside me, binding up my hand, laying it in her bosom, moaning and mourning over it with dove-like sounds. They were not words that came to her, they were sounds more beautiful than speech, infinitely touching, infinitely tender; and yet as I lay there, a thought stung to my heart, a thought wounded me like a sword, a thought, like a worm in a flower, profaned the holiness of my love. Yes, they were beautiful sounds, and they were inspired by human tenderness; but was their beauty human?

All day I lay there. For a long time the cries of that nameless female thing, as she struggled with her half-witted whelp, resounded through the house, and pierced me with despairing sorrow and disgust. They were the death-cry of my love; my love was murdered; it was not only dead, but an offence to me; and yet, think as I pleased, feel as I must, it still swelled within me like a storm of sweetness, and my heart melted at her looks and touch. This horror that had sprung out, this doubt upon Olalla, this savage and bestial strain that ran not only through the whole behaviour of her family, but found a place in the very foundations and story of our love—though it appalled, though it shocked and sickened me, was yet not of power to break the knot of my infatuation.

When the cries had ceased, there came a scraping at the door, by which I knew Felipe was without; and Olalla went and spoke to him— I know not what. With that exception, she stayed close beside me, now kneeling by my bed and fervently praying, now sitting with her eyes upon mine. So then, for these six hours I drank in her beauty, and silently perused the story in her face. I saw the golden coin hover on her breaths; I saw her eyes darken and brighten, and still speak no language but that of an unfathomable kindness; I saw the faultless face, and, through the robe, the lines of the faultless body. Night came at last, and in the growing darkness of the chamber, the sight of her slowly melted; but even then the touch of her smooth hand lingered in mine and talked with me. To lie thus in deadly weakness and drink in the traits of the beloved, is to reawake to love from whatever shock of disillusion. I reasoned with myself; and I shut my eyes on horrors, and again I was very bold to accept the worst. What mattered it, if that imperious sentiment survived; if her eyes still beckoned and attached me; if now, even as before, every fibre of my dull body yearned and turned to her? Late on in the night some strength revived in me, and I spoke:—

"Olalla," I said, "nothing matters; I ask nothing; I am content; I love you."

She knelt down awhile and prayed, and I devoutly respected her devotions. The moon had begun to shine in upon one side of each of the three windows, and make a misty clearness in the room, by which I saw her indistinctly. When she rearose she made the sign of the cross.

"It is for me to speak," she said, "and for you to listen. I know; you can but guess. I prayed, how I prayed for you to leave this place. I begged it of you, and I know you would have granted me even this; or if not, O let me think so!"

"I love you," I said.

"And yet you have lived in the world," she said; after a pause, "you are a man and wise; and I am but a child. Forgive me, if I seem to teach, who am as ignorant as the trees of the mountain; but those who learn much do but skim the face of knowledge; they seize the laws, they conceive the dignity of the design—the horror of the living fact fades from their memory. It is we who sit at home with evil who remember, I think, and are warned and pity. Go, rather, go now, and keep me in mind. So I shall have a life in the cherished places of your memory: a life as much my own, as that which I lead in this body."

"I love you," I said once more; and reaching out my weak hand, took hers, and carried it to my lips, and kissed it. Nor did she resist, but winced a little; and I could see her look upon me with a frown that was not unkindly, only sad and baffled. And then it seemed she made a call upon her resolution; plucked my hand towards her, herself at the same time leaning somewhat forward, and laid it on the beating of her heart. "There," she cried, "you feel the very footfall of my life. It only moves for you; it is yours. But is it even mine? It is mine indeed to offer you, as I might take the coin from my neck, as I might break a live branch from a tree, and give it you. And yet not mine! I dwell, or I think I dwell (if I exist at all), somewhere apart, an impotent prisoner, and carried about and deafened by a mob that I disown. This capsule, such as throbs against the sides of animals, knows you at a touch for its master; ay, it loves you! But my soul, does my soul? I think not; I know not, fearing to ask. Yet when you spoke to me your words were of the soul; it is of the soul that you ask—it is only from the soul that you would take me."

"Olalla," I said, "the soul and the body are one, and mostly so in love. What the body chooses, the soul loves; where the body clings, the soul cleaves; body for body, soul to soul, they come together at God's signal; and the lower part (if we can call aught low) is only the footstool and foundation of the highest."

"Have you," she said, "seen the portraits in the house of my fathers? Have you looked at my mother or at Felipe? Have your eyes never rested on that picture that hangs by your bed? She who sat for it died ages ago; and she did evil in her life. But, look again: there is my hand to the least line, there are my eyes and my hair. What is mine, then, and what am I? If not a curve in this poor body of mine (which you love, and for the sake of which you dotingly dream that you love me) not a gesture that I can frame, not a tone of my voice, not any look from my eyes, no, not even now when I speak to him I love, but has belonged to others? Others, ages dead, have wooed other men with my eyes; other men have heard the pleading of the same voice that now sounds in your ears. The hands of the dead are in my bosom; they move me, they pluck me, they guide me; I am a puppet at their command; and I but reinform features and attributes that have long been laid aside from evil in the quiet of the grave. Is it me you love, friend? or the race that made me? The girl who does not know and cannot answer for the least portion of herself? or the stream of which she is a transitory eddy, the tree of which she is the passing fruit? The race exists; it is old, it is ever young, it carries its eternal destiny in its bosom; upon it, like waves upon the sea, individual succeeds to individual, mocked with a semblance of self-control, but they are nothing. We speak of the soul, but the soul is in the race."

"You fret against the common law," I said. "You rebel against the voice of God, which he has made so winning to convince, so imperious to command. Hear it, and how it speaks between us! Your hand clings to mine, your heart leaps at my touch, the unknown elements of which we are compounded awake and run together at a look; the clay of the earth remembers its independent life and yearns to join us; we are drawn together as the stars are turned about in space, or as the tides ebb and flow, by things older and greater than we ourselves."

"Alas!" she said, "what can I say to you? My fathers, eight hundred years ago, ruled all this province: they were wise, great, cunning, and cruel; they were a picked race of the Spanish; their flags led in war; the king called them his cousin; the people, when the rope was slung for them or when they returned and found their hovels smoking, blasphemed their name. Presently a change began. Man has risen; if he has sprung from the brutes, he can descend again to the same level. The breath of weariness blew on their humanity and the cords relaxed; they began to go down; their minds fell on sleep, their passions awoke in gusts, heady and senseless like the wind in the gutters of the mountains; beauty was still handed down, but no longer the guiding wit nor the human heart; the seed passed on, it was wrapped in flesh, the flesh covered the bones, but they were the bones and the flesh of brutes, and their mind was as the mind of flies. I speak to you as I dare; but you have seen for yourself how the wheel has gone backward with my doomed race. I stand, as it were, upon a little rising ground in this desperate descent, and see both before and behind, both what we have lost and to what we are condemned to go farther downward. And shall I— I that dwell apart in the house of the dead, my body, loathing its ways—shall I repeat the spell? Shall I bind another spirit, reluctant as my own, into this bewitched and tempest-broken tenement that I now suffer in? Shall I hand down this cursed vessel of humanity, charge it with fresh life as with fresh poison, and dash it, like a fire, in the faces of posterity? But my vow has been given; the race shall cease from off the earth. At this hour my brother is making ready; his foot will soon be on the stair; and you will go with him and pass out of my sight for ever. Think of me sometimes as one to whom the lesson of life was very harshly told, but who heard it with courage; as one who loved you indeed, but who hated herself so deeply that her love was hateful to her; as one who sent you away and yet would have longed to keep you for ever; who had no dearer hope than to forget you, and no greater fear than to be forgotten."

She had drawn towards the door as she spoke, her rich voice sounding softer and farther away; and with the last word she was gone, and I lay alone in the moonlit chamber. What I might have done had not I lain bound by my extreme weakness, I know not; but as it was there fell upon me a great and blank despair. It was not long before there shone in at the door the ruddy glimmer of a lantern, and Felipe coming, charged me without a word upon his shoulders, and carried me down to the great gate, where the cart was waiting. In the moonlight the hills stood out sharply, as if they were of cardboard; on the glimmering surface of the plateau, and from among the low trees which swung together and sparkled in the wind, the great black cube of the residencia stood out bulkily, its mass only broken by three dimly lighted windows in the northern front above the gate. They were Olalla's windows, and as the cart jolted onwards I kept my eyes fixed upon them till, where the road dipped into a valley, they were lost to my view for ever. Felipe walked in silence beside the shafts, but from time to time he would check the mule and seem to look back upon me; and at length drew quite near and laid his hand upon my head. There was such kindness in the touch, and such a simplicity, as of the brutes, that tears broke from me like the bursting of an artery.

"Felipe," I said, "take me where they will ask no questions."

He said never a word, but he turned his mule about, end for end, retraced some part of the way we had gone, and, striking into another path, led me to the mountain village, which was, as we say in Scotland, the kirkton of that thinly peopled district. Some broken memories dwell in my mind of the day breaking over the plain, of the cart stopping, of arms that helped me down, of a bare room into which I was carried, and of a swoon that fell upon me like sleep.

The next day and the days following the old priest was often at my side with his snuffbox and prayer book, and after a while, when I began to pick up strength, he told me that I was now on a fair way to recovery, and must as soon as possible hurry my departure; whereupon, without naming any reason, he took snuff and looked at me sideways. I did not affect ignorance; I knew he must have seen Olalla. "Sir," said I, "you know that I do not ask in wantonness. What of that family?"

He said they were very unfortunate; that it seemed a declining race, and that they were very poor and had been much neglected.

"But she has not," I said. "Thanks, doubtless, to yourself, she is instructed and wise beyond the use of women."

"Yes," he said; "the Señorita is well-informed. But the family has been neglected."

"The mother?" I queried.

"Yes, the mother too," said the Padre, taking snuff. "But Felipe is a well-intentioned lad."

"The mother is odd?" I asked.

"Very odd," replied the priest.

"I think, sir, we beat about the bush," said I. "You must know more of my affairs than you allow. You must know my curiosity to be justified on many grounds. Will you not be frank with me?"

"My son," said the old gentleman, "I will be very frank with you on matters within my competence; on those of which I know nothing it does not require much discretion to be silent. I will not fence with you, I take your meaning perfectly; and what can I say, but that we are all in God's hands, and that His ways are not as our ways? I have even advised with my superiors in the church, but they, too, were dumb. It is a great mystery."

"Is she mad?" I asked.

"I will answer you according to my belief. She is not," returned the Padre, "or she was not. When she was young—God help me, I fear I neglected that wild lamb—she was surely sane; and yet, although it did not run to such heights, the same strain was already notable; it had been so before her in her father, ay, and before him, and this inclined me, perhaps, to think too lightly of it. But these things go on growing, not only in the individual but in the race."

"When she was young," I began, and my voice failed me for a moment, and it was only with a great effort that I was able to add, "was she like Olalla?"

"Now God forbid!" exclaimed the Padre. "God forbid that any man should think so slightingly of my favourite penitent. No, no; the Señorita (but for her beauty, which I wish most honestly she had less of) has not a hair's resemblance to what her mother was at the same age. I could not bear to have you think so; though, Heaven knows, it were, perhaps, better that you should."

At this, I raised myself in bed, and opened my heart to the old man; telling him of our love and of her decision, owning my own horrors, my own passing fancies, but telling him that these were at an end; and with something more than a purely formal submission, appealing to his judgment.

He heard me very patiently and without surprise; and when I had done, he sat for some time silent. Then he began: "The church," and instantly broke off again to apologise. "I had forgotten, my child, that you were not a Christian," said he. "And indeed, upon a point so highly unusual, even the church can scarce be said to have decided. But would you have my opinion? The Señorita is, in a matter of this kind, the best judge; I would accept her judgment."

On the back of that he went away, nor was he thenceforward so assiduous in his visits; indeed, even when I began to get about again, he plainly feared and deprecated my society, not as in distaste but much as a man might be disposed to flee from the riddling sphynx. The villagers, too, avoided me; they were unwilling to be my guides upon the mountain. I thought they looked at me askance, and I made sure that the more superstitious crossed themselves on my approach. At first I set this down to my heretical opinions; but it began at length to dawn upon me that if I was thus redoubted it was because I had stayed at the residencia. All men despise the savage notions of such peasantry; and yet I was conscious of a chill shadow that seemed to fall and dwell upon my love. It did not conquer, but I may not deny that it restrained my ardour.

Some miles westward of the village there was a gap in the sierra, from which the eye plunged direct upon the residencia; and thither it became my daily habit to repair. A wood crowned the summit; and just where the pathway issued from its fringes, it was overhung by a considerable shelf of rock, and that, in its turn, was surmounted by a crucifix of the size of life and more than usually painful in design. This was my perch; thence, day after day, I looked down upon the plateau, and the great old house, and could see Felipe, no bigger than a fly, going to and fro about the garden. Sometimes mists would draw across the view, and be broken up again by mountain winds; sometimes the plain slumbered below me in unbroken sunshine; it would sometimes be all blotted out by rain. This distant post, these interrupted sights of the place where my life had been so strangely changed, suited the indecision of my humour. I passed whole days there, debating with myself the various elements of our position; now leaning to the suggestions of love, now giving an ear to prudence, and in the end halting irresolute between the two.

One day, as I was sitting on my rock, there came by that way a somewhat gaunt peasant wrapped in a mantle. He was a stranger, and plainly did not know me even by repute; for, instead of keeping the other side, he drew near and sat down beside me, and we had soon fallen in talk. Among other things he told me he had been a muleteer, and in former years had much frequented these mountains; later on, he had followed the army with his mules, had realised a competence, and was now living retired with his family.

"Do you know that house?" I inquired, at last, pointing to the residencia, for I readily wearied of any talk that kept me from the thought of Olalla.

He looked at me darkly and crossed himself.

"Too well," he said, "it was there that one of my comrades sold himself to Satan; the Virgin shield us from temptations! He has paid the price; he is now burning in the reddest place in Hell!"

A fear came upon me; I could answer nothing; and presently the man resumed, as if to himself: "Yes," he said, "O yes, I know it. I have passed its doors. There was snow upon the pass, the wind was driving it; sure enough there was death that night upon the mountains, but there was worse beside the hearth. I took him by the arm, Señor, and dragged him to the gate; I conjured him, by all he loved and respected, to go forth with me; I went on my knees before him in the snow; and I could see he was moved by my entreaty. And just then she came out on the gallery, and called him by his name; and he turned, and there was she standing with a lamp in her hand and smiling on him to come back. I cried out aloud to God, and threw my arms about him, but he put me by, and left me alone. He had made his choice; God help us. I would pray for him, but to what end? there are sins that not even the Pope can loose."

"And your friend," I asked, "what became of him?"

"Nay, God knows," said the muleteer. "If all be true that we hear, his end was like his sin, a thing to raise the hair."

"Do you mean that he was killed?" I asked.

"Sure enough, he was killed," returned the man. "But how? Ay, how? But these are things that it is sin to speak of."

"The people of that house..." I began.

But he interrupted me with a savage outburst. "The people?" he cried. "What people? There are neither men nor women in that house of Satan's! What? have you lived here so long, and never heard?" And here he put his mouth to my ear and whispered, as if even the fowls of the mountain might have overheard and been stricken with horror.

What he told me was not true, nor was it even original; being, indeed, but a new edition, vamped up again by village ignorance and superstition, of stories nearly as ancient as the race of man. It was rather the application that appalled me. In the old days, he said, the church would have burned out that nest of basilisks; but the arm of the church was now shortened; his friend Miguel had been unpunished by the hands of men, and left to the more awful judgment of an offended God. This was wrong; but it should be so no more. The Padre was sunk in age; he was even bewitched himself; but the eyes of his flock were now awake to their own danger; and some day—ay, and before long—the smoke of that house should go up to heaven.

He left me filled with horror and fear. Which way to turn I knew not; whether first to warn the Padre, or to carry my ill-news direct to the threatened inhabitants of the residencia. Fate was to decide for me; for, while I was still hesitating, I beheld the veiled figure of a woman drawing near to me up the pathway. No veil could deceive my penetration; by every line and every movement I recognised Olalla; and keeping hidden behind a corner of the rock, I suffered her to gain the summit. Then I came forward. She knew me and paused, but did not speak; I, too, remained silent; and we continued for some time to gaze upon each other with a passionate sadness.

"I thought you had gone," she said at length. "It is all that you can do for me—to go. It is all I ever asked of you. And you still stay. But do you know, that every day heaps up the peril of death, not only on your head, but on ours? A report has gone about the mountain; it is thought you love me, and the people will not suffer it."

I saw she was already informed of her danger, and I rejoiced at it. "Olalla," I said, "I am ready to go this day, this very hour, but not alone."

She stepped aside and knelt down before the crucifix to pray, and I stood by and looked now at her and now at the object of her adoration, now at the living figure of the penitent, and now at the ghastly, daubed countenance, the painted wounds, and the projected ribs of the image. The silence was only broken by the wailing of some large birds that circled sidelong, as if in surprise or alarm, about the summit of the hills. Presently Olalla rose again, turned towards me, raised her veil, and, still leaning with one hand on the shaft of the crucifix, looked upon me with a pale and sorrowful countenance.

"I have laid my hand upon the cross," she said. "The Padre says you are no Christian; but look up for a moment with my eyes, and behold the face of the Man of Sorrows. We are all such as He was—the inheritors of sin; we must all bear and expiate a past which was not ours; there is in all of us—ay, even in me—a sparkle of the divine. Like Him, we must endure for a little while, until morning returns bringing peace. Suffer me to pass on upon my way alone; it is thus that I shall be least lonely, counting for my friend Him who is the friend of all the distressed; it is thus that I shall be the most happy, having taken my farewell of earthly happiness, and willingly accepted sorrow for my portion."

I looked at the face of the crucifix, and, though I was no friend to images, and despised that imitative and grimacing art of which it was a rude example, some sense of what the thing implied was carried home to my intelligence. The face looked down upon me with a painful and deadly contraction; but the rays of a glory encircled it, and reminded me that the sacrifice was voluntary. It stood there, crowning the rock, as it still stands on so many highway sides, vainly preaching to passers-by, an emblem of sad and noble truths: that pleasure is not an end, but an accident; that pain is the choice of the magnanimous; that it is best to suffer all things and do well. I turned and went down the mountain in silence; and when I looked back for the last time before the wood closed about my path, I saw Olalla still leaning on the crucifix.

THE TREASURE OF FRANCHARD

CHAPTER I

By the dying mountebank

They had sent for the doctor from Bourron before six. About eight some villagers came round for the performance, and were told how matters stood. It seemed a liberty for a mountebank to fall ill like real people, and they made off again in dudgeon. By ten Madame Tentaillon was gravely alarmed, and had sent down the street for Doctor Desprez.

The Doctor was at work over his manuscripts in one corner of the little dining room, and his wife was asleep over the fire in another, when the messenger arrived.

"Sapristi!" said the Doctor, "you should have sent for me before. It was a case for hurry." And he followed the messenger as he was, in his slippers and skullcap.

The inn was not thirty yards away, but the messenger did not stop there; he went in at one door and out by another into the court, and then led the way by a flight of steps beside the stable, to the loft where the mountebank lay sick. If Doctor Desprez were to live a thousand years, he would never forget his arrival in that room; for not only was the scene picturesque, but the moment made a date in his existence.

We reckon our lives, I hardly know why, from the date of our first sorry appearance in society, as if from a first humiliation; for no actor can come upon the stage with a worse grace. Not to go further back, which would be judged too curious, there are subsequently many moving and decisive accidents in the lives of all, which would make as logical a period as this of birth. And here, for instance, Doctor Desprez, a man past forty, who had made what is called a failure in life, and was moreover married, found himself at a new point of departure when he opened the door of the loft above Tentaillon's stable.

It was a large place, lighted only by a single candle set upon the floor. The mountebank lay on his back upon a pallet; a large man, with a Quixotic nose inflamed with drinking. Madame Tentaillon stooped over him, applying a hot water and mustard embrocation to his feet; and on a chair close by sat a little fellow of eleven or twelve, with his feet dangling. These three were the only occupants, except the shadows. But the shadows were a company in themselves; the extent of the room exaggerated them to a gigantic size, and from the low position of the candle the light struck upwards and produced deformed foreshortenings. The mountebank's profile was enlarged upon the wall in caricature, and it was strange to see his nose shorten and lengthen as the flame was blown about by draughts. As for Madame Tentaillon, her shadow was no more than a gross hump of shoulders, with now and again a hemisphere of head. The chair legs were spindled out as long as stilts, and the boy sat perched atop of them, like a cloud, in the corner of the roof.

It was the boy who took the Doctor's fancy. He had a great arched skull, the forehead and the hands of a musician, and a pair of haunting eyes. It was not merely that these eyes were large, or steady, or the softest ruddy brown. There was a look in them, besides, which thrilled the Doctor, and made him half uneasy. He was sure he had seen such a look before, and yet he could not remember how or where. It was as if this boy, who was quite a stranger to him, had the eyes of an old friend or an old enemy. And the boy would give him no peace; he seemed profoundly indifferent to what was going on, or rather abstracted from it in a superior contemplation, beating gently with his feet against the bars of the chair, and holding his hands folded on his lap. But, for all that, his eyes kept following the Doctor about the room with a thoughtful fixity of gaze. Desprez could not tell whether he was fascinating the boy, or the boy was fascinating him. He busied himself over the sick man: he put questions, he felt the pulse, he jested, he grew a little hot and swore: and still, whenever he looked round, there were the brown eyes waiting for his with the same inquiring, melancholy gaze.

At last the Doctor hit on the solution at a leap. He remembered the look now. The little fellow, although he was as straight as a dart, had the eyes that go usually with a crooked back; he was not at all deformed, and yet a deformed person seemed to be looking at you from below his brows. The Doctor drew a long breath, he was so much relieved to find a theory (for he loved theories) and to explain away his interest.

For all that, he despatched the invalid with unusual haste, and, still kneeling with one knee on the floor, turned a little round and looked the boy over at his leisure. The boy was not in the least put out, but looked placidly back at the Doctor.

"Is this your father?" asked Desprez.

"Oh, no," returned the boy; "my master."

"Are you fond of him?" continued the Doctor.

"No, sir," said the boy.

Madame Tentaillon and Desprez exchanged expressive glances.

"That is bad, my man," resumed the latter, with a shade of sternness. "Every one should be fond of the dying, or conceal their sentiments; and your master here is dying. If I have watched a bird a little while stealing my cherries, I have a thought of disappointment when he flies away over my garden wall, and I see him steer for the forest and vanish. How much more a creature such as this, so strong, so astute, so richly endowed with faculties! When I think that, in a few hours, the speech will be silenced, the breath extinct, and even the shadow vanished from the wall, I who never saw him, this lady who knew him only as a guest, are touched with some affection."

The boy was silent for a little, and appeared to be reflecting.

"You did not know him," he replied at last. "He was a bad man."

"He is a little pagan," said the landlady. "For that matter, they are all the same, these mountebanks, tumblers, artists, and what not. They have no interior."

But the Doctor was still scrutinising the little pagan, his eyebrows knotted and uplifted.

"What is your name?" he asked.

"Jean-Marie," said the lad.

Desprez leaped upon him with one of his sudden flashes of excitement, and felt his head all over from an ethnological point of view.

"Celtic, Celtic!" he said.

"Celtic!" cried Madame Tentaillon, who had perhaps confounded the word with hydrocephalous. "Poor lad! is it dangerous?"

"That depends," returned the Doctor grimly. And then once more addressing the boy: "And what do you do for your living, Jean-Marie?" he inquired.

"I tumble," was the answer.

"So! Tumble?" repeated Desprez. "Probably healthful. I hazard the guess, Madame Tentaillon, that tumbling is a healthful way of life. And have you never done anything else but tumble?"

"Before I learned that, I used to steal," answered Jean-Marie gravely.

"Upon my word!" cried the doctor. "You are a nice little man for your age. Madame, when my *confrère* comes from Bourron, you will communicate my unfavourable opinion. I leave the case in his hands; but of course, on any alarming symptom, above all if there should be a sign of rally, do not hesitate to knock me up. I am a doctor no longer, I thank God; but I have been one. Good night, madame. Good sleep to you, Jean-Marie."

Chapter II

Morning talk

Doctor Desprez always rose early. Before the smoke arose, before the first cart rattled over the bridge to the day's labour in the fields, he was to be found wandering in his garden. Now he would pick a bunch of grapes; now he would eat a big pear under the trellice; now he would draw all sorts of fancies on the path with the end of his cane; now he would go down and watch the river running endlessly past the timber landing place at which he moored his boat. There was no time, he used to say, for making theories like the early morning. "I rise earlier than any one else in the village," he once boasted. "It is a fair consequence that I know more and wish to do less with my knowledge."

The Doctor was a connoisseur of sunrises, and loved a good theatrical effect to usher in the day. He had a theory of dew, by which he could predict the weather. Indeed, most things served him to that end: the sound of the bells from all the neighbouring villages, the smell of the forest, the visits and the behaviour of both birds and fishes, the look of the plants in his garden, the disposition of cloud, the colour of the light, and last, although not least, the arsenal of meteorological instruments in a louvre-boarded hutch upon the lawn. Ever since he had settled at Gretz, he had been growing more and more into the local meteorologist, the unpaid champion of the local climate. He thought at first there was no place so healthful in the arrondissement. By the end of the second year, he protested there was none so wholesome in the whole department. And for some time before he met Jean-Marie he had been prepared to challenge all France and the better part of Europe for a rival to his chosen spot.

"Doctor," he would say—"doctor is a foul word. It should not be used to ladies. It implies disease. I remark it, as a flaw in our civilisation, that we have not the proper horror of disease. Now I, for my part, have washed my hands of it; I have renounced my laureation; I am no doctor; I am only a worshipper of the true goddess Hygieia. Ah, believe me, it is she who has the cestus! And here, in this exiguous hamlet, has she placed her shrine: here she dwells and lavishes her gifts; here I walk with her in the early morning, and she shows me how strong she has made the peasants, how fruitful she has made the fields, how the trees grow up tall and comely under her eyes, and the fishes in the river become clean and agile at her presence.—Rheumatism!" he would cry, on some malapert interruption, "O, yes, I believe we do have a little rheumatism. That could hardly be avoided, you know, on a river. And of course the place stands a little low; and the meadows are marshy, there's no doubt. But, my dear sir, look at Bourron! Bourron stands high. Bourron is close to the forest; plenty of ozone there, you would say. Well, compared with Gretz, Bourron is a perfect shambles."

The morning after he had been summoned to the dying mountebank, the Doctor visited the wharf at the tail of his garden, and had a long look at the running water. This he called prayer; but whether his adorations were addressed to the goddess Hygieia or some more orthodox deity, never plainly appeared. For he had uttered doubtful oracles, sometimes declaring that a river was the type of bodily health, sometimes extolling it as the great moral preacher, continually preaching peace, continuity, and diligence to man's tormented spirits. After he had watched a mile or so of the clear water running by before his eyes, seen a fish or two come to the surface with a gleam of silver, and sufficiently admired the long shadows of the trees falling half across the river from the opposite bank, with patches of moving sunlight in between, he strolled once more up the garden and through his house into the street, feeling cool and renovated.

The sound of his feet upon the causeway began the business of the day; for the village was still sound asleep. The church tower looked very airy in the sunlight; a few birds that turned about it, seemed to swim in an atmosphere of more than usual rarity; and the Doctor, walking in long transparent shadows, filled his lungs amply, and proclaimed himself well contented with the morning.

On one of the posts before Tentaillon's carriage entry he espied a little dark figure perched in a meditative attitude, and immediately recognised Jean-Marie.

"Aha!" he said, stopping before him humorously, with a hand on either knee. "So we rise early in the morning, do we? It appears to me that we have all the vices of a philosopher."

The boy got to his feet and made a grave salutation.

"And how is our patient?" asked Desprez.

It appeared the patient was about the same.

"And why do you rise early in the morning?" he pursued.

Jean-Marie, after a long silence, professed that he hardly knew.

"You hardly know?" repeated Desprez. "We hardly know anything, my man, until we try to learn. Interrogate your consciousness. Come, push me this inquiry home. Do you like it?"

"Yes," said the boy slowly; "yes, I like it."

"And why do you like it?" continued the Doctor. "(We are now pursuing the Socratic method.) Why do you like it?"

"It is quiet," answered Jean-Marie; "and I have nothing to do; and then I feel as if I were good."

Doctor Desprez took a seat on the post at the opposite side. He was beginning to take an interest in the talk, for the boy plainly thought before he spoke, and tried to answer truly. "It appears you have a taste for feeling good," said the Doctor. "Now, there you puzzle me extremely; for I thought you said you were a thief; and the two are incompatible."

"Is it very bad to steal?" asked Jean-Marie.

"Such is the general opinion, little boy," replied the Doctor.

"No; but I mean as I stole," explained the other. "For I had no choice. I think it is surely right to have bread; it must be right to have bread, there comes so plain a want of it. And then they beat me cruelly if I returned with nothing," he added. "I was not ignorant of right and wrong; for before that I had been well taught by a priest, who was very kind to me." (The Doctor made a horrible grimace at the word "priest.") "But it seemed to me, when one had nothing to eat and was beaten, it was a different affair. I would not have stolen for tartlets, I believe; but any one would steal for baker's bread."

"And so I suppose," said the Doctor, with a rising sneer, "you prayed God to forgive you, and explained the case to Him at length."

"Why, sir?" asked Jean-Marie. "I do not see."

"Your priest would see, however," retorted Desprez.

"Would he?" asked the boy, troubled for the first time. "I should have thought God would have known."

"Eh?" snarled the Doctor.

"I should have thought God would have understood me," replied the other. "You do not, I see; but then it was God that made me think so, was it not?"

"Little boy, little boy," said Dr. Desprez, "I told you already you had the vices of philosophy; if you display the virtues also, I must go. I am a student of the blessed laws of health, an observer of plain and temperate nature in her common walks; and I cannot preserve my equanimity in presence of a monster. Do you understand?"

"No, sir," said the boy.

"I will make my meaning clear to you," replied the doctor. "Look there at the sky—behind the belfry first, where it is so light, and then up and up, turning your chin back, right to the top of the dome, where it is already as blue as at noon. Is not that a beautiful colour? Does it not please the heart? We have seen it all our lives, until it has grown in with our familiar thoughts. Now," changing his tone, "suppose that sky to become suddenly of a live and fiery amber, like the colour of clear coals, and growing scarlet towards the top—I do not say it would be any the less beautiful; but would you like it as well?"

"I suppose not," answered Jean-Marie.

"Neither do I like you," returned the Doctor, roughly. "I hate all odd people, and you are the most curious little boy in all the world."

Jean-Marie seemed to ponder for a while, and then he raised his head again and looked over at the Doctor with an air of candid inquiry. "But are not you a very curious gentleman?" he asked.

The Doctor threw away his stick, bounded on the boy, clasped him to his bosom, and kissed him on both cheeks. "Admirable, admirable imp!" he cried. "What a morning, what an hour for a theorist of forty-two! No," he continued, apostrophising heaven, "I did not know such boys existed; I was ignorant they made them so; I had doubted of my race; and now! It is like," he added, picking up his stick, "like a lovers' meeting. I have bruised my favourite staff in that moment of enthusiasm. The injury, however, is not grave." He caught the boy looking at him in obvious wonder, embarrassment, and alarm. "Hullo!" said he, "why do you look at me like that? Egad, I believe the boy despises me. Do you despise me, boy?"

"O, no," replied Jean-Marie, seriously; "only I do not understand."

"You must excuse me, sir," returned the Doctor, with gravity; "I am still so young. O, hang him!" he added to himself. And he took his seat again and observed the boy sardonically. "He has spoiled the quiet of my morning," thought he. "I shall be nervous all day, and have a febricule when I digest. Let me compose myself." And so he dismissed his preoccupations by an effort of the will which he had long practised, and let his soul roam abroad in the contemplation of the morning. He inhaled the air, tasting it critically as a connoisseur tastes a vintage, and prolonging the expiration with hygienic gusto. He counted the little flecks of cloud along the sky. He followed the movements of the birds round the church tower—making long sweeps, hanging poised, or turning airy somersaults in fancy, and beating the wind with imaginary pinions. And in this way he regained peace of mind and animal composure, conscious of his limbs, conscious of the sight of his eyes, conscious that the air had a cool taste, like a fruit, at the top of his throat; and at last, in complete abstraction, he began to sing. The Doctor had but one air—"Malbrouck s'en va-t-en guerre"; even with that he was on terms of mere politeness; and his musical exploits were always reserved for moments when he was alone and entirely happy.

He was recalled to earth rudely by a pained expression on the boy's face. "What do you think of my singing?" he inquired, stopping in the middle of a note; and then, after he had waited some little while and received no answer, "What do you think of my singing?" he repeated, imperiously.

"I do not like it," faltered Jean-Marie.

"Oh, come!" cried the Doctor. "Possibly you are a performer yourself?"

"I sing better than that," replied the boy.

The Doctor eyed him for some seconds in stupefaction. He was aware that he was angry, and blushed for himself in consequence, which made him angrier. "If this is how you address your master!" he said at last, with a shrug and a flourish of his arms.

"I do not speak to him at all," returned the boy. "I do not like him."

"Then you like me?" snapped Doctor Desprez, with unusual eagerness.

"I do not know," answered Jean-Marie.

The Doctor rose. "I shall wish you a good morning," he said. "You are too much for me. Perhaps you have blood in your veins, perhaps celestial ichor, or perhaps you circulate nothing more gross than respirable air; but of one thing I am inexpugnably assured:—that you are no human being. No, boy"—shaking his stick at him—"you are not a human being. Write, write it in your memory—'I am not a human being—I have no pretension to be a human being—I am a dive, a dream, an angel, an acrostic, an illusion—what you please, but not a human being.' And so accept my humble salutations and farewell!"

And with that the Doctor made off along the street in some emotion, and the boy stood, mentally gaping, where he left him.

CHAPTER III

The adoption

Madame Desprez, who answered to the Christian name of Anastasie, presented an agreeable type of her sex; exceedingly wholesome to look upon, a stout *brune,* with cool smooth cheeks, steady, dark eyes, and hands that neither art nor nature could improve. She was the sort of person over whom adversity passes like a summer cloud; she might, in the worst of conjunctions, knit her brows into one vertical furrow for a moment, but the next it would be gone. She had much of the placidity of a contented nun; with little of her piety, however; for

Anastasie was of a very mundane nature, fond of oysters and old wine, and somewhat bold pleasantries, and devoted to her husband for her own sake rather than for his. She was imperturbably good-natured, but had no idea of self-sacrifice. To live in that pleasant old house, with a green garden behind and bright flowers about the window, to eat and drink of the best, to gossip with a neighbour for a quarter of an hour, never to wear stays or a dress except when she went to Fontainebleau shopping, to be kept in a continual supply of racy novels, and to be married to Doctor Desprez and have no ground of jealousy, filled the cup of her nature to the brim. Those who had known the Doctor in bachelor days, when he had aired quite as many theories, but of a different order, attributed his present philosophy to the study of Anastasie. It was her brute enjoyment that he rationalised and perhaps vainly imitated.

Madame Desprez was an artist in the kitchen, and made coffee to a nicety. She had a knack of tidiness, with which she had infected the Doctor; everything was in its place; everything capable of polish shone gloriously; and dust was a thing banished from her empire. Aline, their single servant, had no other business in the world but to scour and burnish. So Doctor Desprez lived in his house like a fatted calf, warmed and cosseted to his heart's content.

The midday meal was excellent. There was a ripe melon, a fish from the river in a memorable Béarnaise sauce, a fat fowl in a fricassee, and a dish of asparagus, followed by some fruit. The Doctor drank half a bottle *plus* one glass, the wife half a bottle *minus* the same quantity, which was a marital privilege, of an excellent Côte-Rôtie, seven years old. Then the coffee was brought, and a flask of Chartreuse for madame, for the Doctor despised and distrusted such decoctions; and then Aline left the wedded pair to the pleasures of memory and digestion.

"It is a very fortunate circumstance, my cherished one," observed the Doctor—"this coffee is adorable—a very fortunate circumstance upon the whole—Anastasie, I beseech you, go without that poison for today; only one day, and you will feel the benefit, I pledge my reputation."

"What is this fortunate circumstance, my friend?" inquired Anastasie, not heeding his protest, which was of daily recurrence.

"That we have no children, my beautiful," replied the Doctor. "I think of it more and more as the years go on, and with more and more gratitude towards the Power that dispenses such afflictions. Your health, my darling, my studious quiet, our little kitchen delicacies, how they would all have suffered, how they would all have been sacrificed! And for what? Children are the last word of human imperfection. Health flees before their face. They cry, my dear; they put vexatious questions; they demand to be fed, to be washed, to be educated, to have their noses blown; and then, when the time comes, they break our hearts, as I break this piece of sugar. A pair of professed egoists, like you and me, should avoid offspring, like an infidelity."

"Indeed!" said she; and she laughed. "Now, that is like you—to take credit for the thing you could not help."

"My dear," returned the Doctor, solemnly, "we might have adopted."

"Never!" cried madame. "Never, Doctor, with my consent. If the child were my own flesh and blood, I would not say no. But to take another person's indiscretion on my shoulders, my dear friend, I have too much sense."

"Precisely," replied the Doctor. "We both had. And I am all the better pleased with our wisdom, because—because——" He looked at her sharply.

"Because what?" she asked, with a faint premonition of danger.

"Because I have found the right person," said the Doctor firmly, "and shall adopt him this afternoon."

Anastasie looked at him out of a mist. "You have lost your reason," she said; and there was a clang in her voice that seemed to threaten trouble.

"Not so, my dear," he replied; "I retain its complete exercise. To the proof: instead of attempting to cloak my inconsistency, I have, by way of preparing you, thrown it into strong relief. You will there, I think, recognise the philosopher who has the ecstasy to call you wife. The fact is, I have been reckoning all this while without an accident. I never thought to find a son of my own. Now, last night, I found one. Do not unnecessarily alarm yourself, my dear; he is not a drop of blood to me that I know. It is his mind, darling, his mind that calls me father."

"His mind!" she repeated with a titter between scorn and hysterics. "His mind, indeed! Henri, is this an idiotic pleasantry, or are you mad? His mind! And what of my mind?"

"Truly," replied the Doctor with a shrug, "you have your finger on the hitch. He will be strikingly antipathetic to my ever beautiful Anastasie. She will never understand him; he will never understand her. You married the animal side of my nature, dear; and it is on the spiritual side that I find my affinity for Jean-Marie. So much so, that, to be perfectly frank, I stand in some awe of him myself. You will easily perceive that I am announcing a calamity for you. Do not," he broke out in tones of real solicitude—"do not give way to tears after a meal, Anastasie. You will certainly give yourself a false digestion."

Anastasie controlled herself. "You know how willing I am to humour you," she said, "in all reasonable matters. But on this point——"

"My dear love," interrupted the Doctor, eager to prevent a refusal, "who wished to leave Paris? Who made me give up cards, and the opera, and the boulevard, and my social relations, and all that was my life before I knew you? Have I been faithful? Have I been obedient? Have I not borne my doom with cheerfulness? In all honesty, Anastasie, have I not a right to a stipulation on my side? I have, and you know it. I stipulate my son."

Anastasie was aware of defeat; she struck her colours instantly. "You will break my heart," she sighed.

"Not in the least," said he. "You will feel a trifling inconvenience for a month, just as I did when I was first brought to this vile hamlet; then your admirable sense and temper will prevail, and I see you already as content as ever, and making your husband the happiest of men."

"You know I can refuse you nothing," she said, with a last flicker of resistance; "nothing that will make you truly happier. But will this? Are you sure, my husband? Last night, you say, you found him! He may be the worst of humbugs."

"I think not," replied the Doctor. "But do not suppose me so unwary as to adopt him out of hand. I am, I flatter myself, a finished man of the world; I have had all possibilities in view; my plan is contrived to meet them all. I take the lad as stable boy. If he pilfer, if he grumble, if he desire to change, I shall see I was mistaken; I shall recognise him for no son of mine, and send him tramping."

"You will never do so when the time comes," said his wife; "I know your good heart."

She reached out her hand to him, with a sigh; the Doctor smiled as he took it and carried it to his lips; he had gained his point with greater ease than he had dared to hope; for perhaps the twentieth time he had proved the efficacy of his trusty argument, his Excalibur, the hint of a return to Paris. Six months in the capital, for a man of the Doctor's antecedents and relations, implied no less a calamity than total ruin. Anastasie had saved the remainder of his fortune by keeping him strictly in the country. The very name of Paris put her in a blue fear; and she would have allowed her husband to keep a menagerie in the back garden, let alone adopting a stable boy, rather than permit the question of return to be discussed.

About four of the afternoon, the mountebank rendered up his ghost; he had never been conscious since his seizure. Doctor Desprez was present at his last passage, and declared the farce over. Then he took Jean-Marie by the shoulder and led him out into the inn garden where there was a convenient bench beside the river. Here he sat him down and made the boy place himself on his left.

"Jean-Marie," he said very gravely, "this world is exceedingly vast; and even France, which is only a small corner of it, is a great place for a little lad like you. Unfortunately it is full of eager, shouldering people moving on; and there are very few bakers' shops for so many eaters. Your master is dead; you are not fit to gain a living by yourself; you do not wish to steal? No. Your situation then is undesirable; it is, for the moment, critical. On the other hand, you behold in me a man not old, though elderly, still enjoying the youth of the heart and the intelligence; a man of instruction; easily situated in this world's affairs; keeping a good table:—a man, neither as friend nor host, to be despised. I offer you your food and clothes, and to teach you lessons in the evening, which will be infinitely more to the purpose for a lad of your stamp than those of all the priests in Europe. I propose no wages, but if ever you take a thought to leave me, the door shall be open, and I will give you a hundred francs to start the world upon. In return, I have an old horse and chaise, which you would very speedily learn to clean and keep in order. Do not hurry yourself to answer, and take it or leave it as you judge aright. Only remember this, that I am no sentimentalist or charitable person, but a man who lives rigorously to himself; and that if I make the proposal, it is for my own ends—it is because I perceive clearly an advantage to myself. And now, reflect."

"I shall be very glad. I do not see what else I can do. I thank you, sir, most kindly, and I will try to be useful," said the boy.

"Thank you," said the Doctor warmly, rising at the same time and wiping his brow, for he had suffered agonies while the thing hung in the wind. A refusal, after the scene at noon, would have placed him in a ridiculous light before Anastasie. "How hot and heavy is the evening, to be sure! I have always had a fancy to be a fish in summer, Jean-Marie, here in the Loing beside Gretz. I should lie under a waterlily and listen to the bells, which must sound most delicately down below. That would be a life—do you not think so too?"

"Yes," said Jean-Marie.

"Thank God you have imagination!" cried the Doctor, embracing the boy with his usual effusive warmth, though it was a proceeding that seemed to disconcert the sufferer almost as much as if he had been an English schoolboy of the same age. "And now," he added, "I will take you to my wife."

Madame Desprez sat in the dining room in a cool wrapper. All the blinds were down, and the tile floor had been recently sprinkled with water; her eyes were half shut, but she affected to be reading a novel as they entered. Though she was a bustling woman, she enjoyed repose between whiles and had a remarkable appetite for sleep.

The Doctor went through a solemn form of introduction, adding, for the benefit of both parties, "You must try to like each other for my sake."

"He is very pretty," said Anastasie. "Will you kiss me, my pretty little fellow?"

The Doctor was furious, and dragged her into the passage. "Are you a fool, Anastasie?" he said. "What is all this I hear about the tact of women? Heaven knows, I have not met with it in my experience. You address my little philosopher as if he were an infant. He must be spoken to with more respect, I tell you; he must not be kissed and Georgy-porgy'd like an ordinary child."

"I only did it to please you, I am sure," replied Anastasie; "but I will try to do better."

The Doctor apologised for his warmth. "But I do wish him," he continued, "to feel at home among us. And really your conduct was so idiotic, my cherished one, and so utterly and distantly out of place, that a saint might have been pardoned a little vehemence in disapproval. Do, do try—if it is possible for a woman to understand young people—but of course it is not, and I waste my breath. Hold your tongue as much as possible at least, and observe my conduct narrowly; it will serve you for a model."

Anastasie did as she was bidden, and considered the Doctor's be-haviour. She observed that he embraced the boy three times in the course of the evening, and managed generally to confound and abash the little fellow out of speech and appetite. But she had the true wom-anly heroism in little affairs. Not only did she refrain from the cheap revenge of exposing the Doctor's errors to himself, but she did her best to remove their ill-effect on Jean-Marie. When Desprez went out for his last breath of air before retiring for the night, she came over to the boy's side and took his hand.

"You must not be surprised nor frightened by my husband's man-ners," she said. "He is the kindest of men, but so clever that he is some-times difficult to understand. You will soon grow used to him, and then you will love him, for that nobody can help. As for me, you may be sure, I shall try to make you happy, and will not bother you at all. I think we should be excellent friends, you and I. I am not clever, but I am very good-natured. Will you give me a kiss?"

He held up his face, and she took him in her arms and then began to cry. The woman had spoken in complaisance; but she had warmed to her own words, and tenderness followed. The Doctor, entering, found them enlaced: he concluded that his wife was in fault; and he was just beginning, in an awful voice, "Anastasie——," when she looked up at him, smiling, with an upraised finger; and he held his peace, wonder-ing, while she led the boy to his attic.

CHAPTER IV

The education of a philosopher

The installation of the adopted stable boy was thus happily effected, and the wheels of life continued to run smoothly in the Doctor's house. Jean-Marie did his horse and carriage duty in the morning; sometimes helped in the housework; sometimes walked abroad with the Doctor, to drink wisdom from the fountainhead; and was intro-duced at night to the sciences and the dead tongues. He retained his singular placidity of mind and manner; he was rarely in fault; but he made only a very partial progress in his studies, and remained much of a stranger in the family.

The Doctor was a pattern of regularity. All forenoon he worked on his great book, the "Comparative Pharmacopœia, or Historical Dictionary of all Medicines," which as yet consisted principally of slips of paper and pins. When finished, it was to fill many personable volumes, and to combine antiquarian interest with professional utility. But the Doctor was studious of literary graces and the picturesque; an anecdote, a touch of manners, a moral qualification, or a sounding epithet was sure to be preferred before a piece of science; a little more, and he would have written the "Comparative Pharmacopœia" in verse! The article "Mummia," for instance, was already complete, though the remainder of the work had not progressed beyond the letter A. It was exceedingly copious and entertaining, written with quaintness and colour, exact, erudite, a literary article; but it would hardly have afforded guidance to a practising physician of today. The feminine good sense of his wife had led her to point this out with uncompromising sincerity; for the Dictionary was duly read aloud to her, betwixt sleep and waking, as it proceeded towards an infinitely distant completion; and the Doctor was a little sore on the subject of mummies, and sometimes resented an allusion with asperity.

After the midday meal and a proper period of digestion, he walked, sometimes alone, sometimes accompanied by Jean-Marie; for madame would have preferred any hardship rather than walk.

She was, as I have said, a very busy person, continually occupied about material comforts, and ready to drop asleep over a novel the instant she was disengaged. This was the less objectionable, as she never snored or grew distempered in complexion when she slept. On the contrary, she looked the very picture of luxurious and appetising ease, and woke without a start to the perfect possession of her faculties. I am afraid she was greatly an animal, but she was a very nice animal to have about. In this way, she had little to do with Jean-Marie; but the sympathy which had been established between them on the first night remained unbroken; they held occasional conversations, mostly on household matters; to the extreme disappointment of the Doctor, they occasionally sallied off together to that temple of debasing superstition, the village church; madame and he, both in their Sunday's best, drove twice a month to Fontainebleau and returned laden with purchases; and in short, although the Doctor still continued to regard them as irreconcilably antipathetic, their relation was as intimate, friendly, and confidential as their natures suffered.

I fear, however, that in her heart of hearts, madame kindly despised and pitied the boy. She had no admiration for his class of virtues; she liked a smart, polite, forward, roguish sort of boy, cap in hand, light of foot, meeting the eye; she liked volubility, charm, a little vice—the promise of a second Doctor Desprez. And it was her indefeasible belief that Jean-Marie was dull. "Poor dear boy," she had said once, "how sad it is that he should be so stupid!" She had never repeated that remark, for the Doctor had raged like a wild bull, denouncing the brutal bluntness of her mind, bemoaning his own fate to be so unequally mated with an ass, and, what touched Anastasie more nearly, menacing the table china by the fury of his gesticulations. But she adhered silently to her opinion; and when Jean-Marie was sitting, stolid, blank, but not unhappy, over his unfinished tasks, she would snatch her opportunity in the Doctor's absence, go over to him, put her arms about his neck, lay her cheek to his, and communicate her sympathy with his distress. "Do not mind," she would say; "I, too, am not at all clever, and I can assure you that it makes no difference in life."

The Doctor's view was naturally different. That gentleman never wearied of the sound of his own voice, which was, to say the truth, agreeable enough to hear. He now had a listener, who was not so cynically indifferent as Anastasie, and who sometimes put him on his mettle by the most relevant objections. Besides, was he not educating the boy? And education, philosophers are agreed, is the most philosophical of duties. What can be more heavenly to poor mankind than to have one's hobby grow into a duty to the State? Then, indeed, do the ways of life become ways of pleasantness. Never had the Doctor seen reason to be more content with his endowments. Philosophy flowed smoothly from his lips. He was so agile a dialectician that he could trace his nonsense, when challenged, back to some root in sense, and prove it to be a sort of flower upon his system. He slipped out of antinomies like a fish, and left his disciple marvelling at the rabbi's depth.

Moreover, deep down in his heart the Doctor was disappointed with the ill-success of his more formal education. A boy, chosen by so acute an observer for his aptitude, and guided along the path of learning by so philosophic an instructor, was bound, by the nature of the universe, to make a more obvious and lasting advance. Now Jean-Marie was slow in all things, impenetrable in others; and his power of forgetting was fully on a level with his power to learn. Therefore the Doctor cherished his peripatetic lectures, to which the boy attended, which he generally appeared to enjoy, and by which he often profited.

Many and many were the talks they had together; and health and moderation proved the subject of the Doctor's divagations. To these he lovingly returned.

"I lead you," he would say, "by the green pastures. My system, my beliefs, my medicines, are resumed in one phrase—to avoid excess. Blessed nature, healthy, temperate nature, abhors and exterminates excess. Human law, in this matter, imitates at a great distance her provisions; and we must strive to supplement the efforts of the law. Yes, boy, we must be a law to ourselves and for our neighbours—lex armata—armed, emphatic, tyrannous law. If you see a crapulous human ruin snuffing, dash from him his box! The judge, though in a way an admission of disease, is less offensive to me than either the doctor or the priest. Above all the doctor—the doctor and the purulent trash and garbage of his pharmacopœia! Pure air—from the neighbourhood of a pinetum for the sake of the turpentine—unadulterated wine, and the reflections of an unsophisticated spirit in the presence of the works of nature—these, my boy, are the best medical appliances and the best religious comforts. Devote yourself to these. Hark! there are the bells of Bourron (the wind is in the north, it will be fair). How clear and airy is the sound! The nerves are harmonised and quieted; the mind attuned to silence; and observe how easily and regularly beats the heart! Your unenlightened doctor would see nothing in these sensations; and yet you yourself perceive they are a part of health.—Did you remember your cinchona this morning? Good. Cinchona also is a work of nature; it is, after all, only the bark of a tree which we might gather for ourselves if we lived in the locality.—What a world is this! Though a professed atheist, I delight to bear my testimony to the world. Look at the gratuitous remedies and pleasures that surround our path! The river runs by the garden end, our bath, our fishpond, our natural system of drainage. There is a well in the court which sends up sparkling water from the earth's very heart, clean, cool, and, with a little wine, most wholesome. The district is notorious for its salubrity; rheumatism is the only prevalent complaint, and I myself have never had a touch of it. I tell you—and my opinion is based upon the coldest, clearest processes of reason—if I, if you, desired to leave this home of pleasures, it would be the duty, it would be the privilege, of our best friend to prevent us with a pistol bullet."

One beautiful June day they sat upon the hill outside the village. The river, as blue as heaven, shone here and there among the foliage. The indefatigable birds turned and flickered about Gretz church tower. A healthy wind blew from over the forest, and the sound of innumerable thousands of treetops and innumerable millions on millions of green leaves was abroad in the air, and filled the ear with something between whispered speech and singing. It seemed as if every blade of grass must hide a cigale; and the fields rang merrily with their music, jingling far and near as with the sleigh bells of the fairy queen. From their station on the slope the eye embraced a large space of poplar'd plain upon the one hand, the waving hilltops of the forest on the other, and Gretz itself in the middle, a handful of roofs. Under the bestriding arch of the blue heavens, the place seemed dwindled to a toy. It seemed incredible that people dwelt, and could find room to turn or air to breathe, in such a corner of the world. The thought came home to the boy, perhaps for the first time, and he gave it words.

"How small it looks!" he sighed.

"Ay," replied the Doctor, "small enough now. Yet it was once a walled city; thriving, full of furred burgesses and men in armour, humming with affairs;—with tall spires, for aught that I know, and portly towers along the battlements. A thousand chimneys ceased smoking at the curfew bell. There were gibbets at the gate as thick as scarecrows. In time of war, the assault swarmed against it with ladders, the arrows fell like leaves, the defenders sallied hotly over the drawbridge, each side uttered its cry as they plied their weapons. Do you know that the walls extended as far as the Commanderie? Tradition so reports. Alas, what a long way off is all this confusion—nothing left of it but my quiet words spoken in your ear—and the town itself shrunk to the hamlet underneath us! By and by came the English wars—you shall hear more of the English, a stupid people, who sometimes blundered into good—and Gretz was taken, sacked, and burned. It is the history of many towns; but Gretz never rose again; it was never rebuilt; its ruins were a quarry to serve the growth of rivals; and the stones of Gretz are now erect along the streets of Nemours. It gratifies me that our old house was the first to rise after the calamity; when the town had come to an end, it inaugurated the hamlet."

"I, too, am glad of that," said Jean-Marie.

"It should be the temple of the humbler virtues," responded the Doctor with a savoury gusto. "Perhaps one of the reasons why I love my little hamlet as I do, is that we have a similar history, she and I. Have I told you that I was once rich?"

"I do not think so," answered Jean-Marie. "I do not think I should have forgotten. I am sorry you should have lost your fortune."

"Sorry?" cried the Doctor. "Why, I find I have scarce begun your education after all. Listen to me! Would you rather live in the old Gretz or in the new, free from the alarms of war, with the green country at the door, without noise, passports, the exactions of the soldiery, or the jangle of the curfew bell to send us off to bed by sundown?"

"I suppose I should prefer the new," replied the boy.

"Precisely," returned the Doctor; "so do I. And, in the same way, I prefer my present moderate fortune to my former wealth. Golden mediocrity! cried the adorable ancients; and I subscribe to their enthusiasm. Have I not good wine, good food, good air, the fields and the forest for my walk, a house, an admirable wife, a boy whom I protest I cherish like a son? Now, if I were still rich, I should indubitably make my residence in Paris—you know Paris—Paris and Paradise are not convertible terms. This pleasant noise of the wind streaming among leaves changed into the grinding Babel of the street, the stupid glare of plaster substituted for this quiet pattern of greens and greys, the nerves shattered, the digestion falsified—picture the fall! Already you perceive the consequences; the mind is stimulated, the heart steps to a different measure, and the man is himself no longer. I have passionately studied myself—the true business of philosophy. I know my character as the musician knows the ventages of his flute. Should I return to Paris, I should ruin myself gambling; nay, I go further—I should break the heart of my Anastasie with infidelities."

This was too much for Jean-Marie. That a place should so transform the most excellent of men transcended his belief. Paris, he protested, was even an agreeable place of residence. "Nor when I lived in that city did I feel much difference," he pleaded.

"What!" cried the Doctor. "Did you not steal when you were there?"

But the boy could never be brought to see that he had done anything wrong when he stole. Nor, indeed, did the Doctor think he had; but that gentleman was never very scrupulous when in want of a retort.

"And now," he concluded, "do you begin to understand? My only friends were those who ruined me. Gretz has been my academy, my sanatorium, my heaven of innocent pleasures. If millions are offered me, I wave them back: *Retro, Sathanas!*—Evil one, begone! Fix your mind on my example; despise riches, avoid the debasing influence of cities. Hygiene—hygiene and mediocrity of fortune—these be your watchwords during life!"

The Doctor's system of hygiene strikingly coincided with his tastes; and his picture of the perfect life was a faithful description of the one he was leading at the time. But it is easy to convince a boy, whom you supply with all the facts for the discussion. And besides, there was one thing admirable in the philosophy, and that was the enthusiasm of the philosopher. There was never any one more vigorously determined to be pleased; and if he was not a great logician, and so had no right to convince the intellect, he was certainly something of a poet, and had a fascination to seduce the heart. What he could not achieve in his customary humour of a radiant admiration of himself and his circumstances, he sometimes effected in his fits of gloom.

"Boy," he would say, "avoid me today. If I were superstitious, I should even beg for an interest in your prayers. I am in the black fit; the evil spirit of King Saul, the hag of the merchant Abudah, the personal devil of the mediæval monk, is with me—is in me," tapping on his breast. "The vices of my nature are now uppermost; innocent pleasures woo me in vain; I long for Paris, for my wallowing in the mire. See," he would continue, producing a handful of silver, "I denude myself, I am not to be trusted with the price of a fare. Take it, keep it for me, squander it on deleterious candy, throw it in the deepest of the river—I will homologate your action. Save me from that part of myself which I disown. If you see me falter, do not hesitate; if necessary, wreck the train! I speak, of course, by a parable. Any extremity were better than for me to reach Paris alive."

Doubtless the Doctor enjoyed these little scenes, as a variation in his part; they represented the Byronic element in the somewhat artificial poetry of his existence; but to the boy, though he was dimly aware of their theatricality, they represented more. The Doctor made perhaps too little, the boy possibly too much, of the reality and gravity of these temptations.

One day a great light shone for Jean-Marie. "Could not riches be used well?" he asked.

"In theory, yes," replied the Doctor. "But it is found in experience that no one does so. All the world imagine they will be exceptional when they grow wealthy; but possession is debasing, new desires spring up; and the silly taste for ostentation eats out the heart of pleasure."

"Then you might be better if you had less," said the boy.

"Certainly not," replied the Doctor; but his voice quavered as he spoke.

"Why?" demanded pitiless innocence.

Doctor Desprez saw all the colours of the rainbow in a moment; the stable universe appeared to be about capsizing with him. "Because," said he—affecting deliberation after an obvious pause—"because I have formed my life for my present income. It is not good for men of my years to be violently dissevered from their habits."

That was a sharp brush. The Doctor breathed hard, and fell into taciturnity for the afternoon. As for the boy, he was delighted with the resolution of his doubts; even wondered that he had not foreseen the obvious and conclusive answer. His faith in the Doctor was a stout piece of goods. Desprez was inclined to be a sheet in the wind's eye after dinner, especially after Rhone wine, his favourite weakness. He would then remark on the warmth of his feeling for Anastasie, and with inflamed cheeks and a loose, flustered smile, debate upon all sorts of topics, and be feebly and indiscreetly witty. But the adopted stable boy would not permit himself to entertain a doubt that savoured of ingratitude. It is quite true that a man may be a second father to you, and yet take too much to drink; but the best natures are ever slow to accept such truths.

The Doctor thoroughly possessed his heart, but perhaps he exaggerated his influence over his mind. Certainly Jean-Marie adopted some of his master's opinions, but I have yet to learn that he ever surrendered one of his own. Convictions existed in him by divine right; they were virgin, unwrought, the brute metal of decision. He could add others indeed, but he could not put away; neither did he care if they were perfectly agreed among themselves; and his spiritual pleasures had nothing to do with turning them over or justifying them in words. Words were with him a mere accomplishment, like dancing. When he was by himself, his pleasures were almost vegetable. He would slip into the woods towards Achères, and sit in the mouth of a cave among grey birches. His soul stared straight out of his eyes; he did not move or think; sunlight, thin shadows moving in the wind, the edge of firs against the sky, occupied and bound his faculties. He was pure unity, a spirit wholly abstracted. A single mood filled him, to which all the objects of sense contributed, as the colours of the spectrum merge and disappear in white light.

So while the Doctor made himself drunk with words, the adopted stable boy bemused himself with silence.

CHAPTER V

Treasure trove

The Doctor's carriage was a two-wheeled gig with a hood; a kind of vehicle in much favour among country doctors. On how many roads has one not seen it, a great way off between the poplars!—in how many village streets, tied to a gatepost! This sort of chariot is affected—particularly at the trot—by a kind of pitching movement to and fro across the axle, which well entitles it to the style of a Noddy. The hood describes a considerable arc against the landscape, with a solemnly absurd effect on the contemplative pedestrian. To ride in such a carriage cannot be numbered among the things that appertain to glory; but I have no doubt it may be useful in liver complaint. Thence, perhaps, its wide popularity among physicians.

One morning early, Jean-Marie led forth the Doctor's noddy, opened the gate, and mounted to the driving seat. The Doctor followed, arrayed from top to toe in spotless linen, armed with an immense flesh-coloured umbrella, and girt with a botanical case on a baldric; and the equipage drove off smartly in a breeze of its own provocation. They were bound for Franchard, to collect plants, with an eye to the "Comparative Pharmacopœia."

A little rattling on the open roads, and they came to the borders of the forest and struck into an unfrequented track; the noddy yawed softly over the sand, with an accompaniment of snapping twigs. There was a great, green, softly murmuring cloud of congregated foliage overhead. In the arcades of the forest the air retained the freshness of the night. The athletic bearing of the trees, each carrying its leafy mountain, pleased the mind like so many statues; and the lines of the trunk led the eye admiringly upward to where the extreme leaves sparkled in a patch of azure. Squirrels leaped in mid air. It was a proper spot for a devotee of the goddess Hygieia.

"Have you been to Franchard, Jean-Marie?" inquired the Doctor. "I fancy not."

"Never," replied the boy.

"It is ruin in a gorge," continued Desprez, adopting his expository voice; "the ruin of a hermitage and chapel. History tells us much of Franchard; how the recluse was often slain by robbers; how he lived on a most insufficient diet; how he was expected to pass his days in prayer. A letter is preserved, addressed to one of these solitaries by the superior of his order, full of admirable hygienic advice; bidding him go from his book to praying, and so back again, for variety's sake, and when he was weary of both to stroll about his garden and observe the honey bees. It is to this day my own system. You must often have remarked me leaving the 'Pharmacopœia'—often even in the middle of a phrase—to come forth into the sun and air. I admire the writer of that letter from my heart; he was a man of thought on the most important subjects. But, indeed, had I lived in the Middle Ages (I am heartily glad that I did not) I should have been an cremite myself—if I had not been a professed buffoon, that is. These were the only philosophical lives yet open: laughter or prayer; sneers, we might say, and tears. Until the sun of the Positive arose, the wise man had to make his choice between these two."

"I have been a buffoon, of course," observed Jean-Marie.

"I cannot imagine you to have excelled in your profession," said the Doctor, admiring the boy's gravity. "Do you ever laugh?"

"Oh, yes," replied the other. "I laugh often. I am very fond of jokes."

"Singular being!" said Desprez. "But I divagate (I perceive in a thousand ways that I grow old). Franchard was at length destroyed in the English wars, the same that levelled Gretz. But—here is the point—the hermits (for there were already more than one) had foreseen the danger and carefully concealed the sacrificial vessels. These vessels were of monstrous value, Jean-Marie—monstrous value—priceless, we may say; exquisitely worked, of exquisite material. And now, mark me, they have never been found. In the reign of Louis Quatorze some fellows were digging hard by the ruins. Suddenly—tock!—the spade hit upon an obstacle. Imagine the men looking one to another; imagine how their hearts bounded, how their colour came and went. It was a coffer, and in Franchard the place of buried treasure! They tore it open like famished beasts. Alas! it was not the treasure; only some priestly robes, which, at the touch of the eating air, fell upon themselves and instantly wasted into dust. The perspiration of these good fellows turned cold upon them, Jean-Marie. I will pledge my reputation, if there was anything like a cutting wind, one or other had a pneumonia for his trouble."

"I should like to have seen them turning into dust," said Jean-Marie. "Otherwise, I should not have cared so greatly."

"You have no imagination," cried the Doctor. "Picture to yourself the scene. Dwell on the idea—a great treasure lying in the earth for centuries: the material for a giddy, copious, opulent existence not employed; dresses and exquisite pictures unseen; the swiftest galloping horses not stirring a hoof, arrested by a spell; women with the beautiful faculty of smiles, not smiling; cards, dice, opera singing, orchestras, castles, beautiful parks and gardens, big ships with a tower of sailcloth, all lying unborn in a coffin—and the stupid trees growing overhead in the sunlight, year after year. The thought drives one frantic."

"It is only money," replied Jean-Marie. "It would do harm."

"O, come!" cried Desprez, "that is philosophy; it is all very fine, but not to the point just now. And besides, it is not 'only money,' as you call it; there are works of art in the question; the vessels were carved. You speak like a child. You weary me exceedingly, quoting my words out of all logical connection, like a parroquet."

"And at any rate, we have nothing to do with it," returned the boy submissively.

They struck the Route Ronde at that moment; and the sudden change to the rattling causeway combined, with the Doctor's irritation, to keep him silent. The noddy jigged along; the trees went by, looking on silently, as if they had something on their minds. The Quadrilateral was passed; then came Franchard. They put up the horse at the little solitary inn, and went forth strolling. The gorge was dyed deeply with heather; the rocks and birches standing luminous in the sun. A great humming of bees about the flowers disposed Jean-Marie to sleep, and he sat down against a clump of heather, while the Doctor went briskly to and fro, with quick turns, culling his simples.

The boy's head had fallen a little forward, his eyes were closed, his fingers had fallen lax about his knees, when a sudden cry called him to his feet. It was a strange sound, thin and brief; it fell dead, and silence returned as though it had never been interrupted. He had not recognised the Doctor's voice; but, as there was no one else in all the valley, it was plainly the Doctor who had given utterance to the sound. He looked right and left, and there was Desprez, standing in a niche between two boulders, and looking round on his adopted son with a countenance as white as paper.

"A viper!" cried Jean-Marie, running towards him. "A viper! You are bitten!"

The Doctor came down heavily out of the cleft, and advanced in silence to meet the boy, whom he took roughly by the shoulder.

"I have found it," he said, with a gasp.

"A plant?" asked Jean-Marie.

Desprez had a fit of unnatural gaiety, which the rocks took up and mimicked. "A plant!" he repeated scornfully. "Well—yes—a plant. And here," he added suddenly, showing his right hand, which he had hitherto concealed behind his back—"here is one of the bulbs."

Jean-Marie saw a dirty platter, coated with earth.

"That?" said he. "It is a plate!"

"It is a coach and horses," cried the Doctor. "Boy," he continued, growing warmer, "I plucked away a great pad of moss from between these boulders, and disclosed a crevice; and when I looked in, what do you suppose I saw? I saw a house in Paris with a court and garden, I saw my wife shining with diamonds, I saw myself a deputy, I saw you— well, I—I saw your future," he concluded, rather feebly. "I have just discovered America," he added.

"But what is it?" asked the boy.

"The Treasure of Franchard," cried the Doctor; and, throwing his brown straw hat upon the ground, he whooped like an Indian and sprang upon Jean-Marie, whom he suffocated with embraces and bedewed with tears. Then he flung himself down among the heather and once more laughed until the valley rang.

But the boy had now an interest of his own, a boy's interest. No sooner was he released from the Doctor's accolade than he ran to the boulders, sprang into the niche, and, thrusting his hand into the crevice, drew forth one after another, encrusted with the earth of ages, the flagons, candlesticks, and patens of the hermitage of Franchard. A casket came last, tightly shut and very heavy.

"O, what fun!" he cried.

But when he looked back at the Doctor, who had followed close behind and was silently observing, the words died from his lips. Desprez was once more the colour of ashes; his lip worked and trembled; a sort of bestial greed possessed him.

"This is childish," he said. "We lose precious time. Back to the inn, harness the trap, and bring it to yon bank. Run for your life, and remember—not one whisper. I stay here to watch."

Jean-Marie did as he was bid, though not without surprise. The noddy was brought round to the spot indicated; and the two gradually transported the treasure from its place of concealment to the boot below the driving seat. Once it was all stored the Doctor recovered his gaiety.

"I pay my grateful duties to the genius of this dell," he said. "O, for a live coal, a heifer, and a jar of country wine! I am in the vein for sacrifice, for a superb libation. Well, and why not? We are at Franchard. English pale ale is to be had—not classical, indeed, but excellent. Boy, we shall drink ale."

"But I thought it was so unwholesome," said Jean-Marie, "and very dear besides."

"Fiddle-de-dee!" exclaimed the Doctor gaily. "To the inn!"

And he stepped into the noddy, tossing his head, with an elastic, youthful air. The horse was turned, and in a few seconds they drew up beside the palings of the inn garden.

"Here," said Desprez—"here, near the table, so that we may keep an eye upon things."

They tied the horse, and entered the garden, the Doctor singing, now in fantastic high notes, now producing deep reverberations from his chest. He took a seat; rapped loudly on the table, assailed the waiter with witticisms; and when the bottle of Bass was at length produced, far more charged with gas than the most delirious champagne, he filled out a long glassful of froth and pushed it over to Jean-Marie. "Drink," he said; "drink deep."

"I would rather not," faltered the boy, true to his training.

"What?" thundered Desprez.

"I am afraid of it," said Jean-Marie: "my stomach——"

"Take it or leave it," interrupted Desprez fiercely; "but understand it once for all—there is nothing so contemptible as a precisian."

Here was a new lesson! The boy sat bemused, looking at the glass but not tasting it, while the Doctor emptied and refilled his own, at first with clouded brow, but gradually yielding to the sun, the heady, prickling beverage, and his own predisposition to be happy.

"Once in a way," he said at last, by way of a concession to the boy's more rigorous attitude, "once in a way, and at so critical a moment, this ale is a nectar for the gods. The habit, indeed, is debasing; wine, the juice of the grape, is the true drink of the Frenchman, as I have often had occasion to point out; and I do not know that I can blame you for refusing this outlandish stimulant. You can have some wine and cakes. Is the bottle empty? Well, we will not be proud; we will have pity on your glass."

The beer being done, the Doctor chafed bitterly while Jean-Marie finished his cakes. "I burn to be gone," he said, looking at his watch. "Good God, how slow you eat!" And yet to eat slowly was his own particular prescription, the main secret of longevity!

His martyrdom, however, reached an end at last; the pair resumed their places in the buggy, and Desprez, leaning luxuriously back, announced his intention of proceeding to Fontainebleau.

"To Fontainebleau?" repeated Jean-Marie.

"My words are always measured," said the Doctor. "On!"

The Doctor was driven through the glades of paradise; the air, the light, the shining leaves, the very movements of the vehicle, seemed to fall in tune with his golden meditations; with his head thrown back, he dreamed a series of sunny visions, ale and pleasure dancing in his veins. At last he spoke.

"I shall telegraph for Casimir," he said. "Good Casimir! a fellow of the lower order of intelligence, Jean-Marie, distinctly not creative, not poetic; and yet he will repay your study; his fortune is vast, and is entirely due to his own exertions. He is the very fellow to help us to dispose of our trinkets, find us a suitable house in Paris, and manage the details of our installation. Admirable Casimir, one of my oldest comrades! It was on his advice, I may add, that I invested my little fortune in Turkish bonds; when we have added these spoils of the mediæval church to our stake in the Mahometan empire, little boy, we shall positively roll among doubloons, positively roll! Beautiful forest," he cried, "farewell! Though called to other scenes, I will not forget thee. Thy name is graven in my heart. Under the influence of prosperity I become dithyrambic, Jean-Marie. Such is the impulse of the natural soul; such was the constitution of primæval man. And I—well, I will not refuse the credit—I have preserved my youth like a virginity; another, who should have led the same snoozing, countryfied existence for these years, another had become rusted, become stereotype; but I, I praise my happy constitution, retain the spring unbroken. Fresh opulence and a new sphere of duties find me unabated in ardour and only more mature by knowledge. For this prospective change, Jean-Marie—it may probably have shocked you. Tell me now, did it not strike you as an inconsistency? Confess—it is useless to dissemble—it pained you?"

"Yes," said the boy.

"You see," returned the Doctor, with sublime fatuity, "I read your thoughts! Nor am I surprised—your education is not yet complete; the higher duties of men have not been yet presented to you fully. A hint—till we have leisure—must suffice. Now that I am once more in possession of a modest competence; now that I have so long prepared myself in silent meditation, it becomes my superior duty to proceed to Paris. My scientific training, my undoubted command of language, mark me out for the service of my country. Modesty in such a case would be a snare. If sin were a philosophical expression, I should call it sinful. A man must not deny his manifest abilities, for that is to evade his obligations. I must be up and doing; I must be no skulker in life's battle."

So he rattled on, copiously greasing the joint of his inconsistency with words; while the boy listened silently, his eyes fixed on the horse, his mind seething. It was all lost eloquence; no array of words could unsettle a belief of Jean-Marie's; and he drove into Fontainebleau filled with pity, horror, indignation, and despair.

In the town Jean-Marie was kept a fixture on the driving seat, to guard the treasure; while the Doctor, with a singular, slightly tipsy airiness of manner, fluttered in and out of cafés, where he shook hands with garrison officers, and mixed an absinthe with the nicety of old experience; in and out of shops, from which he returned laden with costly fruits, real turtle, a magnificent piece of silk for his wife, a preposterous cane for himself, and a képi of the newest fashion for the boy; in and out of the telegraph office, whence he despatched his telegram, and where three hours later he received an answer promising a visit on the morrow; and generally pervaded Fontainebleau with the first fine aroma of his divine good humour.

The sun was very low when they set forth again; the shadows of the forest trees extended across the broad white road that led them home; the penetrating odour of the evening wood had already arisen, like a cloud of incense, from that broad field of treetops; and even in the streets of the town, where the air had been baked all day between white walls, it came in whiffs and pulses, like a distant music. Halfway home, the last gold flicker vanished from a great oak upon the left; and when they came forth beyond the borders of the wood, the plain was already sunken in pearly greyness, and a great, pale moon came swinging skyward through the filmy poplars.

The Doctor sang, the Doctor whistled, the Doctor talked. He spoke of the woods, and the wars, and the deposition of dew; he brightened and babbled of Paris; he soared into cloudy bombast on the glories of the political arena. All was to be changed; as the day departed, it took with it the vestiges of an outworn existence, and tomorrow's sun was to inaugurate the new. "Enough," he cried, "of this life of maceration!" His wife (still beautiful, or he was sadly partial) was to be no longer buried; she should now shine before society. Jean Marie would find the world at his feet; the roads open to success, wealth, honour, and posthumous renown. "And O, by the way," said he, "for God's sake keep your tongue quiet! You are, of course, a very silent fellow; it is a quality I gladly recognise in you—silence, golden silence! But this is a matter of gravity. No word must get abroad; none but the good Casimir is to be trusted; we shall probably dispose of the vessels in England."

"But are they not even ours?" the boy said, almost with a sob—it was the only time he had spoken.

"Ours in this sense, that they are nobody else's," replied the Doctor. "But the State would have some claim. If they were stolen, for instance, we should be unable to demand their restitution; we should have no title; we should be unable even to communicate with the police. Such is the monstrous condition of the law.* It is a mere instance of what remains to be done, of the injustices that may yet be righted by an ardent, active, and philosophical deputy."

Jean-Marie put his faith in Madame Desprez; and as they drove forward down the road from Bourron, between the rustling poplars, he prayed in his teeth, and whipped up the horse to an unusual speed. Surely, as soon as they arrived, madame would assert her character, and bring this waking nightmare to an end.

Their entrance into Gretz was heralded and accompanied by a most furious barking; all the dogs in the village seemed to smell the treasure in the noddy. But there was no one in the street, save three lounging landscape painters at Tentaillon's door. Jean-Marie opened the green gate and led in the horse and carriage; and almost at the same moment Madame Desprez came to the kitchen threshold with a lighted lantern; for the moon was not yet high enough to clear the garden walls.

"Close the gates, Jean-Marie!" cried the Doctor, somewhat unsteadily alighting. "Anastasie, where is Aline?"

"She has gone to Montereau to see her parents," said madame.

"All is for the best!" exclaimed the Doctor fervently. "Here, quick, come near to me; I do not wish to speak too loud," he continued. "Darling, we are wealthy!"

"Wealthy!" repeated the wife.

"I have found the Treasure of Franchard," replied her husband. "See, here are the first fruits; a pineapple, a dress for my ever-beautiful—it will suit her—trust a husband's, trust a lover's, taste! Embrace me, darling! This grimy episode is over; the butterfly unfolds its painted wings. Tomorrow Casimir will come; in a week we may be in Paris—happy at last! You shall have diamonds. Jean-Marie, take it out of the boot, with religious care, and bring it piece by piece into the dining room. We shall have plate at table! Darling, hasten and prepare this turtle; it will be a whet—it will be an addition to our meagre ordinary. I myself will proceed to the cellar. We shall have a bottle of that little Beaujolais you like, and finish with the Hermitage; there are still three bottles left. Worthy wine for a worthy occasion."

*Let it be so, for my tale! [R.L.S.]

"But, my husband; you put me in a whirl," she cried. "I do not comprehend."

"The turtle, my adored, the turtle!" cried the doctor; and he pushed her towards the kitchen, lantern and all.

Jean-Marie stood dumfounded. He had pictured to himself a different scene—a more immediate protest, and his hope began to dwindle on the spot.

The Doctor was everywhere, a little doubtful on his legs, perhaps, and now and then taking the wall with his shoulder; for it was long since he had tasted absinthe, and he was even then reflecting that the absinthe had been a misconception. Not that he regretted excess on such a glorious day, but he made a mental memorandum to beware; he must not, a second time, become the victim of a deleterious habit. He had his wine out of the cellar in a twinkling; he arranged the sacrificial vessels, some on the white tablecloth, some on the sideboard, still crusted with historic earth. He was in and out of the kitchen, plying Anastasie with vermouth, heating her with glimpses of the future, estimating their new wealth at ever larger figures; and before they sat down to supper, the lady's virtue had melted in the fire of his enthusiasm, her timidity had disappeared; she, too, had begun to speak disparagingly of the life at Gretz; and as she took her place and helped the soup, her eyes shone with the glitter of prospective diamonds.

All through the meal, she and the Doctor made and unmade fairy plans. They bobbed and bowed and pledged each other. Their faces ran over with smiles; their eyes scattered sparkles, as they projected the Doctor's political honours and the lady's drawing-room ovations.

"But you will not be a Red!" cried Anastasie.

"I am Left Centre to the core," replied the Doctor.

"Madame Gastein will present us—we shall find ourselves forgotten," said the lady.

"Never," protested the Doctor. "Beauty and talent leave a mark."

"I have positively forgotten how to dress," she sighed.

"Darling, you make me blush," cried he. "Yours has been a tragic marriage!"

"But your success—to see you appreciated, honoured, your name in all the papers, that will be more than pleasure—it will be heaven!" she cried.

"And once a week," said the Doctor, archly scanning the syllables, "once a week—one good little game of baccarat?"

"Only once a week?" she questioned, threatening him with a finger.

"I swear it by my political honour," cried he.

"I spoil you," she said, and gave him her hand.

He covered it with kisses.

Jean-Marie escaped into the night. The moon swung high over Gretz. He went down to the garden end and sat on the jetty. The river ran by with eddies of oily silver, and a low, monotonous song. Faint veils of mist moved among the poplars on the farther side. The reeds were quietly nodding. A hundred times already had the boy sat, on such a night, and watched the streaming river with untroubled fancy. And this perhaps was to be the last. He was to leave this familiar hamlet, this green, rustling country, this bright and quiet stream; he was to pass into the great city; his dear lady mistress was to move bedizened in saloons; his good, garrulous, kind-hearted master to become a brawling deputy; and both be lost for ever to Jean-Marie and their better selves. He knew his own defects; he knew he must sink into less and less consideration in the turmoil of a city life, sink more and more from the child into the servant. And he began dimly to believe the Doctor's prophecies of evil. He could see a change in both. His generous incredulity failed him for this once; a child must have perceived that the Hermitage had completed what the absinthe had begun. If this were the first day, what would be the last? "If necessary, wreck the train," thought he, remembering the Doctor's parable. He looked round on the delightful scene; he drank deep of the charmed night air, laden with the scent of hay. "If necessary, wreck the train," he repeated. And he rose and returned to the house.

Chapter VI

A criminal investigation, in two parts

The next morning there was a most unusual outcry in the Doctor's house. The last thing before going to bed, the Doctor had locked up some valuables in the dining-room cupboard; and behold, when he rose again, as he did about four o'clock, the cupboard had been broken open, and the valuables in question had disappeared. Madame and Jean-Marie were summoned from their rooms, and appeared in hasty toilets; they found the Doctor raving, calling the heavens to witness and avenge his injury, pacing the room barefooted, with the tails of his nightshirt flirting as he turned.

"Gone!" he said; "the things are gone, the fortune gone! We are paupers once more. Boy! what do you know of this? Speak up, sir, speak up. Do you know of it? Where are they?" He had him by the arm, shaking him like a bag, and the boy's words, if he had any, were jolted forth in inarticulate murmurs. The Doctor, with a revulsion from his own violence, set him down again. He observed Anastasie in tears. "Anastasie," he said, in quite an altered voice, "compose yourself, command your feelings. I would not have you give way to passion like the vulgar. This—this trifling accident must be lived down. Jean-Marie, bring me my smaller medicine chest. A gentle laxative is indicated."

And he dosed the family all round, leading the way himself with a double quantity. The wretched Anastasie, who had never been ill in the whole course of her existence, and whose soul recoiled from remedies, wept floods of tears as she sipped, and shuddered, and protested, and then was bullied and shouted at until she sipped again. As for Jean-Marie, he took his portion down with stoicism.

"I have given him a less amount," observed the Doctor, "his youth protecting him against emotion. And now that we have thus parried any morbid consequences, let us reason."

"I am so cold," wailed Anastasie.

"Cold!" cried the Doctor. "I give thanks to God that I am made of fiercer material. Why, madam, a blow like this would set a frog into a transpiration. If you are cold, you can retire; and, by the way, you might throw me down my trousers. It is chilly for the legs."

"Oh, no!" protested Anastasie; "I will stay with you."

"Nay, madam, you shall not suffer for your devotion," said the Doctor. "I will myself fetch you a shawl." And he went upstairs and returned more fully clad and with an armful of wraps for the shivering Anastasie. "And now," he resumed, "to investigate this crime. Let us proceed by induction. Anastasie, do you know anything that can help us?" Anastasie knew nothing. "Or you, Jean-Marie?"

"Not I," replied the boy steadily.

"Good," returned the Doctor. "We shall now turn our attention to the material evidences. (I was born to be a detective; I have the eye and the systematic spirit.) First, violence has been employed. The door was broken open; and it may be observed, in passing, that the lock was dear indeed at what I paid for it: a crow to pluck with Master Goguelat. Second, here is the instrument employed, one of our own table knives, one of our best, my dear; which seems to indicate no preparation on the part of the gang—if gang it was. Thirdly, I observe that nothing has been removed except the Franchard dishes and the casket; our own silver has been minutely respected. This is wily; it shows intelligence, a knowledge of the code, a desire to avoid legal consequences. I argue from this fact that the gang numbers persons of respectability—outward, of course, and merely outward, as the robbery proves. But I argue, second, that we must have been observed at Franchard itself by some occult observer, and dogged throughout the day with a skill and patience that I venture to qualify as consummate. No ordinary man, no occasional criminal, would have shown himself capable of this combination. We have in our neighbourhood, it is far from improbable, a retired bandit of the highest order of intelligence."

"Good heaven!" cried the horrified Anastasie. "Henri, how can you?"

"My cherished one, this is a process of induction," said the Doctor. "If any of my steps are unsound, correct me. You are silent? Then do not, I beseech you, be so vulgarly illogical as to revolt from my conclusion. We have now arrived," he resumed, "at some idea of the composition of the gang—for I incline to the hypothesis of more than one—and we now leave this room, which can disclose no more, and turn our attention to the court and garden. (Jean-Marie, I trust you are observantly following my various steps; this is an excellent piece of education for you.) Come with me to the door. No steps on the court; it is unfortunate our court should be paved. On what small matters hang the destiny of these delicate investigations! Hey! What have we here? I have led you to the very spot," he said, standing grandly backward and indicating the green gate. "An escalade, as you can now see for yourselves, has taken place."

Sure enough, the green paint was in several places scratched and broken; and one of the panels preserved the print of a nailed shoe. The foot had slipped, however, and it was difficult to estimate the size of the shoe, and impossible to distinguish the pattern of the nails.

"The whole robbery," concluded the Doctor, "step by step, has been reconstituted. Inductive science can no further go."

"It is wonderful," said his wife. "You should indeed have been a detective, Henri. I had no idea of your talents."

"My dear," replied Desprez, condescendingly, "a man of scientific imagination combines the lesser faculties; he is a detective just as he is a publicist or a general; these are but local applications of his special talent. But now," he continued, "would you have me go further? Would you have me lay my finger on the culprits—or rather, for I cannot promise quite so much, point out to you the very house where they consort? It may be a satisfaction, at least it is all we are likely to get, since we are denied the remedy of law. I reach the further stage in this way. In order to fill my outline of the robbery, I require a man likely to be in the forest idling, I require a man of education, I require a man superior to considerations of morality. The three requisites all centre in Tentaillon's boarders. They are painters, therefore they are continually lounging in the forest. They are painters, therefore they are not unlikely to have some smattering of education. Lastly, because they are painters, they are probably immoral. And this I prove in two ways. First, painting is an art which merely addresses the eye; it does not in any particular exercise the moral sense. And second, painting, in common with all the other arts, implies the dangerous quality of imagination. A man of imagination is never moral; he outsoars literal demarcations and reviews life under too many shifting lights to rest content with the invidious distinctions of the law!"

"But you always say—at least, so I understood you"—said madame, "that these lads display no imagination whatever."

"My dear, they displayed imagination, and of a very fantastic order, too," returned the Doctor, "when they embraced their beggarly profession. Besides—and this is an argument exactly suited to your intellectual level—many of them are English and American. Where else should we expect to find a thief?—And now you had better get your coffee. Because we have lost a treasure, there is no reason for starving. For my part, I shall break my fast with white wine. I feel unaccountably heated and thirsty today. I can only attribute it to the shock of the discovery. And yet, you will bear me out, I supported the emotion nobly."

The Doctor had now talked himself back into an admirable humour; and as he sat in the arbour and slowly imbibed a large allowance of white wine and picked a little bread and cheese with no very impetuous appetite, if a third of his meditations ran upon the missing treasure, the other two-thirds were more pleasingly busied in the retrospect of his detective skill.

About eleven Casimir arrived; he had caught an early train to Fontainebleau, and driven over to save time; and now his cab was stabled at Tentaillon's, and he remarked, studying his watch, that he could spare an hour and a half. He was much the man of business, decisively spoken, given to frowning in an intellectual manner. Anastasie's born brother, he did not waste much sentiment on the lady, gave her an English family kiss, and demanded a meal without delay.

"You can tell me your story while we eat," he observed. "Anything good today, Stasie?"

He was promised something good. The trio sat down to table in the arbour, Jean-Marie waiting as well as eating, and the Doctor recounted what had happened in his richest narrative manner. Casimir heard it with explosions of laughter.

"What a streak of luck for you, my good brother," he observed, when the tale was over. "If you had gone to Paris, you would have played dick-duck-drake with the whole consignment in three months. Your own would have followed; and you would have come to me in a procession like the last time. But I give you warning—Stasie may weep and Henri ratiocinate—it will not serve you twice. Your next collapse will be fatal. I thought I had told you so, Stasie? Hey? No sense?"

The Doctor winced and looked furtively at Jean-Marie; but the boy seemed apathetic.

"And then again," broke out Casimir, "what children you are—vicious children, my faith! How could you tell the value of this trash? It might have been worth nothing, or next door."

"Pardon me," said the Doctor. "You have your usual flow of spirits, I perceive, but even less than your usual deliberation. I am not entirely ignorant of these matters."

"Not entirely ignorant of anything ever I heard of," interrupted Casimir, bowing, and raising his glass with a sort of pert politeness.

"At least," resumed the Doctor, "I gave my mind to the subject—that you may be willing to believe—and I estimated that our capital would be doubled." And he described the nature of the find.

"My word of honour!" said Casimir, "I half believe you! But much would depend on the quality of the gold."

"The quality, my dear Casimir, was——" And the Doctor, in default of language, kissed his finger-tips.

"I would not take your word for it, my good friend," retorted the man of business. "You are a man of very rosy views. But this robbery," he continued "this robbery is an odd thing. Of course I pass over your nonsense about gangs and landscape painters. For me, that is a dream. Who was in the house last night?"

"None but ourselves," replied the Doctor.

"And this young gentleman?" asked Casimir, jerking a nod in the direction of Jean-Marie.

"He too"—the Doctor bowed.

"Well; and, if it is a fair question, who is he?" pursued the brother-in-law.

"Jean-Marie," answered the Doctor, "combines the functions of a son and stable boy. He began as the latter, but he rose rapidly to the more honourable rank in our affections. He is, I may say, the greatest comfort in our lives."

"Ha!" said Casimir. "And previous to becoming one of you?"

"Jean-Marie has lived a remarkable existence; his experience has been eminently formative," replied Desprez. "If I had had to choose an education for my son, I should have chosen such another. Beginning life with mountebanks and thieves, passing onward to the society and friendship of philosophers, he may be said to have skimmed the volume of human life."

"Thieves?" repeated the brother-in-law, with a meditative air.

The Doctor could have bitten his tongue out. He foresaw what was coming, and prepared his mind for a vigorous defence.

"Did you ever steal yourself?" asked Casimir, turning suddenly on Jean-Marie, and for the first time employing a single eyeglass which hung round his neck.

"Yes, sir," replied the boy, with a deep blush.

Casimir turned to the others with pursed lips, and nodded to them meaningly. "Hey?" said he; "how is that?"

"Jean-Marie is a teller of the truth," returned the Doctor, throwing out his bust.

"He has never told a lie," added madame. "He is the best of boys."

"Never told a lie, has he not?" reflected Casimir. "Strange, very strange. Give me your attention, my young friend," he continued. "You knew about this treasure?"

"He helped to bring it home," interposed the Doctor.

"Desprez, I ask you nothing but to hold your tongue," returned Casimir. "I mean to question this stable boy of yours; and if you are so certain of his innocence, you can afford to let him answer for himself. Now, sir," he resumed, pointing his eyeglass straight at Jean-Marie. "You knew it could be stolen with impunity? You knew you could not be prosecuted? Come! Did you, or did you not?"

"I did," answered Jean-Marie, in a miserable whisper. He sat there changing colour like a revolving pharos, twisting his fingers hysterically, swallowing air, the picture of guilt.

"You knew where it was put?" resumed the inquisitor.

"Yes," from Jean-Marie.

"You say you have been a thief before," continued Casimir. "Now how am I to know that you are not one still? I suppose you could climb the green gate?"

"Yes," still lower, from the culprit.

"Well, then, it was you who stole these things. You know it, and you dare not deny it. Look me in the face! Raise your sneak's eyes, and answer!"

But in place of anything of that sort Jean-Marie broke into a dismal howl and fled from the arbour. Anastasie, as she pursued to capture and reassure the victim, found time to send one Parthian arrow— "Casimir, you are a brute!"

"My brother," said Desprez, with the greatest dignity, "you take upon yourself a licence———"

"Desprez," interrupted Casimir, "for Heaven's sake be a man of the world. You telegraph me to leave my business and come down here on yours. I come, I ask the business, you say 'Find me this thief!' Well, I find him; I say 'There he is!' You need not like it, but you have no manner of right to take offence."

"Well," returned the Doctor, "I grant that; I will even thank you for your mistaken zeal. But your hypothesis was so extravagantly monstrous———"

"Look here," interrupted Casimir; "was it you or Stasie?"

"Certainly not," answered the Doctor.

"Very well; then it was the boy. Say no more about it," said the brother-in-law, and he produced his cigar case.

"I will say this much more," returned Desprez: "if that boy came and told me so himself, I should not believe him; and if I did believe him, so implicit is my trust, I should conclude that he had acted for the best."

"Well, well," said Casimir, indulgently. "Have you a light? I must be going. And by the way, I wish you would let me sell your Turks for you. I always told you, it meant smash. I tell you so again. Indeed, it was partly that that brought me down. You never acknowledge my letters—a most unpardonable habit."

"My good brother," replied the Doctor blandly, "I have never denied your ability in business; but I can perceive your limitations."

"Egad, my friend, I can return the compliment," observed the man of business. "Your limitation is to be downright irrational."

"Observe the relative position," returned the Doctor with a smile. "It is your attitude to believe through thick and thin in one man's judgment—your own. I follow the same opinion, but critically and with open eyes. Which is the more irrational?—I leave it to yourself."

"O, my dear fellow!" cried Casimir, "stick to your Turks, stick to your stable boy, go to the devil in general in your own way and be done with it. But don't ratiocinate with me—I cannot bear it. And so, ta-ta. I might as well have stayed away for any good I've done. Say good-bye from me to Stasie, and to the sullen hang-dog of a stable boy, if you insist on it; I'm off."

And Casimir departed. The Doctor, that night, dissected his character before Anastasie. "One thing, my beautiful," he said, "he has learned one thing from his lifelong acquaintance with your husband: the word *ratiocinate*. It shines in his vocabulary, like a jewel in a muck-heap. And, even so, he continually misapplies it. For you must have observed he uses it as a sort of taunt, in the sense of *to ergotise*, implying, as it were—the poor, dear fellow!—a vein of sophistry. As for his cruelty to Jean-Marie, it must be forgiven him—it is not his nature, it is the nature of his life. A man who deals with money, my dear, is a man lost."

With Jean-Marie the process of reconciliation had been somewhat slow. At first he was inconsolable, insisted on leaving the family, went from paroxysm to paroxysm of tears; and it was only after Anastasie had been closeted for an hour with him, alone, that she came forth, sought out the Doctor, and, with tears in her eyes, acquainted that gentleman with what had passed.

"At first, my husband, he would hear of nothing," she said. "Imagine! if he had left us! what would the treasure be to that? Horrible treasure, it has brought all this about! At last, after he has sobbed his very heart out, he agrees to stay on a condition—we are not to mention this matter, this infamous suspicion, not even to mention the robbery. On that agreement only, the poor, cruel boy will consent to remain among his friends."

"But this inhibition," said the Doctor, "this embargo—it cannot possibly apply to me?"

"To all of us," Anastasie assured him.

"My cherished one," Desprez protested, "you must have misunderstood. It cannot apply to me. He would naturally come to me."

"Henri," she said, "it does; I swear to you it does."

"This is a painful, a very painful circumstance," the Doctor said, looking a little black. "I cannot affect, Anastasie, to be anything but justly wounded. I feel this, I feel it, my wife, acutely."

"I knew you would," she said. "But if you had seen his distress! We must make allowances, we must sacrifice our feelings."

"I trust, my dear, you have never found me averse to sacrifices," returned the Doctor very stiffly.

"And you will let me go and tell him that you have agreed? It will be like your noble nature," she cried.

So it would, he perceived—it would be like his noble nature! Up jumped his spirits, triumphant at the thought. "Go, darling," he said nobly, "reassure him. The subject is buried; more—I make an effort, I have accustomed my will to these exertions—and it is forgotten."

A little after, but still with swollen eyes and looking mortally sheepish, Jean-Marie reappeared and went ostentatiously about his business. He was the only unhappy member of the party that sat down that night to supper. As for the Doctor, he was radiant. He thus sang the requiem of the treasure:—

"This has been, on the whole, a most amusing episode," he said. "We are not a penny the worse—nay, we are immensely gainers. Our philosophy has been exercised; some of the turtle is still left—the most wholesome of delicacies; I have my staff, Anastasie has her new dress,

Jean-Marie is the proud possessor of a fashionable képi. Besides, we had a glass of Hermitage last night; the glow still suffuses my memory. I was growing positively niggardly with that Hermitage, positively niggardly. Let me take the hint: we had one bottle to celebrate the appearance of our visionary fortune; let us have a second to console us for its occultation. The third I hereby dedicate to Jean-Marie's wedding breakfast."

CHAPTER VII

The fall of the house of Desprez.

The Doctor's house has not yet received the compliment of a description, and it is now high time that the omission were supplied, for the house is itself an actor in the story, and one whose part is nearly at an end. Two stories in height, walls of a warm yellow, tiles of an ancient ruddy brown diversified with moss and lichen, it stood with one wall to the street in the angle of the Doctor's property. It was roomy, draughty, and inconvenient. The large rafters were here and there engraven with rude marks and patterns; the handrail of the stair was carved in countrified arabesque; a stout timber pillar, which did duty to support the dining room roof, bore mysterious characters on its darker side, runes, according to the Doctor; nor did he fail, when he ran over the legendary history of the house and its possessors, to dwell upon the Scandinavian scholar who had left them. Floors, doors, and rafters made a great variety of angles; every room had a particular inclination; the gable had tilted towards the garden, after the manner of a leaning tower, and one of the former proprietors had buttressed the building from that side with a great strut of wood, like the derrick of a crane. Altogether, it had many marks of ruin; it was a house for the rats to desert; and nothing but its excellent brightness—the window-glass polished and shining, the paint well scoured, the brasses radiant, the very prop all wreathed about with climbing flowers—nothing but its air of a well-tended, smiling veteran, sitting, crutch and all, in the sunny corner of a garden, marked it as a house for comfortable people to inhabit. In poor or idle management it would soon have hurried into the blackguard stages of decay. As it was, the whole family loved it, and the Doctor was never better inspired than when he narrated its imaginary story and drew the character of its successive masters, from the Hebrew merchant who had re-edified its walls after the sack of the town, and past the mysterious engraver of the runes, down to the long-headed, dirty-handed boor from whom he had himself acquired it at a ruinous expense. As for any alarm about its security, the idea had never presented itself. What had stood four centuries might well endure a little longer.

Indeed, in this particular winter, after the finding and losing of the treasure, the Desprez' had an anxiety of a very different order, and one which lay nearer their hearts. Jean-Marie was plainly not himself. He had fits of hectic activity, when he made unusual exertions to please, spoke more and faster, and redoubled in attention to his lessons. But these were interrupted by spells of melancholia and brooding silence, when the boy was little better than unbearable.

"Silence," the Doctor moralised—"you see, Anastasie, what comes of silence. Had the boy properly unbosomed himself, the little disappointment about the treasure, the little annoyance about Casimir's incivility, would long ago have been forgotten. As it is, they prey upon him like a disease. He loses flesh, his appetite is variable and, on the whole, impaired. I keep him on the strictest regimen, I exhibit the most powerful tonics; both in vain."

"Don't you think you drug him too much?" asked madame, with an irrepressible shudder.

"Drug?" cried the Doctor; "I drug? Anastasie, you are mad!"

Time went on, and the boy's health still slowly declined. The Doctor blamed the weather, which was cold and boisterous. He called in his *confrère* from Bourron, took a fancy for him, magnified his capacity, and was pretty soon under treatment himself—it scarcely appeared for what complaint. He and Jean-Marie had each medicine to take at different periods of the day. The Doctor used to lie in wait for the exact moment, watch in hand. "There is nothing like regularity," he would say, fill out the doses, and dilate on the virtues of the draught; and if the boy seemed none the better, the Doctor was not at all the worse.

Gunpowder Day, the boy was particularly low. It was scowling, squally weather. Huge broken companies of cloud sailed swiftly overhead; raking gleams of sunlight swept the village, and were followed by intervals of darkness and white, flying rain. At times the wind lifted up its voice and bellowed. The trees were all scourging themselves along the meadows, the last leaves flying like dust.

The Doctor, between the boy and the weather, was in his element; he had a theory to prove. He sat with his watch out and a barometer in front of him, waiting for the squalls and noting their effect upon the human pulse. "For the true philosopher," he remarked delightedly, "every fact in nature is a toy." A letter came to him; but, as its arrival coincided with the approach of another gust, he merely crammed it into his pocket, gave the time to Jean-Marie, and the next moment they were both counting their pulses as if for a wager.

At nightfall the wind rose into a tempest. It besieged the hamlet, apparently from every side, as if with batteries of cannon; the houses shook and groaned; live coals were blown upon the floor. The uproar and terror of the night kept people long awake, sitting with pallid faces giving ear.

It was twelve before the Desprez family retired. By half-past one, when the storm was already somewhat past its height, the Doctor was awakened from a troubled slumber, and sat up. A noise still rang in his ears, but whether of this world or the world of dreams he was not certain. Another clap of wind followed. It was accompanied by a sickening movement of the whole house, and in the subsequent lull Desprez could hear the tiles pouring like a cataract into the loft above his head. He plucked Anastasie bodily out of bed.

"Run!" he cried, thrusting some wearing apparel into her hands; "the house is falling! To the garden!"

She did not pause to be twice bidden; she was down the stair in an instant. She had never before suspected herself of such activity. The Doctor meanwhile, with the speed of a piece of pantomime business, and undeterred by broken shins, proceeded to rout out Jean-Marie, tore Aline from her virgin slumbers, seized her by the hand, and tumbled downstairs and into the garden, with the girl tumbling behind him, still not half awake.

The fugitives rendezvous'd in the arbour by some common instinct. Then came a bull's-eye flash of struggling moonshine, which disclosed their four figures standing huddled from the wind in a raffle of flying drapery, and not without a considerable need for more. At the humiliating spectacle Anastasie clutched her nightdress desperately about her and burst loudly into tears. The Doctor flew to console her; but she elbowed him away. She suspected everybody of being the general public, and thought the darkness was alive with eyes.

Another gleam and another violent gust arrived together; the house was seen to rock on its foundation, and, just as the light was once more eclipsed, a crash which triumphed over the shouting of the wind announced its fall, and for a moment the whole garden was alive with skipping tiles and brickbats. One such missile grazed the Doctor's ear; another descended on the bare foot of Aline, who instantly made night hideous with her shrieks.

By this time the hamlet was alarmed, lights flashed from the windows, hails reached the party, and the Doctor answered, nobly contending against Aline and the tempest. But this prospect of help only awakened Anastasie to a more active stage of terror.

"Henri, people will be coming," she screamed in her husband's ear.

"I trust so," he replied.

"They cannot. I would rather die," she wailed.

"My dear," said the Doctor reprovingly, "you are excited. I gave you some clothes. What have you done with them?"

"Oh, I don't know—I must have thrown them away! Where are they?" she sobbed.

Desprez groped about in the darkness. "Admirable!" he remarked; "my grey velveteen trousers! This will exactly meet your necessities."

"Give them to me!" she cried fiercely; but as soon as she had them in her hands her mood appeared to alter—she stood silent for a moment, and then pressed the garment back upon the Doctor. "Give it to Aline," she said—"poor girl."

"Nonsense!" said the Doctor. "Aline does not know what she is about. Aline is beside herself with terror; and at any rate, she is a peasant. Now I am really concerned at this exposure for a person of your housekeeping habits; my solicitude and your fantastic modesty both point to the same remedy—the pantaloons." He held them ready.

"It is impossible. You do not understand," she said with dignity.

By this time rescue was at hand. It had been found impracticable to enter by the street, for the gate was blocked with masonry, and the nodding ruin still threatened further avalanches. But between the Doctor's garden and the one on the right hand there was that very picturesque contrivance—a common well; the door on the Desprez' side had chanced to be unbolted, and now, through the arched aperture a man's bearded face and an arm supporting a lantern were introduced into the world of windy darkness, where Anastasie concealed her woes. The light struck here and there among the tossing apple boughs, it glinted on the grass; but the lantern and the glowing face became the centre of the world. Anastasie crouched back from the intrusion.

"This way!" shouted the man. "Are you all safe?"

Aline, still screaming, ran to the newcomer, and was presently hauled head-foremost through the wall.

"Now, Anastasie, come on; it is your turn," said the husband.

"I cannot," she replied.

"Are we all to die of exposure, madame?" thundered Doctor Desprez.

"You can go!" she cried. "Oh, go, go away! I can stay here; I am quite warm."

The Doctor took her by the shoulders with an oath.

"Stop!" she screamed. "I will put them on."

She took the detested lendings in her hand once more; but her repulsion was stronger than shame. "Never!" she cried, shuddering, and flung them far away into the night.

Next moment the Doctor had whirled her to the well. The man was there and the lantern; Anastasie closed her eyes and appeared to herself to be about to die. How she was transported through the arch she knew not; but once on the other side she was received by the neighbour's wife, and enveloped in a friendly blanket.

Beds were made ready for the two women, clothes of very various sizes for the Doctor and Jean-Marie; and for the remainder of the night, while madame dozed in and out on the borderland of hysterics, her husband sat beside the fire and held forth to the admiring neighbours. He showed them, at length, the causes of the accident; for years, he explained, the fall had been impending; one sign had followed another, the joints had opened, the plaster had cracked, the old walls bowed inward; last, not three weeks ago, the cellar door had begun to work with difficulty in its grooves. "The cellar!" he said, gravely shaking his head over a glass of mulled wine. "That reminds me of my poor vintages. By a manifest providence the Hermitage was nearly at an end. One bottle—I lose but one bottle of that incomparable wine. It had been set apart against Jean-Marie's wedding. Well, I must lay down some more; it will be an interest in life. I am, however, a man somewhat advanced in years. My great work is now buried in the fall of my humble roof; it will never be completed—my name will have been writ in water. And yet you find me calm—I would say cheerful. Can your priest do more?"

By the first glimpse of day the party sallied forth from the fireside into the street. The wind had fallen, but still charioted a world of troubled clouds; the air bit like frost; and the party, as they stood about the ruins in the rainy twilight of the morning, beat upon their breasts and blew into their hands for warmth. The house had entirely fallen, the walls outward, the roof in; it was a mere heap of rubbish, with here and there a forlorn spear of broken rafter. A sentinel was placed over the ruins to protect the property, and the party adjourned to Tentaillon's to break their fast at the Doctor's expense. The bottle circulated somewhat freely; and before they left the table it had begun to snow.

For three days the snow continued to fall, and the ruins, covered with tarpaulin and watched by sentries, were left undisturbed. The Desprez' meanwhile had taken up their abode at Tentaillon's. Madame spent her time in the kitchen, concocting little delicacies, with the admiring aid of Madame Tentaillon, or sitting by the fire in thoughtful abstraction. The fall of the house affected her wonderfully little; that blow had been parried by another; and in her mind she was continually fighting over again the battle of the trousers. Had she done right? Had she done wrong? And now she would applaud her determination; and anon, with a horrid flush of unavailing penitence, she would regret the trousers. No juncture in her life had so much exercised her judgment. In the meantime the Doctor had become vastly pleased with his situation. Two of the summer boarders still lingered behind the rest, prisoners for lack of a remittance; they were both English, but one of them spoke French pretty fluently, and was, besides, a humorous, agile-minded fellow, with whom the Doctor could reason by the hour, secure of comprehension. Many were the glasses they emptied, many the topics they discussed.

"Anastasie," the Doctor said on the third morning, "take an example from your husband, from Jean-Marie! The excitement has done more for the boy than all my tonics, he takes his turn as sentry with positive gusto. As for me, you behold me. I have made friends with the Egyptians; and my Pharaoh is, I swear it, a most agreeable companion. You alone are hipped. About a house—a few dresses? What are they in comparison to the 'Pharmacopœia'—the labour of years lying buried below stones and sticks in this depressing hamlet? The snow falls; I shake it from my cloak! Imitate me. Our income will be impaired, I grant it, since we must rebuild; but moderation, patience, and philosophy will gather about the hearth. In the meanwhile, the Tentaillons are obliging; the table, with your additions, will pass; only the wine is execrable—well, I shall send for some today. My Pharaoh will be gratified to drink a decent glass; aha! and I shall see if he possesses that acme of organisation—a palate. If he has a palate, he is perfect."

"Henri," she said, shaking her head, "you are a man; you cannot understand my feelings; no woman could shake off the memory of so public a humiliation."

The Doctor could not restrain a titter. "Pardon me, darling," he said; "but really, to the philosophical intelligence, the incident appears so small a trifle. You looked extremely well——"

"Henri!" she cried.

"Well, well, I will say no more," he replied. "Though, to be sure, if you had consented to indue—*À propos*," he broke off, "and my trousers! They are lying in the snow—my favourite trousers!" And he dashed in quest of Jean-Marie.

Two hours afterwards the boy returned to the inn with a spade under one arm and a curious sop of clothing under the other.

The Doctor ruefully took it in his hands. "They have been!" he said. "Their tense is past. Excellent pantaloons, you are no more! Stay, something in the pocket," and he produced a piece of paper. "A letter! ay, now I mind me; it was received on the morning of the gale, when I was absorbed in delicate investigations. It is still legible. From poor, dear Casimir! It is as well," he chuckled, "that I have educated him to patience. Poor Casimir and his correspondence—his infinitesimal, timorous, idiotic correspondence!"

He had by this time cautiously unfolded the wet letter; but, as he bent himself to decipher the writing, a cloud descended on his brow.

"Bigre!" he cried, with a galvanic start.

And then the letter was whipped into the fire, and the Doctor's cap was on his head in the turn of a hand.

"Ten minutes! I can catch it, if I run," he cried. "It is always late. I go to Paris. I shall telegraph."

"Henri! what is wrong?" cried his wife.

"Ottoman Bonds!" came from the disappearing Doctor; and Anastasie and Jean-Marie were left face to face with the wet trousers. Desprez had gone to Paris, for the second time in seven years; he had gone to Paris with a pair of wooden shoes, a knitted spencer, a black blouse, a country nightcap, and twenty francs in his pocket. The fall of the house was but a secondary marvel; the whole world might have fallen and scarce left his family more petrified.

Chapter VIII

The wages of philosophy

On the morning of the next day, the Doctor, a mere spectre of himself, was brought back in the custody of Casimir. They found Anastasie and the boy sitting together by the fire; and Desprez, who had exchanged his toilette for a ready-made rig-out of poor materials, waved his hand as he entered, and sank speechless on the nearest chair. Madame turned direct to Casimir.

"What is wrong?" she cried.

"Well," replied Casimir, "what have I told you all along? It has come. It is a clean shave, this time; so you may as well bear up and make the best of it. House down, too, eh? Bad luck, upon my soul."

"Are we—are we—ruined?" she gasped.

The Doctor stretched out his arms to her. "Ruined," he replied, "you are ruined by your sinister husband."

Casimir observed the consequent embrace through his eyeglass; then he turned to Jean-Marie. "You hear?" he said. "They are ruined; no more pickings, no more house, no more fat cutlets. It strikes me, my friend, that you had best be packing; the present speculation is about worked out." And he nodded to him meaningly.

"Never!" cried Desprez, springing up. "Jean-Marie, if you prefer to leave me, now that I am poor, you can go; you shall receive your hundred francs, if so much remains to me. But if you will consent to stay"—the Doctor wept a little—"Casimir offers me a place—as clerk," he resumed. "The emoluments are slender, but they will be enough for three. It is too much already to have lost my fortune; must I lose my son?"

Jean-Marie sobbed bitterly, but without a word.

"I don't like boys who cry," observed Casimir. "This one is always crying. Here! you clear out of this for a little; I have business with your master and mistress, and these domestic feelings may be settled after I am gone. March!" and he held the door open.

Jean-Marie slunk out, like a detected thief.

By twelve they were all at table but Jean-Marie.

"Hey?" said Casimir. "Gone, you see. Took the hint at once."

"I do not, I confess," said Desprez, "I do not seek to excuse his absence. It speaks a want of heart that disappoints me sorely."

"Want of manners," corrected Casimir. "Heart, he never had. Why, Desprez, for a clever fellow, you are the most gullible mortal in creation. Your ignorance of human nature and human business is beyond belief. You are swindled by heathen Turks, swindled by vagabond children, swindled right and left, upstairs and downstairs. I think it must be your imagination. I thank my stars I have none."

"Pardon me," replied Desprez, still humbly, but with a return of spirit at sight of a distinction to be drawn; "pardon me, Casimir. You possess, even to an eminent degree, the commercial imagination. It was the lack of that in me—it appears it is my weak point—that has led to these repeated shocks. By the commercial imagination the financier forecasts the destiny of his investments, marks the falling house——"

"Egad," interrupted Casimir: "our friend the stable boy appears to have his share of it."

The Doctor was silenced; and the meal was continued and finished principally to the tune of the brother-in-law's not very consolatory conversation. He entirely ignored the two young English painters, turning a blind eyeglass to their salutations, and continuing his remarks as if he were alone in the bosom of his family; and with every second word he ripped another stitch out of the air balloon of Desprez's vanity. By the time coffee was over the poor Doctor was as limp as a napkin.

"Let us go and see the ruins," said Casimir.

They strolled forth into the street. The fall of the house, like the loss of a front tooth, had quite transformed the village. Through the gap the eye commanded a great stretch of open snowy country, and the place shrank in comparison. It was like a room with an open door. The sentinel stood by the green gate, looking very red and cold, but he had a pleasant word for the Doctor and his wealthy kinsman.

Casimir looked at the mound of ruins, he tried the quality of the tarpaulin. "H'm," he said, "I hope the cellar arch has stood. If it has, my good brother, I will give you a good price for the wines."

"We shall start digging tomorrow," said the sentry. "There is no more fear of snow."

"My friend," returned Casimir sententiously, "you had better wait till you get paid."

The Doctor winced, and began dragging his offensive brother-in-law towards Tentaillon's. In the house there would be fewer auditors, and these already in the secret of his fall.

"Hullo!" cried Casimir, "there goes the stable boy with his luggage; no, egad, he is taking it into the inn."

And sure enough, Jean-Marie was seen to cross the snowy street and enter Tentaillon's, staggering under a large hamper.

The Doctor stopped with a sudden, wild hope.

"What can he have?" he said. "Let us go and see." And he hurried on.

"His luggage, to be sure," answered Casimir. "He is on the move—thanks to the commercial imagination."

"I have not seen that hamper for—for ever so long," remarked the Doctor.

"Nor will you see it much longer," chuckled Casimir; "unless, indeed, we interfere. And by the way, I insist on an examination."

"You will not require," said Desprez, positively with a sob; and, casting a moist, triumphant glance at Casimir, he began to run.

"What the devil is up with him, I wonder?" Casimir reflected; and then, curiosity taking the upper hand, he followed the Doctor's example and took to his heels.

The hamper was so heavy and large, and Jean-Marie himself so little and so weary, that it had taken him a great while to bundle it upstairs to the Desprez' private room; and he had just set it down on the floor in front of Anastasie, when the Doctor arrived, and was closely followed by the man of business. Boy and hamper were both in a most sorry plight; for the one had passed four months underground in a certain cave on the way to Achères, and the other had run about five miles as hard as his legs would carry him, half that distance under a staggering weight.

"Jean-Marie," cried the Doctor, in a voice that was only too seraphic to be called hysterical, "is it——? It is!" he cried. "O, my son, my son!" And he sat down upon the hamper and sobbed like a little child.

"You will not go to Paris now," said Jean-Marie sheepishly.

"Casimir," said Desprez, raising his wet face, "do you see that boy, that angel boy? He is the thief; he took the treasure from a man unfit to be entrusted with its use; he brings it back to me when I am sobered and humbled. These, Casimir, are the Fruits of my Teaching, and this moment is the Reward of my Life."

"*Tiens,*" said Casimir.

Binding for the English edition of
Island Nights' Entertainments (LONDON, 1893).

ISLAND NIGHTS'
ENTERTAINMENTS

THE BEACH OF FALESÁ

To Three Old Shipmates among the Islands

Harry Henderson
Ben Hird
Jack Buckland

Their Friend
R.L.S.

CHAPTER I

A South Sea Bridal

I saw that island first when it was neither night nor morning. The moon was to the west, setting but still broad and bright. To the east, and right amidships of the dawn, which was all pink, the daystar sparkled like a diamond. The land breeze blew in our faces and smellt strong of wild lime and vanilla: other things besides, but these were the most plain; and the chill of it set me sneezing. I should say I had been for years on a low island near the line, living for the most part solitary among natives. Here was a fresh experience; even the tongue would be quite strange to me; and the look of these woods and mountains, and the rare smell of them, renewed my blood.

The captain blew out the binnacle lamp.

"There," said he, "there goes a bit of smoke, Mr Wiltshire, behind the break of the reef. That's Falesá where your station is, the last village to the east; nobody lives to windward, I don't know why. Take my glass, and you can make the houses out."

I took the glass; and the shores leaped nearer, and I saw the tangle of the woods and the breach of the surf, and the brown roofs and the black insides of houses peeped among the trees.

"Do you catch a bit of white there to the east'ard?" the captain continued. "That's your house. Coral built, stands high, verandah you could walk on three abreast: best station in the South Pacific. When old Adams saw it, he took and shook me by the hand.—'I've dropped into a soft thing here,' says he.—'So you have,' says I, 'and time too!' Poor Johnny! I never saw him again but the once, and then he had changed his tune—couldn't get on with the natives, or the whites, or something; and the next time we came round, there he was dead and buried. I took and put up a bit of a stick to him: 'John Adams, *obit* eighteen and sixty eight. Go thou and do likewise.' I missed that man; I never could see much harm in Johnny."

"What did he die of?" I inquired.

"Some kind of a sickness," says the captain. "It appears it took him sudden. Seems he got up in the night, and filled up on PainKiller and Kennedy's Discovery: no go—he was booked beyond Kennedy. Then he had tried to open a case of gin; no go again—not strong enough. Then he must have turned to and run out on the verandah, and capsized over the rail. When they found him the next day, he was clean crazy—carried on all the time about somebody watering his copra. Poor John!"

"Was it thought to be the island?" I asked.

"Well, it was thought to be the island, or the trouble, or something," he replied. "I never could hear but what it was a healthy place. Our last man, Vigours, never turned a hair. He left because of the beach; said he was afraid of Black Jack and Case and Whistling Jimmie, who was still alive at the time but got drowned soon afterward when drunk. As for old Captain Randall, he's been here any time since eighteen forty, forty five. I never could see much harm in Billy, nor much change. Seems as if he might live to be old Kafoozleum. No, I guess its healthy."

"There's a boat coming now," said I. "She's right in the pass; looks to be a sixteen foot whale; two white men in the stern sheets."

"That's the boat that drowned Whistling Jimmie!" cried the captain. "Let's see the glass. Yes: that's Case, sure enough, and the darkie. They've got a gallows bad reputation, but you know what a place the beach is for talking. My belief, that Whistling Jimmie was the worst of the trouble; and he's gone to glory, you see. What'll you bet they ain't after gin? Lay you five to two they take six cases."

Marriage scene from "The Beach of Falesá," *Island Nights' Entertainments.*
Illustration by Gordon Browne first appeared in the
Illustrated London News, July 2, 1892.

When these two traders came aboard I was pleased with the looks of them at once; or rather, with the looks of both, and the speech of one. I was sick for white neighbours after my four years at the line, which I always counted years of prison; getting tabooed, and going down to the Speak House to see and get it taken off; buying gin, and going on a break, and then repenting; sitting in my house at night with the lamp for company; or walking on the beach and wondering what kind of a fool to call myself for being where I was. There were no other whites upon my island; and when I sailed to the next, rough customers made the most of the society. Now to see these two when they came aboard, was a pleasure. One was a negro to be sure; but they were both rigged out smart in striped pyjamas and straw hats, and Case would have passed muster in a city. He was yellow and smallish; had a hawk's nose to his face, pale eyes, and his beard trimmed with scissors. No man knew his country, beyond he was of English speech; and it was clear he came of a good family and was splendidly educated. He was accomplished too; played the accordion first rate; and give him a piece of string or a cork or a pack of cards, and he could show you tricks equal to any professional. He could speak when he chose fit for a drawing room; and when he chose he could blaspheme worse than a Yankee boatswain and talk smut to sicken a kanaka. The way he thought would pay best at the moment, that was Case's way; and it always seemed to come natural and like as if he was born to it. He had the courage of a lion and the cunning of a rat; and if he's not in Hell today, there's no such place. I know but one good point to the man; that he was fond of his wife and kind to her. She was a Sāmoa woman, and dyed her hair red, Sāmoa style; and when he came to die (as I have to tell of) they found one strange thing, that he had made a will like a christian and the widow got the lot. All his, they said, and all Black Jack's, and the most of Billy Randall's in the bargain; for it was Case that kept the books. So she went off home in the schooner *Manu'a*, and does the lady to this day in her own place.

But of all this, on that first morning, I knew no more than a fly. Case used me like a gentleman and like a friend, made me welcome to Falesá, and put his services at my disposal, which was the more helpful from my ignorance of the native. All the early part of the day, we sat drinking better acquaintance in the cabin, and I never heard a man talk more to the point. There was no smarter trader, and none dodgier, in the islands. I remember one bit of advice he gave that morning, and one yarn he told. The bit of advice was this. "Whenever you get hold of any money," says he—"any christian money, I mean—the first thing to do is to fire it up to Sydney to the bank. It's only a temptation to a copra merchant; some day, he'll be in a row with the other traders, and he'll get his shirt out and buy copra with it. And the name of the man that buys copra with gold is Damfool," says he. That was the advice; and this was the yarn, which might have opened my eyes to the danger of that man for a neighbour, if I had been anyway suspicious. It seems Case was trading somewhere in the Ellices. There was a man Miller a Dutchman there, who had a strong hold with the natives and handled the bulk of what there was. Well one fine day a schooner got wrecked in the lagoon, and Miller bought her (the way these things are usually managed) for an old song, which was the ruin of him. For having a lot of trade on hand that had cost him practically nothing, what does he do but begin cutting rates? Case went round to the other traders. "Wants to lower prices?" says Case. "All right, then. He has five times the turn-over of any one of us; if buying at a loss is the game, he stands to lose five times more. Let's give him the bed rock; let's bilge the———!" And so they did, and five months after, Miller had to sell out his boat and station, and begin again somewhere in the Carolines.

All this talk suited me, and my new companion suited me, and I thought Falesá seemed to be the right kind of a place; and the more I drank, the lighter my heart. Our last trader had fled the place at half an hour's notice, taking a chance passage in a labour ship from up west; the captain, when he came, had found the station closed, the keys left with the native pastor, and a letter from the runaway confessing he was fairly frightened of his life. Since then the firm had not been represented and of course there was no cargo; the wind besides was fair, the captain hoped he could make his next island by dawn, with a good tide; and the business of landing my trade was gone about lively. There was no call for me to fool with it, Case said; nobody would touch my things, everyone was honest in Falesá, only about chickens or an odd knife or an odd stick of tobacco; and the best I could do was to sit quiet till the vessel left, then come straight to his house, see old Captain Randall, the father of the Beach, take pot luck, and go home to sleep when it got dark. So it was high noon, and the schooner was under way, before I set my foot on shore at Falesá.

I had a glass or two on board, I was just off a long cruise and the ground heaved under me like a ship's deck. The world was like all new painted; my foot went along to music; Falesá might have been Fiddler's Green, if there is such a place, and more's the pity if there isn't! It was good to foot the grass, to look aloft at the green mountains, to see the men with their green wreaths and the women in their bright dresses, red and blue. On we went, in the strong sun and the cool shadow, liking both; and all the children in the town came trotting after with their shaven heads and their brown bodies, and raising a thin kind of a cheer in our wake, like crowing poultry.

"By the by," says Case, "we must get you a wife."

"That's so," said I, "I had forgotten."

There was a crowd of girls about us, and I pulled myself up and looked among them like a Bashaw. They were all dressed out for the sake of the ship being in; and the women of Falesá are a handsome lot to see. If they have a fault, they are a trifle broad in the beam; and I was just thinking so when Case touched me.

"That's pretty," says he.

I saw one coming on the other side alone. She had been fishing; all she wore was a chemise, and it was wetted through, and a cutty sark at that. She was young and very slender for an island maid, with a long face, a high forehead, and a sly, strange, blindish look between a cat's and a baby's.

"Who's she?" said I. "She'll do."

"That's Uma," said Case, and he called her up and spoke to her in the native. I didn't know what he said; but when he was in the midst, she looked up at me quick and timid like a child dodging a blow; then down again; and presently smiled. She had a wide mouth, the lips and the chin cut like any statue's; and the smile came out for a moment and was gone. There she stood with her head bent and heard Case to an end; spoke back in the pretty Polynesian voice, looking him full in the face; heard him again in answer; and then with an obeisance started off. I had just a share of the bow, but never another shot of her eye; and there was no more word of smiling.

"I guess it's all right," said Case. "I guess you can have her. I'll make it square with the old lady. You can have your pick of the lot for a plug of tobacco," he added, sneering.

I suppose it was the smile stuck in my memory, for I spoke back sharp. "She doesn't look that sort," I cried.

"I don't know that she is," said Case. "I believe she's as right as the mail. Keeps to herself, don't go round with the gang, and that. O, no, don't you misunderstand me—Uma's on the square." He spoke eager I thought, and that surprised and pleased me. "Indeed," he went on, "I shouldn't make so sure of getting her, only she cottoned to the cut of your jib. All you have to do is to keep dark and let me work the mother my own way; and I'll bring the girl round to the captain's for the marriage."

I didn't care for the word marriage, and I said so.

"O, there's nothing to hurt in the marriage," says he. "Black Jack's the chaplain."

By this time we had come in view of the house of these three white men; for a negro is counted a white man—and so is a Chinese! a strange idea, but common in the islands. It was a board house with a strip of ricketty verandah. The store was to the front, with a counter, scales and the poorest possible display of trade: a case or two of tinned meats; a barrel of hard bread; a few bolts of cotton stuff, not to be compared with mine; the only thing well represented being the contraband—fire arms and liquor. "If these are my only rivals," thinks I, "I should do well in Falesá." Indeed there was only the one way they could touch me, and that was with the guns and drink.

In the back room was old Captain Randall, squatting on the floor native fashion, fat and pale, naked to the waist, gray as a badger and his eyes set with drink. His body was covered with gray hair and crawled over by flies; one was in the corner of his eye—he never heeded; and the mosquitoes hummed about the man like bees. Any clean-minded man would have had the creature out at once and buried him; and to see him, and think he was seventy, and remember he had once commanded a ship, and come ashore in his smart togs, and talked big in bars and consulates, and sat in club verandahs, turned me sick and sober.

He tried to get up when I came in, but that was hopeless; so he reached me a hand instead and stumbled out some salutation.

"Papa's pretty full this morning," observed Case. "We've had an epidemic here; and Captain Randall takes gin for a prophylactic—don't you, papa?"

"Never took such thing my life!" cried the captain, indignantly. "Take gin for my health's sake, Mr Wha's-ever-your-name. 'S a precaution'ry measure."

"That's all right, papa," said Case. "But you'll have to brace up. There's going to be a marriage, Mr Wiltshire here is going to get spliced."

The old man asked to whom.

"To Uma," said Case.

"Uma?" cried the captain. "Wha's he want Uma for? 'S he come here for his health, anyway? Wha' 'n hell's he want Uma for?"

"Dry up papa," said Case. "'Tain't you that's to marry her. I guess you're not her godfather and godmother; I guess Mr Wiltshire's going to please himself."

With that he made an excuse to me that he must move about the marriage, and left me alone with the poor wretch that was his partner and (to speak truth) his gull. Trade and station belonged both to Randall; Case and the negro were parasites; they crawled and fed upon him like the flies, he none the wiser. Indeed I have no harm to say of Billy Randall, beyond the fact that my gorge rose at him, and the time I now passed in his company was like a nightmare.

The room was stifling hot and full of flies; for the house was dirty and low and small, and stood in a bad place, behind the village, in the borders of the bush, and sheltered from the trade. The three men's beds were on the floor, and a litter of pans and dishes. There was no standing furniture, Randall, when he was violent, tearing it to laths. There I sat, and had a meal which was served us by Case's wife; and there I was entertained all day by that remains of man, his tongue stumbling among low old jokes and long old stories, and his own wheezy laughter always ready, so that he had no sense of my depression. He was nipping gin all the while; sometimes he fell asleep and awoke again whimpering and shivering; and every now and again he would ask me why in Hell I wanted to marry Uma. "My friend," I was telling myself all day, "you must not be an old gentleman like this."

It might be four in the afternoon perhaps, when the backdoor was thrust slowly open, and a strange old native woman crawled into the house almost on her belly. She was swathed in black stuff to her heels; her hair was gray in swatches; her face was tattooed, which was not the practise in that island; her eyes big and bright and crazy. These she fixed upon me with a wrapt expression that I saw to be part acting; she said no plain word, but smacked and mumbled with her lips, and hummed aloud, like a child over its Christmas pudding. She came straight across the house heading for me, and as soon as she was alongside, caught up my hand and purred and crooned over it like a great cat. From this she slipped into a kind of song.

"Who in the devil's this?" cried I, for the thing startled me.

"It's Faavao," says Randall, and I saw he had hitched along the floor into the farthest corner.

"You ain't afraid of her?" I cried.

"Me 'fraid!" cried the captain. "My dear friend, I defy her! I don't let her put her foot in here. Only I suppose 's diff'ent today for the marriage. 'S Uma's mother."

"Well, suppose it is, what's she carrying on about?" I asked, more irritated, perhaps more frightened than I cared to show; and the captain told me she was making up a quantity of poetry in my praise because I was to marry Uma. "All right, old lady," says I, with rather a failure of a laugh. "Anything to oblige. But when you're done with my hand, you might let me know."

She did as though she understood; the song rose into a cry and stopped; the woman crouched out of the house the same way that she came in, and must have plunged straight into the bush, for when I followed her to the door she had already vanished.

"These are rum manners," said I.

"'S a rum crowd," said the captain, and to my surprise he made the sign of the cross on his bare bosom.

"Hillo!" says I, "are you a papist?"

He repudiated the idea with contempt. "Hard-shell Baptis'," said he. "But, my dear friend, the papists got some good ideas too; and tha' 's one of 'em. You take my advice, and whenever you come across Uma or Faavao or Vigours or any of that crowd, you take a leaf out o' the priests, and do what I do: savvy?" says he, repeated the sign, and winked his dim eye at me. "No, sir!" he broke out again, "no papists here!" and for a long time entertained me with his religious opinions.

I must have been taken with Uma from the first, or I should certainly have fled from that house and got into the clean air, and the clean sea or some convenient river. Though it's true I was committed to Case; and besides I could never have held my head up in that island, if I had run from a girl upon my wedding night.

The sun was down, the sky all on fire and the lamp had been some-time lighted, when Case came back with Uma and the negro. She was dressed and scented; her kilt was of fine tapa, looking richer in the folds than any silk; her bust, which was of the colour of dark honey, she wore bare only for some half a dozen necklaces of seeds and flowers; and behind her ears and in her hair, she had the scarlet flowers of the hybiscus. She showed the best bearing for a bride conceivable, serious and still; and I thought shame to stand up with her in that mean house and before that grinning negro. I thought shame I say; for the mountebank was dressed with a big paper collar, the book he made believe to read from was an odd volume of a novel, and the words of his service not fit to be set down. My conscience smote me when we joined hands; and when she got her certificate, I was tempted to throw up the bargain and confess. Here is the document: it was Case that wrote it, signatures and all, in a leaf out of the ledger.

This is to certify that *Uma* daughter of *Faavao* of Falesá island of _____, is illegally married to *Mr John Wiltshire* for one night, and Mr John Wiltshire is at liberty to send her to hell next morning.

> John Blackamoor
> Chaplain to the Hulks.

Extracted from the register
 by William T. Randall
 Master Mariner.

That was a nice paper to put in a girl's hand and see her hide away like gold. A man might easily feel cheap for less. But it was the practise in these parts, and (as I told myself) not the least the fault of us White Men but of the missionaries. If they had let the natives be, I had never needed this deception, but taken all the wives I wished, and left them when I pleased, with a clear conscience.

The more ashamed I was, the more hurry I was in to be gone; and our desires thus jumping together, I made the less remark of a change in the traders. Case had been all eagerness to keep me; now, as though he had attained a purpose, he seemed all eagerness to have me go. Uma, he said, could show me to my house, and the three bade us farewell indoors.

The night was nearly come; the village smellt of trees, and flowers and the sea, and breadfruit cooking; there came a fine roll of sea from the reef, and from a distance, among the woods and houses, many pretty sounds of men and children. It did me good to breathe free air; it did me good to be done with the captain and see, instead, the creature at my side. I felt for all the world as though she were some girl at home in the old country, and forgetting myself for the minute, took her hand to walk with. Her fingers nestled into mine; I heard her breathe deep and quick; and all at once she caught my hand to her face and pressed it there. "You good!" she cried, and ran ahead of me, and stopped and looked back and smiled, and ran ahead of me again; thus guiding me through the edge of the bush and by a quiet way to my own house.

The truth is Case had done the courting for me in style; told her I was mad to have her and cared nothing for the consequence; and the poor soul, knowing that which I was still ignorant of, believed it every word, and had her head nigh turned with vanity and gratitude. Now of all this I had no guess; I was one of those most opposed to any nonsense about native women, having seen so many whites eaten up by their wives' relatives and made fools of in the bargain; and I told myself I must make a stand at once and bring her to her bearings. But she looked so quaint and pretty as she ran away and then awaited me, and the thing was done so like a child or a kind dog, that the best I could do was just to follow her whenever she went on, to listen for the fall of her bare feet, and to watch in the dusk for the shining of her body. And there was another thought came in my head. She played kitten with me now when we were alone; but in the house she had carried it the way a countess might, so proud and humble. And what with her dress—for all there was so little of it, and that native enough—what with her fine tapa and fine scents, and her red flowers and seeds that were quite as bright as jewels, only larger—it came over me she was a kind of a countess really, dressed to hear great singers at a concert, and no even mate for a poor trader like myself.

She was the first in the house; and while I was still without, I saw a match flash and the lamplight kindle in the windows. The station was a wonderful fine place, coral built, with quite a wide verandah, and the main room high and wide. My chests and cases had been piled in, and made rather of a mess; and there, in the thick of the confusion, stood Uma by the table, awaiting me. Her shadow went all the way up behind her into the hollow of the iron roof; she stood against it bright, the lamplight shining on her skin. I stopped in the door, and she looked at me, not speaking, with eyes that were eager and yet daunted. Then she touched herself on the bosom. "Me— your wifie," she said. It had never taken me like that before; but the want of her took and shook all through me, like the wind in the luff of a sail.

I could not speak, if I had wanted; and if I could, I would not. I was ashamed to be so much moved about a native; ashamed of the marriage too, and the certificate she had treasured in her kilt; and I turned aside and made believe to rummage among my cases. The first thing I lighted on was a case of gin, the only one that I had brought; and partly for the girl's sake, and partly for horror of the recollection of old Randall, took a sudden resolve. I prized the lid off; one by one, I drew the bottles with a pocket corkscrew, and sent Uma out to pour the stuff from the verandah.

She came back after the last, and looked at me puzzled like.

"Why you do that?" she asked.

"No good," said I, for I was now a little better master of my tongue. "Man he drink, he no good."

She agreed with this but kept considering. "Why you bring him?" she asked presently. "Suppose you no want drink, you no bring him, I think."

"That's all right," said I. "One time I want drink too much; now no want. You see I no savvy I get one little wifie. Suppose I drink gin, my little wifie he 'fraid."

To speak to her kindly was about more than I was fit for; I had made my vow I would never let on to weakness with a native; and I had nothing for it but to stop.

She stood looking gravely down at me where I sat by the open case. "I think you good man," she said. And suddenly she had fallen before me on the floor. "I belong you all-e-same pig!" she cried.

CHAPTER II

The ban

I came on the verandah just before the sun rose on the morrow. My house was the last on the east; there was a cape of woods and cliffs behind that hid the sunrise. To the west, a swift cold river ran down, and beyond was the green of the village, dotted with cocoapalms and breadfruits and houses. The shutters were some of them down and some open; I saw the mosquito bars still stretched, with shadows of people new wakened sitting up inside; and all over the green others were stalking silent, wrapped in their many-coloured sleeping clothes like Bedouins in bible pictures. It was mortal still and solemn and chilly; and the light of the dawn on the lagoon was like the shining of a fire.

But the thing that troubled me was nearer hand. Some dozen young men and children made a piece of a half circle, flanking my house; the river divided them, some were on the near side, some on the far, and one on a boulder in the midst, and they all sat silent, wrapped in their sheets, and stared at me and my house as straight as pointer dogs. I thought it strange as I went out. When I had bathed and come back again, and found them all there, and two or three more along with them, I thought it stranger still. What could they see to gaze at in my house? I wondered, and went in.

But the thought of these starers stuck in my mind, and presently I came out again. The sun was now up, but it was still behind the cape of woods: say quarter of an hour had come and gone. The crowd was greatly increased, the far bank of the river was lined for quite a way; perhaps thirty grown folk, and of children twice as many, some standing, some squatted on the ground, and all staring at my house. I have seen a house in a South Sea village thus surrounded, but then a trader was thrashing his wife inside, and she singing out. Here was nothing: the stove was alight, the smoke going up in a Christian manner; all was shipshape and Bristol fashion. To be sure, there was a stranger come; but they had a chance to see that stranger yesterday and took it quiet enough. What ailed them now? I leaned my arms on the rail and stared back. Devil a wink they had in them. Now and then I could see the children chatter, but they spoke so low not even the hum of their speaking came my length. The rest were like graven images; they stared at me, dumb and sorrowful, with their bright eyes; and it came upon me things would look not much different, if I were on the platform of the gallows, and these good folk had come to see me hanged.

I felt I was getting daunted, and began to be afraid I looked it, which would never do. Up I stood, made believe to stretch myself, came down the verandah stair, and strolled towards the river. There went a short buzz from one to the other, like what you hear in theatres when the curtain goes up; and some of the nearest gave back the matter of a pace. I saw a girl lay one hand on a young man and make a gesture upward with the other; at the same time she said something in the native with a gasping voice. Three little boys sat beside my path, where I must pass within three feet of them. Wrapped in their sheets, with their shaved heads and bits of topknots, and queer faces, they looked like figures on a chimneypiece. Awhile they sat their ground, solemn as judges; I came up hand over fist, doing my five knots, like a man that meant business; and I thought I saw a sort of a wink and gulp in the three faces. Then one jumped up (he was the farthest off) and ran for his mammy. The other two, trying to follow suit, got foul, came to ground together bawling, wriggled right out of their sheets—and in a moment there were all three of them, two mother naked, scampering for their lives and singing out like pigs. The natives, who would never let a joke slip even at a burial, laughed and let up, as short as a dog's bark.

They say it scares a man to be alone. No such thing. What scares him in the dark or the high bush, is that he can't make sure, and there might be an army at his elbow. What scares him worst is to be right in the midst of a crowd, and have no guess of what they're driving at. When that laugh stopped, I stopped too. The boys had not yet made their offing; they were still on the full stretch going the one way, when I had already gone about ship and was sheering off the other. Like a fool I had come out, doing my five knots; like a fool I went back again. It must have been the funniest thing to see; and what knocked me silly, this time no one laughed; only one old woman gave a kind of pious moan, the way you have heard dissenters in their chapels at the sermon.

"I never saw such damfool kanakas as your people here," I said once to Uma, glancing out of the window at the starers.

"Savvy nothing," says Uma, with a kind of a disgusted air that she was good at.

And that was all the talk we had upon the matter; for I was put out, and Uma took the thing so much as a matter of course, that I was fairly ashamed.

All day, off and on, now fewer and now more, the fools sat about the west end of my house and across the river, waiting for the show, whatever that was—fire to come down from heaven, I suppose, and consume me bones and baggage. But by evening, like real islanders, they had wearied of the business; and got away and had a dance instead in the big house of the village, where I heard them singing and clapping hands till maybe ten at night; and the next day, it seemed they had forgotten I existed. If fire had come down from heaven or the earth opened and swallowed me, there would have been nobody to see the sport or take the lesson, or whatever you like to call it. But I was to find they hadn't forgot either, and kept an eye lifting for phenomena over my way.

I was hard at it both these days getting my trade in order, and taking stock of what Vigours had left. This was a job that made me pretty sick, and kept me from thinking on much else. Ben had taken stock the trip before, I knew I could trust Ben; but it was plain somebody had been making free in the meantime. I found I was out by what might easy cover six months salary and profit; and I could have kicked myself all round the village to have been such a blamed ass, sitting boozing with that Case, instead of attending to my own affairs and taking stock.

However, there's no use crying over spilt milk. It was done now and couldn't be undone. All I could do was to get what was left of it, and my new stuff (my own choice) in order, to go round and get after the rats and cockroaches, and to fix up that store regular Sydney style. A fine show I made of it; and the third morning, when I had lit my pipe and stood in the doorway and looked in—and turned and looked far up the mountain, and saw the cocoanuts waving, and footed up the tons of copra—and over the village green and saw the island dandies, and reckoned up the yards of print they wanted for their kilts and dresses—I felt as if I was in the right place to make a fortune, and go home again, and start a public house. There was I sitting in that verandah, in as handsome a piece of scenery as you could find, a splendid sun, and a fine, fresh healthy trade that stirred up a man's blood like seabathing; and the whole thing was clean gone from me, and I was dreaming England, which is after all a nasty, cold, muddy hole, with not enough light to see to read by—and dreaming the looks of my public, by a kant of a broad highroad like an avenue and with the sign on a green tree.

So much for the morning, but the day passed and the devil any one looked near me, and from all I knew of natives in other islands, I thought this strange. People laughed a little at our firm, and their fine stations, and at this station of Falesá in particular: all the copra in the district wouldn't pay for it (I had heard them say) in fifty years; which I supposed was an exaggeration. But when the day went and no business came at all, I began to get down-hearted, and about three in the afternoon, I went out for a stroll to cheer me up. On the green I saw a white man coming with a cassock on, by which and by the face of him, I knew he was a priest. He was a good natured old soul to look at, gone a little grizzled, and so dirty you could have written with him on a piece of paper.

"Good day, sir," says I.

He answered me eagerly in native.

"Don't you speak any English?" said I.

"Franch," says he.

"Well," said I, "I'm sorry, but I can't do anything there."

He tried me awhile in the French, and then again in native, which he seemed to think was the best chance. I made out he was after more than passing the time of day with me, but had something to communicate, and I listened the harder. I heard the names of Adams and Case and of Randall—Randall the oftenest; and the word "poison" or something like it; and a native word that he said very often. I went home repeating it to myself.

"What does *fussy-ocky* mean?" I asked of Uma, for that was as near as I could come to it.

"Make dead," said she.

"The devil it does!" says I. "Did ever you hear that Case had poisoned Johnny Adams?"

"Every man he savvy that," says Uma, scornful like. "Give him white sand—bad sand. He got the bottle still. Suppose he give you gin, you no take him."

Now I had heard much the same sort of story in other islands, and the same white powder always to the front, which made me think the less of it. For all that I went over to Randall's place, to see what I could pick up, and found Case on the door step cleaning a gun.

"Good shooting here?" says I.

"A one," says he. "The bush is full of all kinds of birds. I wish copra was as plenty," says he, I thought slyly, "but there don't seem anything doing."

I could see Black Jack in the store serving a customer.

"That looks like business, though," said I.

"That's the first sale we've made in three weeks," said he.

"You don't tell me?" says I. "Three weeks? Well, well."

"If you don't believe me," he cries, a little hot, "you can go and look at the copra house. It's half empty to this blesséd hour."

"I shouldn't be much the better for that, you see," says I. "For all I can tell, it might have been whole empty yesterday."

"That's so," says he, with a bit of a laugh.

"By the by," I said, "what sort of a party is that priest? Seems rather a friendly sort."

At this Case laughed right out loud. "Ah," says he, "I see what ails you now! Galuchet's been at you." *Father Galoshes* was the name he went by mostly, but Case always gave it the French quirk, which was another reason we had for thinking him above the common.

"Yes, I have seen him," I says. "I made out he didn't think much of you or Captain Randall."

"That he don't!" says Case. "It was the trouble about poor Adams. The last day, when he lay dying, there was young Buncombe round. Ever met Buncombe?"

I told him no.

"He's a cure, is Buncombe!" laughs Case. "Well, Buncombe took it in his head that as there was no other clergyman about, bar kanaka pastors, we ought to call in Father Galuchet, and have the old man administered and take the sacrament. It was all the same to me, you may suppose; but I said I thought Adams was the fellow to consult. He was jawing away about watered copra and a sight of foolery. 'Look here,' I said. 'You're pretty sick. Would you like to see Galoshes?' He sat right up on his elbow. 'Get the priest,' says he, 'get the priest, don't let me die here like a dog.' He spoke kind of fierce and eager, but sensible enough; there was nothing to say against that; so we sent and asked Galuchet if he would come. You bet he would! He jumped in his dirty linen at the thought of it. But we had reckoned without Papa. He's a hard-shell Baptist, is Papa; no papists need apply; and he took and locked the door. Buncombe told him he was bigoted, and I thought he would have had a fit. 'Bigoted!' he says. 'Me bigoted? Have I lived to hear it from a jackanapes like you?' And he made for Buncombe, and I had to hold them apart—and there was Adams in the middle, gone luny again and carrying on about copra like a born fool. It was good as the play, and I was about knocked out of time with laughing, when all of a sudden Adams sat up, clapped his hands to his chest, and went into the horrors. He died hard, did John Adams," says Case with a kind of a sudden sternness.

"And what became of the priest?" I asked.

"The priest?" says Case. "O, he was hammering on the door outside, and crying on the natives to come and beat it in, and singing out it was a soul he wished to save, and that. He was in a hell of a taking was the priest. But what would you have? Johnny had slipped his cable; no more Johnny in the market! and the administration racket clean played out. Next thing, word came to Randall the priest was praying upon Johnny's grave. Papa was pretty full, and got a club, and lit out straight for the place; and there was Galoshes on his knees, and a lot of natives looking on. You wouldn't think papa cared that much about anything, unless it was liquor; but he and the priest stuck to it two hours, slanging each other in native; and every time Galoshes tried to kneel down, papa went for him with the club. There never were such larks in Falesá. The end of it was that Captain Randall knocked over with some kind of a fit or stroke, and the priest got in his goods after all. But he was the angriest priest you ever heard of; and complained to the chiefs about the outrage, as he called it. That was no account, for our chiefs are protestant here; and anyway he had been making trouble about the drum for morning school, and they were glad to give him a wipe. Now he swears old Randall gave Adams poison or something, and when the two meet they grin at each other like baboons."

He told this story as natural as could be, and like a man that enjoyed the fun; though now I come to think of it after so long, it seems rather a sickening yarn. However Case never set up to be soft, only to be square and hearty and a man all round; and to tell the truth, he puzzled me entirely.

I went home, and asked Uma if she were a *Popey,* which I had made out to be the native word for catholics.

"E le ai!" says she—she always used the native when she meant "no" more than usually strong, and indeed there's more of it. "No good, popey," she added.

Then I asked her about Adams and the priest, and she told me much the same yarn in her own way. So that I was left not much farther on; but inclined upon the whole, to think the bottom of the matter was the row about the sacrament, and the poisoning only talk.

The next day was a Sunday, when there was no business to be looked for. Uma asked me in the morning if I was going to "pray"; I told her she bet not; and she stopped home herself with no more words. I thought this seemed unlike a native, and a native woman, and a woman that had new clothes to show off; however, it suited me to the ground and I made the less of it. The queer thing was that I came next door to going to church after all, a thing I'm little likely to forget. I had turned out for a stroll, and heard the hymn tune up. You know how it is; if you hear folk singing, it seems to draw you; and pretty soon I found myself alongside the church. It was a little long low place, coral built, rounded off at both ends like a whale boat, a big native roof on the top of it, windows without sashes and doorways without doors. I stuck my head into one of the windows, and the sight was so new to me—for things went quite different in the islands I was acquainted with—that I stayed and looked on. The congregation sat on the floor on mats, the women on one side, the men on the other; all rigged out to kill, the women with dresses and trade hats, the men in white jackets and shirts. The hymn was over; the pastor, a big, buck kanaka, was in the pulpit preaching for his life; and by the way he wagged his hand, and worked his voice, and made his points, and seemed to argue with the folk, I made out he was a gun at the business. Well, he looked up suddenly and caught my eye; and I give you my word he staggered in the pulpit. His eyes bulged out of his head, his hand rose and pointed at me like as if against his will, and the sermon stopped right there.

It isn't a fine thing to say for yourself, but I ran away; and if the same kind of a shock was given me, I should run away again tomorrow. To see that palavering kanaka struck all of a heap at the mere sight of me, gave me a feeling as if the bottom had dropped out of the world. I went right home, and stayed there, and said nothing. You might think I would tell Uma, but that was against my system. You might have thought I would have gone over and consulted Case; but the truth was I was ashamed to speak of such a thing, I thought everyone would blurt out laughing in my face. So I held my tongue, and thought all the more, and the more I thought, the less I liked the business.

By Monday night, I got it clearly in my head I must be tabooed. A new store to stand open two days in a village, and not a man or woman come to see the trade, was past believing.

"Uma," said I, "I think I'm tabooed."

"I think so," said she.

I thought awhile whether I should ask her more, but it's a bad idea to set natives up with any notion of consulting them, so I went to Case. It was dark, and he was sitting alone, as he did mostly, smoking on the stairs.

"Case," said I, "here's a queer thing. I'm tabooed."

"O, fudge!" says he. "'Tain't the practise in these islands."

"That may be, or it mayn't," said I. "It's the practise where I was before; you can bet I know what it's like; and I tell it you for a fact: I'm tabooed."

"Well," said he, "what have you been doing?"

"That's what I want to find out," said I.

"O, you can't be," said he; "it ain't possible. However I'll tell you what I'll do; just to put your mind at rest, I'll go round and find out for sure. Just you waltz in and talk to papa."

"Thank you," I said, "I'd rather stay right out here on the verandah: your house is so close."

"I'll call papa out here, then," says he.

"My dear fellow," I says, "I wish you wouldn't. The fact is I don't take to Mr Randall."

Case laughed, took a lantern from the store, and set out into the village. He was gone perhaps quarter of an hour; and he looked mighty serious when he came back.

"Well," said he, clapping down the lantern on the verandah steps, "I would never have believed it. I don't know where the impudence of these kanakas 'll go next, they seem to have lost all idea of respect for whites. What we want is a man of war: a German, if we could—they know how to manage kanakas."

"I *am* tabooed then?" I cried.

"Something of the sort," said he. "It's the worst thing of the kind I've heard of yet. But I'll stand by you, Wiltshire, man to man. You come round here tomorrow about nine and we'll have it out with the chiefs. They're afraid of me; or they used to be, but their heads are so big by now I don't know what to think. Understand me, Wiltshire, I don't count this your quarrel," he went on with a great deal of resolution; "I count it all of our quarrel, I count it the White Man's Quarrel, and I'll stand to it through thick and thin, and there's my hand on it."

"Have you found out what's the reason?" I asked.

"Not yet," said Case. "But we'll fix them down tomorrow."

Altogether I was pretty well pleased with his attitude, and almost more the next day when we met to go before the chiefs, to see him so stern and resolved. The chiefs awaited us in one of their big oval houses, which was marked out to us from a long way off by the crowd about the caves, a hundred strong if there was one, men, women and children. Many of the men were on their way to work and wore green wreaths; and it put me in thoughts of the first of May at home. This crowd opened and buzzed about the pair of us as we went in, with a sudden angry animation. Five chiefs were there, four mighty stately men, the fifth old and puckered. They sat on mats in their white kilts and jackets; they had fans in their hands like fine ladies; and two of the younger ones wore catholic medals, which gave me matter of reflection. Our place was set and the mats laid for us over against these grandees on the near side of the house; the midst was empty; the crowd, close at our backs, murmured and craned and jostled to look on, and the shadows of them tossed in front of us on the clean pebbles of the floor. I was just a hair put out by the excitement of the commons, but the quiet, civil appearance of the chiefs reassured me: all the more when their spokesman began and made a long speech in a low tone of voice, sometimes waving his hand toward Case, sometimes toward me, and sometimes knocking with his knuckles on the mat. One thing was clear: there was no sign of anger in the chiefs.

"What's he been saying?" I asked, when he had done.

"O, just that they're glad to see you, and they understand by me you wish to make some kind of a complaint, and you're to fire away, and they'll do the square thing."

"It took a precious long time to say that," said I.

"O, the rest was sawder and *bonjour* and that," says Case—"you know what kanakas are!"

"Well, they don't get much *bonjour* out of me," said I. "You tell them who I am. I'm a white man, and a British Subject, and no end of a big chief at home; and I've come here to do them good and bring them civilisation; and no sooner have I got my trade sorted out, than they go and taboo me and no one dare come near my place! Tell them I don't mean to fly in the face of anything legal; and if what they want's a present, I'll do what's fair. I don't blame any man looking out for himself, tell them, for that's human nature; but if they think they're going to come any of their native ideas over me, they'll find themselves mistaken. And tell them plain, that I demand the reason of this treatment as a White Man and a British Subject."

That was my speech. I know how to deal with kanakas; give them plain sense and fair dealing, and I'll do them that much justice, they knuckle under every time. They haven't any real government or any real law, that's what you've got to knock into their heads; and even if they had, it would be a good joke if it was to apply to a white man. It would be a strange thing if we came all this way and couldn't do what we pleased. The mere idea has always put my monkey up, and I rapped my speech out pretty big. Then Case translated it, or made believe to, rather; and the first chief replied, and then a second and a third, all in the same style, easy and genteel but solemn underneath. Once a question was put to Case, and he answered it, and all hands (both chiefs and commons) laughed out loud and looked at me. Last of all, the puckered old fellow and the big young chief that spoke first, started in to put Case through a kind of catechism. Sometimes I made out that Case was trying to fence, and they stuck to him like hounds, and the sweat ran down his face, which was no very pleasant sight to me; and at some of his answers, the crowd moaned and murmured, which was a worse hearing. It's a cruel shame I knew no native; for (as I now believe) they were asking Case about my marriage, and he must have had a tough job of it to clear his feet. But leave Case alone: he had the brains to run a parliament.

"Well, is that all?" I asked, when a pause came.

"Come along," says he, mopping his face. "I'll tell you outside."

"Do you mean they won't take the taboo off?" I cried.

"It's something queer," said he. "I'll tell you outside. Better come away."

"I won't take it at their hands," cried I. "I ain't that kind of a man. You don't find me turn my back on a parcel of kanakas."

"You'd better," said Case.

He looked at me with a signal in his eye; and the five chiefs looked at me civilly enough but kind of pointed; and the people looked at me and craned and jostled. I remembered the folks that watched my house, and how the pastor had jumped in his pulpit at the bare sight of me; and the whole business seemed so out of the way that I rose and followed Case. The crowd opened again to let us through, but wider than before, the children on the skirts running and singing out; and as we two white men walked away, they all stood and watched us.

"And now," said I, "what is all this about?"

"The truth is I can't rightly make it out myself. They have a down on you," says Case.

"Taboo a man because they have a down on him!" I cried. "I never heard the like."

"It's worse than that, you see," said Case. "You ain't tabooed, I told you that couldn't be. The people won't go near you, Wiltshire; and there's where it is."

"They won't go near me? What do you mean by that? Why won't they go near me?" I cried.

Case hesitated. "Seems they're frightened," says he, in a low voice.

I stopped dead short. "Frightened?" I repeated. "Are you gone crazy, Case? What are they frightened of?"

"I wish I could make out," Case answered, shaking his head. "Appears like one of their tomfool superstitions. That's what I don't cotton to," he said; "it's like the business about Vigours."

"I'd like to know what you mean by that, and I'll trouble you to tell me," says I.

"Well, you know, Vigours lit out and left all standing," said he. "It was some superstition business—I never got the hang of it—but it began to look bad before the end."

"I've heard a different story about that," said I, "and I had better tell you so. I heard he ran away because of you."

"O, well, I suppose he was ashamed to tell the truth," says Case; "I guess he thought it silly. And it's a fact that I packed him off. 'What would you do, old man?' says he—'Get,' says I, 'and not think twice about it.' I was the gladdest kind of man to see him clear away. It ain't my notion to turn my back on a mate when he's in a tight place; but there was that much trouble in the village that I couldn't see where it might likely end. I was a fool to be so much about with Vigours. They cast it up to me today; didn't you hear Maea—that's the young chief, the big one—ripping out about 'Vika'? That was him they were after; they don't seem to forget it, somehow."

"This is all very well," said I, "but it don't tell me what's wrong; it don't tell me what they're afraid of—what their idea is."

"Well, I wish I knew," said Case. "I can't say fairer than that."

"You might have asked, I think," says I.

"And so I did," says he; "but you must have seen for yourself, unless you're blind, that the asking got the other way. I'll go as far as I dare for another white man; but when I find I'm in the scrape myself, I think first of my own bacon. The loss of me is I'm too good natured. And I'll take the freedom of telling you, you show a queer kind of gratitude to a man who's got into all this mess along of your affairs."

"There's a thing I'm thinking of," said I. "You were a fool to be so much about with Vigours. One comfort, you haven't been much about with me. I notice you've never been inside my house. Own up, now: you had word of this before?"

"It's a fact I haven't been," said he. "It was an oversight, and I'm sorry for it, Wiltshire. But about coming now, I'll be quite plain."

"You mean you won't?" I asked.

"Awfully sorry, old man, but that's the size of it," says Case.

"In short, you're afraid?" says I.

"In short, I'm afraid," says he.

"And I'm still to be tabooed for nothing?" I asked.

"I tell you you're not tabooed," said he. "The kanakas won't go near you, that's all. And who's to make 'em? We traders have a lot of gall, I must say; we make these poor kanakas take back their laws, and take up their taboos, and that, whenever it happens to suit us. But you don't mean to say you expect a law obliging people to deal in your store whether they want to or not? You don't mean to tell me you've got the gall for that? And if you had, it would be a queer thing to propose to me. I would just like to point out to you, Wiltshire, that I'm a trader myself."

"I don't think I would talk of gall if I was you," said I. "Here's about what it comes to, as well as I can make out. None of the people are to trade with me, and they're all to trade with you. You're to have the copra, and I'm to go to the devil and shake myself. And I don't know any native, and you're the only man here worth mention that speaks English, and you have the gall to up and hint to me my life's in danger, and all you've got to tell me is, you don't know why?"

"Well, it *is* all I have to tell you," said he. "I don't know; I wish I did."

"And so you turn your back and leave me to myself: is that the position?" says I.

"If you like to put it nasty," says he. "I don't put it so. I say merely I'm going to keep clear of you, or if I don't I'll get in danger for myself."

"Well," said I, "you're a nice kind of a white man!"

"O, I understand you're riled," said he. "I would be myself. I can make excuses."

"All right," I said, "go and make excuses somewhere else. Here's my way, there's yours."

With that we parted, and I went straight home, in a holy temper, and found Uma trying on a lot of trade goods like a baby.

"Here," I said, "you quit that foolery. Here's a pretty mess to have made—as if I wasn't bothered enough anyway! And I thought I told you to get dinner?"

And then I believe I gave her a bit of the rough side of my tongue, as she deserved. She stood up at once, like a sentry to his officer; for I must say she was always well brought up and had a great respect for whites.

"And now," says I, "you belong round here, you're bound to understand this. What am I tabooed for anyway? or if I ain't tabooed, what makes the folks afraid of me?"

She stood and looked at me with eyes like saucers.

"You no savvy?" she gasps at last.

"No," said I. "How would you expect me to? We don't have any such craziness where I come from."

"Ese no tell you?" she asked again.

(*Ese* was the name the natives had for Case; it may mean foreign, or extraordinary; or it might mean a mummy apple; but most like it was only his own name misheard and put in the kanaka spelling.)

"Not much!" said I.

"Damn Ese," she cried.

You might think it was funny to hear this kanaka girl come out with a big swear. No such thing. There was no swearing in her; no, nor anger; she was beyond anger, and meant the word simple and serious. She stood there straight as she said it; I cannot justly say that ever I saw a woman look like that before or after, and it struck me mum. Then she made a kind of an obeisance, but it was the proudest kind, and threw her hands out open.

"I 'shamed," she said. "I think you savvy. Ese he tell me you savvy, he tell me you no mind—tell me you love me too much. Taboo belong me," she said, touching herself on the bosom, as she had done upon our wedding night. "Now I go 'way, taboo he go 'way too. Then you get too much copra. You like more better, I think. Tofá, alii," says she in the native—"Farewell, chief!"

"Hold on," I cried. "Don't be in such a blamed hurry."

She looked at me sidelong with a smile. "You see, you get copra," says she, the same as you might offer candies to a child.

"Uma," said I, "hear reason. I didn't know, and that's a fact; and Case seems to have played it pretty mean upon the pair of us. But I do know now, and I don't mind: I love you too much. You no go 'way, you no leave me, I too much sorry."

"You no love me!" she cried, "you talk me bad words!" And she threw herself in a corner on the floor, and began to cry.

Well, I'm no scholar, but I wasn't born yesterday, and I thought the worst of that trouble was over. However, there she lay—her back turned, her face to the wall—and shook with sobbing like a little child, so that her feet jumped with it. It's strange how it hits a man when he's in love; for there's no use mincing things; kanaka and all, I was in love with her, or just as good. I tried to take her hand, but she would none of that. "Uma," I said, "there's no sense in carrying on like this. I want you stop here, I want my little wifie, I tell you true."

"No tell me true!" she sobbed.

"All right," says I, "I'll wait till you're through with this." And I sat right down beside her on the floor, and set to smoothe her hair with my hand. At first she wriggled away when I touched her; then she seemed to notice me no more; then her sobs grew gradually less and presently stopped; and the next thing I knew, she raised her face to mine.

"You tell me true? You like me stop?" she asked.

"Uma," I said, "I would rather have you than all the copra in the South Seas," which was a very big expression, and the strangest thing was that I meant it.

She threw her arms about me, sprang close up, and pressed her face to mine in the island way of kissing, so that I was all wetted with her tears and my heart went out to her wholly. I never had anything so near me as this little brown bit of a girl. Many things went together and all helped to turn my head. She was pretty enough to eat; it seemed she was my only friend in that queer place; I was ashamed that I had spoken rough to her; and she was a woman, and my wife, and a kind of a baby besides that I was sorry for; and the salt of her tears was in my mouth. And I forgot Case and the natives; and I forgot that I knew nothing of the story, or only remembered it to banish the re-membrance; and I forgot that I was to get no copra and so could make no livelihood; and I forgot my employers, and the strange kind of ser-vice I was doing them, when I preferred my fancy to their business; and I forgot even that Uma was no true wife of mine, but just a maid beguiled, and that in a pretty shabby style. But that is to look too far on. I will come to that part of it next.

It was late before we thought of getting dinner. The stove was out, and gone stone-cold; but we fired up after awhile, and cooked each a dish, helping and hindering each other, and making a play of it like children. I was so greedy of her nearness that I sat down to dinner with my lass upon my knee, made sure of her with one hand, and ate with the other. Ay, and more than that. She was the worst cook I suppose God made; the things she set her hand to, it would have sickened an entire horse to eat of; yet I made my meal that day on Uma's cookery, and can never call to mind to have been better pleased.

I didn't pretend to myself, and I didn't pretend to her. I saw I was clean gone; and if she was to make a fool of me, she must. And I sup-pose it was this that set her talking, for now she made sure that we were friends. A lot she told me, sitting in my lap and eating my dish, as I ate hers, from foolery: a lot about herself and her mother and Case, all which would be very tedious and fill sheets if I set it down in Beach de

Mar, but which I must give a hint of in plain English—and one thing about myself, which had a very big effect on my concerns, as you are soon to hear.

It seems she was born in one of the Line islands; had been only two or three years in these parts, where she had come with a white man who was married to her mother and then died; and only the one year in Falesá. Before that, they had been a good deal on the move, trekking about after the white man, who was one of these rolling stones that keep going round after a soft job. They talk about looking for gold at the end of a rainbow; but if a man wants an employment that'll last him till he dies, let him start out on the soft-job hunt. There's meat and drink in it too, and beer and skittles; for you never hear of them starving and rarely see them sober; and as for steady sport, cockfighting isn't in the same county with it. Anyway, this beachcomber carried the woman and her daughter all over the shop, but mostly to out of the way islands, where there were no police and he thought perhaps the soft-job hung out. I've my own view of this old party; but I was just as glad he had kept Uma clear of Apia and Papeete and these flash towns. At last he struck Fale-alii on this island, got some trade the Lord knows how! muddled it all away in the usual style, and died worth next to nothing, bar a bit of land at Falesá that he had got for a bad debt, which was what put it in the minds of the mother and daughter to come there and live. It seems Case encouraged them all he could, and helped to get their house built. He was very kind those days, and gave Uma trade, and there is no doubt he had his eye on her from the beginning. However, they had scarce settled, when up turned a young man, a native, and wanted to marry her. He was a small chief, and had some fine mats and old songs in his family, and was "very pretty," Uma said; and altogether it was an extraordinary match for a penniless girl and an out-islander.

At the first word of this, I got downright sick with jealousy.

"And you mean to say you would have married him!" I cried.

"Ioe," says she. "I like too much!"

"Well!" I said. "And suppose I had come round after?"

"I like you more better now," said she. "But suppose I marry Ioane, I one good wife. I no common kanaka: good girl!" says she.

Well, I had to be pleased with that; but I promise you I didn't care about the business one little bit, and liked the end of that yarn better than the beginning. For it seems this proposal of marriage was the start of all the trouble. It seems, before that, Uma and her mother had been looked down upon of course for kinless folk and out-islanders, but nothing to hurt; and even when Ioane came forward there was less trouble at first than might have been looked for. And then all of a sudden, about six months before my coming, Ioane backed out and left that part of the island, and from that day to this, Uma and her mother had found themselves alone. None called at their house, none spoke to them on the roads. If they went to church, the other women drew their mats away and left them in a clear place by themselves. It was a regular excommunication, like what you read of in the middle ages; and the cause or sense of it beyond guessing. It was some *tala pepelo*, Uma said, some lie, some calumny; and all she knew of it was that the girls who had been jealous of her luck with Ioane used to twit her with his desertion, and cry out, when they met her alone in the woods, that she would never be married. "They tell me no man he marry me. He too much 'fraid," she said.

The only soul that came about them after this desertion was Master Case; even he was chary of showing himself, and turned up mostly by night; and pretty soon he began to table his cards and make up to Uma. I was still sore about Ioane, and when Case turned up in the same line of business, I cut up downright rough.

"Well," I said sneering, "and I suppose you thought Case 'very pretty' and 'liked too much.' "

"Now you talk silly," said she. "White man he come here, I marry him all-e-same kanaka; very well then, he marry me all-e-same white woman. Suppose he no marry, he go 'way, woman he stop. All-e-same thief; empty hand, Tonga-heart—no can love! Now you come marry me; you big heart—you no 'shamed island girl. That thing I love you for too much. I proud."

I don't know that ever I felt sicker all the days of my life. I laid down my fork and I put away "the island girl"; I didn't seem somehow to have any use for either; and I went and walked up and down in the house, and Uma followed me with her eyes, for she was troubled, and small wonder! But troubled was no word for it with me; I so wanted, and so feared, to make a clean breast of the sweep that I had been.

And just then there came a sound of singing out of the sea; it sprang up suddenly clear and near, as the boat turned the headland; and Uma, running to the window, cried out it was "Misi" come upon his rounds.

I thought it was a strange thing I should be glad to have a missionary; but if it was strange, it was still true.

"Uma," said I, "you stop here in this room, and don't budge a foot out of it till I come back."

CHAPTER III

The missionary

As I came out on the verandah, the mission boat was shooting for the mouth of the river. She was a long whale boat painted white; a bit of an awning astern; a native pastor crouched on the wedge of poop, steering; some four and twenty paddles flashing and dipping, true to the boat-song; and the missionary under the awning, in his white clothes, reading in a book, and set him up! It was pretty to see and hear; there's no smarter sight in the islands than a missionary boat with a good crew and a good pipe to them; and I considered it for half a minute with a bit of envy perhaps, and then strolled towards the river.

From the opposite side there was another man aiming for the same place, but he ran and got there first. It was Case; doubtless his idea was to keep me apart from the missionary who might serve me as interpreter; but my mind was upon other things, I was thinking how he had jockeyed us about the marriage, and tried his hand on Uma before; and at the sight of him, rage flew in my nostrils.

"Get out of that, you low, swindling thief!" I cried.

"What's that you say?" says he.

I gave him the word again, and rammed it down with a good oath. "And if ever I catch you within six fathoms of my house," I cried, "I'll clap a bullet in your measly carcase."

"You must do as you like about your house," said he, "where I told you I have no thought of going. But this is a public place."

"It's a place where I have private business," said I. "I have no idea of a hound like you eavesdropping, and I give you notice to clear out."

"I don't take it though," says Case.

"I'll show you, then," said I.

"We'll have to see about that," said he.

He was quick with his hands, but he had neither the height nor the weight, being a flimsy creature alongside a man like me; and besides I was blazing to that height of wrath that I could have bit into a chisel. I gave him first the one and then the other, so that I could hear his head rattle and crack, and he went down straight.

"Have you had enough?" cries I. But he only looked up white and blank, and the blood spread upon his face like wine upon a napkin. "Have you had enough?" I cried again. "Speak up, and don't lie malingering there, or I'll take my feet to you!"

He sat up at that, and held his head—by the look of him you could see it was spinning—and the blood poured on his pyjamas.

"I've had enough for this time," says he, and he got up staggering and went off by the way that he had come.

The boat was close in; I saw the missionary had laid his book to one side, and I smiled to myself. "He'll know I'm a man, anyway," thinks I.

This was the first time, in all my years in the Pacific, I had ever exchanged two words with any missionary; let alone asked one for a favour. I didn't like the lot, no trader does; they look down upon us and make no concealment; and besides they're partly kanakaised, and suck up with natives instead of with other white men like themselves. I had on a rig of clean, striped pyjamas, for of course I had dressed decent to go before the chiefs; but when I saw the missionary step out of his boat in the regular uniform, white duck clothes, pith helmet, white shirt and tie, and yellow boots to his feet, I could have bunged stones at him. As he came nearer, queering me pretty curious (because of the fight I suppose) I saw he looked mortal sick, for the truth was he had a fever on and had just had a chill in the boat.

"Mr Tarleton, I believe?" says I, for I had got his name.

"And you, I suppose, are the new trader?" says he.

"I want to tell you first that I don't hold with missions," I went on, "and that I think you and the likes of you do a sight of harm, filling up the natives with old wives' tales and bumptiousness."

"You are perfectly entitled to your opinions," says he, looking a bit ugly, "but I have no call to hear them."

"It so happens that you've got to hear them," I said. "I'm no missionary nor missionary lover; I'm no kanaka nor favourer of kanakas: I'm just a trader, I'm just a common, low, god-damned white man and

British subject, the sort you would like to wipe your boots on. I hope that's plain."

"Yes, my man," said he. "It's more plain than creditable. When you are sober, you'll be sorry for this."

He tried to pass on, but I stopped him with my hand. The kanakas were beginning to growl; guess they didn't like my tone, for I spoke to that man as free as I would to you.

"Now you can't say I've deceived you," said I, "and I can go on. I want a service, I want two services in fact; and if you care to give me them, I'll perhaps take more stock in what you call your christianity."

He was silent for a moment. Then he smiled. "You are rather a strange sort of man," says he.

"I'm the sort of a man God made me," says I. "I don't set up to be a gentleman," I said.

"I am not quite so sure," said he. "And what can I do for you, Mr——?"

"Wiltshire," I says, "though I'm mostly called Welsher; but Wiltshire is the way it's spellt, if the people on the beach could only get their tongues about it. And what do I want? Well, I'll tell you the first thing. I'm what you call a sinner—what I call a sweep—and I want you to help me make it up to a person I've deceived."

He turned and spoke to his crew in the native. "And now I am at your service," said he, "but only for the time my crew are dining. I must be much farther down the coast before night. I was delayed at Papa-mālūlū till this morning, and I have an engagement in Fale-alii tomorrow night."

I led the way to my house in silence and rather pleased with myself for the way I had managed the talk, for I like a man to keep his self-respect.

"I was sorry to see you fighting," says he.

"O, that's part of a yarn I want to tell you," I said. "That's service number two. After you've heard it, you'll let me know whether you're sorry or not."

We walked right in through the store, and I was surprised to find Uma had cleared away the dinner things. This was so unlike her ways, that I saw she had done it out of gratitude, and liked her the better. She and Mr Tarleton called each other by name, and he was very civil to her seemingly. But I thought little of that; they can always find civility for a kanaka; it's us white men they lord it over. Besides I didn't want much Tarleton just then: I was going to do my pitch.

"Uma," said I, "give us your marriage certificate." She looked put out. "Come," said I. "You can trust me. Hand it up."

She had it about her person as usual; I believe she thought it was a pass to heaven, and if she died without having it handy she would go to hell. I couldn't see where she put it the first time, I couldn't see now where she took it from; it seemed to jump in her hand like that Blavatsky business in the papers. But it's the same way with all island women, and I guess they're taught it when young.

"Now," said I, with the certificate in my hand, "I was married to this girl by Black Jack the negro. The certificate was wrote by Case, and it's a dandy piece of literature, I promise you. Since then I've found that there's a kind of cry in the place against this wife of mine, and so long as I keep her, I cannot trade. Now what would any man do in my place, if he was a man?" I said. "The first thing he would do is this, I guess." And I took and tore up the certificate and bunged the pieces on the floor.

"*Aué!*" cried Uma, and began to clap her hands, but I caught one of them in mine.

"And the second thing that he would do," said I, "if he was what I would call a man, and you would call a man, Mr Tarleton, is to bring the girl right before you or any other missionary, and to up and say: 'I was wrong married to this wife of mine, but I think a heap of her, and now I want to be married to her right.' Fire away, Mr Tarleton. And I guess you'd better do it in native; it'll please the old lady," I said, giving her the proper name of a man's wife upon the spot.

So we had in two of the crew to witness, and were spliced in our own house; and the parson prayed a good bit, I must say, but not so long as some, and shook hands with the pair of us.

"Mr Wiltshire," he says, when he had made out the lines and packed off the witnesses, "I have to thank you for a very lively pleasure. I have rarely performed the marriage ceremony with more grateful emotions."

That was what you would call talking. He was going on besides with more of it, and I was ready for as much taffy as he had in stock, for I felt good. But Uma had been taken up with something half through the marriage, and cut straight in.

"How your hand he get hurt?" she asked.

"You ask Case's head, old lady," says I.

She jumped with joy, and sang out.

"You haven't made much of a christian of this one," says I to Mr Tarleton.

"We didn't think her one of our worst," says he, "when she was at Fale-alii; and if Uma bears malice, I shall be tempted to fancy she has good cause."

"Well, there we are at service number two," said I. "I want to tell you our yarn, and see if you can let a little daylight in."

"Is it long?" he asked.

"Yes," I said, "it's a goodish bit of a yarn."

"Well, I'll give you all the time I can spare," says he, looking at his watch. "But I must tell you fairly I haven't eaten since five this morning; and unless you can let me have something, I am not likely to eat again before seven or eight tonight."

"By God, we'll give you dinner!" I cried.

I was a little caught up at my swearing, just when all was going straight; and so was the missionary I suppose, but he made believe to look out of the window and thanked us.

So we ran him up a bit of a meal. I was bound to let the old lady have a hand in it, to show off; so I deputised her to brew the tea. I don't think I ever met such tea as she turned out. But that was not the worst, for she got round with the salt-box, which she considered an extra European touch, and turned my stew into sea water. Altogether, Mr Tarleton had a devil of a dinner of it; but he had plenty entertainment by the way, for all the while that we were cooking, and afterwards when he was making believe to eat, I kept posting him up on Master Case and the beach of Falesá, and he putting questions that showed he was following close.

"Well," said he at last, "I am afraid you have a dangerous enemy. This man Case is very clever and seems really wicked. I must tell you I have had my eye on him for nearly a year, and have rather had the worst of our encounters. About the time when the last representative of your firm ran so suddenly away, I had a letter from Namu, the native pastor, begging me to come to Falesá at my earliest convenience, as his flock were all 'adopting catholic practices.' I had great confidence in Namu; I fear it only shows how easily we are deceived. No one could hear him preach and not be persuaded he was a man of extraordinary parts. All our islanders easily acquire a kind of eloquence, and can roll out and illustrate with a great deal of vigour and fancy secondhand sermons; but Namu's sermons are his own, and I cannot deny that I have found them means of grace. Moreover he has a keen curiosity in secular things, does not fear work, is clever at carpentering, and has made himself so much respected among the neighbouring pastors that we call him, in a jest which is half serious, the Bishop of the East. In short I was proud of the man; all the more puzzled by his letter; and took occasion to come this way. The morning before my arrival, Vigours had been set on board the *Lion,* and Namu was perfectly at his ease, apparently ashamed of his letter, and quite unwilling to explain it. This of course I could not allow; and he ended by confessing that he had been much concerned to find his people using the sign of the cross, but since he had learned the explanation his mind was satisfied. For Vigours had the Evil Eye, a common thing in a country of Europe called Italy, where men were often struck dead by that kind of devil; and it appeared the sign of the cross was a charm against its power.

" 'And I explain it, Misi,' said Namu in this way. 'The country in Europe is a Popey country, and the devil of the Evil Eye may be a catholic devil, or at least used to catholic ways. So then I reasoned thus; if this sign of the cross were used in a Popey manner, it would be sinful; but when it is used only to protect men from a devil, which is a thing harmless in itself, the sign too must be harmless. For the sign is neither good nor bad, even as a bottle is neither good nor bad. But if the bottle be full of gin, the gin is bad; and if the sign be made in idolatry, so is the idolatry bad.' And very like a native pastor, he had a text apposite about the casting out of devils.

" 'And who has been telling you about the Evil Eye?' I asked.

"He admitted it was Case. Now I am afraid you will think me very narrow, Mr Wiltshire, but I must tell you I was displeased, and cannot think a trader at all a good man to advise or have an influence upon my pastors. And besides there had been some flying talk in the country of old Adams and his being poisoned, to which I had paid no great heed; but it came back to me at the moment.

" 'And is this Case a man of sanctified life?' I asked.

"He admitted he was not; for though he did not drink, he was profligate with women and had no religion.

" 'Then,' said I, 'I think the less you have to do with him the better.'

"But it is not easy to have the last word with a man like Namu; he was ready in a moment with an illustration. 'Misi,' said he, 'you have told me there were wise men, not pastors, not even holy, who knew many things useful to be taught, about trees for instance, and beasts, and to print books, and about the stones that are burned to make knives of. Such men teach you in your college, and you learn from them, but take care not to learn to be unholy. Misi, Case is my college.'

"I knew not what to say. Mr Vigours had evidently been driven out of Falesá by the machinations of Case and with something not very unlike the collusion of my pastor. I called to mind it was Namu who had reassured me about Adams and traced the rumour to the ill will of the priest. And I saw I must inform myself more thoroughly from an impartial source. There is an old rascal of a chief here, Faiaso, whom I daresay you saw today at the council; he has been all his life turbulent and sly, a great fomenter of rebellions, and a thorn in the side of the mission and the island. For all that he is very shrewd, and except in politics or about his own misdemeanours, a teller of the truth. I went to his house, told him what I had heard, and besought him to be frank. I do not think I had ever a more painful interview. Perhaps you will understand me, Mr Wiltshire, if I tell you that I am perfectly serious in these old-wives' tales with which you reproached me, and as anxious to do well for these islands as you can be to please and to protect your pretty wife. And you are to remember that I thought Namu a paragon, and was proud of the man as one of the first ripe fruits of the mission. And now I was informed that he had fallen in a sort of dependence upon Case. The beginning of it was not corrupt; it began doubtless in fear and respect produced by trickery and pretence; but I was shocked to find that another element had been lately added, that Namu helped himself in the store, and was believed to be deep in Case's debt. Whatever the trader said, that Namu believed with trembling. He was not alone in this; many in the village lived in a similar subjection; but Namu's case was the most influential, it was through Namu Case had wrought most evil; and with a certain following among the chiefs, and the pastor in his pocket, the man was as good as master of the village. You know something of Vigours and Adams; but perhaps you have never heard of old Underhill, Adams's predecessor. He was a quiet, mild old fellow, I remember, and we were told he had died suddenly: white men die very suddenly in Falesá. The truth, as I now heard it, made my blood run cold. It seems he was struck with a general palsy, all of him dead but one eye, which he continually winked. Word was started that the helpless old man was now a devil; and this vile fellow Case worked upon the natives' fears, which he professed to share, and pretended he durst not go into the house alone. At last a grave was dug, and the living body buried at the far end of the village. Namu, my pastor, whom I had helped to educate, offered up prayer at the hateful scene.

"I felt myself in a very difficult position. Perhaps too it was my duty to have denounced Namu and had him deposed; perhaps I think so now; but at the time, it seemed less clear. He had a great influence, it might prove greater than mine. The natives are prone to superstition; perhaps by stirring them up, I might but ingrain and spread these dangerous fancies. And Namu besides, apart from this novel and accursed influence, was a good pastor, an able man and spiritually minded. Where should I look for a better? how was I to find as good? At that moment with Namu's failure fresh in my view, the work of my life appeared a mockery; hope was dead in me; I would rather repair such tools as I had, than go abroad in quest of others that must certainly prove worse; and a scandal is, at the best, a thing to be avoided when humanly possible. Right or wrong then, I determined on a quiet course. All that night I denounced and reasoned with the erring pastor; twitted him with his ignorance and want of faith; twitted him with his wretched attitude, making clean the outside of the cup and platter, callously helping at a murder, childishly flying in excitement about a few childish, unnecessary and inconvenient gestures; and long before day, I had him on his knees and bathed in tears of what seemed a genuine repentance. On Sunday I took the pulpit in the morning and preached from First Kings, nineteenth, on the fire, the earthquake and the voice: distinguishing the true spiritual power, and referring with such plainness as I dared to recent events in Falesá. The effect produced was great; and it was much increased, when Namu rose in his turn, and confessed that he had been wanting in faith and conduct, and was convinced of sin. So far, then, all was well; but there was one unfortunate circumstance. It was nearing the time of our 'May' in the island, when the native contributions to the mission are received; it fell in my duty to make a notification on the subject; and this gave my enemy his chance, by which he was not slow to profit.

"News of the whole proceedings must have been carried to Case as soon as church was over; and the same afternoon he made an occasion to meet me in the midst of the village. He came up with so much intentness and animosity that I felt it would be damaging to avoid him.

" 'So,' says he in native, 'here is the holy man. He has been preaching against me, but that was not in his heart. He has been preaching upon the love of God, but that was not in his heart—it was between his teeth. Will you know what was in his heart?' cries he. 'I will show it you.' And making a snatch at my head, he made believe to pluck out a dollar, and held it in the air.

"There went that rumour through the crowd with which Polynesians receive a prodigy. As for myself, I stood amazed. The thing was a common, conjuring trick, which I have seen performed at home a score of times; but how was I to convince the villagers of that? I wished I had learned legerdemain instead of Hebrew, that I might have paid the fellow out with his own coin. But there I was, I could not stand there silent, and the best that I could find to say was weak.

" 'I will trouble you not to lay hands on me again,' said I.

" 'I have no such thought,' said he, 'nor will I deprive you of your dollar. Here it is,' he said, and flung it at my feet. I am told it lay where it fell three days."

"I must say it was well played," said I.

"O, he is clever," said Mr Tarleton, "and you can now see for yourself how dangerous. He was a party to the horrid death of the paralytic; he is accused of poisoning Adams; he drove Vigours out of the place by lies that might have led to murder; and there is no question but he has now made up his mind to rid himself of you. How he means to try, we have no guess; only be sure it's something new. There is no end to his readiness and invention."

"He gives himself a sight of trouble," says I. "And after all, what for?"

"Why, how many tons of copra may they make in this district?" asked the missionary.

"I daresay as much as sixty tons," says I.

"And what is the profit to the local trader?" he asked.

"You may call it three pounds," said I.

"Then you can reckon for yourself how much he does it for," said Mr Tarleton. "But the more important thing is to defeat him. It is clear he spread some report against Uma, in order to isolate and have his wicked will of her; failing of that, and seeing a new rival come upon the scene, he used her in a different way. Now the first point to find out is about Namu. Uma, when people began to leave you and your mother alone, what did Namu do?"

"Stop away all-e-same," says Uma.

"I fear the dog has returned to his vomit," said Mr Tarleton. "And now what am I to do for you? I will speak to Namu, I will warn him he is observed; it will be strange if he allow anything to go on amiss, when he is put upon his guard. At the same time, this precaution may fail, and then you must turn elsewhere. You have two people at hand to whom you might apply. There is first of all the priest, who might protect you by the catholic interest; they are a wretchedly small body, but they count two chiefs. And then there is old Faiaso. Ah, if it had been some years ago, you would have needed no one else; but his influence is much reduced, it has gone into Maea's hands, and Maea, I fear, is one of Case's jackalls. In fine, if the worst comes to the worst, you must send up or come yourself to Fale-alii, and though I am not due at this end of the island for a month, I will see what can be done."

So Mr Tarleton said farewell; and half an hour later, the crew were singing and the paddles flashing in the missionary boat.

Chapter IV

Devil-work

Near a month went by without much doing. The same night of our marriage, Galoshes called round, made himself mighty civil, and got into a habit of dropping in about dark and smoking his pipe with the family. He could talk to Uma of course, and started to teach me native and French at the same time. He was a kind old buffer, though the dirtiest you would wish to see, and he muddled me up with foreign languages worse than the tower of Babel.

That was one employment we had, and it made me feel less lonesome; but there was no profit in the thing; for though the priest came and sat and yarned, none of his folks could be enticed into my store; and if it hadn't been for the other occupation I struck out, there wouldn't have been a pound of copra in the house. This was the idea: Fa'avao (Uma's mother) had a score of bearing trees. Of course, we could get no labour, being all as good as tabooed. And the two women and I turned to and made copra with our own hands. It was copra to make your mouth water, when it was done—I never understood how much the natives cheated me till I had made that four hundred pounds of my own hand—and it weighed so light, I felt inclined to take and water it myself.

When we were at the job, a good many kanakas used to put in the best of the day looking on, and once that nigger turned up. He stood back with the natives, and laughed, and did the big don and the funny dog, till I began to get riled.

"Here, you, nigger!" says I.

"I don't address myself to you, sah," says the nigger. "Only speak to gen'le'um."

"I know," says I, "but it happens I was addressing myself to you, Mr Black Jack. And all I want to know is just this: did you see Case's figurehead about a week ago?"

"No, sah," says he.

"That's all right, then," says I; "for I'll show you the own brother to it, only black, in the inside of about two minutes."

And I began to walk towards him, quite slow and my hands down; only there was trouble in my eye, if anybody took the pains to look.

"You're a low, obstropulous fellow, sah," says he.

"You bet!" says I.

By that time he thought I was about as near as was convenient, and lit out so it would have done your heart good to see him travel. And that was all I saw of that precious gang, until what I am about to tell you.

It was one of my chief employments these days to go pot-hunting in the woods, which I found (as Case had told me) very rich in game. I have spoken of the cape, which shut up the village and my station from the east. A path went about the end of it, and led into the next bay. A strong wind blew here daily, and as the line of the barrier reef stopped at the end of the cape, a heavy surf ran on the shores of the bay. A little cliffy hill cut the valley in two parts, and stood close on the beach; and at high water the sea broke right on the face of it, so that all passage was stopped. Woody mountains hemmed the place all round; the barrier to the east was particularly steep and leafy; the lower parts of it, along the sea, falling in sheer black cliffs streaked with cinnabar; the upper part lumpy with the tops of the great trees. Some of the trees were bright green, and some red, and the sand of the beach as black as your shoes. Many birds hovered round the bay, some of them snow white; and the flying-fox (or vampire) flew there in broad daylight, gnashing its teeth.

For a long while I came as far as this shooting and went no farther. There was no sign of any path beyond; and the cocoapalms in the front of the foot of the valley were the last this way. For the whole "eye" of the island, as natives call the windward end, lay desert. From Falesá round about to Papa-mālūlū, there was neither house, nor man, nor planted fruit tree; and the reef being mostly absent and the shores bluff, the sea beat direct among crags, and there was scarce a landing place.

I should tell you that after I began to go in the woods, although no one offered to come near my store, I found people willing enough to pass the time of day with me where nobody could see them. And as I had begun to pick up native, and most of them had a word or two of English, I began to hold little odds and ends of conversation, not to much purpose, to be sure, but they took off the worst of the feeling. For it's a miserable thing to be made a leper of.

It chanced one day, towards the end of the month, that I was sitting in this bay in the edge of the bush, looking east, with a kanaka. I had given him a fill of tobacco, and we were making out to talk as best we could; indeed he had more English than most.

I asked him if there was no road going eastward.

"One time one road," said he. "Now he dead."

"Nobody he go there?" I asked.

"No good," said he. "Too much devil he stop there."

"Oho!" says I, "got-um plenty devil, that bush?"

"Man devil, woman devil: too much devil," said my friend. "Stop there all-e-time. Man he go there, no come back."

I thought, if this fellow was so well posted on devils and spoke of them so free, which is not common, I had better fish for a little information about myself and Uma.

"You think me one devil?" I asked.

"No think devil," said he soothingly. "Think all-e-same fool."

"Uma, she devil?" I asked again.

"No, no; no devil; devil stop bush," said the young man.

I was looking in front of me across the bay, and I saw the hanging front of the woods pushed suddenly open, and Case with a gun in his hand step forth into the sunshine on the black beach. He was got up in light pyjamas, near white, his gun sparkled, he looked mighty conspicuous; and the land crabs scuttled from all round him to their holes.

"Hullo, my friend," says I, "you no talk all-e-same true. Ese he go, he come back."

"Ese no all-e-same; Ese *Tiapolo*," says my friend; and with a good bye, slunk off among the trees.

I watched Case all round the beach, where the tide was low; and let him pass me on the homeward way to Falesá. He was in deep thought; and the birds seemed to know it, trotting quite near him on the sand or wheeling and calling in his ears. Where he passed nearest me, I could see by the working of his lips that he was talking in to himself, and what pleased me mightily, he had still my trademark on his brow. I tell you the plain truth, I had a mind to give him a gunfull in his ugly mug, but I thought better of it.

All this time, and all the time I was following home, I kept repeating that native word, which I remembered by "Polly, put the kettle on and make us all some tea": tea-a-pollo.

"Uma," says I, when I got back, "what does Tiapolo mean?"

"Devil," says she.

"I thought *aitu* was the word for that?" I said.

"*Aitu* 'nother kind of devil," said she; "stop bush, eat kanaka. Tiapolo big-chief devil, stop home; all-e-same Christian devil."

"Well then," said I. "I'm no farther forward. How can Case be Tiapolo?"

"No all-e-same," said she. "Ese belong Tiapolo; Tiapolo too much like; Ese all-e-same his son. Suppose Ese he wish something, Tiapolo he make him."

"That's mighty convenient for Ese," says I. "And what kind of things does he make for him?"

Well, out came a rigmarole of all sorts of stories, many of which (like the dollar he took from Mr Tarleton's head) were plain enough to me, but others I could make nothing of; and the thing that most surprised the kanakas was what surprised me least: namely, that he could go in the desert among all the *aitus*. Some of the boldest, however, had accompanied him, and had heard him speak with the dead and give them orders, and safe in his protection, had returned unscathed. Some said he had a church there where he worshipped Tiapolo, and Tiapolo appeared to him; others swore there was no sorcery at all, that he performed his miracles by the power of prayer, and the church was no church but a prison in which he had confined a dangerous *aitu*. Namu had been in the bush with him once, and returned glorifying God for these wonders. Altogether I began to have a glimmer of the man's position, and the means by which he had acquired it, and though I saw he was a tough nut to crack, I was noways cast down.

"Very well," said I, "I'll have a look at Master Case's place of worship myself, and we'll see about the glorifying."

At this time Uma fell in a terrible taking; if I went in the high bush, I should never return; none could go there but by the protection of Tiapolo.

"I'll chance it on God's," said I. "I'm a good sort of a fellow, Uma, as fellows go; and I guess God'll con me through."

She was silent for awhile. "I think," said she, mighty solemn; and then presently: "Victoreea he big chief?"

"You bet," said I.

"He like you too much?" she asked again.

I told her with a grin I believed the old lady was rather partial to me.

"All right," said she. "Victoreea he big chief, like you too much; no can help you here in Falesá; no can do, too far off. Maea he small chief; stop here; suppose he like you, make you all right. All-e-same God and Tiapolo. God he big chief, got too much work. Tiapolo he small chief, he like too much make-see, work very hard."

"I'll have to hand you over to Mr Tarleton," said I. "Your theology's out of its bearings, Uma."

However we stuck at this business all the evening, and with the stories she told me of the desert and its dangers, she came near frightening herself into a fit. I don't remember half a quarter of them of course, for I paid little heed; but two come back to me kind of clear.

About six miles up the coast there is a sheltered cove, they call *Fanga-anaana*, "the haven full of caves." I've seen it from the sea myself, as near as I could get my boys to venture in; and it's a little strip of yellow sand. Black cliffs overhang it full of the black mouths of caves, great trees overhang the cliffs and dangle down lianas, and in one place, about the middle, a big brook pours over in a cascade. Well, there was a boat going by here with six young men of Falesá, "all very pretty," Uma said, which was the loss of them. It blew strong, there was a heavy head sea; and by the time they opened Fanga-anaana, and saw the white cascade and the shady beach, they were all tired and thirsty, and their water had run out. One proposed to land and get a drink; and being reckless fellows, they were all of the same mind except the youngest. Lotu was his name; he was a very good young gentleman and very wise; and he held out they were crazy, telling them the place was given over to spirits and devils and the dead, and there were no living folk nearer than six miles the one way and maybe twelve the other. But they laughed at his words; and being five to one, pulled in, beached the boat, and landed. It was a wonderful pleasant place, Lotu said, and the water excellent. They walked round the beach, but could see nowhere any way to mount the cliffs, which made them easier in their mind; and at last they sat down to make a meal on the food they had brought with them. They were scarce set, when there came out of the mouth of one of the black caves six of the most beautiful ladies ever seen; they had flowers in their hair, and the most beautiful breasts, and necklaces of scarlet seeds; and began to jest with these young gentlemen, and the young gentlemen to jest back with them, all but Lotu. As for Lotu, he saw there could be no living women in such a place, and ran, and flung himself in the bottom of the boat, and covered his face, and prayed. All the time the business lasted, Lotu made one clean break of prayer; and that was all he knew of it, until his friends came back, and made him sit up, and they put to sea again out of the bay, which was now quite desert, and no word of the six ladies. But what frightened Lotu worst, not one of the five remembered anything of what had passed, but they were all like drunken men, and sang and laughed in the boat, and skylarked. The wind freshened and came squally, the sea rose extraordinary high; it was such weather as any man in the islands would have turned his back to and fled home to Falesá; but these five were like crazy folk, and cracked on all sail, and drove their boat into the seas. Lotu went to the bailing; none of the others thought to help him, but sang and skylarked and carried on, and spoke singular things beyond a man's comprehension, and laughed out loud when they said them. So the rest of that day,

Lotu bailed for his life in the bottom of the boat, and was all drenched with sweat and cold sea water; and none heeded him. Against all expectation, they came safe in a dreadful tempest to Papa-mālūlū, where the palms were singing out and the cocoanuts flying like cannonballs about the village green; and the same night the five young gentlemen sickened and spoke never a reasonable word until they died.

"And do you mean to tell me you can swallow a yarn like that?" I asked.

She told me the thing was well known, and with handsome young men alone, it was even common. But this was the only case where five had been slain the same day and in a company by the love of the women devils; and it had made a great stir in the island; and she would be crazy if she doubted.

"Well anyway," says I, "you needn't be frightened about me. I've got no use for the women devils; you're all the women I want, and all the devil too, old lady."

To that she answered there were other sorts, and she had seen one with her own eyes. She had gone one day alone to the next bay, and perhaps got too near the margin of the bad place. The boughs of the high bush overshadowed her from the kant of the hill; but she herself was outside in a flat place, very stony and growing full of young mummy apples, four and five feet high. It was a dark day in the rainy season; and now there came squalls that tore off the leaves and sent them flying, and now it was all still as in a house. It was in one of these still times, that a whole gang of birds and flying-foxes came pegging out of the bush like creatures frightened. Presently after she heard a rustle nearer hand, and saw coming out of the margin of the trees among the mummy-apples, the appearance of a lean, gray, old boar. It seemed to think as it came, like a person; and all of a sudden, as she looked at it coming, she was aware it was no boar but a thing that was a man with a man's thoughts. At that she ran, and the pig after her, and as the pig ran it hollered aloud, so that the place rang with it.

"I wish I had been there with my gun," said I. "I guess the pig would have hollered so as to surprise himself."

But she told me a gun was of no use with the like of these, which were the spirits of the dead.

Well, this kind of talk put in the evening, which was the best of it; but of course it didn't change my notion; and the next day, with my gun and a good knife, I set off upon a voyage of discovery. I made as near as I could for the place where I had seen Case come out; for if it was true he had some kind of establishment in the bush, I reckoned I should find a path. The beginning of the desert was marked off by a wall—to call it so, for it was more of a long mound of stones; they say it reaches right across the island, but how they know it is another question, for I doubt if anyone has made the journey in a hundred years; the natives sticking chiefly to the sea and their little colonies along the coast, and that part being mortal high and steep and full of cliffs. Up to the west side of the wall, the ground has been cleared, and there are cocoapalms, and mummy-apples, and guavas, and lots of sensitive. Just across, the bush begins outright; high bush at that: trees going up like the masts of ships, and ropes of liana hanging down like a ship's rigging, and nasty orchids growing in the forks like funguses. The ground, where there was no underwood, looked to be a heap of boulders. I saw many green pigeons which I might have shot, only I was there with a different idea; a number of butterflies flopped up and down along the ground like dead leaves; sometimes I would hear a bird calling, sometimes the wind overhead, and always the sea along the coast.

But the queerness of the place, it's more difficult to tell of; unless to one who has been alone in the high bush himself. The brightest kind of a day, it is always dim down there. A man can see to the end of nothing; whichever way he looks, the wood shuts up, one bough folding with another, like the fingers of your hand; and whenever he listens, he hears always something new—men talking, children laughing, the strokes of an axe a far way ahead of him, and sometimes a sort of quick, stealthy scurry near at hand that makes him jump and look to his weapons. It's all very well for him to tell himself that he's alone, bar trees and birds; he can't make out to believe it: whichever way he turns, the whole place seems to be alive and looking on. Don't think it was Uma's yarns that put me out; I don't value native talk a fourpenny piece: it's a thing that's natural in the bush, and that's the end of it.

As I got near the top of the hill, for the ground of the wood goes up in this place steep as a ladder, the wind began to sound straight on, and the leaves to toss and switch open and let in the sun. This suited me better; it was the same noise all the time and nothing to startle. Well, I had got to a place where there was an underwood of what they call wild cocoanut—mighty pretty with its scarlet fruits—when there came a sound of singing in the wind that I thought I had never heard the like of. It was all very fine to tell myself it was the branches; I knew better. It was all very fine to tell myself it was a bird; I knew never a bird that sang like that. It rose, and swelled, and died away, and swelled again; and now I thought it was like some one weeping, only prettier; and now I thought it was like harps; and there was one thing I made sure of, it was a sight too sweet to be wholesome in a place like that. You may laugh if you like; but I declare I called to mind the six young ladies that came, with their scarlet necklaces, out of the cave at Fanga-anaana, and wondered if they sang like that. We laugh at the natives and their superstitions; but see how many traders take them up, splendidly educated white men, that have been bookkeepers (some of them) and clerks in the old country! It's my belief a superstition grows up in a place like the different kinds of weeds; and as I stood there, and listened to that wailing, I twittered in my shoes.

You may call me a coward to be frightened; I thought myself brave enough to go on ahead. But I went mighty carefully, with my gun cocked, spying all about me like a hunter, fully expecting to see a handsome young woman sitting somewhere in the bush, and fully determined (if I did) to try her with a charge of duckshot. And sure enough I had not gone far, when I met with a queer thing. The wind came on the top of the wood in a strong puff, the leaves in front of me burst open, and I saw for a second something hanging in a tree. It was gone in a wink, the puff blowing by and the leaves closing. I tell you the truth; I had made up my mind to see an *aitu;* and if the thing had looked like a pig or a woman, it wouldn't have given me the same turn. The trouble was that it seemed kind of square; and the idea of a square thing that was alive and sang, knocked me sick and silly. I must have stood quite a while; and I made pretty certain it was right out of the same tree that the singing came. Then I began to come to myself a bit.

"Well," says I, "if this is really so, if this is a place where there are square things that sing, I'm gone up anyway. Let's have my fun for my money."

But I thought I might as well take the off-chance of a prayer being any good; so I plumped on my knees and prayed out loud; and all the time I was praying, the strange sounds came out of the tree, and went up and down, and changed, for all the world like music; only you could see it wasn't human—there was nothing there that you could whistle.

As soon as I had made an end in proper style, I laid down my gun, stuck my knife between my teeth, walked right up to that tree, and began to climb. I tell you my heart was like ice. But presently, as I went up, I caught another glimpse of the thing, and that relieved me, for I thought it seemed woundy like a box; and when I had got right up to it, I near fell out of the tree with laughing. A box it was, sure enough, and a candle box at that, with the brand upon the side of it; and it had banjo strings stretched so as to sound when the wind blew. I believe they call the thing a Tyrolean harp, whatever that may mean.

"Well, Mr Case," said I, "you've frightened me once. But I defy you to frighten me again," I says, and slipped down the tree, and set out again to find my enemy's head office, which I guessed would not be far away.

The undergrowth was thick in this part. I couldn't see before my nose, and must burst my way through by main force and ply the knife as I went, slicing the cords of the lianas and slashing down whole trees at a blow. I call them trees for the bigness, but in truth they were just big weeds and sappy to cut through like a carrot. From all this crowd and kind of vegetation, I was just thinking to myself the place might have once been cleared, when I came on my nose over a pile of stones, and saw in a moment it was some kind of a work of man. The Lord knows when it was made or when deserted; for this part of the island has lain undisturbed since long before the whites came. A few steps beyond, I hit into the path I had been always looking for. It was narrow but well beaten, and I saw that Case had plenty of disciples. It seems indeed it was a piece of fashionable boldness to venture up here with the trader; and a young man scarce reckoned himself grown, till he had got his breech tattooed for one thing, and seen Case's devils for another. This is mighty like kanakas; but if you look at it another way, it's mighty like white folks too.

A bit along the path, I was brought to a clean stand and had to rub my eyes. There was a wall in front of me, the path passing it by a gap; it was tumble down and plainly very old, but built of big stones very well laid; and there is no native alive today upon that island that could dream of such a piece of building. Along all the top of it was a line of queer figures, idols, or scare-crows, or what not. They had carved and painted faces, ugly to view; their eyes and teeth were of shell; their hair and their bright clothes blew in the wind, and some of them worked with the tugging. There are islands up west, where they make these kinds of figures till today; but if ever they were made in this island, the practise and the very recollection of it are now long forgotten. And the singular thing was that all these bogies were as fresh as toys out of a shop.

Then it came in my mind what Case had let out to me the first day, that he was a good forger of island curiosities: a thing by which so many traders turn an honest penny. And with that I saw the whole business, and how this display served the man a double purpose: first of all to season his curiosities, and then to frighten those that came to visit him.

But I should tell you (what made the thing more curious) that all the time the Tyrolean harps were harping round me in the trees, and even while I looked a green and yellow bird (that I suppose was building) began to tear the hair off the head of one of the figures.

A little farther on, I found the last curiosity of the museum. The first I saw of it was a longish mound of earth with a twist to it. Digging off the earth with my hands, I found underneath tarpaulin stretched on boards, so that this was plainly the roof of a cellar. It stood right on the top of the hill, and the entrance was on the far side, between two rocks, like the entrance to a cave. I went in as far as the bend, and looking round the corner, saw a shining face. It was big and ugly like a pantomime mask, and the brightness of it waxed and dwindled, and at times it smoked.

"Oho," says I, "luminous paint!"

And I must say I rather admired the man's ingenuity. With a box of tools and a few mighty simple contrivances, he had made out to have a devil of a temple. Any poor kanaka brought up here in the dark, with the harps whining all round him, and shown that smoking face in the bottom of a hole, would make no kind of doubt but he had seen and heard enough devils for a lifetime. It's easy to find out what kanakas think. Just go back to yourself anyway round from ten to fifteen years old, and there's an average kanaka. There are some pious, just as there are pious boys; and the most of them, like the boys again, are middling honest and yet think it rather larks to steal, and are easy scared and rather like to be so. I remembered a boy I was at school with at home, who played the Case business. He didn't know anything, that boy; he couldn't do anything; he had no luminous paint and no Tyrolean harps; he just boldly said he was a sorcerer, and frightened us out of our boots, and we loved it. And then it came in my mind how the master had once flogged that boy, and the surprise we were all in to see the sorcerer catch it and bum like anybody else. Thinks I to myself: "I must find some way of fixing it so for Master Case." And the next moment I had my idea.

I went back by the path which, when once you had found it, was quite plain and easy walking; and when I stepped out on the black sands, who should I see but Master Case himself? I cocked my gun and held it handy; and we marched up and passed without a word, each keeping the tail of his eye on the other; and no sooner had we passed, than we each wheeled round like fellows drilling and stood face to face. We had each taken the same notion in his head, you see, that the other fellow might give him the load of a gun in the stern.

"You've shot nothing," says Case.

"I'm not on the shoot today," says I.

"Well, the devil go with you for me," says he.

"The same to you," says I.

But we stuck just the way we were; no fear of either of us moving.

Case laughed. "We can't stop here all day, though," said he.

"Don't let me detain you," says I.

He laughed again. "Look here, Wiltshire, do you think me a fool?" he asked.

"More of a knave if you want to know," says I.

"Well, do you think it would better me to shoot you here on this open beach?" said he, "because I don't. Folks come fishing every day. There may be a score of them up the valley now, making copra; there may be half a dozen on the hill behind you after pigeons; they might be watching us this minute, and I shouldn't wonder. I give you my word I don't want to shoot you. Why should I? You don't hinder me any; you haven't got one pound of copra but what you made with your own hands like a negro slave. You're vegetating, that's what I call it; and I don't care where you vegetate, nor yet how long. Give me your word you don't mean to shoot me, and I'll give you a lead and walk away."

"Well," said I, "you're frank and pleasant, ain't you? and I'll be the same. I don't mean to shoot you today. Why should I? This business is beginning; it ain't done yet, Mr Case. I've given you one turn already, I can see the marks of my knuckles on your head to this blooming hour; and I've more cooking for you. I'm not a paralee like Underhill; my name ain't Adams and it ain't Vigours; and I mean to show you that you've met your match."

"This is a silly way to talk," said he. "This is not the talk to make me move on with."

"All right," said I. "Stay where you are. I ain't in any hurry, and you know it. I can put in the day on this beach, and never mind. I ain't got any copra to bother with. I ain't got any luminous paint to see to."

I was sorry I said that last, but it whipped out before I knew. I could see it took the wind out of his sails, and he stood and stared at me with his brow drawn up. Then I suppose he made up his mind he must get to the bottom of this.

"I take you at your word," says he, and turned his back, and walked right into the devil's bush.

I let him go of course, for I had passed my word. But I watched him as long as he was in sight, and after he was gone, lit out for cover as lively as you would want to see, and went the rest of the way home under the bush. For I didn't trust him sixpenceworth. One thing I saw: I had been ass enough to give him warning; and that which I meant to do, I must do at once.

You would think I had had about enough excitement for one morning; but there was another turn waiting me. As soon as I got far enough round the cape to see my house, I made out there were strangers there; a little farther, and no doubt about it, there were a couple of armed sentries squatting at my door. I could only suppose the trouble about Uma must have come to a head, and the station been seized. For aught I could think Uma was taken up already, and these armed men were waiting to do the like by me.

However, as I came nearer, which I did at top speed, I saw there was a third native sitting on the verandah like a guest, and Uma was talking with him like a hostess. Nearer still I made out it was the big young chief Maea, and that he was smiling away and smoking; and what was he smoking?—none of your European cigarettes fit for a cat; not even the genuine, big, knock-me-down native article, that a fellow can really put in the time with, if his pipe is broke; but a cigar, and one of my Mexicans at that, that I could swear to. At sight of this, my heart started beating; and I took a wild hope in my head that the trouble was over, and Maea had come round.

Uma pointed me out to him, as I came up, and he met me at the head of my own stairs like a thorough gentleman.

"Vilivili," said he, which was the best they could make of my name, "I pleased."

There is no doubt when an island chief wants to be civil he can do it. I saw the way things were from the word go. There was no call for Uma to say to me: "He no 'fraid Ese now; come bring copra." I tell you I shook hands with that kanaka like as if he was the best white man in Europe.

The fact was Case and he had got after the same girl, or Maea suspected it and concluded to make hay of the trader on the chance. He had dressed himself up, got a couple of his retainers cleaned and armed to kind of make the thing more public, and just waiting till Case was clear of the village, came round to put the whole of his business my way. He was rich as well as powerful, I suppose that man was worth fifty thousand nuts per annum. I gave him the price of the beach and a quarter cent better, and as for credit, I would have advanced him the inside of the store and the fittings besides, I was so pleased to see him. I must say he bought like a gentleman: rice and tins and biscuit enough for a week's feast, and stuffs by the bolt. He was agreeable besides; he had plenty fun to him; and we cracked jests together, mostly through Uma for interpreter, because he had mighty little English, and my native was still off colour. One thing I made out: he could never really have thought much harm of Uma; he could never have been really frightened, and must just have made believe from dodginess and because he thought Case had a strong pull in the village and could help him on.

This set me thinking that both he and I were in a tightish place. What he had done was to fly in the face of the whole village, and the thing might cost him his authority. More than that, after my talk with Case on the beach, I thought it might very well cost me my life. Case had as good as said he would pot me if ever I got copra; he would come home to find the best business in the village had changed hands; and the best thing I thought I could do was to get in first with the potting.

"See here, Uma," says I, "tell him I'm sorry I made him wait, but I was looking at Case's Tiapolo store in the bush."

"He want savvy if you no 'fraid?" translated Uma.

I laughed out. "Not much!" says I. "Tell him the place is a blooming toyshop! Tell him in England we give these things to the kids to play with."

"He want savvy if you hear devil sing?" she asked next.

"Look here," I said, "I can't do it now because I've got no banjo strings in stock; but the next time the ship comes round, I'll have one of these same contraptions right here in my verandah, and he can see for himself how much devil there is to it. Tell him, as soon as I can get the strings, I'll make one for his picaninnies. The name of the concern is a Tyrolean harp; and you can tell him the name means in English, that nobody but damfools give a cent for it."

This time he was so pleased he had to try his English again. "You talk true?" says he.

"Rather!" said I. "Talk all-e-same Bible. Bring out a Bible here, Uma, if you've got such a thing, and I'll kiss it. Or I'll tell you what's better still," says I, taking a header. "Ask him if he's afraid to go up there himself by day."

It appeared he wasn't; he could venture as far as that by day and in company.

"That's the ticket, then!" said I. "Tell him the man's a fraud and the place foolishness, and if he'll go up there tomorrow, he'll see all that's left of it. But tell him this, Uma, and mind he understands it; if he gets talking, it's bound to come to Case and I'm a dead man. I'm playing his game, tell him, and if he says one word, my blood will be at his door and be the damnation of him here and after."

She told him, and he shook hands with me up to the hilts, and says he: "No talk. Go up tomollow. You my friend?"

"No, sir!" says I. "No such foolishness. I've come here to trade, tell him, and not to make friends. But as to Case, I'll send that man to glory."

So off Maea went, pretty well pleased, as I could see.

CHAPTER V

Night in the bush

Well, I was committed now; Tiapolo had to be smashed up before next day; and my hands were pretty full, not only with preparations, but with argument. My house was like a mechanics' debating society; Uma was so made up that I shouldn't go into the bush by night, or that if I did I was never to come back again. You know her style of arguing, you've had a specimen about Queen Victoria and the devil; and I leave you to fancy if I was tired of it before dark.

At last, I had a good idea; what was the use of casting my pearls before her? I thought: some of her own chopped hay would be likelier to do the business.

"I'll tell you what, then," said I. "You fish out your bible, and I'll take that up along with me. That'll make me right."

She swore a bible was no use.

"That's just your blamed kanaka ignorance," said I. "Bring the bible out."

She brought it, and I turned to the title page where I thought there would likely be some English, and so there was. "There!" said I. "Look at that! *'London: printed for the British and Foreign Bible Society, Blackfriars'*; and the date, which I can't read, owing to its being in these X's. There's no devil in hell can look near the Bible Society, Blackfriars. Why, you silly!" I said, "how do you suppose we get along with our own *aitus* at home? All Bible Society!"

"I think you no got any," said she. "White man he tell me you no got."

"Sounds likely, don't it?" I asked. "Why would these islands all be chock full of them, and none in Europe?"

"Well, you no got breadfruit," said she.

I could have tore my hair. "Now, look here, old lady," said I, "you dry up, for I'm tired of you. I'll take the bible, which'll put me as straight as the mail; and that's the last word I've got to say."

The night fell extraordinary dark, clouds coming up with sundown and overspreading all; not a star showed; there was only an end of a moon, and that not due before the small hours. Round the village, what with the lights and the fires in the open houses and the torches of many fishers moving on the reef, it kept as gay as an illumination; but the sea and the mountains and woods were all clean gone. I suppose it might be eight o'clock when I took the road, loaden like a donkey. First there was that bible, a book as big as your head, which I had let myself in for by my own tomfoolery. Then there was my gun and knife and lantern and patent matches, all necessary. And then there was the real plant of the affair in hand, a mortal weight of gunpowder, a pair of dynamite fishing-bombs, and two or three pieces of slow match that I had hauled out of the tin cases and spliced together the best way I could; for the match was only trade stuff, and a man would be crazy that trusted it. Altogether, you see, I had the materials of a pretty good blow up. Expense was nothing to me; I wanted that thing done right.

As long as I was in the open, and had the lamp in my house to steer by, I did well. But when I got to the path, it fell so dark I could make no headway, walking into trees and swearing there, like a man looking for the matches in his bedroom. I knew it was risky to light up; for my lantern would be visible all the way to the point of the cape; and as no one went there after dark, it would be talked about and come to Case's ears. But what was I to do? I had either to give the business over and lose caste with Maea, or light up, take my chance, and get through the thing the smartest I was able.

As long as I was on the path, I walked hard; but when I came to the black beach, I had to run. For the tide was now nearly flowed; and to get through with my powder dry between the surf and the steep hill, took all the quickness I possessed. As it was even, the wash caught me to the knees and I came near falling on a stone. All this time, the hurry I was in, and the free air and smell of the sea, kept my spirits lively; but when I was once in the bush and began to climb the path, I took it easier. The fearsomeness of the wood had been a good bit rubbed off for me by Master Case's banjo strings and graven images; yet I thought it was a dreary walk, and guessed, when the disciples went up there, they must be badly scared. The light of the lantern, striking among all these trunks, and forked branches, and twisted rope's-ends of lianas, made the whole place, or all that you could see it, a kind of a puzzle of turning shadows. They came to meet you, solid and quick like giants, and then span off and vanished; they hove up over your head like clubs, and flew away into the night like birds. The floor of the bush glimmered with dead wood, the way the matchbox used to shine after you had struck a lucifer. Big cold drops fell on me from the branches overhead like sweat. There was no wind to mention, only a little icy breath of a land breeze that stirred nothing; and the harps were silent.

The first landfall I made was when I got through the bush of wild cocoanuts, and came in view of the bogies on the wall. Mighty queer they looked by the shining of the lantern, with their painted faces, and shell eyes, and their clothes and their hair hanging. One after another I pulled them all up and piled them in a bundle on the cellar roof, so as they might go to glory with the rest. Then I chose a place behind one of the big stones at the entrance, buried my powder and the two shells, and arranged my match along the passage. And then I had a look at the smoking head, just for good-bye. It was doing fine.

"Cheer up," says I. "You're booked."

It was my first idea to light up and be getting homeward; for the darkness, and the glimmer of the dead wood, and the shadows of the lantern made me lonely. But I knew where one of the harps hung; it seemed a pity it shouldn't go with the rest; and at the same time I couldn't help letting on to myself that I was mortal tired of my employment and would like best to be at home and have the door shut. I stepped out of the cellar, and argued it fore and back. There was a sound of the sea far down below me on the coast; nearer hand, not a leaf stirred; I might have been the only living creature this side Cape Horn. Well, as I stood there thinking, it seemed the bush woke and became full of little noises. Little noises they were, and nothing to hurt— a bit of a crackle, a bit of a brush—but the breath jumped right out of me and my throat went as dry as a biscuit. It wasn't Case I was afraid of, which would have been common sense; I never thought of Case; what took me, as sharp as the cholic, was the old wives' tales, the devil-women and the man-pigs. It was the toss of a penny whether I should run; but I got a purchase on myself, and stepped out, and held up the lantern (like a fool) and looked all round.

In the direction of the village and the path, there was nothing to be seen; but when I turned inland, it's a wonder to me I didn't drop. There—coming right up out of the desert and the bad bush—there, sure enough, was a devil-woman, just the way I had figured she would look. I saw the light shine on her bare arms and her bright eyes. And there went out of me a yell so big that I thought it was my death.

"Ah! No sing out!" says the devil-woman, in a kind of a high whisper. "Why you talk big voice? Put out light! Ese he come."

"My God Almighty, Uma, is that you?" says I.

"Ioe," says she. "I come quick. Ese here soon."

"You come alone?" I asked. "You no 'fraid?"

"Ah, too much 'fraid!" she whispered, clutching me. "I think die."

"Well," says I, with a kind of a weak grin, "I'm not the one to laugh at you, Mrs Wiltshire, for I'm about the worst scared man in the South Pacific myself."

She told me in two words what brought her. I was scarce gone, it seems, when Faavao came in; and the old woman had met Black Jack running as hard as he was fit from our house to Case's. Uma neither spoke nor stopped, but lit right out to come and warn me. She was so close at my heels that the lantern was her guide across the beach, and afterwards, by the glimmer of it in the trees, she got her line up hill. It was only when I had got to the top or was in the cellar, that she wandered—Lord knows where!—and lost a sight of precious time, afraid to call out lest Case was at the heels of her, and falling in the bush so that she was all knocked and bruised. That must have been when she got too far to the southward, and how she came to take me in the flank at last, and frighten me beyond what I've got the words to tell of.

Well, anything was better than a devil-woman; but I thought her yarn serious enough. Black Jack had no call to be about my house, unless he was set there to watch; and it looked to me as if my tomfool word about the paint and perhaps some chatter of Maea's had got us all in a clove hitch. One thing was clear: Uma and I were here for the night; we daren't try to go home before day, and even then it would be safer to strike round up the mountain and come in by the back of the village, or we might walk into an ambuscade. It was plain too that the mine should be sprung immediately, or Case might be in time to stop it.

I marched into the tunnel, Uma keeping tight hold of me, opened my lantern and lit the match. The first length of it burned like a spill of paper; and I stood stupid, watching it burn, and thinking we were going aloft with Tiapolo, which was none of my views. The second took to a better rate, though faster than I cared about; and at that I got my wits again, hauled Uma clear of the passage, blew out and dropped the lantern; and the pair of us groped our way into the bush until I thought it might be safe, and lay down together by a tree.

"Old lady," I said, "I won't forget this night. You're a trump, and that's what's wrong with you."

She humped herself close up to me. She had run out the way she was with nothing on but her kilt; and she was all wet with the dews and the sea on the black beach, and shook straight on with cold and the terror of the dark and the devils.

"Too much 'fraid," was all she said.

The far side of Case's hill goes down near as steep as a precipice into the next valley. We were on the very edge of it, and I could see the dead wood shine and hear the sea sound far below. I didn't care about the position, which left me no retreat, but I was afraid to change. Then I saw I had made a worse mistake about the lantern, which I should have left lighted, so that I could have had a crack at Case when he stepped into the shine of it. And even if I hadn't had the wit to do that, it seemed a senseless thing to leave the good lantern to blow up with the graven images; the thing belonged to me, after all, and was worth money, and might come in handy. If I could have trusted the match, I might have run in still and rescued it. But who was going to trust the match? You know what trade is; the stuff was good enough for kanakas to go fishing with, where they've got to look lively anyway, and the most they risk is only to have their hand blown off; but for any one that wanted to fool around a blow-up like mine, that match was rubbish.

Altogether, the best I could do was to lie still, see my shot gun handy, and wait for the explosion. But it was a solemn kind of a business; the blackness of the night was like solid; the only thing you could see was the nasty, bogy glimmer of the dead wood, and that showed you nothing but itself; and as for sounds, I stretched my ears till I thought I could have heard the match burn in the tunnel, and that bush was as silent as a coffin. Now and then there was a bit of a crack, but whether it was near or far, whether it was Case stubbing his toes within a few yards of me or a tree breaking miles away, I knew no more than the babe unborn.

And then all of a sudden Vesuvius went off. It was a long time coming; but when it came (though I say it that shouldn't) no man could ask to see a better. At first it was just a son of a gun of a row, and a spout of fire, and the wood lighted up so that you could see to read. And then the trouble began. Uma and I were half buried under a waggonful of earth, and glad it was no worse; for one of the rocks at the entrance of the tunnel was fired clean into the air, fell within a couple of fathom of where we lay, and bounded over the edge of the hill, and went pounding down into the next valley. I saw I had rather under-calculated our distance, or overdone the dynamite and powder, which you please.

And presently I saw I had made another slip. The noise of the thing began to die off, shaking the island; the dazzle was over; and yet the night didn't come back the way that I expected. For the whole wood was scattered with red coals and brands from the explosion; they were all round me on the flat, some had fallen below in the valley, and some stuck and flared in the treetops. I had no fear of fire, for these forests are too wet to kindle. But the trouble was that the place was all lit up, not very bright but good enough to get a shot by; and the way the coals were scattered, it was just as likely Case might have the advantage as myself. I looked all round for his white face, you may be sure; but there was not a sign of him. As for Uma, the life seemed to have been knocked right out of her by the bang and blaze of it.

There was one bad point in my game. One of the blessed graven images had come down all afire, hair and clothes and body, not four yards away from me. I cast a mighty noticing glance all round; there was still no Case; and I made up my mind I must get rid of that burning stick before he came, or I should be shot there like a dog.

It was my first idea to have crawled; and then I thought speed was the main thing, and stood half up to make a rush. The same moment, from somewhere between me and the sea, there came a flash and a report, and a rifle bullet screeched in my ear. I swung straight round, and up with my gun. But the brute had a Winchester; and before I could as much as see him, his second shot knocked me over like a ninepin. I seemed to fly in the air, then came down by the run and lay half a minute silly; and then I found my hands empty and my gun had flown over my head as I fell. It makes a man mighty wide awake to be in the kind of box that I was in. I scarce knew where I was hurt, or whether I was hurt or not, but turned right over on my face to crawl after my weapon. Unless you have tried to get about with a smashed leg, you don't know what pain is, and I let a howl out like a bullock's.

This was the unluckiest noise that ever I made in my life. Up to then, Uma had stuck to her tree like a sensible woman, knowing she would be only in the way. But as soon as she heard me sing out, she ran forward—the Winchester cracked again—and down she went.

I had sat up, leg and all, to stop her; but when I saw her tumble, I clapped down again where I was, lay still, and felt the handle of my knife. I had been scurried and put out before. No more of that for me; he had knocked over my girl, I had got to fix him for it; and I lay there and gritted my teeth, and footed up the chances. My leg was broke, my gun was gone, Case had still ten shots in his Winchester, it looked a kind of hopeless business. But I never despaired nor thought upon despairing: that man had got to go.

For a goodish bit, not one of us let on. Then I heard Case begin to move nearer in the bush, but mighty careful. The image had burned out; there were only a few coals left here and there; and the wood was main dark, but had a kind of a low glow in it like a fire on its last legs. It was by this that I made out Case's head looking at me over a big tuft of ferns; and at the same time the brute saw me and shouldered his Winchester. I lay quite still and as good as looked into the barrel; it was my last chance; but I thought my heart would have come right out of its bearings. Then he fired. Lucky for me it was no shot gun, for the bullet struck within an inch of me and knocked the dirt in my eyes.

Just you try and see if you can lie quiet, and let a man take a sitting shot at you, and miss you by a hair! But I did, and lucky too. Awhile Case stood with the Winchester at the port-arms; then he gave a little laugh to himself, and stepped round the ferns.

"Laugh!" thought I. "If you had the wit of a louse, you would be praying!"

I was all as taut as a ship's hauser or the spring of a watch; and as soon as he came within reach of me, I had him by the ankle, plucked the feet right out from under him, laid him out, and was upon the top of him, broken leg and all, before he breathed. His Winchester had gone the same road as my shot gun; it was nothing to me; I defied him now. I'm a pretty strong man anyway, but I never knew what strength was till I got hold of Case. He was knocked out of time by the rattle he came down with, and threw up his hands together, more like a frightened woman, so that I caught both of them with my left. This wakened him up, and he fixed his teeth in my forearm like a weasel. Much I cared! My leg gave me all the pain I had any use for; and I drew my knife, and got it in the place.

"Now," said I, "I've got you; and you're gone up, and a good job too. Do you feel the point of that? That's for Underhill. And there's for

Adams. And now here's for Uma, and that's going to knock your blooming soul right out of you."

With that, I gave him the cold steel for all I was worth. His body kicked under me like a spring sofa; he gave a dreadful kind of a long moan, and lay still.

"I wonder if you're dead. I hope so," I thought, for my head was swimming. But I wasn't going to take chances; I had his own example too close before me for that; and I tried to draw the knife out to give it him again. The blood came over my hands, I remember, hot as tea; and with that I fainted clean away and fell with my head on the man's mouth.

When I came to myself, it was pitch dark; the cinders had burned out, there was nothing to be seen but the shine of the dead wood; and I couldn't remember where I was, nor why I was in such pain, nor what I was all wetted with. Then it came back; and the first thing I attended to was to give him the knife again a half a dozen times up to the handle. I believe he was dead already; but it did him no harm and did me good.

"I bet you're dead now," I said, and then I called to Uma.

Nothing answered; and I made a move to go and grope for her, fouled my broken leg, and fainted again.

When I came to myself the second time, the clouds had all cleared away except a few that sailed there, white as cotton. The moon was up, a tropic moon. The moon at home turns a wood black; but even this old butt-end of a one showed up that forest as green as by day. The night birds—or rather they're a kind of early morning bird—sang out with their long, falling notes like nightingales. And I could see the dead man that I was still half resting on, looking right up into the sky with his open eyes, no paler than when he was alive; and a little way off, Uma tumbled on her side. I got over to her the best way I was able; and when I got there, she was broad awake and crying and sobbing to herself with no more noise than an insect. It appears she was afraid to cry out loud, because of the *aitus*. Altogether she was not much hurt, but scared beyond belief; she had come to her senses a long while ago, cried out to me, heard nothing in reply, made out we were both dead, and had lain there ever since, afraid to budge a finger. The ball had ploughed up her shoulder; and she had lost a main quantity of blood; but I soon had that tied up the way it ought to be with the tail of my shirt and a scarf I had on, got her head on my sound knee and my back against a trunk, and settled down to wait for morning. Uma was for neither use nor ornament; and could only clutch hold of me, and shake, and cry; I don't suppose there was ever anybody worse scared, and to do her justice, she had had a lively night of it. As for me, I was in a good bit of pain and fever, but not so bad when I sat still; and every time I looked over to Case, I could have sung and whistled. Talk about meat and drink! to see that man lying there dead as a herring filled me full.

The night birds stopped after a while; and then the light began to change, the east came orange, the whole wood began to whirr with singing like a musical box, and there was the broad day.

I didn't expect Maea for a long while yet; and indeed I thought there was an off chance he might go back on the whole idea and not come at all. I was the better pleased when, about an hour after daylight, I heard sticks smashing and a lot of kanakas laughing and singing out to keep their courage up. Uma sat up quite brisk at the first word of it; and presently we saw a party come stringing out of the path, Maea in front and behind him a white man in a pith helmet. It was Mr Tarleton who had turned up late last night in Falesá, having left his boat and walked the last stage with a lantern.

They buried Case upon the field of glory, right in the hole where he had kept the smoking head. I waited till the thing was done; and Mr Tarleton prayed, which I thought tomfoolery, but I'm bound to say he gave a pretty sick view of the dear departed's prospects, and seemed to have his own ideas of hell. I had it out with him afterwards, told him he had scamped his duty, and what he had ought to have done was to up like a man and tell the kanakas plainly Case was damned, and a good riddance; but I never could get him to see it my way. Then they made me a litter of poles and carried me down to the station. Mr Tarleton set my leg, and made a regular missionary splice of it, so that I limp to this day. That done, he took down my evidence, and Uma's, and Maea's, wrote it all out fair, and had us sign it; and then he got the chiefs and marched over to Papa Randall's to seize Case's papers.

All they found was a bit of a diary, kept for a good many years, and all about the price of copra and chickens being stolen and that; and the books of the business, and the will I told you of in the beginning, by both of which the whole thing (stock lock and barrel) appeared to belong to the Sāmoa woman. It was I that bought her out, at a mighty reasonable figure, for she was in a hurry to get home. As for Randall and the black, they had to tramp; got into some kind of a station on the Papa-mālūlū side; did very bad business, for the truth is neither of the pair was fit for it; and lived mostly on fish, which was the means of Randall's death. It seems there was a nice shoal in one day, and papa went after them with dynamite; either the match burned too fast or papa was full, or both, but the shell went off (in the usual way) before he threw it; and where was papa's hand? Well, there's nothing to hurt in that; the islands up north are all full of one-handed men, like the parties in the *Arabian Nights;* but either Randall was too old, or he drank too much, and the short and the long of it was that he died. Pretty soon after, the nigger was turned out of the islands for stealing from white men, and went off to the west, where he found men of his own colour, in case he liked that, and the men of his own colour took and ate him at some kind of a corroborree and I'm sure I hope he was to their fancy!

So there was I left alone in my glory at Falesá; and when the schooner came round I filled her up and gave her a deck cargo half as high as the house. I must say Mr Tarleton did the right thing by us; but he took a meanish kind of a revenge.

"Now, Mr Wiltshire," said he, "I've put you all square with everybody here. It wasn't difficult to do, Case being gone; but I have done it, and given my pledge besides that you will deal fairly with the natives. I must ask you to keep my word."

Well, so I did. I used to be bothered about my balances; but I reasoned it out this way. We all have queerish balances, and the natives all know it and water their copra in a proportion; so that it's fair all round. But the truth is, it did use to bother me; and though I did well in Falesá, I was half-glad when the firm moved me on to another station, where I was under no kind of a pledge, and could look my balances in the face.

As for the old lady, you know her as well as I do. She's only the one fault: if you don't keep your eye lifting, she would give away the roof off the station. Well, it seems it's natural in kanakas. She's turned a powerful big woman now, and could throw a London bobby over her shoulder. But that's natural in kanakas too; and there's no manner of doubt that she's an A one wife.

Mr Tarleton's gone home, his trick being over; he was the best missionary I ever struck, and now it seems he's parsonizing down Somerset ways. Well, that's best for him; he'll have no kanakas there to get luny over.

My public house? Not a bit of it, nor ever likely; I'm stuck here, I fancy; I don't like to leave the kids, you see; and there's no use talking—they're better here than what they would be in a white man's country. Though Ben took the eldest up to Auckland, where he's being schooled with the best. But what bothers me is the girls. They're only half castes of course; I know that as well as you do, and there's nobody thinks less of half castes than I do; but they're mine, and about all I've got; I can't reconcile my mind to their taking up with kanakas, and I'd like to know where I'm to find them whites?

THE BOTTLE IMP

NOTE—*Any student of that very unliterary product, the English drama of the early part of the century, will here recognise the name and the root idea of a piece once rendered popular by the redoubtable O. Smith. The root idea is there and identical, and yet I hope I have made it a new thing. And the fact that the tale has been designed and written for a Polynesian audience may lend it some extraneous interest nearer home.*—R. L. S.

There was a man of the Island of Hawaii, whom I shall call Keawe; for the truth is, he still lives, and his name must be kept secret; but the place of his birth was not far from Honaunau, where the bones of Keawe the Great lie hidden in a cave. This man was poor, brave, and active; he could read and write like a schoolmaster; he was a first-rate mariner besides, sailed for some time in the island steamers, and steered a whaleboat on the Hamakua coast. At length it came in Keawe's mind to have a sight of the great world and foreign cities, and he shipped on a vessel bound to San Francisco.

This is a fine town, with a fine harbour, and rich people uncountable; and, in particular, there is one hill which is covered with palaces. Upon this hill Keawe was one day taking a walk with his pocket full of money, viewing the great houses upon either hand with pleasure. "What fine houses these are!" he was thinking, "and how happy must those people be who dwell in them, and take no care for the morrow!" The thought was in his mind when he came abreast of a house that was smaller than some others, but all finished and beautified like a toy; the steps of that house shone like silver, and the borders of the garden bloomed like garlands, and the windows were bright like diamonds; and Keawe stopped and wondered at the excellence of all he saw. So stopping, he was aware of a man that looked forth upon him through a window so clear that Keawe could see him as you see a fish in a pool upon the reef. The man was elderly, with a bald head and a black beard; and his face was heavy with sorrow, and he bitterly sighed. And the truth of it is, that as Keawe looked in upon the man, and the man looked out upon Keawe, each envied the other.

All of a sudden, the man smiled and nodded, and beckoned Keawe to enter, and met him at the door of the house.

"This is a fine house of mine," said the man, and bitterly sighed. "Would you not care to view the chambers?"

So he led Keawe all over it, from the cellar to the roof, and there was nothing there that was not perfect of its kind, and Keawe was astonished.

"Truly," said Keawe, "this is a beautiful house; if I lived in the like of it, I should be laughing all day long. How comes it, then, that you should be sighing?"

"There is no reason," said the man, "why you should not have a house in all points similar to this, and finer, if you wish. You have some money, I suppose?"

"I have fifty dollars," said Keawe; "but a house like this will cost more than fifty dollars."

The man made a computation. "I am sorry you have no more," said he, "for it may raise you trouble in the future; but it shall be yours at fifty dollars."

"The house?" asked Keawe.

"No, not the house," replied the man; "but the bottle. For, I must tell you, although I appear to you so rich and fortunate, all my fortune, and this house itself and its garden, came out of a bottle not much bigger than a pint. This is it."

And he opened a lockfast place, and took out a round-bellied bottle with a long neck; the glass of it was white like milk, with changing rainbow colours in the grain. Withinsides something obscurely moved, like a shadow and a fire.

"This is the bottle," said the man; and, when Keawe laughed, "You do not believe me?" he added. "Try, then, for yourself. See if you can break it."

So Keawe took the bottle up and dashed it on the floor till he was weary; but it jumped on the floor like a child's ball, and was not injured.

"This is a strange thing," said Keawe. "For by the touch of it, as well as by the look, the bottle should be of glass."

Original illustration by W. Hatherell for "The Bottle Imp,"
Island Nights' Entertainments.

"Of glass it is," replied the man, sighing more heavily than ever; "but the glass of it was tempered in the flames of hell. An imp lives in it, and that is the shadow we behold there moving: or so I suppose. If any man buy this bottle the imp is at his command; all that he desires—love, fame, money, houses like this house, ay, or a city like this city—all are his at the word uttered. Napoleon had this bottle, and by it he grew to be the king of the world; but he sold it at the last, and fell. Captain Cook had this bottle, and by it he found his way to so many islands; but he, too, sold it, and was slain upon Hawaii. For, once it is sold, the power goes and the protection; and unless a man remain content with what he has, ill will befall him."

"And yet you talk of selling it yourself?" Keawe said.

"I have all I wish, and I am growing elderly," replied the man. "There is one thing the imp cannot do—he cannot prolong life; and, it would not be fair to conceal from you, there is a drawback to the bottle; for if a man die before he sells it, he must burn in hell forever."

"To be sure, that is a drawback and no mistake," cried Keawe. "I would not meddle with the thing. I can do without a house, thank God; but there is one thing I could not be doing with one particle, and that is to be damned."

"Dear me, you must not run away with things," returned the man. "All you have to do is to use the power of the imp in moderation, and then sell it to someone else, as I do to you, and finish your life in comfort."

"Well, I observe two things," said Keawe. "All the time you keep sighing like a maid in love, that is one; and, for the other, you sell this bottle very cheap."

"I have told you already why I sigh," said the man. "It is because I fear my health is breaking up; and, as you said yourself, to die and go to the devil is a pity for anyone. As for why I sell so cheap, I must explain to you there is a peculiarity about the bottle. Long ago, when the devil brought it first upon earth, it was extremely expensive, and was sold first of all to Prester John for many millions of dollars; but it cannot be sold at all, unless sold at a loss. If you sell it for as much as you paid for it, back it comes to you again like a homing pigeon. It follows that the price has kept falling in these centuries, and the bottle is now remarkably cheap. I bought it myself from one of my great neighbours on this hill, and the price I paid was only ninety dollars. I could sell it for as high as eighty-nine dollars and ninety-nine cents, but not a penny dearer, or back the thing must come to me. Now, about this there are two bothers. First, when you offer a bottle so singular for eighty odd dollars, people suppose you to be jesting. And second—but there is no hurry about that—and I need not go into it. Only remember it must be coined money that you sell it for."

"How am I to know that this is all true?" asked Keawe.

"Some of it you can try at once," replied the man. "Give me your fifty dollars, take the bottle, and wish your fifty dollars back into your pocket. If that does not happen, I pledge you my honour I will cry off the bargain and restore your money."

"You are not deceiving me?" said Keawe.

The man bound himself with a great oath.

"Well, I will risk that much," said Keawe, "for that can do no harm." And he paid over his money to the man, and the man handed him the bottle.

"Imp of the bottle," said Keawe, "I want my fifty dollars back." And sure enough he had scarce said the word before his pocket was as heavy as ever.

"To be sure this is a wonderful bottle," said Keawe.

"And now good-morning to you, my fine fellow, and the devil go with you for me!" said the man.

"Hold on," said Keawe, "I don't want any more of this fun. Here, take your bottle back."

"You have bought it for less than I paid for it," replied the man, rubbing his hands. "It is yours now; and, for my part, I am only concerned to see the back of you." And with that he rang for his Chinese servant, and had Keawe shown out of the house.

Now, when Keawe was in the street, with the bottle under his arm, he began to think. "If all is true about this bottle, I may have made a losing bargain," thinks he. "But perhaps the man was only fooling me." The first thing he did was to count his money; the sum was exact—forty-nine dollars American money, and one Chili piece. "That looks like the truth," said Keawe. "Now I will try another part."

The streets in that part of the city were as clean as a ship's decks, and though it was noon, there were no passengers. Keawe set the bottle in the gutter and walked away. Twice he looked back, and there was the milky, round-bellied bottle where he left it. A third time he looked back, and turned a corner; but he had scarce done so, when something knocked upon his elbow, and behold! it was the long neck sticking up; and as for the round belly, it was jammed into the pocket of his pilot-coat.

"And that looks like the truth," said Keawe.

The next thing he did was to buy a corkscrew in a shop, and go apart into a secret place in the fields. And there he tried to draw the cork, but as often as he put the screw in, out it came again, and the cork as whole as ever.

"This is some new sort of cork," said Keawe, and all at once he began to shake and sweat, for he was afraid of that bottle.

On his way back to the port side, he saw a shop where a man sold shells and clubs from the wild islands, old heathen deities, old coined money, pictures from China and Japan, and all manner of things that sailors bring in their sea chests. And here he had an idea. So he went in and offered the bottle for a hundred dollars. The man of the shop laughed at him at the first, and offered him five; but, indeed, it was a curious bottle—such glass was never blown in any human glass-works, so prettily the colors shone under the milky white, and so strangely the shadow hovered in the midst; so, after he had disputed awhile after the manner of his kind, the shopman gave Keawe sixty silver dollars for the thing, and set it on a shelf in the midst of his window.

"Now," said Keawe, "I have sold that for sixty which I bought for fifty—or, to say truth, a little less, because one of my dollars was from Chili. Now I shall know the truth upon another point."

So he went back on board his ship, and, when he opened his chest, there was the bottle, and had come more quickly than himself. Now Keawe had a mate on board whose name was Lopaka.

"What ails you?" said Lopaka, "that you stare in your chest?"

They were alone in the ship's forecastle, and Keawe bound him to secrecy, and told all.

"This is a very strange affair," said Lopaka; "and I fear you will be in trouble about this bottle. But there is one point very clear—that you are sure of the trouble, and you had better have the profit in the bargain. Make up your mind what you want with it; give the order, and if it is done as you desire, I will buy the bottle myself; for I have an idea of my own to get a schooner, and go trading through the islands."

"That is not my idea," said Keawe; "but to have a beautiful house and garden on the Kona Coast, where I was born, the sun shining in at the door, flowers in the garden, glass in the windows, pictures on the walls, and toys and fine carpets on the tables, for all the world like the house I was in this day—only a story higher, and with balconies all about like the King's palace; and to live there without care and make merry with my friends and relatives."

"Well," said Lopaka, "let us carry it back with us to Hawaii; and if all comes true, as you suppose, I will buy the bottle, as I said, and ask a schooner."

Upon that they were agreed, and it was not long before the ship returned to Honolulu, carrying Keawe and Lopaka, and the bottle. They were scarce come ashore when they met a friend upon the beach, who began at once to condole with Keawe.

"I do not know what I am to be condoled about," said Keawe.

"Is it possible you have not heard," said the friend, "your uncle—that good old man—is dead, and your cousin—that beautiful boy—was drowned at sea?"

Keawe was filled with sorrow, and, beginning to weep and to lament, he forgot about the bottle. But Lopaka was thinking to himself, and presently, when Keawe's grief was a little abated, "I have been thinking," said Lopaka. "Had not your uncle lands in Hawaii, in the district of Kaü?"

"No," said Keawe, "not in Kaü: they are on the mountainside—a little way south of Hookena."

"These lands will now be yours?" asked Lopaka.

"And so they will," says Keawe, and began again to lament for his relatives.

"No," said Lopaka, "do not lament at present. I have a thought in my mind. How if this should be the doing of the bottle? For here is the place ready for your house."

"If this be so," cried Keawe, "it is a very ill way to serve me by killing my relatives. But it may be, indeed; for it was in just such a station that I saw the house with my mind's eye."

"The house, however, is not yet built," said Lopaka.

"No, nor like to be!" said Keawe; "for though my uncle has some coffee and ava and bananas, it will not be more than will keep me in comfort; and the rest of that land is the black lava."

"Let us go to the lawyer," said Lopaka; "I have still this idea in my mind."

Now, when they came to the lawyer's, it appeared Keawe's uncle had grown monstrous rich in the last days, and there was a fund of money.

"And here is the money for the house!" cried Lopaka.

"If you are thinking of a new house," said the lawyer, "here is the card of a new architect, of whom they tell me great things."

"Better and better!" cried Lopaka. "Here is all made plain for us. Let us continue to obey orders."

So they went to the architect, and he had drawings of houses on his table.

"You want something out of the way," said the architect. "How do you like this?" and he handed a drawing to Keawe.

Now, when Keawe set eyes on the drawing, he cried out aloud, for it was the picture of his thought exactly drawn.

"I am in for this house," thought he. "Little as I like the way it comes to me, I am in for it now, and I may as well take the good along with the evil."

So he told the architect all that he wished, and how he would have that house furnished, and about the pictures on the wall and the knick-knacks on the tables; and he asked the man plainly for how much he would undertake the whole affair.

The architect put many questions, and took his pen and made a computation; and when he had done he named the very sum that Keawe had inherited.

Lopaka and Keawe looked at one another and nodded.

"It is quite clear," thought Keawe, "that I am to have this house, whether or no. It comes from the devil, and I fear I will get little good by that; and of one thing I am sure, I will make no more wishes as long as I have this bottle. But with the house I am saddled, and I may as well take the good along with the evil."

So he made his terms with the architect, and they signed a paper; and Keawe and Lopaka took ship again and sailed to Australia; for it was concluded between them they should not interfere at all, but leave the architect and the bottle imp to build and to adorn that house at their own pleasure.

The voyage was a good voyage, only all the time Keawe was holding in his breath, for he had sworn he would utter no more wishes, and take no more favours from the devil. The time was up when they got back. The architect told them that the house was ready, and Keawe and Lopaka took a passage in the *Hall*, and went down Kona way to view the house, and see if all had been done fitly according to the thought that was in Keawe's mind.

Now, the house stood on the mountainside, visible to ships. Above, the forest ran up into the clouds of rain; below, the black lava fell in cliffs, where the kings of old lay buried. A garden bloomed about that house with every hue of flowers; and there was an orchard of papaia on the one hand and an orchard of breadfruit on the other, and right in front, toward the sea, a ship's mast had been rigged up and bore a flag. As for the house, it was three stories high, with great chambers and broad balconies on each. The windows were of glass, so excellent that it was as clear as water and as bright as day. All manner of furniture adorned the chambers. Pictures hung upon the wall in golden frames: pictures of ships, and men fighting, and of the most beautiful women, and of singular places; nowhere in the world are there pictures of so bright a colour as those Keawe found hanging in his house. As for the knick-knacks, they were extraordinary fine; chiming clocks and musical boxes, little men with nodding heads, books filled with pictures, weapons of price from all quarters of the world, and the most elegant puzzles to entertain the leisure of a solitary man. And as no one would care to live in such chambers, only to walk through and view them, the balconies were made so broad that a whole town might have lived upon them in delight; and Keawe knew not which to prefer, whether the back porch, where you got the land breeze, and looked upon the orchards and the flowers, or the front balcony, where you could drink the wind of the sea, and look down the steep wall of the mountain and see the *Hall* going by once a week or so between Hookena and the hills of Pele, or the schooners plying up the coast for wood and ava and bananas.

When they had viewed all, Keawe and Lopaka sat on the porch.

"Well," said Lopaka, "is it all as you designed?"

"Words cannot utter it," said Keawe. "It is better than I dreamed, and I am sick with satisfaction."

"There is but one thing to consider," said Lopaka; "all this may be quite natural, and the bottle imp have nothing whatever to say to it. If

I were to buy the bottle, and got no schooner after all, I should have put my hand in the fire for nothing. I gave you my word, I know; but yet I think you would not grudge me one more proof."

"I have sworn I would take no more favours," said Keawe. "I have gone already deep enough."

"This is no favour I am thinking of," replied Lopaka. "It is only to see the imp himself. There is nothing to be gained by that, and so nothing to be ashamed of; and yet, if I once saw him, I should be sure of the whole matter. So indulge me so far, and let me see the imp; and, after that, here is the money in my hand, and I will buy it."

"There is only one thing I am afraid of," said Keawe. "The imp may be very ugly to view; and if you once set eyes upon him you might be very undesirous of the bottle."

"I am a man of my word," said Lopaka. "And here is the money betwixt us."

"Very well," replied Keawe. "I have a curiosity myself. So come, let us have one look at you, Mr. Imp."

Now as soon as that was said, the imp looked out of the bottle, and in again, swift as a lizard; and there sat Keawe and Lopaka turned to stone. The night had quite come, before either found a thought to say or voice to say it with; and then Lopaka pushed the money over and took the bottle.

"I am a man of my word," said he, "and had need to be so, or I would not touch this bottle with my foot. Well, I shall get my schooner and a dollar or two for my pocket; and then I will be rid of this devil as fast as I can. For to tell you the plain truth, the look of him has cast me down."

"Lopaka," said Keawe, "do not you think any worse of me than you can help; I know it is night, and the roads bad, and the pass by the tombs an ill place to go by so late, but I declare since I have seen that little face, I cannot eat or sleep or pray till it is gone from me. I will give you a lantern, and a basket to put the bottle in, and any picture or fine thing in all my house that takes your fancy;—and be gone at once, and go sleep at Hookena with Nahinu."

"Keawe," said Lopaka, "many a man would take this ill; above all, when I am doing you a turn so friendly, as to keep my word and buy the bottle; and for that matter, the night and the dark, and the way by the tombs, must be all tenfold more dangerous to a man with such a sin upon his conscience, and such a bottle under his arm. But for my part, I am so extremely terrified myself, I have not the heart to blame you. Here I go then; and I pray God you may be happy in your house, and I fortunate with my schooner, and both get to heaven in the end in spite of the devil and his bottle."

So Lopaka went down the mountain; and Keawe stood in his front balcony, and listened to the clink of the horse's shoes, and watched the lantern go shining down the path, and along the cliff of caves where the old dead are buried; and all the time he trembled and clasped his hands, and prayed for his friend, and gave glory to God that he himself was escaped out of that trouble.

But the next day came very brightly, and that new house of his was so delightful to behold that he forgot his terrors. One day followed another, and Keawe dwelt there in perpetual joy. He had his place on the back porch; it was there he ate and lived, and read the stories in the Honolulu newspapers; but when anyone came by they would go in and view the chambers and the pictures. And the fame of the house went far and wide; it was called *Ka-Hale Nui*—the Great House—in all Kona; and sometimes the Bright House, for Keawe kept a Chinaman, who was all day dusting and furbishing; and the glass, and the gilt, and the fine stuffs, and the pictures, shone as bright as the morning. As for Keawe himself, he could not walk in the chambers without singing, his heart was so enlarged; and when ships sailed by upon the sea, he would fly his colours on the mast.

So time went by, until one day Keawe went upon a visit as far as Kailua to certain of his friends. There he was well feasted; and left as soon as he could the next morning, and rode hard, for he was impatient to behold his beautiful house; and, besides, the night then coming on was the night in which the dead of old days go abroad in the sides of Kona; and having already meddled with the devil, he was the more chary of meeting with the dead. A little beyond Honaunau, looking far ahead, he was aware of a woman bathing in the edge of the sea; and she seemed a well-grown girl, but he thought no more of it. Then he saw her white shift flutter as she put it on, and then her red holoku; and by the time he came abreast of her she was done with her toilet, and had come up from the sea, and stood by the track side in her red holoku, and she was all freshened with the bath, and her eyes shone and were kind. Now Keawe no sooner beheld her than he drew rein.

"I thought I knew everyone in this country," said he. "How comes it that I do not know you?"

"I am Kokua, daughter of Kiano," said the girl, "and I have just returned from Oahu. Who are you?"

"I will tell you who I am in a little," said Keawe, dismounting from his horse, "but not now. For I have a thought in my mind, and if you knew who I was, you might have heard of me, and would not give me a true answer. But tell me, first of all, one thing: Are you married?"

At this Kokua laughed out aloud. "It is you who ask questions," she said. "Are you married yourself?"

"Indeed, Kokua, I am not," replied Keawe, "and never thought to be until this hour. But here is the plain truth. I have met you here at the roadside, and I saw your eyes, which are like the stars, and my heart went to you as swift as a bird. And so now, if you want none of me, say so, and I will go on to my own place; but if you think me no worse than any other young man, say so, too, and I will turn aside to your father's for the night, and tomorrow I will talk with the good man."

Kokua said never a word, but she looked at the sea and laughed.

"Kokua," said Keawe, "if you say nothing, I will take that for the good answer; so let us be stepping to your father's door."

She went on ahead of him, still without speech; only sometimes she glanced back and glanced away again, and she kept the strings of her hat in her mouth.

Now, when they had come to the door, Kiano came out on his verandah, and cried out and welcomed Keawe by name. At that the girl looked over, for the fame of the great house had come to her ears; and, to be sure, it was a great temptation. All that evening they were very merry together; and the girl was as bold as brass under the eyes of her parents, and made a mock of Keawe, for she had a quick wit. The next day he had a word with Kiano, and found the girl alone.

"Kokua," said he, "you made a mock of me all the evening; and it is still time to bid me go. I would not tell you who I was, because I have so fine a house, and I feared you would think too much of that house and too little of the man that loves you. Now you know all, and if you wish to have seen the last of me, say so at once."

"No," said Kokua; but this time she did not laugh, nor did Keawe ask for more.

This was the wooing of Keawe; things had gone quickly; but so an arrow goes, and the ball of a rifle swifter still, and yet both may strike the target. Things had gone fast, but they had gone far also, and the thought of Keawe rang in the maiden's head; she heard his voice in the breach of the surf upon the lava, and for this young man that she had seen but twice she would have left father and mother and her native islands. As for Keawe himself, his horse flew up the path of the mountain under the cliff of tombs, and the sound of the hoofs, and the sound of Keawe singing to himself for pleasure, echoed in the caverns of the dead. He came to the Bright House, and still he was singing. He sat and ate in the broad balcony, and the Chinaman wondered at his master, to hear how he sang between the mouthfuls. The sun went down into the sea, and the night came; and Keawe walked the balconies by lamplight, high on the mountains, and the voice of his singing startled men on ships.

"Here am I now upon my high place," he said to himself. "Life may be no better; this is the mountain top; and all shelves about me toward the worse. For the first time I will light up the chambers, and bathe in my fine bath with the hot water and the cold, and sleep alone in the bed of my bridal chamber."

So the Chinaman had word, and he must rise from sleep and light the furnaces; and as he wrought below, beside the boilers, he heard his master singing and rejoicing above him in the lighted chambers. When the water began to be hot the Chinaman cried to his master, and Keawe went into the bathroom; and the Chinaman heard him sing as he filled the marble basin, and heard him sing, and the singing broken, as he undressed; until of a sudden, the song ceased. The Chinaman listened, and listened; he called up the house to Keawe to ask if all were well, and Keawe answered him "Yes," and bade him to go bed; but there was no more singing in the Bright House; and all night long, the Chinaman heard his master's feet go round and round the balconies without repose.

Now the truth of it was this: as Keawe undressed for his bath, he spied upon his flesh a patch like a patch of lichen on a rock, and it was then that he stopped singing. For he knew the likeness of that patch, and knew that he was fallen in the Chinese Evil.

Now, it is a sad thing for any man to fall into this sickness. And it would be a sad thing for anyone to leave a house so beautiful and so commodious, and depart from all his friends to the north coast of

Molokai, between the mighty cliff and the sea-breakers. But what was that to the case of the man Keawe, he who had met his love but yesterday, and won her but that morning, and now saw all his hopes break, in a moment, like a piece of glass?

Awhile he sat upon the edge of the bath; then sprang, with a cry, and ran outside; and to and fro, to and fro, along the balcony, like one despairing.

"Very willingly could I leave Hawaii, the home of my fathers," Keawe was thinking. "Very lightly could I leave my house, the high-placed, the many-windowed, here upon the mountains. Very bravely could I go to Molokai, to Kalaupapa by the cliffs, to live with the smitten and to sleep there, far from my fathers. But what wrong have I done, what sin lies upon my soul, that I should have encountered Kokua coming cool from the sea-water in the evening? Kokua, the soul ensnarer! Kokua, the light of my life! Her may I never wed, her may I look upon no longer, her may I no more handle with my loving hand; and it is for this, it is for you, O Kokua! that I pour my lamentations!"

Now you are to observe what sort of a man Keawe was, for he might have dwelt there in the Bright House for years, and no one been the wiser of his sickness; but he reckoned nothing of that, if he must lose Kokua. And again, he might have wed Kokua even as he was; and so many would have done, because they have the souls of pigs; but Keawe loved the maid manfully, and he would do her no hurt and bring her in no danger.

A little beyond the midst of the night, there came in his mind the recollection of that bottle. He went round to the back porch, and called to memory the day when the devil had looked forth; and at the thought ice ran in his veins.

"A dreadful thing is the bottle," thought Keawe, "and dreadful is the imp, and it is a dreadful thing to risk the flames of hell. But what other hope have I to cure my sickness or to wed Kokua? What!" he thought, "would I beard the devil once, only to get me a house, and not face him again to win Kokua?"

Thereupon he called to mind it was the next day the *Hall* went by on her return to Honolulu. "There must I go first," he thought, "and see Lopaka. For the best hope that I have now is to find that same bottle I was so pleased to be rid of."

Never a wink could he sleep; the food stuck in his throat; but he sent a letter to Kiano, and about the time when the steamer would be coming, rode down beside the cliff of the tombs. It rained; his horse went heavily; he looked up at the black mouths of the caves, and he envied the dead that slept there and were done with trouble; and called to mind how he had galloped by the day before, and was astonished. So he came down to Hookena, and there was all the country gathered for the steamer as usual. In the shed before the store they sat and jested and passed the news; but there was no matter of speech in Keawe's bosom, and he sat in their midst and looked without on the rain falling on the houses, and the surf beating among the rocks, and the sighs arose in his throat.

"Keawe of the Bright House is out of spirits," said one to another. Indeed, and so he was, and little wonder.

Then the *Hall* came, and the whaleboat carried him on board. The afterpart of the ship was full of Haoles who had been to visit the volcano, as their custom is; and the midst was crowded with Kanakas, and the forepart with wild bulls from Hilo and horses from Kaü; but Keawe sat apart from all in his sorrow, and watched for the house of Kiano. There it sat, low upon the shore in the black rocks, and shaded by the cocoa palms, and there by the door was a red holoku, no greater than a fly, and going to and fro with a fly's busyness. "Ah, queen of my heart," he cried, "I'll venture my dear soul to win you!"

Soon after, darkness fell, and the cabins were lit up, and the Haoles sat and played at the cards and drank whiskey as their custom is; but Keawe walked the deck all night; and all the next day, as they steamed under the lee of Maui or of Molokai, he was still pacing to and fro like a wild animal in a menagerie.

Towards evening they passed Diamond Head, and came to the pier of Honolulu. Keawe stepped out among the crowd and began to ask for Lopaka. It seemed he had become the owner of a schooner—none better in the islands—and was gone upon an adventure as far as Pola-Pola or Kahiki; so there was no help to be looked for from Lopaka. Keawe called to mind a friend of his, a lawyer in the town (I must not tell his name), and inquired of him. They said he was grown suddenly rich, and had a fine new house upon Waikiki shore; and this put a thought in Keawe's head, and he called a hack and drove to the lawyer's house.

The house was all brand new, and the trees in the garden no greater than walking-sticks, and the lawyer, when he came, had the air of a man well pleased.

"What can I do to serve you?" said the lawyer.

"You are a friend of Lopaka's," replied Keawe, "and Lopaka purchased from me a certain piece of goods that I thought you might enable me to trace."

The lawyer's face became very dark. "I do not profess to misunderstand you, Mr. Keawe," said he, "though this is an ugly business to be stirring in. You may be sure I know nothing, but yet I have a guess, and if you would apply in a certain quarter I think you might have news."

And he named the name of a man, which, again, I had better not repeat. So it was for days, and Keawe went from one to another, finding everywhere new clothes and carriages, and fine new houses and men everywhere in great contentment, although, to be sure, when he hinted at his business their faces would cloud over.

"No doubt I am upon the track," thought Keawe. "These new clothes and carriages are all the gifts of the little imp, and these glad faces are the faces of men who have taken their profit and got rid of the accursed thing in safety. When I see pale cheeks and hear sighing, I shall know that I am near the bottle."

So it befell at last that he was recommended to a Haole in Beritania Street. When he came to the door, about the hour of the evening meal, there were the usual marks of the new house, and the young garden, and the electric light shining in the windows; but when the owner came, a shock of hope and fear ran through Keawe; for here was a young man, white as a corpse, and black about the eyes, the hair shedding from his head, and such a look in his countenance as a man may have when he is waiting for the gallows.

"Here it is, to be sure," thought Keawe, and so with this man he noways veiled his errand. "I am come to buy the bottle," said he.

At the word, the young Haole of Beritania Street reeled against the wall.

"The bottle!" he gasped. "To buy the bottle!" Then he seemed to choke, and seizing Keawe by the arm carried him into a room and poured out wine in two glasses.

"Here is my respects," said Keawe, who had been much about with Haoles in his time. "Yes," he added, "I am come to buy the bottle. What is the price by now?"

At that word the young man let his glass slip through his fingers, and looked upon Keawe like a ghost.

"The price," says he; "the price! You do not know the price?"

"It is for that I am asking you," returned Keawe. "But why are you so much concerned? Is there anything wrong about the price?"

"It has dropped a great deal in value since your time, Mr. Keawe," said the young man, stammering.

"Well, well, I shall have the less to pay for it," says Keawe. "How much did it cost you?"

The young man was as white as a sheet. "Two cents," said he.

"What?" cried Keawe, "two cents? Why, then, you can only sell it for one. And he who buys it———" The words died upon Keawe's tongue; he who bought it could never sell it again, the bottle and the bottle imp must abide with him until he died, and when he died must carry him to the red end of hell.

The young man of Beritania Street fell upon his knees. "For God's sake buy it!" he cried. "You can have all my fortune in the bargain. I was mad when I bought it at that price. I had embezzled money at my store; I was lost else; I must have gone to jail."

"Poor creature," said Keawe, "you would risk your soul upon so desperate an adventure, and to avoid the proper punishment of your own disgrace; and you think I could hesitate with love in front of me. Give me the bottle, and the change which I make sure you have all ready. Here is a five-cent piece."

It was as Keawe supposed; the young man had the change ready in a drawer; the bottle changed hands, and Keawe's fingers were no sooner clasped upon the stalk than he had breathed his wish to be a clean man. And, sure enough, when he got home to his room, and stripped himself before a glass, his flesh was whole like an infant's. And here was the strange thing: he had no sooner seen this miracle, than his mind was changed within him, and he cared naught for the Chinese Evil, and little enough for Kokua; and had but the one thought, that here he was bound to the bottle imp for time and for eternity, and had no better hope but to be a cinder for ever in the flames of hell. Away ahead of him he saw them blaze with his mind's eye, and his soul shrank, and darkness fell upon the light.

When Keawe came to himself a little, he was aware it was the night when the band played at the hotel. Thither he went, because he feared to be alone; and there, among happy faces, walked to and fro, and heard the tunes go up and down, and saw Berger beat the measure, and all the while he heard the flames crackle, and saw the red fire burning in the bottomless pit. Of a sudden the band played *Hiki-ao-ao;* that was a song that he had sung with Kokua, and at the strain courage returned to him.

"It is done now," he thought, "and once more let me take the good along with the evil."

So it befell that he returned to Hawaii by the first steamer, and as soon as it could be managed he was wedded to Kokua, and carried her up the mountain side to the Bright House.

Now it was so with these two, that when they were together, Keawe's heart was stilled; but so soon as he was alone he fell into a brooding horror, and heard the flames crackle, and saw the red fire burn in the bottomless pit. The girl, indeed, had come to him wholly; her heart leapt in her side at sight of him, her hand clung to his; and she was so fashioned from the hair upon her head to the nails upon her toes that none could see her without joy. She was pleasant in her nature. She had the good word always. Full of song she was, and went to and fro in the Bright House, the brightest thing in its three stories, carolling like the birds. And Keawe beheld and heard her with delight, and then must shrink upon one side, and weep and groan to think upon the price that he had paid for her; and then he must dry his eyes, and wash his face, and go and sit with her on the broad balconies, joining in her songs, and, with a sick spirit, answering her smiles.

There came a day when her feet began to be heavy and her songs more rare; and now it was not Keawe only that would weep apart, but each would sunder from the other and sit in opposite balconies with the whole width of the Bright House betwixt. Keawe was so sunk in his despair, he scarce observed the change, and was only glad he had more hours to sit alone and brood upon his destiny, and was not so frequently condemned to pull a smiling face on a sick heart. But one day, coming softly through the house, he heard the sound of a child sobbing, and there was Kokua rolling her face upon the balcony floor, and weeping like the lost.

"You do well to weep in this house, Kokua," he said. "And yet I would give the head off my body that you (at least) might have been happy."

"Happy!" she cried. "Keawe, when you lived alone in your Bright House, you were the word of the island for a happy man; laughter and song were in your mouth, and your face was as bright as the sunrise. Then you wedded poor Kokua; and the good God knows what is amiss in her—but from that day you have not smiled. Oh!" she cried, "what ails me? I thought I was pretty, and I knew I loved him. What ails me that I throw this cloud upon my husband?"

"Poor Kokua," said Keawe. He sat down by her side, and sought to take her hand; but that she plucked away. "Poor Kokua," he said, again. "My poor child—my pretty. And I had thought all this while to spare you! Well, you shall know all. Then, at least, you will pity poor Keawe; then you will understand how much he loved you in the past—that he dared hell for your possession—and how much he loves you still (the poor condemned one), that he can yet call up a smile when he beholds you."

With that, he told her all, even from the beginning.

"You have done this for me?" she cried. "Ah, well, then what do I care!"—and she clasped and wept upon him.

"Ah, child!" said Keawe, "and yet, when I consider of the fire of hell, I care a good deal!"

"Never tell me," said she; "no man can be lost because he loved Kokua, and no other fault. I tell you, Keawe, I shall save you with these hands, or perish in your company. What! you loved me and gave your soul, and you think I will not die to save you in return?"

"Ah, my dear! you might die a hundred times, and what difference would that make?" he cried, "except to leave me lonely till the time comes of my damnation?"

"You know nothing," said she. "I was educated in a school in Honolulu; I am no common girl. And I tell you, I shall save my lover. What is this you say about a cent? But all the world is not American. In England they have a piece they call a farthing, which is about half a cent. Ah! sorrow!" she cried, "that makes it scarcely better, for the buyer must be lost, and we shall find none so brave as my Keawe! But, then, there is France; they have a small coin there which they call a centime, and these go five to the cent or thereabout. We could not do better. Come, Keawe, let us go to the French islands; let us go to Tahiti, as fast as ships can bear us. There we have four centimes, three centimes, two centimes, one centime; four possible sales to come and go on; and two of us to push the bargain. Come, my Keawe! kiss me, and banish care. Kokua will defend you."

"Gift of God!" he cried. "I cannot think that God will punish me for desiring aught so good! Be it as you will, then; take me where you please: I put my life and my salvation in your hands."

Early the next day Kokua was about her preparations. She took Keawe's chest that he went with sailoring; and first she put the bottle in a corner; and then packed it with the richest of their clothes and the bravest of the knick-knacks in the house. "For," said she, "we must seem to be rich folks, or who will believe in the bottle?" All the time of her preparation she was as gay as a bird; only when she looked upon Keawe, the tears would spring in her eye, and she must run and kiss him. As for Keawe, a weight was off his soul; now that he had his secret shared, and some hope in front of him, he seemed like a new man, his feet went lightly on the earth, and his breath was good to him again. Yet was terror still at his elbow; and ever and again, as the wind blows out a taper, hope died in him, and he saw the flames toss and the red fire burn in hell.

It was given out in the country they were gone pleasuring to the States, which was thought a strange thing, and yet not so strange as the truth, if any could have guessed it. So they went to Honolulu in the *Hall,* and thence in the *Umatilla* to San Francisco with a crowd of Haoles, and at San Francisco took their passage by the mail brigantine, the *Tropic Bird,* for Papeete, the chief place of the French in the south islands. Thither they came, after a pleasant voyage, on a fair day of the Trade Wind, and saw the reef with the surf breaking, and Motuiti with its palms, and the schooner riding within-side, and the white houses of the town low down along the shore among green trees, and overhead the mountains and the clouds of Tahiti, the wise island.

It was judged the most wise to hire a house, which they did accordingly, opposite the British Consul's, to make a great parade of money, and themselves conspicuous with carriages and horses. This it was very easy to do, so long as they had the bottle in their possession; for Kokua was more bold than Keawe, and, whenever she had a mind, called on the imp for twenty or a hundred dollars. At this rate they soon grew to be remarked in the town; and the strangers from Hawaii, their riding and their driving, the fine holokus and the rich lace of Kokua, became the matter of much talk.

They got on well after the first with the Tahitian language, which is indeed like to the Hawaiian, with a change of certain letters; and as soon as they had any freedom of speech, began to push the bottle. You are to consider it was not an easy subject to introduce; it was not easy to persuade people you were in earnest, when you offered to sell them for four centimes the spring of health and riches inexhaustible. It was necessary besides to explain the dangers of the bottle; and either people disbelieved the whole thing and laughed, or they thought the more of the darker part, became overcast with gravity, and drew away from Keawe and Kokua, as from persons who had dealings with the devil. So far from gaining ground, these two began to find they were avoided in the town; the children ran away from them screaming, a thing intolerable to Kokua; Catholics crossed themselves as they went by; and all persons began with one accord to disengage themselves from their advances.

Depression fell upon their spirits. They would sit at night in their new house, after a day's weariness, and not exchange one word, or the silence would be broken by Kokua bursting suddenly into sobs. Sometimes they would pray together; sometimes they would have the bottle out upon the floor, and sit all evening watching how the shadow hovered in the midst. At such times they would be afraid to go to rest. It was long ere slumber came to them, and, if either dozed off, it would be to wake and find the other silently weeping in the dark, or, perhaps, to wake alone, the other having fled from the house and the neighbourhood of that bottle, to pace under the bananas in the little garden, or to wander on the beach by moonlight.

One night it was so when Kokua awoke. Keawe was gone. She felt in the bed and his place was cold. Then fear fell upon her, and she sat up in bed. A little moonshine filtered through the shutters. The room was bright, and she could spy the bottle on the floor. Outside it blew high, the great trees of the avenue cried aloud, and the fallen leaves rattled in the verandah. In the midst of this Kokua was aware of another sound; whether of a beast or of a man she could scarce tell, but it was as sad as death, and cut her to the soul. Softly she arose, set the door ajar, and looked forth into the moonlit yard. There, under the bananas, lay Keawe, his mouth in the dust, and as he lay he moaned.

It was Kokua's first thought to run forward and console him; her second potently withheld her. Keawe had borne himself before his wife like a brave man; it became her little in the hour of weakness to intrude upon his shame. With the thought she drew back into the house.

"Heaven!" she thought, "how careless have I been—how weak! It is he, not I, that stands in this eternal peril; it was he, not I, that took the curse upon his soul. It is for my sake, and for the love of a creature of so little worth and such poor help, that he now beholds so close to him the flames of hell—ay, and smells the smoke of it, lying without there in the wind and moonlight. Am I so dull of spirit that never till now I have surmised my duty, or have I seen it before and turned aside? But now, at least, I take up my soul in both the hands of my affection; now I say farewell to the white steps of heaven and the waiting faces of my friends. A love for a love, and let mine be equalled with Keawe's! A soul for a soul, and be it mine to perish!"

She was a deft woman with her hands, and was soon apparelled. She took in her hands the change—the precious centimes they kept ever at their side; for this coin is little used, and they had made provision at a Government office. When she was forth in the avenue clouds came on the wind, and the moon was blackened. The town slept, and she knew not whither to turn till she heard one coughing in the shadow of the trees.

"Old man," said Kokua, "what do you here abroad in the cold night?"

The old man could scarce express himself for coughing, but she made out that he was old and poor, and a stranger in the island.

"Will you do me a service?" said Kokua. "As one stranger to another, and as an old man to a young woman, will you help a daughter of Hawaii?"

"Ah," said the old man. "So you are the witch from the eight islands, and even my old soul you seek to entangle. But I have heard of you, and defy your wickedness."

"Sit down here," said Kokua, "and let me tell you a tale." And she told him the story of Keawe from the beginning to the end.

"And now," said she, "I am his wife, whom he bought with his soul's welfare. And what should I do? If I went to him myself and offered to buy it, he would refuse. But if you go, he will sell it eagerly; I will await you here; you will buy it for four centimes, and I will buy it again for three. And the Lord strengthen a poor girl!"

"If you meant falsely," said the old man, "I think God would strike you dead."

"He would!" cried Kokua. "Be sure he would. I could not be so treacherous—God would not suffer it."

"Give me the four centimes and await me here," said the old man.

Now, when Kokua stood alone in the street, her spirit died. The wind roared in the trees, and it seemed to her the rushing of the flames of hell; the shadows tossed in the light of the streetlamp, and they seemed to her the snatching hands of evil ones. If she had had the strength, she must have run away, and if she had had the breath she must have screamed aloud; but, in truth, she could do neither, and stood and trembled in the avenue, like an affrighted child.

Then she saw the old man returning, and he had the bottle in his hand.

"I have done your bidding," said he, "I left your husband weeping like a child; tonight he will sleep easy." And he held the bottle forth.

"Before you give it me," Kokua panted, "take the good with the evil—ask to be delivered from your cough."

"I am an old man," replied the other, "and too near the gate of the grave to take a favour from the devil. But what is this? Why do you not take the bottle? Do you hesitate?"

"Not hesitate!" cried Kokua. "I am only weak. Give me a moment. It is my hand resists, my flesh shrinks back from the accursed thing. One moment only!"

The old man looked upon Kokua kindly. "Poor child!" said he, "you fear; your soul misgives you. Well, let me keep it. I am old, and can never more be happy in this world, and as for the next——"

"Give it me!" gasped Kokua. "There is your money. Do you think I am so base as that? Give me the bottle."

"God bless you, child," said the old man.

Kokua concealed the bottle under her holoku, said farewell to the old man, and walked off along the avenue, she cared not whither. For all roads were now the same to her, and led equally to hell. Sometimes she walked, and sometimes ran; sometimes she screamed out loud in the night, and sometimes lay by the wayside in the dust and wept. All that she had heard of hell came back to her; she saw the flames blaze, and she smelt the smoke, and her flesh withered on the coals.

Near day she came to her mind again, and returned to the house. It was even as the old man said—Keawe slumbered like a child. Kokua stood and gazed upon his face.

"Now, my husband," said she, "it is your turn to sleep. When you wake it will be your turn to sing and laugh. But for poor Kokua, alas! that meant no evil—for poor Kokua no more sleep, no more singing, no more delight, whether in earth or heaven."

With that she lay down in the bed by his side, and her misery was so extreme that she fell in a deep slumber instantly.

Late in the morning her husband woke her and gave her the good news. It seemed he was silly with delight, for he paid no heed to her distress, ill though she dissembled it. The words stuck in her mouth, it mattered not; Keawe did the speaking. She ate not a bite, but who was to observe it? for Keawe cleared the dish. Kokua saw and heard him, like some strange thing in a dream; there were times when she forgot or doubted, and put her hands to her brow; to know herself doomed and hear her husband babble, seemed so monstrous.

All the while Keawe was eating and talking, and planning the time of their return, and thanking her for saving him, and fondling her, and calling her the true helper after all. He laughed at the old man that was fool enough to buy that bottle.

"A worthy old man he seemed," Keawe said. "But no one can judge by appearances. For why did the old reprobate require the bottle?"

"My husband," said Kokua, humbly, "his purpose may have been good."

Keawe laughed like an angry man.

"Fiddle-de-dee!" cried Keawe. "An old rogue, I tell you; and an old ass to boot. For the bottle was hard enough to sell at four centimes; and at three it will be quite impossible. The margin is not broad enough, the thing begins to smell of scorching—brr!" said he, and shuddered. "It is true I bought it myself at a cent, when I knew not there were smaller coins. I was a fool for my pains; there will never be found another: and whoever has that bottle now will carry it to the pit."

"O my husband!" said Kokua. "Is it not a terrible thing to save oneself by the eternal ruin of another? It seems to me that I could not laugh. I would be humbled. I would be filled with melancholy. I would pray for the poor holder."

Then Keawe, because he felt the truth of what she said, grew the more angry. "Heighty-teighty!" cried he. "You may be filled with melancholy if you please. It is not the mind of a good wife. If you thought at all of me, you would sit shamed."

Thereupon he went out, and Kokua was alone.

What chance had she to sell that bottle at two centimes? None, she perceived. And if she had any, here was her husband hurrying her away to a country where there was nothing lower than a cent. And here—on the morrow of her sacrifice—was her husband leaving her and blaming her.

She would not even try to profit by what time she had, but sat in the house, and now had the bottle out and viewed it with unutterable fear, and now, with loathing, hid it out of sight.

By and by, Keawe came back, and would have her take a drive.

"My husband, I am ill," she said. "I am out of heart. Excuse me, I can take no pleasure."

Then was Keawe more wroth than ever. With her, because he thought she was brooding over the case of the old man; and with himself, because he thought she was right, and was ashamed to be so happy.

"This is your truth," cried he, "and this your affection! Your husband is just saved from eternal ruin, which he encountered for the love of you—and you can take no pleasure! Kokua, you have a disloyal heart."

He went forth again furious, and wandered in the town all day. He met friends, and drank with them; they hired a carriage and drove into the country, and there drank again. All the time Keawe was ill at ease, because he was taking this pastime while his wife was sad, and because he knew in his heart that she was more right than he; and the knowledge made him drink the deeper.

Now there was an old brutal Haole drinking with him, one that had been a boatswain of a whaler, a runaway, a digger in gold mines, a convict in prisons. He had a low mind and a foul mouth; he loved to drink and to see others drunken; and he pressed the glass upon Keawe. Soon there was no more money in the company.

"Here, you!" says the boatswain, "you are rich, you have been always saying. You have a bottle or some foolishness."

"Yes," says Keawe, "I am rich; I will go back and get some money from my wife, who keeps it."

"That's a bad idea, mate," said the boatswain. "Never you trust a petticoat with dollars. They're all as false as water; you keep an eye on her."

Now, this word struck in Keawe's mind; for he was muddled with what he had been drinking.

"I should not wonder but she was false, indeed," thought he. "Why else should she be so cast down at my release? But I will show her I am not the man to be fooled. I will catch her in the act."

Accordingly, when they were back in town, Keawe bade the boatswain wait for him at the corner, by the old calaboose, and went forward up the avenue alone to the door of his house. The night had come again; there was a light within, but never a sound; and Keawe crept about the corner, opened the back door softly, and looked in.

There was Kokua on the floor, the lamp at her side; before her was a milk-white bottle, with a round belly and a long neck; and as she viewed it, Kokua wrung her hands.

A long time Keawe stood and looked in the doorway. At first he was struck stupid; and then fear fell upon him that the bargain had been made amiss, and the bottle had come back to him as it came at San Francisco; and at that his knees were loosened, and the fumes of the wine departed from his head like mists off a river in the morning. And then he had another thought; and it was a strange one, that made his cheeks to burn.

"I must make sure of this," thought he.

So he closed the door, and went softly round the corner again, and then came noisily in, as though he were but now returned. And, lo! by the time he opened the front door no bottle was to be seen; and Kokua sat in a chair and started up like one awakened out of sleep.

"I have been drinking all day and making merry," said Keawe. "I have been with good companions, and now I only come back for money, and return to drink and carouse with them again."

Both his face and voice were as stern as judgment, but Kokua was too troubled to observe.

"You do well to use your own, my husband," said she, and her words trembled.

"O, I do well in all things," said Keawe, and he went straight to the chest and took out money. But he looked besides in the corner where they kept the bottle, and there was no bottle there.

At that the chest heaved upon the floor like a sea-billow, and the house span about him like a wreath of smoke, for he saw he was lost now, and there was no escape. "It is what I feared," he thought. "It is she who has bought it."

And then he came to himself a little and rose up; but the sweat streamed on his face as thick as the rain and as cold as the well-water.

"Kokua," said he, "I said to you today what ill became me. Now I return to carouse with my jolly companions," and at that he laughed a little quietly. "I will take more pleasure in the cup if you forgive me."

She clasped his knees in a moment; she kissed his knees with flowing tears.

"O," she cried, "I asked but a kind word!"

"Let us never one think hardly of the other," said Keawe, and was gone out of the house.

Now, the money that Keawe had taken was only some of that store of centime pieces they had laid in at their arrival. It was very sure he had no mind to be drinking. His wife had given her soul for him, now he must give his for hers; no other thought was in the world with him.

At the corner, by the old calaboose, there was the boatswain waiting.

"My wife has the bottle," said Keawe, "and, unless you help me to recover it, there can be no more money and no more liquor tonight."

"You do not mean to say you are serious about that bottle?" cried the boatswain.

"There is the lamp," said Keawe. "Do I look as if I was jesting?"

"That is so," said the boatswain. "You look as serious as a ghost."

"Well, then," said Keawe, "here are two centimes; you must go to my wife in the house, and offer her these for the bottle, which (if I am not much mistaken) she will give you instantly. Bring it to me here, and I will buy it back from you for one; for that is the law with this bottle, that it still must be sold for a less sum. But whatever you do, never breathe a word to her that you have come from me."

"Mate, I wonder are you making a fool of me?" asked the boatswain.

"It will do you no harm if I am," returned Keawe.

"That is so, mate," said the boatswain.

"And if you doubt me," added Keawe, "you can try. As soon as you are clear of the house, wish to have your pocket full of money, or a bottle of the best rum, or what you please, and you will see the virtue of the thing."

"Very well, Kanaka," says the boatswain. "I will try; but if you are having your fun out of me, I will take my fun out of you with a belaying pin."

So the whaler-man went off up the avenue; and Keawe stood and waited. It was near the same spot where Kokua had waited the night before; but Keawe was more resolved, and never faltered in his purpose; only his soul was bitter with despair.

It seemed a long time he had to wait before he heard a voice singing in the darkness of the avenue. He knew the voice to be the boatswain's; but it was strange how drunken it appeared upon a sudden.

Next, the man himself came stumbling into the light of the lamp. He had the devil's bottle buttoned in his coat; another bottle was in his hand; and even as he came in view he raised it to his mouth and drank.

"You have it," said Keawe. "I see that."

"Hands off!" cried the boatswain, jumping back. "Take a step near me, and I'll smash your mouth. You thought you could make a cat's-paw of me, did you?"

"What do you mean?" cried Keawe.

"Mean?" cried the boatswain. "This is a pretty good bottle, this is; that's what I mean. How I got it for two centimes I can't make out; but I'm sure you shan't have it for one."

"You mean you won't sell?" gasped Keawe.

"No, *sir!*" cried the boatswain. "But I'll give you a drink of the rum, if you like."

"I tell you," said Keawe, "the man who has that bottle goes to hell."

"I reckon I'm going anyway," returned the sailor; "and this bottle's the best thing to go with I've struck yet. No, sir!" he cried again, "this is my bottle now, and you can go and fish for another."

"Can this be true?" Keawe cried. "For your own sake, I beseech you, sell it me!"

"I don't value any of your talk," replied the boatswain. "You thought I was a flat; now you see I'm not; and there's an end. If you won't have a swallow of the rum, I'll have one myself. Here's your health, and good-night to you!"

So off he went down the avenue towards town, and there goes the bottle out of the story.

But Keawe ran to Kokua light as the wind; and great was their joy that night; and great, since then, has been the peace of all their days in the Bright House.

THE ISLE OF VOICES

Keola was married with Lehua, daughter of Kalamake, the wise man of Molokai, and he kept his dwelling with the father of his wife. There was no man more cunning than that prophet; he read the stars, he could divine by the bodies of the dead and by the means of evil creatures; he would go alone into the highest parts of the mountain, into the region of the hobgoblins, and there he would lay snares to entrap the spirits of the ancient. For this reason no man was more consulted in all the Kingdom of Hawaii; prudent people bought and sold and married and laid out their lives by his counsels; and the King had him twice to Kona to seek the treasures of Kamehameha. Neither was any man more feared: of his enemies, some had dwindled in sickness by the virtue of his incantations, and some had been spirited away, the life and the clay both, so that folk looked in vain for so much as a bone of their bodies. It was rumoured that he had the art or the gift of the old heroes; men had seen him at night upon the mountains, stopping from one cliff to the next; they had seen him walking in the high forest, and his head and shoulders were above the trees. This Kalamake was a strange man to see; he was come of the best blood in Molokai and Maui, of a pure descent; and yet he was more white to look upon than any foreigner, his hair the colour of dry grass, and his eyes red and very blind; so that "Blind as Kalamake that can see across tomorrow," was a byword in the islands.

Of all these doings of his father-in-law, Keola knew a little by the common repute; a little more he suspected; and the rest ignored. But there was one thing troubled him. Kalamake was a man that spared for nothing, whether to eat or to drink or to wear; and for all, he paid in bright new dollars. "Bright as Kalamake's dollars," was another saying in the Eight Isles. Yet he neither sold, nor planted, nor took hire—only now and then for his sorceries—and there was no source conceivable for so much silver coin.

It chanced one day Keola's wife was gone upon a visit to Kaunakakai on the lee side of the island, and the men were forth at the sea fishing. But Keola was an idle dog; and he lay in the verandah, and watched the surf beat on the shore and the birds fly about the cliff. It was a chief thought with him always: the thought of the bright dollars. When he lay down to bed, he would be wondering why they were so many; and when he woke at morn, he would be wondering why they were all new; and the thing was never absent from his mind. But this day of all days, he made sure in his heart of some discovery. For it seems he had observed the place where Kalamake kept his treasure, which was a lockfast desk against the parlour wall, under the print of Kamehameha the fifth and a photograph of Queen Victoria with her crown; and it seems again that, no later than the night before, he found occasion to look in, and behold! the bag lay there empty. And this was the day of the steamer; he could see her smoke off Kalaupapa; and she must soon arrive with a month's goods, tinned salmon and gin and all manner of rare luxuries, for Kalamake.

"Now if he can pay for his goods today," Keola thought, "I shall know for certain that the man is a warlock, and the dollars come out of the devil's pocket."

While he was so thinking, there was his father-in-law behind him, looking vexed.

"Is that the steamer?" he asked.

"Yes," said Keola. "She has but to call at Pelekunu, and then she will be here."

"There is no help for it, then," returned Kalamake, "and I must take you in my confidence, Keola, for the lack of anyone better. Come here within the house."

So they stepped together into the parlour, which was a very fine room, papered and hung with prints, and furnished with a rocking chair and a table and a sofa in the European style; there was a shelf of books besides, and a family bible in the midst of the table, and the lockfast writing-desk against the wall; so that anyone could see it was the house of a man of substance.

Kalamake made Keola close the shutters of the windows, while he himself locked all the doors and set open the lid of the desk. From this he brought forth a pair of necklaces hung with charms and shells, a bundle of dried herbs and the dried leaves of trees, and a green branch of palm.

"What I am about," said he, "is a thing beyond wonder. The men of old were wise; they wrought marvels, and this among the rest; but that was at night, in the dark, under the fit stars and in the desert. The same will I do here in my own house and under the plain eye of day."

So saying, he put the bible under the cushion of the sofa so that it was all covered, brought out from the same place a mat of a wonderful fine texture, and heaped the herbs and leaves on sand in a tin pan. And then he and Keola put on the necklaces, and took their stand upon the opposite corners of the mat.

"The time comes," said the warlock. "Be not afraid."

With that he set flame to the herbs, and began to mutter and wave the branch of palm. At first the light was dim because of the closed shutters; but the herbs caught strongly afire, and the flames beat upon Keola, and the room glowed with the burning; and next the smoke rose and made his head swim and his eyes darken, and the sound of Kalamake muttering ran in his ears. And suddenly, to the mat on which they were standing, came a snatch or twitch, that seemed to be more swift than lightning. In the same wink, the room was gone and the house, the breath all beaten from Keola's body. Volumes of sun rolled upon his eyes and head; and he found himself transported to a beach of the sea, under a strong sun, with a great surf roaring: he and the warlock standing there on the same mat speechless, gasping and grasping at one another, and passing their hands before their eyes.

"What was this?" cried Keola, who came to himself the first, because he was the younger. "The pang of it was like death."

"It matters not," panted Kalamake. "It is now done."

"And, in the name of God, where are we?" cries Keola.

"That is not the question," replied the sorcerer. "Being here, we have matter in our hands, and that we must attend to. Go—while I recover my breath—into the borders of the wood, and bring me the leaves of such and such a herb, and such and such a tree, which you will find to grow there plentifully: three handfuls of each. And be speedy. We must be home again before the steamer comes; it would seem strange if we had disappeared." And he sat on the sand and panted.

Keola went up the beach, which was of shining sand and coral, strewn with singular shells; and he thought in his heart: "How do I not know this beach? I will come here again and gather shells." In front of him was a line of palms against the sky, not like the palms of the Eight Islands, but tall and fresh and beautiful, and hanging out withered fans like gold among the green; and he thought in his heart: "It is strange I should not have found this grove. I will come here again, when it is warm, to sleep." And he thought: "How warm it has grown suddenly!" for it was winter in Hawaii and the day had been chill. And he thought also: "Where are the gray mountains? and where is the high cliff with the hanging forest and the wheeling birds?" And the more he considered, the less he might conceive in what quarter of the islands he was fallen.

In the border of the grove, where it met the beach, the herb was growing, but the tree farther back. Now, as Keola went toward the tree, he was aware of a young woman who had nothing on her body but a belt of leaves. "Well!" thought Keola, "they are not very particular about their dress in this part of the country." And he paused, supposing she would observe him and escape; and seeing that she still looked before her, stood and hummed aloud. Up she leaped at the sound; her face was ashen; she looked this way and that, and her mouth gaped with the terror of her soul. But it was a strange thing that her eyes did not rest upon Keola.

"Good day," said he. "You need not be so frightened, I will not eat you."

And he had scarce opened his mouth before the young woman fled into the bush.

"These are strange manners," thought Keola, and not thinking what he did, ran after her.

As she ran, the girl kept crying in some speech that was not practised in Hawaii; yet some of the words were the same, and he knew she kept calling and warning others. And presently he saw more people running, men, women and children one with another, all running and crying, like people at a fire. And with that, he began to grow afraid himself, and returned to Kalamake, bringing the leaves. Him he told what he had seen.

"You must pay no heed," said Kalamake. "All this is like a dream and shadows: all will disappear and be forgotten."

"It seemed none saw me," said Keola.

"And none did," replied the sorcerer. "We walk here in the broad sun invisible by reason of these charms. Yet they hear us; and therefore it is well to speak softly as I do."

With that he made a circle round the mat with stones, and in the midst he set the leaves. "It will be your part," said he, "to keep the leaves alight, and feed the fire slowly. While they blaze (which is but for a little moment) I must do my errand; and before the ashes blacken, the same power that brought us carries us away. Be ready now with the match; and do you call me in good time lest the flame burn out, and I be left." As soon as the leaves caught, the sorcerer leaped like a deer out of the circle, and began to race along the beach like a hound that has been bathing: as he ran, he kept stooping to snatch shells; and it seemed to Keola that they glittered as he took them. The leaves blazed with a clear flame that consumed them swiftly; and presently Keola had but a handful left, and the sorcerer was far off, running and stooping. "Back!" cried Keola. "Back! the leaves are near done." At that, Kalamake turned, and if he had run before, now he flew. But fast as he ran, the leaves burned faster. The flame was ready to expire, when with a great leap he bounded on the mat; the wind of his leaping blew it out; and with that the beach was gone, and the sun, and the sea; and they stood once more in the dimness of the shuttered parlour, and were once more shaken and blinded; and on the mat betwixt them, lay a pile of shining dollars. Keola ran to the shutters; and there was the steamer tossing in the swell close in.

The same night Kalamake took his son-in-law apart, and gave him five dollars in his hand. "Keola," said he, "if you are a wise man (which I am doubtful of) you will think you slept this afternoon on the verandah, and dreamed as you were sleeping. I am a man of few words, and I have for my helpers people of short memories."

Never a word more said Kalamake, nor referred again to that affair.

But it ran all the while in Keola's head; if he were lazy before, he would now do nothing. "Why should I work?" thought he, "when I have a father-in-law who makes dollars of sea-shells?" Presently his share was spent, and he spent it all upon fine clothes. And then he was sorry. "For," thought he, "I had done better to have bought a concertina, with which I might have entertained myself all day long." And then he began to grow vexed with Kalamake. "This man has the soul of a dog," thought he. "He can gather dollars when he pleases on a beach, and he leaves me to pine for a concertina! Let him beware; I am no child, I am as cunning as he, and hold his secret." With that he spoke to his wife, Lehua, and complained of her father's manners.

"I would let my father be," said Lehua. "He is a dangerous man to cross."

"I care that for him!" cried Keola, and snapped his fingers. "I have him by the nose, I can make him do what I please." And he told Lehua the story.

But she shook her head. "You may do what you like," said she. "But as sure as you thwart my father, you will be no more heard of. Think of this person, and that person; think of Hua, who was a noble of the House of Representatives and went to Honolulu every year; and not a bone or a hair of him was found. Remember Kamau, and how he wasted to a thread, so that his wife lifted him with one hand. Keola, you are a baby in my father's hands; he will take you with his thumb and finger, and eat you like a shrimp."

Now Keola was truly very much afraid of Kalamake, but he was vain too; and these words of his wife incensed him. "Very well," said he. "If that is what you think of me, I will show how much you are deceived." And he went straight to where his father-in-law was sitting in the parlour.

"Kalamake," said he, "I want a concertina."

"Do you indeed?" said Kalamake.

"Yes," said he, "and I may as well tell you plainly, I mean to have it. A man who picks up dollars on the beach can certainly afford a concertina."

"I had no idea you had so much spirit," replied the sorcerer. "I thought you were a timid, useless lad, and I cannot describe how much pleased I am to find I was mistaken. Now, I begin to think I may have found an assistant and successor in my difficult business. A concertina? You shall have the best in Honolulu. And tonight, as soon as it is dark, you and I will go and find the money."

"Shall we return to the beach?" asked Keola.

"No, no," replied Kalamake; "you must begin to learn more of my secrets. Last time, I taught you to pick shells; this time I shall teach you to catch fish. Are you strong enough to launch Pili's boat?"

"I think I am," returned Keola. "But why should we not take your own, which is afloat already?"

"I have a reason, which you will understand thoroughly before to-morrow," says Kalamake. "Pili's boat is the better suited for my purpose. So, if you please, let us meet there as soon as it is dark. And in the meanwhile, let us keep our own counsel, for there is no cause to let the family into our business."

Honey is not more sweet than was the voice of Kalamake; and Keola could scarce contain his satisfaction. "I might have had my concertina weeks ago," thought he, "and there is nothing needed in this world but a little courage." Presently after, he spied Lehua weeping, and was half in a mind to tell her all was well. "But no," thinks he. "I shall wait till I can show her the concertina; we shall see what the chit will do then. Perhaps she will understand in the future that her husband is a man of some intelligence."

As soon as it was dark, father- and son-in-law launched Pili's boat and set the sail. There was a great sea, and it blew strong from the leeward; but the boat was swift and light and dry, and skimmed the waves. The wizard had a lantern, which he lit and held with his finger through the ring; and the two sat in the stern, and smoked cigars, of which Kalamake had always a provision, and spoke like friends of magic, and the great sums of money which they could make by its exercise, and what they should buy first, and what second. And Kalamake talked like a father.

Presently he looked all about, and above him at the stars, and back at the island, which was already three parts sunk under the sea; and he seemed to consider ripely his position.

"Look!" says he. "There is Molokai already far behind us, and Maui like a cloud; and by the bearing of these three stars I know I am come where I desire. This part of the sea is called the Sea of the Dead. It is in this place extraordinary deep, and the floor is all covered with the bones of men, and in the holes of this part gods and goblins keep their habitation. The flow of the sea is to the north, stronger than a shark can swim; and any man, who shall here be thrown out of a ship, it bears away like a wild horse into the uttermost ocean. Presently he is spent and goes down, and his bones are scattered with the rest, and the gods devour his spirit."

Fear came on Keola at the words; and he looked, and by the light of the stars and the lantern, the warlock seemed to change.

"What ails you?" cried Keola, quick and sharp.

"It is not I who am ailing," said the wizard; "but there is one here very sick."

With that he changed his grasp upon the lantern; and behold, as he drew his finger from the ring, the finger stuck and the ring was burst; and his hand was grown to be of the bigness of three.

At that sight Keola screamed and covered his face.

But Kalamake held up the lantern. "Look rather at my face!" said he. And his head was huge as a barrel; and still he grew and grew as a cloud grows on a mountain, and Keola sat before him screaming, and the boat raced on the great seas.

"And now," said the wizard, "what do you think about that concertina? and are you sure you would not rather have a flute? No?" says he. "That is well, for I do not like my family to be changeable of purpose. But I begin to think I had better get out of this paltry boat; for my bulk swells to a very unusual degree, and if we are not the more careful, she will presently be swamped."

With that, he threw his legs over the side. Even as he did so, the greatness of the man grew thirty fold and forty fold as swift as sight or thinking; so that he stood in the deep seas to the armpits, and his head and shoulders rose like a high isle, and the swell beat and burst upon his bosom as it beats and breaks against a cliff. The boat ran still to the north, but he reached out his hand, and took the gunwale by the finger and thumb, and broke the side like a biscuit, and Keola was spilled into the sea. And the pieces of the boat, the sorcerer crushed in the hollow of his hand and flung miles away into the night.

"Excuse me taking the lantern," said he; "for I have a long wade before me, and the land is far, and the bottom of the sea uneven, and I feel the bones under my toes."

And he turned and went off walking with great strides; and as often as Keola sank in the trough, he could see him no longer; but as often as he was heaved upon the crest, there he was striding and dwindling, and he held the lamp high over his head, and the waves broke white about him as he went.

Since first the islands were fished out of the sea, there was never a man so terrified as this Keola. He swam indeed, but he swam as puppies swim when they are cast in to drown, and knew not wherefore. He could but think of the hugeness of the swelling of the warlock, of that face which was great as a mountain, of those shoulders that were broad as an isle, and of the seas that beat on them in vain. He thought too of the concertina, and shame took hold upon him; and of the dead men's bones, and fear shook him.

Of a sudden he was aware of something dark against the stars that tossed, and a light below, and a brightness of the cloven sea; and he heard speech of men. He cried out aloud and a voice answered; and in a twinkling the bows of a ship hung above him on a wave like a thing balanced, and swooped down. He caught with his two hands in the chains of her, and the next moment was buried in the rushing seas, and the next hauled on board by seamen.

They gave him gin and biscuit and dry clothes; and asked him how he came where they found him, and whether the light which they had seen was the lighthouse, Lae o Ka Laau. But Keola knew white men are like children and only believe their own stories; so about himself, he told them what he pleased, and as for the light (which was Kalamake's lantern) he vowed he had seen none.

This ship was a schooner bound for Honolulu, and then to trade in the low islands; and by a very good chance for Keola, she had lost a man off the bowsprit in a squall. It was no use talking, Keola durst not stay in the Eight Islands. Word goes so quickly, and all men are so fond to talk and carry news, that if he hid on the north end of Kauai or in the south end of Kaü, the wizard would have wind of it before a month, and he must perish. So he did what seemed the most prudent, and shipped sailor in the place of the man who had been drowned.

In some ways the ship was a good place. The food was extraordinary rich and plenty, with biscuits and salt beef every day, and pea soup and puddings made of flour and suet twice a week, so that Keola grew fat. The captain also was a good man, and the crew no worse than other whites. The trouble was the mate, who was the most difficult man to please Keola ever met with, and beat and cursed him daily both for what he did and what he did not. The blows that he dealt were very sore, for he was strong; and the words he used were very unpalatable, for Keola was come of a good family and accustomed to respect. And what was the worst of all, whenever Keola found a chance to sleep, there was the mate awake and stirring him up with a rope's end. Keola saw it would never do; and he made up his mind to run away.

They were about a month out from Honolulu when they made the land. It was a fine starry night, the sea was smooth as well as the sky fair, it blew a steady trade; and there was the island on their weather bow, a ribbon of palm trees lying flat along the sea. The captain and the mate looked at it with the night glass, and named the name of it, and talked of it, beside the wheel where Keola was steering. It seemed it was an isle where no traders came. By the captain's way, it was an isle besides where no man dwelt; but the mate thought otherwise.

"I don't give a cent for the directory," said he. "I've been past here one night in the schooner *Eugénie;* it was just such a night as this; they were fishing with torches, and the beach was thick with lights like a town."

"Well, well," says the captain, "it's steep-to, that's the great point; and there ain't any outlying dangers by the chart; so we'll just hug the lee side of it. Keep her ramping full, don't I tell you!" he cried to Keola, who was listening so hard that he forgot to steer.

And the mate cursed him, and swore that Kanaka was for no use in the world, and if he got started after him with a belaying pin, it would be a cold day for Keola.

And so the captain and mate lay down on the house together, and Keola was left to himself. "This island will do very well for me," he thought. "If no traders deal there, the mate will never come. And as for Kalamake, it is not possible he can ever get as far as this." With that he kept edging the schooner nearer in. He had to do this quietly; for it was the trouble with these white men, and above all with the mate, that you could never be sure of them; they would all be sleeping sound or else pretending, and if a sail shook, they would jump to their feet and fall on you with a rope's end. So Keola edged her up little by little, and kept all drawing. And presently the land was close on board, and the sound of the sea on the sides of it grew loud.

With that, the mate sat up suddenly upon the house. "What are you doing?" he roars. "You'll have the ship ashore!"

And he made one bound for Keola, and Keola made another clean over the rail and plump into the starry sea. When he came up again, the schooner had payed off on her true course, and the mate stood by the wheel himself, and Keola heard him cursing. The sea was smooth under the lee of the island; it was warm besides; and Keola had his sailor's knife, so he had no fear of sharks. A little way before him, the trees stopped; there was a break in the line of the land, like the mouth of a harbour; and the tide, which was then flowing, took him up and carried him through. One minute he was without: and the next within, and floated there in a wide shallow water bright with ten thousand stars, and all about him was the ring of the land with its string of palm trees. And he was amazed, because this was a kind of island he had never heard of.

The time of Keola in that place was in two periods: the period when he was alone; and the period when he was there with the tribe. At first he sought everywhere, and found no man; only some houses standing in a hamlet and the marks of fires. But the ashes of the fires were cold and the rains had washed them away; and the winds had blown, and some of the huts were overthrown. It was here he took his dwelling; and he made a fire drill, and a shell hook, and fished and cooked his fish, and climbed after green cocoanuts, the juice of which he drank, for in all the isle there was no water. The days were long to him, and the nights terrifying. He made a lamp of cocoa shell, and drew the oil of the ripe nuts, and made a wick of fibre; and when evening came, he closed up his hut, and lit his lamp, and lay and trembled till morning. Many a time he thought in his heart he would have been better in the bottom of the sea, his bones rolling there with the others.

All this while he kept by the inside of the island, for the huts were on the shore of the lagoon, and it was there the palms grew best, and the lagoon itself abounded with good fish. And to the other side, he went once only, and looked but the once at the beach of the ocean, and came away shaking. For the look of it, with its bright sand, and strewn shells, and strong sun and surf, went sore against his inclination. "It cannot be," he thought, "and yet it is very like. And how do I know? These white men, although they pretend to know where they are sailing, must take their chance like other people. So that after all we may have sailed in a circle, and I may be quite near to Molokai, and this may be the very beach where my father-in-law gathers his dollars." So after that he was prudent, and kept to the landside.

It was perhaps a month later, when the people of the place arrived, the fill of six great boats. They were a fine race of men, and spoke a tongue that sounded very different from the tongue of Hawaii, but so many of the words were the same that it was not difficult to understand. The men besides were very courteous, and the women very towardly: and they made Keola welcome, and built him a house, and gave him a wife; and what surprised him the most, he was never sent to work with the young men.

And now Keola had three periods. First he had a period of being very sad, and then he had a period when he was pretty merry. Last of all came the third, when he was the most terrified man in the four oceans.

The cause of the first period was the girl he had to wife. He was in doubt about the island; and he might have been in doubt about the speech, of which he had heard so little when he came there with the wizard on the mat. But about his wife there was no mistake conceivable, for she was the same girl that ran from him crying in the wood. So he had sailed all this way, and might as well have stayed in Molokai; and had left home and wife and all his friends, for no other cause but to escape his enemy; and the place he had come to was that wizard's haunting ground, and the place where he walked invisible. It was at this period when he kept the most close to the lagoon side, and as far as he dared, abode in the cover of his hut.

The cause of the second period was talk he heard from his wife and the chief islanders. Keola himself said little; he was never so sure of his new friends, for he judged they were too civil to be wholesome; and since he had grown better acquainted with his father-in-law, the man was grown more cautious. So he told them nothing of himself; but only his name and descent, and that he came from the Eight Islands, and what fine islands these were, and about the King's palace in Honolulu, and how he was a chief friend of the King and the missionaries. But he put many questions, and learned much. The island where he was was called the Isle of Voices; it belonged to the tribe, but they made their home upon another three hours' sail to the southward. There they lived and had their permanent houses, and it was a rich island, where were eggs and chickens and pigs, and ships came trading with rum and tobacco. It was there the schooner had gone after Keola deserted; there, too, the mate had died, like a fool of a white man as he was. It seems, when the ship came, it was the beginning of the sickly season in that isle, when the fish of the lagoon are poisonous, and all who eat of them swell up and die. The mate was told of it; he saw the boats preparing, because in that season the people leave that island and sail to the Isle of Voices. But he was a fool of a white man, who would believe no stories but his own; and he caught one of these fish, cooked it and ate it, and swelled up and died: which was good news to Keola. As for the Isle of Voices, it lay solitary the more part of the year; only now and then a boat's crew came for copra; and in the bad season, when the fish at the main isle were poisonous, the tribe dwelt there in a body. It had its name from a marvel. For it seemed the seaside of it was all beset with invisible devils; day and night, you heard them talking one with another in strange tongues; day and night little fires blazed up and were extinguished on the beach; and what was the cause of these doings no man might conceive. Keola asked them, if it were the same in their own island where they stayed? and they told him no, not there; nor yet in any other of some hundred isles that lay all about them in that sea; but it was a thing peculiar to the Isle of Voices. They told him also that these fires and voices were ever on the seaside and in the seaward fringes of the wood; and a man might dwell by the lagoon two thousand years (if he could live so long) and never be anyway troubled. And even on the seaside the devils did no harm, if let alone. Only once a chief had cast a spear at one of the voices, and the same night he fell out of a cocoanut palm and was killed.

Keola thought a good bit with himself. He saw he would be all right when the tribe returned to the main island; and right enough where he was, if he kept by the lagoon; yet he had a mind to make things righter, if he could. So he told the high chief he had once been in an isle that was pestered the same way, and the folk had found a means to cure that trouble. "There was a tree growing in the bush there," says he, "and it seems these devils came to get the leaves of it. So the people of the isle cut down the tree wherever it was found, and the devils came no more." They asked what kind of tree this was, and he showed them the tree of which Kalamake burned the leaves. They found it hard to believe, yet the idea tickled them. Night after night the old men debated it in their councils; but the high chief (though he was a brave man) was afraid of the matter, and reminded them daily of the chief who cast a spear against the voices and was killed; and the thought of that brought all to a stand again.

Though he could not yet bring about the destruction of the trees, Keola was well enough pleased, and began to look about him, and take pleasure in his days. And among other things he was the kinder to his wife, so that the girl began to love him greatly. One day he came to the hut, and she lay on the ground lamenting.

"Why," said Keola, "what is wrong with you now?"

She declared it was nothing.

The same night she woke him. The lamp burned very low but he saw by her face she was in sorrow.

"Keola," she said, "put your ear to my mouth that I may whisper, for none must hear us. Two days before the boats begin to be got ready, go you to the seaside of the isle and lie in a thicket. We shall choose that place beforehand, you and I, and hide food, and every night I shall come near by there singing. So when a night comes, and you do not hear me, you shall know we are clean gone out of the island, and you may come forth again in safety."

The soul of Keola died within him. "What is this?" he cried. "I cannot live among devils. I will not be left behind upon this isle. I am dying to leave it."

"You will never leave it alive, my poor Keola," said the girl. "For to tell you the truth, my people are eaters of men; but this they keep secret. And the reason they will kill you before we leave is because, in our island, ships come, and Donat-Kimaran comes and talks for the French, and there is a white trader there in a house with a verandah, and a catechist. O, that is a fine place indeed! The trader has barrels filled with flour; and a French warship once came in the lagoon and gave everybody wine and biscuit. Ah, my poor Keola, I wish I could take you there, for great is my love to you, and it is the finest place in the seas except Papeete."

So now Keola was the most terrified man in the four oceans. He had heard tell of eaters of men in the south islands, and the thing had always been a fear to him; and here it was knocking at his door. He had heard besides, by travellers, of their practices, and how when they are in a mind to eat a man, they cherish and fondle him like a mother with a favourite baby. And he saw this must be his own case; and that was why he had been housed, and fed, and wived, and liberated from all work, and why the old men and the chiefs discoursed with him like a person of weight. So he lay on his bed and railed upon his destiny, and the flesh curdled on his bones.

The next day the people of the tribe were very civil as their way was. They were elegant speakers, and they made beautiful poetry, and jested at meals so that a missionary must have died laughing. It was little enough Keola cared for their fine ways; all he saw was the white teeth shining in their mouths, and his gorge rose at the sight; and when they were done eating, he went and lay in the bush like a dead man. The next day it was the same, and then his wife followed him.

"Keola," she said, "if you do not eat, I tell you plainly you will be killed and cooked tomorrow. Some of the old chiefs are murmuring already. They think you are fallen sick and must lose flesh."

With that Keola got to his feet, and anger burned in him.

"It is little I care one way or the other," said he. "I am between the devil and the deep sea. Since die I must, let me die the quickest way; and since I must be eaten at the best of it, let me rather be eaten by hobgoblins than by men. Farewell," said he, and he left her standing, and walked to the seaside of that island.

It was all bare in the strong sun; there was no sign of man, only the beach was trodden; and all about him as he went, the voices talked and whispered, and the little fires sprang up and burned down. All tongues of the earth were spoken there, the French, the Dutch, the Russian, the Tamil, the Chinese. Whatever land knew sorcery, there were some of its people whispering in Keola's ear. That beach was thick as a cried fair, yet no man seen; and as he walked he saw the shells vanish before him, and no man to pick them up. I think the devil would have been afraid to be alone in such a company; but Keola was past fear and courted death. When the fires sprang up, he charged for them like a bull; bodiless voices called to and fro, unseen hands poured sand upon the flames; and they were gone from the beach before he reached them. "It is plain Kalamake is not here," he thought, "or I must have been killed long since." With that he sat him down in the margin of the wood, for he was tired, and put his chin upon his hands. The business before his eyes continued; the beach babbled with voices, and the fires sprang up and sank, and the shells vanished and were renewed again even while he looked. "It was a by-day when I was here before," he thought. "For it was nothing to this." And his head was dizzy with the thought of these millions and millions of dollars, and all these hundreds and hundreds of persons culling them upon the beach and flying in the air higher and swifter than eagles. "And to think how they have fooled me with their talk of mints," says he, "and that money was made there! when it is clear that all the new coin in the world is gathered on these sands! But I will know better the next time," said he. And at last, he knew not very well how or when, sleep fell on Keola and he forgot the island and all his sorrows.

Early the next day, before the sun was yet up, a bustle woke him. He awoke in fear, for he thought the tribe had caught him napping; but it was no such matter. Only, on the beach in front of him, the bodiless voices called and shouted one upon another, and it seemed they all passed, and swept beside him, up the coast of the island.

"What is afoot now?" thinks Keola; and it was plain to him it was something beyond ordinary. For the fires were not lighted nor the shells taken, but the bodiless voices kept posting up the beach and hailing, dying away, and others following, and by the sound of them these wizards should be angry. "It is not me they are angry at," thought Keola, "for they pass me close." As when hounds go by, or horses in a race, or city folk coursing to a fire, and all men join and follow after: so it was now with Keola; and he knew not what he did, nor why he did it, but there, lo and behold! he was running with the voices!

So he turned one point of the island, and this brought him in view of a second; and there he remembered the wizard trees to have been growing by the score together in a wood. From this point there went up a hubbub of men crying not to be described; and by the sound of them, those that he ran with shaped their course for the same quarter. A little nearer, and there began to mingle with the outcry the crash of many axes. And at this a thought came at last into his mind, that the high chief had consented, that the men of the tribe had set to cutting down these trees, that word had gone about the isle from sorcerer to sorcerer, and these were all now assembling to defend their trees. Desire of strange things swept him on. He posted with the voices, crossed the beach, and came into the borders of the wood, and stood astonished. One tree had fallen; others were part hewed away. There was the tribe clustered. They were back to back, and bodies lay and blood flowed among their feet. The hue of fear was on all their faces; their voices went up to heaven shrill as a weasel's cry. Have you seen a child, when he is all alone and has a wooden sword, and fights, leaping and hewing, with the empty air? Even so the man-eaters huddled back to back, and heaved up their axes, and laid on, and screamed as they laid on, and behold! no man to contend with them! Only here and there, Keola saw an axe swinging over against them without hands; and time and again a man of the tribe would fall before it, clove in twain or burst asunder, and his soul sped howling.

For awhile Keola looked upon this prodigy like one that dreams, and then fear took him by the midst as sharp as death, that he should behold such doings. Even in that same flash, the high chief of the clan espied him standing, and pointed and called out his name; thereat the whole tribe saw him also, and their eyes flashed and their teeth clashed. "I am too long here," thought Keola; and ran forth out of the wood and down the beach, not caring whither.

"Keola!" said a voice close by upon the empty sand.

"Lehua! is that you?" he cried, and gasped, and looked in vain for her; but by the eyesight, he was stark alone.

"I saw you pass before," the voice answered. "But you would not hear me. Quick, get the leaves and herbs, and let us flee."

"You are there with the mat?" he asked.

"Here, at your side," said she, and he felt her arms about him. "Quick! the leaves and the herbs, before my father can get back!"

So Keola ran for his life, and fetched the wizard fuel; and Lehua guided him back, and set his feet upon the mat, and made the fire. All the time of its burning, the sound of the battle towered out of the wood; the wizards and the man-eaters hard at fight; the wizards, the viewless ones, roaring out aloud like bulls upon a mountain, and the men of the tribe replying shrill and savage out of the terror of their souls. And all the time of the burning Keola stood there, and listened, and shook, and watched how the unseen hands of Lehua poured the leaves. She poured them fast, and the flame burned high, and scorched Keola's hams; and she speeded and blew the burning with her breath. The last leaf was eaten, the flame fell, and the shock followed, and there were Keola and Lehua in the room at home.

Now when Keola could see his wife at last, he was mighty pleased. And he was mighty pleased to be home again in Molokai, and sit down beside a bowl of *poi*—for they make no poi on board ships and there was none in the Isle of Voices—and he was out of the body with pleasure to be clean escaped out of the hands of the eaters of men. But there was another matter not so clear, and Lehua and Keola talked of it all night, and were troubled. There was Kalamake left upon the isle; if, by the blessing of God, he could but stick there, all were well; but should he escape and return to Molokai, it would be an ill day for his daughter and her husband. They spoke of his gift of swelling, and whether he could wade that distance in the seas. But Keola knew by this time where that island was, and that is to say, in the Low or Dangerous Archipelago; so they fetched the atlas, and looked upon the distance in the map, and by what they could make of it, it seemed a far way for an old gentleman to walk. Still it would not do to make too sure of a warlock like Kalamake, and they determined at last to take counsel of a white missionary.

So the first one that came by, Keola told him everything. And the missionary was very sharp on him for taking the second wife in the low island, but for all the rest, he vowed he could make neither head nor tail of it. "However," says he, "if you think this money of your father's ill gotten, my advice to you would be to give some of it to the lepers and some to the missionary fund; and as for this extraordinary rigmarole, you cannot do better than keep it to yourselves." But he warned the police at Honolulu that, by all he could make out, Kalamake and Keola had been coining false money, and it would not be amiss to watch them.

Keola and Lehua took his advice, and gave many dollars to the lepers and the fund. And no doubt the advice must have been good, for from that day to this, Kalamake has never more been heard of. But whether he was slain in the battle by the trees, or whether he is still kicking his heels upon the Isle of Voices, who shall say?

UNCOLLECTED
STORIES

An Old Song

Lieutenant-Colonel John Falconer broke the traditions of his family by entering the army, and his whole youth was expensive and disastrous. He was near being asked to leave his regiment; he was in trouble about the mess funds; he was deplorably in debt; when his aunt sent him a religious tract, it was returned with a pen and ink commentary in a blunt, military style. By these flashes and reverberations his stormy existence was from time to time revealed to his family at home; and as he never wrote between whiles, a letter from India denoted a new scrape.

Suddenly, at the age of thirty, he was converted at a revival meeting. From that moment he was a changed man. It was his principal boast that he had not once omitted or shortened his devotions since that day, and for those who knew his previous habits, the pretension was imposing in the extreme. At the same time that he became religious he developed a sense of duty, and turned into a good officer. Falconer was counted a trusty man; Napier swore by him; his men feared and admired him in equal parts.

When his father died, and he found himself the last of the family besides two nephews, he took it to be his duty to go home and supervise his nephews and the estate. An unpleasant duty was to him what stolen pleasures are to others: it was his passion; he flung himself into it headlong; and the more unpleasant it was, the higher his pride rose as he performed it. To live at Grangehead, to take care of an estate, to be pestered with a pair of playful urchins, to give up his regiment— this was the best thing of the sort he had yet encountered, the raciest piece of self-sacrifice conceivable, the very pink of martyrdom; and on his homeward voyage Colonel Falconer was a prey to all the delights of what we may call Black Happiness.

His old Aunt Rebecca (who had sent him the tract in former days) still survived in a cottage at Hampstead; she had received in the meantime the two nephews; and so the Colonel's first visit was to her.

Aunt Rebecca was much moved when she saw the new arrival descend with a grave demeanour from a hansom cab. He was very tall, upright, and muscular, with a dash of the trooper—a sort of flavour of sword exercise about his carriage. His face was the colour of genuine Indian curry; his moustache heavy, and quite white; his eyebrows black, bushy, and singularly immobile. About his mouth there lurked a hard expression that was imposing, but a little doubtful; it smacked of the soldier. The Colonel was not a hypocrite, mind you.

Aunt Rebecca was all in a flutter, but he kissed her on the left eyebrow, asked after her in a harrowing voice, and generally put her at her ease again. He sat down, and they began talking of family bereavements.

"My father was not irreligious, of course," said the Colonel, "but he scarcely seemed a man of vital piety."

"He died with great joy," said Miss Rebecca, answering the question which the other had been afraid to put.

"Thank God," said the Colonel, with stentorian fervour. "I behaved ill to him, Aunt Rebecca. I was a very hardened young man."

"Indeed, you were a very charming one, John, and always my favourite; so bright and kindly, and such a bonny boy. You are handsomer now, perhaps, but the fire has gone out of you."

"I'm afraid it was wild-fire," said the Colonel, gloomily. "Where are these children?"

Aunt Rebecca fetched them in, and explained them, like a demonstrator in a museum. "This is John, and this is Malcolm. John is the cleverer of the two; but Malcolm's a clinging sort of child, with such a sweet temper"; and so forth, as only an old maid can.

"Which is the elder?" inquired the Colonel.

"John is three weeks older," replied the old lady. "It's not much."

"And then he's of the elder branch. That's as it should be; he shall have Grangehead, Aunt Rebecca."

"Oh, do you think that's quite necessary?" she inquired, a little chopfallen, in the interest of the clinging child with the sweet temper. It was the first time she had crossed the Colonel's path. I may add it was the last. He was not angry; he had no wish to terrify the harmless lady; but when the man's spirit rose, as it always did at a thought of opposition, his voice rose along with it; and the mere volume of sound was appalling to the frail old dame.

"Primogeniture is the law of the land!" he bawled; "and"—he was going to have added it was the law of God, but thought better of this flight. "And a very good thing too," he substituted. "However, I don't bind myself; I shall test the children thoroughly."

"I thought he was a soldier?" demanded John, in the tone of one who has paid for his seat and means to have his entertainment.

"So I am, little man," said the Colonel.

"Where's your sword, then?"

"There's nobody here to fight with; nobody but kind aunties and good little boys. But you shall see my sword some of these days, and a case of pistols. Would you like to be a soldier?"

"That I would!" replied the child.

"So you shall, I hope," answered the Colonel, with emotion; "one of Christ's soldiers."

It was plain he had taken a fancy to John.

CHAPTER II

The whole party moved to Grangehead. It was a rambling old house, most of it only one story high, and none of it higher than two; it seemed to have been built at odd times, and it was difficult to tell where the mansion stopped and the offices began. The grounds were overgrown with hollies and laurels. In summer many fungi prospered in the thicket, and breathed out faint odours upon passersby; but there were also many lilacs which beautified and perfumed the place in spring. A large paddock, almost large enough to justify the name of "park" by which it went, was the playground of the two boys; there was besides a belfry over the gate of the stableyard, a great range of roof to clamber on, a draw-well under an old yew in a dark part of the shrubbery, and many other romantic accidents such as youth delights in. A broken-spirited tutor disposed of their mornings.

The Colonel himself was in his element. He accepted office as elder in the parish church, where his grand manners imparted a flavour of ritual to the boldest ceremonies of Scotch Presbyterianism. He was hand and glove with the subjected clergyman, and his big voice ruled in the Kirk Session. Once in a while, of a Saturday or Sunday evening, he would give a little lecture in the school-room; when he would now besiege the obdurate with denunciations, now delight the simple with soldierly anecdotes and barrack sentiment. It was a mystery to all how Colonel Falconer managed to be so blunt, and plain, and guileless, and simple-hearted as he did on these occasions; for, personally, he was quite a man of the world. He would even throw in a broad Scotch accent on an occasion. It was at these moments that cynical friends discussed the expression of his mouth. But the commonalty were vastly pleased. This man, who had imbued himself all over in the blood of persons of colour, and made a reputation in the army, proved, when put to the touch before a critical audience in the school-room of Grangehead, no great theologian after all, but a plain Christian who was most fitted to touch the hearts of children. That was somehow agreeable to all the hinds. It was concluded that the Colonel was a manly Christian; that was his variety in the local classification.

Poor old Miss Rebecca had been ordered up to Grangehead to help with the children. She soon withered; the Colonel rode her down, horse and van, so to speak. His iron nerves, his cruelly resounding voice, his abrupt decisions, the company and regimental devotions in which she had to take part under his eye—all these things preyed upon her like a disease. Colonel Falconer was her ideal; she had no fault to find with him. But she pined in his neighbourhood—a malady incident to maids—and passed away.

The Colonel was inconsolable; and thenceforward he was a little harsher to the boys. He had always been harsh, without ever being unkind, if you can understand that. The boys were not afraid of him in any deep sense, even loved him after a fashion; but they were shudderingly averse to his society. He was rude to them on principle; he made their lives as dull and bitter as he could, because he thought that was best for them, and he imagined he had so disenchanted existence, that there were no pleasures within their reach, except the pleasures of religion. He reckoned without boyhood, without the paddock, without the roof, without the draw-well in the shrubbery, without the fungi all summer under the laurels, without the sun, and winds, and seasons. The Colonel did his best; but it is easier to command any conceivable number of sepoys than to take the interest and poetry out of young people's lives.

John was a boy with what is called a deep nature—that is to say, he began to mature very early; wrote hymns and other performances, which he hid away in a confusion if anyone approached; was addicted to long meditation, and showed at times a morose and flighty character. Altogether, a boy to be looked after, with plenty of predisposition to evil, and all the passions impending. Malcolm was easy-going, and a little shallow; he had petty selfishnesses, for which John made way with rather a grand air; but then he could put his pride in his pocket to appease others, and had a winning way.

There never was any doubt but John should inherit. He was a boy after the Colonel's heart proud, brave, gloomy, and with a natural talent for religion. Accordingly, he was affianced to Miss Mary Rolland, a girl of his own age, and heiress of the next estate. Mary and John understood their position; and they were always great friends. As soon as John was of age, they were to be married.

CHAPTER III

John was eighteen on the 12th of May, 18—. It was adorable weather. All the lilacs were in flower and all the birds were in love about the gardens of Grangehead; the wind smelt of spring. Mary Rolland and her father had dined with the Falconers, and the whole party strolled into the garden; for there was no loitering over wine at the Colonel's table.

"No, sir, I will not let that pass," roared the host. "It is a matter of principle; I will not bate an ace on it."

"My dear sir," replied Mr. Rolland, "my very dear sir, pardon me for saying so, but, indeed, you take this rather warmly. I believe I may say I am a man of principle myself. I have never paltered or temporised; but I must make distinctions."

"I make no distinctions," answered the Colonel, "in matters of principle. Is it a matter of principle, yes or no?"

"Christian liberty," began Mr. Rolland.

"Don't let me hear the phrase," interrupted the Colonel.

"I believe it is unimpeachably orthodox," replied the other, somewhat nettled. "I believe I could name authorities. Indeed, if I am not mistaken, it occurs in the Bible. Malcolm, will you fetch a testament?"

"It has been abused, Mr. Rolland. People have wrested it to their own damnation. Humble Christians should reverence it as a mystery; not bandy it about in disputations." There was a flush under the curry-coloured cheek; the Colonel was on his war charger for the evening.

"Come away, Mary," whispered John, pettishly. "There'll be no end to this sort of thing."

They went up a path among the evergreens, somewhat dark already, but closed at the far end by a piece of golden sky. The cover was musical on either side. Mary walked slowly, looking on the ground; John, who kept half a step in advance, could not keep his eyes from her. She seemed to have changed; there was more meaning, more life, more blood about her; from a pale, wiry slip of a girl, she had blossomed and spread, and become soft and rich, and foreign-looking. John was confused.

At the end of the path there was an open space with a seat, and a low parapet wall overlooking a public highway, and a great prospect of wood and meadow, bounded to the north by a range of hills. A river glittered along the plain in broken segments. The outline of the hills was bitten into the luminous sky. Clouds of birds passed to and fro between the clumps of plantation.

"Have you written any more poetry?" asked John.

"No." She spoke in a constrained voice; it was a lie, and she lied clumsily, being still very young.

"You promised you would write something for my birthday."

"I found I couldn't," she said.

There was a pause. "I am so glad we are going to be married," he said, blankly. It elicited no answer, and she did not take her eyes off the distant view. John sighed. "I am so fond of—of looking at sunsets," he said. The speech came in two in the middle, and the end was patently not the proper sequel of the beginning.

"So am I," she answered, with a sort of fervour.

"I wonder what has come over us. One would think we weren't happy," he remarked.

"Oh! but I am happy."

"So am I," he said, in his turn, "very happy—very happy"; and he repeated the words vacantly several times. They had never been sparing of caresses to each other, since their nurses had taught them to kiss; and so he was confounded when, on trying to take her hand, he found it withdrawn from him nervously. He waited abashed for some moments, and then he made a sort of effort, for he was frightened at the restraint and the disorder of his own feelings, and wished to do something which should break the spell and bring them back to natural terms of intercourse. He tried to kiss her. She sprang back in a commotion, turned white and red, and then white again, and stood a little way off, silent and seemingly indignant.

"She must hate me," thought John. He was no great doctor in the schools of love; he was better up in the catechism, poor lad.

It was a relief to both when they heard Mr. Rolland calling for Mary, and they returned in silence to the lawn.

He walked so far home with them, on her father's invitation; and the old gentleman spoke with him very kindly by the way. Mary was quite silent; but her colour was a little heightened, and her eyes, which seemed no longer to avoid his gaze, looked very bright and soft.

Tall gates of iron, and an approach of lilacs, gave admission to Grangehead. The approach was buried in transparent shadow. A single blackbird fluted vaingloriously among the lilacs, a sweet smell of evening was abroad upon the air, the view was bounded by the sharp outline of the laurel thickets, and the gables of the house imprinted on the luminous west. Malcolm, with his head bent forward and his hands clasped behind his back, was pacing the gravel with slow, uneven footsteps. He affected not to hear John's approach, for he did not turn. But John overtook him, and in schoolboy fashion threw his arm about his neck. Malcolm shook him off.

"Leave me alone," he said, testily.

"Why, what's wrong with you, Malcolm?" said John.

"I want to be alone."

"Oh, by all means!" said John, and he passed him several steps in a fling of ruffled vanity. But he came to his better self in a moment. Malcolm was certainly moved beyond his custom, and it was not an occasion to be nice on points of etiquette, so John came back. "Tell me what's wrong with you, Malcolm?" he repeated, "there's a good lad! Tell me what's wrong?"

"I never said anything to you, did I?" returned the other in a flash. "I can die, but I won't whine. You've got everything else—you've got the estate, and Mary, and everything—you may leave me my own company."

John was dumbfounded.

"Malcolm, Malcolm," he cried, "you know very well that what's mine is yours. You know very well we're to share and share alike. Do you think I could be happy and leave you out? You know me better than that."

"It's not the estate," said Malcolm with a sob. "It's the girl, man—it's the girl!" and he covered his face passionately with his hands.

John became grave. "Do you love her?" he asked.

"Do I not!" replied the other, throwing up his arms with a wild gesture. "Love her? Do I not!" He was very young.

A number of ugly thoughts presented themselves simultaneously at the door of John's mind. He suffered a furious spasm of the under lip. "Does she love you?" he demanded.

"Do you think she loves you?" returned his cousin, with something like a sneer.

It was a Scotch answer, as people say in the North; but it sent John into the depths of despair. Everything was plain enough now; Mary hated him, as he had imagined. She loved Malcolm. They loved each other. In all likelihood there was an understanding between them. He was no more than an absurd and hateful obstacle in the lives of the two persons who were dearest to him.

Malcolm had made the answer in a tiff, and because he could say nothing more to the purpose. He had no reason to suppose Mary loved him. She seemed fond enough of his society, indeed; but then they usually conversed of John. He began to repent. "It's not the estate," he repeated, with a whimper; "it's only Mary I mind; I can't live without her. But I can die," he added, cheerfully.

"The two go together, my boy," replied John. "You must have both or neither—both or neither." He shook his head mechanically for a long time. He was maturing a great scheme of self-sacrifice with hereditary gusto. The blood of wrong-headed old Covenanters, the blood of the Colonel was working darkly in his heart.

Suddenly a bell interrupted the stillness with a precipitate, undignified clangour. The blackbird flew away. It was the signal for family worship. John took Malcolm's hand solemnly.

"Malcolm," he said, "we are nearer than most brothers. I'll do all I can for you."

CHAPTER IV

Family worship at Grangehead was an affair of great precision. All the servants were expected to attend, morning and evening. The Colonel read aloud a chapter from the Old Testament and one from the New, and delivered a long prayer extempore. His voice was loud and hurried, as if he was calling a roll before proceeding to business; and of course the servants never listened. When the prayer was over, breakfast began in the morning; and at night everyone was expected to retire. On the evening of his birthday John requested a private interview with his uncle.

The Colonel looked at him sharply, and then bade him follow him to the study, where he took a chair himself, and motioned his nephew to another. But John preferred to stand.

"Well, what is it?"

"I understand, Sir," began John, "that I am to succeed you in the property; and I wished—"

"I don't choose to discuss these matters," said the Colonel; "above all, with you. In the meantime you are one of my nephews, and no more. Is that all?"

"Indeed, Sir, you do not understand me. You must allow me to explain. It is a matter of conscience."

"Oh, if it's a matter of conscience!" said the Colonel; and he made an urbane movement with his hand.

"Malcolm is in love with Mary, Sir," said John.

"Well?" bawled the Colonel.

"He cannot marry her unless he is to have the property," continued John; "and for my part I would rather not have it. I would far sooner make a way in the world for myself. I wish to be independent, and owe everything to my own spirit; and there is no fear of me. I could be a clergyman and save souls, or a soldier like you, or go to a colony; there is no fear of that. And think, Sir, what it would be for poor Malcolm to lose all he cares about in the world; and for me, if I had taken it all away from him!"

"I thought you liked the girl yourself," said the Colonel.

"I do." John's mouth was very dry.

The Colonel jumped up and shook John by the hand.

"You're a fine fellow, Sir," he cried. "I honour you for every word you've said. You're a nephew after my own heart, and I believe after God's. But as to what you say, of course it's nonsense. I leave the property to please myself and for God's glory, and for neither your pleasure nor Malcolm's; and you must take it, as I took it, as a talent. Yes, lad," he added, "that's the word that will make it all come easily to you. A talent—perhaps a cross. Bear it for His sake." And he brought his hand down upon John's shoulder with kindly violence.

"But Malcolm," began John.

"Go to bed," cried the Colonel. "I forgive you, but I'll hear no more of it. And mind you pray against spiritual pride. I know you; you're a fine lad; but there lies your stumbling-block. You wish to play the martyr." People will spy their own foibles through chain-mail.

Of course John was bitterly indignant. All this praise rankled in his conscience, and made him suspicious of his own sincerity. If it were only to reinstate his self-respect, he must consummate the sacrifice. Moreover, the Colonel's last insinuation was too near the truth not to be galling. But he dared not struggle further, and said "Good night," leaving the Colonel to thank God upon his knees for his nephew's excellence.

In his own room he threw the window open, and sat down to nurse his desperate determination. The flush had died out of the west; the night was full of stars; troops of dark trees huddled together in the twilight and rocked in faint airs. From the stable court he could hear the watch-dog jangle his chain, or a wakeful horse moving in the stall. He contemplated the stars with imbecility. Sometimes he walked about the room; sometimes he sat down again and began eloquent letters; often he fell bitterly to prayer. The whole subject had gone beyond his control into the region of the imagination, where it worked and fermented, and cast up a fine froth of mock heroics. He would make everybody else happy, and be himself supremely miserable. They should wallow in luxuries; he would live on dry bread in a garret. If he made enough for superfluity, it should be forwarded secretly to add some infinitesimal detail to their felicity. Sometimes a pale face would be seen in the shrubbery; the children would flee from it with screams, while the unknown benefactor made his escape unnoticed. At last he would die on a pallet; everybody would troop around him with tears and apologies, and his grave would be daily visited by those whom he had served.

This sort of fanfaronade was often interrupted by transports of genuine feeling. The boy's love for Mary had roots in his soul, and at times he was beside himself at the thought of losing her.

About three in the morning, as he was leaning out of the window, a train passed many miles off under the range of hills. Just before the sound of its passage died out of earshot, the long shrill scream of the whistle ascended towards the stars. I wonder whether people who were young in the days of stage-coaches and guards'-horns, know what a trouble is brought into the minds of wakeful youth by the sound of a railway whistle. A lad is shown all the kingdoms of the earth in a vision; and, although he is eminently happy where he is, with loving friends and a half-written poem in his desk, he positively despises himself because he is not going somewhere else. You may imagine what it was to John. Thank God! he had the world before him; he would begin anew, and carve out something noble for a career.

He dozed a little in a chair, and was wakened by horrible dreams. His ears were filled with Babel; he was thrust hither and thither in a crowd of vile spectres, and heard the Colonel calling upon him from an incalculable distance. When he awoke, the light of the candle dazzled and distressed him, and he was afraid of the shadows.

Some time before sunrise he suddenly burst out bleeding at the nose, and had hard ado to get it staunched. He soaked his clothes by holding a wet sponge to the nape of his neck, and the coolness gratified so much that he took a bath. This seemed to clear his head and steady his nerves; the more acute symptoms of fever passed away; and he slipped out into the garden in the dawn, with something like composure in his heart.

He walked for a while in the approach, and made some very impassioned verses to Mary, to Malcolm, to his own heart, to God for strength, to the sunrise; all of which he forgot as soon as he had made them, although that was no great matter. He went and sat on the parapet where he had been last night with Mary. The stones were wet with dew; mists were scattered on the plain; there was a great lowing of cattle and bleating of sheep; women with pails and whistling plough-lads began to go by underneath him on the public road. Here he prayed very heartily, wept a good deal, and, for two moments, was near giving up his intention. But the bell for prayers cut in upon this mood, played havoc with his disordered nerves, and called back the dark perversity upon his soul. The harm that is done by ugly bells ill-rung is not to be computed.

CHAPTER V

At breakfast John ate nothing, and drank a great deal of strong tea, which was very bad for him. There never was much talk at this meal, except on Sundays; during the week the Colonel had the papers to read, and a considerable correspondence besides, and the cousins usually brought a book to table. But on this particular morning the Colonel went twice out of his way to address an agreeable remark to John, and looked at him covertly from time to time with much affection; for he had been thinking his nephew over, and was vastly pleased with him. John answered roughly and sourly. The idea of speaking pleasantly over a breakfast-table to a hero and a martyr!

The cover was removed, and John was pretending to read the newspaper over the fire, when his uncle returned with a letter in his hand. He had a very kind look in his eyes as he spoke.

"Take this letter to Hutton, please" (Hutton was Mr. Rolland's place), "and wait an answer."

It was now the moment for action. John drew himself together with a great effort; he did not raise his head from the paper.

"Thank you," he answered, quietly, "I prefer staying where I am."

If a thunderbolt had fallen upon Grangehead, it would have discomposed the Colonel less. John could see him over the edge of the paper. He stood quite still, but the immovable eyebrows went up, and his whole face underwent a swift and rather ghastly change. He seemed about to speak, but he thought better of it, went to the window, and looked out for perhaps a minute and a half. Then he turned to John and addressed him once more.

"I am not sure whether you heard me. I desired you to take this letter to Hutton. I am not in the habit of repeating my commands." Thus far he spoke firmly, and in his usual loud voice; but there he seemed to take fright, and added hurriedly, and in an unsteady tone, "You can take a horse, if you like, John."

Even John, full as he was of heroic and satanic humours, was shocked at his uncle's condescension; his heart yearned to him, and he longed to throw himself on his knees and avow all. It is so hard to insult a person you have respected all your life! But the devil was uppermost.

"I think I said I should prefer to remain where I am," he answered.

"Oh, very well," said the Colonel; and he left the room.

John had expected a blow. He was frightened and elated at the turn affairs had taken, and prayed fervently.

In the meantime Malcolm had repented of last night's scene, in which he felt he had played a childish and perhaps a questionably honest part; and he desired heartily to make it up to John in kindness. He came into the dining room with a penitent but cheerful spirit, and took a seat on the opposite side of the hearth.

"About Mary——," he began.

"Hold your tongue!" returned John. It was a discharge of nervous force, purely involuntary, and directed at no one in particular. The moment it had taken place he felt relieved, and sought to remove the effect. "I beg your pardon, I did not hear what you were saying; I'm a little out of sorts this morning," he explained.

Malcolm stared.

"It was only about Mary and what we said last night," he continued.

"I shall see that you are happy," replied the other, grandly. "Make yourself easy. You have appealed to me, and it is now my business."

"You needn't take it quite so high," said Malcolm. "I'm very much obliged to you, of course; but it's my business too, and I mean to explain——"

"I'm not in the humour for explanations," interrupted John.

"I'll say my say if I choose."

"You'll say it to yourself then." And John rose.

"John," said Malcolm, "I beg your pardon if I spoke rudely. Indeed, I didn't mean. And I really do wish a word with you."

"You may leave me my own company," answered John, mimicking his cousin's voice.

"Oh, well, you may go and be blanked, for me!" flashed Malcolm. "You're a blanked civil fellow, indeed! I wish you were dead!"

"I wouldn't swear if I were you, young man," observed John.

Malcolm flung out of the room in a fine temper, and John heard him slamming doors all about the house, until a stentorian summons and a rumble of reprimand from the Colonel's study re-established peace. John felt very strangely. Thank God, he had quarrelled with everybody now! He was on the high seas of martyrdom. Malcolm was to be happy, thanks to him; and no one would suspect his heroism. I think he positively hated Malcolm; he would almost as soon have sought him out and strangled him, as gone on with the sacrifice that was to make him happy. His brain was in a whirl. He took a road on chance, and walked furiously. The trees danced on either side; the world reeled. Sometimes he was so dazzled he could see nothing; again, a corner of the road stood out before him in a sort of sickly distinctness; it seemed to mean something; it had something to do with his trouble, and he stared at it and hated it. The poor lad was in a fever.

In the course of this aimless walk he hit upon the county town, and, being consumed with thirst, he entered the hotel. The commercial room was occupied by a single personage—a pallid, red-haired, fat young bagman, seated by the fire, with a long tumbler of some beverage at his elbow. John sat as far away from him as he could, picked up a railway time-table, and turned over the pages without seeing a word. When the waiter came for his order, he pointed silently to the bagman's glass.

"Same as that gentleman, Sir? Yes, Sir," said the waiter.

Now it happened for John's sins that the drink he had thus innocently commanded is one of the most insinuating mixtures in the world. Gin and gingerbeer, neither of them remarkable by themselves, become when mixed not only very agreeable, but exceptionally intoxicating. John was mightily pleased; his throat tingled, his brain cleared; the names of stations in the time-table became suddenly legible, and he gave himself over to a confused sort of luxury, picturing what sort of places these should be, and how the penniless martyr, John Falconer, should visit them one after another, and meet with singular adventures by the way. I think, as he got on with the second glass, there were even beautiful faces taking part in these adventures. For not only his love for Malcolm, but his love for Mary also, had suffered from the rivalry of Black Happiness and the violent dislocation of his hopes and prospects.

He did not reach Grangehead until the bell was ringing for dinner. He was aware of a distressing heat in his face, a noise in his ears, and a blur before his eyes. He had eaten nothing all day, had drunk more than was good for him, and still suffered from an unquenchable thirst. He took his place at table, dusty and disordered as he was; and his first action was to fill his glass with sherry and drink it off. The taste offended him, and he felt his head ache dully as he swallowed it; but he was too inexperienced to understand that he was getting drunk; he only knew that he was very ill, which was quite as it ought to be, and would bring on the reconciliation scene beside the pallet all the sooner.

The Colonel never addressed him. Malcolm, who felt that John was in disgrace, but attributed it merely to his unparalleled conduct in not coming home to luncheon, was also a little shy of speaking to him. As for their tiff in the morning, Malcolm had long ago forgiven that.

Towards the end of dinner the sherry began to operate, and John took the lead in the conversation.

"This is a hateful place—Grangehead," he volunteered, cheerfully.

The Colonel looked at him sharply.

"There's no life," he continued; "no v'riety. Young men should see th' world."

Malcolm was alarmed, and telegraphed to him to be silent; but he could not understand the hint, or, if he did, resented it. The Colonel listened with growing attention: the wind was rising in that quarter.

"It's not good, whatever you may think," John proceeded, "for young men of tal'nt to be shut up with 'n old man, whoever he is."

He poured sherry into his tumbler and drank it off. He then looked at the empty tumbler with a maudlin laugh.

"'T occurs to me," he began, "—'t occurs to me—." And he stopped and smiled.

"It occurs to me, Sir," bawled the Colonel, "that you're the worse of drink."

John contemplated his uncle in a vacillating way.

"Tha' 's a lie," he remarked; and then, repeating it with a giggle, as if he had said rather a good thing, "Tha' 's a lie," said he, "tha' 's a lie."

Malcolm and the Colonel rose at the same moment, the former with some idea of interference. The Colonel whipped John out of his chair, and swept him irresistibly to the front door. Three stone steps, with a bit of iron railing on either hand, joined the level of the gravel plot to the level of the entrance hall. Standing on the top of these, the Colonel gave his nephew so smart an impulsion that he descended the stairs at one step, alighted on his left foot, fell thence on his right knee, and finally sprawled at full length upon the gravel.

"Let me see no more of you," shouted the Colonel. "I bar my door against you for ever. I am done with you for time and eternity. God forgive you as I do"; and all unconscious of the irony of his last prayer, he re-entered the house, and shut the door.

John lay as he had fallen in a stupor. Meantime, the sun began to turn the west into a lake of gold, and the blackbird sang among the lilacs as before.

CHAPTER VI

Malcolm was left alone in the dining room in a pitiful situation. He could understand from such sounds as reached him that John had been turned bodily out of doors, and that the Colonel had retired to brood in his private room. Grangehead and Mary were both his own, and yet I assure you he gave neither of them one thought. His mind was full of his cousin, and what could be done to bring about a reconciliation. He finished his wine mechanically. An hour went over his head, and he was still drawing patterns on the plate before him, when an alarmed servant peeped in, and asked if she might take away the things. This shook him into a resolution, and he went straight to his uncle. You must remember that Malcolm had never been the favourite nephew, and even when all went well, would have thought twice before he ventured on a similar intrusion.

The Colonel had neglected to turn up his reading-lamp on entering, so that the room was in twilight and filled with large shadows. He sat at the table, with his head on his hand and his face wholly shaded; even when Malcolm entered and addressed him, he gave no sign of life.

"Sir," said Malcolm, "I trust there is nothing serious between you and John."

"My dear boy," returned the Colonel, with his hand still over his brow, "I have been expecting you; you may spare me the rest of your expostulations, which I can very well imagine for myself. You have mentioned the name of a person whom I once loved, but between him and me, there is an end of everything. I am a sinful man, perhaps a hard one; at least I did my best to be kind to him. But now he has provoked me beyond the power of God to make me forgive him, and I blot him out of my memory for ever. You see how it is," he resumed, after a moment's pause. "Out of consideration for yourself and out of respect for me, you will have to avoid this subject in the future. And remember, you must try and humour me now, for you are all I have left."

He motioned him away, and Malcolm durst not hesitate. As he closed the door he thought he overheard the sound of a groan; and this impressed and terrified him more than ever. He sat on the stairs with his head in his hands, and tried to think. But he could make nothing of it; the pillars of the earth were moved, natural laws were all suspended. The human mind cannot change its base of operations fast enough for certain sweeping catastrophes.

He rose at last and cautiously opened the front door. It was getting very dark; but he could see something darker on the gravel. It lay so still that his heart began to misgive him dreadfully, and he stole down the steps and nearer to the body. He could hear stertorous breathing, now and then rising into a snore, and breaking off again; and as his alarm was quieted, its place was taken by contempt and some disgust.

As he returned to the house, Grangehead and Mary had become at least agreeable features in the background. He was getting reconciled to the new order of things, and sought rather to improve than to alter it. Out of his own savings and those of John (for they kept their money together) he made a purse of about thirty pounds. This he put into one pocket of a large, warm driving-coat, balancing it in the other with John's Bible. And thus equipped he returned to the figure on the gravel.

"John!" he said; "John!"

John answered with a snort. Every fibre of Malcolm's Puritanical body shuddered in revolt; and throwing the coat over his cousin, he fled back into the house.

There never was a night like that at Grangehead. There was no tea and no family worship. Mr. John slept on the gravel; Mr. Malcolm slept by the dining room fire; and the Colonel sat up in his own room in meditation and religious exercise.

Chapter VII

The Colonel hung his head from that day forward. He turned suddenly and surprisingly bald; his face seemed to have shrunken and fallen in; and there were broken tones in his voice. Malcolm never uttered John's name in his uncle's presence; but he thought of him often enough as he looked upon these changes. The old man had been stabbed to the heart—slower or faster, he was dying.

There could be no doubt that he kept himself acquainted with John's life, and would have grasped at any excuse to make up the difference and get his favourite nephew home again. But John's conduct was of a nature to pain the Colonel deeply; every bulletin must have been another cowardly blow on his white head; and though he assisted his nephew underhand, neither his pride nor his principle would allow him to kill the fatted calf for such an unregenerate prodigal.

The end came, when the two lads were in their twenty-first year— John writing leader notes in a London newspaper, and Malcolm agreeably conscious of his approaching marriage with Mary Rolland. The Colonel took to bed rather suddenly. It was wild, windy weather, and the sky was full of flying vapours. He had been looking out of the window all the afternoon, and towards dusk he called Malcolm and pointed to the labouring trees and the dead leaves whirling in the open.

"I'm too old and tired for this sort of thing," he said; "I think I'll go to bed." He looked at Malcolm queerly. "I don't mean to get up again," he added; and he kept his word. All the time of his illness he complained grievously of the sound of the wind; for the weather continued broken, and he would speak much of the perils of sailors, and be overheard praying for lawful travellers by sea and land.

At last one afternoon he bade Malcolm light the candles, prop him up with pillows, and bring him his despatch-box.

"I put it off, and put it off, God help me!" he said; "and I'm just afraid I put it off too long."

Malcolm set the box on his lap.

"Here is the key, Sir," he said.

"It's the last time I shall use it," said the Colonel, holding up the key with a smile. "It's strange, strange to think of." A horrible gust howled in the chimney, and the house quaked. "I wish I could be spared this wind; nevertheless, not my will, but Thine! I'm as full of fancies as a girl," he added, opening the box. "It's a poor account of an old soldier, Malcolm; but we all show the white feather towards the end; the lamp burns low, you see, and the blood runs cold. I've been in sharp affairs in my day, both on sea and land, and many a time I thought I had come to my last hour; but I never knew our need of a Divine Helper until now. I don't mind a stand-up fight; but this lying here in the dark brings a man to his marrow-bones." He had been turning over the papers during these last words, and now produced a sealed envelope. "Aye, here it is," he went on. "And now, Malcolm, mark what I say. I don't wish to open up old sores. I once thought of telling you the story; but it would do no good, and things are best as they are. So I take this way. What is in this envelope refers to—to one whom I have not mentioned for some years. I wish you to know that I loved that person as if he had been my own son, born out of my loins. Yet I was hard on him—very hard, and I pray God's forgiveness."

Malcolm's face was streaming with tears. All the time he had known the Colonel stern and gloomy, merely set off his present mood, and rendered it more touching. The bystander, besides confessing present sympathy, accused himself of injustice in the past.

"No, uncle," he cried, "you never were hard; you were only too good."

"Hush!" said the old man. "This is no time for flattery. I am going where I shall hear the truth plump and plain. I was a hard, proud man; I was hard on my father, I was hard on you, and I was very hard on him. If ever a man needed the merits of Another, here he lies, Malcolm— here he lies. And now, when you see John, you're to tell him that I forgave him, and asked his forgiveness. Don't forget the last. And if ever you should be tempted to quarrel with him, or if ever you have it in your power to do him a service and hesitate to do it, or if ever he does you an injury that you can't forgive, open this envelope, read the letter twice over—twice, mark you—and then down on your knees before your Maker for His guiding Spirit. And remember this, I've tried being a hard man, and you see the kind of death-bed it has brought me to; be you easy, Malcolm—mind and be you easy!"

He stopped exhausted, for he had been speaking with some vehemence.

"But how should I quarrel with John?" asked Malcolm; "or why should he do me an injury?"

"I don't very well know; but circumstances are a great thing," answered the Colonel, philosophically.

"Uncle," objected Malcolm, "you are putting a secret into my life. Let me open the envelope at once, or as soon as—I mean—"

"As soon as I am dead!" the Colonel continued for him. "I have told you already when you may open it, and I don't go back from my word. These are my orders, Sir. I always was a peremptory man; of course I know little or nothing about a future state, and speak under correction; but I rather suspect I shall be a very peremptory spirit." This with a grim smile. "Now you understand. Take away the box, and leave me alone for awhile, like a good fellow."

In the course of the week the old man's mind began to wander. He commanded Sepoy regiments with great pluck, and addressed meetings in the school-room on religious topics. He talked much about John; and sometimes returned on the escapades of his own wild youth in a manner that profoundly afflicted and humiliated Malcolm as he watched alone by the bed. Towards the end he was clearer and very composed, said good-bye to everyone about the house, warning them against hardness and pride; and finally surrendered his sword between six and seven o'clock of a black, tempestuous evening, amidst the genuine grief of many who had only feared him while alive.

Malcolm stood over the fire that same night with the sealed envelope in his hand; now he was in a mind to burn it, and be done with all uncertainty; now he had his finger under the flap to tear it open. But it was an act of disloyalty to the dead, from which his sense of honour recoiled. Nor was this sentiment unhelped by circumstances. The candles winked and flickered in the draughts, and peopled the room with moving shadows, which seemed to spy upon him from behind; and the noise of the winds raving round the house in the darkness, chilled his blood and inclined him to superstitious terrors. He did not really imagine that the spirit of the dead Colonel on his Indian war-horse came charging up the approach with every gust; but somehow it struck him as not being a nice sort of evening for the business. And so he put the envelope into a casket by itself, locked it, and, venturing forth in all this uproar of the elements, threw the key into the draw-well in the shrubbery.

He felt relieved that very moment. The truth is, he had a shrewd guess of what the secret was, and dreaded nervously to learn that he was right. For some days longer the uncertainty haunted him; but by the end of a month he had practically lived it down, and before he had made all ready for the reception of his wife, the idea only recurred to him as a passing curiosity when he had nothing else to think about.

CHAPTER VIII

At first John had to swim very hard for existence; indeed, I scarcely understand how he kept his head above water at all. But he made friends, and the friends got him on to a newspaper in some subaltern capacity. When that newspaper failed, he found another more readily; and thus, like a man walking on a hill-side where every foothold breaks away as he quits it, he went on from journal to journal, as one after another silently expired. I don't think he ever was connected with one that kept alive above a year.

He had written a large volume of poetry about himself and Mary Rolland and Malcolm, in delicately veiled allusion. I am told it scanned very well, and contained quite a surprising number of invocations to the Deity, and, comparatively speaking, no punctuation. And yet somehow it went against the heart of the publishing interest, and remained in manuscript. John took to being rather cynical and worldly, sneered at poetry, and daresay'd, over public-house tables, that he would turn his attention to politics one of these days, and change the face of Europe.

He lived from hand to mouth; and the hand was not always spotless, which fostered his cynicism. To a man in an abject situation, a good twanging snarl is a sort of moral pinch of snuff, and pulls his nerves together. From quite an early period he looked back with some contempt upon the episode of his departure. The hollow parts of it, the swollen vanity, were apparent at a glance; and he used to laugh at himself, not quite heartily perhaps, when he fell thinking of old days. I don't think the laugh was quite genuine, because he very often had a glass of something after one of these attacks of solitary merriment. But then, of course, wine and laughter go together by rights.

He heard with sincere affliction of his uncle's death. A little while after, and the news of Malcolm's marriage followed. He was in great form that evening, and made some capital hits—above all, when he "stood" the company all round, and in a little humorous speech explained this unusual prodigality. His aunt had died, and in spite of the machinations of his wicked cousin, he was about to lead to the altar a young lady of remarkable attractions and great wealth. He made everybody die with laughing as he described this heroine, and expatiated on his own transports; and when it was done he laughed a very great deal over it himself, although he had preserved his gravity inimitably throughout. So you see John was quite a gay young fellow when he was twenty-one.

When he was well on in his thirties, another newspaper foundered under his feet. He was a confirmed prodigal, and when the pay stopped had not a halfpenny to call his own. He walked home through the Park, with his hands in his pockets, very glad to think that he had no longer any obligation to produce copy, and not much concerned about his empty purse, for he had the true Bohemian feeling—I don't know whether to call it an incredulity or a faith—about money. He got into conversation with some children (he was always fond of the young); through them he scraped acquaintance with the nurserymaid; then he fell in tow with an old man covered with sham jewellery, who whiled away some time in a very humorous manner; and finally night began to overtake him without much prospect of dinner. Like the prodigal son, he began to reflect upon his circumstances; and suddenly a thought occurred to him, and he exclaimed, with a laugh, "Egad, I'll go visit my cousins in the country."

He made up his kit in the course of the next day, and borrowed some money among his penniless acquaintance. It was not enough to carry him to his journey's end, and he accomplished the last score of miles on foot. He was weary, and it was already dark when he reached the iron gate and the approach of lilacs. He drew near the house with more emotion than he had anticipated; his heart beat painfully; and after he had pulled the bell he felt inclined to run away.

Malcolm and his wife were sitting over the fire. She was about some needlework, and he had just given vent to a portentous yawn, when the servant brought in a soiled visiting card.

"Mr. John Falconer," read Malcolm. "God bless me!"

"Of all places in the world," cried Mary, "what should bring him here?"

"We must see him, of course," observed the husband.

"It is most annoying—after so many years!" said the wife.

"Show Mr. Falconer in."

He was not going to be welcomed with much warmth, it would appear. The fact is, both Malcolm and Mary had reasons of their own. On his part, John was recuperating his cynicism on the doorstep; and when he was asked to follow the servant, instead of seeing his cousin come towards him with open arms, he felt as if a leading article were too good for mankind.

When he came to the door of the room, he stopped with a painful impression. The room and the two people seemed unchanged. A gush of regret and love came over him in a moment, and all his hard thoughts melted and disappeared. Nor was he more struck with their unchanged looks than they with the pitiful alteration that had overtaken him in his knotless and arduous existence. They had been preserved in a bottle of Domestic Spirits; he had been blown about with all winds. He was bald, haggard, and lean. And when he dashed forward and caught each of them by a hand, and cried, "Malcolm!—Mary!—Malcolm!" their hearts thawed towards him, and they wrung him by the hand, and made as much of him as if they had been longing for his return.

"My uncle's dead?" he asked, suddenly, as if he had heard some rumour, but desired corroboration.

"Eighteen years ago last winter," answered Malcolm. "He died asking your forgiveness."

"Eighteen—eighteen years ago!" John repeated. "And my forgiveness! Why, God help us all, is that not strange?"

He looked so dazed and half-crazy that Malcolm tried to alter the tenor of his thoughts; but he stuck to his point.

"He must have been changed," he said; "greatly changed. I would give my hand off, now, to have seen him before he died. He was a grand old man, our uncle, Colonel Falconer; God rest his soul, he was a grand old man! And yourselves," he added, with a sudden and most engaging change of manner; "tell me how happy you are, and exaggerate if you can. You know you're the only two old friends that I possess in this big world. Tell me about the children, Mary!"

It was long past twelve before Mary retired, and nearer four than three when her lord followed her. And the next day John was domesticated at Grangehead; no one would listen to any talk of limitation; here was a family which had been scattered by an unkind fate, and was now happily reunited.

CHAPTER IX

There was plenty for John to do. Among these quite idle people another idler seemed rather a busy personage. He addicted himself, from constitutional considerations, to gardening—gardening being taken in its usual amateur sense of digging potatoes for ten minutes in the forenoon, and hanging round all the evening with a straw hat and a watering-pot. He recommended a course of reading for the oldest boy, comprising some slashing Radical works which took Malcolm's breath away. And with the young children he was always charming. He would sit on a garden seat the whole summer day, smoking a clay pipe and telling them stories; every now and then it would be, "Run away and give Jane my very respectful compliments, and ask her to be so very polite as send me out a glass of beer."

He had many perplexing ways. It was impossible to guess when he might go to bed or when he might rise. He could not be trusted with the slightest message; he would sometimes insult visitors on controversial topics; and he firmly refused to go to church, which made a great scandal throughout the parish. The most charitable verdict was one by an emphatic middle-aged maiden lady, who had read all sorts of books, from "Erechtheus" to "Lothair," and so acquired a second-hand acquaintance with life. "He is quite a literary man, my dear," she explained. "They are generally rather French in their habits."

In the meanwhile a great revolution was happening in John's mind. He no longer looked back with a sneer upon his own heroics: he took them in deadly earnest; he shunned the parapet wall where he had sat with Mary; he had dark, fitful humours, and affected long and solitary walks. Malcolm was sorry to remark these symptoms; poor John was so eccentric!

One day a careless servant let the rope fall into the draw-well. John had always liked clambering and start fits of exercise; he descended the well, and came up with the rope sure enough, but also with a little key sorely rusted. By the look of it, it must have lain for many years on the ledge where his hand had encountered it. Malcolm and he were alone in that cool, damp corner under the laurels and the yew; at the end of a path some way off they could see the sun lying bright and solid on the open; and this increased their grateful sense of shadow.

Malcolm was upset when John showed him the key. "This is a very extraordinary providence," he said, with some solemnity; "this key has not reappeared for nothing. I threw it down on purpose."

"Let us throw it in again," answered John; and he was preparing to suit the action to the words, when Malcolm caught his arm.

"No, no; give it me!" he said. "Since it has come back, God's will be done."

"I say," said John, sitting down on the edge of the well and folding his arms, "this won't do. It's true you have a tendency to pious ejaculation, a substitute for a trick you used to have in old days. But that particular form means business. It means 'here's something I don't like at any possible price, and I decline dealing.' It means 'God's will be done, and in the meantime I'll do all I can to see that it isn't.' It means as near as may be 'damn it!' Explain yourself."

"John, John! I'm afraid you've lost all your religion."

"Why, as to that, I'm rather afraid I have. But I'm after the key just now. Is it the key of Bluebeard's cellar, or of the subterranean passage which connects this ruinous pile with the seacoast? You're looking down in the mouth, man. Throw it into the well, and defy augury."

"I feel down in the mouth," answered Malcolm. "John," he added, lowering his voice, "do you believe in special providences?"

"Certainly not," answered John.

"Well, I sometimes do, and this—mark my words—this is one."

"This? Which?" demanded John; "the key, or the well? or—or me, perhaps? Am I a special providence? I've been a special correspondent often enough."

"The whole occurrence," answered Malcolm; "the—the circumstance. It is providential, John, and it means mischief."

"As far as I can find out," replied the other, "providence generally does."

"That is the kind of talk that a man repents when he comes to die," observed Malcolm, sententiously.

"I didn't mean to shock you. It was merely a criticism of how people use their words. As for the subject itself, I decline jurisdiction. I know nothing of it, and care about as much."

"You don't believe in a providence at all, I fancy."

"My God! how can I—with my life?" asked John.

"I can—with mine," returned Malcolm, rosily.

John sneered.

"I have no doubt I could do so too," said he, "if I had plenty of money and a wife and a litter of children. But then, you see, I haven't."

"I suppose you might have had them if you'd chosen," answered Malcolm, pettishly.

"Well, do you know, I rather suppose I might," said John; and he stared the other strangely between the eyes.

"I shall never understand you, John."

"I don't suppose you ever will."

And the pair separated; Malcolm went into the house with the key, and it was John's hour for gardening.

CHAPTER X

Mary was an admirable Woman, and all that. At the same time she was not altogether a fool. She used to make poetry with John in the days of their engagement; since then she had read the History of England (which is more than the reader can say), a cookery book, a work on crochet, a vast quantity of novels and newspapers, and "How I Found Livingstone," by Mr. Stanley. In fact, she was quite literary in her tastes. She had a strong, good head, a quiet and perfectly inflexible character, and no knowledge of the world. She was almost entirely engrossed by maternity; her husband had become the father of her children.

John she regarded somewhat in the light of an under-nursery-maid, who was also a pleasant companion for herself. She unmercifully abused his good-will, and never imagined that she was not conferring favours.

One day she and John were taking care of the two youngest at that seat beside the parapet which John was so careful to avoid when he was alone. Mary settled herself luxuriously in one corner and got her work ready.

"Now, if we had a book, you might read to me; that would be nice," she said.

"Shall I fetch one?" he asked.

"Oh, no; never mind. We can talk, and that'll do just as well. Charlie, come back; do you hear me? There's that wretched child on the parapet, John; do take him away."

"I came here the morning I left Grangehead, for ever, as I thought," said John, returning to his seat. "It was before dawn, and you couldn't see much across the road; it was like looking into my future. And I made a great many good resolutions, nearly all of which I have broken."

"How very like you!" she said.

"Isn't it?"

"And what were they all about?"

"A great many things. I was never to return to Grangehead for one."

"I'm glad you've broken that!"

"I was always to be sober and say my prayers, for another."

"I'm afraid you've broken that, too."

"And then I was never to love anyone but you," he went on.

"Oh, oh!" she said, "and that was the first to go!"

"I have never said so," he answered. "I never said I had broken them all." She stole a glance at him; he was looking straight before him on the ground.

"I've dropped my worsted!" she said. "How stupid! Will you pick it up? Thanks."

John was a little huffed; he sat and brooded, while Mary talked easily of this or that, teething or measles, the doctor's wife or the clergyman's maiden sister.

"The clergyman's an ass," broke in John.

"How do you know, when you never go to hear him?"

"Didn't he dine here? And the doctor, too? He's another ass."

"Do you think we are all asses, then—we people in the country?" she asked.

"All but you, upon my word."

"And Malcolm?"

"Malcolm? Oh, Malcolm's a different thing. I was an ass myself, as long as I lived here; and I've carried the panniers ever since in consequence. It's a poor thing to start in life with empty pockets and a broken heart! Ah, Mary! you don't know what a business it is to leave all that you love in the world and go out among strangers. Do you remember"—he had grown warm now—"do you remember the last evening we were here? It was such a beautiful evening! I thought you hated me, and it decided my life."

She smiled. He had been banished Grangehead for insulting the Colonel while drunk; that was what had decided his life.

"You were a very silly fellow," she said. "Why was I to hate you? I never hated anybody, far less an old friend like you."

"You hadn't written some verses for my birthday, as you promised. And—and you wouldn't let me kiss you."

"I have no doubt I was quite right," she said, decisively. "May I trouble you to look after Charlie? he is on the wall again. And, oh! I think I will ask you to fetch a book; it will be so nice to be read to."

She was alarmed and angry; even through her treble armour of innocence, pride, and selfishness she became aware that this man still loved her. It was insulting, it was cruel of him to refer to the time of their engagement. And in such a way, too! It was an indignity—it was almost a disgrace. She felt hot all over. "I wish," she exclaimed, fervently, "I wish he had never come back. How are we ever to get rid of him without a scene?"

As John was coming back with the book, he met her rustling down the alley in great pomp, with a child in each hand. She had changed her mind; she would go into the house and rest; and she dismissed him with a queenly inclination.

John was furious; he went away and walked. By a sort of instinct he took the same road as on a former occasion, and found himself at the county town. He dined at the inn, and spent the evening in a corner of the smoking-room, drinking and sneering to himself at the conversation of the other guests. On one occasion he interfered with a few pleasant words, which nearly brought about a fight. The quarrel was adjusted after a fashion, and somewhat as spilt wine is covered with a napkin; he refused to apologise, and the whole company turned their backs on him. He was vastly pleased at this, and redoubled his cynicism.

It was quite late when he got home; the servants had gone to bed, and Malcolm opened the door himself. John, with his hands in his trousers pockets, regarded him offensively, as he put up the chain and shot the bolts.

"You are late," said Malcolm, quietly.

But John only made answer with an affected laugh, and went away upstairs without salutation.

CHAPTER XI

The next morning it rained heavily. John was later than usual; and while he was sitting alone over breakfast, Malcolm came in and took a chair. He seemed embarrassed.

"My dear John," he began, "if I say anything on the subject, you will believe it is entirely for your own good; but last night I could not help thinking—"

"My dear Malcolm," interrupted John, "I had had a glass. Why, why beat about the bush?"

"You admit it; I am glad of that. Now, do allow me to say one word. You should strive against this tendency. It has done you harm enough. Make an effort."

John was irritated.

"I live here on your charity, of course," he said; "and the position is enviable. But you can have no more idea of what there is in my heart than of what goes on in the farthest of the stars. You often enough admit that you do not understand me; try to act upon the idea. I drank too much last night. Do you know why? Because I like drinking? Because I was in high spirits, perhaps? Man, you know nothing of sorrow."

"You may be as sorrowful as you please," objected Malcolm. "I am grieved to hear of it. I trust it's through no fault of mine; but surely, surely, that's no reason for—well, for—"

"For making a beast of myself?" suggested John. "Enough of this," he added, rising from the table. "I understand your feeling in this matter. You cannot have a drunkard in the house; of course not. I am not going to promise amendment; I do not aspire so high. But you shall be rid of me today."

"You are speaking in anger, John; in irritation, at least. Do you remember our talk in the avenue on the night of your eighteenth birthday? You said then, what we had often agreed before, that we were to share our fortunes."

"Green-sickness—romantic boys," said John, with a wave of his hand.

"You did not think so then, when you had all to expect; nor do I think so now that all is mine. Of course, I have a family; of course, our plans were a little Utopian. But believe me, John, you are doing me the greatest favour in your power by staying here. I respect myself more highly."

"Oh, if it comes to that—" said John, with a laugh.

"You'll stay?" asked Malcolm, holding out his hand.

"As you will," replied John, taking it carelessly. "I own I like my ease; I like gardening and country butter, and the pride of independence I can do without. Besides," with a sudden change of manner, "who should have a better right than I?" And with that he went away.

Malcolm shook his head. "He is not cordial," he thought. "There is something between us. I wish I had held my tongue; and yet I can't have him staggering in here at all hours of the morning."

John went upstairs to a long, low apartment, part lumber-room, part play-room. A considerable library had been brought by Mary Rolland from Hutton at the time of her father's death, but it had never been unpacked until John arrived and offered his services. He went about it leisurely enough; he dallied and lingered over it as a good occupation for wet mornings; and if he ever was two hours on end over his task, for an hour and a-half of that he would be sitting on the floor with some curious book.

The packing-cases were at one end of the room behind a screen; quite at the other end was the fireplace. In about half an hour Mary came in and took a seat by the hearth. John put his head round the end of the screen, wished her a good morning somewhat coldly, and disappeared again. She could hear him take the books out of the case, and lay them on the floor; now and then he cleared his throat. Outside, the rain fell plump and steady; the fire had been lit in honour of the wet day, and the flames prattled pleasantly and the cinders sometimes dropped into the ash-pit. Mary was idly conscious of all these noises: they served her instead of a train of reflection to enliven her work.

John had been silent for some time; he had plainly found something of interest and begun to read, when Mary was startled by a strange sound from behind the screen. It was something between a gasp and a groan. "What's wrong with him now?" she wondered; but complete silence followed, broken only by the rain and the fire. She became a little uneasy in spite of herself, and again heartily wished that John had never returned to Grangehead.

At last, and rather suddenly, John rose, came round the screen, and advanced towards her with a paper in his hand. But he was no longer the same man; he looked twenty years older—or was it twenty years younger?

"Did you write that?" he asked, hoarsely, as he handed her the paper.

It contained some girlish verses. They were headed, *"To my dear John, on his eighteenth birthday, 12th May, 18—,"* and began, "Oh, my dear John, I am so fond of you." It was not the quality of the verse, however, that called the blood up to Mary Falconer's cheek. Her matronly pride was touched; she resented John's emotion like a slur.

"Suppose I did," she answered, as she threw it straight into the fire; "what of that?"

"Then you did love me?" he went on.

"You know very well we were engaged," she answered. "I hope I have always known my duty" (this with a tremor); "as long as I was engaged to you, of course I had no thought of anyone else. I cannot conceive what you mean by these questions. It is most unfeeling—most rude."

John gazed at her with a desolate look in his eyes. "If I had only known!" he said; "if I had only, only known!" And then he was silent for awhile. "But you love your husband now?" he demanded, with sudden fierceness.

"I shall ask you to leave the room, Mr. Falconer," she said, quivering all over, and making a fine picture of indignation.

"Thank God for that! thank God for that!" he answered, with a sort of laugh. She was unable to move, or she would have quitted the room herself; he looked her all over from head to foot, then he looked into the fire; a little stream of blood began to trickle out of one nostril (he kept the old tendency), but he did not seem to observe the circumstance. At last he turned and went away without a word. At the top of the stairs she heard him slip and fall; he lay for perhaps half a minute; then he picked himself up, went heavily down the steps, and she heard the door close behind him, as he went out.

She recovered herself almost at once. "Scene or no scene," she determined, "he shall not be two days longer in this house." She had no pity for him; she was conscious of nothing but the offence and the awkwardness. So she determined to be rid of him anyhow; and she was perfectly right. She sought her husband at once.

CHAPTER XII

Poor Malcolm! here was a position, with a vengeance. As he sat, with his uncle's last letter open on his knee, and his wife's words still ringing in his ears, I wonder whether he was not really the most unfortunate of the two. I am sure he thought so himself. What could have tempted John to behave in so absurd a manner? How was he to guess that he had come home drunk on purpose? What was the good of making a kettle of fish like this, instead of letting things go to the devil quietly in their own way? "Oh!" he cried, finding his old impropriety of expression in the disturbance of the moment, "confound all your heroes!"

John had a very dismal walk in the rain, and came back from it with the settled intention of leaving Grangehead that evening. The situation could not be prolonged either with dignity or comfort. He asked the servant for Mr. Falconer, and was directed to the library.

Malcolm caught sight of him as he entered, dropped his eyes guiltily upon the table, and made a great show of writing. John walked backwards and forwards behind him, like a caged beast; he, too, had prepared his speech, but there was a ball in his throat. He cleared his throat repeatedly, and at length said—

"John!"

He was rather afraid it had been inaudible, and so he repeated it.

"Eh?" said John, stopping suddenly in his walk.

It was so fiercely spoken, that Malcolm was a little flustered.

"I only wished a word with you," he answered apologetically.

"Ah!" said John.

Malcolm looked at the paper on which he had been scribbling his own name over and over again to keep up the feint of correspondence. He read all these repetitions from beginning to end, and seemed to feel refreshed. To the last signature he appended his address in a very careful style of penmanship. Then he cleared his throat as if he were going to begin, and fell to examining the nib of the pen upon his thumb-nail.

"Suppose you were to go on," suggested John.

"Oh, I say, John," Malcolm dashed into it, with a gasp, "I'm very sorry, and—and all that, particularly after what took place this morning; but my wife thinks you had better go away after all—in fact, she insists upon it. Personally, I'm very much disappointed; but of course this kind of thing will happen, I suppose; and—and of course very disagreeable it is. In short—"

He wiped his brow. All his prepared eloquence had deserted him. He was hopelessly entangled, and felt like an imbecile. A curious flame caught his eye and fascinated him at once. He kept staring at it with all his might, telling himself he was thinking what to say next, and not doing so. As he thus sat stupefied, he became conscious, by some electric sympathy, that John was nearer him than he had been, and raised his head with a sudden movement. Their eyes met in the mirror. John's face was deformed with hatred, and in an instant Malcolm's was stricken into the scarcely less hideous image of fear. As they waited, watching each other in the mirror with contracted eyelids, John's hate seemed to increase in proportion with Malcolm's terror, until they looked like a couple of lost spirits.

Malcolm was the first to throw off the spell. With something like a cry he leaped up and turned about as if to defend himself. If he had sat still, nothing in all likelihood would have happened; but his own action courted an onslaught. Before he had half-faced round, he was forced back against the table; the table upset and, being a light thing, broke in twain between the legs; and the two men fell among its ruins into the hearth. Malcolm was underneath, and his head struck sharply against the iron grate.

When he came to himself, his shirt was loosed, his brow had been wet with ink in default of water, and he was propped upon John's knee.

"Do you feel better?" asked John.

"Why, what's wrong? Why am I here? Where's Mary?"

"Oh, Mary's all right!" answered John, bitterly; "and you're not much worse. You've broken your head, and serve you right! And now, if you please, we'll say good-bye." He laid Malcolm's head on the floor, and rose to his feet. At the door he turned, and added, in a kinder tone, "Good-bye, old man." And with that he was gone.

Malcolm had brown paper and vinegar applied to the back of his head, and was rather sulky all that evening. It rained without intermission, and the roads in that part of the country were hardly passable for travellers on foot.

The Story of a Lie

Chapter I

Introduces the Admiral

When Dick Naseby was in Paris he made some odd acquaintances; for he was one of those who have ears to hear, and can use their eyes no less than their intelligence. He made as many thoughts as Stuart Mill; but his philosophy concerned flesh and blood, and was experimental as to its method. He was a type hunter among mankind. He despised small game and insignificant personalities, whether in the shape of dukes or bagmen, letting them go by like seaweed; but show him a refined or powerful face, let him hear a plangent or a penetrating voice, fish for him with a living look in some one's eye, a passionate gesture, a meaning and ambiguous smile, and his mind was instantaneously awakened. "There was a man, there was a woman," he seemed to say, and he stood up to the task of comprehension with the delight of an artist in his art.

And indeed, rightly considered, this interest of his was an artistic interest. There is no science in the personal study of human nature. All comprehension is creation; the woman I love is somewhat of my handiwork; and the great lover, like the great painter, is he that can so embellish his subject as to make her more than human, whilst yet by a cunning art he has so based his apotheosis on the nature of the case that the woman can go on being a true woman, and give her character free play, and show littleness, or cherish spite, or be greedy of common pleasures, and he continue to worship without a thought of incongruity. To love a character is only the heroic way of understanding it. When we love, by some noble method of our own or some nobility of mien or nature in the other, we apprehend the loved one by what is noblest in ourselves. When we are merely studying an eccentricity, the method of our study is but a series of allowances. To begin to understand is to begin to sympathize; for comprehension comes only when we have stated another's faults and virtues in terms of our own. Hence the proverbial toleration of artists for their own evil creations. Hence, too, it came about that Dick Naseby, a high-minded creature, and as scrupulous and brave a gentleman as you would want to meet, held in a sort of affection the various human creeping things whom he had met and studied.

One of these was Mr. Peter Van Tromp, an English-speaking, two-legged animal of the international genus, and by profession of general and more than equivocal utility. Years before he had been a painter of some standing in a colony, and portraits signed "Van Tromp" had celebrated the greatness of colonial governors and judges. In those days he had been married, and driven his wife and infant daughter in a pony trap. What were the steps of his declension? No one exactly knew. Here he was at least, and had been any time these past ten years, a sort of dismal parasite upon the foreigner in Paris.

It would be hazardous to specify his exact industry. Coarsely followed, it would have merited a name grown somewhat unfamiliar to our ears. Followed as he followed it, with a skilful reticence, in a kind of social chiaroscuro, it was still possible for the polite to call him a professional painter. His lair was in the Grand Hotel and the gaudiest cafés. There he might be seen jotting off a sketch with an air of some inspiration; and he was always affable, and one of the easiest of men to fall in talk withal. A conversation usually ripened into a peculiar sort of intimacy, and it was extraordinary how many little services Van Tromp contrived to render in the course of six and thirty hours. He occupied a position between a friend and a courier, which made him worse than embarrassing to repay. But those whom he obliged could always buy one of his villainous little pictures, or, where the favors had been prolonged and more than usually delicate, might order and pay for a large canvas, with perfect certainty that they would hear no more of the transaction.

Among resident artists he enjoyed celebrity of a nonprofessional sort. He had spent more money—no less than three individual fortunes, it was whispered—than any of his associates could ever hope to gain. Apart from his colonial career, he had been to Greece in a brigantine with four brass carronades; he had traveled Europe in a chaise and four, drawing bridle at the palace doors of German princes; queens of song and dance had followed him like sheep and paid his tailor's bills. And to behold him now, seeking small loans with plaintive condescension, sponging for breakfast on an art student of nineteen, a fallen Don Juan who had neglected to die at the propitious hour, had a color of romance for young imaginations. His name and his bright past, seen through the prism of whispered gossip, had gained him the nickname of *The Admiral.*

Dick found him one day at the receipt of custom, rapidly painting a pair of hens and a cock in a little water color sketching box, and now and then glancing at the ceiling like a man who should seek inspiration from the muse. Dick thought it remarkable that a painter should choose to work over an absinthe in a public café, and looked the man over. The aged rakishness of his appearance was set off by a youthful costume; he had disreputable gray hair and a disreputable, sore, red nose; but the coat and the gesture, the outworks of the man, were still designed for show. Dick came up to his table and inquired if he might look at what the gentleman was doing. No one was so delighted as the Admiral.

"A bit of a thing," said he. "I just dash them off like that. I—I dash them off," he added with a gesture.

"Quite so," said Dick, who was appalled by the feebleness of the production.

"Understand me," continued Van Tromp; "I am a man of the world. And yet—once an artist always an artist. All of a sudden a thought takes me in the street; I become its prey; it's like a pretty woman; no use to struggle; I must—dash it off."

"I see," said Dick.

"Yes," pursued the painter; "it all comes easily, easily to me; it is not my business; it's a pleasure. Life is my business—life—this great city,

Paris—Paris after dark—its lights, its gardens, its odd corners. Aha!" he cried, "to be young again! The heart is young, but the heels are leaden. A poor, mean business, to grow old! Nothing remains but the *coup d'œil*, the contemplative man's enjoyment, Mr.——," and he paused for the name.

"Naseby," returned Dick.

The other treated him at once to an exciting beverage, and expatiated on the pleasure of meeting a compatriot in a foreign land; to hear him you would have thought they had encountered in Central Africa. Dick had never found any one take a fancy to him so readily, nor show it in an easier or less offensive manner. He seemed tickled with him as an elderly fellow about town might be tickled by a pleasant and witty lad; he indicated that he was no precisian, but in his wildest times had never been such a blade as he thought Dick. Dick protested, but in vain. This manner of carrying an intimacy at the bayonet's point was Van Tromp's stock-in-trade. With an older man he insinuated himself; with youth he imposed himself, and in the same breath imposed an ideal on his victim, who saw that he must work up to it or lose the esteem of this old and vicious patron. And what young man can bear to lose a character for vice?

At last, as it grew toward dinner time, "Do you know Paris?" asked Van Tromp.

"Not so well as you, I am convinced," said Dick.

"And so am I," returned Van Tromp gaily.

"Paris! My young friend—you will allow me?—when you know Paris as I do, you will have seen Strange Things. I say no more; all I say is, Strange Things. We are men of the world, you and I, and in Paris, in the heart of civilized existence. This is an opportunity, Mr. Naseby. Let us dine. Let me show you where to dine."

Dick consented. On the way to dinner the Admiral showed him where to buy gloves, and made him buy them; where to buy cigars, and made him buy a vast store, some of which he obligingly accepted. At the restaurant he showed him what to order, with surprising consequences in the bill. What he made that night by his percentages it would be hard to estimate. And all the while Dick smilingly consented, understanding well that he was being done, but taking his losses in the pursuit of character, as a hunter sacrifices his dogs. As for the Strange

Things, the reader will be relieved to hear that they were no stranger than might have been expected, and he may find things quite as strange without the expense of a Van Tromp for guide. Yet he was a guide of no mean order, who made up for the poverty of what he had to show by a copious, imaginative commentary.

"And such," said he with a hiccup, "such is Paris."

"Pooh!" said Dick, who was tired of the performance.

The Admiral hung an ear, and looked up sidelong with a glimmer of suspicion.

"Good night," said Dick; "I'm tired."

"So English!" cried Van Tromp, clutching him by the hand. "So English! So *blasé!* Such a charming companion! Let me see you home."

"Look here," returned Dick, "I have said good night, and now I'm going. You're an amusing old boy; I like you, in a sense; but here's an end of it for tonight. Not another cigar, not another grog, not another percentage out of me."

"I beg your pardon!" cried the Admiral with dignity.

"Tut, man!" said Dick; "you're not offended; you're a man of the world, I thought. I've been studying you, and it's over. Have I not paid for the lesson? *Au revoir.*"

Van Tromp laughed gaily, shook hands up to the elbows, hoped cordially they would meet again and that often, but looked after Dick as he departed with a tremor of indignation. After that they two not unfrequently fell in each other's way, and Dick would often treat the old boy to breakfast on a moderate scale and in a restaurant of his own selection. Often, too, he would lend Van Tromp the matter of a pound, in view of that gentleman's contemplated departure for Australia; there would be a scene of farewell almost touching in character, and a week or a month later they would meet on the same boulevard without surprise or embarrassment. And in the mean time Dick learned more about his acquaintance on all sides; heard of his yacht, his chaise and four, his brief season of celebrity amid a more confiding population, his daughter, of whom he loved to whimper in his cups, his sponging, parasitical, nameless way of life; and with each new detail something that was not merely interest nor yet altogether affection grew up in his mind toward this disreputable stepson of the arts. Ere he left Paris Van Tromp was one of those whom he entertained to a farewell supper; and the old gentleman made the speech of the evening, and then fell below the table, weeping, smiling, paralyzed.

CHAPTER II

A letter to the papers

Old Mr. Naseby had the sturdy, untutored nature of the upper middle class. The universe seemed plain to him. "The thing's right," he would say, or "the thing's wrong"; and there was an end of it. There was a contained, prophetic energy in his utterances, even on the slightest affairs; he *saw* the damned thing; if you did not, it must be from perversity of will; and this sent the blood to his head. Apart from this, which made him an exacting companion, he was one of the most upright, hot-tempered, hot-headed old gentlemen in England. Florid, with white hair, the face of an old Jupiter, and the figure of an old fox-hunter, he enlivened the vale of Thyme from end to end on his big, cantering chestnut.

He had a hearty respect for Dick as a lad of parts. Dick had a respect for his father as the best of men, tempered by the politic revolt of a youth who has to see to his own independence. Whenever the pair argued, they came to an open rupture; and arguments were frequent, for they were both positive, and both loved the work of the intelligence. It was a treat to hear Mr. Naseby defending the Church of England in a volley of oaths, or supporting ascetic morals with an enthusiasm not entirely innocent of port wine. Dick used to wax indignant, and none the less so because, as his father was a skilful disputant, he found himself not seldom in the wrong. On these occasions, he would redouble in energy, and declare that black was white, and blue yellow, with much conviction and heat of manner; but in the morning such a license of debate weighed upon him like a crime, and he would seek out his father, where he walked before breakfast on a terrace overlooking all the vale of Thyme.

"I have to apologize, sir, for last night—" he would begin.

"Of course you have," the old gentleman would cut in cheerfully. "You spoke like a fool. Say no more about it."

"You do not understand me, sir. I refer to a particular point. I confess there is much force in your argument from the doctrine of possibilities."

"Of course there is," returned his father. "Come down and look at the stables. Only," he would add, "bear this in mind, and do remember that a man of my age and experience knows more about what he is saying than a raw boy."

He would utter the word "boy" even more offensively than the average of fathers, and the light way in which he accepted these apologies cut Richard to the heart. The latter drew slighting comparisons, and remembered that he was the only one who ever apologized. This gave him a high station in his own esteem, and thus contributed indirectly to his better behavior; for he was scrupulous as well as high-spirited, and prided himself on nothing more than on a just submission.

So things went on until the famous occasion when Mr. Naseby, becoming engrossed in securing the election of a sound party candidate to Parliament, wrote a flaming letter to the papers. The letter had about every demerit of party letters in general: it was expressed with the energy of a believer; it was personal; it was a little more than half unfair, and about a quarter untrue. The old man did not mean to say what was untrue, you may be sure; but he had rashly picked up gossip, as his prejudice suggested, and now rashly launched it on the public with the sanction of his name.

"The Liberal candidate," he concluded, "is thus a public turncoat. Is that the sort of man we want? He has been given the lie, and has swallowed the insult. Is that the sort of man we want? I answer, No! with all the force of my conviction, I answer, *No!*"

And then he signed and dated the letter with an amateur's pride, and looked to be famous by the morrow.

Dick, who had heard nothing of the matter, was up first on that inauspicious day, and took the journal to an arbor in the garden. He found his father's manifesto in one column; and in another a leading article. "No one that we are aware of," ran the article, "had consulted Mr. Naseby on the subject, but if he had been appealed to by the whole body of electors, his letter would be none the less ungenerous and unjust to Mr. Dalton. We do not choose to give the lie to Mr. Naseby, for we are too well aware of the consequences; but we shall venture instead to print the facts of both cases referred to by this red-hot partizan in another portion of our issue. Mr. Naseby is of course a large proprietor in our neighborhood; but fidelity to facts, decent feeling, and English grammar, are all of them qualities more important than the possession of land. Mr. N——is doubtless a great man; in his large gardens and that half mile of greenhouses, where he has probably ripened his intellect and temper, he may say what he will to his hired vassals, but (as the Scotch say):

here
He maunna think to domineer.

"Liberalism," continued the anonymous journalist, "is of too free and sound a growth," &c.

Richard Naseby read the whole thing from beginning to end; and a crushing shame fell upon his spirit. His father had played the fool; he had gone out noisily to war, and come back with confusion. The moment that his trumpets sounded, he had been disgracefully unhorsed. There was no question as to the facts; they were one and all against the Squire. Richard would have given his ears to have suppressed the issue; but as that could not be done, he had his horse saddled, and furnishing himself with a convenient staff, rode off at once to Thymebury.

The editor was at breakfast in a large, sad apartment. The absence of furniture, the extreme meanness of the meal, and the haggard, bright-eyed, consumptive look of the culprit, unmanned our hero; but he clung to his stick, and was stout and war-like.

"You wrote the article in this morning's paper?" he demanded.

"You are young Mr. Naseby? I *published* it," replied the editor, rising.

"My father is an old man," said Richard; and then with an outburst, "And a damned sight finer fellow than either you or Dalton!" He stopped and swallowed; he was determined that all should go with regularity. "I have but one question to put to you, sir," he resumed. "Granted that my father was misinformed, would it not have been more decent to withhold the letter and communicate with him in private?"

"Believe me," returned the editor, "that alternative was not open to me. Mr. Naseby told me in a note that he had sent his letter to three other journals, and in fact threatened me with what he called exposure if I kept it back from mine. I am really concerned at what has happened; I sympathize and approve of your emotion, young gentleman; but the attack on Mr. Dalton was gross, very gross, and I had no choice but to offer him my columns to reply. Party has its duties, sir," added the scribe, kindling, as one who should propose a sentiment; "and the attack was gross."

Richard stood for half a minute digesting the answer; and then the god of fair play came uppermost in his heart, and murmuring "Good morning," he made his escape into the street.

His horse was not hurried on the way home, and he was late for breakfast. The Squire was standing with his back to the fire in a state bordering on apoplexy, his fingers violently knitted under his coat tails. As Richard came in, he opened and shut his mouth like a codfish, and his eyes protruded.

"Have you seen that, sir?" he cried, nodding toward the paper.

"Yes, sir," said Richard.

"Oh, you've read it, have you?"

"Yes, I have read it," replied Richard, looking at his foot.

"Well," demanded the old gentleman, "and what have you to say to it, sir?"

"You seem to have been misinformed," said Dick.

"Well? What then? Is your mind so sterile, sir? Have you not a word of comment? no proposal?"

"I fear, sir, you must apologize to Mr. Dalton. It would be more handsome, indeed it would be only just, and a free acknowledgment would go far—" Richard paused, no language appearing delicate enough to suit the case.

"That is a suggestion which should have come from me, sir," roared the father. "It is out of place upon your lips. It is not the thought of a loyal son. Why, sir, if my father had been plunged in such deplorable circumstances, I should have thrashed the editor of that vile sheet within an inch of his life. I should have thrashed the man, sir. It would have been the action of an ass; but it would have shown that I had the blood and the natural affections of a man. Son? You are no son, no son of mine, sir!"

"Sir!" said Dick.

"I'll tell you what you are, sir," pursued the Squire. "You're a Benthamite. I disown you. Your mother would have died for shame; there was no modern cant about your mother; she thought—she said to me, sir—I'm glad she's in her grave, Dick Naseby. Misinformed! Misinformed, sir? Have you no loyalty, no spring, no natural affections? Are you clockwork, hey? Away! This is no place for you. Away!" (waving his hands in the air) "Go away! Leave me!"

At this moment Dick beat a retreat in a disarray of nerves, a whistling and clamor of his own arteries, and in short in such a final bodily disorder as made him alike incapable of speech or hearing. And in the midst of all this turmoil, a sense of unpardonable injustice remained graven in his memory.

CHAPTER III

In the Admiral's name

There was no return to the subject. Dick and his father were henceforth on terms of coldness. The upright old gentleman grew more upright when he met his son, buckrammed with immortal anger; he asked after Dick's health, and discussed the weather and the crops with an appalling courtesy; his pronunciation was *point-de-vice,* his voice was distant, distinct, and sometimes almost trembling with suppressed indignation.

As for Dick, it seemed to him as if his life had come abruptly to an end. He came out of his theories and clevernesses; his premature man-of-the-worldness, on which he had prided himself on his travels, "shrank like a thing ashamed" before this real sorrow. Pride, wounded honor, pity and respect tussled together daily in his heart; and now he was within an ace of throwing himself upon his father's mercy, and now of slipping forth at night and coming back no more to Naseby House. He suffered from the sight of his father, nay, even from the neighborhood of this familiar valley, where every corner had its legend, and he was besieged with memories of childhood. If he fled into a new land, and among none but strangers, he might escape his destiny, who knew? and begin again lightheartedly. From that chief peak of the hills, that now and then, like an uplifted finger, shone in an arrow of sunlight through the broken clouds, the shepherd in clear weather might perceive the shining of the sea. There, he thought, was hope. But his heart failed him when he saw the Squire; and he remained. His fate was not that of the voyager by sea and land; he was to travel in the spirit, and begin his journey sooner than he supposed.

For it chanced one day that his walk led him into a portion of the uplands which was almost unknown to him. Scrambling through some rough woods, he came out upon a moorland reaching toward the hills. A few lofty Scotch firs grew hard by upon a knoll; a clear fountain near the foot of the knoll sent up a miniature streamlet which meandered in the heather. A shower had just skimmed by, but now the sun shone brightly, and the air smelt of the pines and the grass. On a stone under the trees sat a young lady sketching. We have learned to think of women in a sort of symbolic transfiguration, based on clothes; and one of the readiest ways in which we conceive our mistress is as a composite thing, principally petticoats. But humanity has triumphed over clothes; the look, the touch of a dress has become alive; and the woman who stitched herself into these material integuments, has now permeated right through and gone out to the tip of her skirt. It was only a black dress that caught Dick Naseby's eye; but it took possession of his mind, and all other thoughts departed. He drew near and the girl turned around. Her face startled him; it was a face he wanted; and he took it in at once like breathing air.

"I beg your pardon," he said, taking off his hat, "you are sketching."

"Oh!" she exclaimed, "for my own amusement. I despise the thing."

"Ten to one you do yourself injustice," returned Dick. "Besides, it's a freemasonry. I sketch myself, and you know what that implies."

"No. What?" she asked.

"Two things," he answered. "First, that I am no very difficult critic, and second, that I have a right to see your picture."

She covered the block with both her hands. "Oh no," she said; "I am ashamed."

"Indeed, I might give you a hint," said Dick. "Although no artist myself, I have known many; in Paris I had many for friends, and used to prowl among studios."

"In Paris?" she cried, with a leap of light into her eyes. "Did you ever meet Mr. Van Tromp?"

"I? Yes. Why, you are not the Admiral's daughter, are you?"

"The Admiral? Do they call him that?" she cried. "Oh, how nice, how nice of them! It is the younger men who call him so, is it not?"

"Yes," said Dick, somewhat heavily.

"You can understand now," she said, with an unspeakable accent of contented and noble-minded pride, "why it is I do not choose to show my sketch. Van Tromp's daughter! The Admiral's daughter! I delight in that name. The Admiral! And so you know my father?"

"Well," said Dick, "I met him often; we were even intimate. He may have mentioned my name—Naseby."

"He writes so little. He is so busy, so devoted to his art! I have had a half wish," she added laughing, "that my father was a plainer man, whom I could help—to whom I could be a credit; but only sometimes, you know, and with only half my heart. For a great painter! You have seen his works?"

"I have seen some of them," returned Dick; "they—they are very nice."

She laughed aloud. "Nice?" she repeated. "I see you don't care much for art."

"Not much," he admitted; "but I know that many people are glad to buy Mr. Van Tromp's pictures."

"Call him the Admiral!" she cried. "It sounds kindly and familiar; and I like to think that he is appreciated and looked up to by young painters. He has not always been appreciated; he had a cruel life for many years; and when I think"—there were tears in her eyes—"when I think of that, I feel inclined to be a fool," she broke off. "And now I shall go home. You have filled me full of happiness; for think, Mr. Naseby, I have not seen my father since I was six years old; and yet he is in my thoughts all day! You must come and call on me; my aunt will be delighted, I am sure; and then you will tell me all—all about my father, will you not?"

Dick helped her to get her sketching traps together; and when all was ready she gave Dick her hand and a frank return of pressure.

"You are my father's friend," she said; "we shall be great friends too. You must come and see me soon."

Then she was gone down the hillside at a run; and Dick stood by himself in a state of some bewilderment and even distress. There were elements of laughter in the business; but the black dress, and the face that belonged to it, and the hand that he had held in his, inclined him to a serious view. What was he, under the circumstances, called upon to do? Perhaps to avoid the girl? Well, he would think about that. Perhaps to break the truth to her? Why, ten to one, such was her infatuation, he would fail. Perhaps to keep up the illusion, to color the raw facts; to help her to false ideas, while yet not plainly stating falsehoods? Well, he would see about that; he would also see about avoiding the girl. He saw about this last so well, that the next afternoon beheld him on his way to visit her.

In the meantime the girl had gone straight home, light as a bird, tremulous with joy, to the little cottage where she lived alone with a maiden aunt; and to that lady, a grim, sixty years old Scotchwoman, with a nodding head, communicated news of her encounter and invitation.

"A friend of his?" cried the aunt. "What like is he? What did ye say was his name?"

She was dead silent, and stared at the old woman darkling. Then very slowly, "I said he was my father's friend; I have invited him to my house, and come he shall," she said; and with that she walked off to her room, where she sat staring at the wall all the evening. Miss M'Glashan, for that was the aunt's name, read a large Bible in the kitchen with some of the joys of martyrdom.

It was perhaps half-past three when Dick presented himself, rather scrupulously dressed, before the cottage door; he knocked, and a voice bade him enter. The kitchen, which opened directly off the garden, was somewhat darkened by foliage; but he could see her as she approached from the far end to meet him. This second sight of her surprised him. Her strong black brows spoke of temper easily aroused and hard to quiet; her mouth was small, nervous and weak; there was something dangerous and sulky underlying, in her nature, much that was honest, compassionate, and even noble.

"My father's name," she said, "has made you very welcome."

And she gave him her hand, with a sort of curtsey. It was a pretty greeting, although somewhat mannered; and Dick felt himself among the gods. She led him through the kitchen to a parlor, and presented him to Miss M'Glashan.

"Esther," said the aunt, "see and make Mr. Naseby his tea."

And as soon as the girl was gone upon this hospitable intent, the old woman crossed the room and came quite near to Dick as if in menace.

"Ye know that man?" she asked in an imperious whisper.

"Mr. Van Tromp?" said Dick. "Yes, I know him."

"Well, and what brings ye here?" she said. "I couldn't save the mother—her that's dead—but the bairn!" She had a note in her voice that filled poor Dick with consternation. "Man," she went on, "what is it now? Is it money?"

"My dear lady," said Dick, "I think you misinterpret my position. I am young Mr. Naseby of Naseby House. My acquaintance with Mr. Van Tromp is really very slender; I am only afraid that Miss Van Tromp has exaggerated our intimacy in her own imagination. I know positively nothing of his private affairs, and do not care to know. I met him casually in Paris—that is all."

Miss M'Glashan drew a long breath. "In Paris?" she said. "Well, and what do you think of him?—what do ye think of him?" she repeated, with a different scansion, as Richard, who had not much taste for such a question, kept her waiting for an answer.

"I found him a very agreeable companion," he said.

"Ay," said she, "did ye! And how does he win his bread?"

"I fancy," he gasped, "that Mr. Van Tromp has many generous friends."

"I'll warrant!" she sneered; and before Dick could find more to say, she was gone from the room.

Esther returned with the tea things, and sat down.

"Now," she said cosily, "tell me all about my father."

"He"—stammered Dick, "he is a very agreeable companion."

"I shall begin to think it is more than you are, Mr. Naseby," she said, with a laugh. "I am his daughter, you forget. Begin at the beginning, and tell me all you have seen of him, all he said and all you answered. You must have met somewhere; begin with that."

So with that he began: how he had found the Admiral painting in a café; how his art so possessed him that he could not wait till he got home to—well, to dash off his idea; how (this in reply to a question) his idea consisted of a cock crowing and two hens eating corn; how he was fond of cocks and hens; how this did not lead him to neglect more ambitious forms of art; how he had a picture in his studio of a Greek subject which was said to be remarkable from several points of view; how no one had seen it nor knew the precise site of the studio in which it was being vigorously though secretly confected; how (in answer to a suggestion) this shyness was common to the Admiral, Michelangelo, and others; how they (Dick and Van Tromp) had struck up an acquaintance at once, and dined together that same night; how he (the Admiral) had once given money to a beggar; how he spoke with effusion of his little daughter; how he had once borrowed money to send her a doll—a trait worthy of Newton, she being then in her nineteenth year at least; how, if the doll never arrived (which it appeared it never did), the trait was only more characteristic of the highest order of creative intellect; how he was—no, not beautiful—striking, yes, Dick would go so far, decidedly striking in appearance; how his boots were made to lace and his coat was black, not cutaway, a frock; and so on, and so on by the yard. It was astonishing how few lies were necessary. After all, people exaggerated the difficulty of life. A little steering, just a touch of the rudder now and then, and with a willing listener there is no limit to the domain of equivocal speech. Sometimes Miss M'Glashan made a freezing sojourn in the parlor; and then the task seemed unaccountably more difficult; but to Esther, who was all eyes and ears, her face alight with interest, his stream of language flowed without break or stumble, and his mind was ever fertile in ingenious evasions and—

What an afternoon it was for Esther!

"Ah!" she said at last, "it's good to hear all this! My aunt, you should know, is narrow and too religious; she can not understand an artist's life. It does not frighten me," she added grandly; "I am an artist's daughter."

With that speech, Dick consoled himself for his imposture; she was not deceived so grossly after all; and then if a fraud, was not the fraud piety itself?—and what could be more obligatory than to keep alive in the heart of a daughter that filial trust and honor which, even although misplaced, became her like a jewel of the mind? There might be another thought, a shade of cowardice, a selfish desire to please; poor Dick was merely human; and what would you have had him do?

CHAPTER IV

Esther on the filial relation

A month later Dick and Esther met at the stile beside the crossroads; had there been any one to see them but the birds and summer insects, it would have been remarked that they met after a different fashion from the day before. Dick took her in his arms, and their lips were set together for a long while. Then he held her at arm's length, and they looked straight into each other's eyes.

"Esther!" he said;—you should have heard his voice!

"Dick!" said she.

"My darling!"

It was some time before they started for their walk; he kept an arm about her, and their sides were close together as they walked; the sun, the birds, the west wind running among the trees, a pressure, a look, the grasp tightening round a single finger, these things stood them in lieu of thought and filled their hearts with joy. The path they were following led them through a wood of pine trees carpeted with heather and blueberry, and upon this pleasant carpet, Dick, not without some seriousness, made her sit down.

"Esther!" he began, "there is something you ought to know. You know my father is a rich man, and you would think, now that we love each other, we might marry when we pleased. But I fear, darling, we may have long to wait, and shall want all our courage."

"I have courage for anything," she said, "I have all I want; with you and my father, I am so well off, and waiting is made so happy, that I could wait a lifetime and not weary."

He had a sharp pang at the mention of the Admiral. "Hear me out," he continued. "I ought to have told you this before; but it is a thought I shrink from; if it were possible, I should not tell you even now. My poor father and I are scarce on speaking terms."

"Your father," she repeated, turning pale.

"It must sound strange to you; but yet I cannot think I am to blame," he said. "I will tell you how it happened."

"Oh, Dick!" she said, when she had heard him to an end, "how brave you are, and how proud. Yet I would not be proud with a father. I would tell him all."

"What!" cried Dick, "go in months after, and brag that I had meant to thrash the man, and then didn't. And why? Because my father had made a bigger ass of himself than I supposed. My dear, that's nonsense."

She winced at his words and drew away. "But when that is all he asks," she pleaded. "If he only knew that you had felt that impulse, it would make him so proud and happy. He would see you were his own son after all, and had the same thoughts and the same chivalry of spirit.

And then you did yourself injustice when you spoke just now. It was because the editor was weak and poor and excused himself, that you repented your first determination. Had he been a big red man, with whiskers, you would have beaten him—you know you would—if Mr. Naseby had been ten times more committed. Do you think, if you can tell it to me, and I understand at once, that it would be more difficult to tell it to your own father, or that he would not be more ready to sympathize with you than I am? And I love you, Dick; but then he is your father."

"My dear," said Dick, desperately, "you do not understand; you do not know what it is to be treated with daily want of comprehension and daily small injustices, through childhood and boyhood and manhood, until you despair of a hearing, until the thing rides you like a nightmare, until you almost hate the sight of the man you love, and who's your father after all. In short, Esther, you don't know what it is to have a father, and that's what blinds you."

"I see," she said musingly, "you mean that I am fortunate in my father. But I am not so fortunate after all; you forget, I do not know him; it is you who know him; he is already more your father than mine." And here she took his hand. Dick's heart had grown as cold as ice. "But I am sorry for you, too," she continued, "it must be very sad and lonely."

"You misunderstand me," said Dick, chokingly. "My father is the best man I know in all this world; he is worth a hundred of me, only he doesn't understand me, and he can't be made to."

There was a silence for a while. "Dick," she began again, "I am going to ask a favor, it's the first since you said you loved me. May I see your father—see him pass, I mean, where he will not observe me?"

"Why?" asked Dick.

"It is a fancy; you forget, I am romantic about fathers."

The hint was enough for Dick; he consented with haste, and full of hang-dog penitence and disgust, took her down by a back way and planted her in the shrubbery, whence she might see the Squire ride by to dinner. There they both sat silent, but holding hands, for nearly half an hour. At last the trotting of a horse sounded in the distance, the park gates opened with a clang, and then Mr. Naseby appeared, with stooping shoulders and a heavy, bilious countenance, languidly rising to the trot. Esther recognized him at once; she had often seen him before, though with her huge indifference for all that lay outside the circle of her love, she had never so much as wondered who he was; but now she recognized him, and found him ten years older, leaden and springless, and stamped by an abiding sorrow.

"Oh, Dick, Dick!" she said, and the tears began to shine upon her face as she hid it in his bosom; his own fell thickly too. They had a sad walk home, and that night, full of love and good counsel, Dick exerted every art to please his father, to convince him of his respect and affection, to heal up this breach of kindness, and reunite two hearts. But alas! the Squire was sick and peevish; he had been all day glooming over Dick's estrangement—for so he put it to himself, and now with growls, cold words, and the cold shoulder, he beat off all advances, and entrenched himself in a just resentment.

Chapter V

The prodigal father makes his debut at home

That took place upon a Tuesday. On the Thursday following, as Dick was walking by appointment, earlier than usual, in the direction of the cottage, he was appalled to meet in the lane a fly from Thymebury, containing the human form of Miss M'Glashan. The lady did not deign to remark him in her passage, her face was suffused with tears, and expressed much concern for the packages by which she was surrounded. He stood still, and asked himself what this circumstance might portend. It was so beautiful a day that he was loth to forecast evil, yet something must perforce have happened at the cottage, and that of a decisive nature; for here was Miss M'Glashan on her travels, with a small patrimony in brown paper parcels, and the old lady's bearing implied hot battle and unqualified defeat. Was the house to be closed against him? Was Esther left alone, or had some new protector made his appearance from among the millions of Europe? It is the character of love to loathe the near relative of the loved one; chapters in the history of the human race have justified this feeling, and the conduct of uncles, in particular, has frequently met with censure from the independent novelist. Miss M'Glashan was now seen in the rosy colors of regret; whoever succeeded her, Dick felt the change would be for the worse. He hurried forward in this spirit; his anxiety grew upon him with every step; as he entered the garden a voice fell upon his ear, and he was once more arrested, not this time by doubt, but by indubitable certainty of ill.

The thunderbolt had fallen; the Admiral was here.

Dick would have retreated, in the panic terror of the moment; but Esther kept a bright lookout when her lover was expected. In a twinkling she was by his side, brimful of news and pleasure, too glad to notice his embarrassment, and in one of those golden transports of exultation which transcend not only words but caresses. She took him by the end of the fingers (reaching forward to take them, for her great preoccupation was to save time), she drew him toward her, pushed him past her in the door, and planted him face to face with Mr. Van Tromp, in a suit of French country velveteens and with a remarkable carbuncle on his nose. Then, as though this was the end of what she could endure in the way of joy, Esther turned and ran out of the room.

The two men remained looking at each other with some confusion on both sides. Van Tromp was naturally the first to recover; he put out his hand with a fine gesture.

"And you know my little lass, my Esther?" he said. "This is pleasant, this is what I have conceived of home. A strange word for the old rover; but we all have a taste for home and the homelike, disguise it how we may. It has brought me here, Mr. Naseby," he concluded, with an intonation that would have made his fortune on the stage, so just, so sad, so dignified, so like a man of the world and a philosopher, "and you see a man who is content."

"I see," said Dick.

"Sit down," continued the parasite, setting the example. "Fortune has gone against me. (I am just siruping a little brandy—after my journey.) I was going down, Mr. Naseby; between you and me, I was *décavé*; I borrowed fifty francs, smuggled my valise past the concierge—a work of considerable tact—and here I am!"

"Yes," said Dick; "and here you are." He was quite idiotic.

Esther, at this moment reentered the room.

"Are you glad to see him?" she whispered in his ear, the pleasure of her voice almost bursting through the whisper into song.

"Oh, yes," said Dick, "very."

"I knew you would be," she replied; "I told him how you loved him."

"Help yourself," said the Admiral, "help yourself; and let us drink to a new existence."

"To a new existence," repeated Dick; and he raised the tumbler to his lips, but set it down untasted. He had had enough of novelties for one day.

Esther was sitting on a stool beside her father's feet, holding her knees in her arms, and looking with pride from one to the other of her two visitors. Her eyes were so bright that you were never sure if there were tears in them or not; little voluptuous shivers ran about her body; sometimes she nestled her chin into her throat, sometimes threw back her head, with ecstasy; in a word, she was in that state when it is said of people that they cannot contain themselves for happiness. It would be hard to exaggerate the agony of Richard.

And, in the meantime, Van Tromp ran on interminably.

"I never forget a friend," said he, "nor yet an enemy: of the latter, I never had but two—myself and the public; and I fancy I have had my vengeance pretty freely out of both." He chuckled. "But those days are done. Van Tromp is no more. He was a man who had successes; I believe you knew I had successes—to which we shall refer no farther," pulling down his neckcloth with a smile. "That man exists no more: by an exercise of will I have destroyed him. There is something like it in the poets. First, a brilliant and conspicuous career—the observed, I may say, of all observers, including the bum-baily: and then, presto! a quiet, sly, old, rustic *bonhomme,* cultivating roses. In Paris, Mr. Naseby—"

"Call him Richard, father," said Esther.

"Richard, if he will allow me. Indeed, we are old friends, and now near neighbors; and apropos, how are we off for neighbors, Richard? The cottage stands, I think, upon your father's land—a family which I respect—and the wood, I understand, is Lord Trevanion's. Not that I care; I am an old Bohemian. I have cut society with a cut direct; I cut it when I was prosperous, and now I reap my reward, and can cut it with dignity in my declension. These are our little *amours propres,* my daughter: your father must respect himself. Thank you, yes; just a leetle, leetle, tiny—thanks, thanks; you spoil me. But, as I was saying, Richard, or was about to say, my daughter has been allowed to rust; her aunt was a mere duenna; hence, in parenthesis, Richard, her distrust of me; my nature and that of the duenna are poles asunder—poles! But, now that I am here, now that I have given up the fight, and live henceforth for one only of my works—I have the modesty to say it is my best—my daughter—well, we shall put all that to rights. The neighbors, Richard?"

Dick was understood to say that there were many good families in the Vale of Thyme.

"You shall introduce us," said the Admiral.

Dick's shirt was wet; he made a lumbering excuse to go; which Esther explained to herself by a fear of intrusion, and so set down to the merit side of Dick's account, while she proceeded to detain him.

"Before our walk?" she cried. "Never! I must have my walk."

"Let us all go," said the Admiral, rising.

"You do not know that you are wanted," she cried, leaning on his shoulder with a caress. "I might wish to speak to my old friend about my new father. But you shall come today, you shall do all you want; I have set my heart on spoiling you."

"I will take just *one* drop more," said the Admiral, stooping to help himself to brandy. "It is surprising how this journey has fatigued me. But I am growing old, I am growing old, I am growing old, and—I regret to add— bald."

He cocked a white wide-awake coquettishly upon his head—the habit of the lady-killer clung to him; and Esther had already thrown on her hat, and was ready, while he was still studying the result in a mirror: the carbuncle had somewhat painfully arrested his attention.

"We are papa now; we must be respectable," he said to Dick, in explanation of his dandyism: and then he went to a bundle and chose himself a staff. Where were the elegant canes of his Parisian epoch? This was a support for age, and designed for rustic scenes. Dick began to see and appreciate the man's enjoyment in a new part, when he saw how carefully he had "made it up." He had invented a gait for this first country stroll with his daughter, which was admirably in key. He walked with fatigue; he leaned upon the staff; he looked round him with a sad, smiling sympathy on all that he beheld; he even asked the name of a plant, and rallied himself gently for an old townbird, ignorant of nature. "This country life will make me young again," he sighed. They reached the top of the hill toward the first hour of evening; the sun was descending heaven, the color had all drawn into the west; the hills were modeled in their least contour by the soft, slanting shine; and the wide moorlands, veined with glens and hazel woods, ran west and north in a hazy glory of light. Then the painter awakened in Van Tromp.

"Gad, Dick," he cried, "what value!"

An ode in four hundred lines would not have seemed so touching to Esther; her eyes filled with happy tears; yes, here was the father of whom she had dreamed, whom Dick had described; simple, enthusiastic, unworldly, kind, a painter at heart, and a fine gentleman in manner.

And just then the Admiral perceived a house by the wayside, and something depending over the house door which might be construed as a sign by the hopeful and thirsty.

"Is that," he asked, pointing with his stick, "an inn?"

There was a marked change in his voice, as though he attached importance to the inquiry. Esther listened, hoping she should hear wit or wisdom.

Dick said it was.

"You know it?" inquired the Admiral.

"I have passed it a hundred times, but that is all," replied Dick.

"Ah," said Van Tromp, with a smile, and shaking his head; "you are not an old campaigner; you have the world to learn. Now I, you see, find an inn so very near my own home, and my first thought is—my neighbors. I shall go forward and make my neighbor's acquaintance; no, you needn't come; I shall not be a moment."

And he walked off briskly toward the inn, leaving Dick alone with Esther on the road.

"Dick," she exclaimed, "I am so glad to get a word with you; I am so happy, I have such a thousand things to say; and I want you to do me a favor. Imagine, he has come without a paintbox, without an easel; and I want him to have all. I want you to get them for me in Thymebury. You saw, this moment, how his heart turned to painting. They can't live without it," she added; meaning perhaps Van Tromp and Michelangelo.

Up to that moment, she had observed nothing amiss in Dick's behavior. She was too happy to be curious; and his silence, in presence of the great and good being whom she called her father, had seemed both natural and praiseworthy. But now that they were alone, she became conscious of a barrier between her lover and herself, and alarm sprang up in her heart.

"Dick," she cried, "you don't love me."

"I do that," he said heartily.

"But you are unhappy; you are strange; you—you are not glad to see my father," she concluded, with a break in her voice.

"Esther," he said, "I tell you that I love you; if you love me, you know what that means, and that all I wish is to see you happy. Do you think I cannot enjoy your pleasures? Esther, I do. If I am uneasy, if I am alarmed, if—. Oh, believe me, try and believe in me," he cried, giving up argument with perhaps a happy inspiration.

But the girl's suspicions were aroused; and though she pressed the matter no farther (indeed, her father was already seen returning), it by no means left her thoughts. At one moment she simply resented the selfishness of a man who had obtruded his dark looks and passionate language on her joy; for there is nothing that a woman can less easily forgive than the language of a passion which, even if only for the moment, she does not share. At another, she suspected him of jealousy against her father; and for that, although she could see excuses for it, she yet despised him. And at least, in one way or the other, here was the dangerous beginning of a separation between two hearts. Esther found herself at variance with her sweetest friend; she could no longer look into his heart and find it written in the same language as her own; she could no longer think of him as the sun which radiated happiness upon her life, for she had turned to him once, and he had breathed upon her black and chilly, radiated blackness and frost. To put the whole matter in a word, she was beginning, although ever so slightly, to fall out of love.

CHAPTER VI

The prodigal father goes on from strength to strength

We will not follow all the steps of the Admiral's return and installation, but hurry forward toward the catastrophe, merely chronicling by the way a few salient incidents, wherein we must rely entirely upon the evidence of Richard, for Esther to this day has never opened her mouth upon this trying passage of her life, and as for the Admiral— well, that naval officer, although still alive, and now more suitably installed in a seaport town where he has a telescope and a flag in his front garden, is incapable of throwing the slightest gleam of light upon the affair. Often and often has he remarked to the present writer: "If I know what it was all about, sir, I'll be——" in short, be what I hope he will not. And then he will look across at his daughter's portrait, a photograph, shake his head with an amused appearance, and mix himself another grog by way of consolation. Once I have heard him go farther, and express his feelings with regard to Esther in a single but eloquent word. "A minx, sir," he said, not in anger, rather in amusement; and he cordially drank her health upon the back of it. His worst enemy must admit him to be a man without malice; he never bore a grudge in his life, lacking the necessary taste and industry of attention.

Yet it was during this obscure period that the drama was really performed; and its scene was in the heart of Esther, shut away from all eyes. Had this warm, upright, sullen girl been differently used by destiny, had events come upon her even in a different succession, for some things lead easily to others, the whole course of this tale would have been changed, and Esther never would have run away. As it was, through a series of acts and words of which we know but few, and a series of thoughts which any one may imagine for himself, she was awakened in four days from the dream of a life.

The first tangible cause of disenchantment was when Dick brought home a painter's arsenal on Friday evening. The Admiral was in the chimney-corner, once more "sirupping" some brandy and water, and Esther sat at the table at work. They both came forward to greet the new arrival; and the girl, relieving him of his monstrous burden, proceeded to display her offerings to her father. Van Tromp's countenance fell several degrees; he became quite querulous.

"God bless me," he said; and then, "I must really ask you not to interfere, child," in a tone of undisguised hostility.

"Father," she said, "forgive me; I knew you had given up your art——"

"Oh, yes!" cried the Admiral; "I've done with it to the judgment day!"

"Pardon me again," she said firmly, "but I do not, I cannot think that you are right in this. Suppose the world is unjust, suppose that no one understands you, you have still a duty to yourself. And, oh, don't spoil the pleasure of your coming home to me; show me that you can be my father and yet not neglect your destiny. I am not like some daughters; I will not be jealous of your art, and I will try to understand it."

The situation was odiously farcical. Richard groaned under it; he longed to leap forward and denounce the humbug. And the humbug himself? Do you fancy he was easier in his mind? I am sure, on the other hand, that he was acutely miserable; and he betrayed his sufferings by a perfectly silly and undignified access of temper, during which he broke his pipe in several places, threw his brandy and water in the fire, and employed words which were very plain, although the drift of them was somewhat vague. It was of very brief duration. Van Tromp was himself again, and in a most delightful humor within three minutes of the first explosion.

"I am an old fool," he said frankly. "I was spoiled when a child. As for you, Esther, you take after your mother; you have a morbid sense of duty, particularly for others; strive against it, my dear—strive against it. And as for the pigments, well, I'll use them, some of these days; and to show that I'm in earnest, I'll get Dick here to prepare a canvas."

Dick was put to this menial task forthwith, the Admiral not even watching how he did it, but quite occupied with another grog and a pleasant vein of talk.

A little after Esther arose, and making some pretext, good or bad, went off to bed. Dick was left hobbled by the canvas and was subjected to Van Tromp for about an hour.

The next day, Saturday, it is believed that little intercourse took place between Esther and her father; but toward the afternoon Dick met the latter returning from the direction of the inn, where he had struck up quite a friendship with the landlord. Dick wondered who paid for these excursions, and at the thought that the reprobate must get his pocket money where he got his board and lodging, from poor Esther's generosity, he had it almost in his heart to knock the old gentleman down. He, on his part, was full of airs and graces and geniality.

"Dear Dick," he said, taking his arm, "this is neighborly of you; it shows your tact to meet me when I had a wish for you. I am in pleasant spirits; and it is then that I desire a friend."

"I am glad to hear you are so happy," retorted Dick bitterly. "There's certainly not much to trouble you."

"No," assented the Admiral, "not much. I got out of it in time; and here—well, here everything pleases me. I am plain in my tastes. Apropos, you have never asked me how I liked my daughter?"

"No," said Dick roundly; "I certainly have not."

"Meaning you will not. And why, Dick? She is my daughter, of course; but then I am a man of the world and a man of taste, and perfectly qualified to give an opinion with impartiality—yes, Dick, with impartiality. Frankly, I am not disappointed in her. She has good looks; she has them from her mother. So I may say I *chose* her looks. She is devoted, quite devoted to me—"

"She is the best woman in the world!" broke out Dick.

"Dick," cried the Admiral, stopping short; "I have been expecting this. Let us—let us go back to the Trevanion Arms, and talk this matter out over a bottle."

"Certainly not," said Dick. "You have had far too much already."

The parasite was on the point of resenting this; but a look at Dick's face, and some recollections of the terms on which they had stood in Paris, came to the aid of his wisdom and restrained him.

"As you please," he said, "although I don't know what you mean— nor care. But let us walk, if you prefer it. You are still a young man; when you are my age—But, however, to continue. You please me, Dick; you have pleased me from the first; and to say truth, Esther is a trifle fantastic, and will be better when she is married. She has means of her own, as of course you are aware. They come, like the looks, from her poor, dear, good creature of a mother. She was blessed in her mother. I mean she shall be blessed in her husband, and you are the man, Dick, you and not another. This very night I will sound her affections."

Dick stood aghast.

"Mr. Van Tromp, I implore you," he said; "do what you please with yourself, but for God's sake, let your daughter alone."

"It is my duty," replied the Admiral, "and between ourselves, you rogue, my inclination too. I am as matchmaking as a dowager. It will be more discreet for you to stay away tonight. Farewell. You leave your case in good hands; I have the tact of these little matters by heart; it is not my first attempt."

All arguments were in vain; the old rascal stuck to his point; nor did Richard conceal from himself how seriously this might injure his prospects, and he fought hard. Once there came a glimmer of hope. The Admiral again proposed an adjournment to the "Trevanion Arms," and when Dick had once more refused, it hung for a moment in the balance whether or not the old toper would return there by himself. Had he done so, of course, Dick could have taken to his heels, and warned Esther of what was coming, and of how it had begun. But the Admiral, after a pause, decided for the brandy at home, and made off in that direction.

We have no details of the sounding.

Next day the Admiral was observed in the parish church, very properly dressed. He found the places, and joined in response and hymn, as to the manner born; and his appearance, as he intended it should, attracted some attention among the worshippers. Old Naseby, for instance, had observed him.

"There was a drunken-looking blackguard opposite us in church," he said to his son as they drove home; "do you know who he was."

"Some fellow—Van Tromp, I believe," said Dick.

"A foreigner, too!" observed the Squire.

Dick could not sufficiently congratulate himself on the escape he had effected. Had the Admiral met him with his father, what would have been the result? And could such a catastrophe be long postponed? It seemed to him as if the storm were nearly ripe; and it was so more nearly than he thought.

He did not go to the cottage in the afternoon, withheld by fear and shame; but when dinner was over at Naseby House, and the Squire had gone off into a comfortable doze, Dick slipped out of the room, and ran across country, in part to save time, in part to save his own courage from growing cold; for he now hated the notion of the cottage or the Admiral, and if he did not hate, at least he feared to think of Esther. He had no clue to her reflections; but he could not conceal from his own heart that he must have sunk in her esteem, and the spectacle of her infatuation galled him like an insult.

He knocked and was admitted. The room looked very much as on his last visit, with Esther at the table and Van Tromp beside the fire; but the expression of the two faces told a very different story. The girl was paler than usual; her eyes were dark, the color seemed to have faded from round about them, and her swiftest glance was as intent as a stare. The appearance of the Admiral, on the other hand, was rosy, and flabby, and moist; his jowl hung over his shirt collar, his smile was loose and wandering, and he had so far relaxed the natural control of his eyes, that one of them was aimed inward, as if to watch the growth of the carbuncle. We are warned against bad judgments; but the Admiral was certainly not sober. He made no attempt to rise when Richard entered, but waved his pipe flightily in the air, and gave a leer of welcome. Esther took as little notice of him as might be.

"Aha! Dick!" cried the painter. "I've been to church; I have, upon my word. And I saw you there, though you didn't see me. And I saw a devilish pretty woman, by Gad. If it were not for this baldness, and a kind of crapulous air I can't disguise from myself—if it weren't for this and that and t'other thing—I—I've forgot what I was saying. Not that that matters, I've heaps of things to say. I'm in a communicative vein tonight. I'll let out all my cats, even unto seventy times seven. I'm in what I call *the* stage, and all I desire is a listener, although he were deaf, to be as happy as Nebuchadnezzar."

Of the two hours which followed upon this it is unnecessary to give more than a sketch. The Admiral was extremely silly, now and then amusing, and never really offensive. It was plain that he kept in view the presence of his daughter, and chose subjects and a character of language that should not offend a lady. On almost any other occasion Dick would have enjoyed the scene. Van Tromp's egotism, flown with drink, struck a pitch above mere vanity. He became candid and explanatory; sought to take his auditors entirely into his confidence, and tell them his inmost conviction about himself. Between his self-knowledge, which was considerable, and his vanity, which was immense, he had created a strange hybrid animal, and called it by his own name. How he would plume his feathers over virtues which would have gladdened the heart of Cæsar or St. Paul; and anon, complete his own portrait with one of those touches of pitiless realism which the satirist so often seeks in vain.

"Now, there's Dick," he said, "he's shrewd; he saw through me the first time we met, and told me so—told me so to my face, which I had the virtue to keep. I bear you no malice for it, Dick; you were right; I am a humbug."

You may fancy how Esther quailed at this new feature of the meeting between her two idols.

And then, again, in a parenthesis:

"That," said Van Tromp, "was when I had to paint those dirty daubs of mine."

And a little further on, laughingly said perhaps, but yet with an air of truth:

"I never had the slightest hesitation in sponging upon any human creature."

Thereupon Dick got up.

"I think perhaps," he said, "we had better all be thinking of going to bed." And he smiled with a feeble and deprecatory smile.

"Not at all," cried the Admiral, "I know a trick worth two of that. Puss here," indicating his daughter, "shall go to bed; and you and I will keep it up till all's blue."

Thereupon Esther arose in sullen glory. She had sat and listened for two mortal hours while her idol defiled himself and sneered away his godhead. One by one, her illusions had departed. And now he wished to order her to bed in her own house! now he called her Puss! now, even as he uttered the words, toppling on his chair, he broke the stem of his tobacco pipe in three! Never did the sheep turn upon her shearer with a more commanding front. Her voice was calm, her enunciation a little slow, but perfectly distinct, and she stood before him as she spoke, in the simplest and most maidenly attitude.

"No," she said, "Mr. Naseby will have the goodness to go home at once, and you will go to bed."

The broken fragments of pipe fell from the Admiral's fingers; he seemed by his countenance to have lived too long in a world unworthy of him; but it is an odd circumstance, he attempted no reply, and sat thunderstruck, with open mouth.

Dick she motioned sharply toward the door, and he could only obey her. In the porch, finding she was close behind him, he ventured to pause and whisper, "You have done right."

"I have done as I pleased," she said. "Can he paint?"

"Many people like his paintings," returned Dick in stifled tones; "I never did; I never said I did," he added, fiercely defending himself before he was attacked.

"I ask you if he can paint. I will not be put off. Can he paint?" she repeated.

"No," said Dick.

"Does he even like it?"

"Not now, I believe."

"And he is drunk?"—she leaned upon the word with hatred.

"He has been drinking."

"Go," she said, and was turning to reenter the house when another thought arrested her. "Meet me tomorrow morning at the stile," she said.

"I will," replied Dick.

And then the door closed behind her, and Dick was alone in the darkness. There was still a chink of light above the sill, a warm, mild glow behind the window; the roof of the cottage and some of the banks and hazels were defined in denser darkness against the sky; but all else was formless, breathless, and noiseless like the pit. Dick remained as she had left him, standing squarely on one foot and resting only on the toe of the other, and as he stood he listened with his soul. The sound of a chair pushed sharply over the floor startled his heart into his mouth; but the silence which had thus been disturbed settled back again at once upon the cottage and its vicinity. What took place during this interval is a secret from the world of men; but when it was over the voice of Esther spoke evenly and without interruption for perhaps half a minute, and as soon as that ceased heavy and uncertain footfalls crossed the parlor and mounted lurching up the stairs.

The girl had tamed her father, Van Tromp had gone obediently to bed; so much was obvious to the watcher in the road. And yet he still waited, straining his ears, and with terror and sickness at his heart; for if Esther had followed her father, if she had even made one movement in this great conspiracy of men and nature to be still, Dick must have had instant knowledge of it from his station before the door; and if she had not moved, must she not have fainted? or might she not be dead?

He could hear the cottage clock deliberately measure out the seconds; time stood still with him; an almost superstitious terror took command of his faculties; at last, he could bear no more, and, springing through the little garden in two bounds, he put his face against the window.

The blind, which had not been drawn fully down, left an open chink about an inch in height along the bottom of the glass, and the whole parlor was thus exposed to Dick's investigation. Esther sat upright at the table, her head resting on her hand, her eyes fixed upon the candle. Her brows were slightly bent, her mouth slightly open; her whole attitude so still and settled that Dick could hardly fancy that she breathed. She had not stirred at the sound of Dick's arrival. Soon after, making a considerable disturbance amid the vast silence of the night, the clock lifted up its voice, whined for a while like a partridge, and then eleven times hooted like a cuckoo. Still Esther continued immovable and gazed upon the candle. Midnight followed, and then one of the morning; and still she had not stirred, nor had Richard Naseby dared to quit the window. And then about half-past one, the candle she had been thus intently watching flared up into a last blaze of paper, and she leaped to her feet with an ejaculation, looked about her once, blew out the light, turned round, and was heard rapidly mounting the staircase in the dark.

Dick was left once more alone to darkness and to that dulled and dogged state of mind when a man thinks that misery must now have done her worst, and is almost glad to think so. He turned and walked slowly toward the stile; she had told him no hour, and he was determined, whenever she came, that she should find him waiting. As he got there the day began to dawn, and he leaned over a hurdle and beheld the shadows flee away. Up went the sun at last out of a bank of clouds that were already disbanding in the east; a herald wind had already sprung up to sweep the leafy earth and scatter the congregated dew drops. "Alas!" thought Dick Naseby, "how can any other day come so distastefully to me?" He still wanted his experience of the morrow.

CHAPTER VII

The elopement

It was probably on the stroke of ten, and Dick had been half asleep for some time against the bank, when Esther came up the road carrying a bundle. Some kind of instinct, or perhaps the distant light footfalls, recalled him, while she was still a good way off, to the possession of his faculties, and he half raised himself and blinked upon the world. It took him some time to recollect his thoughts. He had awakened with a certain blank and childish sense of pleasure, like a man who had received a legacy overnight, but this feeling gradually died away, and was then suddenly and stunningly succeeded by a conviction of the truth. The whole story of the past night sprang into his mind with every detail, as by an exercise of the direct and speedy sense of sight, and he arose from the ditch and, with rueful courage, went to meet his love.

She came up to him walking steady and fast, her face still pale, but to all appearance perfectly composed; and she showed neither surprise, relief, nor pleasure at finding her lover on the spot. Nor did she offer him her hand.

"Here I am," said he.

"Yes," she replied; and then, without a pause or any change of voice, "I want you to take me away," she added.

"Away?" he repeated. "How? Where?"

"Today," she said. "I do not care where it is, but I want you to take me away."

"For how long? I do not understand," gasped Dick.

"I shall never come back here any more," was all she answered.

Wild words uttered, as these were, with perfect quiet of manner and voice, exercise a double influence on the hearer's mind. Dick was confounded; he recovered from astonishment only to fall into doubt and alarm. He looked upon her frozen attitude, so discouraging for a lover to behold, and recoiled from the thoughts which it suggested.

"To me?" he asked. "Are you coming to me, Esther?"

"I want you to take me away," she repeated with weary impatience. "Take me away—take me away from here."

The situation was not sufficiently defined. Dick asked himself with concern whether she were altogether in her right wits. To take her away, to marry her, to work off his hands for her support, Dick was content to do all this; yet he required some show of love upon her part. He was not one of those tough-hided and small-hearted males who would marry their love at the point of the bayonet rather than not marry her at all. He desired that a woman should come to his arms with an attractive willingness, if not with ardor. And Esther's bearing was more that of despair than that of love. It chilled him and taught him wisdom.

"Dearest," he urged, "tell me what you wish, and you shall have it; tell me your thoughts, and then I can advise you. But to go from here without a plan, without forethought, in the heat of a moment, is madder than madness, and can help nothing. I am not speaking like a man, but I speak the truth; and I tell you again, the thing's absurd, and wrong, and hurtful."

She looked at him with a lowering, languid look of wrath.

"So you will not take me?" she said. "Well, I will go alone."

And she began to step forward on her way. But he threw himself before her.

"Esther, Esther!" he cried.

"Let me go—don't touch me—what right have you to interfere? Who are you, to touch me?" she flashed out, shrill with anger.

Then, being made bold by her violence, he took her firmly, almost roughly, by the arm, and held her while he spoke.

"You know well who I am, and what I am, and that I love you. You say I will not help you; but your heart knows the contrary. It is you who will not help me; for you will not tell me what you want. You see—or you could see, if you took the pains to look—how I have waited here all night to be ready at your service. I only asked information; I only urged and beg you to consider; and I still urge you to think better of your fancies. But if your mind is made up, so be it; I will beg no longer; I give you my orders; and I will not allow—not allow you to go hence alone."

She looked at him for a while with cold, unkind scrutiny like one who tries the temper of a tool.

"Well, take me away, then," she said with a sigh

"Good," said Dick. "Come with me to the stables; there we shall get the pony trap and drive to the junction. Tonight you shall be in London. I am yours so wholly that no words can make me more so; and, besides, you know it, and the words are needless. May God help me to be good to you, Esther—may God help me! for I see that you will not."

So, without more speech, they set out together, and were already got some distance from the spot ere he observed that she was still carrying the handbag. She gave it up to him, passively, but when he offered her his arm, merely shook her head and pursed up her lips. The sun shone clearly and pleasantly; the wind was fresh and brisk upon their faces, and smelled racily of woods and meadows. As they went down into the valley of the Thyme, the babble of the stream rose into the air like a perennial laughter. On the faraway hills, sunburst and shadow raced along the slopes and leaped from peak to peak. Earth, air and water, each seemed in better health and had more of the shrewd salt of life in them than upon ordinary mornings; and from east to west, from the lowest glen to the height of heaven, from every look and touch and scent, a human creature could gather the most encouraging intelligence as to the durability and spirit of the universe.

Through all this walked Esther, picking her small steps like a bird, but silent and with a cloud under her thick eyebrows. She seemed insensible, not only of nature, but of the presence of her companion. She was altogether engrossed in herself, and looked neither to right nor to left, but straight before her on the road. When they came to the bridge, however, she halted, leaned on the parapet, and stared for a moment at the clear, brown pool, and swift, transient snowdrift of the rapids.

"I am going to drink," she said; and descended the winding footpath to the margin.

There she drank greedily in her hands and washed her temples with water. The coolness seemed to break, for an instant, the spell that lay upon her; for, instead of hastening forward again in her dull, indefatigable tramp, she stood still where she was, for near a minute, looking straight before her. And Dick, from above on the bridge, where he stood to watch her, saw a strange, equivocal smile dawn slowly on her face and pass away again at once and suddenly, leaving her as grave as ever; and the sense of distance, which it is so cruel for a lover to endure, pressed with every moment more heavily on her companion. Her thoughts were all secret; her heart was locked and bolted; and he stood without, vainly wooing her with his eyes.

"Do you feel better?" asked Dick, as she at last rejoined him; and after the constraint of so long a silence, his voice sounded foreign to his own ears.

She looked at him for an appreciable fraction of a minute ere she answered, and when she did, it was in the monosyllable—"Yes."

Dick's solicitude was nipped and frosted. His words died away on his tongue. Even his eyes, despairing of encouragement, ceased to attend on hers. And they went on in silence through Kirton hamlet, where an old man followed them with his eyes, and perhaps envied them their youth and love; and across the Ivy beck where the mill was splashing and grumbling low thunder to itself in the checkered shadow of the dell, and the miller before the door was beating flour from his hands as he whistled a modulation; and up by the high spinney, whence they saw the mountains upon either hand; and down the hill again to the back courts and offices of Naseby House. Esther had kept ahead all the way, and Dick plodded obediently in her wake; but as they neared the stables, he pushed on and took the lead. He would have preferred her to await him in the road while he went on and brought the carriage back, but after so many repulses and rebuffs he lacked courage to offer the suggestion. Perhaps, too, he felt it wiser to keep his convoy within sight. So they entered the yard in Indian file, like a tramp and his wife.

The groom's eyebrows rose as he received the order for the pony phaeton, and kept rising during all his preparations. Esther stood bolt upright and looked steadily at some chickens in the corner of the yard. Master Richard himself, thought the groom, was not in his ordinary; for in truth, he carried the handbag like a talisman, and either stood listless, or set off suddenly walking in one direction after another with brisk, decisive footsteps. Moreover he had apparently neglected to wash his hands, and bore the air of one returning from a prolonged nutting ramble. Upon the groom's countenance there began to grow up an expression as of one about to whistle. And hardly had the carriage turned the corner and rattled into the high road with this inexplicable pair than the whistle broke forth—prolonged, and low and tremulous; and the groom, already so far relieved, vented the rest of his surprise in one simple English word, friendly to the mouth of Jacktar and the sooty pitman, and hurried to spread the news round the servants' hall of Naseby House. Luncheon would be on the table in little beyond an hour; and the Squire, on sitting down, would hardly fail to ask for Master Richard. Hence, as the intelligent reader can foresee, this groom has a part to play in the imbroglio.

Meantime, Dick had been thinking deeply and bitterly. It seemed to him as if his love had gone from him, indeed, yet gone but a little way; as if he needed but to find the right touch or intonation, and her heart would recognize him and be melted. Yet he durst not open his mouth, and drove in silence till they had passed the main park gates and turned into the crosscut lane along the wall. Then it seemed to him as if it must be now, or never.

"Can't you see you are killing me?" he cried. "Speak to me, look at me, treat me like a human man."

She turned slowly and looked him in the face with eyes that seemed kinder. He dropped the reins and caught her hand, and she made no resistance, although her touch was unresponsive. But when, throwing one arm round her waist, he sought to kiss her lips, not like a lover indeed, not because he wanted to do so, but as a desperate man who puts his fortunes to the touch, she drew away from him, with a knot in her forehead, backed and shied about fiercely with her head, and pushed him from her with her hand. Then there was no room left for doubt, and Dick saw, as clear as sunlight, that she had a distaste or nourished a grudge against him.

"Then you don't love me?" he said, drawing back from her, he also, as though her touch had burnt him; and then, as she made no answer, he repeated with another intonation, imperious and yet still pathetic, "You don't love me, *do* you, *do* you?"

"I don't know," she replied. "Why do you ask me? Oh, how should I know? It has all been lies together—lies, and lies, and lies!"

He cried her name sharply, like a man who has taken a physical hurt, and that was the last word that either of them spoke until they reached Thymebury Junction.

This was a station isolated in the midst of moorlands, yet lying on the great upline to London. The nearest town, Thymebury itself, was seven miles distant along the branch they call the Vale of Thyme Railway. It was now nearly half an hour past noon, the down train had just gone by, and there would be no more traffic at the junction until half-past three, when the local train comes in to meet the up express at a quarter before four. The stationmaster had already gone off to his garden, which was half a mile away in a hollow of the moor; a porter, who was just leaving, took charge of the phaeton, and promised to return it before night to Naseby House; only a deaf, snuffy, and stern old man remained to play propriety for Dick and Esther.

Before the phaeton had driven off, the girl had entered the station and seated herself upon a bench. The endless, empty moorlands stretched before her, entirely unenclosed, and with no boundary but the horizon. Two lines of rails, a wagon shed, and a few telegraph posts, alone diversified the outlook. As for sounds, the silence was unbroken save by the chant of the telegraph wires and the crying of the plovers on the waste. With the approach of midday the wind had more and more fallen, it was now sweltering hot and the air trembled in the sunshine.

Dick paused for an instant on the threshold of the platform. Then, in two steps, he was by her side and speaking almost with a sob.

"Esther," he said, "have pity on me. What have I done? Can you not forgive me? Esther, you loved me once—can you not love me still?"

"How can I tell you? How am I to know?" she answered. "You are all a lie to me—all a lie from first to last. You were laughing at my folly, playing with me like a child, at the very time when you declared you loved me. Which was true? was any of it true? or was it all, all a mockery? I am weary trying to find out. And you say I loved you; I loved my father's friend. I never loved, I never heard of, you, until that man came home and I began to find myself deceived. Give me back my father, be what you were before, and you may talk of love indeed!"

"Then you cannot forgive me—cannot?" he asked.

"I have nothing to forgive," she answered. "You do not understand."

"Is that your last word, Esther?" said he, very white and biting his lip to keep it still.

"Yes, that is my last word," replied she.

"Then we are here on false pretenses, and we stay here no longer," he said. "Had you still loved me, right or wrong, I should have taken you away, because then I could have made you happy. But as it is—I must speak plainly—what you propose is degrading to you and an insult to me, and a rank unkindness to your father. Your father may be this or that, but you should use him like a fellow-creature."

"What do you mean?" she flashed. "I leave him my house and all my money; it is more than he deserves. I wonder you dare speak to me about that man. And besides, it is all he cares for; let him take it, and let me never hear from him again."

"I thought you romantic about fathers," he said.

"Is that a taunt?" she demanded.

"No," he replied, "it is an argument. No one can make you like him, but don't disgrace him in his own eyes. He is old, Esther, old and broken down. Even I am sorry for him, and he has been the loss of all I cared for. Write to your aunt; when I see her answer you can leave quietly and naturally, and I will take you to your aunt's door. But in the meantime you must go home. You have no money, and so you are helpless, and must do as I tell you; and believe me, Esther, I do all for your good, and your good only, so God help me."

She had put her hand into her pocket and withdrawn it empty.

"I counted upon you," she wailed.

"You counted rightly then," he retorted. "I will not, to please you for a moment, make both of us unhappy for our lives; and since I can not marry you, we have only been too long away and must go home at once."

"Dick," she cried suddenly, "perhaps I might—perhaps in time—perhaps—"

"There is no perhaps about the matter," interrupted Dick. "I must go and bring the phaeton."

And with that he strode from the station, all in a glow of passion and virtue. Esther, whose eyes had come alive and her cheeks flushed during these last words, relapsed in a second into a state of petrifaction. She remained without motion during his absence, and when he returned suffered herself to be put back into the phaeton, and driven off on the return journey like an idiot or a tired child. Compared with what she was now, her condition of the morning seemed positively natural. She sat white and cold and silent, and there was no speculation in her eyes. Poor Dick flailed and flailed at the pony, and once tried to whistle, but his courage was going down; huge clouds of despair gathered together in his soul, and from time to time their darkness was divided by a piercing flash of longing and regret. He had lost his love—he had lost his love for good.

The pony was tired, and the hills very long and steep, and the air sultrier than ever, for now the breeze began to fail entirely. It seemed as if this miserable drive would never be done, as if poor Dick would never be able to go away and be comfortably wretched by himself; for all his desire was to escape from her presence, and the reproach of her averted looks. He had lost his love, he thought—he had lost his love for good.

They were already not far from the cottage, when his heart again faltered and he appealed to her once more, speaking low and eagerly in broken phrases.

"I cannot live without your love," he concluded.

"I do not understand what you mean," she replied, and I believe with perfect truth.

"Then," said he, wounded to the quick, "your aunt might come and fetch you herself. Of course you can command me as you please. But I think it would be better so."

"Oh, yes," she said wearily, "better so."

This was the only exchange of words between them till about four o'clock; the phaeton, mounting the lane, "opened out" the cottage between the leafy banks. Thin smoke went straight up from the chimney; the flowers in the garden, the hawthorn in the lane, hung down their heads in the heat; the stillness was broken only by the sound of hoofs. For right before the gate a livery servant rode slowly up and down, leading a saddle horse. And in this last Dick shuddered to identify his father's chestnut.

Alas! poor Richard, what should this portend?

The servant, as in duty bound, dismounted and took the phaeton into his keeping; yet Dick thought he touched his hat to him with something of a grin. Esther, passive as ever, was helped out and crossed the garden with a slow and mechanical gait, and Dick, following close behind her, heard from within the cottage his father's voice upraised in an anathema, and the shriller tones of the Admiral responding in the key of war.

CHAPTER VIII
Battle royal

Squire Naseby, on sitting down to lunch, had inquired for Dick, whom he had not seen since the day before at dinner; and the servant answering awkwardly that Master Richard had come back but had gone out again with the pony phaeton, his suspicions became aroused, and he cross-questioned the man until the whole was out.

It appeared from this report that Dick had been going about for nearly a month with a girl in the Vale—a Miss Van Tromp; that she lived near Lord Trevanion's upper wood; that recently Miss Van Tromp's papa had returned home from foreign parts after a prolonged absence; that this papa was an old gentleman, very chatty and free with his money in the public house—whereupon Mr. Naseby's face became encrimsoned; that the papa, furthermore, was said to be an admiral—whereupon Mr. Naseby spat out a whistle brief and fierce as an oath; that Master Dick seemed very friendly with the papa—"God help him!" said Mr. Naseby; that last night Master Dick had not come in, and today he had driven away in the phaeton with the young lady—

"Young woman," corrected Mr. Naseby.

"Yes, sir," said the man, who had been unwilling enough to gossip from the first, and was now cowed by the effect of his communication on the master. "Young woman, sir!"

"Had they luggage?" demanded the Squire.

"Yes, sir."

Mr. Naseby was silent for a moment, struggling to keep down his emotion, and he mastered it so far as to mount into the sarcastic vein, when he was in the nearest danger of melting into the sorrowful.

"And was this—this Van Dunk with them?" he asked, dwelling scornfully upon the name.

The servant believed not, and being eager to shift the responsibility of speech to other shoulders, suggested that perhaps the master had better inquire further from George the stableman in person.

"Tell him to saddle the chestnut and come with me. He can take the gray gelding; for we may ride fast. And then you can take away this trash," added Mr. Naseby, pointing to the luncheon; and he arose, lordly in his anger, and marched forth upon the terrace to await his horse.

There Dick's old nurse shrunk up to him, for the news went like wildfire over Naseby House, and timidly expressed a hope that there was nothing much amiss with the young master.

"I'll pull him through," the Squire said grimly, as though he meant to pull him through a thrashing mill; "I'll save him from this gang; God help him with the next! He has a taste for low company, and no natural affections to steady him. His father was no society for him; he must go fuddling with a Dutchman, Nance, and now he's caught. Let us pray he'll take the lesson," he added more gravely, "but youth is here to make troubles, and age to pull them out again."

Nance whimpered and recalled several episodes of Dick's childhood, which moved Mr. Naseby to blow his nose and shake her hard by the hand; and then, the horse arriving opportunely, to get himself without delay into the saddle and canter off.

He rode straight, hot spur, to Thymebury, where, as was to be expected, he could glean no tidings of the runaways. They had not been seen at the George; they had not been seen at the station. The shadow darkened on Mr. Naseby's face; the junction did not occur to him; his last hope was for Van Tromp's cottage; thither he bade George guide him, and thither he followed, nursing grief, anxiety and indignation in his heart.

"Here it is, sir," said George, stopping.

"What! on my own land!" he cried. "How's this? I let this place to somebody—M'Whirter or M'Glashan."

"Miss M'Glashan was the young lady's aunt, sir, I believe," returned George.

"Aye—dummies," said the Squire. "I shall whistle for my rent, too. Here, take my horse."

The Admiral, this hot afternoon, was sitting by the window with a long glass. He already knew the Squire by sight, and now, seeing him dismount before the cottage and come striding through the garden, concluded without doubt he was there to ask for Esther's hand.

"This is why the girl is not yet home," he thought: "a very suitable delicacy on young Naseby's part."

And he composed himself with some pomp, answered the loud rattle of the riding whip upon the door with a dulcet invitation to enter, and coming forward with a bow and a smile, "Mr. Naseby, I believe," said he.

The Squire came armed for battle; took in his man from top to toe in one rapid and scornful glance, and decided on a course at once. He must let the fellow see that he understood him.

"You are Mr. Van Tromp?" he returned roughly, and without taking any notice of the proffered hand.

"The same, sir," replied the Admiral. "Pray be seated."

"No, sir," said the Squire point-blank, "I will not be seated. I am told that you are an admiral," he added.

"No, sir, I am not an admiral," returned Van Tromp, who now began to grow nettled and enter into the spirit of the interview.

"Then why do you call yourself one, sir?"

"I have to ask your pardon, I do not," says Van Tromp, as grand as the Pope.

But nothing was of avail against the Squire.

"You sail under false colors from beginning to end," he said. "Your very house was taken under a sham name."

"It is not my house. I am my daughter's guest," replied the Admiral. "If it were my house—"

"Well?" said the Squire, "what then? hey?"

The Admiral looked at him nobly, but was silent.

"Look here," said Mr. Naseby, "this intimidation is a waste of time; it is thrown away on me, sir; it will not succeed with me. I will not permit you even to gain time by your fencing. Now, sir, I presume you understand what brings me here."

"I am entirely at a loss to account for your intrusion," bows and waves Van Tromp.

"I will try to tell you, then. I come here as a father"—down came the riding whip upon the table—"I have right and justice upon my side. I understand your calculations, but you calculated without me. I am a man of the world, and I see through you and your maneuvers. I am dealing now with a conspiracy—I stigmatize it as such, and I will expose it and crush it. And now I order you to tell me how far things have gone, and whither you have smuggled my unhappy son."

"My God, sir!" Van Tromp broke out, "I have had about enough of this. Your son? God knows where he is for me! What the devil have I to do with your son? My daughter is out, for the matter of that; I might ask you where she was, and what would you say to that? But this is all midsummer madness. Name your business distinctly, and be off."

"How often am I to tell you?" cried the Squire. "Where did your daughter take my son today in that cursed pony carriage?"

"In a pony carriage?" repeated Van Tromp.

"Yes, sir—with luggage."

"Luggage?"—Van Tromp had turned a little pale.

"Luggage, I said—luggage!" shouted Naseby. "You may spare me this dissimulation. Where's my son? You are speaking to a father, sir, a father."

"But, sir, if this be true," out came Van Tromp in a new key, "it is I who have an explanation to demand."

"Precisely. There is the conspiracy," retorted Naseby. "Oh!" he added, "I am a man of the world. I can see through and through you."

Van Tromp began to understand.

"You speak a great deal about being a father, Mr. Naseby," said he; "I believe you forget that the appellation is common to both of us. I am at a loss to figure to myself, however dimly, how any man—I have not said any gentleman—could so brazenly insult another as you have been insulting me since you entered this house. For the first time I appreciate your base insinuations, and I despise them and you. You were, I am told, a manufacturer; I am an artist; I have seen better days; I have moved in societies where you would not be received, and dined where you would be glad to pay a pound to see me dining. The so-called aristocracy of wealth, sir, I despise. I refuse to help you; I refuse to be helped by you. There lies the door."

And the Admiral stood forth in a halo.

It was then that Dick entered. He had been waiting in the porch for some time back, and Esther had been listlessly standing by his side. He had put out his hand to bar her entrance, and she had submitted without surprise; and though she seemed to listen, she scarcely appeared to comprehend. Dick, on his part, was as white as a sheet; his eyes burned and his lips trembled with anger as he thrust the door suddenly open, introduced Esther with ceremonious gallantry, and stood forward and knocked his hat firmer on his head like a man about to leap.

"What is all this?" he demanded.

"Is this your father, Mr. Naseby?" inquired the Admiral.

"It is," said the young man.

"I make you my compliments," returned Van Tromp.

"Dick!" cried his father, suddenly breaking forth, "it is not too late, is it? I have come here in time to save you. Come, come away with me—come away from this place."

And he fawned upon Dick with his hands.

"Keep your hands off me," cried Dick, not meaning unkindness, but because his nerves were shattered by so many successive miseries.

"No, no," said the old man, "don't repulse your father, Dick, when he has come here to save you. Don't repulse me, my boy. Perhaps I have not been kind to you, not quite considerate, too harsh; my boy, it was not for want of love. Think of old times. I was kind to you then, was I not? When you were a child, and your mother was with us." Mr. Naseby was interrupted by a sort of sob. Dick stood looking at him in a maze. "Come away," pursued the father in a whisper; "you need not be afraid of any consequences. I am a man of the world, Dick; and she can have no claim on you—no claim, I tell you; and we'll be handsome too, Dick—we'll give them a good round figure, father and daughter, and there's an end."

He had been trying to get Dick toward the door, but the latter stood off.

"You had better take care, sir, how you insult that lady," said the son, as black as night.

"You would not choose between your father and your mistress?" said the father.

"What do you call her, sir?" cried Dick, high and clear.

Forbearance and patience were not among Mr. Naseby's qualities.

"I called her your mistress," he shouted, "and I might have called her a—"

"That is an unmanly lie," replied Dick, slowly.

"Dick!" cried the father, "Dick!"

"I do not care," said the son, strengthening himself against his own heart; "I—I have said it, and it is the truth."

There was a pause.

"Dick," said the old man at last, in a voice that was shaken as by a gale of wind, "I am going. I leave you with your friends, sir—with your friends. I came to serve you, and now I go away a broken man. For years I have seen this coming, and now it has come. You never loved me. Now you have been the death of me. You may boast of that. Now I leave you. God pardon you!"

With that he was gone; and the three who remained together heard his horse's hoofs descend the lane. Esther had not made a sign throughout the interview, and still kept silence now that it was over; but the Admiral, who had once or twice moved forward and drawn back again, now advanced for good.

"You are a man of spirit, sir," said he to Dick; "but though I am no friend to parental interference, I will say that you are heavy on the governor." Then he added with a chuckle: "You began, Richard, with a silver spoon, and here you are in the water like the rest. Work, work, nothing like work. You have parts, you have manners; why, with application, you may die a millionaire!"

Dick shook himself. He took Esther by the hand, looking at her mournfully.

"Then this is farewell," he said.

"Yes," she answered. There was no tone in her voice, and she did not return his gaze.

"Forever," added Dick.

"Forever," she repeated mechanically.

"I have had hard measure," he continued. "In time I believe I could have shown you I was worthy, and there was no time long enough to show how much I loved you. But it was not to be. I have lost all."

He relinquished her hand, still looking at her, and she turned to leave the room.

"Why, what in fortune's name is the meaning of all this?" cried Van Tromp. "Esther, come back!"

"Let her go," said Dick, and he watched her disappear with strangely mingled feelings. For he had fallen into that stage when men have the vertigo of misfortune, court the strokes of destiny, and rush toward anything decisive, that it may free them from suspense though at the cost of ruin. It is one of the many minor forms of suicide.

"She did not love me," he said, turning to her father.

"I feared as much," said he, "when I sounded her. Poor Dick, poor Dick! And yet I believe I am as much cut up as you are. I was born to see others happy."

"You forget," returned Dick, with something like a sneer, "that I am now a pauper."

Van Tromp snapped his fingers.

"Tut!" said he; "Esther has plenty for us all."

Dick looked at him with some wonder. It had never dawned upon him that the shiftless, thriftless, worthless, sponging parasite was yet, after all and in spite of all, not mercenary in the issue of his thoughts; yet so it was.

"Now," said Dick, "I must go."

"Go?" cried Van Tromp. "Where? Not one foot, Mr. Richard Naseby. Here you shall stay in the meantime! and—well, and do something practical—advertise for a situation as private secretary—and when you have it, go and welcome. But in the meantime, sir, no false pride; we must stay with our friends; we must sponge a while on Papa Van Tromp, who has sponged so often upon us."

"By God," cried Dick, "I believe you are the best of the lot."

"Dick, my boy," replied the Admiral, winking, "you mark me, I am not the worst."

"Then why," began Dick, and then paused. "But Esther," he began again, once more to interrupt himself. "The fact is, Admiral," he came out with it roundly now, "your daughter wished to run away from you today, and I only brought her back with difficulty."

"In the pony carriage?" asked the Admiral, with the silliness of extreme surprise.

"Yes," Dick answered.

"Why, what the devil was she running away from?"

Dick found the question unusually hard to answer.

"Why," said he, "you know you're a bit of a rip."

"I behave to that girl, sir, like an archdeacon," replied Van Tromp warmly.

"Well—excuse me—but you know you drink," insisted Dick.

"I know that I was a sheet in the wind's eye, sir, once—once only, since I reached this place," retorted the Admiral. "And even then I was fit for any drawing room. I should like you to tell me how many fathers, lay and clerical, go upstairs every day with a face like a lobster and cod's eyes—and are dull, upon the back of it—not even mirth for the money! No, if that's what she runs for, all I say is, let her run."

"You see," Dick tried it again, "she has fancies—"

"Confound her fancies!" cried Van Tromp. "I used her kindly; she had her own way; I was her father. Besides, I had taken quite a liking to the girl, and meant to stay with her for good. But I tell you what it is, Dick, since she has trifled with you—Oh, yes, she did though!—and since her old papa's not good enough for her—the devil take her, say I."

"You will be kind to her at least?" said Dick.

"I never was unkind to a living soul," replied the Admiral. "Firm I can be, but not unkind."

"Well," said Dick, offering his hand, "God bless you, and farewell."

The Admiral swore by all his gods he should not go. "Dick," he said, "you are a selfish dog; you forget your old Admiral. You wouldn't leave him alone, would you?"

It was useless to remind him that the house was not his to dispose of, that being a class of considerations to which his intelligence was closed; so Dick tore himself off by force, and shouting a good-bye, made off along the lane to Thymebury.

Chapter IX

In which the liberal editor reappears as "deus ex machina"

It was perhaps a week later, as old Mr. Naseby sat brooding in his study, that there was shown in upon him, on urgent business, a little hectic gentleman shabbily attired.

"I have to ask pardon for this intrusion, Mr. Naseby," he said; "but I come here to perform a duty. My card has been sent in, but perhaps you may not know, what it does not tell you, that I am the editor of the Thymebury 'Star.' "

Mr. Naseby looked up, indignant.

"I cannot fancy," he said, "that we have much in common to discuss."

"I have only a word to say—one piece of information to communicate. Some months ago, we had—you will pardon my referring to it, it is absolutely necessary—but we had an unfortunate difference as to facts."

"Have you come to apologize?" asked the Squire, sternly.

"No, sir; to mention a circumstance. On the morning in question, your son, Mr. Richard Naseby—"

"I do not permit his name to be mentioned."

"You will, however, permit me," replied the Editor.

"You are cruel," said the Squire. He was right, he was a broken man.

Then the Editor described Dick's warning visit; and how he had seen in the lad's eye that there was a thrashing in the wind, and had escaped through pity only—so the Editor put it—"through pity only, sir. And oh, sir," he went on, "if you had seen him speaking up for you, I am sure you would have been proud of your son. I know I admired the lad myself, and indeed that's what brings me here."

"I have misjudged him," said the Squire. "Do you know where he is?"

"Yes, sir, he lies sick at Thymebury."

"You can take me to him?"

"I can."

"I pray God he may forgive me," said the father.

And he and the Editor made posthaste for the country town.

Next day the report went abroad that Mr. Richard was reconciled to his father and had been taken home to Naseby House. He was still ailing, it was said, and the Squire nursed him like the proverbial woman. Rumor, in this instance, did no more than justice to the truth; and over the sickbed many confidences were exchanged, and clouds that had been growing for years passed away in a few hours, and as fond mankind loves to hope, for ever. Many long talks had been fruitless in external action, though fruitful for the understanding of the pair; but, at last, one showery Tuesday, the Squire might have been observed upon his way to the cottage in the lane.

The old gentleman had arranged his features with a view to self-command, rather than external cheerfulness; and he entered the cottage on his visit of conciliation with the bearing of a clergyman come to announce a death.

The Admiral and his daughter were both within, and both looked upon their visitor with more surprise than favor.

"Sir," said he to Van Tromp, "I am told I have done you much injustice."

There came a little sound in Esther's throat, and she put her hand suddenly to her heart.

"You have, sir; and the acknowledgment suffices," replied the Admiral. "I am prepared, sir, to be easy with you, since I hear you have made it up with my friend Dick. But let me remind you that you owe some apologies to this young lady also."

"I shall have the temerity to ask for more than her forgiveness," said the Squire. "Miss Van Tromp," he continued, "once I was in great distress, and knew nothing of you or your character; but I believe you will pardon a few rough words to an old man who asks forgiveness from his heart. I have heard much of you since then; for you have a fervent advocate in my house. I believe you will understand that I speak of my son. He is, I regret to say, very far from well; he does not pick up as the doctors had expected; he has a great deal upon his mind, and, to tell you the truth, my girl, if you won't help us, I am afraid I shall lose him. Come, now, forgive him! I was angry with him once myself, and I found I was in the wrong. This is only a misunderstanding, like the other, believe me; and with one kind movement, you may give happiness to him, and to me, and to yourself."

Esther made a movement toward the door, but long before she reached it she had broken forth sobbing.

"It is all right," said the Admiral; "I understand the sex. Let me make you my compliments, Mr. Naseby."

The Squire was too much relieved to be angry.

"My dear," said he to Esther, "you must not agitate yourself."

"She had better go up and see him right away," suggested Van Tromp.

"I had not ventured to propose it," replied the Squire. "Les convenances, I believe—"

"Je m'en fiche," cried the Admiral, snapping his fingers. "She shall go and see my friend Dick. Run and get ready, Esther."

Esther obeyed.

"She has not—has not run away again?" inquired Mr. Naseby, as soon as she was gone.

"No," said Van Tromp, "not again. She is a devilish odd girl, though, mind you that."

"But I cannot stomach the man with the carbuncles," thought the Squire.

And this is why there is a new household and a brand-new baby in Naseby Dower House; and why the great Van Tromp lives in pleasant style upon the shores of England; and why twenty-six individual copies of the Thymebury "Star" are received daily at the door of Naseby House.

THE BODY-SNATCHER

Every night in the year, four of us sat in the small parlor of the George at Debenham—the undertaker, and the landlord, and Fettes, and myself. Sometimes there would be more; but blow high, blow low, come rain or snow or frost, we four would be each planted in his own particular armchair. Fettes was an old drunken Scotchman, a man of education obviously, and a man of some property, since he lived in idleness. He had come to Debenham years ago, while still young, and by a mere continuance of living had grown to be an adopted townsman. His blue camlet cloak was a local antiquity, like the church spire. His place in the parlor at the George, his absence from church, his old, crapulous, disreputable vices, were all things of course in Debenham. He had some vague Radical opinions and some fleeting infidelities, which he would now and again set forth and emphasize with tottering slaps upon the table. He drank rum—five glasses regularly every evening; and for the greater portion of his nightly visit to the George sat, with his glass in his right hand, in a state of melancholy alcoholic saturation. We called him the Doctor, for he was supposed to have some special knowledge of medicine, and had been known, upon a pinch, to set a fracture or reduce a dislocation; but beyond these slight particulars, we had no knowledge of his character and antecedents.

One dark winter night—it had struck nine some time before the landlord joined us—there was a sick man in the George, a great neighboring proprietor suddenly struck down with apoplexy on his way to Parliament; and the great man's still greater London doctor had been telegraphed to his bedside. It was the first time that such a thing had happened in Debenham, for the railway was but newly open, and we were all proportionately moved by the occurrence.

"He's come," said the landlord, after he had filled and lighted his pipe.

"He?" said I. "Who?—not the doctor?"

"Himself," replied our host.

"What is his name?"

"Dr. Macfarlane," said the landlord.

Fettes was far through his third tumbler, stupidly fuddled, now nodding over, now staring mazily around him; but at the last word he seemed to awaken, and repeated the name "Macfarlane" twice, quietly enough the first time, but with sudden emotion at the second.

"Yes," said the landlord, "that's his name, Doctor Wolfe Macfarlane."

Fettes became instantly sober; his eyes awoke, his voice became clear, loud, and steady, his language forcible and earnest. We were all startled by the transformation, as if a man had risen from the dead.

"I beg your pardon," he said. "I am afraid I have not been paying much attention to your talk. Who is this Wolfe Macfarlane?" And then, when he had heard the landlord out, "It cannot be, it cannot be," he added; "and yet I would like well to see him face to face."

"Do you know him, Doctor?" asked the undertaker, with a gasp.

"God forbid!" was the reply. "And yet the name is a strange one; it were too much to fancy two. Tell me, landlord, is he old?"

"Well," said the host, "he's not a young man, to be sure, and his hair is white; but he looks younger than you."

"He is older, though; years older. But," with a slap upon the table, "it's the rum you see in my face—rum and sin. This man, perhaps, may have an easy conscience and a good digestion. Conscience! Hear me speak. You would think I was some good, old, decent Christian, would you not? But no, not I; I never canted. Voltaire might have canted if he'd stood in my shoes; but the brains"—with a rattling fillip on his bald head—"the brains were clear and active, and I saw and made no deductions."

"If you know this doctor," I ventured to remark, after a somewhat awful pause, "I should gather that you do not share the landlord's good opinion."

Fettes paid no regard to me.

"Yes," he said, with sudden decision, "I must see him face to face."

There was another pause, and then a door was closed rather sharply on the first floor, and a step was heard upon the stair.

"That's the doctor," cried the landlord. "Look sharp, and you can catch him."

It was but two steps from the small parlor to the door of the old George Inn; the wide oak staircase landed almost in the street; there was room for a Turkey rug and nothing more between the threshold and the last round of the descent; but this little space was every evening brilliantly lit up, not only by the light upon the stair and the great signal lamp below the sign, but by the warm radiance of the bar-room window. The George thus brightly advertised itself to passers-by in the cold street. Fettes walked steadily to the spot, and we, who were hanging behind, beheld the two men meet, as one of them had phrased it, face to face. Dr. Macfarlane was alert and vigorous. His white hair set off his pale and placid, although energetic, countenance. He was richly dressed in the finest of broadcloth and the whitest of linen, with a great gold watch chain, and studs and spectacles of the same precious material. He wore a broad-folded tie, white and speck-led with lilac, and he carried on his arm a comfortable driving coat of fur. There was no doubt but he became his years, breathing, as he did, of wealth and consideration; and it was a surprising contrast to see our parlor sot—bald, dirty, pimpled, and robed in his old camlet cloak—confront him at the bottom of the stairs.

"Macfarlane!" he said somewhat loudly, more like a herald than a friend.

The great doctor pulled up short on the fourth step, as though the familiarity of the address surprised and somewhat shocked his dignity.

"Toddy Macfarlane!" repeated Fettes.

The London man almost staggered. He stared for the swiftest of seconds at the man before him, glanced behind him with a sort of scare, and then in a startled whisper, "Fettes!" he said, "you!"

"Ay," said the other, "me! Did you think I was dead too? We are not so easy shut of our acquaintance."

"Hush, hush!" exclaimed the doctor. "Hush, hush! this meeting is so unexpected—I can see you are unmanned. I hardly knew you, I con-fess, at first; but I am overjoyed—overjoyed to have this opportunity.

For the present it must be how-d'ye-do and good-by in one, for my fly is waiting, and I must not fail the train; but you shall—let me see— yes—you shall give me your address, and you can count on early news of me. We must do something for you, Fettes. I fear you are out at elbows; but we must see to that for auld lang syne, as once we sang at suppers."

"Money!" cried Fettes; "money from you! The money that I had from you is lying where I cast it in the rain."

Dr. Macfarlane had talked himself into some measure of superiority and confidence, but the uncommon energy of this refusal cast him back into his first confusion.

A horrible, ugly look came and went across his almost venerable countenance. "My dear fellow," he said, "be it as you please; my last thought is to offend you. I would intrude on none. I will leave you my address, however—"

"I do not wish it—I do not wish to know the roof that shelters you," interrupted the other. "I heard your name; I feared it might be you; I wished to know if, after all, there were a God; I know now that there is none. Begone!"

He still stood in the middle of the rug, between the stair and doorway; and the great London physician, in order to escape, would be forced to step to one side. It was plain that he hesitated before the thought of this humiliation. White as he was, there was a dangerous glitter in his spectacles; but while he still paused uncertain, he became aware that the driver of his fly was peering in from the street at this unusual scene, and caught a glimpse at the same time of our little body from the parlor, huddled by the corner of the bar. The presence of so many witnesses decided him at once to flee. He crouched together, brushing on the wainscot, and made a dart like a serpent, striking for the door. But his tribulation was not entirely at an end, for even as he was passing Fettes clutched him by the arm and these words came in a whisper, and yet painfully distinct, "Have you seen it again?"

The great rich London doctor cried out aloud with a sharp, throttling cry; he dashed his questioner across the open space, and, with his hands over his head, fled out of the door like a detected thief. Before it had occurred to one of us to make a movement the fly was already rattling toward the station. The scene was over like a dream, but the dream had left proofs and traces of its passage. Next day the servant found the fine gold spectacles broken on the threshold, and that very night we were all standing breathless by the barroom window, and Fettes at our side, sober, pale and resolute in look.

"God protect us, Mr. Fettes!" said the landlord, coming first into possession of his customary senses. "What in the universe is all this? These are strange things you have been saying."

Fettes turned toward us; he looked us each in succession in the face. "See if you can hold your tongues," said he. "That man Macfarlane is not safe to cross; those that have done so already have repented it too late."

And then, without so much as finishing his third glass, far less waiting for the other two, he bade us good-by and went forth, under the lamp of the hotel, into the black night.

We three turned to our places in the parlor, with the big red fire and four clear candles; and as we recapitulated what had passed the first chill of our surprise soon changed into a glow of curiosity. We sat late; it was the latest session I have known in the old George. Each man, before we parted, had his theory that he was bound to prove; and none of us had any nearer business in this world than to track out the past of our condemned companion, and surprise the secret that he shared with the great London doctor. It is no great boast, but I believe I was a better hand at worming out a story than either of my fellows at the George; and perhaps there is now no other man alive who could narrate to you the following foul and unnatural events.

In his young days Fettes studied medicine in the schools of Edinburgh. He had talent of a kind, the talent that picks up swiftly what it hears and readily retains it for its own. He worked little at home; but he was civil, attentive, and intelligent in the presence of his masters. They soon picked him out as a lad who listened closely and remembered well; nay, strange as it seemed to me when I first heard it, he was in those days well favored and pleased by his exterior. There was, at that period, a certain extramural teacher of anatomy, whom I shall here designate by the letter K. His name was subsequently too well known. The man who bore it skulked through the streets of Edinburgh in disguise, while the mob that applauded at the execution of Burke called loudly for the blood of his employer. But Mr. K—— was then at the top of his vogue; he enjoyed a popularity due partly to his own talent and address, partly to the incapacity of his rival, the university professor. The students, at least, swore by his name, and Fettes believed himself, and was believed by others, to have laid the foundations of success when he had acquired the favor of this meteorically famous man. Mr. K—— was a *bon vivant* as well as an accomplished teacher; he liked a sly allusion no less than a careful preparation. In both capacities Fettes enjoyed and deserved his notice, and by the second year of his attendance he held the half-regular position of second demonstrator or subassistant in his class.

In this capacity, the charge of the theater and lecture room devolved in particular upon his shoulders. He had to answer for the cleanliness of the premises and the conduct of the other students, and it was a part of his duty to supply, receive, and divide the various subjects. It was with a view to this last—at that time very delicate—affair that he was lodged by Mr. K—— in the same wynd, and at last in the same building, with the dissecting room. Here, after a night of turbulent pleasures, his hand still tottering, his sight still misty and confused, he would be called out of bed in the black hours before the winter dawn by the unclean and desperate interlopers who supplied the table. He would open the door to these men, since infamous throughout the land. He would help them with their tragic burden, pay them their sordid price, and remain alone, when they were gone, with the unfriendly relics of humanity. From such a scene he would return to snatch another hour or two of slumber, to repair the abuses of the night, and refresh himself for the labors of the day.

Few lads could have been more insensible to the impressions of a life thus passed among the ensigns of mortality. His mind was closed against all general considerations. He was incapable of interest in the fate and fortunes of another, the slave of his own desires and low ambitions. Cold, light, and selfish in the last resort, he had that modicum of prudence, miscalled morality, which keeps a man from inconvenient drunkenness or punishable theft. He coveted, besides, a measure of consideration from his masters and his fellow pupils, and he had no desire to fail conspicuously in the external parts of life. Thus he made it his pleasure to gain some distinction in his studies, and day after day rendered unimpeachable eye-service to his employer, Mr. K——. For his day of work he indemnified himself by nights of roaring, blackguardly enjoyment; and when that balance had been struck, the organ that he called his conscience declared itself content.

The supply of subjects was a continual trouble to him as well as to his master. In that large and busy class, the raw material of the anatomists kept perpetually running out; and the business thus rendered necessary was not only unpleasant in itself, but threatened dangerous consequences to all who were concerned. It was the policy of Mr. K—— to ask no questions in his dealings with the trade. "They bring the body, and we pay the price," he used to say, dwelling on the alliteration—"*quid pro quo.*" And again, and somewhat profanely, "Ask no questions," he would tell his assistants, "for conscience' sake." There was no understanding that the subjects were provided by the crime of murder. Had that idea been broached to him in words, he would have recoiled in horror; but the lightness of his speech upon so grave a matter was, in itself, an offense against good manners, and a temptation to the men with whom he dealt. Fettes, for instance, had often remarked to himself upon the singular freshness of the bodies. He had been struck again and again by the hangdog, abominable looks of the ruffians who came to him before the dawn; and putting things together clearly in his private thoughts, he perhaps attributed a meaning too immoral and too categorical to the unguarded counsels of his master. He understood his duty, in short, to have three branches: to take what was brought, to pay the price, and to avert the eye from any evidence of crime.

One November morning this policy of silence was put sharply to the test. He had been awake all night with a racking toothache—pacing his room like a caged beast or throwing himself in fury on his bed—and had fallen at last into that profound, uneasy slumber that so often follows on a night of pain, when he was awakened by the third or fourth angry repetition of the concerted signal. There was a thin, bright moonshine; it was bitter cold, windy, and frosty; the town had not yet awakened, but an indefinable stir already preluded the noise and business of the day. The ghouls had come later than usual, and they seemed more than usually eager to be gone. Fettes, sick with sleep, lighted them upstairs. He heard their grumbling Irish voices through a dream; and as they stripped the sack from their sad merchandise he leaned dozing, with his shoulder propped against the wall; he had to shake himself to find the men their money. As he did so his eyes lighted on the dead face. He started; he took two steps nearer, with the candle raised.

"God Almighty!" he cried. "That is Jane Galbraith!"

The men answered nothing, but they shuffled nearer the door.

"I know her, I tell you," he continued. "She was alive and hearty yesterday. It's impossible she can be dead; it's impossible you should have got this body fairly."

"Sure, sir, you're mistaken entirely," said one of the men.

But the other looked Fettes darkly in the eyes, and demanded the money on the spot.

It was impossible to misconceive the threat or to exaggerate the danger. The lad's heart failed him. He stammered some excuses, counted out the sum, and saw his hateful visitors depart. No sooner were they gone than he hastened to confirm his doubts. By a dozen unquestionable marks he identified the girl he had jested with the day before. He saw, with horror, marks upon her body that might well betoken violence. A panic seized him, and he took refuge in his room. There he reflected at length over the discovery that he had made; considered soberly the bearing of Mr. K———'s instructions and the danger to himself of interference in so serious a business, and at last, in sore perplexity, determined to wait for the advice of his immediate superior, the class assistant.

This was a young doctor, Wolfe Macfarlane, a high favorite among all the reckless students, clever, dissipated, and unscrupulous to the last degree. He had traveled and studied abroad. His manners were agreeable and a little forward. He was an authority on the stage, skilful on the ice or the links with skate or golf club; he dressed with nice audacity, and, to put the finishing touch upon his glory, he kept a gig and a strong trotting horse. With Fettes he was on terms of intimacy; indeed, their relative positions called for some community of life; and when subjects were scarce the pair would drive far into the country in Macfarlane's gig, visit and desecrate some lonely graveyard, and return before dawn with their booty to the door of the dissecting room.

On that particular morning Macfarlane arrived somewhat earlier than his wont. Fettes heard him, and met him on the stairs, told him his story, and showed him the cause of his alarm. Macfarlane examined the marks on her body.

"Yes," he said with a nod, "it looks fishy."

"Well, what should I do?" asked Fettes.

"Do?" repeated the other. "Do you want to do anything? Least said soonest mended, I should say."

"Someone else might recognize her," objected Fettes. "She was as well known as the Castle Rock."

"We'll hope not," said Macfarlane, "and if anybody does—well, you didn't, don't you see, and there's an end. The fact is, this has been going on too long. Stir up the mud, and you'll get K—— into the most unholy trouble; you'll be in a shocking box yourself. So will I, if you come to that. I should like to know how any one of us would look, or what the devil we should have to say for ourselves in any Christian witness-box. For me, you know there's one thing certain—that, practically speaking, all our subjects have been murdered."

"Macfarlane!" cried Fettes.

"Come now!" sneered the other. "As if you hadn't suspected it yourself!"

"Suspecting is one thing—"

"And proof another. Yes, I know; and I'm as sorry as you are this should have come here," tapping the body with his cane. "The next best thing for me is not to recognize it; and," he added coolly, "I don't. You may, if you please. I don't dictate, but I think a man of the world would do as I do; and I may add, I fancy that is what K—— would look for at our hands. The question is, Why did he choose us two for his assistants? And I answer, because he didn't want old wives."

This was the tone of all others to affect the mind of a lad like Fettes. He agreed to imitate Macfarlane. The body of the unfortunate girl was duly dissected, and no one remarked or appeared to recognize her.

One afternoon, when his day's work was over, Fettes dropped into a popular tavern and found Macfarlane sitting with a stranger. This was a small man, very pale and dark, with coal black eyes. The cut of his features gave a promise of intellect and refinement which was but feebly realized in his manners, for he proved, upon a nearer acquaintance, coarse, vulgar, and stupid. He exercised, however, a very remarkable control over Macfarlane; issued orders like the Great Bashaw; became inflamed at the least discussion or delay, and commented rudely on the servility with which he was obeyed. This most offensive person took a fancy to Fettes on the spot, plied him with drinks, and honored him with unusual confidences on his past career. If a tenth part of what he confessed were true, he was a very loathsome rogue; and the lad's vanity was tickled by the attention of so experienced a man.

"I'm a pretty bad fellow myself," the stranger remarked, "but Macfarlane is the boy—Toddy Macfarlane, I call him. Toddy, order your friend another glass." Or it might be, "Toddy, you jump up and shut the door." "Toddy hates me," he said again. "Oh, yes, Toddy, you do!"

"Don't you call me that confounded name," growled Macfarlane.

"Hear him! Did you ever see the lads play knife? He would like to do that all over my body," remarked the stranger.

"We medicals have a better way than that," said Fettes. "When we dislike a dead friend of ours, we dissect him."

Macfarlane looked up sharply, as though this jest was scarcely to his mind.

The afternoon passed. Gray, for that was the stranger's name, invited Fettes to join them at dinner, ordered a feast so sumptuous that the tavern was thrown in commotion, and when all was done commanded Macfarlane to settle the bill. It was late before they separated; the man Gray was incapably drunk. Macfarlane, sobered by his fury, chewed the cud of the money he had been forced to squander and the slights he had been obliged to swallow. Fettes, with various liquors singing in his head, returned home with devious footsteps and a mind entirely in abeyance. Next day Macfarlane was absent from the class, and Fettes smiled to himself as he imagined him still squiring the intolerable Gray from tavern to tavern. As soon as the hour of liberty had struck he posted from place to place in quest of his last night's companions. He could find them, however, nowhere; so returned early to his rooms, went early to bed, and slept the sleep of the just.

At four in the morning he was awakened by the well-known signal. Descending to the door, he was filled with astonishment to find Macfarlane with his gig, and in the gig one of those long and ghastly packages with which he was so well acquainted.

"What?" he cried. "Have you been out alone? How did you manage?"

But Macfarlane silenced him roughly, bidding him turn to business. When they had got the body upstairs and laid it on the table, Macfarlane made at first as if he were going away. Then he paused and seemed to hesitate; and then, "You had better look at the face," said he, in tones of some constraint. "You had better," he repeated, as Fettes only stared at him in wonder.

"But where, and how, and when did you come by it?" cried the other.

"Look at the face," was the only answer.

Fettes was staggered; strange doubts assailed him. He looked from the young doctor to the body, and then back again. At last, with a start, he did as he was bidden. He had almost expected the sight that met his eyes, and yet the shock was cruel. To see, fixed in the rigidity of death and naked on that coarse layer of sackcloth, the man whom he had left well clad and full of meat and sin upon the threshold of a tavern, awoke, even in the thoughtless Fettes, some of the terrors of the conscience. It was a *cras tibi* which re-echoed in his soul, that two whom he had known should have come to lie upon these icy tables. Yet these were only secondary thoughts. His first concern regarded Wolfe. Unprepared for a challenge so momentous, he knew not how to look his comrade in the face. He durst not meet his eye, and he had neither words nor voice at his command.

It was Macfarlane himself who made the first advance. He came up quietly behind and laid his hand gently but firmly on the other's shoulder.

"Richardson," said he, "may have the head."

Now Richardson was a student who had long been anxious for that portion of the human subject to dissect. There was no answer, and the murderer resumed: "Talking of business, you must pay me; your accounts, you see, must tally."

Fettes found a voice, the ghost of his own: "Pay you!" he cried. "Pay you for that?"

"Why, yes, of course you must. By all means and on every possible account, you must," returned the other. "I dare not give it for nothing, you dare not take it for nothing; it would compromise us both. This is another case like Jane Galbraith's. The more things are wrong the more we must act as if all were right. Where does old K—— keep his money?"

"There," answered Fettes hoarsely, pointing to a cupboard in the corner.

"Give me the key, then," said the other, calmly, holding out his hand.

There was an instant's hesitation, and the die was cast. Macfarlane could not suppress a nervous twitch, the infinitesimal mark of an immense relief, as he felt the key between his fingers. He opened the cupboard, brought out pen and ink and a paperbook that stood in one compartment, and separated from the funds in a drawer a sum suitable to the occasion.

"Now, look here," he said, "there is the payment made—first proof of your good faith: first step to your security. You have now to clinch it by a second. Enter the payment in your book, and then you for your part may defy the devil."

The next few seconds were for Fettes an agony of thought; but in balancing his terrors it was the most immediate that triumphed. Any future difficulty seemed almost welcome if he could avoid a present quarrel with Macfarlane. He set down the candle which he had been carrying all this time, and with a steady hand entered the date, the nature, and the amount of the transaction.

"And now," said Macfarlane, "it's only fair that you should pocket the lucre. I've had my share already. By the bye, when a man of the world falls into a bit of luck, has a few shillings extra in his pocket—I'm ashamed to speak of it, but there's a rule of conduct in the case. No treating, no purchase of expensive class-books, no squaring of old debts; borrow, don't lend."

"Macfarlane," began Fettes, still somewhat hoarsely, "I have put my neck in a halter to oblige you."

"To oblige me?" cried Wolfe. "Oh, come! You did, as near as I can see the matter, what you downright had to do in self-defense. Suppose I got into trouble, where would you be? This second little matter flows clearly from the first. Mr. Gray is the continuation of Miss Galbraith. You can't begin and then stop. If you begin, you must keep on beginning; that's the truth. No rest for the wicked."

A horrible sense of blackness and the treachery of fate seized hold upon the soul of the unhappy student.

"My God!" he cried, "but what have I done? and when did I begin? To be made a class assistant—in the name of reason, where's the harm in that? Service wanted the position; Service might have got it. Would *he* have been where *I* am now?"

"My dear fellow," said Macfarlane, "what a boy you are! What harm *has* come to you? What harm *can* come to you if you hold your tongue? Why, man, do you know what this life is? There are two squads of us—the lions and the lambs. If you're a lamb, you'll come to lie upon these tables like Gray or Jane Galbraith; if you're a lion, you'll live and drive a horse like me, like K——, like all the world with any wit or courage.

You're staggered at the first. But look at K——! My dear fellow, you're clever, you have pluck. I like you, and K—— likes you. You were born to lead the hunt; and I tell you, on my honor and my experience of life, three days from now you'll laugh at all these scarecrows like a high school boy at a farce."

And with that Macfarlane took his departure and drove off up the wynd in his gig to get under cover before daylight. Fettes was thus left alone with his regrets. He saw the miserable peril in which he stood involved. He saw, with inexpressible dismay, that there was no limit to his weakness, and that, from concession to concession, he had fallen from the arbiter of Macfarlane's destiny to his paid and helpless accomplice. He would have given the world to have been a little braver at the time, but it did not occur to him that he might still be brave. The secret of Jane Galbraith and the cursed entry in the daybook closed his mouth.

Hours passed; the class began to arrive; the members of the unhappy Gray were dealt out to one and to another, and received without remark. Richardson was made happy with the head; and before the hour of freedom rang Fettes trembled with exultation to perceive how far they had already gone toward safety.

For two days he continued to watch, with increasing joy, the dreadful process of disguise.

On the third day Macfarlane made his appearance. He had been ill, he said; but he made up for lost time by the energy with which he directed the students. To Richardson in particular he extended the most valuable assistance and advice, and that student, encouraged by the praise of the demonstrator, burned high with ambitious hopes, and saw the medal already in his grasp.

Before the week was out Macfarlane's prophecy had been fulfilled. Fettes had outlived his terrors and had forgotten his abasement. He began to plume himself upon his courage, and had so arranged the story in his mind that he could look back on these events with an unhealthy pride. Of his accomplice he saw but little. They met, of course, in the business of the class; they received their orders together from Mr. K——. At times they had a word or two in private, and Macfarlane was from first to last particularly kind and jovial. But it was plain that he avoided any reference to their common secret;

and even when Fettes whispered to him that he had cast in his lot with the lions and forsworn the lambs, he only signed to him smilingly to hold his peace.

At length an occasion arose which threw the pair once more into a closer union. Mr. K—— was again short of subjects; pupils were eager, and it was a part of this teacher's pretensions to be always well supplied. At the same time there came the news of a burial in the rustic graveyard of Glencorse. Time has little changed the place in question. It stood then, as now, upon a crossroad, out of call of human habitations, and buried fathoms deep in the foliage of six cedar trees. The cries of the sheep upon the neighboring hills, the streamlets upon either hand, one loudly singing among pebbles, the other dripping furtively from pond to pond, the stir of the wind in mountainous old flowering chestnuts, and once in seven days the voice of the bell and the old tunes of the precentor, were the only sounds that disturbed the silence around the rural church. The Resurrection Man—to use a by-name of the period—was not to be deterred by any of the sanctities of customary piety. It was part of his trade to despise and desecrate the scrolls and trumpets of old tombs, the paths worn by the feet of worshipers and mourners, and the offerings and the inscriptions of bereaved affection. To rustic neighborhoods, where love is more than commonly tenacious, and where some bonds of blood or fellowship unite the entire society of a parish, the body-snatcher, far from being repelled by natural respect, was attracted by the ease and safety of the task. To bodies that had been laid in earth, in joyful expectation of a far different awakening, there came that hasty, lamplit, terror-haunted resurrection of the spade and mattock. The coffin was forced, the cerements torn, and the melancholy relics, clad in sackcloth, after being rattled for hours on moonless byways, were at length exposed to uttermost indignities before a class of gaping boys.

Somewhat as two vultures may swoop upon a dying lamb, Fettes and Macfarlane were to be let loose upon a grave in that green and quiet resting-place. The wife of a farmer, a woman who had lived for sixty years, and been known for nothing but good butter and a godly conversation, was to be rooted from her grave at midnight and carried, dead and naked, to that faraway city that she had always honored with her Sunday's best; the place beside her family was to be empty till the crack of doom; her innocent and almost venerable members to be exposed to that last curiosity of the anatomist.

Late one afternoon the pair set forth, well wrapped in cloaks and furnished with a formidable bottle. It rained without remission—a cold, dense, lashing rain. Now and again there blew a puff of wind, but these sheets of falling water kept it down. Bottle and all, it was a sad and silent drive as far as Penicuik, where they were to spend the evening. They stopped once, to hide their implements in a thick bush not far from the churchyard, and once again at the Fisher's Tryst, to have a toast before the kitchen fire and vary their nips of whiskey with a glass of ale. When they reached their journey's end the gig was housed, the horse was fed and comforted, and the two young doctors in a private room sat down to the best dinner and the best wine the house afforded. The lights, the fire, the beating rain upon the window, the cold, incongruous work that lay before them, added zest to their enjoyment of the meal. With every glass their cordiality increased. Soon Macfarlane handed a little pile of gold to his companion.

"A compliment," he said. "Between friends these little d——d accommodations ought to fly like pipe lights."

Fettes pocketed the money, and applauded the sentiment to the echo. "You are a philosopher," he cried. "I was an ass till I knew you. You and K—— between you, by the Lord Harry! but you'll make a man of me."

"Of course, we shall," applauded Macfarlane. "A man? I tell you, it required a man to back me up the other morning. There are some big, brawling, forty-year-old cowards who would have turned sick at the look of the d——d thing; but not you—you kept your head. I watched you."

"Well, and why not?" Fettes thus vaunted himself. "It was no affair of mine. There was nothing to gain on the one side but disturbance, and on the other I could count on your gratitude, don't you see?" And he slapped his pocket till the gold pieces rang.

Macfarlane somehow felt a certain touch of alarm at these unpleasant words. He may have regretted that he had taught his young companion so successfully, but he had no time to interfere, for the other noisily continued in this boastful strain:

"The great thing is not to be afraid. Now, between you and me, I don't want to hang—that's practical; but for all cant, Macfarlane, I was born with a contempt. Hell, God, Devil, right, wrong, sin, crime, and all the old gallery of curiosities—they may frighten boys, but men of the world, like you and me, despise them. Here's to the memory of Gray!"

It was by this time growing somewhat late. The gig, according to order, was brought round to the door with both lamps brightly shining, and the young men had to pay their bill and take the road. They announced that they were bound for Peebles, and drove in that direction till they were clear of the last houses of the town; then, extinguishing the lamps, returned upon their course, and followed a by-road toward Glencorse. There was no sound but that of their own passage, and the incessant, strident pouring of the rain. It was pitch dark; here and there a white gate or a white stone in the wall guided them for a short space across the night; but for the most part it was at a foot pace, and almost groping, that they picked their way through that resonant blackness to their solemn and isolated destination. In the sunken woods that traverse the neighborhood of the burying-ground the last glimmer failed them, and it became necessary to kindle a match and reillumine one of the lanterns of the gig. Thus, under the dripping trees, and environed by huge and moving shadows, they reached the scene of their unhallowed labors.

They were both experienced in such affairs, and powerful with the spade; and they had scarce been twenty minutes at their task before they were rewarded by a dull rattle on the coffin lid. At the same moment Macfarlane, having hurt his hand upon a stone, flung it carelessly above his head. The grave, in which they now stood almost to the shoulders, was close to the edge of the plateau of the graveyard; and the gig lamp had been propped, the better to illuminate their labors, against a tree, and on the immediate verge of the steep bank descending to the stream. Chance had taken a sure aim with the stone. Then came a clang of broken glass; night fell upon them; sounds alternately dull and ringing announced the bounding of the lantern down the bank, and its occasional collision with the trees. A stone or two, which it had dislodged in its descent, rattled behind it into the profundities of the glen; and then silence, like night, resumed its sway; and they might bend their hearing to its utmost pitch, but naught was to be heard except the rain, now marching to the wind, now steadily falling over miles of open country.

They were so nearly at an end of their abhorred task that they judged it wisest to complete it in the dark. The coffin was exhumed and broken open; the body inserted in the dripping sack and carried between them to the gig; one mounted to keep it in its place, and the other, taking the horse by the mouth, groped along by wall and bush until they reached the wider road by the Fisher's Tryst. Here was a faint, diffused radiancy, which they hailed like daylight; by that they pushed the horse to a good pace and began to rattle along merrily in the direction of the town.

They had both been wetted to the skin during their operations, and now, as the gig jumped among the deep ruts, the thing that stood propped between them fell now upon one and now upon the other. At every repetition of the horrid contact each instinctively repelled it with the greatest haste; and the process, natural although it was, began to tell upon the nerves of the companions. Macfarlane made some ill-favored jest about the farmer's wife, but it came hollowly from his lips, and was allowed to drop in silence. Still their unnatural burden bumped from side to side; and now the head would be laid, as if in confidence, upon their shoulders, and now the drenching sackcloth would flap icily about their faces. A creeping chill began to possess the soul of Fettes. He peered at the bundle, and it seemed somehow larger than at first. All over the countryside, and from every degree of distance, the farm dogs accompanied their passage with tragic ululations; and it grew and grew upon his mind that some unnatural miracle had been accomplished, that some nameless change had befallen the dead body, and that it was in fear of their unholy burden that the dogs were howling.

"For God's sake," said he, making a great effort to arrive at speech, "for God's sake, let's have a light!"

Seemingly Macfarlane was affected in the same direction; for, though he made no reply, he stopped the horse, passed the reins to his companion, got down, and proceeded to kindle the remaining lamp. They had by that time got no farther than the cross-road down to Auchenclinny.

The rain still poured as though the deluge were returning, and it was no easy matter to make a light in such a world of wet and darkness. When at last the flickering blue flame had been transferred to the wick and began to expand and clarify, and shed a wide circle of misty brightness round the gig, it became possible for the two young men to see each other and the thing they had along with them. The rain had molded the rough sacking to the outlines of the body underneath; the head was distinct from the trunk, the shoulders plainly modeled; something at once spectral and human riveted their eyes upon the ghastly comrade of their drive.

For some time Macfarlane stood motionless, holding up the lamp. A nameless dread was swathed, like a wet sheet, about the body, and tightened the white skin upon the face of Fettes; a fear that was meaningless, a horror of what could not be, kept mounting to his brain. Another beat of the watch, and he had spoken. But his comrade forestalled him.

"That is not a woman," said Macfarlane in a hushed voice.

"It was a woman when we put her in," whispered Fettes.

"Hold that lamp," said the other. "I must see her face."

And as Fettes took the lamp his companion untied the fastenings of the sack and drew down the cover from the head. The light fell very clear upon the dark, well-molded features and smooth-shaven cheeks of a too familiar countenance, often beheld in dreams of both of these young men. A wild yell rang up into the night; each leaped from his own side into the roadway; the lamp fell, broke, and was extinguished; and the horse, terrified by this unusual commotion, bounded and went off toward Edinburgh at a gallop, bearing along with it, sole occupant of the gig, the body of the dead and long-dissected Gray.

THE MISADVENTURES OF
JOHN NICHOLSON

I

In which John sows the wind

John Varey Nicholson was stupid; yet, stupider men than he are now sprawling in Parliament, and lauding themselves as the authors of their own distinction. He was of a fat habit, even from boyhood, and inclined to a cheerful and cursory reading of the face of life; and possibly this attitude of mind was the original cause of his misfortunes. Beyond this hint philosophy is silent on his career, and superstition steps in with the more ready explanation that he was detested of the gods.

His father—that iron gentleman—had long ago enthroned himself on the heights of the Disruption Principles. What these are (and in spite of their grim name they are quite innocent) no array of terms would render thinkable to the merely English intelligence; but to the Scot they often prove unctuously nourishing, and Mr. Nicholson found in them the milk of lions. About the period when the churches convene at Edinburgh in their annual assemblies, he was to be seen descending the mound in the company of divers red-headed clergymen: these voluble, he only contributing oracular nods, brief negatives, and the austere spectacle of his stretched upper lip. The names of Candlish and Begg were frequently in these interviews, and occasionally the talk ran on the Residuary Establishment and the doings of one Lee. A stranger to the tight little theological kingdom Scotland might have listened and gathered literally nothing. And Mr. Nicholson (who was not a dull man) knew this, and raged at it. He knew there was a vast world outside, to whom Disruption Principles were as the chatter of the treetop apes; the paper brought him chill whiffs from it; he had met Englishmen who had asked lightly if he did not belong to the Church of Scotland and then had failed to be much interested by his elucidation of that nice point; it was an evil, wild, rebellious world, lying sunk in *dozenedness*, for nothing short of a Scot's word will paint this Scotsman's feelings. And when he entered into his own house in Randolph Crescent (south side), and shut the door behind him, his heart swelled with security. Here, at least, was a citadel impregnable by right-hand defections or left-hand extremes. Here was a family where prayers came at the same hour, where the Sabbath literature was unimpeachably selected, where the guest who should have leaned to any false opinion was instantly set down, and over which there reigned all week, and grew denser on Sundays, a silence that was agreeable to his ear, and a gloom that he found comfortable.

Mrs. Nicholson had died about thirty, and left him with three children: a daughter two years, and a son about eight years younger than John; and John himself, the unlucky bearer of a name infamous in English history. The daughter, Maria, was a good girl—dutiful, pious, dull, but so easily startled that to speak to her was quite a perilous enterprise. "I don't think I care to talk about that, if you please," she would say, and strike the boldest speechless by her unmistakable pain; this upon all topics—dress, pleasure, morality, politics, in which the formula was changed to "my papa thinks otherwise," and even religion, unless it was approached with a particular whining tone of voice. Alexander, the younger brother, was sickly, clever, fond of books and drawing, and full of satirical remarks. In the midst of these, imagine that natural, clumsy, unintelligent, and mirthful animal, John; mighty well-behaved in comparison with other lads, although not up to the mark of the house in Randolph Crescent; full of a sort of blundering affection, full of caresses which were never very warmly received; full of sudden and loud laughter which rang out in that still house like curses. Mr. Nicholson himself had a great fund of humor, of the Scots order—intellectual, turning on the observation of men; his own character, for instance—if he could have seen it in another—would have been a rare feast to him; but his son's empty guffaws over a broken plate, and empty, almost lighthearted remarks, struck him with pain as the indices of a weak mind.

Outside the family John had early attached himself (much as a dog may follow a marquis) to the steps of Alan Houston, a lad about a year older than himself, idle, a trifle wild, the heir to a good estate which was still in the hands of a rigorous trustee, and so royally content with himself that he took John's devotion as a thing of course. The intimacy was gall to Mr. Nicholson; it took his son from the house, and he was a jealous parent; it kept him from the office, and he was a martinet; lastly, Mr. Nicholson was ambitious for his family (in which, and the Disruption Principles, he entirely lived), and he hated to see a son play second fiddle to an idler. After some hesitation, he ordered that the friendship should cease—an unfair command, though seemingly inspired by the spirit of prophecy; and John, saying nothing, continued to disobey the order under the rose.

John was nearly nineteen when he was one day dismissed rather earlier than usual from his father's office, where he was studying the practise of the law. It was Saturday; and except that he had a matter of four hundred pounds in his pocket which it was his duty to hand over to the British Linen Company's Bank, he had the whole afternoon at his disposal. He went by Prince's Street enjoying the mild sunshine, and the little thrill of easterly wind that tossed the flags along that terrace of palaces, and tumbled the green trees in the garden. The band was playing down in the valley under the castle; and when it came to the turn of the pipers, he heard their wild sounds with a stirring of the blood. Something distantly martial woke in him; and he thought of Miss Mackenzie, whom he was to meet that day at dinner.

Now, it is undeniable that he should have gone directly to the bank, but right in the way stood the billiard room of the hotel where Alan was almost certain to be found; and the temptation proved too strong. He entered the billiard room, and was instantly greeted by his friend, cue in hand.

"Nicholson," said he, "I want you to lend me a pound or two till Monday."

"You've come to the right shop, haven't you?" returned John. "I have twopence."

"Nonsense," said Alan. "You can get some. Go and borrow at your tailor's; they all do it. Or I'll tell you what: pop your watch."

"Oh, yes, I dare say," said John. "But how about my father?"

"How is he to know? He doesn't wind it up for you at night, does he?" inquired Alan, at which John guffawed. "No, seriously; I am in a fix," continued the tempter. "I have lost some money to a man here. I'll give it to you tonight, and you can get the heirloom out again on Monday. Come; it's a small service, after all. I would do a good deal more for you."

Whereupon John went forth, and pawned his gold watch under the assumed name of John Froggs, 85 Pleasance. But the nervousness that assailed him at the door of that inglorious haunt—a pawnshop—and the effort necessary to invent the pseudonym which, somehow, seemed to him a necessary part of the procedure, had taken more time than he imagined; and when he returned to the billiard room with the spoils, the bank had already closed its doors.

This was a shrewd knock. "A piece of business had been neglected." He heard these words in his father's trenchant voice, and trembled, and then dodged the thought. After all, who was to know? He must carry four hundred pounds about with him till Monday, when the neglect could be surreptitiously repaired; and meanwhile, he was free to pass the afternoon on the encircling divan of the billiard room, smoking his pipe, sipping a pint of ale, and enjoying to the masthead the modest pleasures of admiration.

None can admire like a young man. Of all youth's passions and pleasures, this is the most common and least alloyed; and every flash of Alan's black eyes; every aspect of his curly head; every graceful reach, every easy, standoff attitude of waiting; ay, and down to his shirt-sleeves and wrist-links, were seen by John through a luxurious glory. He valued himself by the possession of that royal friend, hugged himself upon the thought, and swam in warm azure; his own defects, like vanquished difficulties, becoming things on which to plume himself. Only when he thought of Miss Mackenzie there fell upon his mind a shadow of regret; that young lady was worthy of better things than plain John Nicholson, still known among schoolmates by the derisive name of "Fatty"; and he felt, if he could chalk a cue, or stand at ease, with such careless grace as Alan, he could approach the object of his sentiments with a less crushing sense of inferiority.

Before they parted, Alan made a proposal that was startling in the extreme. He would be at Collette's that night about twelve, he said. Why should not John come there and get the money? To go to Collette's was to see life, indeed; it was wrong; it was against the laws; it partook, in a very dingy manner, of adventure. Were it known, it was the sort of exploit that disconsidered a young man for good with the more serious classes, but gave him a standing with the riotous. And yet Collette's was not a hell; it could not come, without vaulting hyperbole, under the rubric of a gilded saloon; and, if it was a sin to go there, the sin was merely local and municipal. Collette (whose name I do not know how to spell, for I was never in epistolary communication with that hospitable outlaw) was simply an unlicensed publican, who gave suppers after eleven at night, the Edinburgh hour of closing. If you belonged to a club you could get a much better supper at the same hour, and lose not a jot in public esteem. But if you lacked that qualification, and were an hungered, or inclined toward conviviality at unlawful hours, Collette's was your only port. You were very ill-supplied. The company was not recruited from the Senate or the Church, though the Bar was very well represented on the only occasion on which I flew in the face of my country's laws, and, taking my reputation in my hand, penetrated into that grim supper house. And Collette's frequenters, thrillingly conscious of wrongdoing and "that two-handed engine (the policeman) at the door," were perhaps inclined to somewhat feverish excess. But the place was in no sense a very bad one; and it is somewhat strange to me, at this distance of time, how it had acquired its dangerous repute.

In precisely the same spirit as a man may debate a project to ascend the Matterhorn or to cross Africa, John considered Alan's proposal, and, greatly daring, accepted it. As he walked home, the thoughts of this excursion out of the safe places of life into the wild and arduous, stirred and struggled in his imagination with the image of Miss Mackenzie—incongruous and yet kindred thoughts, for did not each imply unusual tightening of the pegs of resolution? did not each woo him forth and warn him back again into himself?

Between these two considerations, at least, he was more than usually moved; and when he got to Randolph Crescent, he quite forgot the four hundred pounds in the inner pocket of his greatcoat, hung up the coat, with its rich freight, upon his particular pin of the hatstand; and in the very action sealed his doom.

II

In which John reaps the whirlwind

About half-past ten it was John's brave good fortune to offer his arm to Miss Mackenzie, and escort her home. The night was chill and starry; all the way eastward the trees of the different gardens rustled and looked black. Up the stone gully of Leith Walk, when they came to cross it, the breeze made a rush and set the flames of the streetlamps quavering; and when at last they had mounted to the Royal Terrace, where Captain Mackenzie lived, a great salt freshness came in their faces from the sea. These phases of the walk remained written on John's memory, each emphasized by the touch of that light hand on his arm; and behind all these aspects of the nocturnal city he saw, in his mind's eye, a picture of the lighted drawing room at home where he had sat talking with Flora; and his father, from the other end, had looked on with a kind and ironical smile. John had read the significance of that smile, which might have escaped a stranger. Mr. Nicholson had remarked his son's entanglement with satisfaction, tinged by humor; and his smile, if it still was a thought contemptuous, had implied consent.

At the captain's door the girl held out her hand, with a certain emphasis; and John took it, and kept it a little longer, and said, "Good night, Flora, dear," and was instantly thrown into much fear by his presumption. But she only laughed, ran up the steps, and rang the bell; and while she was waiting for the door to open, kept close in the porch, and talked to him from that point as out of a fortification. She had a knitted shawl over her head; her blue Highland eyes took the light from the neighboring street lamp and sparkled; and when the door opened and closed upon her, John felt cruelly alone.

He proceeded slowly back along the terrace in a tender glow; and when he came to Greenside Church, he halted in a doubtful mind. Over the crown of the Calton Hill, to his left, lay the way to Collette's, where Alan would soon be looking for his arrival, and where he would now have no more consented to go than he would have wilfully wallowed in a bog; the touch of the girl's hand on his sleeve, and the kindly light in his father's eyes, both loudly forbidding. But right before him was the way home, which pointed only to bed, a place of little ease for one whose fancy was strung to the lyrical pitch, and whose not very ardent heart was just then tumultuously moved. The hilltop, the cool air of the night, the company of the great monuments, the sight of the city under his feet, with its hills and valleys and crossing files of lamps, drew him by all he had of the poetic, and he turned that way; and by that quite innocent deflection, ripened the crop of his venial errors for the sickle of destiny.

On a seat on the hill above Greenside he sat for perhaps half an hour, looking down upon the lamps of Edinburgh, and up at the lamps of heaven. Wonderful were the resolves he formed; beautiful and kindly were the vistas of future life that sped before him. He uttered to himself the name of Flora in so many touching and dramatic keys, that he became at length fairly melted with tenderness, and could have sung aloud. At that juncture a certain creasing in his greatcoat caught his ear. He put his hand into his pocket, pulled forth the envelope that held the money, and sat stupefied. The Calton Hill, about this period, had an ill name of nights; and to be sitting there with four hundred pounds that did not belong to him was hardly wise. He looked up. There was a man in a very bad hat a little on one side of him, apparently looking at the scenery; from a little on the other a second nightwalker was drawing very quietly near. Up jumped John. The envelope fell from his hands; he stooped to get it, and at the same moment both men ran in and closed with him.

A little after, he got to his feet very sore and shaken, the poorer by a purse which contained exactly one penny postage stamp, by a cambric handkerchief, and by the all-important envelope.

Here was a young man on whom, at the highest point of loverly exaltation, there had fallen a blow too sharp to be supported alone; and not many hundred yards away his greatest friend was sitting at supper—ay, and even expecting him. Was it not in the nature of man that he should run there? He went in quest of sympathy—in quest of that droll article that we all suppose ourselves to want when in a strait, and have agreed to call advice; and he went, besides, with vague but rather splendid expectations of relief. Alan was rich, or would be so when he came of age. By a stroke of the pen he might remedy this misfortune, and avert that dreaded interview with Mr. Nicholson, from which John now shrunk in imagination as the hand draws back from fire.

Close under the Calton Hill there runs a certain narrow avenue, part street, part by-road. The head of it faces the doors of the prison; its tail descends into the sunless slums of the Low Calton. On one hand it is overhung by the crags of the hill, on the other by an old graveyard. Between these two the roadway runs in a trench, sparsely lighted at night, sparsely frequented by day, and bordered, when it has cleared the place of tombs, by dingy and ambiguous houses. One of these was the house of Collette; and at his door our ill-starred John was presently beating for admittance. In an evil hour he satisfied the jealous inquiries of the contraband hotelkeeper; in an evil hour he penetrated into the somewhat unsavory interior. Alan, to be sure, was there, seated in a room lighted by noisy gas jets, beside a dirty table-cloth, engaged on a coarse meal, and in the company of several tipsy members of the junior bar. But Alan was not sober; he had lost a thousand pounds upon a horse race, had received the news at dinner-time, and was now, in default of any possible means of extrication, drowning the memory of his predicament. He to help John! The thing was impossible; he couldn't help himself.

"If you have a beast of a father," said he, "I can tell you I have a brute of a trustee."

"I'm not going to hear my father called a beast," said John, with a beating heart, feeling that he risked the last sound rivet of the chain that bound him to life.

But Alan was quite good-natured.

"All right, old fellow," said he. "Mos' respec'able man your father." And he introduced his friend to his companions as "old Nicholson the what-d'ye-call-um's son."

John sat in dumb agony. Collette's foul walls and maculate table-linen, and even down to Collette's villainous casters, seemed like objects in a nightmare. And just then there came a knock and a scurrying; the police, so lamentably absent from the Calton Hill, appeared upon the scene; and the party, taken *flagrante delicto,* with their glasses at their elbow, were seized, marched up to the police office, and all duly summoned to appear as witnesses in the consequent case against that arch-shebeener, Collette.

It was a sorrowful and a mightily sobered company that came forth again. The vague terror of public opinion weighed generally on them all; but there were private and particular horrors on the minds of individuals. Alan stood in dread of his trustees, already sorely tried. One of the group was the son of a country minister, another of a judge; John, the unhappiest of all, had David Nicholson to father, the idea of facing whom on such a scandalous subject was physically sickening. They stood awhile consulting under the buttresses of Saint Giles; thence they adjourned to the lodgings of one of the number in North Castle Street, where (for that matter) they might have had quite as good a supper, and far better drink, than in the dangerous paradise from which they had been routed. There, over an almost tearful glass, they debated their position. Each explained he had the world to lose if the affair went on, and he appeared as a witness. It was remarkable what bright prospects were just then in the very act of opening before each of that little company of youths, and what pious consideration for the feelings of their families began now to well from them. Each, moreover, was in an odd state of destitution. Not one could bear his share of the fine; not one but evinced a wonderful twinkle of hope that each of the others (in succession) was the very man who could step in to make good the deficit. One took a high hand; he could not pay his share; if it went to a trial, he should bolt; he had always felt the English Bar to be his true sphere. Another branched out into touching details about his family, and was not listened to. John, in the midst of this disorderly competition of poverty and meanness, sat stunned, contemplating the mountain bulk of his misfortunes.

At last, upon a pledge that each should apply to his family with a common frankness, this convention of unhappy young asses broke up, went down the common stair, and in the gray of the spring morning, with the streets lying dead empty all about them, the lamps burning on into the daylight in diminished luster, and the birds beginning to sound premonitory notes from the groves of the town gardens, went each his own way with bowed head and echoing footfall.

The rooks were awake in Randolph Crescent; but the windows looked down, discreetly blinded, on the return of the prodigal. John's passkey was a recent privilege; this was the first time it had been used; and, oh! with what a sickening sense of his unworthiness he now inserted it into the well-oiled lock and entered that citadel of the proprieties! All slept; the gas in the hall had been left faintly burning to light his return; a dreadful stillness reigned, broken by the deep ticking of the eight-day clock. He put the gas out, and sat on a chair in the hall, waiting and counting the minutes, longing for any human countenance. But when at last he heard the alarm spring its rattle in the lower story, and the servants begin to be about, he instantly lost heart, and fled to his own room, where he threw himself upon the bed.

III

In which John enjoys the harvest home

Shortly after breakfast, at which he assisted with a highly tragical countenance, John sought his father where he sat, presumably in religious meditation, on the Sabbath mornings. The old gentleman looked up with that sour, inquisitive expression that came so near to smiling and was so different in effect.

"This is a time when I do not like to be disturbed," he said.

"I know that," returned John; "but I have—I want—I've made a dreadful mess of it," he broke out, and turned to the window.

Mr. Nicholson sat silent for an appreciable time, while his unhappy son surveyed the poles in the back green, and a certain yellow cat that was perched upon the wall. Despair sat upon John as he gazed; and he raged to think of the dreadful series of his misdeeds, and the essential innocence that lay behind them.

"Well," said the father, with an obvious effort, but in very quiet tones, "what is it?"

"Maclean gave me four hundred pounds to put in the bank, sir," began John; "and I'm sorry to say that I've been robbed of it!"

"Robbed of it?" cried Mr. Nicholson, with a strong rising inflection. "Robbed? Be careful what you say, John!"

"I can't say anything else, sir; I was just robbed of it," said John, in desperation, sullenly.

"And where and when did this extraordinary event take place?" inquired the father.

"On the Calton Hill about twelve last night."

"The Calton Hill?" repeated Mr. Nicholson. "And what were you doing there at such a time of the night?"

"Nothing, sir," says John.

Mr. Nicholson drew in his breath.

"And how came the money in your hands at twelve last night?" he asked sharply.

"I neglected that piece of business," said John, anticipating comment; and then in his own dialect: "I clean forgot all about it."

"Well," said his father, "it's a most extraordinary story. Have you communicated with the police?"

"I have," answered poor John, the blood leaping to his face. "They think they know the men that did it. I dare say the money will be recovered, if that was all," said he, with a desperate indifference, which his father set down to levity but which sprung from the consciousness of worse behind.

"Your mother's watch, too?" asked Mr. Nicholson.

"Oh, the watch is all right!" cried John. "At least, I mean I was coming to the watch—the fact is, I am ashamed to say, I—I pawned the watch before. Here is the ticket; they didn't find that; the watch can be redeemed; they don't sell pledges." The lad panted out these phrases, one after another, like minute guns; but at the last word, which rang in that stately chamber like an oath, his heart failed him utterly and the dreaded silence settled on father and son.

It was broken by Mr. Nicholson picking up the pawn-ticket. "John Froggs, 85 Pleasance," he read; and then turning upon John, with a brief flash of passion and disgust, "Who is John Froggs?" he cried.

"Nobody," said John. "It was just a name."

"An *alias*," his father commented.

"Oh! I think scarcely quite that," said the culprit; "it's a form, they all do it, the man seemed to understand, we had a great deal of fun over the name—"

He paused at that, for he saw his father wince at the picture like a man physically struck; and again there was silence.

"I do not think," said Mr. Nicholson, at last, "that I am an ungenerous father. I have never grudged you money within reason, for any avowable purpose; you had just to come to me and speak. And now I find that you have forgotten all decency and all natural feeling, and actually pawned—pawned—your mother's watch. You must have had some temptation; I will do you the justice to suppose it was a strong one. What did you want with this money?"

"I would rather not tell you, sir," said John. "It will only make you angry."

"I will not be fenced with," cried his father. "There must be an end of disingenuous answers. What did you want with this money?"

"To lend it to Houston, sir," says John.

"I thought I had forbidden you to speak to that young man?" asked the father.

"Yes, sir," said John; "but I only met him."

"Where?" came the deadly question.

And "In a billiard room" was the damning answer. Thus, had John's single departure from the truth brought instant punishment. For no other purpose but to see Alan would he have entered a billiard room; but he had desired to palliate the fact of his disobedience, and now it appeared that he frequented these disreputable haunts upon his own account.

Once more Mr. Nicholson digested the vile tidings in silence; and when John stole a glance at his father's countenance, he was abashed to see the marks of suffering.

"Well," said the old gentleman, at last, "I cannot pretend not to be simply bowed down. I rose this morning what the world calls a happy man—happy, at least, in a son of whom I thought I could be reasonably proud—"

But it was beyond human nature to endure this longer, and John interrupted almost with a scream. "Oh, wheest!" he cried, "that's not all, that's not the worst of it—it's nothing! How could I tell you were proud of me? Oh! I wish, I wish that I had known; but you always said I was such a disgrace! And the dreadful thing is this: we were all taken up last night, and we have to pay Collette's fine among the six, or we'll be had up for evidence—shebeening it is. They made me swear to tell you; but for my part," he cried, bursting into tears, "I just wish that I was dead!" And he fell on his knees before a chair and hid his face.

Whether his father spoke, or whether he remained long in the room or at once departed, are points lost to history. A horrid turmoil of mind and body; bursting sobs; broken, vanishing thoughts, now of indignation, now of remorse; broken elementary whiffs of consciousness, of the smell of the horsehair on the chair bottom, of the jangling of church bells that now began to make day horrible throughout the confines of the city, of the hard floor that bruised his knees, of the taste of tears that found their way into his mouth: for a period of time, the duration of which I cannot guess, while I refuse to dwell longer on its agony, these were the whole of God's world for John Nicholson.

When at last, as by the touching of a spring, he returned again to clearness of consciousness and even a measure of composure, the bells had but just done ringing, and the Sabbath silence was still marred by the patter of belated feet. By the clock above the fire, as well as by these more speaking signs, the service had not long begun; and the unhappy sinner, if his father had really gone to church, might count on near two hours of only comparative unhappiness. With his father, the superlative degree returned infallibly. He knew it by every shrinking fiber in his body, he knew it by the sudden dizzy whirling of his brain, at the mere thought of that calamity. An hour and a half, perhaps an hour and three-quarters, if the doctor was long-winded, and then would begin again that active agony from which, even in the dull ache of the present, he shrunk as from the bite of fire. He saw, in a vision, the family pew, the somnolent cushions, the Bibles, the psalm-books, Maria with her smelling salts, his father sitting spectacled and critical; and at once he was struck with indignation, not unjustly. It was inhuman to go off to church, and leave a sinner in suspense, unpunished, unforgiven. And at the very touch of criticism, the paternal sanctity was lessened; yet the paternal terror only grew; and the two strands of feeling pushed him in the same direction.

And suddenly there came upon him a mad fear lest his father should have locked him in. The notion had no ground in sense; it was probably no more than a reminiscence of similar calamities in childhood, for his father's room had always been the chamber of inquisition and the scene of punishment; but it stuck so rigorously in his mind that he must instantly approach the door and prove its untruth. As he went, he struck upon a drawer left open in the business table. It was the money drawer, a measure of his father's disarray: the money drawer—perhaps a pointing providence! Who is to decide, when even divines differ between a providence and a temptation? or who, sitting calmly under his own vine, is to pass a judgment on the doings of a poor, hunted dog, slavishly afraid, slavishly rebellious, like John Nicholson on that particular Sunday? His hand was in the drawer, almost before his mind had conceived the hope; and rising to his new situation, he wrote, sitting in his father's chair and using his father's blotting pad, his pitiful apology and farewell:

"MY DEAR FATHER:—I have taken the money, but I will pay it back as soon as I am able. You will never hear of me again. I did not mean any harm by anything, so I hope you will try and forgive me. I wish you would say good-by to Alexander and Maria, but not if you don't want to. I could not wait to see you, really. Please try to forgive me. Your affectionate son,

"JOHN NICHOLSON."

The coins abstracted and the missive written, he could not be gone too soon from the scene of these transgressions; and remembering how his father had once returned from church, on some slight illness, in the middle of the second psalm, he durst not even make a packet of a change of clothes. Attired as he was, he slipped from the paternal doors, and found himself in the cool spring air, the thin spring sunshine, and the great Sabbath quiet of the city, which was now only pointed by the cawing of the rooks. There was not a soul in Randolph Crescent, nor a soul in Queensferry Street; in this outdoor privacy and the sense of escape, John took heart again; and with a pathetic sense of leave-taking, he even ventured up the lane and stood a while, a strange peri at the gates of a quaint paradise, by the west end of St. George's Church. They were singing within; and by a strange chance, the tune was "St. George's, Edinburgh," which bears the name, and was first sung in the choir of that church. "Who is this King of Glory?" went the voices from within; and, to John, this was like the end of all Christian observances, for he was now to be a wild man like Ishmael, and his life was to be cast in homeless places and with godless people.

It was thus, with no rising sense of the adventurous, but in mere desolation and despair, that he turned his back on his native city, and set out on foot for California, with a more immediate eye to Glasgow.

IV

The second sowing

It is no part of mine to narrate the adventures of John Nicholson, which were many, but simply his more momentous misadventures, which were more than he desired, and, by human standards, more than he deserved; how he reached California, how he was rooked, and robbed, and beaten and starved; how he was at last taken up by chari-table folk, restored to some degree of self-complacency, and installed as a clerk in a bank in San Francisco, it would take too long to tell; nor in these episodes were there any marks of the peculiar Nicholsonic destiny, for they were just such matters as befell some thousands of other young adventurers in the same days and places. But once posted in the bank, he fell for a time into a high degree of good fortune, which, as it was only a longer way about to fresh disaster, it behooves me to explain.

It was his luck to meet a young man in what is technically called a "dive," and, thanks to his monthly wages, to extricate this new ac-quaintance from a position of present disgrace and possible danger in the future. This young man was the nephew of one of the Nob Hill magnates, who run the San Francisco Stock Exchange, much as more humble adventurers, in the corner of some public park at home, may be seen to perform the simple artifice of pea and thimble: for their own profit, that is to say, and the discouragement of public gambling. It was thus in his power—and, as he was of grateful temper, it was among the things that he desired—to put John in the way of growing rich; and thus, without thought or industry, or so much as even understanding the game at which he played, but by simply buying and selling what he was told to buy and sell, that plaything of fortune was presently at the head of between eleven and twelve thousand pounds, or, as he reck-oned it, of upward of sixty thousand dollars.

How he had come to deserve this wealth, any more than how he had formerly earned disgrace at home, was a problem beyond the reach of his philosophy. It was true that he had been industrious at the bank, but no more so than the cashier, who had seven small children and was vis-ibly sinking in decline. Nor was the step which had determined his ad-vance—a visit to a dive with a month's wages in his pocket—an act of such transcendent virtue, or even wisdom, as to seem to merit the favor of the gods. From some sense of this, and of the dizzy seesaw—heaven-high—hell-deep—on which men sit clutching; or perhaps fearing that the sources of his fortune might be insidiously traced to some root in the field of petty cash, he stuck to his work, said not a word of his new circumstances, and kept his account with a bank in a different quarter of the town. The concealment, innocent as it seems, was the first step in the second tragicomedy of John's existence.

Meanwhile, he had never written home. Whether from diffidence or shame, or a touch of anger, or mere procrastination, or because (as we have seen) he had no skill in literary arts, or because (as I am sometimes tempted to suppose) there is a law in human nature that prevents young men—not otherwise beasts—from the performance of this simple act of piety—months and years had gone by, and John had never written. The habit of not writing, indeed, was already fixed before he had begun to come into his fortune; and it was only the difficulty of breaking this long silence that withheld him from an instant restitution of the money he had stolen or (as he preferred to call it) borrowed.

In vain he sat before paper, attending on Inspiration; that heavenly nymph, beyond suggesting the words "my dear father," remained obstinately silent; and presently John would crumple up the sheet and decide, as soon as he had "a good chance," to carry the money home in person. And this delay, which is indefensible, was his second step into the snares of fortune.

Ten years had passed, and John was drawing near to thirty. He had kept the promise of his boyhood, and was now of a lusty frame, verging toward corpulence; good features, good eyes, a genial manner, a ready laugh, a long pair of sandy whiskers, a dash of an American accent, a close familiarity with the great American joke, and a certain likeness to a R—y—l P—rs—a—ge, who shall remain nameless for me, made up the man's externals as he could be viewed in society. Inwardly, in spite of his gross body and highly masculine whiskers, he was more like a maiden lady than a man of twenty-nine.

It chanced one day, as he was strolling down Market Street on the eve of his fortnight's holiday, that his eye was caught by certain railway bills, and in very idleness of mind he calculated that he might be home for Christmas if he started on the morrow. The fancy thrilled him with desire, and in one moment he decided he would go.

There was much to be done: his portmanteau to be packed, a credit to be got from the bank where he was a wealthy customer, and certain offices to be transacted for that other bank in which he was a humble clerk; and it chanced, in conformity with human nature, that out of all this business it was the last that came to be neglected. Night found him, not only equipped with money of his own, but once more (as on that former occasion) saddled with a considerable sum of other people's.

Now it chanced there lived in the same boarding house a fellow-clerk of his, an honest fellow, with what is called a weakness for drink—though it might, in this case, have been called a strength, for the victim had been drunk for weeks together without the briefest intermission. To this unfortunate John intrusted a letter with an inclosure of bonds, addressed to the bank manager. Even as he did so he thought he perceived a certain haziness of eye and speech in his trustee; but he was too hopeful to be stayed, silenced the voice of warning in his bosom, and with one and the same gesture committed the money to the clerk, and himself into the hands of destiny.

I dwell, even at the risk of tedium, on John's minutest errors, his case being so perplexing to the moralist; but we have done with them now, the roll is closed, the reader has the worst of our poor hero, and I leave him to judge for himself whether he or John has been the less deserving. Henceforth we have to follow the spectacle of a man who was a mere whip-top for calamity; on whose unmerited misadventures not even the humorist can look without pity, and not even the philosopher without alarm.

That same night the clerk entered upon a bout of drunkenness so consistent as to surprise even his intimate acquaintance. He was speedily ejected from the boarding house; deposited his portmanteau with a perfect stranger, who did not even catch his name; wandered he knew not where, and was at last hove-to, all standing, in a hospital at Sacramento. There, under the impenetrable *alias* of the number of his bed, the crapulous being lay for some more days unconscious of all things, and of one thing in particular: that the police were after him. Two months had come and gone before the convalescent in the Sacramento hospital was identified with Kirkman, the absconding San Francisco clerk; even then, there must elapse nearly a fortnight more till the perfect stranger could be hunted up, the portmanteau recovered, and John's letter carried at length to its destination, the seal still unbroken, the inclosure still intact.

Meanwhile, John had gone upon his holidays without a word, which was irregular; and there had disappeared with him a certain sum of money, which was out of all bounds of palliation. But he was known to be careless, and believed to be honest; the manager besides had a regard for him; and little was said, although something was no doubt thought, until the fortnight was finally at an end, and the time had come for John to reappear. Then, indeed, the affair began to look black; and when inquiries were made, and the penniless clerk was found to have amassed thousands of dollars, and kept them secretly in a rival establishment, the stoutest of his friends abandoned him, the books were overhauled for traces of ancient and artful fraud, and though none were found, there still prevailed a general impression of loss. The telegraph was set in motion; and the correspondent of the bank in Edinburgh, for which place it was understood that John had armed himself with extensive credits, was warned to communicate with the police.

Now this correspondent was a friend of Mr. Nicholson's; he was well acquainted with the tale of John's calamitous disappearance from Edinburgh; and putting one thing with another, hasted with the first word of this scandal, not to the police, but to his friend. The old gentleman had long regarded his son as one dead; John's place had been taken, the memory of his faults had already fallen to be one of those old aches, which awaken again indeed upon occasion, but which we can always vanquish by an effort of the will; and to have the long lost resuscitated in a fresh disgrace was doubly bitter.

"Macewen," said the old man, "this must be hushed up, if possible. If I give you a check for this sum, about which they are certain, could you take it on yourself to let the matter rest?"

"I will," said Macewen. "I will take the risk of it."

"You understand," resumed Mr. Nicholson, speaking precisely, but with ashen lips, "I do this for my family, not for that unhappy young man. If it should turn out that these suspicions are correct, and he has embezzled large sums, he must lie on his bed as he has made it." And then looking up at Macewen with a nod, and one of his strange smiles: "Good-by," said he; and Macewen, perceiving the case to be too grave for consolation, took himself off, and blessed God on his way home that he was childless.

V

The prodigal's return

By a little after noon on the eve of Christmas, John had left his portmanteau in the cloakroom, and stepped forth into Prince's Street with a wonderful expansion of the soul, such as men enjoy on the completion of long-nourished schemes. He was at home again, incognito and rich; presently he could enter his father's house by means of the passkey, which he had piously preserved through all his wanderings; he would throw down the borrowed money; there would be a reconciliation, the details of which he frequently arranged; and he saw himself, during the next month, made welcome in many stately houses at many frigid dinner parties, taking his share in the conversation with the freedom of the man and the traveler, and laying down the law upon finance with the authority of the successful investor. But this programme was not to be begun before evening—not till just before dinner, indeed, at which meal the reassembled family were to sit roseate, and the best wine, the modern fatted calf, should flow for the prodigal's return.

Meanwhile he walked familiar streets, merry reminiscences crowding round him, sad ones also, both with the same surprising pathos. The keen, frosty air; the low, rosy, wintry sun; the castle, hailing him like an old acquaintance; the names of friends on doorplates; the sight of friends whom he seemed to recognize, and whom he eagerly avoided, in the streets; the pleasant chant of the north country accent; the dome of St. George's reminding him of his last penitential moments in the lane, and of that King of Glory whose name had echoed ever since in the saddest corner of his memory; and the gutters where he had learned to slide, and the shop where he had bought his skates, and the stones on which he had trod, and the railings in which he had rattled his clachan as he went to school; and all those thousand and one nameless particulars, which the eye sees without noting, which the memory keeps indeed, yet without knowing, and which taken one with another, build up for us the aspect of the place that we call home: all these besieged him, as he went, with both delight and sadness.

His first visit was for Houston, who had a house on Regent's Terrace, kept for him in old days by an aunt. The door was opened (to his surprise) upon the chain, and a voice asked him from within what he wanted.

"I want Mr. Houston—Mr. Alan Houston," said he.

"And who are ye?" said the voice.

"This is most extraordinary," thought John; and then aloud he told his name.

"No young Mr. John?" cried the voice, with a sudden increase of Scotch accent, testifying to a friendlier feeling.

"The very same," said John.

And the old butler removed his defenses, remarking only, "I thocht ye were that man." But his master was not there; he was staying, it appeared, at the house in Murrayfield; and though the butler would have been glad enough to have taken his place and given all the news of the family, John, struck with a little chill, was eager to be gone. Only, the door was scarce closed again, before he regretted that he had not asked about "that man."

He was to pay no more visits till he had seen his father and made all well at home; Alan had been the only possible exception, and John had not time to go as far as Murrayfield. But here he was on Regent's Terrace; there was nothing to prevent him going round the end of the hill, and looking from without on the Mackenzies' house. As he went, he reflected that Flora must now be a woman of near his own age, and it was within the bounds of possibility that she was married; but this dishonorable doubt he dammed down.

There was the house, sure enough; but the door was of another color, and what was this—two doorplates? He drew nearer; the top one bore, with dignified simplicity, the words, "Mr. Proudfoot"; the lower one was more explicit, and informed the passerby that here was likewise the abode of "Mr. J. A. Dunlop Proudfoot, Advocate." The Proudfoots must be rich, for no advocate could look to have much business in so remote a quarter; and John hated them for their wealth and for their name, and for the sake of the house they desecrated with their presence. He remembered a Proudfoot he had seen at school, not known: a little, whey-faced urchin, the despicable member of some lower class. Could it be this abortion that had climbed to be an advocate, and now lived in the birthplace of Flora and the home of John's tenderest memories? The chill that had first seized upon him when he heard of Houston's absence deepened and struck inward. For a moment, as he stood under the doors of that estranged house, and looked east and west along the solitary pavement of the Royal Terrace, where not a cat was stirring, the sense of solitude and desolation took him by the throat, and he wished himself in San Francisco.

And then the figure he made, with his decent portliness, his whiskers, the money in his purse, the excellent cigar that he now lighted, recurred to his mind in consolatory comparison with that of a certain maddened lad who, on a certain spring Sunday ten years before, and in the hour of church-time silence, had stolen from that city by the Glasgow road. In the face of these changes, it were impious to doubt fortune's kindness. All would be well yet; the Mackenzies would be found, Flora, younger and lovelier and kinder than before; Alan would be found, and would have so nicely discriminated his behavior as to have grown, on the one hand, into a valued friend of Mr. Nicholson's, and to have remained, upon the other, of that exact shade of joviality which John desired in his companions. And so, once more, John fell to work discounting the delightful future: his first appearance in the family pew; his first visit to his uncle Greig, who thought himself so great a financier, and on whose purblind Edinburgh eyes John was to let in the dazzling daylight of the West; and the details in general of that unrivaled transformation scene, in which he was to display to all Edinburgh a portly and successful gentleman in the shoes of the derided fugitive.

The time began to draw near when his father would have returned from the office, and it would be the prodigal's cue to enter. He strolled westward by Albany Street, facing the sunset embers, pleased, he knew not why, to move in that cold air and indigo twilight, starred with streetlamps. But there was one more disenchantment waiting him by the way.

At the corner of Pitt Street he paused to light a fresh cigar; the vesta threw, as he did so, a strong light upon his features, and a man about his own age stopped at sight of it.

"I think your name must be Nicholson," said the stranger. It was too late to avoid recognition; and besides, as John was now actually on the way home, it hardly mattered, and he gave way to the impulse of his nature.

"Great Scott!" he cried, "Beatson!" and shook hands with warmth. It scarce seemed he was repaid in kind.

"So you're home again?" said Beatson. "Where have you been all this long time?"

"In the States," said John—"California. I've made my pile though; and it suddenly struck me it would be a noble scheme to come home for Christmas."

"I see," said Beatson. "Well, I hope we'll see something of you now you're here."

"Oh, I guess so," said John, a little frozen.

"Well, ta-ta," concluded Beatson, and he shook hands again and went.

This was a cruel first experience. It was idle to blink facts; here was John home again, and Beatson—Old Beatson—did not care a rush. He recalled Old Beatson in the past—that merry and affectionate lad—and their joint adventures and mishaps, the window they had broken with a catapult in India Place, the escalade of the castle rock, and many another inestimable bond of friendship; and his hurt surprise grew deeper. Well, after all, it was only on a man's own family that he could count; blood was thicker than water, he remembered; and the net result of this encounter was to bring him to the doorstop of his father's house, with tenderer and softer feelings.

The night had come; the fanlight over the door shone bright; the two windows of the dining room where the cloth was being laid, and the three windows of the drawing room where Maria would be waiting dinner, glowed softlier through yellow blinds. It was like a vision of the past. All this time of his absence, life had gone forward with an equal foot, and the fires and the gas had been lighted, and the meal spread, at the accustomed hours. At the accustomed hour, too, the bell had sounded thrice to call the family to worship. And at the thought, a pang of regret for his demerit seized him; he remembered the things that were good and that he had neglected, and the things that were evil and that he had loved; and it was with a prayer upon his lips that he mounted the steps and thrust the key into the keyhole.

He stepped into the lighted hall, shut the door softly behind him, and stood there fixed in wonder. No surprise of strangeness could equal the surprise of that complete familiarity. There was the bust of Chalmers near the stair railings, there was the clothes brush in the accustomed place; and there, on the hatstand, hung hats and coats that must surely be the same as he remembered. Ten years dropped from his life, as a pin may slip between the fingers; and the ocean, and the mountains, and the mines, and crowded marts and mingled races of San Francisco, and his own fortune and his own disgrace, became, for that one moment, the figures of a dream that was over.

He took off his hat, and moved mechanically toward the stand; and there he found a small change that was a great one to him. The pin that had been his from boyhood, where he had flung his balmoral when he loitered home from the Academy, and his first hat when he came briskly back from college or the office—his pin was occupied. "They might have at least respected my pin!" he thought, and he was moved as by a slight, and began at once to recollect that he was here an interloper, in a strange house, which he had entered almost by a burglary, and where at any moment he might be scandalously challenged.

He moved at once, his hat still in his hand, to the door of his father's room, opened it, and entered. Mr. Nicholson sat in the same place and posture as on that last Sunday morning; only he was older, and grayer, and sterner; and as he now glanced up and caught the eye of his son, a strange commotion and a dark flush sprung into his face.

"Father," said John, steadily, and even cheerfully, for this was a moment against which he was long ago prepared, "father, here I am, and here is the money that I took from you. I have come back to ask your forgiveness, and to stay Christmas with you and the children."

"Keep your money," said the father, "and go!"

"Father!" cried John; "for God's sake don't receive me this way. I've come for—"

"Understand me," interrupted Mr. Nicholson; "you are no son of mine; and in the sight of God, I wash my hands of you. One last thing I will tell you; one warning I will give you; all is discovered, and you are being hunted for your crimes; if you are still at large it is thanks to me; but I have done all that I mean to do; and from this time forth I would not raise one finger—not one finger—to save you from the gallows! And now," with a low voice of absolute authority, and a single weighty gesture of the finger, "and now—go!"

VI

The house at Murrayfield

How John passed the evening, in what windy confusion of mind, in what squalls of anger and lulls of sick collapse, in what pacing of streets and plunging into public houses, it would profit little to relate. His misery, if it were not progressive, yet tended in no way to diminish; for in proportion as grief and indignation abated, fear began to take their place. At first, his father's menacing words lay by in some safe drawer of memory, biding their hour. At first, John was all thwarted affection and blighted hope; next bludgeoned vanity raised its head again, with twenty mortal gashes: and the father was disowned even as he had disowned the son. What was this regular course of life, that John should have admired it? what were these clock-work virtues, from which love was absent? Kindness was the test, kindness the aim and soul; and judged by such a standard, the discarded prodigal—now rapidly drowning his sorrows and his reason in successive drams—was a creature of a lovelier morality than his self-righteous father. Yes, he was the better man; he felt it, glowed with the consciousness, and entering a public house at the corner of Howard Place (whither he had somehow wandered) he pledged his own virtues in a glass—perhaps the fourth since his dismissal. Of that he knew nothing, keeping no account of what he did or where he went; and in the general crashing hurry of his nerves, unconscious of the approach of intoxication. Indeed, it is a question whether he were really growing intoxicated, or whether at first the spirits did not even sober him. For it was even as he drained this last glass that his father's ambiguous and menacing words—popping from their hiding place in memory—startled him like a hand laid upon his shoulder. "Crimes, hunted, the gallows." They were ugly words; in the ears of an innocent man, perhaps all the uglier; for if some judicial error were in act against him, who should set a limit to its grossness or to how far it might be pushed? Not John, indeed; he was no believer in the powers of innocence, his cursed experience pointing in quite other ways; and his fears, once wakened, grew with every hour and hunted him about the city streets.

It was, perhaps, nearly nine at night; he had eaten nothing since lunch, he had drunk a good deal, and he was exhausted by emotion, when the thought of Houston came into his head. He turned, not merely to the man as a friend, but to his house as a place of refuge. The danger that threatened him was still so vague that he knew neither what to fear nor where he might expect it; but this much at least seemed undeniable, that a private house was safer than a public inn. Moved by these counsels, he turned at once to the Caledonian Station, passed (not without alarm) into the bright lights of the approach, redeemed his portmanteau from the cloakroom, and was soon whirling in a cab along the Glasgow road. The change of movement and position, the sight of the lamps twinkling to the rear, and the smell of damp and mold and rotten straw which clung about the vehicle, wrought in him strange alternations of lucidity and mortal giddiness.

"I have been drinking," he discovered; "I must go straight to bed, and sleep." And he thanked Heaven for the drowsiness that came upon his mind in waves.

From one of these spells he was awakened by the stoppage of the cab; and, getting down, found himself in quite a country road, the last lamp of the suburb shining some way below, and the high walls of a garden rising before him in the dark. The Lodge (as the place was named) stood, indeed, very solitary. To the south it adjoined another house, but standing in so large a garden as to be well out of cry; on all other sides, open fields stretched upward to the woods of Corstorphine Hill, or backward to the dells of Ravelston, or downward toward the valley of the Leith. The effect of seclusion was aided by the great height of the garden walls, which were, indeed, conventual, and, as John had tested in former days, defied the climbing schoolboy. The lamp of the cab threw a gleam upon the door and the not brilliant handle of the bell.

"Shall I ring for ye?" said the cabman, who had descended from his perch and was slapping his chest, for the night was bitter.

"I wish you would," said John, putting his hand to his brow in one of his accesses of giddiness.

The man pulled at the handle, and the clanking of the bell replied from further in the garden; twice and thrice he did it, with sufficient intervals; in the great, frosty silence of the night, the sounds fell sharp and small.

"Does he expect ye?" asked the driver, with that manner of familiar interest that well became his port-wine face; and when John had told him no, "Well, then," said the cabman, "if ye'll tak' my advice of it, we'll just gang back. And that's disinterested, mind ye, for my stables are in the Glesgie road."

"The servants must hear," said John.

"Hout!" said the driver. "He keeps no servants here, man. They're a' in the town house; I drive him often; it's just a kind of a hermitage, this."

"Give me the bell," said John; and he plucked at it like a man desperate.

The clamor had not yet subsided before they heard steps upon the gravel, and a voice of singular nervous irritability cried to them through the door, "Who are you, and what do you want?"

"Alan," said John, "it's me—it's Fatty—John, you know. I'm just come home, and I've come to stay with you."

There was no reply for a moment, and then the door was opened.

"Get the portmanteau down," said John to the driver.

"Do nothing of the kind," said Alan; and then to John, "Come in here a moment. I want to speak to you."

John entered the garden, and the door was closed behind him. A candle stood on the gravel walk, winking a little in the drafts; it threw inconstant sparkles on the clumped holly, struck the light and darkness to and fro like a veil on Alan's features, and sent his shadow hovering behind him. All beyond was inscrutable; and John's dizzy brain rocked with the shadow. Yet even so, it struck him that Alan was pale, and his voice, when he spoke, unnatural.

"What brings you here tonight?" he began. "I don't want, God knows, to seem unfriendly; but I cannot take you in, Nicholson; I cannot do it."

"Alan," said John, "you've just got to! You don't know the mess I'm in; the governor's turned me out, and I daren't show my face in an inn, because they're down on me for murder or something!"

"For what?" cried Alan, starting.

"Murder, I believe," says John.

"Murder!" repeated Alan, and passed his hand over his eyes. "What was that you were saying?" he asked again.

"That they were down on me," said John. "I'm accused of murder, by what I can make out; and I've really had a dreadful day of it, Alan, and I can't sleep on the roadside on a night like this—at least, not with a portmanteau," he pleaded.

"Hush!" said Alan, with his head on one side; and then, "Did you hear nothing?" he asked.

"No," said John thrilling, he knew not why, with communicated terror. "No, I heard nothing; why?" And then, as there was no answer, he reverted to his pleading: "But I say, Alan, you've just got to take me in. I'll go right away to bed if you have anything to do. I seem to have been drinking; I was that knocked over. I wouldn't turn you away, Alan, if you were down on your luck."

"No?" returned Alan. "Neither will I you, then. Come and let's get your portmanteau."

The cabman was paid, and drove off down the long, lamp-lighted hill, and the two friends stood on the sidewalk beside the portmanteau till the last rumble of the wheels had died in silence. It seemed to John as though Alan attached importance to this departure of the cab; and John, who was in no state to criticize, shared profoundly in the feeling.

When the stillness was once more perfect, Alan shouldered the portmanteau, carried it in, and shut and locked the garden door; and then, once more, abstraction seemed to fall upon him, and he stood with his hand on the key, until the cold began to nibble at John's fingers.

"Why are we standing here?" asked John.

"Eh?" said Alan blankly.

"Why, man, you don't seem yourself," said the other.

"No, I'm not myself," said Alan; and he sat down on the portmanteau and put his face in his hands.

John stood beside him swaying a little, and looking about him at the swaying shadows, the flitting sparkles, and the steady stars overhead, until the windless cold began to touch him through his clothes on the bare skin. Even in his bemused intelligence, wonder began to awake.

"I say, let's come on to the house," he said at last.

"Yes, let's come on to the house," repeated Alan.

And he rose at once, reshouldered the portmanteau, and taking the candle in his other hand, moved forward to the Lodge. This was a long, low building, smothered in creepers; and now, except for some chinks of light between the dining room shutters, it was plunged in darkness and silence.

In the hall Alan lighted another candle, gave it to John, and opened the door of a bedroom.

"Here," said he; "go to bed. Don't mind me, John. You'll be sorry for me when you know."

"Wait a bit," returned John; "I've got so cold with all that standing about. Let's go into the dining room a minute. Just one glass to warm me, Alan."

On the table in the hall stood a glass, and a bottle with a whisky label on a tray. It was plain the bottle had been just opened, for the cork and corkscrew lay beside it.

"Take that," said Alan, passing John the whisky, and then with a certain roughness pushed his friend into the bedroom, and closed the door behind him.

John stood amazed; then he shook the bottle, and, to his further wonder, found it partly empty. Three or four glasses were gone. Alan must have uncorked the bottle of whisky and drank three or four glasses, one after the other, without sitting down, for there was no chair, and that in his own cold lobby on this freezing night! It fully explained his eccentricities, John reflected sagely, as he mixed himself a grog. Poor Alan! He was drunk; and what a dreadful thing was drink, and what a slave to it poor Alan was, to drink in this unsociable, uncomfortable fashion! The man who would drink alone, except for health's sake—as John was now doing—was a man utterly lost. He took the grog out, and felt hazier, but warmer. It was hard work opening the portmanteau and finding his night things; and before he was undressed, the cold had struck home to him once more. "Well," said he; "just a drop more. There's no sense in getting ill with all this other trouble." And presently dreamless slumber buried him.

When John awoke it was day. The low winter sun was already in the heavens, but his watch had stopped, and it was impossible to tell the hour exactly. Ten, he guessed it, and made haste to dress, dismal reflections crowding on his mind. But it was less from terror than from regret that he now suffered; and with his regret there were mingled cutting pangs of penitence. There had fallen upon him a blow, cruel, indeed, but yet only the punishment of old misdoing; and he had rebelled and plunged into fresh sin. The rod had been used to chasten, and he had bit the chastening fingers. His father was right; John had justified him; John was no guest for decent people's houses, and no fit associate for decent people's children. And had a broader hint been needed, there was the case of his old friend. John was no drunkard, though he could at times exceed; and the picture of Houston drinking neat spirits at his hall table struck him with something like disgust. He hung back from meeting his old friend. He could have wished he had not come to him; and yet, even now, where else was he to turn?

These musings occupied him while he dressed, and accompanied him into the lobby of the house. The door stood open on the garden; doubtless, Alan had stepped forth; and John did as he supposed his friend had done. The ground was hard as iron, the frost still rigorous; as he brushed among the hollies, icicles jingled and glittered in their fall; and wherever he went, a volley of eager sparrows followed him. Here were Christmas weather and Christmas morning duly met, to the delight of children. This was the day of reunited families, the day to which he had so long looked forward, thinking to awake in his own bed in Randolph Crescent, reconciled with all men and repeating the footprints of his youth; and here he was alone, pacing the alleys of a wintery garden and filled with penitential thoughts.

And that reminded him: why was he alone? and where was Alan? The thought of the festal morning and the due salutations reawakened his desire for his friend, and he began to call for him by name. As the sound of his voice died away, he was aware of the greatness of the silence that environed him. But for the twittering of the sparrows and the crunching of his own feet upon the frozen snow, the whole windless world of air hung over him entranced, and the stillness weighed upon his mind with a horror of solitude.

Still calling at intervals, but now with a moderated voice, he made the hasty circuit of the garden, and finding neither man nor trace of man in all its evergreen coverts, turned at last to the house. About the house the silence seemed to deepen strangely. The door, indeed, stood open as before; but the windows were still shuttered, the chimneys breathed no stain into the bright air, there sounded abroad none of that low stir (perhaps audible rather to the ear of the spirit than to the ear of the flesh) by which a house announces and betrays its human lodgers. And yet Alan must be there—Alan locked in drunken slumbers, forgetful of the return of day, of the holy season, and of the friend whom he had so coldly received and was now so churlishly neglecting. John's disgust redoubled at the thought; but hunger was beginning to grow stronger than repulsion, and as a step to breakfast, if nothing else, he must find and arouse this sleeper.

He made the circuit of the bedroom quarters. All, until he came to Alan's chamber, were locked from without, and bore the marks of a prolonged disuse. But Alan's was a room in commission, filled with clothes, knicknacks, letters, books, and the conveniences of a solitary man. The fire had been lighted; but it had long ago burned out, and the ashes were stone cold. The bed had been made, but it had not been slept in.

Worse and worse, then; Alan must have fallen where he sat, and now sprawled brutishly, no doubt, upon the dining room floor.

The dining room was a very long apartment, and was reached through a passage; so that John, upon his entrance, brought but little light with him, and must move toward the windows with spread arms, groping and knocking on the furniture. Suddenly he tripped and fell his length over a prostrate body. It was what he had looked for, yet it shocked him; and he marveled that so rough an impact should not have kicked a groan out of the drunkard. Men had killed themselves ere now in such excesses, a dreary and degraded end that made John shudder. What if Alan were dead? There would be a Christmas day!

By this, John had his hand upon the shutters, and flinging them back, beheld once again the blessed face of the day. Even by that light the room had a discomfortable air. The chairs were scattered, and one had been overthrown; the tablecloth, laid as if for dinner, was twitched upon one side, and some of the dishes had fallen to the floor. Behind the table lay the drunkard, still unaroused, only one foot visible to John.

But now that light was in the room, the worst seemed over; it was a disgusting business, but not more than disgusting; and it was with no great apprehension that John proceeded to make the circuit of the table: his last comparatively tranquil moment for that day. No sooner had he turned the corner, no sooner had his eyes alighted on the body, than he gave a smothered, breathless cry, and fled out of the room and out of the house.

It was not Alan who lay there, but a man well up in years, of stern countenance and iron-gray locks; and it was no drunkard, for the body lay in a black pool of blood, and the open eyes stared upon the ceiling.

To and fro walked John before the door. The extreme sharpness of the air acted on his nerves like an astringent, and braced them swiftly. Presently, he not relaxing in his disordered walk, the images began to come clearer and stay longer in his fancy, and next the power of thought came back to him, and the horror and danger of the situation rooted him to the ground.

He grasped his forehead, and staring on one spot of gravel, pieced together what he knew and what he suspected. Alan had murdered some one: possibly "that man" against whom the butler chained the door in Regent's Terrace; possibly another; some one at least; a human soul, whom it was death to slay and whose blood lay spilled upon the floor. This was the reason of the whisky drinking in the passage, of his unwillingness to welcome John, of his strange behavior and bewildered words; this was why he had started at and harped upon the name of murder; this was why he had stood and harkened, or sat and covered his eyes, in the black night. And now he was gone, now he had basely fled; and to all his perplexities and dangers John stood heir.

"Let me think—let me think," he said, aloud, impatiently, even pleadingly, as if to some merciless interrupter. In the turmoil of his wits, a thousand hints and hopes and threats and terrors dinning continuously in his ears, he was like one plunged in the hubbub of a crowd. How was he to remember—he, who had not a thought to spare—that he was himself the author, as well as the theater, of so much confusion? But in hours of trial the junto of man's nature is dissolved, and anarchy succeeds.

It was plain he must stay no longer where he was, for here was a new Judicial Error in the very making. It was not so plain where he must go, for the old Judicial Error, vague as a cloud, appeared to fill the habitable world; whatever it might be, it watched for him, fullgrown, in Edinburgh; it must have had its birth in San Francisco; it stood guard no doubt, like a dragon, at the bank where he should cash his credit; and though there were doubtless many other places, who should say in which of them it was not ambushed? No, he could not tell where he was to go; he must not lose time on these insolubilities. Let him go back to the beginning. It was plain he must stay no longer where he was. It was plain, too, that he must not flee as he was, for he could not carry his portmanteau, and to flee and leave it, was to plunge deeper in the mire. He must go, leave the house unguarded, find a cab, and return—return after an absence? Had he courage for that?

And just then he spied a stain about a hand's breadth on his trouser leg, and reached his finger down to touch it. The finger was stained red; it was blood; he stared upon it with disgust, and awe, and terror, and in the sharpness of the new sensation, fell instantly to act.

He cleansed his finger in the snow, returned into the house, drew near with hushed footsteps to the dining room door, and shut and locked it. Then he breathed a little freer, for here at least was an oaken barrier between himself and what he feared. Next, he hastened to his room, tore off the spotted trousers which seemed in his eyes a link to bind him to the gallows, flung them in a corner, donned another pair, breathlessly crammed his night things into his portmanteau, locked it, swung it with an effort from the ground, and with a rush of relief came forth again under the open heavens.

The portmanteau, being of occidental build, was no featherweight; it had distressed the powerful Alan; and as for John, he was crushed under its bulk, and the sweat broke upon him thickly. Twice he must set it down to rest before he reached the gate; and when he had come so far, he must do as Alan did, and take his seat upon one corner. Here, then, he sat a while and panted; but now his thoughts were sensibly lightened; now, with the trunk standing just inside the door, some part of his dissociation from the house of crime had been effected, and the cabman need not pass the garden wall. It was wonderful how that relieved him; for the house, in his eyes, was a place to strike the most cursory beholder with suspicion, as though the very windows had cried murder.

But there was to be no remission of the strokes of fate. As he thus sat, taking breath in the shadow of the wall and hopped about by sparrows, it chanced that his eye roved to the fastening of the door; and what he saw plucked him to his feet. The thing locked with a spring; once the door was closed, the bolt shut of itself! and without a key, there was no means of entering from without.

He saw himself obliged to one of two distasteful and perilous alternatives; either to shut the door altogether and set his portmanteau out upon the wayside, a wonder to all beholders; or to leave the door ajar, so that any thievish tramp or holiday schoolboy might stray in and stumble on the grisly secret. To the last, as the least desperate, his mind inclined; but he must first insure himself that he was unobserved. He peered out, and down the long road: it lay dead empty. He went to the corner of the by-road that comes by way of Dean; there also not a passenger was stirring. Plainly it was, now or never, the high tide of his affairs; and he drew the door as close as he durst, slipped a pebble in the chink, and made off downhill to find a cab.

Halfway down a gate opened, and a troop of Christmas children sallied forth in the most cheerful humor, followed more soberly by a smiling mother.

"And this is Christmas day!" thought John; and could have laughed aloud in tragic bitterness of heart.

VII

A Tragicomedy in a cab

In front of Donaldson's Hospital, John counted it good fortune to perceive a cab a great way off, and by much shouting and waving of his arm to catch the notice of the driver. He counted it good fortune, for the time was long to him till he should have done forever with the Lodge; and the further he must go to find a cab, the greater the chance that the inevitable discovery had taken place, and that he should return to find the garden full of angry neighbors. Yet when the vehicle drew up he was sensibly chagrined to recognize the port-wine cabman of the night before. "Here," he could but reflect, "here is another link in the Judicial Error."

The driver, on the other hand, was pleased to drop again upon so liberal a fare; and as he was a man—the reader must already have perceived—of easy, not to say familiar, manners, he dropped at once into a vein of friendly talk, commenting on the weather, on the sacred season, which struck him chiefly in the light of a day of liberal gratuities, on the chance which had reunited him to a pleasing customer, and on the fact that John had been (as he was pleased to call it) visibly "on the randan" the night before.

"And ye look dreidful bad the-day, sir, I must say that," he continued. "There's nothing like a dram for ye—if ye'll take my advice of it; and bein' as it's Christmas, I'm no saying," he added with a fatherly smile, "but what I would join ye mysel'."

John had listened with a sick heart.

"I'll give you a dram when we've got through," said he, affecting a sprightliness which sat on him unhandsomely, "and not a drop till then. Business first, and pleasure afterward."

With this promise the jarvey was prevailed upon to clamber to his place and drive, with hideous deliberation, to the door of the Lodge. There were no signs as yet of any public emotion; only, two men stood not far off in talk, and their presence, seen from afar, set John's pulses buzzing. He might have spared himself his fright, for the pair were lost in some dispute of a theological complexion, and with lengthened upper lip and enumerating fingers, pursued the matter of their difference, and paid no heed to John.

But the cabman proved a thorn in the flesh. Nothing would keep him on his perch; he must clamber down, comment upon the pebble in the door (which he regarded as an ingenious but unsafe device), help John with the portmanteau, and enliven matters with a flow of speech, and especially of questions, which I thus condense:

"He'll no be here himsel', will he? No? Well, he's an eccentric man—a fair oddity—if ye ken the expression. Great trouble with his tenants, they tell me. I've driven the fam'ly for years. I drove a cab at his father's waddin'. What'll your name be?—I should ken your face. Baigrey, ye say? There were Baigreys about Gilmerton; ye'll be one of that lot? Then this'll be a friend's portmantie, like? Why? Because the name upon it's Nucholson! Oh, if ye're in a hurry that's another job. Waverley Brig'? Are ye for away?"

So the friendly toper prated and questioned and kept John's heart in a flutter. But to this also, as to other evils under the sun, there came a period; and the victim of circumstances began at last to rumble toward the railway terminus at Waverley Bridge. During the transit, he sat with raised glasses in the frosty chill and moldy fetor of his chariot, and glanced out sidelong on the holiday face of things, the shuttered shops, the crowds along the pavement, much as the rider in the Tyburn cart may have observed the concourse gathering to his execution.

At the station his spirits rose again; another stage of his escape was fortunately ended—he began to spy blue water. He called a railway porter, and bade him carry the portmanteau to the cloakroom: not that he had any notion of delay; flight, instant flight was his design, no matter whither; but he had determined to dismiss the cabman ere he named, or even chose his destination, thus possibly balking the Judicial Error of another link. This was his cunning aim, and now with one foot on the roadway, and one still on the coach step, he made haste to put the thing in practise, and plunged his hand into his trousers pocket.

There was nothing there!

Oh, yes; this time he was to blame. He should have remembered, and when he deserted his bloodstained pantaloons, he should not have deserted along with them his purse. Make the most of his error, and then compare it with the punishment! Conceive his new position, for I lack words to picture it; conceive him condemned to return to that house, from the very thought of which his soul revolted, and once more to expose himself to capture on the very scene of the misdeed; conceive him linked to the moldy cab and the familiar cabman. John cursed the cabman silently, and then it occurred to him that he must stop the incarceration of his portmanteau; that, at least, he must keep close at hand, and he turned to recall the porter. But his reflections, brief as they had appeared, must have occupied him longer than he supposed, and there was the man already returning with the receipt.

Well, that was settled; he had lost his portmanteau also; for the sixpence with which he had paid the Murrayfield Toll was one that had strayed alone into his waistcoat pocket, and unless he once more successfully achieved the adventure of the house of crime, his portmanteau lay in the cloakroom in eternal pawn, for lack of a penny fee. And then he remembered the porter, who stood suggestively attentive, words of gratitude hanging on his lips.

John hunted right and left; he found a coin—prayed God that it was a sovereign—drew it out, beheld a halfpenny, and offered it to the porter.

The man's jaw dropped.

"It's only a halfpenny!" he said, startled out of railway decency.

"I know that," said John piteously.

And here the porter recovered the dignity of man.

"Thank you, sir," said he, and would have returned the base gratuity. But John, too, would none of it; and as they struggled, who must join in but the cabman?

"Hoots, Mr. Baigrey," said he, "you surely forgot what day it is!"

"I tell you I have no change!" cried John.

"Well," said the driver, "and what then? I would rather give a man a shillin' on a day like this than put him off with a derision like a bawbee. I'm surprised at the like of you, Mr. Baigrey!"

"My name is not Baigrey!" broke out John, in mere childish temper and distress.

"You told me it was yoursel'," said the cabman.

"I know I did; and what the devil right had you to ask?" cried the unhappy one.

"Oh, very well," said the driver. "I know my place, if you know yours—if you know yours!" he repeated, as one who should imply grave doubt; and muttered inarticulate thunders, in which the grand old name of gentleman was taken seemingly in vain.

Oh, to have been able to discharge this monster, whom John now perceived, with tardy clear-sightedness, to have begun betimes the festivities of Christmas! But far from any such ray of consolation visiting the lost, he stood bare of help and helpers, his portmanteau sequestered in one place, his money deserted in another and guarded by a corpse; himself, so sedulous of privacy, the cynosure of all men's eyes about the station; and, as if these were not enough mischances, he was now fallen in ill-blood with the beast to whom his poverty had linked him! In ill-blood, as he reflected dismally, with the witness who perhaps might hang or save him! There was no time to be lost; he durst not linger any longer in that public spot; and whether he had recourse to dignity or conciliation, the remedy must be applied at once. Some happily surviving element of manhood moved him to the former.

"Let us have no more of this," said he, his foot once more upon the step. "Go back to where we came from."

He had avoided the name of any destination, for there was now quite a little band of railway folk about the cab, and he still kept an eye upon the court of justice and labored to avoid concentric evidence. But here again the fatal jarvey outmaneuvered him.

"Back to the Ludge?" cried he, in shrill tones of protest.

"Drive on at once!" roared John, and slammed the door behind him, so that the crazy chariot rocked and jingled.

Forth trundled the cab into the Christmas streets, the fare within plunged in the blackness of a despair that neighbored on unconsciousness, the driver on the box digesting his rebuke and his customer's duplicity. I would not be thought to put the pair in competition; John's case was out of all parallel. But the cabman, too, is worth the sympathy of the judicious; for he was a fellow of genuine kindliness and a high sense of personal dignity incensed by drink; and his advances had been cruelly and publicly rebuffed. As he drove, therefore, he counted his wrongs, and thirsted for sympathy and drink. Now, it chanced he had a friend, a publican, in Queensferry Street, from whom, in view of the sacredness of the occasion, he thought he might extract a dram. Queensferry Street lies something off the direct road to Murrayfield. But then there is the hilly crossroad that passes by the valley of the Leith and the Dean Cemetery; and Queensferry Street is on the way to that. What was to hinder the cabman, since his horse was dumb, from choosing the crossroad, and calling on his friend in passing? So it was decided; and the charioteer, already somewhat mollified, turned aside his horse to the right.

John, meanwhile, sat collapsed, his chin sunk upon his chest, his mind in abeyance. The smell of the cab was still faintly present to his senses, and a certain leaden chill about his feet; all else had disappeared in one vast oppression of calamity and physical faintness. It was drawing on to noon—two-and-twenty hours since he had broken bread; in the interval, he had suffered tortures of sorrow and alarm, and been partly tipsy; though it was impossible to say he slept, yet when the cab stopped and the cabman thrust his head into the window, his attention had to be recalled from depths of vacancy.

"If you'll no *stand* me a dram," said the driver, with a well-merited severity of tone and manner, "I dare say ye'll have no objection to my taking one mysel'?"

"Yes—no—do what you like," returned John; and then, as he watched his tormentor mount the stairs and enter the whisky shop, there floated into his mind a sense as of something long ago familiar. At that he started fully awake, and stared at the shop fronts. Yes, he knew them; but when? and how? Long since, he thought; and then, casting his eye through the front glass, which had been recently occluded by the figure of the jarvey, he beheld the treetops of the rookery in Randolph Crescent. He was close to home—home, where he had thought, at that hour, to be sitting in the well-remembered drawing room in friendly converse; and, instead—!

It was his first impulse to drop into the bottom of the cab; his next, to cover his face with his hands. So he sat, while the cabman toasted the publican, and the publican toasted the cabman, and both reviewed the affairs of the nation; so he still sat, when his master condescended to return, and drive off at last downhill, along the curve of Lynedoch Place; but even so sitting, as he passed the end of his father's street, he took one glance from between shielding fingers, and beheld a doctor's carriage at the door.

"Well, just so," thought he; "I'll have killed my father! And this is Christmas day!"

If Mr. Nicholson died, it was down this same road he must journey to the grave; and down this road, on the same errand, his wife had preceded him years before; and many other leading citizens, with the proper trappings, and attendance of the end. And now, in that frosty, ill-smelling, straw-carpeted, and ragged-cushioned cab, with his breath congealing on the glasses, where else was John himself advancing to?

The thought stirred his imagination, which began to manufacture many thousand pictures, bright and fleeting, like the shapes in a kaleidoscope; and now he saw himself, ruddy and comforted, sliding in the gutter; and, again, a little wo-begone, bored urchin tricked forth in crape and weepers, descending this same hill at the foot's pace of mourning coaches, his mother's body just preceding him; and yet again, his fancy, running far in front, showed him his destination—now standing solitary in the low sunshine, with the sparrows hopping on the threshold and the dead man within staring at the roof—and now, with a sudden change, thronged about with white-faced, hand-uplifting neighbors, and the doctor bursting through their midst and fixing his stethoscope as he went, the policeman shaking a sagacious head beside the body. It was to this he feared that he was driving; in the midst of this he saw himself arrive, heard himself stammer faint explanations, and felt the hand of the constable upon his shoulder. Heavens! how he wished he had played the manlier part; how he despised himself that he had fled that fatal neighborhood when all was quiet, and should now be tamely traveling back when it was thronging with avengers!

Any strong degree of passion lends, even to the dullest, the forces of the imagination. And so now he dwelt on what was probably awaiting him at the end of this distressful drive—John, who saw things little, remembered them less, and could not have described them at all, beheld in his mind's eye the garden of the Lodge, detailed as in a map; he went to and fro in it, feeding his terrors; he saw the hollies, the snowy borders, the paths where he had sought Alan, the high, conventual walls, the shut door—what! was the door shut? Ay, truly, he had shut it—shut in his money, his escape, his future life—shut it with these hands, and none could now open it! He heard the snap of the spring lock like something bursting in his brain, and sat astonished.

And then he woke again, terror jarring through his vitals. This was no time to be idle; he must be up and doing, he must think. Once at the end of this ridiculous cruise, once at the Lodge door, there would be nothing for it but to turn the cab and trundle back again. Why, then, go so far? why add another feature of suspicion to a case already so suggestive? why not turn at once? It was easy to say, turn; but whither? He had nowhere now to go to; he could never—he saw it in letters of blood—he could never pay that cab; he was saddled with that cab forever. Oh, that cab! his soul yearned and burned, and his bowels sounded to be rid of it. He forgot all other cares. He must first quit himself of this ill-smelling vehicle and of the human beast that guided it—first do that; do that, at least; do that at once.

And just then the cab suddenly stopped, and there was his persecutor rapping on the front glass. John let it down, and beheld the port-wine countenance inflamed with intellectual triumph.

"I ken wha ye are!" cried the husky voice. "I mind ye now. Ye're a Nucholson. I drove ye to Hermiston to a Christmas party, and ye came back on the box, and I let ye drive."

It is a fact. John knew the man; they had been even friends. His enemy, he now remembered, was a fellow of great good nature—endless good nature—with a boy; why not with a man? Why not appeal to his better side? He grasped at the new hope.

"Great Scott! and so you did," he cried, as if in a transport of delight, his voice sounding false in his own ears. "Well, if that's so, I've something to say to you. I'll just get out, I guess. Where are we, anyway?"

The driver had fluttered his ticket in the eyes of the branch-toll keeper, and they were now brought to on the highest and most solitary part of the by-road. On the left, a row of fieldside trees beshaded it; on the right, it was bordered by naked fallows, undulating downhill to the Queensferry Road; in front, Corstorphine Hill raised its snow-bedabbled, darkling woods against the sky. John looked all about him, drinking the clear air like wine; then his eyes returned to the cabman's face as he sat, not ungleefully, awaiting John's communication, with the air of one looking to be tipped.

The features of that face were hard to read, drink had so swollen them, drink had so painted them, in tints that varied from brick red to mulberry. The small gray eyes blinked, the lips moved, with greed; greed was the ruling passion; and though there was some good nature, some genuine kindliness, a true human touch, in the old toper, his greed was now so set afire by hope, that all other traits of character lay dormant. He sat there a monument of gluttonous desire.

John's heart slowly fell. He had opened his lips, but he stood there and uttered nought. He sounded the well of his courage, and it was dry. He groped in his treasury of words, and it was vacant. A devil of dumbness had him by the throat; the devil of terror babbled in his ears; and suddenly, without a word uttered, with no conscious purpose formed in his will, John whipped about, tumbled over the roadside wall, and began running for his life across the fallows.

He had not gone far, he was not past the midst of the first field, when his whole brain thundered within him, "Fool! You have your watch!" The shock stopped him, and he faced once more toward the cab. The driver was leaning over the wall, brandishing his whip, his face empurpled, roaring like a bull. And John saw (or thought) that he had lost the chance. No watch would pacify the man's resentment now; he would cry for vengeance also. John would be had under the eye of the police; his tale would be unfolded, his secret plumbed, his destiny would close on him at last, and forever.

He uttered a deep sigh; and just as the cabman, taking heart of grace, was beginning at last to scale the wall, his defaulting customer fell again to running, and disappeared into the further fields.

VIII

Singular instance of the utility of passkeys

Where he ran at first, John never very clearly knew; nor yet how long a time elapsed ere he found himself in the by-road near the lodge of Ravelston, propped against the wall, his lungs heaving like bellows, his legs leaden-heavy, his mind possessed by one sole desire—to lie down and be unseen. He remembered the thick coverts round the quarry-hole pond, an untrodden corner of the world where he might surely find concealment till the night should fall. Thither he passed down the lane; and when he came there, behold! he had forgotten the frost, and the pond was alive with young people skating, and the pondside coverts were thick with lookers-on. He looked on a while himself. There was one tall, graceful maiden, skating hand in hand with a youth, on whom she bestowed her bright eyes perhaps too patently; and it was strange with what anger John beheld her. He could have broken forth in curses; he could have stood there, like a mortified tramp, and shaken his fist and vented his gall upon her by the hour—or so he thought; and the next moment his heart bled for the girl. "Poor creature, it's little she knows!" he sighed. "Let her enjoy herself while she can!" But was it possible, when Flora used to smile at him on the Braid ponds, she could have looked so fulsome to a sick-hearted bystander?

The thought of one quarry, in his frozen wits, suggested another; and he plodded off toward Craig Leith. A wind had sprung up out of the northwest; it was cruel keen, it dried him like a fire, and racked his finger-joints. It brought clouds, too; pale, swift, hurrying clouds, that blotted heaven and shed gloom upon the earth. He scrambled up among the hazeled rubbish heaps that surround the caldron of the quarry, and lay flat upon the stones. The wind searched close along the earth, the stones were cutting and icy, the bare hazels wailed about him; and soon the air of the afternoon began to be vocal with those strange and dismal harpings that herald snow. Pain and misery turned in John's limbs to a harrowing impatience and blind desire of change; now he would roll in his harsh lair, and when the flints abraded him, was almost pleased; now he would crawl to the edge of the huge pit and look dizzily down. He saw the spiral of the descending roadway, the steep crags, the clinging bushes, the peppering of snow-wreaths, and far down in the bottom, the diminished crane. Here, no doubt, was a way to end it. But it somehow did not take his fancy.

And suddenly he was aware that he was hungry; ay, even through the tortures of the cold, even through the frosts of despair, a gross, desperate longing after food, no matter what, no matter how, began to wake and spur him. Suppose he pawned his watch? But no, on Christmas day—this was Christmas day!—the pawnshop would be closed. Suppose he went to the public house at Blackhall, and offered the watch, which was worth ten pounds, in payment for a meal of bread and cheese? The incongruity was too remarkable; the good folks would either put him to the door, or only let him in to send for the police. He turned his pockets out one after another; some San Francisco tramcar checks, one cigar, no lights, the passkey to his father's house, a pocket-handkerchief, with just a touch of scent: no, money could be raised on none of these. There was nothing for it but to starve; and after all, what mattered it? That also was a door of exit.

He crept close among the bushes, the wind playing round him like a lash; his clothes seemed as thin as paper, his joints burned, his skin curdled on his bones. He had a vision of a high-lying cattle drive in California, and the bed of a dried stream with one muddy pool, by which the vaqueros had encamped; splendid sun over all, the big bonfire blazing, and strips of cow browning and smoking on a skewer of wood; how warm it was, how savory the steam of scorching meat! And then again he remembered his manifold calamities and burrowed and wallowed in the sense of disgrace and shame. And next he was entering Frank's restaurant in Montgomery Street, San Francisco; he had ordered a pan-stew and venison chops, of which he was immoderately fond, and as he sat waiting, Munroe, the good attendant, brought him a whisky punch; he saw the strawberries float on the delectable cup, he heard the ice chink about the straws. And then he woke again to his detested fate, and found himself sitting, humped together, in the windy combe of quarry refuse—darkness thick about him, thin flakes of snow flying here and there like rags of paper, and the strong shuddering of his body clashing his teeth like a hiccough.

We have seen John in nothing but the stormiest condition; we have seen him reckless, desperate, tried beyond his moderate powers; of his daily self, cheerful, regular, not unthrifty, we have seen nothing; and it may thus be a surprise to the reader, to learn that he was studiously careful of his health. This favorite preoccupation now awoke. If he was to sit there and die of cold, there would be mighty little gained; better the police cell and the chances of a jury trial, than the miserable certainty of death at a dikeside before the next winter's dawn, or death a little later in the gas-lighted wards of an infirmary.

He rose on aching legs, and stumbled here and there among the rubbish heaps, still circumvented by the yawning crater of the quarry; or perhaps he only thought so, for the darkness was already dense, the snow was growing thicker, and he moved like a blind man, and with a blind man's terrors. At last he climbed a fence, thinking to drop into the road, and found himself staggering, instead, among the iron furrows of a plowland, endless, it seemed, as a whole county. And next he was in a wood, beating among young trees; and then he was aware of a house with many lighted windows, Christmas carriages waiting at the doors, and Christmas drivers (for Christmas has a double edge) becoming swiftly hooded with snow. From this glimpse of human cheerfulness, he fled like Cain; wandered in the night, unpiloted, careless of whither he went; fell, and lay, and then rose again and wandered further; and at last, like a transformation scene, behold him in the lighted jaws of the city, staring at a lamp which had already donned the tilted nightcap of the snow. It came thickly now, a "Feeding Storm"; and while he yet stood blinking at the lamp, his feet were buried. He remembered something like it in the past, a streetlamp crowned and caked upon the windward side with snow, the wind uttering its mournful hoot, himself looking on, even as now; but the cold had struck too sharply on his wits, and memory failed him as to the date and sequel of the reminiscence.

His next conscious moment was on the Dean Bridge; but whether he was John Nicholson of a bank in a California street, or some former John, a clerk in his father's office, he had now clean forgotten. Another blank, and he was thrusting his passkey into the door-lock of his father's house.

Hours must have passed. Whether crouched on the cold stones or wandering in the fields among the snow, was more than he could tell; but hours had passed. The finger of the hall clock was close on twelve; a narrow peep of gas in the hall lamp shed shadows; and the door of the back room—his father's room—was open and emitted a warm light. At so late an hour, all this was strange; the lights should have been out, the doors locked, the good folk safe in bed. He marveled at the irregularity, leaning on the hall table; and marveled to find himself there; and thawed and grew once more hungry, in the warmer air of the house.

The clock uttered its premonitory catch; in five minutes Christmas day would be among the days of the past—Christmas!—what a Christmas! Well, there was no use waiting; he had come into that house, he scarce knew how; if they were to thrust him forth again, it had best be done at once; and he moved to the door of the back room and entered.

Oh, well, then he was insane, as he had long believed.

There, in his father's room at midnight, the fire was roaring and the gas blazing; the papers, the sacred papers—to lay a hand on which was criminal—had all been taken off and piled along the floor; a cloth was spread, and a supper laid, upon the business table; and in his father's chair a woman, habited like a nun, sat eating. As he appeared in the doorway, the nun rose, gave a low cry, and stood staring. She was a large woman, strong, calm, a little masculine, her features marked with courage and good sense; and as John blinked at her, a faint resemblance dodged about his memory, as when a tune haunts us, and yet will not be recalled.

"Why, it's John!" cried the nun.

"I dare say I'm mad," said John, unconsciously following King Lear; "but, upon my word, I do believe you're Flora."

"Of course I am," replied she.

"And yet it is not Flora at all," thought John; Flora was slender, and timid, and of changing color, and dewy-eyed; and had Flora such an Edinburgh accent? But he said none of these things, which was perhaps as well. What he said was, "Then why are you a nun?"

"Such nonsense!" said Flora. "I'm a sick-nurse; and I am here nursing your sister, with whom, between you and me, there is precious little the matter. But that is not the question. The point is: How do you come here? and are you not ashamed to show yourself?"

"Flora," said John, sepulchrally, "I haven't eaten anything for three days. Or, at least, I don't know what day it is; but I guess I'm starving."

"You unhappy man!" she cried. "Here, sit down and eat my supper; and I'll just run upstairs and see my patient, not but what I doubt she's fast asleep; for Maria is a *malade imaginaire.*"

With this specimen of the French, not of Stratford-atte-Bowe, but of a finishing establishment in Moray Place, she left John alone in his father's sanctum. He fell at once upon the food; and it is to be supposed that Flora had found her patient wakeful, and been detained with some details of nursing, for he had time to make a full end of all there was to eat, and not only to empty the teapot, but to fill it again from a kettle that was fitfully singing on his father's fire. Then he sat torpid, and pleased, and bewildered; his misfortunes were then half forgotten; his mind considering, not without regret, this unsentimental return to his old love.

He was thus engaged, when that bustling woman noiselessly reentered.

"Have you eaten?" said she. "Then tell me all about it."

It was a long and (as the reader knows) a pitiful story; but Flora heard it with compressed lips. She was lost in none of those questionings of human destiny that have, from time to time, arrested the flight of my own pen; for women, such as she, are no philosophers, and behold the concrete only. And women, such as she, are very hard on the imperfect man.

"Very well," said she, when he had done; "then down upon your knees at once, and beg God's forgiveness."

And the great baby plumped upon his knees, and did as he was bid; and none the worse for that! But while he was heartily enough requesting forgiveness on general principles, the rational side of him distinguished, and wondered if, perhaps, the apology were not due upon the other part. And when he rose again from that becoming exercise, he first eyed the face of his old love, doubtfully, and then taking heart, uttered his protest.

"I must say, Flora," said he, "in all this business, I can see very little fault of mine."

"If you had written home," replied the lady, "there would have been none of it. If you had even gone to Murrayfield reasonably sober, you would never have slept there, and the worst would not have happened. Besides, the whole thing began years ago. You got into trouble, and when your father, honest man, was disappointed, you took the pet, or got afraid, and ran away from punishment. Well, you've had your own way of it, John, and I don't suppose you like it."

"I sometimes fancy I'm not much better than a fool," sighed John.

"My dear John," said she, "not much."

He looked at her, and his eye fell. A certain anger rose within him; here was a Flora he disowned; she was hard; she was of a set color; a settled, mature, undecorative manner; plain of speech, plain of habit—he had come near saying, plain of face. And this changeling called herself by the same name as the many-colored, clinging maid of yore; she of the frequent laughter, and the many sighs, and the kind, stolen glances. And to make all worse, she took the upper hand with him, which (as John well knew) was not the true relation of the sexes. He steeled his heart against this sick-nurse.

"And how do you come to be here?" he asked.

She told him how she had nursed her father in his long illness, and when he died, and she was left alone, had taken to nurse others, partly from habit, partly to be of some service in the world; partly, it might be, for amusement. "There's no accounting for taste," said she. And she told him how she went largely to the houses of old friends, as the need arose; and how she was thus doubly welcome, as an old friend first, and then as an experienced nurse, to whom the doctors would confide the gravest cases.

"And, indeed, it's a mere farce my being here for poor Maria," she continued; "but your father takes her ailments to heart, and I cannot always be refusing him. We are great friends, your father and I; he was very kind to me long ago—ten years ago."

A strange stir came in John's heart. All this while had he been thinking only of himself? All this while, why had he not written to Flora? In penitential tenderness, he took her hand, and to his awe and trouble, it remained in his, compliant. A voice told him this was Flora, after all—told him so quietly, yet with a thrill of singing.

"And you never married?" said he.

"No, John; I never married," she replied.

The hall clock striking two recalled them to the sense of time.

"And now," said she, "you have been fed and warmed, and I have heard your story, and now it's high time to call your brother."

"Oh!" cried John, chap-fallen; "do you think that absolutely necessary?"

"*I* can't keep you here; I am a stranger," said she. "Do you want to run away again? I thought you had enough of that."

He bowed his head under the reproof. She despised him, he reflected, as he sat once more alone; a monstrous thing for a woman to despise a man; and strangest of all, she seemed to like him. Would his brother despise him, too? And would his brother like him?

And presently the brother appeared under Flora's escort; and, standing afar off beside the doorway, eyed the hero of this tale.

"So this is you?" he said, at length.

"Yes, Alick, it's me—it's John," replied the elder brother, feebly.

"And how did you get in here?" inquired the younger.

"Oh, I had my passkey," says John.

"The deuce you had!" said Alexander. "Ah, you lived in a better world! There are no passkeys going now."

"Well, father was always averse to them," sighed John. And the conversation then broke down, and the brothers looked askance at one another in silence.

"Well, and what the devil are we to do?" said Alexander. "I suppose if the authorities got wind of you, you would be taken up?"

"It depends on whether they've found the body or not," returned John. "And then there's that cabman, to be sure!"

"Oh, bother the body!" said Alexander. "I mean about the other thing. That's serious."

"Is that what my father spoke about?" asked John. "I don't even know what it is."

"About your robbing your bank in California, of course," replied Alexander.

It was plain, from Flora's face, that this was the first she had heard of it; it was plainer still, from John's, that he was innocent.

"I!" he exclaimed. "I rob my bank! My God! Flora, this is too much; even you must allow that."

"Meaning you didn't?" asked Alexander.

"I never robbed a soul in all my days," cried John: "except my father, if you call that robbery; and I brought him back the money in this room, and he wouldn't even take it!"

"Look here, John," said his brother; "let us have no misunderstanding upon this. Macewen saw my father; he told him a bank you had worked for in San Francisco was wiring over the habitable globe to have you collared—that it was supposed you had nailed thousands; and it was dead certain you had nailed three hundred. So Macewen said, and I wish you would be careful how you answer. I may tell you also, that your father paid the three hundred on the spot."

"Three hundred?" repeated John. "Three hundred pounds, you mean? That's fifteen hundred dollars. Why, then, it's Kirkman!" he broke out. "Thank Heaven! I can explain all that. I gave them to Kirkman to pay for me the night before I left—fifteen hundred dollars, and a letter to the manager. What do they suppose I would steal fifteen hundred dollars for? I'm rich; I struck it rich in stocks. It's the silliest stuff I ever heard of. All that's needful is to cable to the manager: Kirkman has the fifteen hundred—find Kirkman. He was a fellow clerk of mine, and a hard case; but to do him justice, I didn't think he was as hard as this."

"And what do you say to that, Alick?" asked Flora.

"I say the cablegram shall go tonight!" cried Alexander, with energy. "Answer prepaid, too. If this can be cleared away—and upon my word I do believe it can—we shall all be able to hold up our heads again. Here, you John, you stick down the address of your bank manager. You, Flora, you can pack John into my bed, for which I have no further use tonight. As for me, I am off to the post office, and thence to the High Street about the dead body. The police ought to know, you see, and they ought to know through John; and I can tell them some rigmarole about my brother being a man of highly nervous organization, and the rest of it. And then, I'll tell you what, John—did you notice the name upon the cab?"

John gave the name of the driver, which as I have not been able to command the vehicle, I here suppress.

"Well," resumed Alexander, "I'll call round at their place before I come back, and pay your shot for you. In that way, before breakfast-time, you'll be as good as new."

John murmured inarticulate thanks. To see his brother thus ener-getic in his service moved him beyond expression; if he could not utter what he felt, he showed it legibly in his face; and Alexander read it there, and liked it the better in that dumb delivery.

"But there's one thing," said the latter, "cablegrams are dear; and I dare say you remember enough of the governor to guess the state of my finances."

"The trouble is," said John, "that all my stamps are in that beastly house."

"All your what?" asked Alexander.

"Stamps—money," explained John. "It's an American expression; I'm afraid I contracted one or two."

"I have some," said Flora. "I have a pound note upstairs."

"My dear Flora," returned Alexander, "a pound note won't see us very far, and besides, this is my father's business, and I shall be very much surprised if it isn't my father who pays for it."

"I would not apply to him yet; I do not think that can be wise," ob-jected Flora.

"You have a very imperfect idea of my resources, and none at all of my effrontery," replied Alexander. "Please observe."

He put John from his way, chose a stout knife among the supper things, and with surprising quickness broke into his father's drawer.

"There's nothing easier when you come to try," he observed, pock-eting the money.

"I wish you had not done that," said Flora. "You will never hear the last of it."

"Oh, I don't know," returned the young man; "the governor is human after all. And now, John, let me see your famous passkey. Get into bed, and don't move for any one till I come back. They won't mind you not answering when they knock; I generally don't myself."

IX

In which Mr. Nicholson accepts the principle of an allowance

In spite of the horrors of the day and the tea-drinking of the night, John slept the sleep of infancy. He was awakened by the maid, as it might have been ten years ago, tapping at the door. The winter sunrise was painting the east: and as the window was to the back of the house, it shone into the room with many strange colors of refracted light. Without, the houses were all cleanly roofed with snow; the garden walls were coped with it a foot in height; the greens lay glittering. Yet strange as snow had grown to John during his years upon the Bay of San Francisco, it was what he saw within that most affected him. For it was to his own room that Alexander had been promoted; there was the old paper with the device of flowers, in which a cunning fancy might yet detect the face of Skinny Jim, of the Academy, John's former dominie; there was the old chest of drawers; there were the chairs—one, two, three— three as before. Only the carpet was new, and the litter of Alexander's clothes and books and drawing materials, and a pencil-drawing on the wall, which (in John's eyes) appeared a marvel of proficiency.

He was thus lying, and looking, and dreaming, hanging, as it were, between two epochs of his life, when Alexander came to the door, and made his presence known in a loud whisper. John let him in, and jumped back into the warm bed.

"Well, John," said Alexander, "the cablegram is sent in your name, and twenty words of answer paid. I have been to the cab office and paid your cab, even saw the old gentleman himself, and properly apologized. He was mighty placable, and indicated his belief you had been drinking. Then I knocked up old Macewen out of bed, and explained affairs to him as he sat and shivered in a dressing gown. And before that I had been to the High Street, where they have heard nothing of your dead body, so that I incline to the idea that you dreamed it."

"Catch me!" said John.

"Well, the police never do know anything," assented Alexander; "and at any rate, they have dispatched a man to inquire and to recover your trousers and your money, so that really your bill is now fairly clean; and I see but one lion in your path—the governor."

"I'll be turned out again, you'll see," said John, dismally.

"I don't imagine so," returned the other; "not if you do what Flora and I have arranged; and your business now is to dress, and lose no time about it. Is your watch right? Well, you have a quarter of an hour. By five minutes before the half hour you must be at table, in your old seat, under Uncle Duthie's picture. Flora will be there to keep you countenance; and we shall see what we shall see."

"Wouldn't it be wiser for me to stay in bed?" said John.

"If you mean to manage your own concerns, you can do precisely what you like," replied Alexander; "but if you are not in your place five minutes before the half hour I wash my hands of you, for one."

And thereupon he departed. He had spoken warmly, but the truth is, his heart was somewhat troubled. As he hung over the balusters, watching for his father to appear, he had hard ado to keep himself braced for the encounter that must follow.

"If he takes it well, I shall be lucky," he reflected. "If he takes it ill, why it'll be a herring across John's tracks, and perhaps all for the best. He's a confounded muff, this brother of mine, but he seems a decent soul."

At that stage a door opened below with a certain emphasis, and Mr. Nicholson was seen solemnly to descend the stairs, and pass into his own apartment. Alexander followed, quaking inwardly, but with a steady face. He knocked, was bidden to enter, and found his father standing in front of the forced drawer, to which he pointed as he spoke.

"This is a most extraordinary thing," said he; "I have been robbed!"

"I was afraid you would notice it," observed his son; "it made such a beastly hash of the table."

"You were afraid I would notice it?" repeated Mr. Nicholson. "And, pray, what may that mean?"

"That I was a thief, sir," returned Alexander. "I took all the money in case the servants should get hold of it; and here is the change, and a note of my expenditure. You were gone to bed, you see, and I did not feel at liberty to knock you up; but I think when you have heard the circumstances, you will do me justice. The fact is, I have reason to believe there has been some dreadful error about my brother John; the sooner it can be cleared up the better for all parties; it was a piece of business, sir—and so I took it, and decided, on my own responsibility, to send a telegram to San Francisco. Thanks to my quickness we may hear tonight. There appears to be no doubt, sir, that John has been abominably used."

"When did this take place?" asked the father.

"Last night, sir, after you were asleep," was the reply.

"It's most extraordinary," said Mr. Nicholson. "Do you mean to say you have been out all night?"

"All night, as you say, sir. I have been to the telegraph and the police office, and Mr. Macewen's. Oh, I had my hands full," said Alexander.

"Very irregular," said the father. "You think of no one but yourself."

"I do not see that I have much to gain in bringing back my elder brother," returned Alexander shrewdly.

The answer pleased the old man; he smiled. "Well, well, I will go into this after breakfast," said he.

"I am sorry about the table," said the son.

"The table is a small matter; I think nothing of that," said the father.

"It's another example," continued the son, "of the awkwardness of a man having no money of his own. If I had a proper allowance, like other fellows of my age, this would have been quite unnecessary."

"A proper allowance!" repeated his father, in tones of blighting sarcasm, for the expression was not new to him. "I have never grudged you money for any proper purpose."

"No doubt, no doubt," said Alexander, "but then you see you aren't always on the spot to have the thing explained to you. Last night for instance—"

"You could have wakened me last night," interrupted his father.

"Was it not some similar affair that first got John into a mess?" asked the son, skilfully evading the point.

But the father was not less adroit. "And pray, sir, how did you come and go out of the house?" he asked.

"I forgot to lock the door, it seems," replied Alexander.

"I have had cause to complain of that too often," said Mr. Nicholson. "But still I do not understand. Did you keep the servants up?"

"I propose to go into all that at length after breakfast," returned Alexander. "There is the half hour going; we must not keep Miss Mackenzie waiting."

And greatly daring, he opened the door.

Even Alexander, who, it must have been perceived, was on terms of comparative freedom with his parent; even Alexander had never before dared to cut short an interview in this high-handed fashion. But the truth is the very mass of his son's delinquencies daunted the old gentleman. He was like the man with the cart of apples—this was be-yond him! That Alexander should have spoiled his table, taken his money, stayed out all night, and then coolly acknowledged all, was something undreamed of in the Nicholsonian philosophy, and tran-scended comment. The return of the change, which the old gentleman still carried in his hand, had been a feature of imposing impudence; it had dealt him a staggering blow. Then there was the reference to John's original flight—a subject which he always kept resolutely curtained in his own mind; for he was a man who loved to have made no mistakes, and when he feared he might have made one kept the papers sealed. In view of all these surprises and reminders, and of his son's composed and masterful demeanor, there began to creep on Mr. Nicholson a sickly misgiving.

He seemed beyond his depth; if he did or said anything, he might come to regret it. The young man, besides, as he had pointed out him-self, was playing a generous part. And if wrong had been done—and done to one who was, after, and in spite of, all, a Nicholson—it should certainly be righted.

All things considered, monstrous as it was to be cut short in his in-quiries, the old gentleman submitted, pocketed the change, and fol-lowed his son into the dining room. During these few steps he once more mentally revolted, and once more, and this time finally, laid down his arms: a still, small voice in his bosom having informed him authentically of a piece of news; that he was afraid of Alexander. The strange thing was that he was pleased to be afraid of him. He was proud of his son; he might be proud of him; the boy had character and grit, and knew what he was doing.

These were his reflections as he turned the corner of the dining room door. Miss Mackenzie was in the place of honor, conjuring with a teapot and cozy; and, behold! there was another person present, a large, portly, whiskered man of a very comfortable and respectable air, who now rose from his seat and came forward, holding out his hand.

"Good morning, father," said he.

Of the contention of feeling that ran high in Mr. Nicholson's starched bosom, no outward sign was visible; nor did he delay long to make a choice of conduct. Yet in that interval he had reviewed a great field of possibilities both past and future; whether it was possible he had not been perfectly wise in his treatment of John; whether it was possible that John was innocent; whether, if he turned John out a second time, as his outraged authority suggested, it was possible to avoid a scandal; and whether, if he went to that extremity, it was possible that Alexander might rebel.

"Hum!" said Mr. Nicholson, and put his hand, limp and dead, into John's.

And then, in an embarrassed silence, all took their places; and even the paper—from which it was the old gentleman's habit to suck mortification daily, as he marked the decline of our institutions—even the paper lay furled by his side.

But presently Flora came to the rescue. She slid into the silence with a technicality, asking if John still took his old inordinate amount of sugar. Thence it was but a step to the burning question of the day; and in tones a little shaken, she commented on the interval since she had last made tea for the prodigal, and congratulated him on his return. And then addressing Mr. Nicholson, she congratulated him also in a manner that defied his ill-humor; and from that launched into the tale of John's misadventures, not without some suitable suppressions.

Gradually Alexander joined; between them, whether he would or no, they forced a word or two from John; and these fell so tremulously, and spoke so eloquently of a mind oppressed with dread, that Mr. Nicholson relented. At length even he contributed a question: and before the meal was at an end all four were talking even freely.

Prayers followed, with the servants gaping at this newcomer whom no one had admitted; and after prayers there came that moment on the clock which was the signal for Mr. Nicholson's departure.

"John," said he, "of course you will stay here. Be very careful not to excite Maria, if Miss Mackenzie thinks it desirable that you should see her. Alexander, I wish to speak with you alone." And then, when they were both in the back room: "You need not come to the office today," said he; "you can stay and amuse your brother, and I think it would be respectful to call on Uncle Greig. And by the bye" (this spoken with a certain—dare we say?—bashfulness), "I agree to concede the principle of an allowance; and I will consult with Doctor Durie, who is quite a man of the world and has sons of his own, as to the amount. And, my fine fellow, you may consider yourself in luck!" he added, with a smile.

"Thank you," said Alexander.

Before noon a detective had restored to John his money, and brought news, sad enough in truth, but perhaps the least sad possible. Alan had been found in his own house in Regent's Terrace, under care of the terrified butler. He was quite mad, and instead of going to prison, had gone to Morningside Asylum. The murdered man, it appeared, was an evicted tenant who had for nearly a year pursued his late landlord with threats and insults; and beyond this, the cause and details of the tragedy were lost.

When Mr. Nicholson returned from dinner they were able to put a despatch into his hands: "John V. Nicholson, Randolph Crescent, Edinburgh.—Kirkman has disappeared; police looking for him. All understood. Keep mind quite easy.—Austin." Having had this explained to him, the old gentleman took down the cellar key and departed for two bottles of the 1820 port. Uncle Greig dined there that day, and Cousin Robina, and, by an odd chance, Mr. Macewen; and the presence of these strangers relieved what might have been otherwise a somewhat strained relation. Ere they departed, the family was welded once more into a fair semblance of unity.

In the end of April John led Flora—or, as more descriptive, Flora led John—to the altar, if altar that may be called which was indeed the drawing room and mantelpiece in Mr. Nicholson's house, with the Reverend Dr. Durie posted on the hearthrug in the guise of Hymen's priest.

The last I saw of them, on a recent visit to the north, was at a dinner party in the house of my old friend Gellatly Macbride; and after we had in classic phrase, "rejoined the ladies," I had an opportunity to overhear Flora conversing with another married woman on the much canvassed matter of a husband's tobacco.

"Oh, yes!" said she; "I only allow Mr. Nicholson four cigars a day. Three he smokes at fixed times—after a meal, you know, my dear; and the fourth he can take when he likes with any friend."

"Bravo!" thought I to myself; "this is the wife for my friend John!"

NOTES

The notes to this edition are designed to aid comprehension: the translation of a Scots vocabulary, the identification of technical and rare words or phrases, and the citation of slang, colloquial, or dialectal expressions. Stevenson had an irregular habit of defining Scots terms in the margins, and these are noted here with the initials "R.L.S." in brackets following the gloss. Since his general lexicon was both studied and broad, many other terms may seem exotic to the reader but are readily defined in a standard reference, such as the *OED, Webster's Third New International Dictionary,* or *The Random House Dictionary of the English Language.* I have also cited allusions that may not be immediately apparent or available in a standard encyclopaedia, as well as place names that are accessible only in obscure gazetteers. But as Henry James would have said, the main job of interpretation is the reader's: these notes are simply the provisions for a clear reading of the stories.

At the beginning of his career Stevenson published his short stories in established English magazines like the *Cornhill* and *Temple Bar,* or, in the case of *The Suicide Club* and *The Rajah's Diamond,* in a short-lived polemical journal called *London,* edited by his good friend William Ernest Henley and featuring as one of its contributors George Saintsbury. In a letter written to Saintsbury years later from Samoa, Stevenson recalled those early *London* days: "As the first person who encouraged me to publish my fiction in book form, you may be called the father of my fortunes" ([September 1890], *Letters,* 6:413). Stevenson published three collections of his stories during his lifetime: *New Arabian Nights* (London, 1882), *The Merry Men and*

Other Tales and Fables (London, 1887), and *Island Nights' Entertainments* (London, 1893). The texts in this volume, with the exception of "Markheim," "The Isle of Voices," and "The Beach of Falesá," are drawn from these first English editions. For the first two stories, the texts are the holographs at the Houghton Library and the Rosenbach Museum and Library. There are numerous differences between the holograph and printed versions of both stories, particularly in the matter of punctuation, but also in details of vocabulary and expression. In order to reproduce the manuscripts faithfully, Stevenson's unorthodox use of capitals and lowercase letters has been retained. Emendations have been made in a small number of cases: supplying an absent quotation mark, period, or hyphen; adding or removing an apostrophe; or altering Stevenson's spelling in less than a dozen instances (e.g., *wiegh, niether, nieghbour, siezed, dwellt, Christmass, hasard*). In all cases the emendations conform with the printed versions. For "The Beach at Falesá" the text is that of the holograph manuscript at the Huntington Library, as originally edited by Barry Menikoff and published by Stanford University Press in 1984. *Strange Case of Dr. Jekyll and Mr. Hyde* reproduces the first English edition published by Longmans, Green, and Co. (London, 1886). For "The Story of a Lie," "The Body-Snatcher," and "The Misadventures of John Nicholson," all uncollected in book form during his lifetime, the texts are from the first Vailima edition (P. F. Collier & Son, New York, 1912), which reproduced them from their serial publications. As for "An Old Song," the text reprinted here, with permission, is from the edition prepared by Roger G. Swearingen (Archon Books, Hamden, Connecticut, 1982), who discovered the story in the files of *London* magazine.

New Arabian Nights

THE SUICIDE CLUB

Story of the Young Man with the Cream Tarts

P. 3, L. 15. *temerarious:* unreasonably adventurous; rash, reckless.

P. 7, L. 15. *penny gaff:* a cheap, low music hall or theater (J. S. Farmer and W. E. Henley, *Slang and Its Analogues,* 7 vols. [London, 1890–1904], hereafter cited as F&H).

P. 11, L. 2. *for all who desire to be out of the coil:* "For in that sleep of death what dreams may come, / When we have shuffled off this mortal coil, / Must give us pause" (*Hamlet,* 3.1.65–67).

P. 12, LL. 7–8. *four-wheeler:* a four-wheeled hackney carriage.

P. 14, L. 15. *All Fools'-Day:* April Fools' Day.

P. 20, L. 21. vogue la galère: "come what may" (proverbial).

P. 22, L. 1. *pasteboard:* playing card.

P. 25, L. 12. *devil's dozen:* thirteen, the original baker's dozen, from the number of witches supposed to gather on a sabbath (F&H).

Story of the Physician and the Saratoga Trunk

P. 29, L. 13. *Saratoga trunk:* a very large trunk used for traveling, named after the upstate New York resort (J. S. Farmer, *Americanisms* [London, 1889]).

P. 33, L. 13. *counterjumpers:* a contemptuous term for junior clerks in dry goods stores.

P. 41, L. 27. *bistery:* scalpel.

P. 47, L. 35. *boots:* a hotel servant who cleans boots and offers minor assistance to guests.

P. 49, L. 15. *consumptive marker:* a *marker* keeps score in competitive games; *consumption* was the common term for tuberculosis.

The Adventure of the Hansom Cabs

P. 52, L. 35. *nine days' vitality:* something that causes a sensation for a few days and then passes into oblivion (a nine days' wonder).

P. 55, L. 29. *paletot:* a loose outer coat, or cloak.

P. 56, L. 34. *Manillas:* a cigar (or cheroot) made of tobacco grown in the Philippines.

P. 60, L. 34. *Joshua in the Bible:* "and Joshua chose out thirty thousand mighty men of valour" (Joshua 8:3).

P. 62, L. 35. parc aux cerfs: deer park.

P. 63, L. 4. *postern:* a back or side door separate from the main entrance.

P. 68, L. 29. *"God defend the right!": Richard II,* 1.3.101.

L. 38. *hound of hell:* Cerberus, the watchdog guarding the entrance to the infernal regions.

THE RAJAH'S DIAMOND

Story of the Bandbox

P. 73, L. 27. *Tame Cat:* a woman's "fetch-and-carry" (F&H), or gofer.

P. 74, L. 19. *Mechlin:* delicate lace used for dresses and millinery, produced at Mechlin (Belgium).

P. 83, L. 35. Gloire de Dijons: a variety of tea rose.

P. 84, L. 22. *Rag-fair:* an old clothes market in Houndsditch, an area surrounding the original wall of the City of London.

P. 91, L. 2. *oakum:* loose fiber obtained by untwisting and picking old rope, used in caulking ships' seams and stopping leaks; picking it was an employment of convicts and workhouse inmates.

L. 14. *Bendigo:* a city in central Australia, northwest of Melbourne, founded in 1851 with a rush for gold.

L. 14. *Trincomalee:* a town in Sri Lanka (formerly Ceylon) overlooking a fine natural harbor, contested by the Portuguese, Dutch, French, and English and finally ceded to England in the early nineteenth century.

Story of the Young Man in Holy Orders

P. 91, L. 31. *St. Ambrose:* Ambrose (c. 340–97), early father of the Roman church, noted for oratory, magnanimity, and stainless character.

L. 31. *St. Chrysostom:* Chrysostom (c. 347–407), one of the fathers of the Greek church, patriarch of Constantinople, noted for wide learning and ascetic discipline.

P. 95, L. 21. *Gaboriau:* Emile Gaboriau (1832–1873), French originator of the *roman policier,* or police novel (*L'affaire Lerouge,* 1866).

P. 96, L. 5. *Paley's Evidences:* William Paley (1743–1805), English theologian and clergyman (*Evidences of Christianity,* 1794).

P. 99, L. 15. *old gentleman:* the devil (John Camden Hotten, *The Slang Dictionary: A New Edition* [London, 1874]).

Story of the House with the Green Blinds

P. 110, L. 8. chevaux-de-frise: a line of sharp points (as of spikes or nails) set firmly into the top of a fence or wall.

P. 116, L. 12. *Trichinopoli:* a district and city in southern India.

P. 126, L. 29. *wideawake:* a soft felt hat with a broad brim and low crown.

The Adventure of Prince Florizel and a Detective

P. 135, L. 2. *as Jacob served Laban:* (Genesis 29:15–20).

THE PAVILION ON THE LINKS

P. 137, L. 1. *Fidra:* a rocky islet near North Berwick (Francis Groome, *Ordnance Gazetteer of Scotland,* vol. 3 [Edinburgh, 1883]).

L. 3. *Sea-Wood:* situated in or by the sea.

L. 8. *Easter:* eastern, lying toward the east; common in place names and in names of farms (William Grant, ed., *The Scottish National Dictionary,* 10 vols. [Edinburgh, 1931–1936], hereafter cited as *SND*).

P. 138, L. 2. *German Ocean:* North Sea.

P. 140, L. 10. *Ness:* a promontory, headland; in general used as a place-name.

L. 10. *Bullers:* a loud gurgling noise, the boiling of an eddy or torrent.

P. 143, L. 16. *Floe:* a pool, a marsh, or bay, especially in place names (*SND*).

L. 17. *sea quags:* marshy or boggy spots, especially ones covered with a layer of turf which yields when walked on.

P. 147, L. 36. *policies:* the enclosed grounds of a large country house; the park of an estate (*SND*).

P. 154, LL. 23–24. *the rose-leaf . . . the Princess:* Supersensitivity was considered characteristic of nobility, and tales like Andersen's "The Princess and the Pea" are common, including a Persian story where the princess was in constant pain because a rose leaf "had pressed against her side and had rubbed her skin till the bones showed" (N. M. Penzer, ed., *The Ocean of Story,* vol. 6 [Delhi: Motilal Banarsidass, 1968], 293–94).

P. 157, L. 6. *Wester:* western, lying toward the west, usually in place names (*SND*).

P. 158, L. 37. *black-avised:* dark complexioned (Joseph Wright, *The English Dialect Dictionary,* 6 vols. [Oxford, 1898–1905], hereafter cited as *EDD*).

P. 165, L. 10. *"trump":* first-rate, good-natured person (Hotten, *Slang Dictionary*); in the original *Cornhill* magazine version the text reads: "She's a perfect cock-sparrow, Frank."

L. 30. carbonaro: *Carbonari* were members of a secret political society that originated in Naples during the French occupation (1808–1815); their major aim was the establishment of a republican government.

L. 33. *Tridentino:* the city of Trent in the Tyrolean Alps; in the nineteenth century it was part of Austria, but because it had always been Italian in language and culture, a strong movement developed for union with Italy, which was achieved in 1919.

L. 33. *Parma:* capital of the province of Parma in northern Italy.

P. 169, L. 17. *tan your liver:* "white-livered" means cowardly, mean (F&H).

L. 20. *precisian:* one who is rigidly precise in the observance of rules or forms.

P. 174, L. 11. fey: fated to die, doomed; also, behaving oddly as if bewitched or crazy (*SND*).

L. 18. *millstone:* "It were better for him that a millstone were hanged about his neck, and he cast into the sea, than that he should offend one of these little ones" (Luke 17:2; also, Matthew 18:6; Mark 9:42).

P. 177, L. 11. *tail of his eye:* the outer corner of the eye (F&H).

L. 20. beaux yeux: beautiful eyes.

A LODGING FOR THE NIGHT

P. 187, L. 34. *ballade:* Stevenson's spelling distinguishes between two different poetic forms: "*Ballade* was by precedent the allotted name of certain verses written after old French models [which] had no kinship whatever with the ordinary ballad" (Gleeson White, "Of the Ballade," *Atalanta* 4 [1890–1891]: 303).

P. 189, L. 14. *Elias:* "And it came to pass, as they still went on, and talked, that, behold, there appeared a chariot of fire, and horses of fire, and parted them both asunder; and Elijah went up by a whirlwind into heaven" (2 Kings 2:11).

L. 15. Hominibus impossibile: impossible for men.

L. 27. *The black dog was on his back:* melancholy, depression of spirits (F&H).

P. 192, L. 35. *Henry V. of England:* Henry (1388–1422) was proclaimed king in 1413, fought at Agincourt two years later, and died just before consolidating his victories in France.

P. 196, L. 25. *gripes:* colic or stomach pains (F&H).

P. 201, L. 38. *Man is not a solitary animal:* "And the Lord God said, *It is* not good that the man should be alone; I will make him an helpmeet for him" (Genesis 2:18).

P. 202, L. 1. Cui Deus faeminam tradit: To whom God gives woman.

L. 1. *pantler:* a servant or officer in charge of the bread and the pantry in a great family.

P. 203, L. 19. *linking:* walking smartly and vigorously, passing by quickly (*EDD*).

THE SIRE DE MALÉTROIT'S DOOR

P. 206, L. 33. *bartizan:* any kind of fence, as of stone or wood (*SND*).

L. 37. *weir:* a river dam.

P. 208, L. 16. *debouched:* led out from a narrower to a wider space.

P. 211, L. 10. *damoiseau:* page, squire.

P. 212, L. 27. *messire:* sir (title of honor).

P. 213, L. 7. *groining:* a rib (of wood or stone) designed to cover the projecting edge formed by the intersection of two vaults.

P. 215, L. 32. *Queen Isabeau:* (1371–1435), married Charles VI in 1385, saw
her daughter married to Henry V of England in 1420.

P. 216, L. 17. *salle:* hall; large room.

P. 222, L. 26. *steadings:* the buildings on a farm (*SND*).

PROVIDENCE AND THE GUITAR

P. 224, L. 14. *Molière:* As befits a story of vagabond thespians, there are allusions to classic playwrights of the French theater like Molière and
Beaumarchais, as well as to contemporary actors who were noted for
their Romantic excess (Étienne Mélingue, Antoine Frédérick).

P. 225, L. 14. *tombola:* a kind of lottery game.

L. 15. *art and part:* Scots law term, to be an accomplice in a chargeable
act.

P. 226, L. 26. *Sédan:* at the foot of the Ardennes, near the Belgian border;
scene of a decisive French defeat (1870) during the Franco-Prussian
War and the capture of Napoleon III.

P. 228, L. 15. *"Fichu Commissaire!":* Rotten Commissioner!

P. 229, L. 6. *Maire:* mayor.

L. 13. *"Y a des honnêtes gens partout!":* There are honest people everywhere.

L. 24. *Garde Champêtre:* guard of the field.

P. 233, L. 30. *Eugène Sue:* (1804–1857), popular novelist during the 1830s and
1840s, republican and socialist in his sympathies.

P. 235, LL. 19–21. *Béranger's:—"Commissaire ... ménagère":* Pierre Béranger
(1780–1857), songwriter, lyric poet, ardent republican; "Commissioner! Commissioner! Colin beats his wife."

P. 236, L. 27. *"Sauve qui peut":* Each man for himself.

P. 237, L. 20. *Alceste and Célimène:* protagonists in Molière's *The Misanthrope*.
L. 26. *"Dites ... aller":* Tell me, beautiful young lady, where do you want
to go?

L. 34. *Bezonian:* a raw recruit; a base fellow or wretch.

P. 238, LL. 30–31. *Montrouge, Belleville ... Montmartre:* all sections of what is
now Paris.

P. 242, L. 33. *"Let dogs delight":* "Let dogs delight to bark and bite,/For God
hath made them so"; Isaac Watts (1674–1748), *Divine Songs Attempted
in Easy Language for the use of Children* (1715).

LL. 37–38. *Pierre Dupont's:* Pierre Dupont (1821–1870), popular songwriter, expressed republican and socialistic aspirations.

P. 243, LL. 1–2. *Savez-vous... mois?:* Do you know where May lies, that beautiful month? Stevenson provides his own translation: "Know you the lair of May, the lovely month?"

P. 244, L. 4. *Admetus's sheep... Apollo:* Apollo was sentenced to tend the flocks of Admetus, who, because he was kind to the god, was rewarded by having his flocks increased.

P. 246, L. 23. *"non... que mois!":* no—I will not keep quiet—I can't help it!

P. 248, LL. 22–25. *O mon amante... charmante!:* O my love / O my desire / Let's seize this charming time.

STRANGE CASE OF DR. JEKYLL AND MR. HYDE

P. 255, L. 9. *mortify:* to subdue the appetites by discipline and self-denial.

L. 22. *catholicity:* liberality, inclusiveness.

P. 256, L. 16. *by-street:* a side street, one lying out of the way of the main road.

L. 19. *coquetry:* an affected charm or prettiness, akin to the manner of a coquette.

P. 257, L. 22. *Juggernaut:* a massive inexorable force that crushes whatever is in its path.

P. 260, L. 20. *long tongue:* proverbial, "little can a long tongue conceal," i.e., to talk more than is good for you.

P. 261, L. 22. *fanciful:* not governed by facts, realities, and reason.

L. 22. *immodest:* indecent.

P. 262, L. 38. *Damon and Pythias:* classical figures synonymous with devoted friendship.

P. 264, LL. 13–14. *concourse:* at the gathering of crowds or throngs.

P. 266, L. 15. *the old story of Dr. Fell:* alludes to a seventeenth-century translation of a Latin epigram that was made as a punishment by an Oxford student for his teacher: "I do not love thee, Dr. Fell / The reason why I cannot tell / But this alone I know full well / I do not love thee, Dr. Fell"; it signifies an inexplicable, even visceral antipathy or hatred.

P. 267, L. 25. *pede claudo:* slowly but inevitably.

P. 272, L. 17. *accosted:* approached and spoke to.

P. 274, L. 32. *penny numbers:* the sensational pulp fiction of the day, also called "penny dreadfuls."

P. 277, L. 15. *baize:* a coarsely woven fabric made to imitate felt and used to line furniture.

L. 18. *cheval glass:* a full-length mirror in a frame which may be tilted.

P. 279, L. 19. *circulars:* printed advertisements, announcements, or notices that are widely distributed.

L. 36. *carbuncles:* deep-red gemstones.

P. 289, L. 12. *wrack:* rack, a wind-driven mass of high, often broken clouds.

P. 290, L. 14. *get this through hands:* thoroughly deal with or dispose of this matter.

P. 292, L. 29. *exorbitant:* deviating from the normal or ordinary course (archaic); also, excessive, beyond customary limits.

P. 294, L. 19. *scud:* loose clouds or fragments of cloud driven swiftly by the wind.

P. 295, L. 29. *glazed presses:* cupboards fitted or set with glass windowpanes.

P. 301, L. 6. *farrago:* confused or disordered assemblage of words and ideas.

L. 30. *version book:* a school exercise book.

P. 302, L. 26. *debility of constitution:* weakness or feebleness of mind or temperament.

L. 28. *incipient rigor:* goose bumps.

P. 304, LL. 13–14. *ebullition:* the process of boiling or bubbling up.

L. 28. *prodigy:* something extraordinary or inexplicable; a marvel.

P. 305, LL. 1–2. *injected:* congested.

P. 306, L. 13. *blazoned:* proclaimed, boasted.

P. 307, L. 13. *polity:* civil order, political organization.

LL. 13–14. *multifarious, incongruous:* great diversity or variety; lacking harmony, consistency, or compatibility.

L. 30. *faggots:* a bunch or bundle of sticks tied together and used for fuel.

P. 308, L. 8. *effulgence:* strong radiant light; brilliance.

P. 310, L. 13. *Philippi:* ancient city of Macedonia, whose prisoners were freed by an earthquake that was seen as miraculous (Acts 16:26).

P. 312, L. 25. *swart:* blackish, swarthy.

P. 314, LL. 8–9. *abstinence:* self-restraint or self-denial.

L. 31. *insensibility:* lack of emotional feeling or response; apathy.

L. 33. *insensate:* unfeeling; cruel, harsh, brutal.

THE MERRY MEN AND OTHER TALES AND FABLES

THE MERRY MEN

P. 326, L. 13. *overlooked:* looked over, i.e., inspected, reviewed.

P. 329, L. 3. *a certain saint:* St. Columba (521–597), the "Apostle of Caledonia," established a monastery on the island of Iona in 563.

L. 29. *King Philip:* Philip II of Spain (r. 1556–1598), whose naval Armada was defeated in war with England (1588).

L. 34. *Dr. Robertson:* William Robertson (1721–1793), a distinguished historian of Scotland, England, and America.

P. 330, L. 4. *King Jamie's:* James I (1566–1625), who as James VI was king of Scotland (r. 1567–1603) at the time of the Armada's defeat.

LL. 21–22. *Cameronians:* militant sect of Presbyterians founded by Richard Cameron, a young schoolteacher and field preacher who in 1680 renounced allegiance to Charles II.

P. 332, L. 32. *the killing times:* period in Scottish history (c. 1683–1685) when Presbyterians (or Covenanters) opposed to Charles II were put to death.

P. 333, L. 14. *the peace of God:* "And the peace of God, which passeth all understanding, shall keep your hearts and minds through Christ Jesus" (Philippians 4:7).

P. 334, LL. 20–21. *"And now ... glad":* Metrical Psalm 65 (Kenneth Gelder, ed., *Robert Louis Stevenson: The Scottish Stories and Essays* [Edinburgh: Edinburgh University Press, 1989], 286).

LL. 25–28. *"And in ... wonders see":* Metrical Psalm 107 (Gelder, 286).

P. 336, L. 32. *Cutchull'ns:* Cuchullins or Cuillin Hills, group of rugged and serrated mountain ranges, among the wildest scenery in Scotland, situated on the island of Skye.

L. 33. *Soa:* Soay, an isle separated from Skye by a channel of the same name.

P. 337, L. 11. *Loch Uskevagh ... Benbecula:* Benbecula is a low island in the Outer Hebrides, indented with bays, including Uskevagh on its eastern side.

P. 343, L. 4. *Norwegian city:* Christiana was the name of the capital of Norway, which changed back to its original name, Oslo, in 1925.

P. 349, L. 12. *Eilean Gour:* "Not far from the north-eastern extremity of Coll [an island west of Mull, where David Balfour began his Highland adventures] is the island Eilean-Mhor, uninhabited" (Samuel Lewis, *A Topographical Dictionary of Scotland,* vol. 2 [London, 1846], 544).

P. 352, L. 27. *The mark is on his brow:* a sign or token of imminent death (God's marks).

WILL O' THE MILL

P. 370, L. 6. *coil:* tumult, turmoil.

L. 10. *tumbril:* a two-wheeled cart used to carry ammunition.

L. 22. *dicky:* a seat at the back of a carriage for servants.

P. 374, L. 12. *wagged:* continued, moved along.

P. 376, L. 8. *hipped:* morbidly depressed; low-spirited.

P. 383, L. 2. *shrift:* confession, i.e., admission of sin or wrong for the sake of absolution (archaic).

MARKHEIM

P. 397, LL. 7–8. *as he began to re-arise:* Stevenson wrote "rëarise" in the manuscript, which was altered to "re-arise" in all the printed texts.

P. 399, LL. 1–2. *Bohemian goblets:* By the end of the seventeenth century Bohemian crystal was the most fashionable in Europe.

L. 24. *the image of the dead dealer reinspired:* Stevenson again used the diaeresis in "rëinspired," which was dropped in the printed editions.

P. 400, LL. 30–32. *Brownrigg... Thurtell:* Elizabeth Brownrigg, employed by a London parish to look after its poor pregnant women, was executed in 1767 after savagely abusing a young female apprentice to death; Frederick and Maria Manning murdered a dinner guest and buried him under the kitchen floor (they were executed in 1849); John Thurtell, gambler and son of a prosperous merchant, lured William Weare to a rural cottage and slit his throat when he refused to die after a brutal beating (executed in 1823).

P. 401, L. 17. *dropping cavern:* The printed texts substituted "dripping" for Stevenson's less common word.

P. 402, L. 21. *the defeated tyrant:* Napoleon would fly into fits of rage at small irritations such as losses at chess (George Henry Nettleton, ed., *Specimens of the Short Story* [New York: Henry Holt, 1907], 229).

L. 22. *Napoleon:* The winter of 1812 came unseasonably early and was responsible for much of the disastrous Russian campaign (Nettleton, 229).

P. 403, L. 3. *Sheraton sideboard:* Thomas Sheraton (1751–1806), English furniture maker whose designs were artistically simple and utilitarian.

P. 409, L. 9. *chance-medley:* legal term; unpremeditated wounding or killing in a casual encounter.

THRAWN JANET

P. 410, L. 16. *those hints that Hamlet deprecated:* "To be or not to be" (3.1.55–87)

P. 411, L. 34. *the moderates:* a group of professional clergymen in the late seventeenth century opposed to the traditional Calvinism of the Presbyterians who upheld the Westminster Confession; they controlled the Church of Scotland after 1712.

P. 416, L. 2. *Accuser of the Brethren:* "for the accuser of our brethren is cast down, which accused them before our God day and night" (Revelation 12:10).

OLALLA

P. 420, L. 20. *tatterdemalion:* decayed, broken down; beggarly.

P. 424, L. 3. *Kelpie:* a water demon, in the form of a horse, that haunts rivers and lures the unwary to their deaths.

P. 425, L. 5. *wicket:* a small gate or door; in this case, built into the larger gate.

P. 428, LL. 2–3. *shuttle-witted:* His mind moved back and forth like a shuttle, i.e., his "broken talk" or "disjointed babble."

L. 9. *debauch:* to lead or entice away from duty or obligations (archaic).

P. 432, L. 22. *impoverished:* exhausted in strength or fertility; made sterile.

L. 30. *contrabandista:* smuggler (Spanish).

L. 30. *hebetude:* lethargy, dullness.

P. 434, L. 4. *brandished:* flashed.

P. 438, L. 4. *maceration:* excessive fasting; mortification.

P. 445, L. 38. *insolation:* exposure to the sun's rays.

P. 455, L. 37. *vamped up:* patched together; concocted, fabricated.

P. 456, L. 2. *basilisks:* legendary reptiles whose breath and look were fatal.

THE TREASURE OF FRANCHARD

P. 459, L. 13. *embrocation:* liniment.

P. 461, L. 20. *knock me up:* to arouse or awaken from sleep.

P. 462, L. 18. *laureation:* academic degree; the term for "graduation" in Scottish universities.

L. 20. *cestus:* a woman's belt, especially a symbolic one worn by a bride.

L. 26. *malapert:* impudently bold; saucy.

P. 465, L. 32. *"Malbrouck s'en va-t-en guerre":* "Malbrouck is going to war," the name of a popular song about the Duke of Marlborough.

P. 466, L. 17. *ichor:* in Greek mythology, the ethereal fluid that takes the place of blood in the veins of the gods.

L. 21. *dive:* also *"div,"* an evil spirit or demon in Persian folklore.

L. 30. brune: brunette.

P. 468, L. 38. *hitch:* entanglement, impediment.

P. 473, L. 9. *"Mummia":* mummy, a medicinal preparation sold by pharmacists (obsolete).

P. 475, L. 18. *pinetum:* a plantation of pine trees.

L. 27. *cinchona:* the medicinal bark of a genus of trees native to the Andes.

P. 476, L. 11. *cigale:* cicada.

P. 477, LL. 17–18. *Golden mediocrity:* the common phrase, citing Horace, is "golden mean."

P. 478, L. 31. *homologate:* agree with, sanction; ratify, confirm.

P. 479, L. 22. *a sheet in the wind's eye:* slightly drunk; the proverbial phrase "three sheets in the wind" meaning very drunk.

P. 480, L. 11. *bemused:* here meaning engrossed or lost in thought or reverie.

L. 19. *Noddy:* a small two-wheeled carriage used in Ireland and Scotland.

L. 29. *baldric:* a belt, often ornamented, worn over the shoulder and across the chest, usually supporting a sword or a bugle.

P. 483, L. 2. *simples:* medicinal plants.

P. 484, L. 3. *patens:* shallow round dishes or plates, usually made of silver.

P. 485, L. 4. *precisian:* one who scrupulously adheres to a strict standard of religious observance or morality; formerly synonymous with puritan.

L. 5. *bemused:* here meaning bewildered, confused.

P. 488, L. 32. *whet:* a stimulant that sharpens or makes keen the appetite.

P. 490, L. 15. *bedizened:* dressed or adorned with gaudy vulgarity.

P. 496, L. 12. *pharos:* a lighthouse or beacon to guide seamen.

P. 497, L. 9. *smash:* commercial failure; bankruptcy.

P. 499, L. 6. *occultation:* concealment, i.e., for its being cut off from view.

L. 34. *blackguard:* low, coarse, vicious, and vulgar.

P. 500, L. 2. *re-edified:* rebuilt.

L. 34. *Gunpowder Day:* November 5, the day of the plot to blow up the English Parliament (1605).

P. 505, L. 18. *indue:* or "endue," put on, don, clothe oneself.

L. 33. "Bigre!": Confound it!

ISLAND NIGHTS' ENTERTAINMENTS

THE BEACH OF FALESÁ

P. 513, L. 8. *line:* the equator.

P. 514, L. 9. *stick:* familiar term for mast.

LL. 14–15. *Pain-Killer and Kennedy's Discovery:* patent medicines that had a high alcoholic content.

L. 25. *Black Jack:* sobriquet; a black-jack was a piratical-looking individual or the ensign of a pirate; also, a large, tarred, leather vessel for beer.

L. 25. *Whistling Jimmie:* sobriquet; a whistling-shop was a place where liquor was sold without a license.

L. 31. *pass:* abbreviation of "passage."

L. 32. *stern sheets:* the after part of an open boat, often furnished with seats to accommodate passengers.

L. 35. *gallows:* an intensifier signifying very or exceedingly.

P. 516, L. 21. *Kanaka:* Hawaiian term for "man"; also used pejoratively to signify an indigenous islander.

L. 31. Manu'a: Manua is the easternmost group of islands of the principal range of Samoan islands.

L. 31. *does:* to get on, thrive, flourish.

P. 517, L. 6. *get his shirt out:* get angry.

LL. 10–11. *Miller a Dutchman:* sailors often called all northern Europeans "Dutchmen."

L. 25. *a labour ship:* "blackbirding" was the term for the recruitment of men (often called kidnapping) from the islands of the Western Pacific to work as contract laborers, especially on plantations in Australia.

P. 518, L. 3–4. *Fiddler's Green:* where all good sailors go when they die, a place of fiddling, dancing, rum, and tobacco.

L. 20. *cutty sark:* a short or scanty chemise.

P. 519, LL. 7–8. *the cut of your jib:* the look of your face.

L. 12. *to hurt:* to matter, signify.

L. 35. *full:* drunk.

P. 520, L. 7. *old man:* the term applied to the captain by a crew.

L. 11. *Dry up:* Hush; be quiet.

L. 33. *old gentleman:* the devil.

P. 521, L. 29. *Hard-shell Baptis':* strict and uncompromising, also known as primitive Baptist.

P. 525, L. 9. *mortal:* an intensifier signifying extremely or great.

L. 30. *shipshape and Bristol fashion:* proverbial phrase referring to Bristol in its flourishing days as the chief port on the west coast of England.

L. 33. *Devil a wink:* an indefinite intensifier; e.g., devil of a mess, devil of a row.

P. 528, L. 31. fussy-ocky: *fasioti* in Samoan means to kill someone.

P. 529, L. 27. *Buncombe:* Bunkum, or talking merely for talk's sake; also, non-sense, claptrap.

L. 29. *cure:* an odd or eccentric person; abridged from "curiosity."

P. 530, L. 12. *the horrors:* delirium tremens.

L. 17. *taking:* agitation; a fit of temper.

L. 18. *Johnny had slipped his cable:* to "slip the cable" means to let go of the inboard end and allow the entire cable to run out.

LL. 24–25. *slanging:* abusing in foul language.

L. 28. *goods:* what is expected or required; the real thing.

P. 532, L. 1. *struck all of a heap:* suddenly astonished.

P. 534, L. 5. *sawder:* flattery; wheedling talk.

LL. 14–15. *to come any of their native ideas over me:* "to come over" or "come it over one" is to get the better of someone by craft or guile.

L. 24. *put my monkey up:* rouse one's passion or ill temper.

P. 535, LL. 19–20. *They have a down on you:* "to have a down on" means to dis-like, to regard with suspicion or alarm.

P. 536, L. 20. *bacon:* body.

P. 538, L. 2. *mummy-apple:* mammee apple, a tropical fruit that grows well in Hawaii.

P. 539, L. 38. *Beach de Mar:* the jargon or pidgin of the Western Pacific.

P. 540, L. 14. *beachcomber:* a contemptuous term for someone who hangs about the shore on the lookout for jobs; chiefly applied to runaway seamen and deserters from whalers who lived along the beaches in South America and the South Seas.

L. 18. *Apia and Papeete:* port centers of Samoa and Tahiti where beach-combers and rough seamen congregated.

L. 18. *flash:* low and vulgar; pertaining to thieves and criminals.

L. 32. "Ioe": Yes.

P. 541, L. 22. *cut up downright rough:* become obstreperous and dangerous.

L. 36. *sweep:* a contemptuous term for a low or disreputable man.

P. 543, L. 25. *bunged:* thrown with force.

P. 545, L. 19. "Aué!": Alas!

P. 549, L. 29. *flying:* circulating as a rumor, without definite authority.

P. 551, L. 31. *buffer:* a good-humored or liberal old man.

P. 552, LL. 13–14. *big don and the funny dog:* "don" is a distinguished man, a leader; also, an adept; "funny dog" is a gay or jovial man; a good fellow.

L. 26. *obstropulous:* a corrupt variant of obstreperous.

L. 31. *pot-hunting:* a hunter shooting anything he comes across, having more regard to filling his bag than to the rules of the sport.

P. 556, L. 31. *skylarked:* fooled around, engaged in rough sport or horseplay.
L. 35. *cracked on:* added sail in a strong wind.

P. 559, L. 34. *gone up:* gone to heaven, i.e., dead.

P. 560, L. 8. *woundy:* an intensifier signifying extremely or excessively (obsolete).
L. 12. *Tyrolean harp:* Aeolian harp: a stringed instrument adapted to produce musical sounds on exposure to a current of air.

P. 562, L. 7. *bum:* cry.

P. 567, L. 7. *plant:* a hidden store of goods or valuables.

P. 572, L. 2. *clapped down:* sat down suddenly or abruptly.

P. 574, L. 23. *sick:* spiritually or morally unsound or corrupt (obsolete).

P. 575, L. 37. *trick:* business; dealings.

THE BOTTLE IMP

P. 580, L. 33. *Prester John:* a legendary Christian king and priest of the Middle Ages whose kingdom (believed to be in either Asia or Africa) was associated with marvelous tales.

P. 589, L. 35. *Chinese Evil:* Hawaiian has no word for leprosy; *ma'i Pake* literally means "Chinese disease."

P. 590, LL. 11–12. *the smitten:* Kalaupapa, on the island of Molokai, was the site of Hawaii's leper colony.

P. 594, L. 6. *Berger:* Henry Berger (1844–1929), composer, arranger, and bandmaster of the Royal Hawaiian Military Band.

P. 600, L. 23. *the true helper after all: Kōkua* means help or helper in Hawaiian.

P. 604, L. 36. *a flat:* a fool; a dim-witted person.

THE ISLE OF VOICES

P. 606, L. 1. *Lehua:* The flower of the *ōhia* tree as well as the tree itself, the lehua is now the official flower of the island of Hawaii.
L. 10. *Kamehameha:* Kamehameha I (1758–1819) united the Hawaiian islands in 1809. "Kamehameha the First, founder of the realm of the Eight Islands, was a man properly entitled to the style of Great" (Robert Louis Stevenson, *The South Seas,* in *The Works of Robert Louis Stevenson,* vol. 9 [New York: P. F. Collier, 1912], 171).

P. 615, L. 17. *the directory:* Alexander Findlay, *A Directory for the Navigation of the South Pacific Ocean,* 5th ed. (London, 1884).
L. 18. *it was just such a night as this:* "The moon shines bright. In such a night as this…" (*The Merchant of Venice,* 5.1.1).

L. 20. *steep-to:* said of a coast or shore that rises abruptly from the water.

L. 22. *ramping:* to sail swiftly.

P. 616, L. 5. *payed off:* the movement by which a ship's head falls off from the wind and drops to leeward.

P. 619, L. 27. *Donat-Kimaran:* a minor government official whom Stevenson met in the Paumotu islands, or the Dangerous Archipelago: "my friend Mr. Donat—Donat-Rimarau, 'Donat the much handed'—acting Vice-Resident, present ruler of the archipelago, by far the man of chief importance on the scene, but known besides for one of an unshakable good temper" (Stevenson, *South Seas,* 128).

P. 620, LL. 27–28. *cried fair:* a fair proclaimed in advance by public announcement.

P. 621, L. 1. *by-day:* a day out of the ordinary course, incidental, apart from major events.

UNCOLLECTED STORIES

AN OLD SONG

P. 628, L. 5. *raciest:* the liveliest, the most exhilarating.

L. 6. *pink:* the most perfect condition or degree; the height, extreme.

P. 631, L. 32. *bate an ace:* to make the slightest abatement, i.e., to make any effort to diminish or moderate.

L. 35. *paltered:* equivocated; lied; dealt evasively.

P. 636, L. 13. *talent:* treasure, riches.

P. 637, L. 11. *fanfaronade:* swaggering or empty boasting; bluster.

P. 645, L. 31. *plump:* bluntly, directly, in plain terms.

P. 652, LL. 3–4. *providence generally does:* providence here meaning a disastrous accident, or fatality, regarded as an act of God (obsolete or dialectal).

P. 654, L. 6. *panniers:* large baskets carried in pairs over the back of a beast of burden.

THE STORY OF A LIE

P. 662, L. 23. *declension:* deterioration.

P. 663, L. 8. *carronades:* short cannons chiefly used on ships.

P. 664, L. 4. coup d'œil: "stroke of the eye," a glance that takes in a wide view.

L. 36. *done:* cheated (slang).

P. 670, L. 12. *buckrammed:* made rigid; stiffened, as if with buckram.

P. 671, L. 14. *integuments:* coverings, coatings.

L. 23. *freemasonry:* natural sympathy (i.e., between those with the same passion).

P. 679, L. 27. *siruping:* variant of syrup.

L. 28. *décavé:* cleaned out, ruined, beggared.

P. 680, L. 21. *bum-baily:* contemptuous term for bailiff, sheriff's deputy.

P. 688, L. 10. *let out all my cats:* disclose all my secrets.

P. 689, L. 8. *till all's blue:* until we are very drunk.

P. 694, LL. 31–32. *spinney:* a small wood or grove.

P. 695, L. 11. *nutting:* the act of gathering nuts.

P. 705, L. 35. *rip:* a reckless, dissolute person; a libertine.

THE BODY-SNATCHER

P. 710, L. 9. *camlet:* a fine fabric of silk and wool.

P. 711, L. 12. *mazily:* dizzily, confusedly.

L. 32. *canted:* mouthed pieties.

L. 33. *fillip:* a smart blow, usually with the fist (rare).

P. 713, LL. 4–5. *out at elbows:* ragged, poor.

P. 715, L. 15. *wynd:* a narrow street or passage.

P. 716, L. 35. *Irish voices:* the historical models for the body-snatchers, William Burke and William Hare, emigrated from Ireland to Scotland (Gelder, 284).

P. 718, L. 34. *Bashaw:* earlier form of pasha.

P. 720, L. 10. cras tibi: *hodie mihi, cras tibi*—it is my lot today, yours tomorrow (a line often found in old epitaphs).

P. 723, L. 15. *precentor:* one who directs the singing of a choir or congregation.

LL. 16–17. *by-name:* a secondary name; a nickname.

P. 725, L. 5. *gig:* a light carriage that has one pair of wheels and is drawn by one horse.

P. 726, L. 23. *ululations:* howls, wails; cries of lamentation.

THE MISADVENTURES OF JOHN NICHOLSON

P. 728, L. 2. *sows the wind:* to sow the wind and reap the whirlwind: proverbial, to labor in vain, or in Sir Walter Scott's words, "indiscriminate profusion."

LL. 19–20. *Candlish and Begg:* Edinburgh ministers (Gelder, 287).

P. 729, LL. 13–14. *right-hand defections or left-hand extremes:* a veiled allusion to Patrick Walker, the uncompromising historian of the early Covenanters (Gelder, 287–88).

P. 731, L. 2. *pop:* pawn (slang).

L. 17. *knock:* piece of bad luck.

P. 735, LL. 37–38. *arch-shebeener:* A shebeen is an unlicensed or illegally operated saloon or bar.

P. 739, L. 29. *shebeening:* the illegal selling of liquor.

P. 741, L. 19. *peri:* in Persian folklore, an elf or fairy, originally regarded as evil but later as benevolent and even beautiful.

L. 34. *rooked:* cheated, swindled.

P. 747, L. 29. *abortion:* a malformed or misshapen person.

P. 748, L. 23. *vesta:* a short wooden match.

P. 760, L. 16. *on the randan:* on a spree.

L. 25. *jarvey:* cabdriver.

P. 761, L. 13. *fetor:* stench; offensive smell.

P. 762, L. 24. *derision:* an object of ridicule, a laughingstock.

P. 767, LL. 12–13. *taking heart of grace:* to pluck up courage (proverbial).

P. 769, L. 9. *combe:* a hollow, usually on the flank of a hill.

P. 772, L. 11. *took the pet:* took offence, sulked.

P. 773, L. 11. *chap-fallen:* crestfallen; dejected, dispirited.

P. 777, L. 17. *muff:* a bungler, without skill or aptitude.

Scots Glossary

abune	above, overhead
aik	oak
ava'	at all
back-spang	a legal flaw or loophole; a trick or legal quirk
bairnly	childlike
bannock	a round, flat cake
bawbee	a halfpenny
begude	begun
behoved	be under an obligation or necessity
ben	inside, within
bield	shelter, protection (**bieldy:** sheltered or cosy)
birks	a small wood mainly of birches
bogle	a supernatural being, ugly and terrifying
brae, braes	the (steep or sloping) bank of a river or shore of the sea; a hillside
braw, braws	fine, splendid
bruik	enjoy; enjoy the use or possession of
brunstane	brimstone
brunt	burnt
buckled to	joined to, got going
bullering	roaring, bellowing

by	done, over (of past things)
by ordnar	extraordinary, unusual
cairn	a pyramid of loose stones built as a memorial to the dead; frequently used in place-names
callant	youth, young man
caller	cool; refreshing
cantrip	spell or charm; trick
canty	lively, cheerful; pleasant
carline	old woman (often disparaging); witch
cauld-wamed	cold-blooded
chafts	cheeks
chalmer	chamber, private room
chappin'	stroking
chittered	chattered
clachan	village
claught	caught, seized
claverin'	gossiping
clavers	idle tales; nonsense
clink	of words, to jingle together, rhyme
coats	petticoat; skirt
collieshangie	noisy dispute, uproar
corbie craws	carrion crows, ravens
craig	neck
cuist	threw off
cummers	gossips, scandalmongers; witches
daffin'	playfully
daunton	taunt
daurnae	dare not
deave	weary with talk
deid thraws	death throes
deil	devil
dirl	rattle, reverberate (**play dirl thegether:** chatter or clash together)
dirling	piercing
door cheeks	literally, the doorpost; by synecdoche, the door itself
dowie	melancholy, dismal

dozened	dazed, dulled, stupefied
dozenedness	stupidity, torpor, spiritlessness
duds	clothes
dunt	heavy, dull-sounding blow, knock (**played dunt:** throbbed, quickened)
dwining	wasting away
eldritch	weird, ghostly, unearthly
ettling (at)	aiming at
fashed	troubled, bothered
fause	false
fecht, fechtin'	fight, struggle
feck	quantity
ferlies	marvels, curiosities
fleyed	frightened
forbye	besides, in addition to; except for
forjaskit	exhausted
fuff	hiss
gane	gone
gang	(see **gate** and **gyte**)
gangrel	toad; tramp, vagrant
gart	made, forced
gate	way, path (**gang her ain gate:** go her own way)
gaun	gone; brisk
gear	possessions; movable property, household goods
gey (and)	rather, very
gied	gave
girn	snarl, grimace
girzie	servant maid
glamour	enchantment, magic
glebe	a parish minister's allotted land
gliff	a sudden fright, a scare
glisk	glimpse
gloamin'	twilight, dusk
glowrin'	staring, gazing intently

gousty	dreary, desolate
grogram	a coarse, often stiffened fabric of silk, mohair, or wool, or a blend of these
grue	terror; a shudder of horror or repulsion
gurled	roared (**gurlin':** howling)
gut	a channel or watercourse
gyte	mad, insane (**gang gyte:** went mad)
ha'e, hae	have
hag	a hollow of marshy ground in a moor
han'sel	gift for luck or celebration
hap	hop
hasp	clasp
haud	hold (**neither to haud nor to bind:** beyond control, unable to be restrained)
hinder	**at the hinder end:** finally, ultimately
hirsle	slither
hoot awa	nonsense
howff	a refuge or shelter
howking	rooting, burrowing
hunkers	**sittin' on his hunkers:** squatting down
ilka	each
jaloose, jaloosed	suspect, guessed
keeked	peered, looked sharply
keekit	peeped, watched surreptitiously
ken	know (**ken't:** know it)
kilted	tucked up
kirkton	the town or village in which the church is situated
kittle	tricky, somewhat difficult
knock	clock
kye	cows
laigh	low
lee-lane	solitary, all by oneself
leelang	livelong, whole

leevin'	living
leir	learning, knowledge, lore, doctrine
limmer	loose woman; contemptuous term for a woman
linkin'	moving fast, walking briskly
linn	pool below a waterfall
lown	calm, still
lowp, lowped	leap, leaped
luffed	sailed close to the wind
lug	ear
mad	infuriated; angry, annoyed
maned	moaned
maun; maunnae	must; must not
meddled	interfered with, bothered
mirk	dark, black, gloomy (**mirk nicht**: the dead of night; **mirk as the pit**: dark as a pit or the pit [of hell])
mistrysted	failed to meet, broken faith (with)
muckle	much; large, great (**muckle hell**: the depths of hell)
mutch	a close-fitting cap
napery	table linen
neaps	for neap tides, the smallest tides
neuk	corner
niest	next
noo (the)	just now, at present
ordnar	one's regular portion of (chiefly) food or drink
owercome	refrain
oxter	armpit
partans	edible crabs
pechin'	gasping
pickle	a little, a few
plenished	furnished
preen	fasten
ram-stam	headstrong, heedless
rattons	rats

reishling	whistling
rumm'ld	rumbled
sabbin'	soaking
sair	sore; involving hardship, difficulty; severe, stormy (of the weather)
sark	shift or chemise; shirt
saughs	willows
saut	salt; bitter, painful; the sea
scart	a mark or scrape of a pen
scunner	a feeling of disgust or nausea; a repugnant shudder
seepin'	dripping, soaking (**seep-sabbin:** the noise of running water)
shaw	a small, natural wood; a thicket
shoother	shoulder
sib	relative, related by blood
siccan	such
sinsyne	from that time
skelpt	struck, hit
skirled	screamed, shrieked with fear
skreigh	shriek, screech (also **skreighs, skreighin'**)
slavered	talked nonsense, chattered
slockened	quenched
smoored	smothered; drowned in a bog
sook	flow, current
soum	swim
sowp	sip (used ironically for a draught, a swig)
spang	amount
spars	the bars or rails of a wooden fence or gate
spate	a flood, a rush
speered	asked, questioned (**speiring:** inquiring)
spenster	sea specter
spentacle	spectacle
spunk	spark
spunkies	spirits, will-o'-the-wisps
steeked	shut tight
steer	stir, commotion

stramp	stamping or trampling
stravaguin'	roaming, wandering
syne	since, thereafter, thereupon, next
taed	toad
thae	those
the-day	today
thirled	bound in servitude
thrapples	windpipes
thrawn	twisted, crooked, misshapen; perverse; cross
threep	assert vehemently (**threep it doun their thrapples:** force the point down their throats)
tint	lost, destroyed, or disappeared
tramp-trampin'	washing clothes by treading in soapsuds
uncanny	dangerous, threatening; unlucky, inauspicious; ominous, eerie
unco	strange, unfamiliar; extraordinary, awful; very, exceedingly
unstreakit	not prepared or laid out for burial
upsitten	indifferent
wa'	wall
wale	the choice, the pick, the best
wanchancy	unlucky, inauspicious; dangerous, unreliable
warstlin'	struggling, wrestling
wast	west
waur	worst
wearied	sad; bored, listless
weary fa'	damn!, the devil take
whammled	turned round
wheen	few
wheest	be quiet!
whiles	sometimes, (at) times
wimple	a twist, turn, or winding
win	surmount, proceed
win through	get through

won	reached, arrived at
wud	mad, insane
yam-yammered	clamored, chattered incoherently
yett	gate
yoke on	set on, attack
yowlin'	wailing

STEVENSON IN THE *OED*

A dictionary is a reader's delight and an author's treasure. While one savors it as an enhancement of the reading process, the other depends upon it as an artery for meaning. When Simon Rolles, the luckless cleric, stumbled upon and instantly pocketed the brilliant "crystal" worth a rajah's fortune, he was shrewd enough to know that it was worthless to him unless it was cut. But how to do that? He needed help, but he did not want to go to books. For all his scholarship and study—none of it had helped to advance his career—he was disappointed in what books had to offer. In this he was unlike his creator, for Robert Louis Stevenson not only made books, he lived in them. Old books, new books, philosophy, history, romance, poetry, letters—if it was printed, and told a story, or pointed a moral, and captured his attention, even for a moment, he thought it of value. As a by-product of this incessant reading, Stevenson possessed an extraordinary vocabulary—one often wonders how or where he stored those words—and much of it wound up in his writing. That vocabulary also became a major resource for the people who were engaged in that epic enterprise in the late nineteenth century, the construction of *A New English Dictionary on Historical Principles*, later renamed the *Oxford English Dictionary* and commonly called the *OED*. Stevenson was quoted consistently, for his English, his Scots, his slang and colloquialisms, his archaisms, and occasionally because no other examples could be found. What follows are the words from the short stories that are cited in the original *OED*, and those in the revised Second Edition. An asterisk (*) before a word signifies that it is defined as *rare* or *obsolete* or *archaic*; a dagger (†) indicates that it is the only example listed; and a numeral (²) that the word first appears in the Second Edition of the dictionary.

²accidented	Characterized by uneven surfaces in the landscape.
alight	Aflame, i.e., on fire.
back	*To put one's back into,* i.e., to use all one's strength.
*bitter	I.e., bitterly.
black dog	When a child is sulky, it is said "the black dog is on his back." See Notes.
blistered	Flawed, as if covered with small lumps or blisters.
†bludgeoned	Beaten down or wounded, as with a bludgeon.
†blue fear	variant of *blue funk:* depressed, low-spirited.
boxful	As much as a box will contain.
brandishing	Flashing.
Britisher	A British subject; a native or resident of Great Britain.
broken	Disjointed, disconnected.
capital	*To make capital out of,* i.e., to turn to account.
²carrying it off	Facing or braving it out.
²carrying on	Behaving irrationally and erratically, even raging. Cited twice in the original *OED* for "The Beach of Falesá," and in the Second Edition for *Jekyll and Hyde.*
*characters	I.e., distinctive marks, features, characteristics.
cicatrised	Scarred, marked with scars.
clay	Earthly, material; clay = human body.
²clubbed	Beat or knocked down or killed with a club.
†clumped	Formed into a clump.
coastward	Toward, or in the direction of, the coast.
concealed	Hid, shielded.
*contained	Restrained; self-restrained.
*²continent	That which contains or holds; i.e., vessel.
conventual	Characteristic of a convent.
corded	The cordlike pattern made by a hard or taut muscle.
crystals	Rock crystals or quartz, clear and transparent like ice; also, a colorless transparent diamond.
*delicacy	Something pleasurable; a thing which gives delight.
deranged	Disturbed, interrupted.

detonations	Sudden expressions or eruptions of anger.
devilish	Excessively, devilishly; a coarse intensive.
*†disconsidered	Deprived of consideration or esteem, brought into disrepute.
*discovered	Disclosed or exposed to view something hidden or covered up.
²disgustful	Resulting from or accompanied by disgust.
dissimulated	Hid or disguised under a false appearance; dissembled.
doing well	*To do well:* to prosper, thrive, or succeed.
dozed (over)	*To doze off or over:* to drop off into a doze.
drawled	Uttered or spoken slowly.
dully	Tediously, without interest or spirit.
eager	Pungent, keen, chill.
*effected	Made, constructed.
entr'acte	A dance or piece of music performed between the acts.
†ergotize	To quibble, wrangle (*OED*); to argue logically or sophistically (*Webster's Third*).
escalade	The act of scaling the wall of some fortified or protected place.
face (showed)	*To show one's face:* to put in an appearance.
fallen (to be)	*To fall to be* = to come to be.
²fan-light	A fan-shaped or semicircular window over a door.
†febricule	Anglicized version of *febricula:* a slight and transient fever.
feck	See Scots Glossary.
flattered	Beguiled, charmed.
*†flecked	To force in flecks or patches *into.*
flee	Run away from; abandon.
fleeringly	Mockingly, scornfully.
flirting	Opening out quickly or briskly.
floe	A quicksand. See Notes.
fogged	Covered or enveloped with or as if with fog.
²for	Designating an amount to be received or paid; i.e., *in payment for.*
fortification	The act of providing a defensive barrier.
†fronted (about)	Turned around so as to face in another direction.

²**hailing**	To strike with considerable force like hail in a storm.
hands	*Come to (one's) hands;* to fight hand to hand.
harebrain	I.e., *harebrained,* with no more brain than a hare; reckless or flighty.
[†]**harlequinesque**	Having the style of a harlequin.
heady	Headlong, precipitate, impetuous, violent; passionate, headstrong.
hell	A gambling house.
²**hide-bound**	Narrow or restricted in view; bigoted, obstinately set in opinion.
holoku	(Hawaiian) A long gown with a train, as worn in Hawaii.
hove-to	I.e., *heaved to:* to bring a ship to a standstill.
hunkers	See Scots Glossary.
idol	A visible appearance without substance, an image caused by reflection as in a mirror; an incorporeal phantom.
*[†]**immateriality**	Slightness, flimsiness.
immediateness	Immediacy.
inclination	Affection, liking.
incompetent	An incompetent person.
indices	*Index* = a sign, token, or indication *of* something.
inexpugnably	Invincibly, unconquerably.
²**intake**	The act of taking in from outside; that which is taken in.
^{†2}**ivory-faced**	Combination with *ivory.*
jangled	Discordant, harsh, jarring.
²**join**	To unite, associate, or ally oneself *with* or *to.*
²**Kalmuck**	A member of a Mongolian people living on the northwest slopes of the Caspian Sea.
[†]**key-rack**	Combination with *key.*
kirkton	See Scots Glossary.
knuckly	Having large or prominent knuckles.
Latin Quarter	A district of Paris on the left bank of the Seine, where Latin was spoken in the Middle Ages; site of the university, and the haunt of students and artists.

lean-to	A shed or shelter whose roof leans against another building.
leek	*To eat the leek:* to submit to humiliation under compulsion; cf. Shakespeare, *Henry V,* 5.1.10.
lee-lane	See Scots Glossary.
leir	See Scots Glossary.
²light-headedly	Frivolously, thoughtlessly.
²lot	*The lot* = the whole or entire bunch. *Colloq.*
†loud-spoken	Given to loud speaking.
loverly	Befitting a lover.
†low-bodied	Combination with *low.*
maculate	Marked with spots, blotched.
made (away with)	Put out of the way, i.e., killed.
made (it my pride)	Set down as a law.
masthead (to the)	To the fullest possible extent. *Sc.*
meetings	Gatherings for purposes of entertainment and discussion.
†menially	Like a menial or domestic servant, with a disparaging or contemptuous implication.
miracle	*To a miracle* = extraordinarily well.
misbegotten	Unlawfully conceived; illegitimate; deformed,
†mobile	Constantly in motion.
mortally	Extremely, exceedingly. *Colloq.*
moss	Wet, spongy soil; bog.
most (the)	*The most* = the majority.
mountain bulk	Resembling a mountain, i.e., huge, enormous.
mountebanking	Playing the mountebank, i.e., the charlatan.
*muddy	Morally impure or "dirty."
muffle	Muffling effect; muffled sound.
nameable	Capable of being named, i.e., identifiable.
native	I.e., native language.
nosed	Examined closely.
nut	A question difficult to answer, or a problem hard to solve.
obliterated	Effaced, wiped out or made indistinct.
observatory	A place of observation. The *OED* lists this as a "nonce-use," i.e., applied only for a special occasion, and cites its repeated use in *Kidnapped.*

off chance	A remote or slight chance.
off colour	Not up to the mark, defective, deficient.
ordnar	See Scots Glossary.
outcropping	I.e., *outcrop,* the part of a rock formation that appears at the surface of the ground.
panically	With panic-like fear.
*part (on the other)	Part = *hand.*
*passage	I.e., of people passing.
peep	A tiny speck of light.
peg	In stringed instruments, a pin to which the strings are fastened at one end, and which is turned to adjust the tension in tuning.
*period	*To put a period to:* to terminate, end.
pitching (it)	*To pitch it strong:* to speak forcefully; to deliver a case with a glibness marked by exaggeration.
plangency	The quality of being plangent, i.e., plaintiveness.
planting	Placing or striking firmly and forcibly. *Slang.*
plies	Folds; each of the layers produced by folding cloth; carpets made of two or more interwoven webs.
pointed	Piercing, cutting, stinging.
points	Units in appraisal. Also, marks.
†pot-herbs	I.e., pot plant. *OED* cites "pot-herbs" as an erroneous usage.
propose	To proffer, to offer for acceptance.
provocatively	Stimulating or exciting appetite or lust.
quaver	A shake or tremble in the voice.
quavering	Quivering; shaking or moving with a slight, tremulous motion.
Queer Street	An imaginary street where people in trouble presumably live. *Slang.*
quiet (at)	*More at quiet,* i.e., quieter.
raffle	A confused jumble or tangle.
rag (of a man)	Applied contemptuously to a person.
rancid	Nasty, odious.
rarity	Thinness of composition (of air).
ratiocinate	Reason, i.e., carry on a process of reasoning.

reaping	Cutting down or harvesting (the crop of a field).
recollected	Gathered or summoned up (strength, courage); rallied, recovered by an effort.
reindue	Put on again.
reinform	To invest again with form.
reinspired	Inspired again.
†rëinvasion	A second or another invasion.
rendezvous'd	Assembled.
†rivershed	*River,* with word denoting the course or part of the course of a river.
rose	Stood up from a sitting position.
roseate	Happy, smiling.
rowing	The action of propelling a boat by means of oars. *Fig.*
rubric	Designation, category.
run	A flow or current of water, a strong rush or sweep of the tide.
run (strong)	To course or flow.
†run-the-hedge	A vagabond.
sake	*For old sake's sake:* for the sake of old friendship.
²scission	I.e., *schism,* division, separation.
screwed	Tightened the tension (of a musical string) by turning a screw or key.
†sea quags	Situated in or by the sea. See Notes.
secularly	In a secular manner, i.e., as a lay person.
*†seduction	Seductiveness, alluring quality.
seizing	That seizes the attention; arresting, powerfully impressive.
self-destroyer	I.e., a suicide.
sensitive	The sensitive plant, a shrub having a high degree of irritability.
sheeted (up)	Covered with a sheet of snow.
sickish	Somewhat nauseated, queasy.
slyish	Rather sly; roguish.
smother	Dense or suffocating dust, fog... filling the air.
soum	See Scots Glossary. *Swim or drown:* used in reference to the ordeal of suspected witches.
Spanishly	I.e., like Spanish.
spars	See Scots Glossary.

Speak House	A large hut used as a place of council in the Pacific islands.
†**spire-top**	A tall, tapering structure rising from a tower or roof.
spring (its rattle)	I.e., to sound.
†**squash (nose)**	I.e., having the appearance of being squashed.
stern	I.e., the rear part.
stick out	*To stick out:* to continue resisting, to hold out.
stiff	Unusually high, excessive.
stink	To be abhorrent, offensive.
*****stock**	A stump.
struck	I.e., surrendered.
suicide (Club)	*Attributive.*
superiorly	In a higher or better manner or degree.
sweetly	An intensive used ironically with *pay*.
take (*You ~ me*)	To understand, grasp the meaning of.
third	In proverbial phrase, *the third time's lucky.*
thread	*Worn to the thread:* threadbare.
thread-paper	Long and narrow, slender.
transpires	Passes out or escapes as a vapor from the body.
²**troglodytic**	Resembling a troglodyte, i.e., of or relating to cave dwellers; coarse, brutal, or degraded.
*****truncheon**	A broken or cut-off piece, a fragment.
twilit	Lit by twilight.
twist	The junction of the thighs, the fork.
two-twos	*In two twos:* in a very short time, in a twinkling. *Slang.*
†**ungodly**	Outrageous, dreadful. *Colloq.*
unmanning	To deprive of courage or vigor; to degrade; to emasculate.
vainglorying	Boasting, self-promoting.
vaulting	Reaching for the heights.
view halloa	The shout given by a hunter on seeing a fox break cover.
wale	See Scots Glossary.
warfaring	Warring, militant.
†**whip-top**	I.e., whipping post.
whites	Silver money.
wimple	See Scots Glossary.
*****withinsides**	I.e., inside.

A NOTE ON THE TYPE

The principal text of this Modern Library edition
was set in a digitized version of Janson,
a typeface that dates from about 1690 and was cut by Nicholas Kis,
a Hungarian working in Amsterdam. The original matrices have
survived and are held by the Stempel foundry in Germany.
Hermann Zapf redesigned some of the weights and sizes for Stempel,
basing his revisions on the original design.

MODERN LIBRARY IS ONLINE AT
WWW.MODERNLIBRARY.COM

MODERN LIBRARY ONLINE IS YOUR GUIDE
TO CLASSIC LITERATURE ON THE WEB

THE MODERN LIBRARY E-NEWSLETTER

Our free e-mail newsletter is sent to subscribers, and features sample chapters,
interviews with and essays by our authors, upcoming books, special promotions,
announcements, and news.

To subscribe to the Modern Library e-newsletter, send a blank e-mail to:
sub_modernlibrary@info.randomhouse.com or visit www.modernlibrary.com

THE MODERN LIBRARY WEBSITE

Check out the Modern Library website at
www.modernlibrary.com for:

- The Modern Library e-newsletter
- A list of our current and upcoming titles and series
- Reading Group Guides and exclusive author spotlights
- Special features with information on the classics and other
  paperback series
- Excerpts from new releases and other titles
- A list of our e-books and information on where to buy them
- The Modern Library Editorial Board's 100 Best Novels and
  100 Best Nonfiction Books of the Twentieth Century written
  in the English language
- News and announcements

Questions? E-mail us at modernlibrary@randomhouse.com.
For questions about examination or desk copies, please visit
the Random House Academic Resources site at
www.randomhouse.com/academic